The THIRD GOD

BOOK THREE of
THE STONE DANCE OF THE
CHAMELEON *Trilogy*

RICARDO PINTO

BANTAM BOOKS
LONDON · TORONTO · SYDNEY · AUCKLAND · JOHANNESBURG

TRANSWORLD PUBLISHERS
61–63 Uxbridge Road, London W5 5SA
A Random House Group Company
www.rbooks.co.uk

THE THIRD GOD
A BANTAM BOOK: 9780553815054

First published in Great Britain
in 2009 by Bantam Press
an imprint of Transworld Publishers
Bantam edition published 2010

Addresses for Random House Group Ltd companies outside the UK
can be found at: www.randomhouse.co.uk
The Random House Group Ltd Reg. No. 954009

The Random House Group Ltd supports The Forest Stewardship
Council (FSC), the leading international forest-certification organization.
All our titles that are printed on Greenpeace-approved FSC-certified
paper carry the FSC logo. Our paper procurement policy can be found at
www.rbooks.co.uk/environment

Typeset in 10/12pt Goudy by
Kestrel Data, Exeter, Devon.
Printed in the UK by
CPI Cox & Wyman, Reading, RG1 8EX.

2 4 6 8 10 9 7 5 3 1

To my family

Acknowledgements

In a world where it seems publishers are no longer as fastidious as they once were, Transworld have lavished upon this book the attention of many excellent professionals – from Claire Ward's book jacket design to Elizabeth Dobson's precise copy-editing. Neil Gower has produced another set of beautiful glyphs and Jim Burns has given me a wonderful, vibrant jacket illustration. But it is Simon Taylor who has championed the book, and whose editing has made it considerably more than it would otherwise have been. I am grateful to them all.

Victoria Hobbs has midwived this trilogy with much patience and skill. Jennifer Custer, my other agent, was the first person to read the whole trilogy in one go, and her discerning feedback and much needed enthusiasm was important to me when I was at a low ebb. I want to thank her for reading the final draft as well as Robbie, Sam Edenborough, Remco, Angeline and Simon Bolton.

My quest for completeness was aided by various experts. Of these I would particularly like to thank Ben Harte for the geology that forms the bones of my invented world – the landforms of which determine the flow of the story; David Adger, who produced for me the translations into Quya which I then wrote with glyphs; Dominic Prior, whose mathematics has brought clarity to my own inelegant calculations. Others include Tom Darling for the talk we had on muscle wastage; John Robertson for his insights into military matters; Mark Haillay for his horticultural advice and Paula Rudall for helping me with a problem concerning banyan wood.

Though I have worked in blessed isolation, the internet has allowed me to have much needed virtual work colleagues. Among these are Dean Thompson, Dave Newbert, James Worrall, Dave Scott, Colin Bell, Keith Brunton, Graham Gibson, John Robertson and Adrian Smith. Additionally there was Bob Gillies and Max Gaunt, my T'ai Chi buddies. Special mention needs to be made of Remco van Straten and Angeline Adams who have aided me in so many ways. Finally, I would like to thank those of my readers who have written to me and whose kindness and enthusiasm have been an important support to me throughout the more than ten years it has taken me to write these books.

Sharon Jacobsen helped me, over five years, to unravel the ungordian knot of my own psyche. Without her skill and empathy I doubt if the story could have reached a conclusion that is both natural and true.

Finally, I owe more than can be said to my partner Robbie who has stood by me through this long, long process, even though it often eclipsed anything else and seemed interminable.

The THIRD GOD

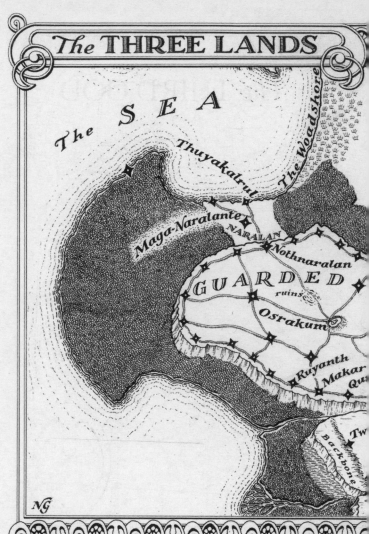

The THREE LANDS

The SEA

The Woadshore

Thuyakalrul

Maga-Naralante

NARALAN

Nothnaralan

GUARDED

ruins

Osrakum

Ruyanth

Makar

Qu

Tw

Backbone

NG

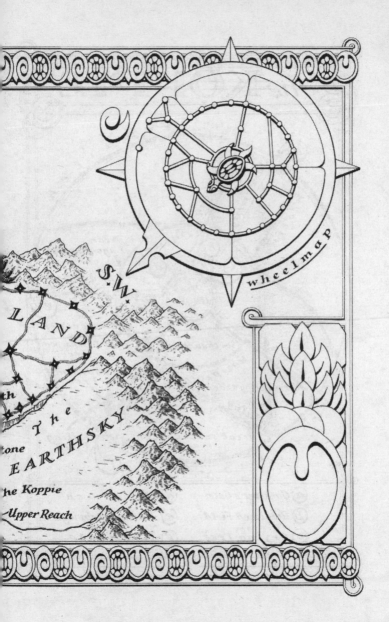

wheelmap

S.W.

LAND
th
The
one
EARTHSKY
he Koppie
Upper Reach

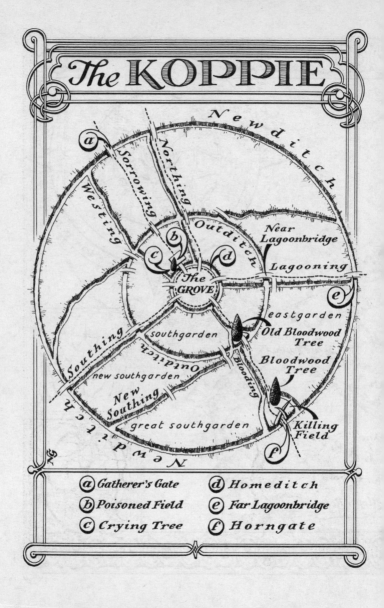

The KOPPIE

Newditch

Westing

Sorrowing

Northing

Outditch

Near
Lagoonbridge

Lagooning

The
GROVE

eastgarden

Old Bloodwood
Tree

Bloodwood
Tree

Southing

southgarden

Outditch

Blooding

new southgarden

New
Southing

great southgarden

Killing
Field

Newditch

(a) **Gatherer's Gate**   (d) **Homeditch**

(b) **Poisoned Field**   (e) **Far Lagoonbridge**

(c) **Crying Tree**   (f) **Horngate**

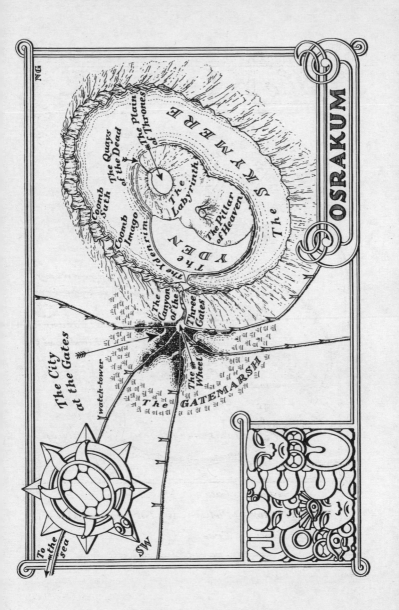

MOTHERING MASK

Salty with tears their mother's milk.
(fragment – origin unknown)

She squeezed the ruby into her left eye socket, felt a pop, then sensed its shape inside her head. A sister stone nestled its cool weight in her palm. Raising it she filled the other socket, then inclined her head. A hard blink settled the stones, shaped to occupy each socket, their spinel axes aligned to give the orbs the appearance of focus. Though the Wise had robbed her of sight, they could not deprive her of this blood-red gaze. Raking the chamber, Ykoriana heard the uneasy movements that it induced among her slaves. She did not allow her lips to smile. Eyes, even of stone, are weapons.

As slaves intruded into every part of her with their unguents, perfume blossomed so that in her mind she escaped from her forbidden house and was walking in a garden. Her nostrils drank in the musk of mummified roses. She became intoxicated by attar of lilies. Spidersilk flowed over her, so finely woven it seemed liquid spilling down her shoulders and breasts, her hips and thighs. She had learned to derive some consolation from sensuousness.

Though it was their daughter her son claimed he was coming to see, he knew well enough that Ykoriana would not allow him near Ykorenthe unless she were safe in her

15

embrace. Molochite knew also that, because he was God Emperor, his mother would have to be cleansed according to the exact procedure demanded by the Law. The Grand Sapient of the Domain of Blood had come himself as usual to oversee the ritual. She felt his presence though he had not yet spoken through his homunculus. All the Wise had earned her hatred, but he most of all, whom she considered chief among her jailors.

This visit was typical of Molochite. He liked to remind her of her vulnerability. He enjoyed humiliating her. Now they rarely met. She could maintain her control over him through intermediaries. She had exploited his lust for her, but now she had a daughter, she only invited him into her bed to renew her dominance. The rest of the time she let him vent his desires where he would. As for his petty defiances, she could bear them. Though he wore the Masks, it was she who ruled.

The women of the House of the Masks had always played a major part in the choosing of a God Emperor, but even as they dropped their blood-rings into the voting urns, they squandered their power by fighting each other. Their ichorous blood would not allow them to yield supremacy to another. This disunity Ykoriana had abolished with her birth. The first female of blood-rank four for generations, her rings cast eight thousand votes. Enough power to dominate the House of the Masks. Enough even to empower her to stand alone, if she chose, against half the assembled might of the Houses of the Great. Power coursed in her veins that all her mothers had dreamed and bred for. What a bitter jest, then, that such power had brought her nothing but suffering.

The Grand Sapient's homunculus murmured and the slaves began loading her with robes of brocade denser than armour. She conquered the familiar fear of being shut in, smothered.

She had been only a girl when her father had died. She had loved her brother Kumatuya, but never forgave him gifting Azurea, their sister, to his lover Suth Sardian. Azurea had died bearing him a son, Carnelian. Grief overcoming policy,

Ykoriana had demanded her brother exile Suth as the price for her votes in his election as God Emperor. In revenge, Kumatuya had had her eyes put out. She had not imagined the Wise would support him. A foolish misjudgement. All who spun out their lives in the forbidden houses of the Chosen had reason to know how much the Wise feared and hated women.

A procession was approaching. They were bringing her daughter. Hastily she reached for what she termed her 'mothering mask' and hid her face behind it. She loathed that mask. She had had it made so as not to scare her daughter. She did not want her child to see her withered face, her ruby eyes. Those baleful stones she wore to express her bitter anger, to terrorize, but, most of all, in defiance of the Wise who had insisted that, as they did, she should wear eyes of jade or obsidian to reflect whichever of the Masks the God Emperor was wearing.

As the procession halted, her ears searched among the tinkling metals, the clink of jewels. When she heard her daughter's faltering steps, it was as if sunlight fell upon Ykoriana's face. She touched the cold gold of her mask to reassure herself that she was hidden. Her fingers traced its kind smile, the small nose, its loving eyes of embedded shell and sky-blue sapphire. Her robes would not allow her to stoop so she had them lift Ykorenthe. Her hands sought her daughter's face. She found the familiar warm curve of her chin with a caress. 'Ykorenthe, my delight,' she said, brightly.

Ykoriana longed to hold the child, but the weight of her sleeves had consumed her strength. Little Ykorenthe's wordless chatter was sweeter than music. Protecting her had become the very heart of Ykoriana's life. She suppressed the familiar longing to see the tiny face. She had been told the girl had her father's beauty. The daughter she had lost, Flama, she too had been beautiful. Time had not dulled the blade of Ykoriana's grief. Her extreme purdah had made her sons Molochite and Osidian Nephron strangers to her, but Flama she had kept as

17

close as the Law permitted. Headstrong, the girl had fought her mother over the election of Kumatuya's successor. Had she been given time, Ykoriana was confident she would have been able to gently poison Flama's love for Nephron. Ykoriana's spies had revealed enough about him for her to have had no illusions about what her role would be should he become the Gods. Flama's blood was ichor in even greater part than Ykoriana's. Nephron would have married his sister and their mother would have been exiled to the depths of the imperial forbidden houses. Still, she had loved Flama enough to risk that fate. It was her other son she had underestimated. Molochite had known Flama's votes would neutralize those his mother could cast for him. Also he had known that his brother was more popular than he, not only in the House of the Masks, but, beyond, among the Great. Fearing to lose, Molochite had murdered his sister. Enraged, Ykoriana had come close to handing him over to the justice of the Wise; that she was no longer so ruled by her passions was what had saved him. Flama was dead and her death had opened a way to power through him.

As she had vacillated, a rumour had spread through Osrakum that it was she who had murdered her daughter. Outrage and indignation had given way to contemplation as she had observed how much this news made her feared. She had learned from the Wise, that fear is the path to dominion. Her enemies had taken advantage of her distraction. In the midst of the turmoil caused by the preparations the households had been making to move up to their palaces high in the Sacred Wall, the Lord Aurum had convened the Clave and there had managed to get Suth elected He-who-goes-before. This appointment she could have thwarted had she had time to mobilize her supporters among the Great. But, on reflection, she had seen Aurum's gambit for what it was, an act of desperation. Let the old fool leave his faction leaderless while he went off on a futile mission to that house of exile in the remote north. The world that mattered, the world she knew, lay within Osrakum's mountain wall. Beyond was nothing more than the squalid barbarism of the Guarded Land. With characteristic eccentricity, Suth had not even chosen to wait out his exile in one of the cities there, but had sailed with his son to some bleak island across the northern sea. She had been, if anything, amused. She had known what Aurum did not, that Suth's exile had long ago been revoked, but that he had chosen not to return.

Still she had taken precautions. Hastily her agents had recruited a minor Lord of the Great, Vennel, to go with Aurum and, with promises of a child brought forth from some woman from her House, she had bought his eyes and ears. When she had received a letter from the fool, she had been less amused. Against her expectations, Suth had returned with Aurum to the Three Lands. Unease had become panic when they had disappeared from the Tower in the Sea. She had feared that, if they reached Osrakum in time, they might influence the Great enough to carry the election for Osidian Nephron. It had been the Hanuses who had offered to organize an attempt to waylay them. She had given those syblings no answer lest she be implicated. They knew that should they fail she would abandon them to the Wise. The syblings' plot had served only to wound Suth. None had accused her, but most had believed she was behind it. Schism between the factions had deepened. Those who had adhered to her candidate, Molochite, had been drawn closer from fear of her: the opposition had been strengthened in equal measure and blossomed once Suth had arrived in Osrakum. She had bent Molochite to negotiating with the Great for his own election. Coercion and seduction had been employed. The final coup of bringing Imago Jaspar over to her cause had made her certain of victory, but her schemes had come to nothing. The voting had gone against her.

Fondling Ykorenthe, Ykoriana smiled behind her mask. While Suth and Aurum had celebrated their triumph, she had snatched victory from their grip. Before the election,

Imago had told her that Osidian Nephron had descended to the Forbidden Garden of the Yden with Suth's son, Carnelian. The parallels between their actions and those of their fathers had disturbed her, but when the votes had gone against Molochite, she had become desperate enough for one last throw. She had already let Molochite into her bed. He had been sniffing after her for years and it had been essential to bind him to her before the imperial power became his. Subverting her purdah, before witnesses, she had allowed him to put a child in her. If it were a daughter and should one day seek to stand against her mother, Ykoriana would be able to prove the child had been conceived before her sire had been made the Gods and thus strip her of her voting rings. That was before Ykoriana came to love her, though she had vowed she would never be so weak again. A loved child was a terrible vulnerability.

She treasured the iron rings she had demanded the Hanuses bring as proof Osidian and his lover were slain. This triumph had brought another when Suth had drawn the Wise into making a fatal error that had put them in her power. Of course they suspected her hand was behind the disappearance but, without proof, they dared not accuse her. Ykoriana had made certain no bodies would ever be found. The Wise had had no choice but to deify Molochite at an Apotheosis. The new God Emperor had inaugurated Their reign by marrying her.

Her daughter's breath was warm against her hand. Ykoriana stroked the little head.

Forcing the Clave to depose Suth had not brought her the pleasure she had anticipated. Aurum she had had impeached. Struggling to save himself, the old fool had revealed to her why it was that Suth had chosen not to return from exile as soon as it had been revoked. Vennel, having failed to solve this riddle for her, had suffered for it. It was this secret that Aurum had used to control Suth during the election, expecting to wield influence over Osidian Nephron once he was God Emperor. The information had not been as valuable to her as the old fool had hoped. She had been minded only to commute his deposal to exile. She smiled, imagining his despair. Denied the heir he craved, he would waste his remaining years far from Osrakum, imprisoned in the desolation of the outer world.

THE LIVING AND THE DEAD

From death shall they awake
who cross the water to the Shadow Isle.
(from the 'Ruáya', the first book of the 'Ilkaya',
part of the holy scriptures of the Chosen)

A gouged eye, the sun hung low above the reddened earth. Carnelian was standing on the porch of the Ancestor House. Once again he had spared Osidian, had listened to that butcher even in the midst of the slaughtered Ochre. Those dear people who had overcome their terror of the Masters to offer him and Osidian sanctuary were now all hanging down there from their sacred mother trees, not even a child spared.

Behind him like his own shadow, he could feel Osidian's malign presence in the Ancestor House. Carnelian glared at the bloodshot sun. Threads of smoke rose tethered to the circling horizon. Osidian claimed these to be a Plainsman sign a thousand years old warning that the Masters had come down to ravage their Earthsky. Carnelian strained his eyes northwards. Was he even certain Aurum was really coming? What of Osidian's claim that only he could defeat him? Carnelian recalled Aurum setting ants alight. As casually would the Master torch men. Carnelian regarded the spear in his hand with which he had intended to take Osidian's life. He slumped. It seemed he was destined always to listen to Osidian's arguments, though their logic always concealed poison.

He looked once more upon the mother trees. He must go down there and submit to the gaze of the dead. He must face Fern's grief though Fern had the right to kill him. Was it only that morning they had been so close? Their friendship was dead with everything else. He moved to the steps that led down to the clearing. First he must return to where he had left Poppy, though he had no idea what he might say to her. Then he would go to Fern and begin making whatever atonement he could.

The Oracle Morunasa was at the foot of the steps with some other Marula. Uncertainty was in his amber eyes as he regarded the spear in Carnelian's fist – the spear he had given him to kill Osidian. Morunasa was desperate to be free of Osidian, but after the profound visions he believed his god had shown him, he dared not do it himself.

Carnelian offered him the spear. 'Where are the hostage children?'

Morunasa registered that its blade was unbloodied. 'Not here, Master.'

Carnelian surveyed the warriors standing round. They would not look at him and seemed afraid. He dismissed a twinge of empathy. Though forced to it by Osidian and the Oracles, it was their hands had strung up the Ochre.

He turned back to Morunasa. 'I don't know what part you played in what happened here, but I do believe that you and your people will suffer for it.'

As he offered the spear again, Morunasa glanced up to the Ancestor House uneasily, then back, penetratingly, at Carnelian, so that he was left feeling they were making some agreement. It was only then the Oracle took back his spear.

At the edge of the clearing, Carnelian hesitated. The horror of what the gloom concealed made his heart pound.

'Poppy,' he whispered to himself, setting her up as a beacon to guide him through the nightmare. He edged into the shadows, afraid to make a sound. Fetor wafted, thick, sickening-sweet. He blessed the slope that rose up to meet the pendant branches, so concealing what lay further down the hill. He crept forward, his right hand sliding and crawling along the Crag rock. He heard furtive splashing up ahead. A figure came into sight, washing at the cistern. Carnelian watched it scoop water then trickle it over its head. As the hands fell the figure saw him; it was Krow. The youth's eyes bulged. He reached down to pluck up some clothing, as if ashamed of his nakedness.

Carnelian moved forward and recognition lit Krow's face with hope.

'Carnie . . .'

Carnelian noticed the dark stains on the clothing he was clutching and frowned. Krow began to tremble. His chin fell. Water dripped from his hair into the dust. Carnelian pushed past him. Just then, he could not bear to know what had caused those stains.

As he passed Akaisha's mother tree, Carnelian averted his gaze. Nevertheless, at the edge of his vision, a corpse seemed to be standing in the gloom. One of his hearthmates. The stench of its rotting smothered him. He doubled up, vomiting, then lurched down the rootstair, his eyes half closed and his feet finding the hollow steps.

The ferngarden was an emerald framed in the gateway. The bright air beckoned him as if he were struggling up through water to breathe it. Stumbling over the earthbridge, he gulped the breeze. Arid musk of fernland laced with acacia and magnolia. He gaped at the sun making a gory end to the day. Turning away, with each blink he printed its turquoise ghost on the ferns.

Poppy? He spun round, checking to see where he was relative to the earthbridge. This was the Bloodgate. He was certain it was here he had made her promise to wait for him. There was no movement but the swaying ferns. What if some Marula had found her? Panic choked him. He had abandoned not only Poppy, but also Fern. What if Osidian had commanded the Marula to leave no one in the Koppie alive?

He took the roots of the stair three at a time, desperate to find Poppy and Fern. Akaisha's mother tree was caging twilight. He came to a halt when he realized her branches were now bare. Squinting, he managed to make out a shape lying in a root hollow like a seed in a pod. Edging closer he first smelled then saw, in its green marbled face, that it was a corpse. He circled it; saw another, then another. Then he spotted one still hanging. His heart jumped when it moved. It was changing shape like a chrysalis erupting. Then it began to fall so that he almost cried out, but it halted, sagging, before reaching the ground and he saw that it was being held; saw it was Fern holding it. He was cutting down the dead.

A smaller shape rose from a crouch. Poppy. She wandered a little, then crouched again. Drawing closer, Carnelian saw she was straightening the body of a child that lay within a root hollow as if asleep. He was grateful the gloom did not allow him to see which one it was of the hearth's children. He watched Poppy's tender movements, unsure what to do, unable to speak. Already she had had to endure the massacre of her own tribe; now this. He wished he could see her face. Surely she must be aware of his presence. She rose. He reached out to touch her, but she pushed his fingers away. A chill spread over his chest. Did she hate him too? Then he felt a hesitant touch, a tiny squeeze, before she moved away to another corpse. The one Fern had been carrying was laid out on the ground. Already he was embracing another. Carnelian, determined to help, found an occupied hollow, crouched, then leaned forward into the sickening aura of decay, feeling for something he could grab hold of.

*   *   *

25

From the direction of the rootstair a figure emerged: Morunasa in his pale Oracle ashes. Carnelian reacted with instinctive outrage when Morunasa set foot upon the hearth's rootearth. The reality sank in of how terribly it had already been violated. He glanced round, expecting Fern to launch himself at the Maruli, but he was laying a body out along a hollow and seemed unaware of Morunasa's presence.

'The Master's sent me to bring you to him.'

That Fern showed no reaction to Morunasa's voice left Carnelian desolate. He would have preferred rage, violence, anything but passivity.

Following Morunasa away from the hearth, he noticed with some alarm a shape skulking. Too squat to be Marula, it could only be Krow. Carnelian did not want to believe that the youth had taken any part in the atrocity, but there was his bloodstained robe, his guilty looks, and so he said nothing as he passed him.

When they reached the stair, he gripped Morunasa's shoulder. As the Maruli came to a halt, Carnelian remembered that what caked the skin of an Oracle was the burnt remains of their human victims. He wiped his hand down his robe, then indicated Fern and Poppy. 'If they're harmed, I'll kill you.'

Morunasa shrugged, and resumed their journey to the Crag.

Osidian sat upon the floor of the Ancestor House that was a mosaic of the bones of Ochre grandmothers. Tiny fetal skulls grinned under his feet. Behind him crouched two Marula warriors with stone blades in their fists. Carnelian noted the shadow welling around Osidian's sunken eyes and at the corners of his thinned lips. His sweat-sheathed, pale skin was spotted with festering wounds. In the firelight, his grin flickered as the maggots inside him feasted: an infestation the Oracles claimed brought communion with their god and that made Osidian one of them. It was only his hunger to annihilate the Ochre that had drawn him from the Isle of Flies before the maggots had had time to pupate.

Morunasa's face showed fear and hatred as he gazed upon Osidian. Carnelian had already determined not to reveal the Maruli's betrayal.

'My Lord,' he said to Osidian and waited for him to focus a frown on him. 'We must cut down the dead.'

Osidian's frown deepened. 'The Ochre shall hang on their trees as a lesson to the other tribes.'

Carnelian grew cold with fear for Fern and Poppy and what he had left them doing. He must save them. Osidian must have chosen the mode of death deliberately, for he knew what Plainsmen believed. His intention was that no Ochre soul should find release through the proper rites, but, perhaps, there was a contradiction in Osidian's goals that could be exploited.

'What lesson do you intend the other tribes to learn, my Lord?'

Osidian grimaced. 'I would have thought that clear enough.'

'That they will be destroyed if they oppose you? You have gone to some lengths to justify this massacre in their eyes.'

'I merely administer the Law-that-must-be-obeyed.' Osidian regarded him balefully. 'It allows no exceptions.'

The implied threat struck Carnelian hard. Whatever transgressions against the Law of the Masters the Ochre might be guilty of, so were Poppy, Fern and all the other Plainsmen of Osidian's tribes. He focused on the moment. 'The Law demands only that they should die; it says nothing about how their bodies are to be disposed of. We have seen how they keep their enemies as huskmen, using them as guards . . .' He still had Osidian's attention. 'But eventually even they are released . . .'

The maggots were gnawing at Osidian's patience. 'I said, they will see them hanging.'

'You have summoned them?'

'They will be here tomorrow if they value their lives.'

'Then they will see your justice but, after, if you were to allow the proper funerary rites, you would only serve to force the lesson deeper by framing it in a show of respect for their ways.'

'When they come, I march north. There will be no time for burials.'

That statement seemed an unscalable wall. Then a way over occurred to Carnelian. 'Fern and I will do it.'

The labour required to save all the souls of his people must surely force Fern to put off any attempt at retribution. It would also provide them all with a channel down which to pour their grief.

Osidian sneered. 'Do you not feel already unclean enough? Besides, surely the barbarian would rather join his tribe in death.'

Fear for Fern overcame Carnelian's distress. 'Would it not be better to force him to live as a permanent reminder to the other tribes of the lesson that you have taught them?'

Osidian considered this a moment, then gave a slight nod. 'We shall let your barbarian boy live until he next defies us.'

The smile that followed showed how certain Osidian was that such a time would come. Carnelian could not let that go unchallenged. 'Do you really want to have his corpse join the others lying between you and me?'

Pain closed Osidian's eyes before he could respond. Carnelian had time to calm himself, to realize he did not want to throw away what he might have gained, but there was another anxiety he could not ignore. He waited for Osidian's attack to subside.

'You really believe you can stop Aurum's legion?'

The shadows in Osidian's face deepened. 'If that becomes necessary . . .'

At first Carnelian did not understand, could see no alternative, then he remembered that Aurum had been, with his

28

father Suth, the prime supporter of Osidian's election. 'You hope he might come over to you?'

'If he becomes convinced I have a chance to regain the Masks.'

Aurum had once before risked all on a not dissimilar gamble. Dread reared in Carnelian at the thought of Osidian in control of a legion. Horrors flashed through his mind, but from these a thought emerged. Possessed of such power, could Osidian resist striking directly at Osrakum before the Wise had a chance to muster a sufficient defence? With the Masters' focus shifted to the Guarded Land, the Plainsmen must surely become a peripheral concern. Then, perhaps, when the gaze of the Wise turned back towards the Earthsky, they might take more measured retribution.

Carnelian made his way back to the hearth nursing the hope that his plan would save Fern. The stench from the dead snuffed this out. He could bear the nausea better than their pendular swing among the creaking cedars.

When he reached Akaisha's rootearth, his eyes could not pierce the darkness beneath the cedar. He yearned for the light that once had radiated from the hearth; its warmth filtering out through the huddle of his hearthmates to welcome him. He remembered how it had illuminated the embracing branches of their mother tree like the rafters of his old room in the Hold. Anger rose in him. All such comforts were now dead. What remained to him was to make amends. He wanted to call out, but it felt to him that his voice would be a desecration. Was it possible Fern and Poppy were sleeping in their hollows among the corpses? Trusting to his feet, he crept forward. It was only when he became aware he was listening out for breathing that he realized this had always been an unconscious part of his navigation. Now the only human sound was his heart, louder even than the creak of the mother tree.

*   *   *

When at last he reached his hollow, he crouched and inched his hand into it. His fingers, touching flesh, recoiled.

'Carnie?' Poppy's terrified whisper.

He slipped in beside her. She clung to him and wept, but he could not weep with her, though he wanted to.

Floating, warm. Soft shapes kiss his outline. Liquid, lapping thick-tongued, coats his skin like honey. Reek of iron, taste of salt. Sinking, he flails. Strikes the logs of tiny limbs bloating sodden. His desperate fingers gouge into children's heads as soft as rotten melons, into tooth-rimmed holes, eye sockets. His grip slips free from slimy flesh. Gasping, he drinks, drowning in a surge of clotting blood.

He woke gulping. Cedar branches formed black veins against a fleshy sky. Render. He had been swimming in render. He remembered the briny soup of pygmy flesh the sartlar had kept in a hollow baobab. His tongue scoured the inside of his mouth anticipating the taste of blood. But in his dream they were children, not pygmies. It felt like an omen. He thought about the children Osidian had taken hostage from his vassal tribes. Morunasa had told him they were not here when he had come with Osidian. Then where were they? The answer was obvious and yet he was surprised. The Ochre had given them back in the hope of winning over the other tribes to their rebellion. Why should that surprise him? Because, like any other Master, he had assumed the Plainsmen incapable of strategy. His shame deepened. Had he helped bring about so much disaster because he had seen everything that was happening as a quarrel between him and Osidian, or as a game?

The dream still saturated his mind. The last time he had had such a nightmare was in the Upper Reach. He remembered a tree with strange, overripe fruit. He heard again the creaking of its burdened branches. Disbelief came with a certainty that that dream had predicted the massacre. Shock that he had not seen its warning gave way to disgust. A warning from where? From whom? A god? He felt polluted. Was he now going to allow himself to become as possessed by dreams as Osidian?

He became aware Poppy was gone. Sitting up, he saw the things occupying the hollows round him with their swollen purple faces veined with green and black: monstrous, familiar strangers. He rose into the aura of their putrefaction. Nauseous, he cast around for Poppy. A scraping was coming from beyond the trunk of the mother tree. He hurried to find someone else alive, but not fast enough to avoid recognizing Koney and Hirane with their greenish baby between them.

With a mattock, Fern was clawing at the black earth of the hearth, revealing red beneath. Poppy was crouched over a corpse. She turned up a blank face as Carnelian approached. He saw who it was she was rouging with ochre: Akaisha, her wrinkles stretched smooth by her ballooning cheeks and forehead. Her face had already been painted the colour of fresh blood. Her belly had a green cast as if she were pregnant with jade. Whin, near her, looked fat, though in life she had been so thin. Fern's wife Sil was there too, her beauty distorted in a net of purple-black veins, their daughter Leaf beside her, a discarded doll. All three had livid collars cut into the flesh of their necks and throats by the ubas that had been used to hang them. Carnelian's hand strayed up to the scar the slavers' ropes had left around his own neck. Osidian was similarly marked. That he might have chosen hanging because of what he himself had suffered numbed Carnelian with hatred.

He watched Fern gouging the earth. Each stroke tore a grunt from his throat. His eyes seemed stones. Carnelian knew where the mattocks were kept and fetched one. Returning, he leapt down into the hole with Fern and began to take out his rage on the earth. A shove threw him out of the hole onto the ground. Carnelian surged to his feet, but Fern's hopeless face cooled his anger. He watched the man who had been his friend return to his digging. 'These were my hearthmates too.'

31

Fern turned cold eyes on him. 'You're not the first to claim that.'

Carnelian struggled to understand what he meant. 'Krow?'

Fern snorted sour laughter. 'He came here claiming that my mother had sent me a message through him.'

Carnelian could make no sense of this.

'I asked him how it could be that, coming here with the Master, he'd had time to talk to my mother.'

Carnelian could not help glancing towards dead Akaisha.

Another snort from Fern, 'Yes, he helped murder her.'

'He told you this?'

'He didn't need to. Guilt reeked off him.'

Carnelian gazed at Fern, not knowing what to say.

'I told him that, once I've saved the souls of my kin, I'm going to kill him.' Fern's lips curled contemptuously. 'He ran away.' He raised his mattock, then brought it down murderously.

In the clear morning light, Carnelian remembered the hope he had had the night before. 'We must save the souls not only of your kin, but of all the Ochre.'

Fern lost the rhythm of his strokes.

'Please let me help.'

The mattock bit again into the red earth.

'Me too,' said Poppy.

Carnelian looked into her face and saw her need. His gaze caught on Akaisha's face, disfigured by the way she had died. She had become merely a thing. He felt the pain of grief rising and forced it down. Anything she might have said to Krow now had more of her in it than her body.

He put his arm around Poppy and drew her away. They stumbled towards the stair. Morning was revealing the grotesquely laden trees. Lime flames were lit along the branches. Drawn to the nearest, he saw it was a fresh young cone. It gave off a green fragrance that cut through the charnel air. It kindled a little hope in his heart.

Poppy grabbed his arm to draw his attention to her. He

looked down into her face so thinned with grief she seemed old. Misery threatened to imprison them. He stroked some of her hair from her mouth and asked her what Krow had said.

'Something about forgiveness.' She shook her head. 'I didn't hear it properly.' She glanced back at Fern and watched the mattock rise and fall. 'He didn't really listen to him.' Her eyes ignited. 'Why should he? Krow's clearly a murderer.'

Carnelian felt there was something unjust in her fierce anger. 'Whatever he did, the Master was behind it.'

She turned her fury on him. 'He could have said no. Even now he does the Master's bidding.' She must have sensed Carnelian's confusion because she added: 'He rides today to the Upper Reach.'

'He told you that?'

'He told Fern, when Fern threatened him.'

Carnelian felt suddenly an urgent need to hear what Akaisha had said. He glanced up at the sky. There might still be time to catch Krow.

Remembering his own expedition to the Upper Reach, Carnelian went to the Southgate. The Westgarden, still in the shadow of the Grove hill, had been turned into a camp. A smoky haze suggested that many fires had recently been dowsed. A few Marula warriors hunched here and there like boulders, but his gaze was drawn down the Southing to where another contingent of Marula were gathered at the Near Southbridge. Thinking this might have something to do with Krow, he set off towards them.

Several of the Marula came to meet him as he approached. He could feel their eyes on him, but any man he looked at turned away. At first he imagined it was that they thought him Osidian, whom they feared. Then he began to sense they were displaying not fear but shame. Their apparent leader was almost as tall as Carnelian, but more slender. The prominent ribs of his beaded corselet made him seem as if he were suffering from famine. His head was bowed. His fellows had drawn away from him. His fingers gripped his spear tighter. Carnelian stood for a moment, trying to work out his feelings towards the man. Pity perhaps. If that, why? Kinship? Carnelian's head jerked back in surprise. He remembered how he had helped teach these warriors how to form a wall of spears that was proof against mounted attack. These men had come up from their Lower Reach to fight for Osidian in obedience to one of their princes. Carnelian could feel the Grove with its atrocities staring at his back. These warriors had murdered his people, but had they had any choice except to do Osidian's bidding?

He regarded the man before him. 'Maruli.'

The man's handsome face came up. They looked at each other. Carnelian wanted to believe it was regret he could see in those bloodshot eyes. 'Where is Krow?' he asked in Vulgate.

The Maruli's brow creased. Carnelian remembered that they spoke no tongue but their own, but he also remembered that Krow, as one of Osidian's commanders, was known by the name of his tribe. 'Twostone?'

The Maruli gave half a nod, then raised a hand to point towards the earthbridge. Carnelian saw a commotion there. Marula with lowered spears were confronting a mass of angry Plainsmen.

He pushed into the back of the Marula hornwall, shoving men from his path, slapping their spears up. As he appeared on the bridge, the Plainsmen began falling to their knees. 'Keep that show of subservience for the Master.'

Confused, the Plainsmen rose and stumbled back across the bridge to let him cross. Looking into their faces he recognized they were Darkcloud; also, they were afraid of him. That cooled his anger, which really had been fear of more bloodshed. 'Who will tell me what's going on here?'

The Plainsmen looked at each other, then some youths stepped forward. Each had his face painted white to demonstrate his devotion to Osidian. 'We've come as the Master commanded,' said one, indicating the press of aquar and drag-cradles filling up the Southing almost to the Newditch. 'Twostone claims we're to set off immediately.' He indicated Krow, who was there among the older men. 'But we won't go anywhere until we hear this from the Master himself.' He pointed accusingly at the Marula. 'And they won't let us pass.' An angry murmur of agreement rose from the Darkcloud behind him.

Carnelian saw the need for answers on every face except Krow's. Their eyes met. Clearly the youth had told them nothing about the massacre. Carnelian wondered again what part Krow had played in that. Perhaps Krow had reason to fear their reaction. At the news they must surely experience the terror Osidian wanted them to, but also anger. They would not dare turn this against the Master. The Marula they hated already, but could do nothing about. But, if they suspected that one of their own had been involved, had turned against the people who had taken him in, who knew what they might do? Carnelian's heart leapt to Krow's defence.

He would satisfy the curiosity of the Plainsmen, but first there were some things he needed to know. 'Where are the hostage children?'

Glances of fear flitted among them.

'I only want to know they're safe.'

The youth who had spoken before spoke again: 'The Ochre gave them back, Master.'

It occurred to Carnelian that the Darkcloud, being an 'ally' tribe, had had no children hostage in the Koppie. 'How do you know this?'

The youth looked at his hands.

'They asked you to join their revolt, didn't they?'

The youth grimaced. He glanced at his fellows, seeking permission, then gave a slow nod. Wide-eyed, he gazed at Carnelian. 'But the Darkcloud sent them away. Every last one of us is loyal to the Master.'

35

Carnelian saw behind the youth how many heads were bowed. They were not telling the truth. He could well imagine the consternation the Ochre emissaries had produced. A desire for freedom would have set the old against the young, women against men. Ultimately, it would have been fear and uncertainty that had dictated their answer to the Ochre. How could they be sure the other tribes would rise with them and not leave them exposed to Osidian's wrath? Then there were the hatreds his conquests had sown among them. As one of the resented Ally tribes the position of the Darkcloud would have been particularly perilous. Carnelian found it hard to blame them. Osidian had had good reason to be confident that, when he marched against the Ochre, no other tribe would come to their aid.

'What does the smoke rising from every koppie across the Earthsky mean to you?'

The white-faced youth looked at Carnelian as if trying to find out what answer he wanted. He gave up. 'Our old people claim, Master, it means the Standing Dead have invaded the Earthsky.'

Carnelian nodded heavily. It was confirmation of what he had hoped they would deny. No doubt this too had played a part in their decision not to join the Ochre. It was time to tell them about the massacre. As he described what had happened, he watched blood drain from their faces.

The youth's eyes were popping. 'All of them?'

'All save Fern, Twostone Poppy . . . and Twostone Krow.'

Deliberately, Carnelian did not turn, but everyone else did, to stare at Krow.

After hearing his news, the Darkcloud were only too glad to flee the Koppie. Carnelian left them to make their preparations while he took Krow aside. The youth would not return his gaze. Carnelian felt no anger towards him, only sad disappointment. 'Akaisha gave you words for Fern?'

Krow glanced up. 'And for you.'

Carnelian heard that with a jolt.

'She called you sister's son.'

Carnelian squinted against tears.

'She committed Fern into your care.'

Krow's voice was as empty of emotion as his face. Carnelian felt the same confusion he had among the Marula. Anger rose in him that he was being denied the release of straightforward hatred. 'What else did she say?'

Krow's brows knitted. 'What she could . . .'

Carnelian could hear in Krow's voice how close to her death she must have been when she had spoken to him.

'Tell me it as she told it to you.'

Krow regarded him, as if he was having difficulty remembering. '"Should you wish to atone for the part you've played in the destruction of the Tribe, then save my son, care for him, protect him from his bitterness, from his lust for revenge."'

'You told Fern this?'

Krow nodded.

Carnelian sensed that the youth had more to say. He waited. Krow seemed to consider something, then decide against it.

'Was there more?' Carnelian asked at last.

Krow shook his head.

Carnelian resisted his urge to judge him. Krow was not the first Plainsman Osidian had corrupted. Carnelian gazed out, seeking some solace in the emerald plain, in the vast blue dome of the sky. 'Why do you go to the Upper Reach?'

'To fetch the salt stored there from the sartlar.'

Their eyes met. Both had grim memories of the place. He thought of asking Krow why he still chose to serve the Master, but decided against it. That might provoke a confession Carnelian was in no position to handle well.

He took his leave, then walked back through the Darkcloud towards the Marula-guarded bridge. Krow's mention of the sartlar had plunged him back into his render nightmare.

*   *   *

37

A smell like burning hair grew stronger as Carnelian approached the hearth. Poppy was standing with her back to him. When he had come close enough, he saw she was looking down into the graves Fern had dug. Women so red they seemed freshly peeled nestled among the snake roots of the mother tree. Fern was gently scooping earth over Koney as if he was washing her. Carnelian felt he was intruding on private intimacy. A thin current of smoke was curling up from a curve of horn charring in some embers: hornblack for the corpses of the men. He returned to watching Fern. He had to prepare him for the coming of the vassal tribes. 'The Master's levies are coming here on their way north.'

'North?' Poppy said.

Her expression of bafflement confused him, until he realized with shock he had not told them of the invasion. It was so deeply branded in his mind, he had assumed everyone knew. He explained to Poppy the meaning of the smoke columns they had seen as they rode towards the Koppie from the Upper Reach.

Poppy gaped. 'Dragons, coming here?'

Carnelian wanted to confess to her this was the reason he had spared Osidian's life, but his eyes were drawn to Fern, who was stroking earth over Koney's face. She sank from sight like the pygmy in the render. Carnelian's confusion became distress.

'Why?' Poppy said.

'Aurum,' said Carnelian, still trying to resolve his feelings.

He felt stupid gazing at Poppy's incomprehension. He could not remember the name the Plainsmen gave him. He shaped the Master's cypher with his hand. 'Hookfork.'

Blood drained from Poppy's face. 'Hookfork?'

It had a cruel sound when she said it. She was seeing something in her mind. 'I grew up fearing him.' Her sight returned. She saw Carnelian. 'Long ago it was he who came with fire to make us slaves. A ravener in a man's shape.'

Grimly, Carnelian considered that. 'As are all the Standing Dead, but still, he's just a man like me.'

Poppy looked incredulous.

'Really. I knew him. He's an old man.'

'A kindly one, no doubt,' said Fern, whom grief seemed to have made old too. 'Is this all you came to say?'

Carnelian hesitated.

Fern frowned.

'The Master means to display the Tribe as a lesson to the others.'

With a trembling hand, Fern returned to scooping earth, cold fury in his eyes.

When the charred horn had cooled enough, Fern began crumbling it into a bowl, then ground it with a mortar. As Carnelian watched him, he listened to the rumble of aquar moving along the Homing. It seemed that the procession of riders would never end.

Earlier, leaving Fern burying his women, Carnelian had climbed to the Crag summit and watched Osidian's vassals arriving from the south and east. Marula at the Outditch bridges had dammed their flood until they had been forced to spill into the ferngardens. At Osidian's command, the Marula had retired with him to the Poisoned Field and the Plainsmen had flowed into the Grove. Seeing how numerous was Osidian's host, Carnelian had begun to believe it possible Aurum could be defeated. He had also reached another, grimmer conclusion: if all had joined the Ochre in revolt, Osidian and his Marula would have been overwhelmed.

Carnelian had returned to Akaisha's mother tree fearing Fern's reaction to this further desecration, all those strangers staring up into the hearths of his tribe, gawping at his people hanging like meat, but Fern had just continued labouring on the rituals, apparently oblivious.

He was now adding fat to the bowl to make a black paste. Carnelian watched him carry the bowl to where the males of their hearth were laid out naked on blankets. Carefully, Fern began to daub his brother Ravan black; the colour of the Skyfather's rain-filled sky. This scene made Carnelian recall another, seemingly so long ago it might have been merely the memory of a dream, when Fern's father and uncle had been laid out similarly. From the moment Fern had set eyes upon Carnelian, his kin had begun to die. None now were left.

Carnelian gazed down the slope and caught glimpses of the riders and aquar rumbling by. Turning back, he edged closer to Fern. The desire to help him was an ache in his chest, but he dare not break his trance, not until Osidian and his host were gone.

Fern did not pause when he was done; he leaned his shoulder into his brother's corpse, working it onto his back. He rose, unsteady under the bloated burden, then staggered off to the rootstair and began climbing it towards the Crag.

'He goes to expose him,' Poppy whispered and Carnelian gave a nod. Itching to help, his hands squeezed each other. Hard as it had been to watch Fern work, it was worse being left there with no distraction but the swing of corpses hanging from the other mother trees. Carnelian crouched over the bowl of hornblack. Its acrid smell was a clean relief from the miasma of decay that clung to the whole hillside.

'I'll be back . . .' Poppy said, then was off after Fern.

Carnelian gazed at the hornblack, trying to work out how Fern might react if he were to return to find him blackening the dead. He looked towards the mother tree and thought how much he now loathed her shade with its aura of death. A patter of feet made him turn to see Poppy running towards him. The look on her face made him run to meet her. She grabbed hold of him, tears smearing the dirt on her face. 'He can't do it . . .'

'Can't do what?'

But she was shaking her head, too distressed to make sense. They rushed up to the clearing under the Ancestor House. Carnelian saw Ravan's corpse draped over the lower steps.

40

Seeing Fern prostrate, his shoulders shuddering, Carnelian ran up to him, reached out, but could not bring himself to touch him, to comfort him. 'I'll take his legs, you take his arms.'

Fern fumbled under Ravan's head, lifting it so that Carnelian could not help looking upon the bloated face, twisted in its death grimace. Black tears had formed in the corners of the sunken eyes. They struggled up the steps. So close, the stench was overpowering. Sick with horror and grief, he longed to reach out to Fern, but he did not know how.

DRAGONS

The terror from a weapon diminishes in proportion
with its use.
(a precept of the Wise of the Domain Legions)

They tended the dead one hearth at a time. Akaisha's was
first, then those that lay in the eastern, upwind part of the
Grove, so that at least they might sleep free of the waft of
putrefaction. Days merging one into another, they worked
their way round the hearths that lined the Blooding and
towards the Southing.

At each hearth, Fern cut down the women first, laying them
out for Poppy to ochre as best she could. Carnelian dug graves
among the roots. The men were next. They made hornblack
overnight. While Poppy applied this, Carnelian and Fern
would carry the corpse she had already blackened up to the
Crag. Dead, the men were heavier than they had been living.
They seemed huge waterskins that they had to wrestle with as
they released foul gas or dribbled slime down their arms and
chests and legs. Though lighter burdens, the boys were heavier
on the heart. When the funerary trestles were piled high, they
laid the corpses on naked rock. The place became submerged
beneath the frenzied wings of scavengers. At first the dead
were picked clean, but with so much carrion, only the choicest
morsels were consumed. The summit became a brown mesh of

bones and tendons, frayed-lipped smiles, skin turned to curling leather by the sun.

There was no spare water in the cistern with which to wash and Osidian had seen fit to maroon them without aquar to fetch more. Their skins became so grimed with putrid matter they began to look and smell like the corpses. The charnel stench tainted everything. They took to sleeping as far apart as possible.

Their work grew harder as the corpses began slipping off their skin. There came a time when Poppy had no need to make the women red. Later, all the dead turned greenish-black and they stopped making hornblack. Ritual faded. Laments ran dry in their throats. By the end, corpses with living eyes, they laboured mindless in a new Isle of Flies Osidian had consecrated for his Marula god with his holocaust.

Osidian's face, burial black. Pits for eyes. The tree burning. Her screaming is the flames, is the branches piercing him like spears. He falls before the swelter of her approach. Ebeny aflame, wild-eyed, masked with blood. No, it is Akaisha mouthing words, her hair, flames beaded with iron. Bloated ochre face mouthing words he cannot, will not hear. Horror of her corpse breath. Her dead lips kiss him, suck him into her. Struggling against her fiery walls squeezing him to blood.

Carnelian woke transfixed by the moon. Osidian dead in the dream, the fire; both seemed omens of defeat. Plainsmen against dragons: he could hear again the mocking laughter of the men who had served in the legions. Such futile defiance would only provoke Aurum's terrible retribution. Only the Wise could have given him a legion. Why else but because they wanted Osidian, alive so that he could accuse his mother. Carnelian was another witness to her crime. The bright stare of the moon possessed him. Cypher of the Wise. The same cool clarity that characterized their thought. Left to them, just enough would be done to restore order in the

43

Earthsky and nothing more. Aurum was the real danger.

The moon was as colourless as the Marula salt Krow was bringing from the Upper Reach. If such a treasure were to fall into Plainsman hands they would cease to provide military service to the Masters. That the Wise would not allow. Greed for its possession would enflame the tribes to wars amongst themselves. It had to be destroyed. But what of the mine it came from?

As his nostrils filled with the reek of death, Carnelian felt his resolve fraying. Who was he to find a way through such a labyrinth? Merely another victim of the forces he had helped unleash.

The corpse they were lugging up to the summit of the Crag was so putrid they had had to wrap it in a blanket to keep it intact. The blanket was soaked through with the fluids weeping from the decomposing flesh. Carnelian and Fern struggled up the last step onto the summit and paused, panting through ubas wound several times over mouth and nose. The glare squeezed their eyes to slits. Ravens hopped, screeching, among the charnel heaps. Even through the layers of cloth the stench was overpowering. They dragged the corpse with a bandy-legged waddle to avoid treading in the dark trail it oozed over the brown-crusted rock. When they found a space they gripped the blanket edge then rolled the corpse free. They averted their eyes, but could still feel the sodden release of weight; were still enveloped in the aura released by its moist collapse. Carnelian let go the blanket as dry retching racked him like a cough. Ravens rushed in to fight over this new feast. Flies eddied like smoke. The dream had stripped his mind of the dullness that had protected him. Under the repeated stabbings of their beaks the corpse was releasing its rot-soft meat. Jet eyes blinked their beads at the root of gore-clotted plumage.

He tore free of that horrid fascination and sent his gaze soaring up into the clean sky. That blue so pure above the corruption of the world restored him to his centre. When he returned his gaze to earth he looked south and west, searching for Krow. That morning he had been doing that every time he came up to the summit. Fernland spread to incandescent lagoons. Acacias, spaced like the towers of the overseers in the Guarded Land, danced languidly in the haze. The only other movement was the slight creeping of the herds along the edge of the lagoons. He saw Fern was gazing northwards and sought the focus of his attention. Carnelian's heart leapt. Riders. The omen of his dream, of his conjectures overwhelmed him with dread. 'Plainsmen . . .' he murmured.

'Marula,' said Fern in a flat tone, looking as if he was barely managing to stay on his feet.

Carnelian almost asked him how he knew, before seeing for himself that they lacked the easy grace of Plainsman riders. Too few to be a rout, they had to be bringing a message from Osidian. If this were verbal, then most likely it would be Morunasa who was the messenger. It was strange that the thought it might be this man he loathed should kindle hope. What would Fern do? Turning, Carnelian saw he was moving away, crouched, towards the steps, dragging the blanket after him. He followed him. Reaching the edge he watched him descend. When Fern reached the clearing below, he turned west. Carnelian sighed relief. They had just carried the last of Mossie's hearth up and the next one they had meant to clear was further down the Westing. It seemed that Fern was intent on ignoring the visitors. If Poppy remained with him, Carnelian might have a chance to tackle Morunasa alone.

He quit the shade to cross the earthbridge. The withering heat was preferable to the region he had just come through. Being the furthest from Akaisha's tree, they had left the Northing and Sorrowing hearths for last. The cedars there were still laden with dead. The air choked with flies.

Unwinding his uba he breathed deep, not caring about the

scorch of the clean air, his gaze fixed on the riders ambling up the Northing in the shade of its magnolias. As they drew closer he could see by the indigo robes that most of them were Oracles. Their leader pulled the cloth down from his nose and mouth.

'We must have water.'

The voice was so hoarse, the face so gaunt, that Carnelian did not at first recognize it was Morunasa.

Ribbons of light writhed up the Crag rock when they pulled back the cistern cover. Morunasa was the first to drink. He downed one bowl and then another, exposing his sharpened teeth in a grimace of relief. He handed the bowl to one of his fellows and looked off among the trees. 'This place feels something like our sacred grove.'

As they had climbed the rootstair from where they had left the aquar and Morunasa's warrior escort, Carnelian had noticed with what frowns of recognition the Oracles had regarded the corpses and the swarming flies.

Morunasa looked at him. 'And you have the look . . . and odour of an offering to our Lord.'

Carnelian glanced down at his body encrusted with filth, but it was the awe in Morunasa's face that made him feel most polluted.

'Perhaps our God has followed us here,' Morunasa said, voicing one of Carnelian's fears.

Another Oracle, reaching awkwardly for the bowl, winced as his sleeves slid down his arms revealing seared flesh, crusted and weeping. Morunasa saw what Carnelian was looking at. 'Dragonfire.'

Turning, Carnelian almost believed he could see flames reflecting in Morunasa's eyes. Dread seeped into him. 'Defeat then?'

'Hookfork invited the Master to negotiate, then betrayed the truce. Many were lost to the firestorm as we covered his escape.'

Remote from Morunasa's voice, Carnelian stood stunned by an outcome even worse than any he had feared. 'How many dead?'

Morunasa's eyes burned. 'Among the Flatlanders?'

'I know the Marula are mortal too.'

Morunasa's glare softened. 'The Flatlanders suffered worse.'

'He's protecting the Marula?'

Morunasa snorted. 'Not from love.'

Carnelian understood. 'He believes you are more fully under his control.'

Morunasa nodded. 'The Flatlanders now have one worse to fear than him.'

'But they still follow him?'

'He persuaded them they must delay the dragons to give their people a chance to get away.'

'Away where?'

'To the mountains.'

'So early in the year? Madness!' Though the heavener hunts Osidian had organized might have provided enough food for the journey, it was still impossible. 'The raveners . . .' he said, feeling revulsion at the idea of exposing so many people to the fernland before the predators had gone east. Day after day as naked prey. Night after night manning rings of fire against the monsters. 'Madness,' he said again. 'They don't even have the aquar they would need to pull the drag-cradles.'

'The tribes will set off once their men return.'

Migration across a land still prowled by raveners with Aurum pursuing them. The image of the old Master torching ants caused dread to rise in Carnelian. Who could survive the coming holocaust? He forced himself to consider what else Morunasa had said. 'Delay? How?'

The Oracle frowned. 'We skirmish with them, encourage them to attempt envelopment, then break out before the dragons can come in to finish us.'

Carnelian began to understand their stooping, their dull eyes. How many times must they have come close to

47

annihilation? The image of Akaisha and Ebeny burning. Cedars lit like torches. Holocaust. He strove to focus his mind. Despair was an indulgence he must not give way to. Aurum was not the only threat. Osidian would have a plan to have his power survive this debacle. What part might these migrations play in his schemes? Carnelian tried to find some hope in the possibility of the tribes fleeing to the mountains, but what was there to stop Aurum pursuing them with fire? The Withering perhaps? Even a legion could not hope to endure such waterless heat. Yes, the Withering might drive Aurum back to the Guarded Land. What then?

Carnelian focused on Morunasa. 'Why've you come?'

'When the salt arrives here from the Upper Reach, he's commanded that you take it to the koppie of the Bluedancing.'

So that was it. Osidian wanted to safeguard the treasure with which he might recruit more Plainsmen. He would fight on until the Earthsky was a lifeless desert. He must be stopped.

Carnelian knew that in what was to come Morunasa could well be pivotal. 'And what's to happen to your people?'

The Oracle considered his answer. 'Our warriors still follow the Master, but this land can no longer be saved.'

But the Upper Reach could be. Carnelian considered whether Morunasa might be hoping to persuade Osidian to retreat there with the Marula. Isolated in the Isle of Flies, Morunasa could hope to overthrow him. Then Morunasa would be free to re-establish the Oracles' cruel dominion over the Lower Reach. Carnelian was not happy about that, but he had to do what he could, not attempt to save the whole world.

Morunasa dipped another bowl into the cistern. 'I've done as he bade me.' He drank another draught, then declared he must return to the Master.

'How many days before the dragons reach here?' Carnelian asked.

Morunasa shrugged. 'Two at most. More easily might he seek to stop the Rains than their advance.'

48

They carried some of the precious water down to the aquar and the warriors. As they drank, greedily, they squinted at the incandescent plain. Most likely, the anxiety in their faces had less to do with returning to the withering heat than with returning to the battlefront.

Watching Morunasa, Carnelian strove to devise some way he might use an alliance with him to help the Plainsmen. Though he and Morunasa might conspire against Osidian, this would not protect the tribes from Aurum, who would soon be in their midst. Fern and Poppy might be saved. He reached out to touch Morunasa's shoulder. The Oracle glanced at Carnelian's hand in surprise.

'Leave me some aquar.'

Morunasa raised an eyebrow. His gaze unfocused then sharpened again. 'I'll leave you one.'

'Leave me two . . . please.'

Something like a smile played over Morunasa's lips. 'I can spare only one.'

He barked a command at one of the Marula warriors. The man glanced at Carnelian, then gave a nod. Morunasa and the rest climbed into their saddle-chairs. Their aquar rose and they began filing through the Northgate. One by one they sped away, pulsing bright and dark as they coursed through the magnolia shadows.

Carnelian regarded the man Morunasa had left behind. He peered along the Homing in the direction in which it was likely Fern and Poppy were working. He would have to go and talk to them. How would they react to the presence of one of the murderers of the Tribe? He had worse news for them. A holocaust was bearing down on them he could see no way to deflect and all he might suggest they could do was to destroy the salt. Beyond that, his only hope now, however thin, was that somehow he could restore the subjugation of the Plainsmen to the Masters.

The Maruli was sneaking glances up the hill at the hanging

dead. He looked distressed. Perhaps it was unjust to hold him responsible for the massacre. What choice had he had, but to obey the Oracles and Osidian? Carnelian caught the man's attention and, together, they set off with the aquar ambling after them.

Poppy stared down at the Maruli standing where Carnelian had left him on the Homing. Mattock in hand, Fern regarded the man with cold malice. Trying to head off a dangerous confrontation Carnelian spoke quickly. 'Morunasa left him here because I asked for an aquar. Whatever he may have done, remember that he's little more than the Master's slave.'

Fern turned on Carnelian, raising the stone blade of his mattock, snarling. 'If he comes anywhere near one of my people I'll kill him.'

Carnelian was relieved Fern was venting his rage through words rather than action. 'I've something to tell you.'

Fern climbed out of the grave he had been digging and advanced on Carnelian. 'What? That Morunasa's come with commands from the Master?'

Carnelian eyed the raised mattock then looked at Poppy. 'Please, Poppy, go to the hearth. I need to talk to Fern alone.'

Holding him with a glare, the girl shook her grimy head. Carnelian saw the lump of ochre like clotted blood in her hand and how gore sheathed her arms. What was he trying to protect her from? He sat on the ground. 'Let's talk then.'

Poppy's eyes softened and she too sank to the ground. Fern lowered the mattock, but remained standing. Carnelian began by admitting that Morunasa had come with instructions from Osidian '. . . to safeguard the salt Krow's bringing from the Upper Reach.'

Poppy struck the ground with her ochre. 'Even now he does whatever the Master tells him.'

Carnelian looked from her face to Fern's. 'The Master's been defeated. He flees before the dragons. They're coming here.'

He watched them pale beneath their masks of filth. With the back of her hand Poppy stirred the cedar needles she had ochred. Fern let his mattock slide to the earth, his gaze rising blind up into the canopy. Carnelian went on to explain what he thought Osidian wanted with the salt and felt guilty relief as he spilled his worry out. 'And so we must do what we can to destroy it.'

Fern impaled him with his dark eyes. 'What does that matter when the Standing Dead are going to turn everything to ash?'

'What does Hookfork want with us?' Poppy said, her childish distress making Carnelian feel he had been wrong after all to let her stay.

'He wants the Master.'

'Why?'

Carnelian could not deny the plea in her eyes. 'Because Hookfork seeks to use the Master against the God in the Mountain.'

Fern's face twisted and he let out a groan. 'I don't understand. How . . . ?'

Preparing to answer that, Carnelian felt how deep had been his betrayal of these people whom he loved. 'Because he's the brother of the God in the Mountain who, treacherously, set himself up in his place.'

The mattock toppled to the ground. Fern sank down open-mouthed. Poppy simply stared. Carnelian watched as the truth of it slowly sank in. Shock turned to agony as Fern realized the part he had played in bringing Osidian and Carnelian into the Earthsky. Carnelian could not let him bear this alone. He reached out, but did not feel he could touch him. 'It was my fault. I kept this from you. I never imagined it would come to this. I was blind. I've always been blind.' The enormity of his failure made his words run dry.

They sat like boulders until Poppy spoke. 'So we must give Hookfork what he wants and then he'll go away.'

As Carnelian nodded, a cold expression came over Fern's face. 'We'll give him a mutilated corpse.'

Carnelian grimaced. 'Dead, the Master's a blunted weapon.'

He tried to explain the politics of Osrakum, but, sitting there amid the rotting dead, even to him it was all incomprehensible. He ended up assuring them that, if Osidian returned to Osrakum, he would be unable to escape the rituals requiring his death. 'And this might turn the eyes of the Standing Dead away from the Earthsky.'

Silence fell again as they all stared blindly, tortured by guilt, by regrets, by grief. Carnelian, sickened, knew he must tell them the rest of it. He did not want to, but it was such weakness that had brought them there. He tried again to find a way round it, but the certainty of Aurum's retribution was as solid as the massacre surrounding him. 'Most likely this will not save the Master's tribes.'

Poppy stabbed him with a look of pure horror. 'Why not?'

Carnelian cast around for some way to make it clear. 'Because Hookfork's at least as cruel as the Master. He'll see the defiance of the Plainsmen as an affront to his pride. He'll feel . . .' Corpse stench was the air they breathed. 'As the Master did here he'll feel the need to avenge the insult to the Standing Dead of your familiarity with him . . . with us.'

He bowed his head. He thought of telling them the Wise might yet restrict Aurum's retribution, but he was sick of peddling false hope. He recoiled as Poppy touched his arm. The look of love in her face released his tears. 'I don't deserve . . .'

She gripped his arm. 'They won't leave you with us, will they?'

He wanted to tell her that Osidian would reveal to Aurum that he was here, that if he returned to Osrakum he could accuse Ykoriana and Molochite, that he would strive to curb Aurum's holocaust, but, ultimately, all he did was shake his head. He wiped his eyes. 'The most that can be done is to

52

bring what's left of the tribes back into submission to the Standing Dead.'

Poppy squeezed his arm. 'Is that why you want to destroy the salt, Carnie?'

He nodded. 'Otherwise who'd go into service in the legions?'

'How do we take the Master alive?'

Carnelian looked at her, then at Fern who was scowling, kneading one foot. 'With Morunasa's help.'

Poppy's mouth became a line and Fern's scowl deepened. She gave a slight nod. 'And the salt?'

'Krow's our best hope there.'

Poppy looked surprised. 'You really think he'll help us?'

'I don't know, but I believe his heart's not the Master's.' Carnelian gazed at Fern, so still, so quiet. 'Though it would be a grim and thankless task, you could play an important part in bringing the tribes back into submission.'

Fern raised his eyes. 'You really believe they'd listen to me, who brought this plague among them?'

Carnelian felt Fern's anguish like a knife. 'You've atoned for whatever mistakes you might have made. None will gainsay this. Your voice will be free from tribal dependence and will carry weight because of your undeniable loss.'

A wind came from the east and stirred the mother trees to murmuring.

Poppy looked distraught. 'Carnie, is there really no way at all you can see how we might avoid more deaths?'

Desolate, Carnelian shook his head. 'No way at all.'

Hollow-eyed, they struggled to complete the burials. The Maruli stayed away from them. Carnelian noticed him, as did Poppy, but if Fern did he gave no sign. It would have made sense to have the man help them, but no one had forgotten Fern's threat.

When darkness forced them to stop they returned, weary, to Akaisha's hearth. It was Carnelian's turn to make the stew.

The evening was growing cold and they huddled round the fire for warmth. Stirring the pot, Carnelian had noticed the Maruli creep up the rootstair where he had been crouched for some time. He felt sorry for him. When the stew was done, Carnelian gave a bowl of it to Poppy and one to Fern, then rose with another cradled in his hands.

'Where're you going?' demanded Fern.

Carnelian indicated the man sitting on the rootstair. 'Since I'm sure he's not welcome at our fire I'm going to give him something to warm him up.'

He did not wait for more, but took the bowl to the Maruli. The man looked up as he approached. His grin was bright as he accepted the bowl. He put it down carefully then turned back and ran his finger twice across his brow. Carnelian did not understand. The man repeated the action. The Maruli was making the sign for ten. Carnelian had daubed numbers on the foreheads of Marula to help train them to fight in horn-walls. He nodded, smiling, and struck himself on the chest. 'Carnie.' He pointed at the man with a questioning nod. The Maruli frowned, then grinned and, placing his hand on his beaded corselet, uttered a syllable.

'Sthax,' echoed Carnelian as best he could.

'Carnie,' the man said and both smiled.

Carnelian returned to the fire to find Fern gone, his bowl on the ground untouched.

Looking miserable, Poppy pointed up towards the Crag.

He found him on the summit: a man shaped from the same darkness as the night. Approaching, he became aware of the focus of Fern's stillness. Carnelian looked out into the blackness. A sky alive with stars overlay the earth's void. He watched, puzzled, but then there was a flicker along the northern horizon. Then another. Dragonfire!

He turned to peer at Fern. His profile was clear enough. Carnelian quelled an impulse to embrace him.

Fern shifted. 'Tomorrow we have to finish.'

Carnelian lingered after Fern left, gazing north, brooding over what was coming their way.

Just before dawn, Carnelian and Fern went to gauge how much was left to be done. Fully three hearths remained. The stinking, rotting masses hanging seemed never to have been people. Both would have liked to walk away. The thought of touching them was unbearable. They returned to their hearth and discussed it with Poppy over breakfast.

'We've never managed more than two hearths in one day,' she said.

Grimly Fern nodded.

'Will you allow the Maruli at least to dig?' Carnelian asked. Both he and Poppy waited anxiously until Fern gave another nod.

As dusk fell what remained of the women of the last hearth lay beneath its earth. Its men laid out in a row had yet to be carried up to the Crag. Fern wanted to keep going, but Carnelian and Poppy would not let him, saying it would be better to finish the work the following morning once they were rested.

When Carnelian took food to Sthax Fern said nothing, but continued to eat his own. Later Carnelian, Fern and Poppy went up to the summit of the Crag. The north remained dark until the moon rose. They made their way to their hollows by its light.

The next day Poppy called down to them when they reached the Crag steps. Looking up, they saw her arms waving against the blue sky. For more than half the morning she had sat as a lookout among the ravens, the flies, the mouldering dead. Carnelian and Fern left the corpse they had been carrying, wrapped in its blanket, and ran up the steps.

Poppy greeted them, wide-eyed. 'Dust.'

They followed her along the path they had cleared among

55

the bones, hunched against the storm of ravens their rush disturbed into the air. She pointed. There, in the north, was a rolling front of dust.

'Saurians?' Carnelian asked.

Squinting, Fern did not answer. Carnelian and Poppy waited, then saw him slowly shake his head.

'If it's a herd it's one larger than any I've ever seen before. Not even heaveners could raise so much dust. Besides, they're coming straight at us.'

Carnelian looked again, his heart pounding. He was too inexperienced to see what Fern was seeing.

'Dragons?' asked Poppy breathlessly.

Fern shook his head again. 'I don't know. I've never seen dragons moving in the Earthsky.'

Carnelian bowed his head. The time to act had come. He looked at Fern. 'How long before they get here?'

'Well before dusk.'

Carnelian looked into the south-west as he had done every time he had come up to the summit that day.

'Are you looking for Krow?' Poppy asked.

Carnelian was about to answer, when he saw a slight disturbance to the west. He grabbed Fern and pulled him round. He stabbed his finger. 'There.'

Fern shaded his eyes with his hand. Carnelian peered but, through the melting air, he could not really be sure there was anything there. 'Well?'

Fern shrugged. 'Could be.'

'It's in the direction of the Darkcloud koppie.'

'Yes,' said Fern. 'It could be drag-cradles.'

Carnelian looked back north. That could only be Aurum and Osidian bringing a storm that would soon break upon the Koppie. West, it was not so clear, but if it was Krow Carnelian knew there was his best chance of stopping the salt from reaching the Koppie.

'If I leave now I could get there and back before the dragons get here.' This was more a question than a statement.

56

Fern looked horrified. 'I can't bring the rest of the dead up here by myself.'

Carnelian grimaced.

'I could help,' said Poppy, a determined look in her eye.

'Even if you had the strength,' said Fern, 'it's not woman's work.'

Glancing west again Carnelian was more and more certain there were riders there. 'Sthax can help you.' Then, seeing Fern's puzzlement: 'The Maruli.'

Fern scowled.

'At this moment I'm more concerned with the living than the dead. If you want to save these last few souls you'll allow Sthax to help you.'

The need to get going overwhelmed Carnelian. Without waiting for an answer, he made for the steps.

The moment he reached the shade of the first mother tree Carnelian freed his face from his uba and breathed deep. After the summit the cedar perfume was so fresh it brought tears to his eyes. As he made his way down the Sorrowing he gazed about him as if he were seeing the Grove for the last time.

Sthax was sitting on a root step. When he heard Carnelian approach he rose, grinning. Carnelian pointed insistently back up towards the Crag. Carnelian watched him climb the root-stair, then ran down to the Childsgate where they had tethered the aquar.

She was there, sunk to the ground, snoozing in the shade. Climbing into her saddle-chair, he made her rise and rode her round to the Southgate. Soon they were coursing down the Southing. When they reached the Newditch, Carnelian glanced back to the Crag, then sent her speeding westwards across the open plain.

There were enough aquar pulling drag-cradles for them to have flattened a road through the ferns. The shape of their saddle-chairs was characteristically Darkcloud and it was Krow riding up in front. They raced forward to meet Carnelian, giving him no time to examine their convoy.

Krow gave a grim nod as he approached. 'Master.'

The Darkcloud round him were less restrained in their greeting. Looking among them Carnelian was pleased to see men he knew and greeted those he did by name, lighting smiles among them.

Noses wrinkled, eyes registered the staining on Carnelian's robes and skin. He had become so accustomed to being filthy he had not considered the impression he would give. Horror and disgust had spread to all their faces.

'I've been working with Ochre Fern and Twostone Poppy to save the souls of the Ochre.' Their looks of compassion made him feel a kinship with them, but there was no time to linger on that. 'The Master's been defeated.'

The Plainsmen gaped, staring, but it was Krow who erupted towards him. 'You lie!'

Carnelian drew back in surprise. 'I assure you, Krow, it's true. Even now he flees before the dragons.' He pointed north.

'Our people have seen dragonfire on the horizon,' said one of the Darkcloud. Several more declared they must return home immediately. Krow was gazing northwards, his face sagging with utter disbelief.

Carnelian raised himself up in his saddle-chair. 'You'll not save your people by hiding in your koppie.'

Their fear turned to anger and they challenged him. In answer he pointed at the drag-cradles. 'First of all you must destroy that salt.'

Outrage turned them into a mob. He shouted them down. 'Listen to me.'

One of their leaders swung his arm back to take in the cradles. 'You'd have us destroy such a vast treasure?'

'It belongs to us all,' cried one.

'We've bought it with our blood,' said another.

58

Their leader bared his teeth. 'We'll take it as our reward for serving the Master.'

Carnelian fought his own rising anger. 'To our shame we've all served the Master.' He could not help glancing back at Krow, who had subsided into his chair. He looked as many of the Darkcloud in the eyes as he could. 'I'm as guilty as any here, but now I say to you it's over. Whatever ambitions the Master put in your hearts, let them go. It's clear for all to see that everything he promised you is turning to dust. Your only hope now is to return to the way things were.'

'To be slaves to the Standing Dead?'

Carnelian fixed the speaker with a glare. 'Do you really believe you've ever been anything else?'

The contempt in his voice cooled their defiance. He pointed at the salt again. 'If you keep that for yourselves, you will earn the envy and hatred of the other tribes. If you share it with them, you might avoid strife for a while, but, ask yourselves, would you or your sons then willingly go into the legions to earn the Gods' salt? If not, how long do you think it would be before the Standing Dead came to find out why you no longer chose to serve them?'

Consternation broke out again, but Carnelian sensed their anger was really fear.

'Let's say we destroy the salt, what then? Would we be protected from those dragons?' Their leader indicated the approaching dust-cloud.

Carnelian had no answer. Even if they managed to give up Osidian, alive, would Aurum return to the Guarded Land without inflicting retribution? Carnelian remembered how much Aurum liked to enforce the Law. All Osidian's tribes had seen him and Carnelian without masks. Just for that the penalty was death.

His doubt was infecting the Plainsmen. He looked to Krow, but there was no help there. Before he knew it he was saying: 'I have a plan that might save you all.'

Their faces lit with hope, but Carnelian, needing time to think, looked away down the convoy. 'First I must see how much salt you've brought.'

He rode his aquar down the flank of the column. There were hundreds of drag-cradles, heavily laden. Overwhelming wealth. Notions of using it himself flitted through his mind. How else was he to make good on his promise to them? How could he save them from Aurum?

Coming to the end of the convoy, he saw its rump, creatures on foot. A mass of matted hair and misshapen bodies clad in verminous rags. Sartlar. Distaste rose in him like bile. His render dream came back to him as he recalled with disgust how they had turned pygmies into broth then fed on them.

He walked his aquar back up the column, the taste of the dream in his mouth. He eyed Aurum's dust-cloud. They were running out of time. He almost cried out as an idea began forming in his mind. It was a narrow, dangerous path, but it might just be a way to salvation. There was no time to analyse it. The leaders of the Darkcloud were waiting for him, Krow among them.

'First we must save the people who are fleeing with the Master before the dragons.'

His certainty stiffened spines. Even Krow became alert.

He gazed towards the Koppie. Osidian would not have told him to send the salt to the Bluedancing koppie unless he thought it safe from Aurum. He had an inkling why that might be true and, for the moment, he would have to build his own plan upon Osidian's.

He looked back at the Darkcloud. 'We'll convene a council of war in the koppie of the Bluedancing.'

Men shifted uneasily, gauging each other's reaction with sidelong glances.

'Will you trust me?'

Many still looked unconvinced.

Krow rode forward, grim, haunted. 'When this Master

led you before didn't he help you save your koppie from the Marula?'

They looked to their leaders, who looked at each other. First one then another began nodding. There was not time for Carnelian to feel triumphant. 'The salt first. We need the drag-cradles cleared to evacuate your people from your koppie.'

Not giving them time to think further he rode back along the convoy and was relieved when they followed him. Everywhere Darkcloud were throwing off the protective blankets to reveal the sparkling white slabs stacked beneath. Carnelian could sense how great was their reluctance to destroy such wealth. 'Unhitch the drag-cradles,' he cried.

He allowed Krow to overtake him. 'Thank you.'

Krow shrugged.

'Will you ride with me?'

Krow nodded.

'Well, then, choose forty of the bravest from among those who least fear the Master.'

Krow jerked a nod then rode away. Carnelian gave his attention to instilling confidence in the Darkcloud leaders. Soon they were bellowing orders. At first the Plainsmen lifted the slabs with care. After the first shattered among the meshing fernroots, more followed. Soon their work of destruction took on a fury of its own. Crystals flashed in the air so that the men in the midst of the destruction seemed to be splashing about in water as they ground shards to powder with their heels. Aquar, lifting heads crowned with startled eye-plumes, shied away from the mayhem.

Carnelian rode back towards the sartlar. As he approached they collapsed to the ground grovelling. This added to his disgust. 'Kor?'

One of the shapeless mounds rose. The hag's disfigured face slipped free of her mane. He had forgotten how fearfully ugly she was. 'Will your people be able to keep up with the riders?'

She bowed her head. 'Master.'

61

He took that for a yes. Pity overcame his loathing. He wondered why Krow had brought the sartlar from the Upper Reach. It seemed unlikely any would survive what was to come.

Hubbub rushed through the convoy towards him. Looking up, he saw everyone gazing towards the Koppie. Smoke was rising from the Crag. Fear clutched him. It was a signal from Fern. He sped back across a frost of salt to the Darkcloud leaders.

'Send messengers to all the tribes. All must do what they can for their own protection, then send representatives to a council of war to be held tonight in the koppie of the Bluedancing. Get your own people there with all the djada and water they can gather. If they stay at home, they'll be trapped between the Backbone and the dragons.'

When he was sure they understood, Carnelian joined Krow and the men he had picked and, with two riderless aquar, led them at full pelt towards the Koppie.

Smoke rising from the Koppie made Carnelian recall the plague sign on his ride to Osrakum. Ravens disturbed by it swarmed the Crag like flies. He saw his dread mirrored on the faces of the Plainsmen round him. All could see these omens of death.

It was past midday when they reached the Newditch. Fern's signal had frayed away on the breeze. The ravens had settled once more to their feasting. Carnelian led the Darkcloud up the Southing. When they neared the Southgate bridge they saw two figures, Fern and Poppy, waiting for them. Sthax gleamed behind them in the gloom under the cedars.

The Darkcloud regarded Fern as if he were a living corpse. One bowed his head. 'May we set foot upon your earth, Ochre Fern?'

Fern gave his leave then turned troubled eyes on Carnelian. 'Marula approach the Koppie, Plainsmen covering their retreat. Auxiliaries pursue them closely and . . . dragons.'

'Any sign of the Master?' Carnelian asked.

'A small group is coming up the Sorrowing.'

Carnelian prayed this would be Osidian with his Oracles. Morunasa was sure to be with him and might be their best hope of taking Osidian without a fight. He turned in his saddle-chair and scanned the grim faces of the Darkcloud. 'We must take the Master alive.'

Colour drained from their faces. Krow looked sick.

'If he escapes, the dragons will lay waste to every koppie many days' ride in all directions. If we manage to get his body, the same. Only if we have him living can we hope to survive. Will you help me?'

The Darkcloud looked to their leaders who, after exchanging glances, reluctantly gave Carnelian their support.

'And you, Krow?'

Chewing his lip the youth gave a nod. Fern stood forward, eyes blazing. 'I'll have nothing to do with this murderer.'

Krow withered under Fern's glare. Carnelian saw with what horror the Darkcloud turned to regard the youth. He had mixed feelings, but owed him a debt. 'Krow, will you take Poppy with you down to the Old Bloodwood Tree and watch over her?'

Poppy began a protest that Carnelian silenced with a look. 'Please, Krow.'

He felt a burst of relief as the youth rode up to Poppy, leaning to offer her his hand. Frowning she took hold of it and he swung her up to sit on his lap. Carnelian asked a couple of Darkcloud to go with them, then, after Fern and Sthax were mounted on the aquar he had brought for them, he led them and the remaining Darkcloud round the Homing to the Childsgate, where they all dismounted. As he directed them to conceal themselves in the shadows Carnelian noticed how the Darkcloud stole furtive glances up the hill, how they whispered to each other, how they trod the carpet of cedar needles as if they were afraid to wake the women lying among the roots of their mother trees.

Through the wicker of the Childsgate Carnelian could see riders coming towards them across the Poisoned Field. He drew back to join Fern and Sthax, then glanced round to make sure the Darkcloud were ready. The gate swung open, flooding light into the Grove that flashed and darkened as several aquar rode through. Quickly Carnelian recognized the leading rider by his frame to be Osidian, who was squinting, still blind in the gloom. Carnelian gestured for the Darkcloud to surround the riders, all Oracles. Stepping to block Osidian's path he pulled his uba down from his mouth.

'Carnelian?' Osidian, wrinkling his nose, made Carnelian aware of how filthy he must look. 'Has Krow arrived with the salt?'

'Where's Morunasa?'

'With the Marula.'

Carnelian had counted on him being with Osidian. What now?

Osidian was frowning. 'There's no time for this. Aurum's almost upon us.' His eyes darted as he became aware of the encircling Darkcloud. He grew enraged. 'Get back, Plainsmen, unless you want my wrath to fall upon your kin.'

Carnelian saw the Darkcloud were wavering but, before he could act, Fern was there, thrusting a spear point to within a hand's breadth of Osidian's face. Osidian started a little then turned upon Carnelian. 'Call off your barbarian boy,' he said in chilling Quya.

The spear point, finding Osidian's throat, scratched blood when he swatted it away.

'Another sound and you die, Master,' hissed Fern through clenched teeth.

Sthax stepped forward with frantic eyes. Carnelian spoke to the Maruli in a soothing tone. When he was sure the man would not interfere, he turned back to Fern. He saw the lust in his face for Osidian's death. 'Fern, we need him alive.' He made a hurried decision. Raising his hand he indicated three of the Darkcloud leaders to remain, then, in a low voice, he told the rest to mount up and take the Oracles back through the gate. The Oracles looked to Osidian for guidance, but Darkcloud spears herded them out of the Grove.

Carnelian was aware of Fern as he addressed Osidian. 'I've destroyed the salt. It's over.'

Osidian's eyes became hooded. 'More treachery, Carnelian?'

Carnelian mastered a burst of anger before he replied. 'I'm only doing what I should've done long ago. If I had, perhaps the Tribe would still be living.'

He turned to Fern. 'Please, Fern, think of what there is to lose.'

Fern clenched his spear tighter, but backed away enough to allow Carnelian to approach Osidian. Close up his skin looked sallow, moist.

'Do you still have the worms in you?' he asked in Quya.

When Osidian looked down at him, Carnelian saw that his eyes were rimmed with shadow. In spite of everything that had happened he did not like seeing him like that. Osidian grinned and his teeth seemed yellow. 'It is not too high a price to speak to a god.'

Carnelian glanced at the three Darkcloud then at Fern. 'I'm going to have to leave the Master in your care.'

As Fern's face crumpled, Carnelian wondered if Osidian would be safe with his friend, but knew he had no choice. 'Be certain, Osidian, that, if you vex him, Fern and these others *will* slay you.'

Osidian seemed not to have heard. His eyes had lost their fire and it was as if he was no longer there. Carnelian did not trust that. He reached up to Osidian's aquar, ready to make it sink should he try to escape. He waited until Fern and the Darkcloud had mounted before signing Sthax to mount. Only then did he himself clamber into his saddle-chair.

'Where're you going?' Fern demanded as Carnelian's aquar rose.

'To persuade Morunasa to save the Plainsmen.'

Fern grimaced. 'What?'

Carnelian did not have time to explain. He made his aquar turn.

'I'll come with you,' cried Fern.

Carnelian looked back. 'I *really* need you to keep the Master safe.'

He saw Fern understood: even weakened as the Master was the Darkcloud might not be able to resist his power of command. When Sthax rode through the gate, Carnelian and his aquar slipped into the light after him.

Their aquar churned ash up from the Poisoned Field as they sped across it and down the Sorrowing. As he crossed the Near Sorrowbridge, he saw a wall of smoke ahead. Rising higher than the Koppie's outer ring of trees, it was approaching like a sandstorm. His feet sent his aquar loping towards it. Soon he was riding parallel to Sthax, then with the Darkcloud, the Oracles in their midst. The faces he could see were stiff with fear. He rode on, watching the smoke fumbling towards them through the trees.

Acrid air caught at their throats as they crossed the last earthbridge out onto the fernland. Behind the billowing mass of smoke rolling towards them lurked mountainous shadows. Carnelian was shocked to find that Aurum had already arrived. Then he was startled when something resembling an arc of lightning came alive behind the veil. A screaming followed, like metal shearing; shrill, unbearable.

Squinting, he searched for Morunasa's Marula. At the foot of the smoke wall a tide of them was mounding towards him in full flight. Just behind the Marula, partially obscured by haze, he saw Osidian's Plainsmen. In close pursuit, a crescent of riders was extending its horns out on either flank: knowing

Osidian had entered the Koppie, Aurum was attempting to encircle it with his auxiliaries.

Looking round, Carnelian saw the Darkcloud, wide-eyed, gaping. He shouted at them, but they seemed deaf. He rode his aquar into their midst, bellowing: 'If you want your people to survive, reach the other tribes.' He pointed at the Plainsmen hurtling towards them. 'Get as many of them as you can to the Bluedancing.'

Some nodded, confused, then in twos and threes they sped off until only the Oracles were left, and Sthax, who was hunched, uneasy in the presence of his masters. Carnelian gestured for him to follow, then sent his aquar like an arrow towards the oncoming Marula. Sthax was soon riding alongside, a crazed grimace on his face. Glancing back, Carnelian saw the Oracles chasing them. He and they were all flying on the wings of a rising gale that was bending the ferns towards Aurum's approaching storm. Thunder grumbled in the earth. Another arc of fire flashed into life, wavering as it slid its flame across the fernland, setting it alight; then, even as its screaming reached them, it sputtered and vanished.

Soon the Marula fleeing towards them were close enough for Carnelian to see their rictus grins. He searched and found, at their heart, the ashen faces of more Oracles. Hurtling towards this core he was aware of the Marula warriors crashing past on either side.

'Morunasa,' he cried, but his voice was snatched away by the gale.

Morunasa's Oracles were almost upon him. He slowed his aquar, spun her round, then made her run back the way he had come, letting Morunasa's Oracles overtake him. Soon when he looked to either side he could see their ashen faces, their yellow eyes wide with terror. He sensed a shape close on his left shoulder. Glancing round, he expected to see Sthax, but it was Morunasa, ravener teeth lining his gape as he shouted something. Carnelian waited until Morunasa had pulled abreast, then leaned across. 'The Master's my prisoner.'

Morunasa shook his head, indicating his ears, then slowed his beast and Carnelian followed suit. They came to a halt together as Marula hurtled past them.

'The Master's my prisoner,' Carnelian shouted. 'Help me and I'll help you get back your Upper Reach.'

Morunasa regarded him with wild eyes. 'What do you want me to do?'

'Take them into the Koppie.'

Morunasa jerked a nod then whipped his aquar off at furious speed. Carnelian looked for Sthax, but he was gone. He sent his aquar after Morunasa's in swift pursuit. The sky was darkening, the ground shaking so violently dust was rising up from the earth. Suddenly his shadow was cast stark in front of him. He felt a burning at his back. He turned, squinting against the glare. A column of fire brighter than the sun was gaining on him. Its scream raped his ears as the fire shuddered away. He gaped slack-jawed as a monster emerged from the murk. It was bearing down on him like a great ship. Horns curved up like ivory figureheads. A leprous tower rose from its back, tapering in tiers, rigged, with a mast that thrust a standard like a sail up into the blackening sky. Another high whining scream shocked Carnelian out of his trance. His hand jerked up to shield his eyes from the fire-flash. Through his fingers he could see more arcing liquid-flame carve glowing curves across the ground. Then the scene was lost in sulphurous billows of smoke. Its black wave rolled over him. He was choking. Coughing, he wiped away stinging tears. His aquar lost the rhythm of her stride. He peered at where they were heading. The Newditch magnolias were rushing up. Riders were leaping the ditch like fish. He gritted his teeth. His aquar leapt. They were in the air, the ditch beneath them. Then she landed with a thump that rattled his skull and they were coursing across the ferngarden with the others. A whine chased him. Almost beyond hearing, its pitch slid down to a fearful shrieking. There was a whoosh, then roar. A wall of heat slammed into him. Turning his cheek into it, eyes welling, he saw the magnolias burning fiercely as they had in his dream.

COUNCIL OF WAR

Enough bees can kill a ravener.
(a precept of the Plainsmen)

As he tore across the ferngardens, leaping two more ditches, Carnelian was relieved to put the Grove between him and the dragons. He caught up with Morunasa in the Southgarden.

'Where's the Master?' cried the Oracle.

'Marshal your warriors. We'll need them to punch a hole through the encirclement.'

Morunasa gauged Carnelian, then swung round in his saddle-chair spitting out instructions in his own language. His Oracles raced away, riding hard to overtake the Marula flight.

He turned back. 'Where?'

Carnelian could feel no thunder in the ground. The dragons must be circling the Koppie to cut them off. He sent his aquar past Morunasa, heading for the Old Bloodwood Tree. They leapt another ditch and careered into a body of riders crammed around the tree. Carnelian urged his aquar towards Fern's. Osidian was there, guarded by Darkcloud. His crazed eyes drilled past Carnelian. 'Morunasa, destroy these unbelievers.'

Carnelian's hand, reaching for his spear, relaxed when he

saw Morunasa shaking his head. 'No, Master. Now I must do what I can to save my people.'

Carnelian addressed Osidian. 'It's not in your interests to impede us further. Even now Aurum is throwing his forces around us to capture you.'

Osidian's head dropped to his chest. Carnelian looked around him. Faces were tight with terror, but he was sure they would obey him. He managed a smile for Poppy sitting with Krow. 'We must go.'

Fern shook his head. 'I'm staying.'

Carnelian took in all the Darkcloud with a glare. 'If the Master's taken your tribe'll be burned alive.' Then to Morunasa: 'Get them through the auxiliaries. Now go!'

Poppy began a protest, but Krow carried them both off after Morunasa and the others as they sped off down the Blooding.

Carnelian knew this delay might hazard his whole plan. He had to get away. 'Fern, come with me. Your mother didn't want you to throw your life away. Live for her.'

Fern's face darkened. 'How dare you quote my—'

At that moment a whining scream drew their eyes towards the Grove. Hissing, the mother trees were leafed with flames. Fern's mouth fell open as he stared, frozen by horror. Carnelian freed his spear and with its haft struck Fern's aquar into motion. Then kicking his own he took the lead and was relieved when the other followed him.

Hurtling down the Blooding Carnelian could see, on the plain, the horns of the auxiliaries' encirclement coming together. Osidian's Plainsmen were a fleeing rabble already beyond their grasp. The Marula looked in better order, but would soon be overtaken by the auxiliaries. He and Fern dodged through the slaughterhouse chaos of the Killing Field. As they reached open fernland, Carnelian was glad to see that Fern seemed more composed. Both saw the Marula slowing, even as the auxiliary encirclement closed ahead of them. Their ranks opened to absorb Osidian and the Darkcloud. Carnelian and Fern coaxed even more speed out of their aquar. Soon there were Marula all around them, every eye focused on the auxiliary line thickening ahead. When the Marula let forth a battlecry, Carnelian joined his voice to theirs. Aquar added their screeching to the tumult. Their charge struck the auxiliaries with a detonation that reverberated through the ground. Their intersection frothed like a breaking wave. Then the auxiliary wall broke and he and the Marula washed through. More auxiliaries crashed into their flanks as the enveloping curve melted into pursuit. Carnelian was losing hope of escape, when trumpets screamed from behind them. He looked round and saw the auxiliaries slowing, disengaging, veering away, but his cry of triumph caught in his throat as he saw that the Grove had become the roots of a tower of smoke that might have been the Marula god rising up in wrath from the earth.

Flattened ferns formed a road that led them to the Bluedancing's outer ditch. Several earthbridges spanned it but of these all but one had collapsed. Carnelian rode across and found himself in a ferngarden similarly trampled. It was larger than any of the Ochre outer gardens. He grew uneasy at the eerie quiet, at how tall the ferns had grown, at the saplings sprung up everywhere. Glancing round, he saw the earthbridge was funnelling the Marula. He did not wait for them all to cross, but rode towards the next ditch with Osidian and his Darkcloud escort, Fern and Morunasa, Krow and Poppy and some Oracles in their wake.

The edges of the next ditch had crumbled. The earth on the other side had been gouged by many claws. Carnelian was reassured. Those fresh red wounds showed that many aquar had crossed there today. At least some of the tribes must have come at his summons.

He jumped his aquar across then scrambled up the other side. A trail led off through another large ferngarden. At its further end rose the hill that was the koppie's heart. Though it was not as lofty as the Ochre's it was wider, its crags spreading as a cliff. What lay beneath surprised him. Though the grove canopy was patchy, it seemed that its mother trees had survived Osidian's arson.

Figures were descending steps from the edge of the grove. He wanted to talk to them and to climb the crags to reassure himself Aurum was not pursuing them.

The steps turned out to be stones set into an earthbridge that curved up to the cedar hill. The ditch it crossed had been cut into the side of the slope and not at its foot. The figures coming down to meet them were Plainsmen.

'Where're your commanders?' Carnelian asked.

They looked at each other, perhaps not understanding Vulgate. One turned to point up at the crags. Carnelian nodded. It made sense that their leaders were up there keeping a lookout. Dismounting, he kept a careful eye on the Plainsmen, who were staring at Osidian being helped out of his saddle-chair. It was reassuring to see the Darkcloud form a cordon round him. Even stooped, Osidian towered in their midst. Carnelian was thankful Osidian was so weakened by his infestation. Others were dismounting, including Morunasa, Krow and Poppy. He followed her glance of concern to Fern, who was still aloft.

'Poppy?'

When she looked at him Carnelian made a gesture and she nodded. Approaching Fern's aquar she stroked its neck to make it kneel, then coaxed Fern to climb out.

Carnelian spoke Osidian's name and, when he raised his head to look, Carnelian indicated the steps with his spear. 'If you would please go first, my Lord.'

Expressionless, Osidian advanced, the Darkcloud around him. The Plainsmen on the steps drew aside, fearfully, watching him ascend. Carnelian asked Morunasa to leave word that the Marula should make their camp before the steps, then followed Osidian.

Two ancient cedars stood guard upon the entrance to the grove. Both had been maimed by fire. Bark was charcoaled up to a great height, and in places had burned away deep enough to expose the heartwood. Some of these scars reached high enough that branches had withered. Those that survived bore needles, but in brushes that hung lopsidedly.

As they climbed a grand rootstair, Carnelian saw with what haunted eyes the Darkcloud and his Plainsman friends looked around them. Ferns had invaded the hearths where the Bluedancing had eaten and talked, had shared their lives. They swamped the hollows in which they had slept, made love. The canopy above was too ragged to keep out the sky. Mutilated, the mother trees could not reach each other to plug the gaps. Carnelian could feel their anguish and the wrath they were drawing up from the earth where their daughters lay. Peering along the rootstairs and paths that split off from the one they climbed, he saw how much bigger this grove was than that of the Ochre. It gave a measure to what had been done when the Bluedancing had been destroyed. Though driven to this crime by Osidian, it was the Ochre who had set the fires. Carnelian saw Fern taking in the destruction and wondered if his friend was feeling that it was for this sin that the Mother had allowed his tribe to suffer such terrible retribution.

The Ancestor House of the Bluedancing seemed a bone boat run aground upon the crags. The flight of steps that climbed to it divided and swept up on either side towards the summit. Carnelian bowed his head as he climbed, feeling the presence of the ancestors weighing down on him. As he passed their House he dared to peer at its ivory traceries, at the buttresses of femurs that anchored it to the rock.

It was a relief to come up into the sky. He breathed deep, seeking to free his heart from despair. Voices made him turn to see Plainsmen hurrying across the rock towards Osidian. Carnelian moved to intercept them. Their whitened faces betrayed them as Osidian's acolytes. They were gaudy with the salt trinkets with which he had seduced them. Carnelian held his spear horizontal in front of him to bar their way. Craning round him to see Osidian, they spoke all at once. Carnelian gleaned enough of what they were saying to answer them. 'It was I who summoned you.'

They fell silent, staring at him. 'At the Master's command?' said one.

Carnelian shook his head slowly. More consternation broke out, but he ignored it. Smoke was rising in the north from the Koppie. Enraged, he silenced their clamour with a glare. Some started to kneel. 'I'll speak when all the tribes have assembled here and not before nightfall.'

Some were brave enough to threaten leaving. Seeing their fear of him, he felt compassion for them. That must have softened his expression for they relaxed a little.

'All must combine their strength if that,' he pointed to the Koppie, 'is not to be the fate for all your homes.'

Defiance left them as they looked upon the Ochre pyre.

'Please go now and set your men to gathering fernwood. We'll meet in council here and will need a good fire to warm us against the coming night.'

Like everyone else Osidian sat upon the summit gazing at the Koppie burning. Carnelian searched his face, looking for satisfaction, anger, a glimpse of cunning, but found nothing. All he saw was Osidian's beauty marred by defeat and the pain and sickness caused by the maggots burrowing in his flesh.

He rose and went to crouch beside Poppy. Grime from the burials grained her skin. She looked up at him. 'Can you really save them from that?'

Though he wanted to take away the fear in her eyes, the most he could say was: 'I hope so.'

She gave him a pale smile then turned her gaze back to the Koppie. Sitting near her, Krow shot him a grim look to which

75

Carnelian responded with a nod before going off to sit beside Fern.

He had chosen a promontory away from the others. His gaze was fixed, sightless, on his burning home. The creases of grief in his face deepened Carnelian's misery. He longed to comfort him, but did not know how. Touch would not reach Fern, nor words. At that moment Fern turned to look at him, tearful as he shook his head. Carnelian's own grief welled up. He understood what Fern's eyes were telling him. Whatever they had had, or could have had, was gone. The dead stood between them like a wall.

Carnelian walked around the rim of the summit on the lookout for more Plainsmen on the plain below, but could see none. He was having to pick his way around funerary trestles bearing bones so sun-bleached they resembled carved limestone. It seemed a sterile imitation of the stinking mess they had left behind in the Koppie. The Koppie. Its dying exerted a horrid fascination over him. He had stood watching past the point where he could bear it. Even now that he had managed to tear free he felt its pull. It was as if the heart of the world was failing.

He was sure he now knew how Osidian had intended to cover his flight with the Marula, picking the salt up on the way. Osidian had coaxed Aurum to the Koppie and offered it up with his Plainsmen as a sacrifice. Osidian had made certain Aurum was aware the Koppie was the centre of his power. From the tattooed hands of the Plainsman veterans he had killed, the old Master would have already learned the names of the tribes defying him. He would know he had now reached within striking distance of their homes. Torching the Koppie was a warning for all to see. Aurum would now make camp in their midst, send messengers with threats and rely on the Plainsmen to bring him Osidian alive. Such methods came naturally to all Masters.

Loathing for Osidian, for Aurum seeped into Carnelian,

swelling into hatred of all the Masters, chief amongst them himself. He and they were responsible for this misery, these atrocities. The Masters were a curse, a cancer that had fed off the world for millennia. Desperate fantasies possessed him that he might find a way to cut out their disease.

Suddenly, Poppy leapt to her feet. Others joined her. Aurum's legion was swarming out from the Koppie like ants fleeing a burning nest. Carnelian watched, heart pounding. Was his reasoning flawed? If Aurum came for them now, all was lost. Across the summit, people were turning to look at him. It was Morunasa who spoke. 'Do we flee?'

Carnelian knew he must hold firm. 'Hookfork moves towards the lagoons. He intends to make a camp and will need water for his host.'

His words appeared to soothe many, but Morunasa, for one, did not seem convinced. As the legion crept across the plain, Carnelian watched, affecting unconcern. Shadows were stretching east when it became clear that Aurum was indeed heading for the lagoons. Carnelian's relief was soured by the realization that Aurum's camp would be sited on the shore where the Ochre had been accustomed to fetch their water.

Plainsman fires formed constellations in the ferngardens, but were a poor imitation of the stars. Carnelian was only intermittently aware of the scuffling and muted voices behind him as the representatives of the tribes came up onto the summit. What he intended to say to them might lead him back to Osrakum, back to his father and the rest of his lost family. It felt like a betrayal that, for so long, they should have been so far from his thoughts. The pattern of lights below resembled any one of so many of the stopping places he had seen from the watch-towers on his way to the election. He was reminded also of when he had stood with his father upon a spur of rock high in the Pillar of Heaven surveying the tributaries gathering on the Plain of Thrones. Both seemed more fairytale than memory.

He gazed north as if his sight might pierce the night all the way to Osrakum. It was the glimmering wheelmap of Aurum's camp that caught his eye. Three concentric rings inscribed into the earth by the ditches Aurum's dragons had ploughed into the fernland. The outer, bright with the fires of the auxiliaries, enclosed a dimmer ring where the dragons formed a wall around a flickering hub. That flicker showed where Aurum and his Lesser Chosen commanders no doubt were enjoying the exquisite pleasures they could not deprive themselves of even on campaign.

The citrine splendour of that camp contrasted with the murky smoulder of the Koppie that appeared, strangely, the same size, so that the two seemed to form a pair of unmatched eyes. The Koppie too was a wheelmap in form. Osidian had been right: in that design the Plainsmen aped the Chosen, but it seemed clear to Carnelian now that it was not a wheelmap, but rather military camps they copied. It saddened him that the Plainsmen had shaped their homes in imitation of the military mechanisms of their oppressors. The thought awoke his longing to free them, instead of which he was going to urge them to return to slavery.

The bonfire roaring behind him was spilling his shadow over the summit edge. He turned to face it and at first could see nothing but its great circle and, for a moment, stood again before his father's hearth in the Hold. That its light must be clearly visible from Aurum's camp thrilled him with fierce defiance. Approaching the flames, he began to be able to see the people gathered round it. Plainsmen, mostly legionary veterans, no doubt chosen by their men because they spoke Vulgate; others were youths, many with white-painted faces that shone too brightly. Here and there he saw some wrinkled faces, ears flaccid without their gleaming ear spools, chests bare without the pectorals; those salt treasures now bedecked the young. As his gaze touched each of these ancients, he gave a nod of respect and was warmed by their cautious smiles. He completed the circuit near him, with Poppy's grim face, and

Fern staring blindly, Osidian at his side, head bowed. Some vestige of the love he had had for Osidian disturbed him, but he crushed it. A part of him yearned for death for them both.

'This fire will bring Hookfork here,' a voice accused.

Carnelian looked for its owner, but could not find him. 'Would you prefer he went to an inhabited koppie? The Ochre dead on the summit of their Crag will confirm what Hookfork already guessed: that their koppie was the centre of the Master's rebellion.' He regarded Osidian with contempt. 'For in that atrocity he will recognize the unmistakable handiwork of one of the Standing Dead.' He scanned their faces. 'Hookfork torched the Koppie of the Ochre as an object lesson. Tomorrow he'll proceed to terrorize the neighbouring koppies.'

A man stood forward. 'Though my tribe feels deep sympathy, how does that concern us? Our koppie's far away and safe.'

Carnelian walked round the fire towards the man, who stepped back, fearful. 'You're sure of that?'

As the man stared back at him Carnelian leaned closer. 'Tell me, have any veterans from your tribe fallen to Hookfork's assaults?'

The man pushed out his chest. 'We've fought as bravely as any here.'

'I don't question that. Did you recover their bodies?'

The man looked uncertain. 'Most of them. Why?'

'Most, but not all? Then Hookfork knows exactly where your koppie lies.' He surveyed the gathering. 'He knows where all your koppies lie.'

'Who betrayed us?' many voices cried out.

'Your dead,' Carnelian said, stoking up their consternation. He returned to the man he had been speaking to. 'Give me your hand.' When the man hesitated, Carnelian reached down and grabbed it. Twisting it open he strove to decipher the service tattoo on his palm. 'The Fireferns.'

The man plucked his hand back, aghast. Carnelian moved

79

round the line grabbing hands, calling out the name of the tribe inscribed on each. Terror spread as men stared at their palms.

Carnelian waited until they had begun to look up. 'I believe I know a way in which you can save all your tribes.'

The hope that lit in many faces struck him in the heart. He could not bear quenching it, but he had to. 'First you must understand something,' he said, gently. A ripple of unease spread around the fire. 'Things will have to return to the way they were.' Fear haunted their eyes. 'You'll have to resume the sending of your children to the Mountain.' He felt their anger rising. 'Surely you must know in your hearts that the great hunts are over for ever? Surely you see that you must return to hunting as your fathers have done or else starve?'

There were some protests, but Carnelian chose to ignore them. 'Your young men *must* return into service in the legions.'

Protest swelled, among which clearly could be heard the phrase: 'Marula salt.'

'I destroyed it all,' Carnelian cried. His words released a gale of shock and disbelief that he bellowed over. 'Even if it hadn't caused strife among you, you must earn your salt in the legions. The Standing Dead would not permit anything else. Surely you can see that? But there's another reason . . .'

As their noise abated, Carnelian pointed at Osidian, who might have been carved salt. 'I couldn't let *him* get his hands on it. With it he could do to other tribes what he's done to you.'

Several men stepped forward. 'We wouldn't have let him.'

'How could you stop him when he made sure to bring the dragons here to destroy you?'

They stared at Osidian, horror turning in some throats to howling rage. 'Kill him,' cried one and was echoed by many others.

Carnelian retreated to stand before Osidian, shielding him

with his body. 'This you must not do,' he bellowed. 'Hookfork must have him alive.'

Krow appeared from the crowd. 'How will that help?'

The youth's fury took Carnelian by surprise. Eyes flaming, Krow advanced on Osidian, listing his crimes, his betrayals, his lies. Osidian, smiling coldly, froze Krow to silence. The youth stared, shaking his head. 'He can't, he mustn't escape our vengeance.'

Carnelian felt a strange kinship to the youth in his distress. 'Krow,' he said, to get his attention, 'I promise you that, if the Master's given to Hookfork, he will die. The Law of the Standing Dead demands it.'

Tears in Krow's eyes had put out their fire. 'I don't understand.'

'Because he's the reason Hookfork is here.'

Krow grimaced, unfocused, lost. Carnelian stood back. 'He is the brother of the God in the Mountain, who hates him.'

Fernwood cracked and sparked in the flames as the Plainsmen gaped, blinking, at Osidian. Murmurous fear began moving among them. Some glanced around, seeking confirmation of Carnelian's claims. Others, who tried to laugh it off, soon fell silent. Osidian's white-faced lieutenants cowered. Carnelian saw they were, after all, only youths whom Osidian had corrupted and he felt sorry for them.

An old woman fixed Carnelian with bleak eyes. 'Then we must give him up.'

'And me with him, my mother,' Carnelian said.

Poppy, gazing at him, looked miserable.

'But that won't be enough. You've rebelled against the Standing Dead. You've looked upon our faces. Either of these sins on their own would provide Hookfork with a pretext to destroy you all.'

He let the horror sink in before he spoke further. 'There may still be a chance to avert total disaster.' Their looks of hope made him pause to re-examine his plan. Could it possibly work? It had to. 'We must draw Hookfork away into the north.

Only then must you give us to him, as close as possible to the Leper Valleys.'

Their frowns demanded an explanation. 'I believe Hookfork will be so greedy to return to the Mountain with his prize that he'll not bother returning here.'

The old woman's frown refused to smooth. 'What if he leaves some of his dragons behind?'

Carnelian saw in his mind's eye the broth Kor and her sartlar had made from the pygmies. 'What is every man, aquar and dragon of a legion fed on? Render. Hookfork's stretched an umbilical cord of its supply all the way from the Guarded Land. Cut that cord and all his forces must retreat. Further, by consuming the render ourselves we'll have no need to deplete the migration djada of the tribes.'

'And what of the Marula, Master?' Morunasa asked.

Carnelian gazed at the Oracle. He and his fellows with their grey faces had sat so quietly he had forgotten them. He glanced at Fern. This part he had not cleared with him because he knew he must put the needs of the Plainsmen before his friend's feelings.

Sthax came unbidden into his mind as he turned back to Morunasa and the other Oracles. Carnelian could think of no way to neutralize their threat except by returning Sthax and all the rest of the Marula warriors into their power. 'You'll take them back with you to the Upper Reach?'

Morunasa bared his ravener teeth. 'You know perfectly well they'll only serve the Master.'

'Disband them. With salt you'll be able to recruit enough Plainsmen to hold the Upper Reach.'

Krow pushed forward, grinning unpleasantly. 'Oh no. They won't be doing that. I cut down the ladder trees.'

Morunasa fixed the youth with such a staring look of horror that it stirred a commotion among the other Oracles.

Plainsmen were crying out. 'Both ladders?'

Krow looked crazed. 'I had the sartlar do it then dig the roots up so there would be no anchors for new ones.'

Carnelian sensed Osidian had deliberately chosen the Darkcloud to accompany Krow. Of all the tribes they had most reason to hate the Marula. 'You did this at the Master's command?'

Krow gave a gleeful nod. 'Now my tribe, the Twostone, is avenged, Maruli,' he said to Morunasa. He looked towards Fern and became only a sad boy. 'The Ochre too.'

Fern sprang at Krow, who fell near enough to the fire to raise a jet of sparks. Fern stood over him. 'Do you really imagine this will clean my kin's blood from your filthy hands?'

Krow stared up at him, petrified. Only when Fern turned away from him did he roll over. As he rose, people moved out of his way as if he were a leper. Carnelian watched the youth slink off and felt regret he had not intervened.

Fern closed on Morunasa, thrusting his face towards him. 'You and your kind murdered my people at the Master's command,' he snarled, close enough that his saliva sprayed Morunasa's face. 'Now it seems he's repaid you as you deserve.'

Carnelian feared Morunasa would launch himself into Fern, but instead he seemed lost in thought. Fern's rage was spreading to the other Plainsmen. As people realized the Marula were trapped in the Earthsky with no hope of reinforcement they began to list the killing they had carried out during Osidian's conquest; the men they had tortured on their Isle of Flies. The Plainsmen were turning into a mob that looked to Fern to lead them. He was still glaring at Morunasa. 'There're ten of us to every one of you, Maruli.'

Though Morunasa did not react, the other Oracles moved around him, baring their teeth at the Plainsmen, hissing. Transfixed, Carnelian considered letting the Plainsmen destroy them. If the Marula had been dangerous before, desperate they were doubly so, but he remembered Sthax's remorse and that most of the Marula had had little choice but to collaborate with Osidian. Pushing in between Fern and Morunasa, he rounded on the baying mob. 'Turning upon each other will only make us easier prey for Hookfork. I've no more liking for these Marula than you but, deprived of the Upper Reach salt, their people will perish.' He glanced at Fern. 'That seems enough revenge for now.'

He became aware Morunasa was regarding him malevolently. Carnelian remembered the promise he had made to him that day. He gazed round at the Plainsmen. 'Besides, if it hadn't been for the Marula today the Master would've fallen into Hookfork's hands and you and all your people would be doomed. In the coming days we'll have need of all the strength we can muster.'

He turned back to Morunasa. 'Will you throw in your lot with us?'

The man gave Carnelian an almost imperceptible nod. Carnelian knew he had merely postponed the confrontation between them. He pulled back. 'He says yes.'

The Plainsmen confronted him with silence.

'Who among you will follow me north?'

No one moved, no one spoke. A chill spread across Carnelian's chest. He had nothing left to say that might persuade them. Lit by the embers, their faces had taken on the colour of the coming bloodbath.

Fern appeared at his side, arm outstretched. 'All day I've had the murderer of my child, my wife, my mother, my kin, the destroyer of all my tribe, within my grasp.' He closed his fingers into a fist. His hand opened again. 'And yet he still lives. I've spared him because I have faith in this Master.

'I don't speak to you for my own sake, for all that I've loved is lost.' Fern's gaze lingered on Carnelian. 'I speak because my mother, even as she was being strung up by that bastard' – Fern stabbed his finger at Osidian, his face deadened with hatred – 'sent me a plea that I should stay alive long enough to help you all survive what she feared was coming.'

Many shrank back from his baleful glare. 'This even though, when she and my tribe sent you back your hostage children and begged you all to rise with them against the

Master, you chose instead to stay at home like cowards.' Few there were able to return Fern's gaze. He indicated Carnelian. 'Follow him or else prepare yourselves for the destruction of all you love.'

Bathed in red light the Plainsmen looked at each other and a few at first, then all, gave Carnelian and Fern reluctant nods of agreement.

Half-sleeping, tortured by dreams, Carnelian was woken by a murmur from the ferngardens below. Rising, he walked to the edge of the summit. A glimmering mass was funnelling into the western rim of the koppie: the Darkcloud tribe arriving at last. It was a relief to see them reaching safety. The torches they carried must have been a poor defence against the raveners prowling the night. He did not want to consider the losses they might have suffered. He reassured himself his decision to bring them here had been the right one. Even if the council had not agreed to his plan, coming to the koppie of the Bluedancing was the best chance the Darkcloud had of making their escape east to the mountains.

He returned to where Fern was crouched, gazing north. His friend had chosen to take the first watch. Carnelian wrapped his blanket more tightly round himself and sank down beside him. Fern's back was ochred by the light of the embers. He looked round and their eyes met. Seeing Fern's bleakness, Carnelian yearned to share his blanket with him as they had once done, but Fern turned away.

Carnelian tried to let the bitter night numb the pain. He sought solace in the stars, in the faint gleam in the east that presaged moon dawn. The rest of the earth was black. Aurum's camp had dimmed so much it took him a while to locate it. The distance that lay between them was some comfort. He drew his blanket up to cover his ears and thought about the next day. His much-reviewed plan seemed stale, improbable. What was he going to do with the Marula? Curse Osidian for having sent Krow to cut down the anchor baobabs. He saw the sartlar chopping at them with their flint axes. That made him remember what he himself had said to Kor the day he had left the Upper Reach: cut the trees down in ten days' time unless you hear from me. The cold night penetrated to his bones. He had been so focused on reaching the Koppie. Then the massacre and the burials had put it clean from his mind. If Osidian had not ordered it, most likely it would have happened anyway. Try as hard as he might to escape it, it always came down to this: he and Osidian were alike. He could no more be free of being a Master than the Plainsmen could escape their oppression.

RAVENERS

With the odour of her blood
She seduced him into devouring her.
(Pre-Quyan fragment)

'We can't wake him.'

Carnelian opened his eyes. It was a moment before he recognized it was Fern's voice. 'What?'

'The Master won't wake.'

Carnelian rose, hugging his blanket against the cold. The hem of the sky was blue, but the sun had still to rise. He followed Fern to where Osidian was lying. Crouching, he took Osidian's shoulder and shook it. Only the slight twitches at the corners of Osidian's mouth and eyes showed he was alive. Darkcloud who had gathered were gazing down at him anxiously. Carnelian sent one to fetch Morunasa.

Fern was regarding Osidian with an expression Carnelian could not read. Carnelian was also in turmoil. If Osidian died they would still be able to draw Aurum north, but his corpse might not be sufficient incentive for the old Master to quit the Earthsky. Aurum might choose to cool his wrath with blood. Carnelian reflected that Osidian near to death might rid them of Aurum even faster: fear of losing his prize would make Aurum speed back to Osrakum in the hope that the Wise might revive him. He became aware of how these calculations were masking his emotions. He was thinking like a Master. He gazed down at Osidian. Feeling the vestige of their love rising in him, he turned away. Poppy was there, watching him. He suddenly had a need to be alone. He made for the northern edge of the summit, wanting to see his enemy.

No predawn light had yet reached Aurum's camp. Carnelian looked down to the ferngardens. Smoke was rising here and there in lazy spirals. He whirled round and, seeing one of the Darkcloud, cried out: 'You there.'

The man came running.

'Go down there and tell them to put out those fires.'

As the man sped off, Carnelian felt a hand on his arm and turned. It was Poppy. What was he going to do with her?

'They're only making breakfast to see us off,' she said.

'I want this place to seem dead enough that Hookfork won't believe we've left anyone behind.'

Gazing at her he knew what he must do, though it would break his heart. There was no place for her in Osrakum. Besides, he could not afford the vulnerability. 'I'll talk to the Elders of the Darkcloud. They'll take care of you until Fern returns. Then you can both choose to stay there or to join some other tribe.'

Expecting tears he was not ready for her icy anger. 'You and Fern are the only kin I feel I have left. Do you really think I'll let you leave me behind?' Though her body was a girl's she was glaring at him with a woman's eyes.

'Ultimately we'll have to part. Where I'm going you can't follow.'

'Then I'll stay with you and Fern as long as I can.'

The massacre had changed her. The burials. Carnelian tried to find another argument. 'We can't afford to have any rider carry you.'

'I agree. I'll need my own aquar. And before you object to that remember I'm a Plainswoman and have been riding longer than you.'

He laughed. 'I can see that I'm not going to win this.'

Poppy was still girl enough to consider for a moment being offended by his laughter, but his smile reassured her. 'So that's settled then. I ride with you.'

Carnelian became grim again, considering what they would be riding into, but he gave a nod.

When Morunasa appeared, Carnelian told the Darkcloud to go down and say their farewells to their kin. They thanked him, clearly relieved there still was time to do so. As Carnelian watched them go he was aware of the pressure of Morunasa's gaze. He felt deeply the part he had played in the disaster that had overtaken Morunasa's people, but stood his ground. The Oracles were every bit as rapacious as the Masters.

He led the Maruli to where Fern was standing over Osidian. 'Will he die?'

Morunasa crouched to peer at Osidian's face. He looked up. 'After the twelfth day no initiate has ever died, but then none has ever left the Isle of Flies before the maggots emerged. It was only seventeen days after he was incepted that the Master came here. He's been pushing himself too hard. I can't be certain what will happen.'

'When will the maggots emerge?'

Morunasa shrugged. 'Most likely . . .' His brows knitted as he calculated '. . . it won't be more than fifty days.'

'He can't ride like this,' said Fern.

'I'll wake him.' Morunasa leaned forward to bring his lips close to Osidian's ear and began whispering.

Osidian frowned, then slowly awoke. He began mumbling. Carnelian strained to make out words. Morunasa cocked his head to listen. His eyes narrowed as if he disliked what he was hearing. As Carnelian brought his face closer Osidian focused on him. 'Carnelian.'

The look of love Osidian gave him caused Carnelian to draw back, embarrassed. 'Can you walk, my Lord?'

Osidian stared up into the sky for some moments then, with

a grunt, rolled over, pushed himself up and rose unsteadily to his feet.

Carnelian turned to Fern. 'He won't be able to walk far. Could you bring an aquar to the foot of the steps?'

Silently Fern moved off while Carnelian and Morunasa helped Osidian.

As they descended the steps the first rays of the sun caught the patchy canopies of the mother trees below. The jade of new cones glowed among the dark brushes. Carnelian felt the fresh odour of resin cleanse his lungs. Hope surprised him, but only served to make him view the Plainsmen below with an aching heart. Hope was a vulnerability he could ill afford.

Fern was waiting with an aquar. When they reached her they helped Osidian clamber into her saddle-chair. They made her rise and led her down through the grove. Crossing the ditch, they descended to the ferngardens where Marula and Plainsmen crowded between the humps of their kneeling mounts. A Maruli – it was Sthax – brought an aquar over to Carnelian. The man gave him a wary look that took in Morunasa. Warned, Carnelian did not greet him. In Sthax's face he could see neither accusation nor grief. It seemed unlikely that the Maruli knew anything about the cut-down baobabs.

Once mounted, Carnelian could see the Darkcloud warriors mingling among their people. Men clung to their children as their mothers and wives embraced them, faces tight from holding back tears. Carnelian noticed sartlar there too. He had forgotten them. Then he became aware that the men from other tribes were gazing at him, tense hope on every face. They needed to have faith in him and so he put aside his doubts. His smile made them sit straighter. He rode down through their ranks. As he passed, aquar rose with a great din. Across the ferngarden he rode, raising a quaking in the ground as they followed him. He jumped the ditch into the outer garden, hearing them surging after him. He resisted the temptation of rushing speed. When he reached the fernland, he turned to watch them pouring out from the koppie after him, and sped off towards Aurum's camp.

The perfect geometries of the military camp were an alien imposition on the fernland. It had none of the yielding curves of a koppie. Its rampart was not softened by living trees but, rather, toothed with stakes. Even the morning gleam of the lagoon behind the camp seemed harsh and brittle. Carnelian's plan to expose himself as bait now seemed childish. The camp was a mechanism devoid of human weakness. He suppressed a surge of fear that any attempt to defy Aurum was madness. The old Master was there at its centre as its directing mind. He must focus on Aurum and not on the terrible power that was an extension of his will.

He began listing what he knew. Aurum would not imagine Osidian had been overthrown. The fire on the Bluedancing crags he would have seen as a sign of Osidian's defiance. This was unlikely to daunt him. Aurum would be confident he controlled the situation. His legion was in the heart of Osidian's Plainsman empire. He could now bring terror to bear on the women of the tribes opposing him, on their children. It was only a matter of time before they would yield Osidian up to him. Yes, Aurum would be confident, but not absolutely so. It was not a barbarian who confronted him, but a Lord of the House of the Masks. Such were not to be casually underestimated.

Carnelian saw with what fear the Plainsmen were surveying the camp. Certain that any movement by Aurum would wake alarm in their ranks, he sank his head and tried to enter the Master's mind. Try as he might he could imagine nothing specific that would unsettle him. Carnelian could taste despair as he began to doubt that even an attack on the render supply would be enough to cause Aurum to abandon his position of dominance among the tribes. Then it came to him: Aurum could have no clear understanding as to why

Osidian had risked so much to delay his southward march. It was unlikely he would know about the Upper Reach salt. Certainly, the delay Osidian had won was too slight to allow him any hope of protecting the koppies that were the source of his power. This point of doubt might be a chink in Aurum's invulnerability. With growing excitement, Carnelian saw that to ride north would be to signal a complete disregard for the dominance of Aurum's position. Such an act he might regard as typical of Osidian's arrogance, but he might also see in it evidence of some factor he was ignorant of. Surely this would cause Aurum's certainty to crumble? Carnelian almost let forth a whoop. He was sure he had him, but he set himself to check his reasoning. So much hung on its slender links. His confidence grew as he found no flaw. Few Masters, Aurum least of all, could conceivably deduce the real reason behind the movement north: compassion. It would never occur to Aurum that any Master, certainly not Osidian, would carry out such a plan merely with the aim of saving some barbarians.

Consternation around him made Carnelian look up. Though too far away for them to make out any detail, Aurum's camp was coming alive. He pushed his left heel into his aquar's neck and she veered away from the camp. The Plainsmen began to wheel behind him.

Fern rode up, angry. 'You've not shown yourself to Hookfork. How will he know the Master is with us?'

Carnelian smiled grimly. 'He knows and he will follow us.'

The sun climbed high enough to steal their shadows. Ahead, lagoons became blinding shards of light. Tramping through the heat had wilted Carnelian's confidence. His spirit had been wounded by the charcoal breeze wafting from the Koppie as they passed it. Even before then he had been constantly craning round, hoping to see the dust tide of Aurum's pursuit, but the shimmering horizon remained stubbornly clear.

A cry brought their whole march to a halt. Carnelian turned his aquar. Thick smoke was rising from the direction of Aurum's camp. He tried to deduce what new devilment this might portend. Then his heart went cold. The koppie of the Woading was on fire. The same realization was spreading panic among the Plainsmen. Before he had time to think, they were mobbing him. Woading fought their way to the front, baying that he had led their people into this disaster. Stunned, striving to calm his aquar, he could give them no answer. Other voices were making themselves heard. They wanted to return. He watched them arguing, shouting, panicking. Had his plan failed already? If he had given Osidian to Aurum, would he have left? Anger displaced his doubts with a memory of Aurum telling him his uncle Crail had died during the mutilation the Master had insisted on. Carnelian relived Aurum slicing open the throat of a Maruli. Aurum was a monster. Even if he had left immediately for Osrakum with Osidian, he would have made sure to leave behind enough dragons to visit retribution on the tribes.

Carnelian forced his aquar in among the Woading. They turned on him, shrieking. Ignoring their threats he bellowed for silence. The tumult faded.

One of the Woading snarled at him: 'We'll kill you. We'll give you to Hookfork in pieces; you and the Master.'

'Do that and every single one of your koppies will be set alight.'

One man rolled his eyes up. 'Father in heaven, but haven't we heard enough of your threats?'

Carnelian saw the utter despair behind the man's rage. 'I don't know if my plan will work,' he said. 'But what choice is there . . . ?' He raised his voice. 'There is no choice. Either we draw the bastard away or else he'll burn your tribes. He'll not be argued with and, even if he gets what he wants, he'll not stop.'

Men gaped at him, bleak-eyed. Several moaned. Tears were blinding them. They turned their backs on him and began to push through the press.

'Where're you going?' Carnelian cried, but they showed

no sign they heard. He tried to think what he could do. If they went back to their koppie Aurum was bound to take some of them alive. They would be unable to avoid betraying Carnelian's plan. Then it would all be over. He glanced around and found Morunasa and the Marula some distance away through the crowd. He could command them to stop the Woading, but that would unleash a bloodbath. Even as he groaned, seeing no way out, his feet were making his aquar slip forward, his hand unhitching his spear. He picked up speed following the Woading. 'If they return all hope is gone.'

Plainsmen stared at him. He raised his spear, crying: 'Woading, I will not let you go.'

One of the men turned and went white seeing Carnelian urging his aquar towards him. Other Woading were turning too. One face distorted with rage. 'Then we'll kill you now.' The man's spear was in his hand. He rode at Carnelian brandishing it. The flanks of their aquar slapped into each other. Their saddle-chairs scraped together. Carnelian ducked and drove his spear into the man's chest. Both he and the man stared at where the haft sprang from his robe, which was darkening with blood. Carnelian's anger left him as he watched the man die. Someone was speaking. Recognizing Fern's voice, he turned. He registered the shock in the faces around him.

'Let's give it until morning. If Hookfork's not come after us by then, we'll send him a message that we will give him the Standing Dead.'

Everyone agreed they should make for the Backbone, where they might camp safe from raveners. Fern announced he knew a fastness where it had been the custom of his tribe to spend the first night of their journeys to Osrakum. When he described it the Darkcloud gave their support. It was a place they used too.

It was nearing dusk when they reached the serried rocks of the Backbone that rose up from the fernland in a seemingly

94

unscalable cliff. Fern and the Darkcloud found paths winding up into it. Though negotiable by aquar these would be too narrow for a ravener to climb.

When they reached the summits they saw a wide slope falling gently into the west, strewn with black boulders. As the sun swelled raw on the horizon they gathered fernwood for fires. Carnelian helped Fern build theirs among some stunted trees in the lee of the Backbone's ragged edge. Afterwards he clambered up to survey the road they had crushed through the ferns. Poppy followed him. 'If Hookfork comes after us he'll have no difficulty finding us.'

Grim, they returned to where Fern was coaxing flames from a nest of roots. Osidian had clambered out from his saddle-chair then climbed a few steps to slump against a rock face. Swathed as he was in his Oracle indigos, all Carnelian could see of him was his narrowed eyes. On the horizon nothing was left of the sun but an incandescent filament that branded his vision for a while after it had disappeared. The slopes around him were dotted with huddles of Plainsmen illuminated by the fires in their midst. Further out, on their own, Marula in rings. It was Fern crisping djada in the flames that drew Carnelian's attention back. The smell evoked times he had spent among the Ochre; happier times. His mind turned reluctantly to the fate of the Woading: another koppie that had suffered holocaust. Hope had once more drained away, leaving nothing but sapping despair.

Poppy called him to eat. As he approached she made a place for him by the fire. She talked brightly, trying to kindle some life in them. 'Are you sure the raveners won't come at us up this slope?'

Fern shook his head almost imperceptibly. Without looking up from the flames, he moved his arm vaguely. 'The Backbone here runs unbroken north and south for a great distance. There's no water west of here and so no herds. Any raveners will come from the east.'

Carnelian read Fern's look of misery as he looked around

95

him. The last time he had been camping here it had been with his tribesmen, all now dead.

Carnelian's eyes snapped open. He could see nothing but the black between the stars. Terror clutched his chest. Raveners had been hunting him in his dreams. Tremors in the ground beneath his back. He sprang up. The slope was peopled by shadow men. The earth under his feet was trembling. A murmur of fear breathed up the slope as if a wind through trees. He scrambled up the incline, slipping, reaching the edge of the Backbone on all fours. Hair rose on his neck. The rising moon was almost blotted out by a spined tower rising black from the earth. Other immensities were sliding forward on either side with a dull clatter of brass. Thin light caught on surfaces, on curves, on infernal machines. The chemical reek of naphtha. Dragons!

Carnelian recoiled, expecting the night at any moment to be turned to day by jetting flame. Losing his footing, he rolled, found his feet, stumbled into their fire, sparking embers into the air. A chaos of rushing figures, men, aquar rising, careering into each other. Poppy tugging at him. Fern was shouting. Carnelian helped him bundle Osidian into a saddle-chair. Then he was clinging to another as its aquar began striding away from him. He heaved himself up. The aquar reeled under him like a boat in a swell. He struggled to find his seat. Flailing around with his feet. Toes found the creature's back. Both soles slapped onto its warm hide. His feet stroked her calm while he scried the darkness for Fern, for Poppy. 'Here,' he heard her cry. He saw her mounted, Fern nearby. Osidian was swept past, carried by his fleeing aquar. Carnelian felt his beast's desire to follow and lifted his feet to let her run unguided.

The moon peering above the Backbone lit their flight into the west. It was the land that slowed them. Its dry watercourses and hummocks made treacherous footing for the

96

aquar. Carnelian's voice carried through the night. It took a while, but he rallied them; their leaders finding him in the moonlight.

'The Backbone'll not hold him long,' said a voice and was answered by a murmur of agreement.

'Hookfork has come after us as Carnie said he would,' Poppy announced.

'So now there's no reason we can't go home,' said one of the Woading.

Voices rose in agreement from among the other tribes. Carnelian was dismayed. Without seeing a substantial force Aurum would not feel the threat of their northward march credible. 'Impossible.'

They answered him with growling anger.

'If Hookfork brings his whole legion against us it's to match our numbers. Should these noticeably decrease I fear he'll leave enough dragons behind to devastate more koppies.'

His argument swayed enough of them to encourage all save the Woading, reluctantly, to agree to go with him. The sight of the Woading riding away reminded many of what it was they might find waiting for them at home when they returned. Resentfully they followed Carnelian north with the sullen Marula.

As the sun rose, Carnelian rode up to a spur of the Backbone, unsure whether he was more afraid of seeing Aurum or of not seeing him. Golden in the dawn, the Earthsky seemed innocent of war. Closing his eyes, he drank in its musky perfume.

'There,' said Fern.

Carnelian opened his eyes. Fern was pointing south to where the Backbone undulated away to haze.

'Dragons?'

Fern nodded. They rode back to join the others.

*　　　*　　　*

97

When they reached a break in the Backbone, they rode through onto the plains then resumed their march. North, always north. Shadows moved round until each aquar was treading on her own. Periodically Carnelian would send scouts up among the rocks to reassure himself Aurum was still following.

They visited a lagoon that lay close to their route. Cautious among the giant saurians drinking there, watching for raveners, they filled their waterskins. Carnelian saw in the dancing incandescence of the water a warning of the dragonfire following them. He soaked his uba then wrung it out. As he rode away, its wet cling cooled his skin, but not his anxiety.

As shadows lengthened eastwards they found, high on the Backbone, another refuge known to one of the tribes: a valley that raised a shield of rock against the Earthsky. Once again, with darkness came fear that they tried to keep at bay by huddling round their fires, their aquar still saddled in a ring around them.

Sitting with Fern and Poppy Carnelian could tell that, like him, they were listening with their bodies for any tremor in the ground. It seemed to him better to confront their fear. 'He intended to take us all alive. Afraid to hurt the Master, he used no fire.' He gouged a crescent in the earth with a stone. He placed the stone within the curve. 'He meant to surround us with his dragons. Probably his auxiliaries would form an outer cordon to seal his trap.'

Poppy shuddered.

Fern looked up. 'He would've taken you and the Master and then . . .'

Carnelian watched the flames dancing in his eyes and nodded.

Poppy patted the earth and smiled. 'It was the Mother's Backbone saved us. She'll keep us safe from Hookfork.'

Carnelian could see how much Poppy wanted to believe

that. It seemed strange to him that the Plainsmen should have an ancient fear of the name Hookfork. Could this really be a memory of some Lord of House Aurum campaigning in the Earthsky? If so then this might reflect another aberration in the history of the Commonwealth. Peering into the flames he tried to see deep into the past to another Carnelian, another Osidian fugitive in the Earthsky. He could not. Such parallel events seemed implausible. What then was the answer to this riddle? His fingers recalled some beadcord they had read in the Library of the Wise: a story of a God Emperor making war on the Plainsmen. That They should leave Osrakum was also forbidden. The conclusion to be drawn from this was startling. There had been a time before the Balance of the Powers had been set up. His hand shaped Aurum's cypher: a horned-ring set upon a staff. A representative of the God Emperor might carry such insignia. He caught glimpses of another world in the flames, of a time before the Great and the House of the Masks were caged in Osrakum by the Law-that-must-be-obeyed. He drew greedily on what comfort there was in that. Perhaps the order of things was not as immutable as he had been taught to believe.

The next morning the dust-cloud Aurum's dragons were raising could be seen rolling up from the south. In punishing heat Carnelian led his host on.

Some time in the afternoon they lost sight of their pursuers. He called a halt and stood anxiously with others on a bluff of the Backbone, searching. Not even the keenest eye could see any sign of the dragons. Fearing some stratagem of Aurum's, some outflanking, worried that if Aurum found them waiting for him he would deduce he was being lured north, Carnelian made his host push on.

When they stopped to make a camp for the night, the southern horizon was still empty. There was a whispering around the hearths. Sharp in every eye was the fear that Hookfork had turned back towards their koppies.

In the morning the Plainsmen lingered at their breakfasts. Watching them eat in silence Carnelian hoped his face did not betray that he shared their fear. On the rocks above their camp, scouts were gazing south. He would have been there with them if he could. Cries from these lookouts made every Plainsman surge to his feet. Carnelian scrambled up with them onto the heights. Relief moved along the ridge like light released by a passing cloud. Carnelian's height allowed him to look over the others' heads to where the Backbone faded into the stirred-up dust of Aurum's pursuit.

By midday they had once again left Aurum behind. Though the Plainsman commanders urged Carnelian to slow their pace he refused. He wanted to force Aurum to continue his night marches to catch up with them.

Later, consternation up ahead made Carnelian ride to the head of their column with Fern. When they saw him men pointed north. Carnelian's heart sank as he saw the hazing touching the Backbone. 'It can't be,' he muttered.

'Not dragons,' Fern said. He looked Carnelian in the eye. 'The cloud is smaller, closer.'

Carnelian saw Fern was right. 'It must be a render convoy.'

Hundreds of pack huimur lumbered by, weighed down by frames like pitched roofs hung with rows of what in size and shape could have been human heads. Their legs were lost in the dust they raised, clouds of which were rolling up into the defiles of the Backbone. Crouching, Carnelian shifted his attention to the escort of riders. Auxiliaries on pacing aquar, lances across their laps, heads sagging. He looked to either side where his men formed a ragged ambush, squatting concealed among the ferns, cradling the heads of their aquar to keep them stretched out upon the ground.

He gave the signal then edged back, clucking to his aquar. He slipped his legs around the pommel and over the crossbar.

Grasping his saddle-chair he put his feet onto her back, encouraging her to rise. Her head came up, flicking from side to side as she blinked to look around her. The jerk of her rolling onto her feet wrenched him fully into the chair. She rocked forward, her hands touched the ground, then she rocked back and thrust him into the air. Carnelian could see others rising all around him, but he did not wait. He freed his spear from its scabbard then launched his aquar at the convoy. He chose a target and watched the man becoming suddenly aware of the threat, reining his mount round, swinging his lance up. Carnelian saw how his charge was threatening to impale him on the auxiliary's bronze blade. Striking the lance with the haft of his spear, he rolled it from his path. He registered the auxiliary's terror as he realized it was a Master coming at him, but then the spear pierced the man's leather cuirass. Carnelian felt momentary resistance then his blade penetrating flesh. It jerked in his hand as it struck a rib. His aquar pulled up, trying to avoid colliding with the auxiliary's. He managed to hold onto his spear. The man grimaced as Carnelian twisted it out. He slumped, blood running down into his lap. Carnelian used his feet to swing his aquar deeper into the melee.

The auxiliary line dissolved into chaos. A few in flight were pursued by Plainsmen but mostly it was riderless aquar that were running away into the ferns. Carnelian turned to the huimur, who were backing away, lowering their heads to present the stumps of their sawn-off horns. Riders astride their necks cowered behind the shields of the monsters' crests. Plainsmen were throwing themselves onto the sloping sides of the wicker frames. Scrabbling up them they struck at the riders with mattocks. Though some managed to put up a fight with their goads, they soon joined the others tumbling to the ground, where they were crunched, screaming, under the huge feet of the huimur.

Astride the necks of the huimur the Plainsmen managed to bring them under control. More men clambered up the frames and began releasing the objects that Carnelian could now see were like huge leather pomegranates. Plainsmen queued up to catch the things. Grinning, a Darkcloud came to offer Carnelian one. It was a bottle of some kind, of leather held in a net of rope. It had a stumpy neck topped with a crown of bony knobs.

'A belly,' the man said.

Another had come up. 'A sac, Master. Enough render in these two,' the veteran indicated the bottles, 'to feed you and your aquar for ten days.'

'Can we tie them on for you, Master?' asked the other.

When Carnelian nodded, they moved to fasten the sacs to the rear pole of his saddle-chair, one on each side. Turning, Carnelian could see how comfortably the sacs nestled between the flank and upper thigh of his beast. As he made her walk he could feel by her gait that they were heavy, but they did not impede her movement.

When everyone had a pair of sacs, Carnelian was asked what he wanted done with the rest.

'Destroy them.'

Whooping, they rode among the huimur slashing at the sacs. The vessels ruptured like stomachs, spilling their soupy contents down the frames. Carnelian curled his nose up at the meaty smell as it soaked into the earth. The Plainsmen struck the haunches of the huimur with the flats of their spears and, bleating, the monsters lumbered off into the plain, spraying ferns brown with render as they went. The poor creatures would not survive long. The odour of the render was sure to draw raveners.

Carnelian gazed south, but could see no evidence that Aurum was following them. Still, without this consignment, Aurum's host would begin to starve. Aurum would have no choice but to follow him north as fast as he could.

Carnelian unhitched one of the sacs from his saddle-chair. He did not like the feeling of the liquid moving under the leather.

He crouched to set it down. He had watched the veterans moving among the Plainsmen and Marula explaining how to open them. Its shape reminded him of the funerary urns. The leather swelled up to form lips: two arcs of bone that bit up through the leather in a series of carved knobs. Within the lips the leather formed a puckered mouth. He pierced this with a flint. The gash released a meaty, salty smell. The knife came out moistened. Gingerly he lifted the sac and held it over a hollow he had scooped in the earth and lined with fern fronds. He tipped the sac and poured render out of a corner of its mouth. Lumps of meat spluttered out, falling into the puddle, splashing him with juice. When he judged there was enough for his aquar he let her feed.

He lugged the sac over to the fire Fern had lit. Sitting down with it between his legs, as he saw others doing, he dipped his flint into the opening and, drawing it out, licked some of the render off it. He grimaced at the salt burn. The taste was even worse than the smell. He forced himself to have some more, but could not manage a third scoop.

Looking up, he saw Poppy and Fern watching him. 'I think I'll finish the djada first.'

Poppy made a face. 'I don't like it either.'

Fern looked down at his sac grimly. 'We'll have to eat it eventually.'

Carnelian nodded. 'But not until we've run out of djada.' The others agreed. Fern demonstrated how twisting some twine from knob to knob across the gash in his sac pulled its lips closed. Carnelian rehitched his sac to his saddle-chair then returned with some djada which he handed out.

As they chewed contentedly Poppy spoke. 'Where's Hookfork?'

Carnelian shrugged. 'I'm sure we'll see him again in the morning.'

Poppy nodded and resumed her chewing.

*　　*　　*

103

Morning brought unease when the lookouts declared they could see no sign of Hookfork. Grumbling, the Plainsmen agreed to follow Carnelian north, though they hung back, their march becoming ragged as men took turns to ride up onto the Backbone to gaze south.

Carnelian's gaze was fixed in the direction they were riding. He dared not turn his head despite being as anxious as the Plainsmen. He feared that if he did so they might refuse to go further.

A rider came up on his flank. Though the man was shrouded against the dust, Carnelian knew it was Fern and saw the worry in his eyes. 'You must give them a reason to go on.'

Carnelian had run out of reasons. He shared the Plainsmen's fear that Aurum had returned south. Before he could vent his irritation Fern said: 'We're near the koppie of the Twostone.'

Carnelian looked at Poppy to see if she had heard this mention of her birthplace, but she was slumped in her saddle-chair and seemed asleep. He surveyed the route ahead. For a while now the Backbone had sunk so that only knobs of rock rose up out of the earth. These rocks no longer offered decent vantage points nor any place well enough defended to make a camp. The Twostone koppie would provide both, but then there was the matter of the massacre of that tribe. He leaned close to Fern. 'What about Poppy . . . Krow?'

Fern frowned. 'Because it's abandoned we'd not be endangering another tribe. The men would be glad to spend a night in a koppie.'

Carnelian worried too about how the Plainsmen might feel towards the Marula once they found themselves at the scene of another of their massacres. He said nothing, however. It was not likely to be something Fern had forgotten. He gave a nod and Fern returned it before swinging his aquar away. He gazed at Poppy, remembering the nightmares she had had about the massacre of her people. What would it do to her, or to Krow, who had seen his tribe left as carrion by Marula? Carnelian looked for the youth. The news spreading down the march was making men gaze north with an eagerness that had been absent for days.

The outer ditch had become a waterhole that held a bright sickle of water. Rain had softened the banks to lips, gouged where saurians had slid down to drink, printed with the huge arrowheads of ravener tracks. Some of the magnolias, gripping the banks, leaned, exposing their roots. Others lay fallen, rotting, bearded with moss.

Glancing at Poppy's fixed expression, at Krow who rode staring at her side, Carnelian led the Plainsmen on a broad front over the ditch into a ferngarden that was being reclaimed by the plain. Once across, Fern rode ahead down the avenue of cone trees towards the two crag teeth that had given this koppie's tribe its name.

The second ditch was as ruined as the first, but when they reached the one that encircled the cedar grove they found that its walls were still held sheer by the roots of the cedar trees. The rampart of the further bank still rose crenellated with earther skulls. The avenue brought them to the opening in that rampart which was still barred by the wicker gate studded with horns, at which a huskman had failed in his duty by letting in the Marula who had sheltered in the koppie and slaughtered the Twostone when they returned from their migration.

Dismounting, Poppy and Krow were first across the earthbridge to the gate. She pushed at the wicker and, when it resisted her, Krow put his shoulder to it and forced it ajar. The two stood for a moment gazing through the gap, then entered the grove. Carnelian followed them, warily, peering up a rootstair into the gloom beneath the mother trees. Hunched, he listened to their creaking. His shoulders only relaxed once he became aware he was searching for corpses hanging.

Poppy glanced at Carnelian then past him. He followed her gaze and saw Fern by the gate.

'Please come in, Fern,' she said.

Almost against his will Fern looked towards Krow, who was surveying the grove as if he were counting each tree, each stone. Poppy reached out and touched Krow gently. When he turned to her, she indicated Fern. Krow flushed when he saw that Fern was waiting for his permission. He gave a nod and Fern entered.

The four of them climbed the hill. They passed the funeral pyre the Marula had made to burn their dead. Its scar lay between the mother trees they had mutilated for firewood.

When they reached the foot of the twin crags, Carnelian eyed the Ancestor House nestling in the fork where they met. He knew that its walls, its floor, its roof contained the bones of Poppy's and Krow's grandmothers and grandfathers. There Oracles had camped, lighting fires upon that sacred floor.

They followed Krow up a stair to the summit of the highest crag. There among the bare funerary trestles they stood to survey the plain. South the Backbone ran away to a scratch. They widened their search east along the southern horizon. Of Aurum and his dragons there was no sign.

Poppy and Krow sat together gazing into the flames. Carnelian watched with concern. Earlier they had crept off, whispering as they pointed things out to each other. When they had returned they had seemed empty of themselves.

Fern was gazing at them with a father's eyes. Becoming aware he was being watched, he focused on kneading his hands. It salved Carnelian's misery a little that, perhaps, Fern was halfway to forgiving Krow. He looked at the trunk of the cedar under whose branches they were sitting. He felt affection for Poppy's mother tree. This hearth, the sleeping hollows, even the water jar nestling between the roots, were very like Akaisha's. He could not remember the last time he had felt so much at home. His gaze lingered on Osidian lying near the fire, twitching.

The whole hill was clothed with Plainsmen. Poppy had given them leave to camp beneath the mother trees and to light fires wherever they could find space. She had even allowed in the small number of sartlar who had managed to keep up with the march. Only the Marula and the aquar were outside the protection of the inner ditch. He was glad Morunasa had accepted this without argument. Even had Poppy been prepared to allow the Marula into the grove Carnelian was sure Krow and Fern would not countenance it.

Carnelian pondered what the next day might bring. If the morning did not reveal some sign Aurum was still pursuing them they would have to return south. He blanked his inner sight to what they might be returning to. He would not allow himself to consider failure until he had to. Instead he clung to the hope that, in destroying the render, he had made it impossible for Aurum not to follow them.

Carnelian was woken by a tremor in the ground. He jumped up, certain Aurum had come for them. Embers lit the shapes of Plainsmen panicking. The grove seemed an ant nest breached. He tried desperately to pierce the cedar canopy to look down into the ferngardens, anticipating at any moment that the night would be lit by dragonfire.

He became aware Poppy was clinging to him. Fern was there in front of him demanding to know what they should do. At his side, Krow looked stunned. Carnelian found his voice. 'We need to quell this disorder and find out what's going on.'

Fern jerked a nod. 'I'll see to the men.'

Carnelian grabbed his shoulder. 'No.' He prised Poppy loose, knelt and looked into her eyes. 'You do it, Poppy. This is your koppie; they'll listen to you.' When she nodded he rose and looked at Krow. 'You too.'

As they sped away Carnelian grabbed Fern's arm and pulled

him off towards a rootstair. Fern broke free. 'What about the Master?'

Carnelian glanced back to Osidian, lying like a corpse in the glow of their hearth. 'Leave him.'

When they reached the rootstair Carnelian stumbled up it, pushing his way through the Plainsmen coming down. He was only distantly aware of Fern barking orders. He was focused on trying to devise a plan that might salvage something. What could they do if dragons were coming across the ferngardens?

As he reached the crag, Fern said: 'Why Poppy?'

Carnelian answered him without turning. 'She'll shame them.'

It took them a while to find the steps they had climbed earlier. Carnelian scaled them on all fours so as not to fall. Reaching the top he almost tripped over one of the funerary trestles. Then he was standing on the edge surveying the night. At first he was tormented by a certainty he could see shapes creeping towards them across the ferngardens. Gradually he convinced himself he was imagining it. Then he noticed a flickering circle to the north. Campfires. It was puzzling. 'It's too small to be a camp.'

'There's another there,' said Fern.

Carnelian saw another circle to the south. Neither was large enough to be a dragon encampment. He walked along the edge gazing out. When he had made a complete circuit, he turned to Fern. 'Earlier, when you woke, you felt it too?'

'Dragons . . . perhaps earthers, though I've never known a herd move in darkness.'

'Raveners?' Carnelian tensed. 'The Marula!'

'The Plainsmen are safe within the ditch,' Fern said, coldly; but then added: 'If there was a ravener among the Marula, we would've heard their screams.'

Carnelian nodded and returned his attention to the fernland. 'He must be out there somewhere.'

Fern walked to the edge and gazed down. The din from the

Plainsman panic was ringing out into the night. 'Perhaps he's waiting for the dawn. You said yourself he wants the Master alive. He'd not risk a night attack.'

Carnelian became lost in pondering what they should do. It would be foolish to assume Aurum had learned nothing from his previous attempt at encirclement. The handover was now being forced on them. Were they far enough north to be certain Aurum would choose to immediately quit the Earthsky with his prize? What about the Plainsmen? Would Aurum let them go?

'Why did you want me up here? I'd be more use down there.'

Carnelian had a notion. Perhaps he could negotiate with Aurum. If he went in person the auxiliaries would have no choice but to take him to their master. He suppressed sympathy for those men who, for setting eyes on him, would suffer death. Perhaps he might be able to convince Aurum that he had come to betray Osidian. Betrayal was something Aurum might believe. Besides, it was not so far from the truth. Could Carnelian persuade Aurum to let the Plainsmen go by saying it was more likely he would get Osidian alive? It was a narrow hope. Then there was the problem of the Marula. The warriors might let Osidian go; Morunasa would not.

'I'll go down then,' Fern said, his voice tinged with anger.

Carnelian rose, apologizing. It was instinct that had made him bring Fern. He now knew why. 'Fern, the only hope we have to save the Plainsmen is through you.'

Fern gave a snort. 'How?'

Carnelian explained his plan. 'They'll follow you out of the trap. I don't know if Hookfork will let them go, but you'll have a chance to break out. I might even be able to send you a signal.'

Fern's head dropped. Carnelian waited, knowing he was talking about them separating for ever. Fern looked up again. 'And Poppy?'

'Take her with you. I'll slip away . . . not say goodbye . . .

She wouldn't go with you if I said goodbye.' Carnelian was surprised he was feeling nothing.

'And the Marula?'

'Leave them to me.'

At that moment they heard a scrabbling from the steps and a figure appeared. It was Morunasa. Carnelian's first feeling was outrage that the man had chosen to defy the ban set on him and his people from entering the grove. His next feeling was anxiety: how much had Morunasa heard? With relief, he realized that he and Fern had been talking in Ochre. Fern was regarding Morunasa with anger, but, since he chose to say nothing, Carnelian decided that, in the circumstances, it was best to let Morunasa's defiance pass.

Morunasa was surveying the night. 'Are we surrounded?'

'I imagine we are,' Carnelian said. He gazed eastwards. 'Dawn's not near yet. We've time to prepare a breakout. Go ready your men.'

'And you?' Fern asked.

'I'll remain here a while alone.'

Carnelian watched them leave before returning to sit upon the rock, where he fell prey to his doubts, his failures and the contemplation of unavoidable loss.

On the summit of the crag, sitting among funerary trestles, Carnelian saw the brightening east. He rose but, however much he strained his tired eyes, he could see nothing of his enemy.

As he waited for dawn others came up, Fern and Morunasa among them. They joined him anxiously watching the creep of light across the land.

'There,' cried one.

All eyes followed his finger south to an encampment of men and aquar. Carnelian scanned the land in an arc. The other encampment was there to the north; but of Aurum and his dragons nothing.

As the Plainsmen began arguing among themselves

110

Carnelian turned desperately to Fern. 'Can you see them?'

Fern shook his head. He raised his eyebrows in a silent question, but Carnelian had no answer for him. He had no idea whatever where Aurum might be. He regarded the two encampments, noting they were equidistant from the koppie. Such a precise deployment had the flavour of a trap. He searched again for the dragons, this time more carefully, seeking out rocks or any fold in the ground where Aurum might be concealed. He gave up, exasperated. A dragon would be hard to hide anywhere, never mind a legion of them and on this plain. He considered that Aurum might have sent his auxiliaries forward to hold them until he arrived. But then what was it that had passed them in the night if not dragons? A saurian herd?

Carnelian gazed north then south. Estimating how far the auxiliaries were from the koppie brought understanding. Their deployment was actually an encirclement. There was no direction in which he and the Plainsmen and Marula could ride out that could avoid them being caught between the two forces of auxiliaries.

One of the Plainsmen confronted him. 'We leave now.'

His fellows echoed him with much nodding. 'Nothing you can say, Master, will change our minds. We're going home.'

When Carnelian turned away, Fern stepped in to argue with them. Carnelian lost awareness of them as he pondered the position of the auxiliaries and the ground that lay between them. East, a lagoon was beginning to burn in the dawn. A breeze seemed to flow from it that was caressing his face with the earth's musk. As he breathed it, an idea began growing in his mind. He let it blossom. He controlled his excitement as he checked it through. Only then did he turn back to the Plainsmen. The look on his face made them fall silent. 'If you go south you'll be caught between them like this.' Clapping his hands made them blink. He silenced their protests with a gesture. 'If you ride east there may be a way to confound them.'

111

If there was doubt in their faces, there was also a wary hope. As Carnelian explained how they could use the Earthsky against the invaders, the Plainsmen began frowning. They looked at each other for support, but none voiced opposition. Fern was looking at him, then he glanced at Morunasa. Carnelian had not forgotten the problem of the Marula. However much Plainsman blood was on their hands, the fate he had in mind for them saddened him. Morunasa had good reason to look uneasy but, for now, he would have no choice other than to go along with the Plainsmen.

As they slaughtered enough aquar Carnelian took Poppy aside to say goodbye to her. He expected tears when he told her that the time for their parting had come, but she gazed at him steadily, saying nothing. So much loss and horror had perhaps made her woman enough to accept the inevitable. When he told her she would be returning south with Fern she gave a slight nod. He felt too numb to kiss her. He was thankful that neither of them cried. Tears might thaw their hearts to grief.

Together they returned to watch the Plainsmen tearing strips from their robes then steeping these in aquar blood. What the Plainsmen did not catch pumping from the creatures' severed throats soaked dark into the earth.

Osidian's back arched as he convulsed, eyes rolling back into his head. Fern gave Carnelian a look he understood. There was something in Osidian's condition that recalled the time they had carried him across the swamp. Carnelian sensed that Fern was seeing an omen in this. He dismissed doubt and crouched to slip his arms under Osidian's back. As Fern took his feet Morunasa appeared. He looked down at Osidian.

'They are eating their way out of him,' he said, pointing.

Carnelian saw with disgust a shape like a finger moving under the skin of Osidian's neck.

'It is always the moment of greatest pain . . . and of the deepest communion with our Lord.'

Carnelian made no attempt to keep from his face his contempt for Morunasa's god. He gave Fern a nod and together they lifted Osidian and carried him to the waiting saddle-chair. When they had settled him in they stepped back and looked at each other. Carnelian searched Fern's face for feeling and saw only confusion. In a short time they would part for ever, but they had lost the ability to talk, never mind touch. He turned away. Besides, neither wished to make a display of their emotions before Morunasa.

The Plainsmen swarmed across the whole arc of the outer ditch from north to south. Hoping to conceal his intentions from the auxiliaries Carnelian had first marshalled them in the inner ferngardens. Once everyone was mounted they had begun to leap the second ditch and fan out over the outer gardens towards the final ditch.

Carnelian glanced over at Osidian convulsing in his saddle-chair. He had made sure to put himself between Osidian and Morunasa. Around them were ranged the Oracles. Marula formed a wall of beaded, gleaming flesh on either side.

As he saw the last Plainsmen scramble up out of the ditch, Carnelian urged his aquar forward and the Marula lurched into movement. The feet of their aquar drummed a rumble into the earth. He held onto his chair as his aquar stumbled down into the ditch. As she scrambled up the other side, he kept an anxious eye on Osidian being shaken around as if he were a full waterskin. Then they were striding over the plain. Turning, he saw the Marula emerging up between the magnolias. He rocked his feet on his aquar's back and she picked up speed. He was relieved to see Osidian's beast keeping pace with his. Ahead, black against the incandescent blade of the lagoon, the Plainsman line was thinning as it widened to shield the body of Marula in its crescent. Fern was there at its centre with Poppy and Krow. Carnelian glanced to his right. Morunasa showed no sign he suspected anything. His yellow eyes trained north then south to where the auxiliaries

113

were moving towards them. Judging their speed, Carnelian gave a grunt of satisfaction. The auxiliaries were not racing to intercept them, but seemed content merely to match their pace. So far so good.

As shadows shortened, Carnelian had watched the two lines of pursuing auxiliaries join. North and south their new line now stretched to match that of the Plainsmen, whose wavefront was separating and reforming around what appeared to be rocks but Carnelian knew to be raveners lazing in the heat. Soon he and the Marula were moving through this region. He too eyed the striped dark mounds nervously. Fear rippled through their ranks whenever one of the monsters stirred. Carnelian breathed more freely when he and the Marula reached the relative safety of the clear ground between the raveners and the earther herds. He watched the wall of Plainsmen encouraging the earthers to lumber off towards the lagoon. It was their experience with herding the creatures that he had used to justify to Morunasa why the Marula must ride behind the Plainsmen. An earther stampede now could wreck his dispositions.

Satisfied that events were proceeding as he had hoped, Carnelian led Morunasa, his Oracles and Osidian back through the ranks of the Marula warriors until there was nothing but open fernland between him and the auxiliaries. He watched their line being disrupted by aquar shying away from raveners. He chewed his lip. He needed the auxiliaries safely on this side of the raveners. Glancing round, he saw Fern had brought the Plainsmen to a halt. Their line now stretched so far that, at either end, the heat made its thread waver away to nothing.

Carnelian resumed watching the auxiliaries approach. Their commanders probably believed they had their quarry trapped against the lagoon. His heart became a war drum as he watched their line smooth. The raveners were now behind them. He made sure everyone was in place. Death was in his hands as he raised them to comb the breeze flowing over him towards the auxiliaries. Behind him there was a flutter like flamingos taking to flight. Glancing round, he saw the Plainsmen holding aloft red pennants, scarlet and russet banners, all tainting the wind with the iron smell of blood.

The auxiliaries were now close enough for their brass collars to stitch a glint along their line. As time stretched, Carnelian began to fear his plan was failing. Suddenly a section of their line buckled as something forced some riders forwards. Then another eruption at a different part of the line. Two more. Squinting, he saw the dark shapes looming up behind each focus of disturbance. Thinned by the distance, he could hear the screaming of men and aquar. Military order dissolved as more and more raveners, woken by the odour of blood in the air, came in to feed. Raggedly, the auxiliary line fled towards him. He looked round the back of his saddle-chair. The Plainsmen seemed ready to leave. He tried to pierce their ranks to see Fern and Poppy one last time. Of course it was hopeless. The Marula were gaping at the oncoming auxiliaries. Carnelian was getting ready to charge when he noticed Osidian's eyes were open, staring. He hardly had time to register this before Osidian's aquar lunged forward. Cries erupted around him. He glimpsed Morunasa's face, frozen in a silent scream as the whole mass of the Marula began sliding forward. Carnelian sent his aquar after Osidian, riding the thunder of the Marula charge.

Osidian struck the auxiliaries like a thunderbolt. Two aquar were flung on their backs. One staggered to her feet with a shattered mess of flesh and wood on her back. Carnelian noticed too late he had not unsheathed his spear. An auxiliary was bearing down on him, bulging eyes in a face marbled with dirt, teeth bared. Carnelian reached to deflect the bronze spearhead slicing towards him. Felt the burn of the shaft rasp his wrist. Then it jammed into the wicker back of his chair. His aquar, turning, snapped the spear, flaring splinters in Carnelian's face. He caught the broken haft and yanked. The auxiliary snarled as his arms pulled taut, trying to keep hold. Carnelian forced the spear butt back into the man's belly, grinding it in until the blood came.

Nearby, Osidian's white Master's face was instilling terror in the auxiliaries as he slid through them gouging, impaling, disembowelling. Carnelian tore his uba from his face. It seemed unfair to unleash such a weapon, but it was necessary he be taken alive. Auxiliaries cringed away from him, shielding their eyes as if blinded by his skin. He pushed his aquar through a space roofed with splintering spears. Snarling, the Marula were breaking them with their hands or lunging at the auxiliaries with their blades. Carnelian watched flesh slice open. Blood drizzled warm onto his forearms, then his face. He reached Osidian easily. The terror of their faces made them invulnerable.

Battlecries, then a shuddering crash as a front of riders struck. Grimly, he turned. Now, enveloped by the auxiliary wings, the Marula would be slain. He sensed the auxiliaries faltering, then gaped in disbelief. It was Plainsmen who had charged into the fight. This was not supposed to happen. Scanning their fury, his eyes snagged on Fern's face. He looked deranged, shouting something, pointing. Carnelian searched in that direction. It was Poppy in the midst of the auxiliaries. He dug his toes so hard into his aquar's back it bucked, but then leapt forward. Unhitching a mattock he swung it, bludgeoning a bloody path, his gaze fixed on Poppy in the very throat of carnage. She saw him coming and cried out. He veered his aquar as he closed on her so that their saddle-chairs slid side by side. He reached over and pulled her onto his lap. As he did so, something stung his arm. He cleared a space around them with his Master's face.

'Krow,' she cried and Carnelian saw the youth had been there protecting her.

'Take her to safety,' cried Krow.

Carnelian longed to help the Plainsmen, but he could feel Poppy warm against his chest. He gave Krow a nod. Behind him the Plainsmen were pressing forward four ranks deep. He groaned, knowing there was only one way out, and urged his aquar into the auxiliaries.

Using their terror of his face to open a path, Carnelian rode with Poppy through the auxiliaries, as untouched as if they had been lepers, but, as they came through into open ground, the aquar suddenly reared up, blinding them with her eye-plumes. He leaned forward and saw a ravener not far away with an aquar in the talons of one foot at which it was tearing. Poppy slipped her feet to the aquar's back, stroked her, soothed her and coaxed her past the monster. More raveners were being drawn by the odour of blood that even Carnelian could now smell wafting on the wind. As he watched the monsters lope towards the heaving wall of the battle, he was desperate to return, to share Fern's fate, Krow's and that of the other Plainsmen. First he had to carry Poppy to safety. That meant taking her back to the koppie.

Soon they were coursing through the ferns having left the raveners behind. As they rode Carnelian grew calm enough to be able to talk. 'Why did Fern lead them in?'

Her head gave a tiny shake against his chest. There was something in the smallness of that movement that made him probe further. He felt her hand upon his arm. Looking up at him she focused on first one of his eyes then the other.

'It might have been my fault, Carnie.'

He must have looked confused for she added: 'When I saw you riding away, I decided that, after all, I would prefer to go with you to the Mountain.'

Some figures were waiting for them on the half-collapsed earthbridge that led into the koppie. Carnelian was surprised to see they were sartlar. As he swept up they fell prostrate on the earth. He made his aquar kneel. Poppy climbed out, then he followed her. As he stood over the sartlar one glanced up. He knew the face. 'Kor?'

The sartlar abased herself. He wondered at her being there, but was relieved. 'Get up.'

The hag rose painfully to stand, head bowed.

'I'm going to leave this girl in your care.'

The sartlar looked up at him. 'Yes, Master.'

The skin of her branded forehead almost made her eyes disappear as she frowned. She was looking at his wrist. He raised it and saw the wound there. It was just a graze. Quick as a snake she reached out and touched him. The graze stung. He raised his hand to strike her, but she cowered back to her knees. Her fear of him made him ashamed of his anger. She raised her face through her lank hair. She had her finger in her mouth. She withdrew it. She indicated his graze. 'Blood.'

Her face had resumed its passive mask. What was she after? The scar around his neck itched. He recalled another sartlar woman, on the road when he had been a slave. He ran his fingers over his scar and remembered the soothing salve she had put on it. Kor was wiping her finger on her rags. Carnelian was anxious to get back to the battle, but he became worried, imagining what might happen to Poppy if they should be defeated. He dismissed this fear. There was nothing else he could do.

Poppy tugged his hand. He could see in her face that she knew where he was going. He bent to kiss her.

'Come back,' she said.

He nodded, told Kor that she and the sartlar must protect Poppy with their lives then, mounting, rode back towards the battle.

He slowed his aquar when he saw riders approaching. Among the indigo of the Oracles, Osidian's pale face seemed made of bone. Beyond them raveners prowled the battlefield. Carnelian felt sick. There was no sign of living Plainsmen nor Marula warriors. He could not believe them all perished. He would not. He waited as calmly as he could for Osidian to reach him.

118

The Master's legs, arms and face were streaked with gore. His eyes burned. 'Be joyous, Carnelian, we are victorious.'

Osidian was shivering. Carnelian could not tell if the agony he was suffering was from a wound or from the maggots. 'The Plainsmen and the Marula?'

Osidian closed his eyes and sank back into his chair. Beside him, Morunasa fixed Carnelian with a baleful look. 'They hunt what remains of the auxiliaries.'

'And you don't?'

Morunasa indicated Osidian. 'The Kissed will soon give birth to the servants of our Lord.'

Carnelian saw with unease the reverence with which the Oracles were regarding Osidian. As Morunasa led them past him, Carnelian searched the horizon, then turned his aquar to follow them back to the koppie. His plan lay in ruins. He dared not consider how many men might have been slain. He no longer knew what was happening.

Carnelian stood guard on the gate waiting for Fern and Krow, counting the survivors. All day they came in, Plainsmen and Marula, exhausted and bloody, but with the stiff backs and raised chins of victors. He asked the Plainsmen for news of Fern. Many told him that, when they had last seen him, he had been dealing death to the auxiliaries.

Carnelian was sitting, morose, when another group came in. He rose and saw with joy that Fern was among them. He ran forward to greet him, but was warned off by the look in his eyes.

'Many good men fell today.'

Carnelian nodded. 'But most have survived.'

'And Poppy?' The speaker was so begrimed with blood that Carnelian did not at first realize it was Krow.

'Safe and unhurt.'

'And the Master?' asked Fern.

'He returned with Morunasa.'

'What now?'

'I don't know.'

Scowling, Fern dismounted and, leaving his aquar in Krow's care, he strode into the grove. Carnelian and the youth exchanged glances, then Carnelian followed Fern.

Ravener screeches carried through the night as the monsters feasted on the wounded and the dead. The Plainsmen cowered, sick with shame that they had abandoned their brethren to such a fate. Poppy whispered to Carnelian that it reminded her of the sounds coming from the Isle of Flies.

Morunasa and the Oracles clustered around Osidian as he groaned, like crows around a corpse. Nauseated, Carnelian watched them minister to Osidian like midwives. When the moon had set, pale maggots as thick as thumbs began wriggling out from the sticky mouths of his wounds. The Oracles cherished them as if they were babies.

BURNT OFFERINGS

Truly the Gods savour sacrifice
But swell not too much Their holocausts
Lest you wake Their greed
And They devour the world.

(*Quyan fragment*)

First light found Carnelian bleary-eyed. He had hardly slept. At first he had been haunted by the maggot births, then he became possessed by the fear that, at any moment, Aurum would fall on them with his dragons. He was exhausted from the continuous effort of listening for the first tremor of an attack. He rose, knuckled his forehead, rubbed his eyes. A gleam from Osidian's body could just be seen through the huddle of the Oracles. Where he had failed to work out Aurum's intentions, Osidian might succeed. As he approached, Morunasa rose to bar his way.

'I must talk to him.'

The Oracle shook his head. 'It's our Lord who must wake him from within his dreams.'

'But we're still in danger. The dragons could be upon us at any time.'

Morunasa frowned. 'What I fear is more terrible than dragons.' He leaned close. 'Can you not feel the presence of our Lord?'

The odour of the Isle of Flies was coming off his ashen skin. Carnelian shuddered, swayed by Morunasa's certainty, finding it easy to sense the Darkness-under-the-Trees pulsing in the gloom. It drove the last fragment of fight out of him. He became too weary to withstand his doubts. The edifices he had constructed with his reason crumbled. An old fear returned. What if Osidian's power revived? What if victory over the auxiliaries were to give him back ascendancy over the Plainsmen?

'The men intend to return to their homes today.' It was Fern approaching.

Carnelian glanced back towards where Osidian lay.

'He can do nothing to stop it.'

'You're so sure?'

Fern gave a solid nod, but Carnelian thought he saw a glimmer of uncertainty in his eyes. Rising commotion and an impression of movement made him notice the whole hillside in motion. In the twilight it was hard to make out individuals.

'First they'll return to the battlefield,' Fern said.

Carnelian nodded. It was good that they should save what they could of their dead.

'I fear Hookfork will be waiting for them,' said Fern.

'I too,' said Carnelian, glad to be able to share his fear with someone. 'But that leaves us with the mystery of what caused the thunder in the night.'

Fern grimaced. 'Could Hookfork have gone north, hoping to trap us?'

'If so why has he allowed us to destroy his auxiliaries?'

'Perhaps he felt it all-important to protect his render supply.'

Carnelian shook his head. 'A few dragons would have sufficed for that.'

Fern's eyes flashed. 'What then?'

Carnelian had an answer, but dared not voice it until he was sure it was not desperation overthrowing reason. Fern's pained frustration drew it out of him. 'Perhaps he's fled back to the Guarded Land.'

'Why would he do that? You told us the Master's the entire focus of his schemes.'

'He is, but Hookfork might fear the Master reaching the Guarded Land before him.'

With effort, Carnelian strove to analyse matters as a Master might. Barbarians were unimportant; even the loss of so many auxiliaries. What mattered was how all this would be perceived in Osrakum. This war was merely the shadow cast by the game being played there between the Powers. The Wise had risked much in attempting to retrieve Osidian: Aurum had risked everything. If Osidian were to make his appearance unfettered, the alignments of the forces would be disrupted. The Wise might be able to regain control, but Aurum would be lucky to salvage anything at all.

Carnelian became aware of Fern's exasperation. He sought to find an end to untie the knot of his analysis for him, then gave up the attempt. 'Politics.'

Seeing Fern grow angry, Carnelian was about to retreat from his Chosen vantage point, when a thought occurred to him. Such an appearance by Osidian might disrupt the nexus of power in Osrakum enough to cause the whole business in the Earthsky, even the sins of the Plainsmen, to be forgotten. He was stunned, certain he was seeing a move in the game. He found himself trying to remember the few things his father had said about how it was played. Why had his father taught him so little?

He focused on Fern's angry frustration. The desire to save him, to save Poppy and the Plainsmen, to atone for the annihilation of the Ochre, all this meant he must learn to play the Masters' game.

He reached out to touch Fern. 'I'm sorry.'

His friend's face collapsed into an expression of confusion. He watched Carnelian's hand withdrawing. 'I've no wish to understand what the Standing Dead might mean by "politics",' he said, his mouth curling with disgust.

Carnelian marshalled his thoughts. 'Nevertheless I'm now convinced Hookfork is leaving or has left the Earthsky.' Though he could not really believe it, he still felt relieved. Something else occurred to him. 'This could provide us with a way to rid the Earthsky of Morunasa and the Marula.'

Fern looked uncertain, but he was watching Carnelian with hope.

'If the Plainsmen knew that Hookfork was gone would they continue to listen to the Master?'

Fern shook his head. 'But why should they believe your conjectures?'

Carnelian saw how impossible it would be to explain his reasoning to the Plainsmen. If Fern was accepting this at all it was from some vestige of faith that he still had in him. Carnelian felt ashamed, humbled that any should still linger in his friend's heart.

He waited for him to speak. Fern looked up. 'You hope the Master will take the Marula with him in pursuit of Hookfork?'

Carnelian pondered this. It was a fair question. 'I believe the faith he and Morunasa have in the Marula god could be enough to make them attempt it.'

Fern stared blindly. 'Most likely they'd be going to their destruction.' He regarded Carnelian. 'And you'll go with him?'

'I must.'

'Then I'll go with you.'

Carnelian wondered what lay behind this decision. He wanted it to be because Fern still felt something for him. The look in Fern's face suggested he might have bleaker motivations.

He smiled grimly. 'And what if you don't die in battle?'

'I'm sure I'll die some other way.'

Their gazes locked; Fern was first to break contact.

'What about Poppy?' Carnelian said, as much as anything else to cover up a feeling of embarrassment.

Fern chewed his lip. 'I believe Krow would want to take care of her . . . be capable even . . .'

'She wouldn't go willingly,' Carnelian said.

Fern shook his head. 'We couldn't force her.'

Carnelian smiled ruefully. 'The last time I tried that she triggered a battle.'

Fern nodded. 'She's earned the right to choose for herself.'

They found Poppy and Krow together watching the Plainsmen stream down through the mother trees towards their aquar. Carnelian studied the two of them as Fern explained the conclusions they had come to. Krow had eyes only for Poppy's face as she nodded, listening. When Fern was done she looked up at Carnelian. She indicated the deserting Plainsmen. 'You're going to tell me I have to leave with them.'

Carnelian exchanged a glance with Fern, whose look of encouragement prompted a shaking of Carnelian's head.

Poppy looked from one to the other and frowned. 'I don't understand what's going on here.'

Fern answered: 'If you choose to go with us it'll almost certainly be to your death.'

She blushed. 'The Mother will protect us.' She looked hard into Carnelian's eyes. 'I'm coming with you.'

'Then I'm coming too,' said Krow.

When they all looked at him his face too changed colour.

'Many tribes would take you in,' Carnelian said.

Krow glanced at Poppy, slowly shaking his head. 'I'll never again be a stranger in a strange tribe.'

Poppy looked at Fern then Carnelian. 'He's right. You're my tribe now.' She turned to Krow. 'You too.'

Krow coloured again and Poppy smiled. 'Well, that's settled then.'

While Carnelian had been sitting on a rock waiting for Osidian to wake, the grove had emptied of Plainsmen. The sound of them riding away had echoed up through the cedars, then silence had fallen. Brooding mostly over Poppy's decision, he had watched the sun chase shadows from under the trees.

When the Oracles stirred he leapt up. They yielded to him when he pushed through them. Osidian, blinking, shaded his sunken eyes with an emaciated arm. Morunasa leaned down and began interrogating him in a tense whisper. The Oracles craned forward, struggling to listen. Osidian shook his head, pushed Morunasa away and, with a groan, sat up.

His face lit up as he saw Carnelian. 'Where . . . ?'

Looking for a moment like the boy in the Yden, though so wasted, he caused Carnelian's heart to trip. 'Do you remember the battle?'

Osidian went blind, looking within himself. 'My Father was there . . .' He frowned. 'Everywhere . . .'

'The Darkness-under-the-Trees?' Morunasa asked, his eyes like flames.

Osidian glanced at him, confused.

Carnelian caught Osidian's gaze with his. 'The auxiliaries were destroyed, my Lord.'

Osidian frowned. 'And Aurum?'

Carnelian ignored Morunasa, who was baring his teeth at their Quya. He felt this was an opportunity to make a move in the game. Carefully he began describing their flight north; Aurum's disappearance; the thunder in the night. He watched with fascination as Osidian's eyes betrayed his struggle to make sense of it all. He fought to suppress a thrill of excitement as he saw the pattern settle in Osidian's mind, certain he was drawing the same conclusions as he had himself. Osidian was now alight with confidence, evident in the smile that he turned on the Oracles. 'Consider the confluence of events. Can you not see the hand of our Lord behind these developments? Is battle . . .' – his eyes burned – 'not one of the clearest instruments of divination?'

As he rose, the Oracles stepped back, awe in their faces. The birthmark on Osidian's forehead creased as the light dimmed in his eyes. 'He was with me and in me and about me.'

He looked into the shadow still lingering around the nearest cedar trunk.

'We must return south before the dragons come,' Morunasa declared, but the way he searched Osidian's face belied his tone of confidence.

Osidian seemed not to hear him. He looked at Carnelian. 'Where are the Plainsmen now?'

Morunasa narrowed his yellow eyes. 'They've deserted you.'

Osidian ignored the Oracle and waited for Carnelian to answer him.

'They've gone to gather their dead from the battlefield,' Carnelian said. 'And then, I believe, they'll go home.'

Osidian frowned. 'I need them to come with me.'

'Go where, my Lord?' Carnelian said, playing the game and then striving to forget that he knew the answer, to keep his face from betraying him.

Osidian looked around him. 'Where are the aquar?'

Carnelian knew he could say nothing more without revealing himself. He looked to Morunasa, urging him to say what he could not. Almost as if under his control the man obliged. 'With our Lord behind you what need have we of the Plainsmen? We're still yours, my Master.'

Osidian would not be deflected. 'We ride to the battlefield.'

Carnelian nodded and followed him as he strode off to the nearest rootstair. When Fern joined them, Carnelian dared not look him in the eye and clung on to Fern's belief that the Plainsmen would not be swayed by Osidian's words.

Carnelian covered his mouth and nose against the fetid air. The ground was foul with corpses. Everywhere ferns were trampled, clotted with dried blood. Dense, swirling mats of flies gave twitching life to the dead. The sky was darkened by wheeling clouds of ravens, by sky-saurians gliding in arcs. The raveners had left, perhaps having eaten their fill. However other, smaller scavengers swarmed the battlefield. Against such numbers the attempts the Plainsmen were making with their whirling bullroarers to drive them from their feast were futile.

As he rode Carnelian's gaze snagged on a glint here, another there. His eyes found the brass of a service collar bright among the dun and rusty carnage. Its familiar gleam and colour made him turn to see its like around Fern's throat. He regarded the vastness of the slaughter. He had so easily fallen into thinking of the auxiliaries as merely an extension of Aurum's malice. Now he was seeing them as men. Each had been recruited from some tribe that was probably not so different from those of the Earthsky. The next Plainsman he passed he stared at. Hunched, the man was picking his way through the mesh of arms and legs, searching. Carnelian scrutinized his face. Its sadness and the misery in the darting eyes was not restricted to his own people. So close, the man could not help seeing that the rage he had sought to turn against the Standing Dead had fallen on men like himself. Carnelian felt the confidence he had drawn from his plotting leak away. This was another massacre: a slaughter of brother by brother. All his defences crumbled. He drank in the horror unmediated by excuses, by judgement, by any consideration of context. A sort of wonder rose in him, a bleak, surprised contemplation of how it was that he and his kind could wreak so much horror, but pass through it unscathed.

Voices raised in anger broke through his trauma. Morunasa was shouting and other Oracles were joining their commands to his. At first Carnelian could not understand their anger, but then he saw the Marula streaming across the battlefield, defiantly gathering up their own dead.

A bellow drew all attention to its source. Osidian rode in among them brandishing a spear. In stentorian tones he summoned the leaders of the Plainsmen to attend him. For a moment everyone stared, as stunned as Carnelian, but then his heart died as he saw men, from all across the plain, disengage from what they were doing and begin trudging towards the Master. Morose, Carnelian urged his aquar forward.

Even before anyone had reached him Osidian began haranguing them. 'There's no time to gather the dead!'

Carnelian was appalled by the depth and volume of his voice. He was transfixed by the wasted beauty of his face so bright against a halo of flies. Enringed by Plainsmen Osidian raked their ranks with his emerald gaze. 'We must fly north.'

Carnelian tore his eyes away from him, expecting to see awe in the faces round him. Instead there were only frowns of confusion. He noticed that not a single face was painted. He realized he could not remember the last time he had seen a whitened face among the Plainsmen. Osidian continued to explain that Hookfork was fleeing north. That if they reached the Leper Valleys before him they would achieve victory. That the victory they had won the day before was as nothing to that which awaited them should they obey him now. Carnelian watched the Plainsman faces sour. His heart leapt as they began to turn away. Osidian, confident of triumph, was blind to his audience. Carnelian almost felt sorry for him. When Osidian became aware, with a look of surprise, that he was losing them, the pitch of his voice rose and he tried to buy them with promises. Shriller and shriller it grew as more and more of them turned their backs on him. Even his wrath when it came was not enough to turn their tide. His threats indeed produced some sour laughter. The joy that had burned up into Carnelian's chest quickly turned to ice. The Plainsmen had ceased to fear the Standing Dead. They had seen behind their mask, had seen them weak, had seen they were just men. At that moment their power seemed fallible, broken at their feet. Carnelian recognized with chill horror that this was what the Wise feared most. Before the cancer of such a liberation from fear should spread through the body of the Commonwealth, the Wise would strike to eradicate it, to cut out even the memory of such freedom.

Contemplating this bleak scenario, he was slow to notice

that it was Morunasa now speaking, not Osidian. The Oracle, realizing that Aurum's threat was receding and having witnessed the desertion of the Plainsmen, clearly felt confident enough to voice his own demands. He was describing a vision of the theocracy Osidian could build in the south. How he could bring the Marula up from the failing ruin of the Lower Reach. How he could build a new power centred on the Isle of Flies. A new power with which he could conquer the Earthsky and bring all under the sway of the god they both served.

As Morunasa fell silent Carnelian focused on Osidian. His thinned lips began distorting. 'You believe, Morunasa, that, offered a way back to the heart of the world, I would be content to bury myself in the squalor of this wilderness?'

Morunasa looked for a moment as if he had been slapped, then quickly hooded his amber glare.

'Your Lower Reach is dead,' Osidian said. 'Be thankful you have your lives and, if you follow me, I will make a place for you and your god at the heart of the world.'

As Morunasa seemed to ponder this a while, Carnelian sensed how desperate the man was in spite of all his bravado.

Morunasa fixed Osidian with baleful eyes. 'That is not enough, Master.' He indicated the receding Plainsmen. 'Now that they reject you, all the power that remains to you are our Marula.' He glanced at the other Oracles. 'And we are the key to them.'

Osidian gazed northwards as if he were seeing all the way to Osrakum. Morunasa watched him. Perhaps it was doubt bringing a twitch to the corner of his mouth. 'The Marula here will not follow you much longer. They must be told what's befallen their people, their kin. Then you must give them a reason to follow you.'

Carnelian saw it was Morunasa who most needed a reason. The other Oracles fretted, not understanding what was being said, but sensing the tension. At last Osidian turned. 'What reason would suffice?'

'An obvious one: you must promise to save our people.'

Osidian smiled. 'You believe I can?'

Morunasa nodded. 'The Masters know how to wed bronze to rock. You can build a new, imperishable ladder between the Upper and Lower Reaches.'

And there it was, Carnelian thought. Morunasa had had no choice but to reveal how dependent he was on Osidian, who clearly had known this already. His smile seemed carved upon his bony face. 'We couldn't permit your salt to disrupt our economy.'

Morunasa frowned.

'Further, the Isle of Flies would have to become a vassal of the Labyrinth.'

Morunasa's frown deepened as he looked at his knees. He raised his yellow eyes. 'We must have freedom to run our affairs as we wish.'

'We'll allow you enough salt to meet the needs of the Lower Reach and to hire enough Plainsmen to defend the Upper Reach.'

'Is there more?'

'You will send me a tithe of Marula children.' Osidian smiled. 'I have a whim to make myself a guard of black men.'

Slowly, Morunasa gave a nod of defeat.

Carnelian approached Osidian. 'I will go with you, my Lord.'

Osidian glared at him. 'From whence comes such unexpected loyalty?'

Carnelian shrugged. 'To remain here would serve only to bring down more disaster upon these people. Besides, it was the Ochre that I loved.' He could see the Tribe in the battlefield dead.

Morunasa was arguing with the other Oracles.

'I had hoped to free you from this unseemly . . . attachment.'

Carnelian saw Osidian was ready for a fight, but he would not allow himself to be goaded. 'I have motives of my own, Osidian. I wish harm to come to my Lord Aurum.'

131

Osidian's eyebrows rose. 'Indeed?'

'I do not believe you will regain your throne, but there is a chance that we shall reach the Guarded Land.' He smiled. 'I imagine that, were news to reach Osrakum that the Lord Nephron has been sighted, it might cause some consternation, some realignment of the Powers.'

Osidian looked suddenly serious. 'Not only would my mother be discomfited but, most likely, Aurum would fall victim to the wrath of the Wise.'

Carnelian nodded. 'Be aware I seek to bring as much mayhem as I can to Osrakum.'

'In the hope that thus you might make the Wise forget to punish your precious Plainsmen?'

Carnelian let the question hang unanswered as he watched the Oracles riding among the Marula. Where they passed, there rose a wailing. Many of the warriors turned to glare at the two Masters. Carnelian was glad of their hatred. It was well deserved. He found no consolation from knowing that the Marula were now suffering something like the same loss they had inflicted on others.

He turned to Osidian, making no attempt to hide his feelings. 'Surely the massacre of the Ochre is punishment enough?' Osidian's face was unreadable. Carnelian turned away again to watch the Plainsmen gathering their dead. 'Their fate will become a myth of horror and warning among all the tribes,' he said.

He felt a touch on his arm and found that Osidian was regarding him with something like hope in his eyes. 'Then we are once more on the same side?'

Carnelian suppressed revulsion; he had to play the game. 'Fern, Poppy and Krow are coming with me. In the unlikely circumstance that we win I intend to induct them safely into my House.'

Anger and sadness mingled in Osidian's expression, but he lifted his hand in acquiescence.

They became aware Morunasa was approaching. He looked

grim. 'They'll follow you, Master. But, be warned, we'll hold you to our agreement.'

Osidian controlled anger at being addressed thus. 'Make ready to ride north.'

Morunasa almost smiled as he shook his head. 'They'll not leave until they've burned their dead.'

He was demonstrating to them both that they were not going to command unquestioning obedience. The Marula might need Osidian, but he was in their power.

As they watched him ride off, Osidian said: 'I wish there were a way to communicate with the creatures other than through that man.'

Carnelian glanced at Osidian, uneasy. Marching north with the Marula it was not only Osidian and he who would be in their power, but also his loved ones. And Osidian was right: it was not the warriors who were the real danger, but their masters, the Oracles. It must surely be possible to find a way to speak to the warriors direct.

Marula corpses being thrown on pyres were pumping smoke up into a sky choked with scavengers. The Plainsmen were loading their dead onto drag-cradles they had improvised from the battlefield debris. Tending to the dead seemed such familiar work that Carnelian was drawn to help. What held him back was his reluctance to diminish the Masters any further in Marula eyes.

His thoughts turned to the auxiliaries, and what their beliefs might have been. That their bodies should be left for the scavengers would doubtless be as abhorrent to them as to the Plainsmen or the Marula. Eventually he sent for Kor and her sartlar and set them to piling the auxiliary dead upon blazing saddle-chairs. Soon they were adding their smoke to that of the Marula.

Weary, burdened by loss, as night approached men collapsed among the smouldering pyres. The reek of smoke, of roasting flesh was close enough to the smell of food to bring nausea. At least the fires kept the raveners at bay.

Carnelian rose. Overnight the horror of the battlefield seemed to have seeped into his bones. Raveners nosing round had haunted his half-waking dreams. He peered at the smoke-choked dawn. Huddled in twos and threes the Marula were grimacing at the bony grins of their charring dead. He wandered among them, but could not find the one he sought.

Osidian had the Marula scour the battlefield for the bronze-bladed lances of the auxiliaries with which to replace their flint-headed spears. After that it was a drawn-out struggle to gather them and get them mounted. As the Oracles marshalled them, Carnelian watched Osidian ride up. Osidian indicated the Mother's Backbone with his spear. 'There lies the road my Father made for us.'

Carnelian said nothing as Osidian rode ahead, but glanced to where drag-cradles were pulling away into the south. Gazing at the hunched Plainsmen he knew he would never see any of them again. He looked for Poppy and Fern and Krow. When he found them, his feelings of love for them conflicted with his conviction that they were all riding to certain ruin.

Mangled ferns formed the wake left by the passage of Aurum's dragons. Dung rose in hills along that route. Poppy complained about how much they stank. 'Like ravener shit,' she said, her face twisting.

'By feeding them render,' Fern said, 'the Standing Dead make them akin to raveners.'

Osidian drove them hard through the blistering day. His eyes, revealed in the slit of his indigo swathings, were always fixed on the wavering horizon. It was a race, but not one that Carnelian or the others were certain they wanted to win.

As dusk fell the pace slackened. Eventually they came to a halt and found a place up among the Backbone rocks to make a camp. People sat round their fires in morbid silence.

Even before dawn Osidian had them mounted and trudging northwards. It was around midday when they began to see the horizon ahead, banded with shimmering white. With each passing moment this mirage solidified. As they looked for a spot to make camp, Carnelian watched the band turn pink then bloody purple. Gazing thus on the cliff edge of the Guarded Land he could not help feeling a yearning to see his father and his family again.

In the still morning air the Guarded Land was solid, undeniable. Its cliff formed the pale foundations of the sky. As everyone packed up, Carnelian spotted some sartlar and wondered what those creatures must be feeling at seeing again the land of their bondage. He watched Fern and Poppy and Krow frown as they stole glances at the cliff. In their faces and those of the Marula he saw his own doubts and fears reflected. Only Osidian's eyes burned as if gazing upon some long-lost lover. Soon he had them mounted and coursing northwards again, their shadows spindling away towards the vertebrae of the Backbone. As the shadows shortened, the sun began to melt the Guarded Land into a shimmering vision that rose ever higher as they rode.

Cresting a ridge Carnelian lifted his feet from his aquar's back. As she slowed he stared. The slope plunged down into a land veined with rivers. These braided eastwards into a single channel: a torrent that issued from a canyon where the cliffs of the Guarded Land closed upon the slopes of the Earthsky. Westwards the land fanned out, undulating, sparkling with water, spreading to hazy distance. On the edge of delight he felt unease. The greens should have been more vibrant. There was a greying, like mould tainting the skin of a lime. Blackened patches. Scars disfigured the canopies. Everywhere he could see signs of fire. Of flame-pipes.

*   *   *

They wound down a wide gully. Trees towered on either side. Gouged scree showed where the dragons had gone before them. Soon they were riding into a deepening twilight. Sky was banished to shifting diamond cracks high among the branches. The air moistened like breath. Moss carpeted the slopes and boulders. Lichens furred trunks and twigs. They followed a tunnel, edged with splintered branches, that had been ripped through the forest by something massive. The only sounds were aquar footfalls muffled in the moss. Carnelian could not rid himself of a feeling of impending doom.

At last it began growing brighter up ahead. The air was acid with a reek of charcoal. His eyes took some moments adjusting to the light. He became aware that a sinister autumn had come to these forests. The ground was scattered with the ghosts of leaves. Trees were skeletal and black. The feet of the aquar were churning up a mist of ash. This was a world so wan it felt as if the capacity to see colour had drained from his sight.

They came to a river soapy with ash. After crossing it they climbed a path lined with posts. As they neared this fence Carnelian's dread flared into full horror. Melted, grinning, to each post was what was left of a human being.

That was only the first avenue of charred bodies. In that ashen land such fences were common. Villages were thickets of charcoal stumps on the edges of black fields. Drifts of ash like grey snow banked here and there. The cliff of the Guarded Land was a vague, leprous wall. Even the sky seemed bone. The Oracles with their ash-rubbed skin seemed natural inhabitants of that sere land. Soon pale powder floating on the air had turned their march into a procession of wraiths. Terribly white, Osidian urged them on, driven by an inner vision that seemed to make him blind to the devastation. Hope leached from Carnelian's heart. Anything beyond this dead world must be an illusion. Life and vigour were a fantasy; atrocity the only truth.

Darkness found them on a hill overlooking the ruins of a village edging a black stream. The gold of the fires they lit seemed counterfeit. That dead world drew Carnelian away from the warmth. He drifted down the hill. Burnt trees had become the roots of the encroaching night. His footsteps faltered as his nostrils caught a whiff of cooked meat, of decay. Passing down an avenue of charred corpses, he could feel their eyeless sockets watching him. Despair claimed him. Would he never escape the Isle of Flies? Was he doomed to witness its malice infecting the world? Was he, perhaps, a carrier of its contagion?

Some doorpost stumps tempted him to enter the circle of a hovel. Ash buried his feet with each step. His toe struck something. He crouched, tentatively feeling for it though he feared it might be some gruesome remains. Something smooth. A lump with small wheels at the corners. A toy, then. He searched the twilight, hearing the echoes of children playing. Ghostly memories of life. He put the toy down carefully and left the house.

As he approached the black water the path sank into mud churned deep by the crossing of the dragons. Warped boards stretched between posts formed a fragile causeway zigzagging out through the reeds. The gurgle of the stream seemed unnaturally remote. A heron lifting heavily into the air flapped away, pale, along the stream.

He felt a tremor in the boards beneath his feet. Turning, he could just make out a small figure approaching.

'Carnie,' it breathed.

'Poppy.'

She came to nestle into his hip. He caressed the warm, stubbly swelling of her head.

'Why?' she murmured.

'This destruction?' He contemplated all the death he had seen, all the suffering and wasted lives. 'The Standing Dead need no more reason than does a plague.'

'It must end,' she said, an edge of pleading in her voice.

Carnelian desperately wanted it to end, wanted desperately to make it end, but he was powerless. Resistance was self-indulgence. Every act of defiance led only to more victims. He was so weary he could not believe his heart still beat. His knees wanted to buckle. He would fall into the reeds. Slip into the dark water, drown. But release would not be so easily found. It seemed that his atonement was to be doomed to watch everything he loved die.

Poppy, starting, awakened his senses. Reeds were parting. A sighing as something pushed through them. A shadow growing solid. Carnelian, reliving the night he and Osidian were captured in the Yden, scoured the twilight. The causeway was too narrow for them both to run back along it. He crouched to put his mouth to her ear. 'Run,' he growled.

She clung to him, but he prised her off. He shoved her away. 'Run!' Poppy's face was a blur, then disappeared. He felt her footfalls thumping off and turned to face the shadow. A black boat. He backed away, feeling for the boards behind him with his heels. The causeway gave a judder as the boat struck it. Figures swarmed off it. Carnelian gritted his teeth. His fists flashed as he struck at them. Hard contact skinning knuckles. An outline crumpling. A cry. A splash. He threw them off as they came at him. Shapeless creatures hissing, growling. Despair became rage. He strode forward clubbing at them. Poppy's voice rose keening far away. Then something smashed into his head. He was on his knees, hands pale against the rough wood, receding.

THE LEPER

Purity abhors pollution.
Control of the boundary where these meet
Is control over those who wish to cross it.
(*a precept of the Wise of the Domain Immortality*)

Slipping through glooms roofed with fronds. Each peeping star a needle in his eye. The dull ache in his head threading each fleeting awakening like a bead. Curves rubbing raw his ear, shoulder, hip, ankle. Was he still curled in the womb of the funerary urn? Unhuman heads dipped over him. Murmuring voices. Repeating rhythm of a ferryman poling. Drifting into the harbours of the dead. A woman's voice. The sky's first blush of dawn turned bloody. Suddenly all was a blue so bright it burned him like ice. Carnelian lost his grip on consciousness, slipping back into a darkness haunted by the recent passing of some horror.

Feeling her leaning over him, he opened his eyes. A shape pulled back, oil light flickering over the slopes of its shrouds. It had a head of sorts, a glint of eyes. Carnelian's attention wandered off over rock surfaces that sagged into columns. Moving, the shape drew his gaze back to it. He tried to make sense of what it might be. 'Where . . . ?' he managed.

'Deep in the caves of my people,' the shape said with

139

a husky, female voice. 'In the heart of our camp, far from help.'

Carnelian's head was throbbing. He tried to lift a hand, but it was tethered.

The shape shambled forward, eyes like distant flames. 'You'll not escape us.'

'Who?'

'What does that matter? One of your victims.'

Carnelian heard in her voice her appalling crisis of loss.

'We've sent word to the other refuges. Soon they'll begin to arrive. We didn't want to waste you. It would've been greedy to keep you all for ourselves.' The woman's eyes glittered as they gazed at him. They seemed to linger greedily. She shook her shrouded head. 'We lack your skill at torture, but we'll do our best. I'm sure we'll manage to make it last long enough for everyone to get their fill.'

Animal fear welled up in Carnelian. 'Why?'

The eyes flashed. 'Why? You ask me that? We offered you submission. We grovelled before you. Gave you everything we had.' The voice was swelling the pain in his head. 'Vowed everything. We even worshipped you!'

The cry echoed around the cave then died. The woman rose and Carnelian saw from her movement that, under her shrouds, she had human proportions. He could see no flesh, no hands, no feet. Even the eyes had disappeared into the narrow slit in the swaddling of cloth strips.

'Did you feel invulnerable on your dragon? Did you laugh as you watched our people impaled? Did you revel at your feasts lit by the bodies of my people as they burned alive?'

Carnelian remembered the charred remains. 'Lepers?' he muttered, growing cold.

The shrouded head turned as if to listen. 'What was that?'

'Were they Lepers?'

'Yes, just filthy lepers,' the Leper agreed, 'and you're a Master, but still you will dance for our amusement.'

The Leper turned away, her shrouds sighing as they dragged

on the floor. When silence fell, Carnelian tried his strength against his bonds, but struggling only served to make them bite deeper into his wrists and ankles. Phantasms of shadow were fluttering in crannies in the rock. The Leper thought him Aurum's ally. Anger burned up in him that he was to die in Aurum's place. Thoughts of never seeing Fern or Poppy again caused his mind to falter with despair. Images merged, divided. He saw the Lepers burning, impaled, and they merged with the Ochre dead. He had made it all happen. Akaisha burned beneath the arches of her tree. Aurum, a pillar of ice, did not melt even a tear. No, the cold beauty was Osidian's. He saw his own face in Osidian's; Osidian's in his. Even aged Aurum's. All cut from the same ice. Each guilty of the other's crimes.

Afloat on a black sea oppressed by glowering sky. Terror slicing through the depths. Is that dawn spreading livid across the waves? Spume turns to choking dust. Whirling towers of it like smoke. Becalmed upon rusty dunes, he stoops to scoop a handful of red earth. Itching palm. Worms sliming into his honeycomb flesh.

Carnelian woke bucking. He calmed down, heart pounding, letting the dream drain away.

The Leper was there. He shuddered at her touch as she cleaned him like a baby. Her skin rasped against his thighs, his buttocks. Wiping him with leprosy. Trapped between waking horror and his dreams Carnelian had nowhere left to flee.

The shrouds rose over him. Water dribbled into his mouth, trickled down his cheek then neck. 'Drink.'

A lip of rough earthenware opened his mouth wider, clinked against his teeth. 'Drink.'

A choking flood. He arched his back, spluttering.

'You're not what I expected,' said the Leper once his coughing had subsided.

Carnelian imagined all kinds of faces deep in the black

141

mouth of her hood: deformities more hideous than the sartlar Kor's.

'You don't believe you will die?'

Carnelian did and longed for it, as the only remaining way out. The Leper leaned close enough for Carnelian to see bandages stretched over a mouth and chin and all the way up the bridge of a nose. The eyes were remote stars reflected in a midnight sea.

'I'm wrong. I can feel your fear.' The bandages deformed as the Leper spoke. 'Beg for your life!'

The scene lost cohesion, dissolved.

'You'll beg sure enough when we torture you.'

Carnelian felt he was overhearing a faraway conversation.

'I saw many plead as they were broken. Cut, crushed, impaled, burned. You watch it, because you can't turn away. Hard to believe they could still be alive. A mere rag of a thing, blood and piss and shit leaking away, but still watching its tormentor with animal eyes, pouring a scream so sharp it's nothing more than a gasp.'

Silence. A silence that made Carnelian come back, that made the Leper solid again.

'Stripped of your power you're not so different from us.' She lifted a shrouded arm from which hung a ball of stained cloth. 'You foul yourself as a man does.' The arm dropped. 'Though your beauty is unearthly; your eyes. I can see why you hide behind a mask. Your face is more terrifying than leprosy. But don't imagine that weakness . . .' The Leper waved an arm over Carnelian. 'It won't save you. My people were more helpless than you look now. We'll show you we can be as merciless.'

Silence and Carnelian enduring it, trying to stay in the cave.

'Why did you do it? We offered you submission.'

Carnelian tried to find words.

The Leper jabbed a foot into his ribs. 'Why?'

Carnelian moistened his mouth to speak. 'Do Masters need a reason to be cruel?'

                        *   *   *

The Leper was there again. 'Where've you hidden your auxiliaries?'

Carnelian strung the words together. Auxiliaries?

'You're hoping we'll go back to our homes. You call us
vermin. Extermination is a Master's word.'

Carnelian remembered the pyres and the stench of death
in his nostrils as familiar as his own smell.

Light thrust into his face, searing his eyes closed.
'Where?'

Carnelian tried to turn away, but fingers digging into his
cheek forced his head back.

'Dead,' he said, moving his jaw against the Leper's grip. 'All
dead.'

The grip released. 'Do you take us for fools?'

'It's true.'

'You expect me to believe that?'

'We killed them all.'

'What're you talking about?'

Carnelian tried to describe the battle as he recalled it, in
snatches. As each jewel-bright impression flashed into his
mind he tried to hook words to it. He fell silent, aching for
his loved ones.

'Are you trying to tell me the Plainsmen defeated you?'

Carnelian registered the Leper's incredulity as it mixed
with his confusion. Clarity came as a vision of a landscape
columned by rising smoke.

'Are you?'

Carnelian managed a nod.

'All were destroyed?'

'All,' Carnelian said, as memory dug its roots into him.
Pyres burned the smiling dead. Trees burned. The Koppie
Crag with darkness coiled around it like a snake. Poppy's
face striped by tears. Flashes of light, smothering dark, faces,
familiar, strange. The living and the dead. Enmeshing memory
and dream.

When he surfaced again in the cave the Leper was gone. A lamp guttering was causing shadows in the walls to shudder like mourners.

'You were travelling with Marula. We followed you. We're sure they had no brass around their necks.'

Carnelian groaned. 'I told you before: the auxiliaries are all dead.'

The Leper shifted her shapeless shrouds. 'There was a girl with you, a Plainsman girl.'

Carnelian's heart leapt. 'Poppy.'

'Your slave?'

Carnelian tried to shake his head.

'Why weren't you wearing a mask? Why the rags? Were you disguised? It doesn't make sense.'

Carnelian began rambling, discovering his past even as he was coining it into words.

'Living with them? You were living with Plainsmen?'

Carnelian brought the Leper into focus. 'They gave us sanctuary.' That last word chimed like a bell, then he was overwhelmed with loss, with the horror of what he had allowed to happen.

'Why are you crying?' said the Leper, her voice huskier with alarm.

Carnelian staunched his tears. The dead demanded not tears, but atonement.

'Sanctuary from whom?'

Carnelian responded to the gentleness in the Leper's voice. 'Other Masters.'

Carnelian sensed her surprise.

'You fought with the Plainsmen against the auxiliaries?' she whispered. 'You were fighting the Master who is our enemy . . . ?'

'Aurum,' Carnelian said, tasting the syllables as if his breath had become that of a corpse.

'Au-rum,' the Leper repeated. 'It's strange to know our

144

enemy by name.' She leaned towards him. 'You hate him too. I can see it in your face.'

'I hate all the Masters. All.'

The Leper waited for the echoes to fade. 'But him most of all.'

Carnelian almost explained how Aurum had had his uncle put to death, but that did not feel right. The Lepers had primacy when it came to loss at Aurum's hand.

'Then you weren't involved in . . . in the atrocities . . . ?'

Carnelian managed a dry chuckle, almost a cough. 'You're wrong. I am involved. Aurum came down here searching for . . . for me.'

The shrouded head nodded. 'But if he's your enemy why are you prepared to die in his place?'

Carnelian grew suddenly fatigued, worn out, despairing that he could not find enough energy to confess his crimes.

His buttocks were raw. The discomfort he could bear, but he was enough himself to feel the humiliation of being cleaned like a baby. When the Leper had finished she brought a bowl of water to his lips. He drank, trying to pierce the shadow in her shrouds.

'There's no need for you to have to keep doing this,' he said. He lifted his ankles to show their bindings. 'Loose me then I can relieve myself decently.'

The Leper drew back. 'So you can try to escape?'

Carnelian's heart leapt at the thought of rejoining his people. He shook his head. He had been a prisoner for days; they must be long gone.

'Even if you managed to pass through our caves, you'd be lost in our land. We'd hunt you down.'

Carnelian smiled. 'Well then.'

The Leper looked down her cowl at him for a while. 'Roll over.'

Carnelian did as he was told. He felt her working at the knots and bore the pain as the rope peeled away from his wounded flesh. His arms seemed wood as he brought them round in front of him. He grimaced as he saw his wrists; the colours of bronze and so swollen that they did not seem to belong to him at all. He sat up to watch the Leper free his legs. Her bandaged hands were nimble. He imagined the skin beneath the bandages with its sores, its thickened plaques. It quickened fear in him that he must now be a leper.

When his feet came loose, he gingerly drew them apart, grimacing at the ache and stiffness.

The Leper laughed. 'You'll have difficulty standing on those, never mind escaping.'

Her laughter was a warm sound. Not meant unkindly. Relief perhaps.

'What're you called?' he said.

The Leper regarded him in her motionless way. 'Lily.'

His face must have betrayed his surprise because she added: 'Do you think a leper has no right to a pretty name?'

Carnelian shrugged, discomfited.

'And you?' Lily said.

Carnelian told her and was charmed by how she pronounced it. 'Do you wear those shrouds even among your own kind?'

Lily turned her head to one side. 'Why do you ask?'

Carnelian shrugged. 'I'm not sure.'

'Perhaps it's because I'm monstrously disfigured.'

'I've seen much disfigurement.'

He sensed her anger in the cast of her shoulders. 'How like a Master that you should only be capable of seeing this from your own perspective.'

Carnelian was stung by this rebuke, not least because it was justified. 'I'm sorry.'

'A Master apologizing to a leper?' She laughed. 'Incredibly, you seem to have the capacity for pity. Keep it for yourself, Master.'

Her bandaged hands rose to her cowl. As she pulled it back, a cascade of white hair was released that, for a moment, blinded Carnelian to anything else. It was not old woman's hair, but thick and lustrous. Then he saw her skin, rosy, pale as one of the Chosen. There was something strange about her eyes. She held his gaze and he saw they were the colour of watered blood.

'You like my eyes?'

Carnelian could not think what to say.

Lily began to unwrap the lower half of her face. Each unwinding showed more of a wide, flat nose. He tensed, fearing the ragged wound of a mouth that would make a mockery of her strange beauty. Her lips appeared, a washed-out coral, but unflawed.

The last bandage fell away from her small chin. Her eyebrows and lashes were white. Carnelian gazed, mesmerized. 'You're beautiful . . .'

Her eyes darkened. 'Who did the Enemy, Au-rum, kill? Someone you loved?'

Carnelian told her about Crail, then: 'And you?'

She looked puzzled. 'Is it possible all Masters are like you under their masks?'

Carnelian frowned. 'No. Most of them are like Aurum. Pray you never see him unmasked. The atrocities against your people he carried out with indifference or for his amusement.'

Lily's eyes grew dark as roses. 'Lust for revenge withers my heart; the hearts of all the Lepers. He murdered everyone I loved.'

On the cave wall, shadows played out the scenes of torture and death that Carnelian had witnessed the Masters inflicting; that he had inflicted.

'You're not to blame.'

Carnelian turned on her. 'You don't know that!'

Her shock chased away his anger. 'My actions, my inaction, have brought disaster on those I've loved. I was a fool to believe I could escape what I am. We're a cancer.'

Lily nodded. 'One for which there is no cure.'

'Perhaps,' Carnelian said, not seeing her, seeing only Osidian's face, Aurum's, the sheer, invulnerable ramparts of Osrakum. 'I would cut it out and burn it if I could find a way.'

He became aware of how intensely Lily was looking at him. 'I believe you would.'

She chewed her lip. Carnelian waited, knowing she wanted to tell him something. She made her decision. 'Your Marula are looking for you.'

'What do you mean?'

'They search the Valleys for you.'

Carnelian had been certain that the Marula, driven by Osidian's obsession with reaching the Guarded Land before Aurum, must be far away by now. 'Have they done violence to your people?'

Lily shook her head. 'Though they threaten it if you're not returned.'

Such restraint on Osidian's part made Carnelian uneasy. 'You shouldn't trust him.'

'Him?'

'They're led by another Master who's more like Aurum than he's like me.'

'But he too is Au-rum's enemy?'

Carnelian considered this. 'For the moment.' When it came to wars between themselves, Masters were driven more by whatever might bring political advantage than by their feelings.

'So you don't want to be given back to him?'

Carnelian probed Lily's red eyes. He thought of Fern and of Poppy. He thought of playing the game. 'You told me your people are being gathered to watch me die.'

'They are, but it's not you they really hate.'

'One Master will seem to them very much like another.'

'That's true, but I now believe you are different.'

Lily offered him a shroud. She looked angry at his hesitation. 'Take it. Put it on – or are you too proud?'

148

Carnelian regarded the rags. To take them was to confirm what he already knew. He might prefer death to living as a leper. He imagined Poppy shunning him, Fern. 'I don't think I can return.'

'Why not?' she demanded.

He indicated the shrouds she was holding out to him.

She looked puzzled. Then her white eyebrows rose. 'You mean as a leper?'

Grimly, Carnelian nodded.

To his surprise Lily threw back her head and laughed. 'I thought you would've noticed I'm clean.'

Carnelian stared at her. 'But . . . why then do you wear a shroud?' Before she had a chance to answer he knew it already. 'A disguise . . .'

'A leper's all but invisible to the Clean. As an object of horror we're almost invulnerable. They may cast stones, but that's just fear. We slip through their cities like shadows.'

Carnelian felt as if she had given him the gift of life. When she offered him the shrouds again, he took them and she helped him put them on.

They crept through the darkness along the edge of a river. Though Lily held a lamp aloft it cast little light. Carnelian felt his way with feet and hands. Then the rock fell away, opening into a cavern, its ceiling low enough to force him to stoop. A diamond-bright slot oozed light in from the outside. Squinting, Carnelian could make out furtive movements. Soon they were passing through an encampment. Chambers had been made by hanging rugs from the rock. Within these lurked thickly shrouded shapes. As he drew closer to the source of light Carnelian almost had to close his eyes against its intensity. People shuffled like ghosts. They drew away from his path as if it were he who was a leper.

When they reached the entrance of the cave Carnelian had to turn his back on the flood of light. His head ached. He felt dizzy.

Lily touched his arm. 'Are you strong enough?'

'I just need some time for my eyes to adjust.'

Looking back into the cavern, he could see people more clearly. Hunched, bony women. Tiny mounds of filthy cloth from which children's limbs projected as thin as sticks.

'Where're your men?' he said.

'I lied to you. Most died defending their families.' She pulled at his arm. 'Come on.'

Lily led him down to the bank. There, concealed under some ferns, was a boat sewn from bundled reeds. Carnelian helped her launch it on the stream. The water was a braided mirror to the fully risen sun. Its rays sliced into his head. The slow rocking of the boat soothed him. A gentle breeze cooled his face as they drifted along the bank. Squinting, he could see Lily using a pole to keep them from running aground.

When he offered to take the pole, she shook her head. 'I'll do it better.'

He slept and, when he woke, he found they were pushing through a dense weave of stems. Gnats threaded the air. Fish darted glinting in the shadowed water. Sometimes the boat would drift into pools along whose banks he glimpsed giants shifting slowly, their movements hissing a sway into the reeds.

Their stream eddied suddenly into a great, winding river. With her full weight Lily poled them towards the northern bank where they could move hidden within tunnels of rushes. Glancing up-river he caught glimpses of an immense gorge.

Soon Lily was poling them down a branch channel that swelled into a water meadow paved with lotus pads and golden hyacinth. The pads squealed as the prow parted them. He tried to talk to her, but she seemed not to hear him. Her shrouds streaked with sweat, she kept the boat slicing through the green.

*　　*　　*

When she pointed over his head, he swivelled round and peered into the twilight. An island rose where the river forked ahead. For a moment he could see nothing out of the ordinary, but then he noticed a thread of rising smoke. He turned back to her, heart beating hard. 'My people?'

She nodded.

He watched her as she punted. Her strength belied her apparent fragility. He glanced over the prow. Osidian would be there, Fern and Poppy and Krow. A part of him longed to see them; another misgave at the thought. The truth was that he felt too exhausted, too drained to take on again the burden of their expectations, of his need to seek atonement.

He looked at Lily. 'How long has it been?'

'Since we captured you? Eight days.'

'So long?' He realized that Osidian must have abandoned his pursuit of Aurum. He considered what this implied about the situation he was going into. Something occurred to him. 'How did you know where to find them?'

Lily raised her pole, then, throwing her weight onto it, drove it deep into the water. 'There're many Leper eyes in these valleys.'

'The camp will be fortified; the Marula guards jumpy. It might be better if you were to leave me at some distance and let me walk in.'

'You think you're strong enough for that?'

He imagined stumbling through the undergrowth, in the darkness.

Lily drew the pole up. 'It might be better if we make our own camp on the opposite shore. I can take you over in the morning.'

Carnelian agreed.

He helped Lily pull the boat up from the water. She lifted a bundle from the stern then made off up the slope. Carnelian followed her, dizzy, his feet snagging on roots. Several times he had to stop to free his shrouds from thorns.

151

They came to a small clearing lit dimly by the darkening sky. Lily found a place to sit. Barely seeing her, he sat nearby. 'I suppose we shouldn't make a fire.'

'They'd see it. Put your hands out.'

Carnelian did so. They hovered, faint, but visible enough for Lily to see them. He felt something falling onto his palms. Bringing it up to his nose he sniffed it. A smoky, cooked smell. Fernroot of some kind. He bit off a piece and chewed. It was floury and faintly sweet.

'This morning a rumour reached us that the Ringwall's been closed,' said Lily.

'All of it?' he asked, confused.

'At least that part running above us.'

He thought about it. Aurum might have closed the border to stop Osidian getting into the Guarded Land.

'Au-rum's doing?'

'Probably,' Carnelian said.

'Why would he do that? Is it to keep you from returning?'

Carnelian's instinct was to deny this, but the lie caught in his throat.

'Why with his dragons does he fear two Masters and a band of Marula mercenaries?'

Carnelian could only answer that if he told her who Osidian was.

'I'm also curious as to why he came down here in the first place. Though there are legends describing a time when the Masters brought fire and ruin down from the Guarded Land, no Leper living can remember such a thing.'

'He came to put down a Plainsman rebellion.'

'Then it had nothing to do with you being among them?'

Carnelian saw that no lie he could come up with would make sense of everything Lily knew. Further, he could not clearly understand why it was that he wanted to keep the truth from her. So he launched into some kind of account of how he and Osidian had ended up in the Earthsky, of what

152

had happened there, of why they had come with Marula into the Leper Valleys.

'I still don't understand why you're so important to him.'

'It's not me, but the other Master that Aurum seeks.' Carnelian went on to tell her why. When he was done, there was silence between them.

'You expect me to believe that this other Master is actually the God in the Mountain?'

Carnelian shook his head. As he tried to explain divine election, he became increasingly aware of her exasperation. 'Do you have any other theory that fits what you know?'

'So you believe Au-rum acts according to the wishes of the current God?'

'Actually I believe the opposite is likely to be true.'

Lily groaned. 'But if he were to capture this other Master, this fallen god, Au-rum would triumph, right?'

'He might be allowed back into the Mountain. I'm sure that's what he desires above all else.'

'And if the fallen god were to reach the Guarded Land he'd cause Au-rum ruin? Perhaps even overthrow the God in the Mountain?'

'The God in the Mountain's unassailable. He has count-less legions. The Mountain is a fortress none could take, but there's a possibility that, should he reach the Guarded Land, he could disrupt the currents of power of the Commonwealth. This I've worked for, will work for, in the hope it will cause the Masters enough confusion that they'll forget the Plainsmen defied them in open rebellion.'

'And Au-rum?'

'He'd fall prey to the God in the Mountain.'

A rasping rhythm of insect calls filled the night. Lily suggested they should settle down to sleep.

Lily shook Carnelian awake. Her red eyes were gazing down at him. She pulled her shrouds over her head and rose. He spent some moments gazing up at the blueing sky. His body ached all over. Groaning, he rose, then plodded down the slope after Lily's pale form.

When they reached the boat they pushed it down into the water and then she held it for him as he clambered aboard. Soon she was poling them away from the bank.

The water was a grey mirror. Night still lingered among the reeds. Winged shapes flitted across the dawn sky.

Lily made one last, slow punt to nudge the boat into the bank. Standing leaning on her pole she seemed a kharon boatman with his steering oar.

'So this is goodbye then?' he said.

She nodded, her face, even her eyes hidden beneath her shrouds. He waited, but there was nothing more. He rose, steadied himself on the prow and swung onto the shore. When he looked back, the boat was already beginning to edge away. He felt suddenly alone and realized he was sorry that he would never see Lily again. He raised his hand in a half-hearted gesture, then watched as she disappeared among the reeds.

Walking along the bank brought Carnelian into view of the camp: a wound in the forest edged about by a crude palisade. Smoke was rising in a dozen spires. According to Lily, he had been away eight days. Time enough for Aurum to make the pass to Makar secure. In lingering, Osidian had thrown away any chance he might have had to overtake Aurum and, with that, the failure of his schemes was all but assured. Reluctant to confront what awaited him there, Carnelian felt like turning round. It might still be possible to catch up with Lily. No, his fate lay before him, for good or ill.

As he approached the camp a cry went up. Marula sprang to the palisade. Carnelian made for a gateway and found it barred by a hedge of lances. There was fear in their faces as they stared at him. Eyes widened as he threw back his cowl. The bronze points wavered and began to rise. He marched forward and a gap opened in their ranks. Soon he was among them, breathing their stale sweat. He saw with what fearfulness they drew away from him. It was not him they feared, but the contagion they believed he carried. One stood out as being braver than the others: Carnelian recognized him as Sthax. He was wondering how to react when a tall, ash-grey man appeared in his path. Carnelian forgot everything else. 'Aren't you pleased to see me, Morunasa?'

The Oracle seemed impassive, but his yellow eyes betrayed a mix of emotion Carnelian could not read. There was an increase in the hubbub. He knew it was Osidian approaching even before he came into sight. A darker figure followed just behind him; a smaller one pushed past them both. Seeing it was Poppy running to greet him, Carnelian grinned. Krow, rushing forward, caught her. She struggled, but fell still when Osidian advanced.

The emerald intensity of his eyes was a shock.

'Are you clean?'

Carnelian saw the fear for him there was in Osidian's face. It humbled and confused him. He nodded. Osidian searched Carnelian's eyes, uncertain.

'I am clean, my Lord,' Carnelian said, in Quya.

Osidian's shoulders fell. He came so close Carnelian felt uncomfortable, but he did not flinch when Osidian leaned forward to kiss him. Osidian gave him one last, intense look then turned away crying out: 'Morunasa, we leave immediately.'

Poppy was there, beaming at him, tearful. Carnelian knelt, opening his arms, and she ran into them. She nuzzled him, wetting his throat with her tears as she rattled out the fears she had had for him, how long they had searched, how she had never given up hope. Looking over her shoulder, Carnelian saw Krow gazing at her, hesitating as to whether he should come to greet him or wait. Next to Krow, standing like a post, was Fern. Carnelian thought his eyes cold. Upset, he gave all his attention to Poppy. By the time he looked up again, Fern had disappeared into the maelstrom of the Marula breaking camp.

They rode across the island. The villages they came to had been abandoned but, though the roofs of their huts had been burned, the circles of their mud walls were still intact. Trees still shaded the paths. There were some dead, but these hung rotting from trees among ferngardens still fresh and green.

They waded water meadows following underwater roads whose routes were marked by posts. Eventually they came up out of the water, where a track led up to a ridge. It was only when they crested this that they saw, below, the black swathe of devastation branded deep into the earth. Soon they were once more riding through a grey land spined by charcoaled stumps, down avenues of the impaled dead. Where the dragons had passed they had left the earth scarred. The rest of the day was a slog along a black road made by flame-pipes.

In deepening dusk they made camp on the edge of a valley. While some Marula cleared the ground others began to erect a palisade. Osidian told Carnelian he wanted to talk. They passed through a perimeter of aquar being fed to the heart of the camp where Oracles were setting fires. At the centre of this space was a hearth already lit. Osidian sat down, his eyes on the flames teasing smoke from wood and dry ferns. When Carnelian joined him, Osidian proceeded to question him about the Lepers. Carnelian did not feel it a betrayal to tell him what he knew.

As he described the pitiful refugees he had witnessed, Osidian nodded. 'They hate Aurum?'

'Venomously.'

'Could we use this hate? Would they fight for us?'

Carnelian did not like the direction Osidian was taking. 'I told you already I saw no men, just women, children.'

'Was my Lord then overpowered and captured by women or children?'

Carnelian had to admit that this was unlikely, though he had only indistinct memories of his capture.

'You learned nothing else at all?'

Carnelian followed his instinct to pass on the information he had gleaned from Lily. 'The Lepers told me the Ringwall above here has been closed.'

Osidian's eyes pierced him. 'How could they know this?'

Carnelian shrugged. 'They told me word had come down the river to them.' He saw how hard Osidian was taking this news. 'You should not have waited here for me.'

Osidian regarded him, emotions shifting in his eyes. 'It was already too late to reach the pass before Aurum.'

Carnelian was surprised to feel disappointment. Did he really want to believe that Osidian had chosen to abandon his campaign for love of him? He focused on what was important. 'Then you know it's hopeless.'

Osidian frowned. 'We shall go on. We will reach the pass tomorrow.'

'Why go on? If it is not Aurum who has closed the Ringwall then it is the Wise. Either way the Commonwealth will be impenetrable.'

Osidian's birthmark folded deeper into his frown. 'We shall see.'

Under the licking onslaught of the flames the tangle of firewood was collapsing.

Morunasa appeared. 'Master, you wanted to check the perimeter.'

Osidian rose. He looked down at Carnelian. 'Tonight I would rather that my Lord should sleep at my fire.'

It was the sadness in Osidian's face that made Carnelian agree. He watched him move away with Morunasa, then turned back to the fire and saw in it a vision of what would happen should they try to force the Pass against dragons.

He punched the earth. 'No!'

'Who are you talking to, Carnie?'

It was Poppy approaching. Anxiety jumped from his face to hers. 'What's the matter?'

157

He reached out to catch her wrist. Drew her to his side. 'Nothing.'

She looked at him, puzzled, then said: 'Do you have dreams?'

He humphed. 'Oh yes, I have dreams.' But he did not want to talk about them, especially with her. 'Where's Fern?'

'Out there,' she said, pointing with her chin. 'I left him with Krow.'

Carnelian smiled at her. 'Krow's turning out to be nicer than you thought, isn't he?'

Poppy looked down, chewing her lip. 'I suppose.' She looked up. 'I came here to tell you what's been happening and to find out what you've been up to.'

'You go first,' he said.

She began describing what had happened on the night he was taken. 'The Master's rage was terrifying. He sent the Marula searching for you in all directions.'

Carnelian remembered her cries.

'In the morning his rage had cooled, but it was still burning in his eyes.'

She gazed at him and he nodded, knowing exactly what she meant. 'The Master said that, if the Lepers thought they'd suffered from Hookfork's dragons, they'd soon learn they could suffer much worse at his hands. It was Fern who told him to go easy. He suggested we should use the terror they'd suffered to our advantage. Numbed by horror and loss, the Lepers might respond better to kindness.

'I think it was seeing how frantic Fern was that made the Master listen to him.'

'Frantic?'

'Don't let his coldness fool you, he was frantic.'

'How do you know?'

'Well, for one thing, the two of them worked on getting you back, together, like brothers.'

Carnelian found this overwhelming. Poppy saw the change come upon him and took his hand. 'They both love you.'

By the time Osidian and Morunasa came back with some of the other Oracles Poppy had gone. Carnelian had been trying to work out how he felt. He watched Osidian approach and reminded himself of what he had done to the Ochre. Whatever else he felt, that could never be forgiven.

He addressed Osidian in Quya. 'My Lord, is the perimeter secure enough to defend us against Aurum's return?'

Osidian gazed at him as if he were holding an internal debate. 'If he comes with huimur alone we can escape him.'

'What if he has obtained more auxiliaries?'

'Well, then we will find ourselves in a difficult position. Nevertheless my calculations suggest we still have a few days' grace. Enough time, perhaps, to force our way up to Makar.'

The next morning, Carnelian, having saddled his aquar, went to look for Fern. He found him adjusting the girth on his saddle-chair. Fern glanced up as he approached, then returned to what he was doing. Carnelian watched him, searching for an opening to conversation.

'Poppy told me how you worked with the Master to try and get me back.'

'It was either that or watch him prey on some other poor bastards,' Fern said, without turning.

Carnelian stared at his back. Desiring to touch him. 'Was that the only reason?' he said, then grimaced, longing to take the words back.

Fern whirled round. 'What do you want from me?'

Carnelian could look into his brown eyes now. There was anger there, but also a vulnerability, as if Fern were caught in a trap he could not escape. Carnelian yearned to help him free himself, but did not know how. 'I'm not sure.'

Lunging forward, Fern kissed him. 'There. Do you feel better? Now both of us have proved we don't care if you're a leper.'

Carnelian stared. Fern vaulted into the saddle-chair, then

touched his feet to the aquar's neck. The creature rose, forcing Carnelian to step back. As he watched it pound away he frowned, confused.

After crossing a stretch of marshy water their march brought them up onto the hump of an island. For the rest of the morning they journeyed along its spine, keeping parallel to the silver band of the cliffs of the Guarded Land. They were still following Aurum's ashen road.

The sun was at its highest when the land began to sink down into a vast swamp, on the other side of which they could see the gaping maw in the white cliff. Green land ran up into the narrowing throat, greying until it became the pale thread that led up to Makar.

Earth softened to mud as they descended towards the swamp. Soon they were wading, water up to their saddle-chairs, following the winding route marked through the water lilies by posts. Here and there they would pass a mound covered with the charcoal ruins of some hamlet whose inhabitants' tattered remains spiked the road posts, grinning like Oracles.

At last they began to leave the pools behind. Ahead the cliffs of the Guarded Land rose white and scabrous in the afternoon. They followed the high ground west towards the gaping Pass.

Shadows were stretching when they turned north riding directly for the Pass. The ground became scrubby and strewn with rocks the colour of bad teeth. As the Pass widened to receive them, the cliffs that framed it rose higher still, so that Carnelian felt he and the Marula were shrinking. Soon the pale boulders surrounding them were so large that, even riding, they could no longer see over them. Larger still they grew, becoming cliffs in their own right. The Guarded Land had risen up to fill the sky with ramparts etched by deepening shade. Then shadow fell on them like a tidal wave. The sun was shut off by sheer, forbidding rock. The Marula shivered. Carnelian wound his uba around his face.

They marched on in twilight, though behind them the land was still soaked in gold by the westering sun. When even this began to darken Osidian called a halt.

They made a camp among some boulders. The Marula sent foraging came back with roots like snakes. The fires cheered them. Some dared to turn their backs upon the Pass. Others faced it, though they sank their heads so as not to see it. Carnelian gazed into its abyss of darkness. Somewhere up there was Aurum and his dragons. The Pass had a look about it of the canyon that led up into Osrakum, though it was impossible to imagine that a smiling lake encircled with palaces lay within its black depths.

In the dawn, men eyed the Pass nervously. Osidian sent word round that they should hone their weapons. Carnelian watched the Marula sharpening the bronze of their stolen blades and made a show of doing it himself, though he failed to see how lances would be effective against dragonfire. At least it distracted everyone from the coming trial. He ran his finger along the edge of his spearhead, imagining what the day ahead might bring. He was a victim to his hopes and fears. Glancing up, he saw Poppy working hard on some flint she had found. Fear for her choked him.

At last Osidian ordered them to mount. Soon they were filtering up through the boulders into the black throat of the Pass, the sartlar, as usual, at the end of the column. Narrower and narrower the Pass became. Closer and closer its limestone ramparts. The sun bathed the valley behind them, but they were denied its light and heat. A chill wind blew constantly in their faces carrying a bleak odour of remote, empty places. Scree skittered constantly down from above. The scrabbling their aquar made upon the chalky paths was echoed by the cliffs, so that it seemed their march was haunted by other, invisible riders. The walls on either side were filled with caves like empty eye sockets or toothless, gaping maws. Occasionally they crossed the mouth of a tributary canyon down which sunlight could be seen glowing; some were only a narrow slit, others wider, choked with boulders or rotten with caves.

Then light caught the ragged summit of the western cliff. It burned lower, chasing shadows from the strata, turning the whole cliff brilliant white. Down it came until it reached the canyon floor. A tidal wave of incandescence broke over them. The sun was on their backs. Carnelian loosened his robe, delighting in the warmth seeping back into his bones, but the heat kept building. Breathless, the wind fell silent. The air began to melt, the cliffs to dance. Soon it was unbearable and they had to seek shelter in caves.

Some nibbled at djada, some fed from sacs. Carnelian sipped water from a skin, squinting out at the featureless blaze, trying to sear the fear from his heart.

They waited for the shadow to slip back across the canyon floor. They waited until its stone was cool enough to stand on. Then they resumed their march, the breeze returning to waft in their faces, to lift and flutter their robes like flags.

Day was failing when they saw ahead a fork in the Pass. Its walls had been drawing in steadily to squeeze the sky above into a luminous strip. The sun was just gilding the craggy heights of the eastern wall. Carnelian was as weary as his aquar. Around him the Marula sagged in their chairs, their mounts plodding forward with drooping necks. He lifted his head to examine the canyons of the fork as they approached. The right and narrower of the two had a steep, irregular floor. The left was wide with a smooth floor and gloomy almost to the brim. He squinted, trying to pierce its shadows. Something caught his eye: a regularity like the crenellations of a city wall. He resolved the shapes into towers supported by great black masses. His cry of warning was drowned out by a harsh, metallic braying that reverberated so deafeningly in the Pass it seemed the limestone cliffs must shatter and fall.

'Dragons,' Carnelian breathed as the trumpet echoes faded. He gaped at the line of monsters stretched across the Pass.

'Their pipes are unlit,' Osidian cried. 'Ride between them!'

With that he launched himself towards the dragon line. Morunasa bellowed out a command that was taken up by the other Oracles. They kicked their aquar forward. Reluctantly the Marula followed them. Through his feet Carnelian felt his aquar keen to shoal with her kind. He let her go, casting glances from side to side. Fern overtook him. Poppy and Krow were looking to him.

'After them, we have no choice.'

Then he had to give attention to his aquar's increasing pace. He rolled with her strides. Riding the rhythm he could look up and face the dragons. Dim massing of shadows, they seemed more like the columns of the Labyrinth than creatures of flesh. Their towers with banner masts and rigging seemed incongruously delicate machines. His eyes detected a fraying above them. 'Smoke,' he groaned. 'Their pipes *are* lit,' he cried, but his warning was lost in their rushing charge.

A coughing came from somewhere above, then lightning. Night became day. Shrill screaming. Gobbets of fire spitting through the air. Incandescent arcs. Black masses mushrooming suddenly into great rolling clouds in which danced shards of sun. The reek of naphtha made his nose run, his throat raw. A rotting sulphurous stench. And heat, a furnace heat that beat in waves upon his face. His aquar stumbled, thrashed her neck from side to side. He struggled to make out the shapes of men and riders. Scratches of their cries engulfed by another chorus of shrieking fire that lit up the world. He urged his aquar forward; saw Osidian, terrible, with flamelight living in his eyes as he commanded everyone to advance. Carnelian located Morunasa and veered his aquar towards him. 'Retreat,' he cried. 'Back.'

Morunasa's face was lurid with reflected light. Just as he turned to face Carnelian, he disappeared behind blossoming, rolling blackness. Carnelian felt more than saw the Marula flee. The dragons hung before him, horned, their great white eyes blindly staring, their towers reflecting the firestorm. Osidian's pale face was coming towards him, distorted by rage. 'Where're they going, the cowards?'

Carnelian was allowing his aquar to turn away from the heat when he heard a voice he knew. He searched for it. Located Fern, who was struggling to force his aquar into the dragonfire. The creature fought his control and he half fell, half tumbled out of his saddle-chair. Stumbling to his feet he confronted the dragons with arms upraised.

Carnelian was slipping away from him as his aquar picked up speed. There was no stopping her. He threw himself out of his chair, was kicked up by her rising knee, flew through the blazing night. It seemed as if the curling flames were his wings. Then the ground slammed into him.

He lay dazed, feeling thunder and the detonations through his ribs and jaw. He pushed himself up. Fire spirits uncurled like serpents, spun like acrobats. Fern's voice drew him. Carnelian could see him dwarfed by the pillars of smoke, in the path of a blade of quivering light. He lunged towards him. Felt heat peeling his skin, turning his eyes to leather. In front of him Fern arched his back as the flame roared towards him. His hair was crisping. He danced and twitched in a shower of sparks. He threw his arms up to deflect the light and screamed. Carnelian reached out for him, gazing into the sun. He clutched his body. Pulled its weight onto him.

Slumped under what was left of Fern, Carnelian staggered away from the inferno.

BARGAINS

Sexual attraction is a dangerous and chaotic force. If we were
not free of it the mirror-like clarity of our thought would be
stirred to opacity. Though this force cannot be excised from
the Chosen it can and must be controlled. The incarceration
of fertile females, while it ensures the accuracy of the blood
calculus, as importantly constrains the sexual force between
the genders to run along channels that we control and
supervise. The fraction of the force that remains at least
partially unconstrained between females within a forbidden
house is a small and measurable factor. Far more dangerous
is the fraction that remains unconstrained between males
and for which no effective system of control has yet been
devised. This free sexuality is to be considered dangerous
in the extreme. It has the potential to severely disrupt the
astrological calculus with the consequence that our
ability to project our thought into the future
could become fatally compromised.

(*extract from a beadcord manual of the Wise of the Domain Blood*)

A sickening odour of cooked meat was wafting over him as
he rolled with the gentle pace. A sinking feeling, then cool
hands lifting him. Carnelian rolled his head and saw Sthax.
He smiled.

*   *   *

The profile of the rock under his back was forcing him to lie a little twisted. In the dim light he could just make out a ceiling of fractured stone. He was waking from another awful dream. Was he still among the Lepers? He jerked as he remembered Fern burning in the flames. The movement released a stinging pain on his arms, his shoulders, his cheek. Enduring it he rolled over and saw a familiar, small shape stooping. 'Where?'

It turned, and was Poppy, her face in the moonlight blank with fear. She rushed to him. 'How do you feel?'

'Fern?'

A grimace squeezed tears from her eyes.

Carnelian sat up, reeled. 'Not dead?'

Poppy shook her head, shrugged, tried a smile. She helped him get up. He leaned on her as he took some steps to where a body was lying naked on the rock. It had Fern's face with lips blistered and hair burned away, but it was not his body. What lay there was swollen. Carnelian fell to his knees beside him and dared to touch him. Fern's left arm had the texture of dead leaves. Carnelian edged in close to peer at his face. He winced at the cooked smell coming off his flesh.

Poppy knelt on the other side of Fern. 'We've poured water on his burns. We don't know what else to do.'

He glanced up and saw her despair. Then back down at Fern's face. He put his ear to Fern's mouth. 'He breathes.'

He straightened up, staring, stunned by the disaster. A small inner voice said: Are you surprised?

Poppy was there in front of him. 'You're burned too.'

Carnelian looked down at his arms. They stung. His robe was charred, but the skin beneath seemed unbroken. He glanced back at Fern.

'You saved him. You brought him out of the fire. We brought you here.'

'We?'

'Marula.'

'Sthax?'

Poppy nodded. 'He was one of them.'

166

Carnelian looked around him at the cave they were in.

A shadow loomed over them. 'What now, Master?'

It was Morunasa. Carnelian was overcome by a surge of rage. 'Why ask me?'

'The Master won't speak to me.'

Carnelian rose and saw shadowy forms scattered through the cave. 'Where is he?'

Morunasa walked off and Carnelian followed him. As they wound through the cave, scared faces turned up to watch them pass. One man whimpered, another embraced him with a long, trembling arm. Leaving them behind, they came to the mouth of the cave. The moonlight made the Pass seem a delicate picture engraved on glass. Osidian, leaning against a rock, seemed part of it.

Carnelian moved round to stand in front of him. Osidian's gaze rose. 'You countermanded my order.'

Carnelian felt sick. 'What?'

'You sent the Marula back.'

Carnelian groaned. 'Do you really imagine the aquar would have ridden through that firestorm?'

Osidian glanced at Morunasa, who was making no attempt to hide his resentment of their use of Quya. 'I would have thought it would suit you to have the Marula dead.'

'I no longer know what I want.'

Osidian nodded as if this were some great wisdom. 'It is time to admit defeat.'

Carnelian stared at him. It felt as if the last prop holding him up had been pulled away. Though he had never believed in Osidian's plan, opposition to it had defined his own. 'So that is it, you are simply going to give up?'

Osidian glanced up the Pass. 'I will wait here for Aurum. I want to die in Osrakum.'

Carnelian looked at him with contempt. 'Never a thought for anyone but yourself.'

Osidian looked around as if wounded. 'You can come with me. The Wise will punish you, but you will survive.'

Carnelian looked back into the cave. 'And these others?'

Osidian shrugged. 'I do not imagine my Lord Aurum will let them live, but you can try to bring some with you.'

Slow anger simmered in Carnelian. 'I will not so easily abandon them.' He turned to Morunasa. 'Oracle, at first light, we'll leave this infernal canyon.'

'And go where, Master?'

Carnelian felt suddenly so tired it was an effort to remain standing. 'I don't know. I really don't know. Perhaps we might find some Lepers and get some help for our wounded.'

He gazed at Osidian. 'Stay here by yourself if you want.'

He walked back into the cave. When he reached Fern he sank down, drawing Poppy towards him and putting his arm around her.

Before he led the Marula out from the caves Carnelian waited until the sky was bright enough to light the Pass. In spite of the care with which he and Krow had loaded Fern into his saddle-chair, with each step his aquar took, he jigged like a doll. Many Marula were nursing livid burns. Some were crammed two to a saddle-chair. Aquar that had been badly scorched had become uncontrollable. Looking back along the line, Carnelian saw not a military force but a mob of mauled and beaten men.

As the morning passed, the wind following them seemed to urge them to greater speed. Still, he was not keen to risk the wounded on the uneven ground. Allowing his aquar to find her own route down he had plenty of time to think. Osidian was there, riding at his side, brooding. Carnelian nonetheless thought it unlikely Osidian would change his mind: he meant to give himself up to Aurum. Carnelian knew he should be thankful Osidian was not bent on returning to the Earthsky, but all he could feel was resentment. It sickened him that Aurum had won. The Lepers would have no justice. Unbearably, the destruction of the Ochre would become nothing more than an incidental occurrence utterly peripheral to the political

168

upheaval their absence from Osrakum had caused. It was as if everything he and Osidian had suffered, all the destruction they had brought about, all the atrocities, were to become nothing more than an inelegantly played gambit in a game of Three. With Osidian's capture and return to Osrakum Aurum and the Wise would have pulled off a major coup. As for him he was a minor piece. Depending on the movements of the major pieces he might end up merely chastised. His House would lose influence. Ultimately, he would be returned to the splendours and luxuries of his palaces. The massacres in the Earthsky and the Leper Valleys would merely elicit some small adjustments in the tributary lists and some measured reprisals of terror against the errant tribes. The ripples that had spread out from Osrakum would undulate away to nothing. Order would return. Everything would be as it had always been. How he yearned to stay behind somewhere, anywhere that he could live in peace with Fern and Poppy, but this desire had been shown for the madness that it was. He had no place out here among the subjects of the Commonwealth. What little he could still do he must endeavour to do well.

Fern's wounds needed urgent attention. The only possible source of help was the Lepers, but even if, somehow, he could contact them and they not only had the means to help, but chose to, where would Fern live out the rest of his days?

Poppy was riding nearby, Krow beside her. There was some hope there. The youth seemed to love her and, in time, she might forgive him. Carnelian tried to visualize scenarios in which they could return to the Earthsky, find a tribe, resume the pattern of their lives his coming had nearly obliterated. He could see nothing but the difficulties. Lily came into his mind. Her people had suffered terrible loss too, and defilement. Among them, his friends might be able to find a refuge; in time, even happiness. This was something that was possible and that might be within his power to arrange. But he was forgetting the Marula. Morunasa's control of them was now the greatest threat. If he found out what Osidian was planning

169

to do, he would have his people slaughter them all. Carnelian's gaze took in the Marula warriors riding all around him. They must be kept busy long enough to get his loved ones to safety. He realized he was searching for Sthax. What good would finding him do? The Maruli was as much a creature of the Oracles as the rest of his fellows. As for Osidian and himself, he cared not a jot. If anything, he drew pleasure from how their deaths might still ruin the game Aurum and the Wise were playing.

He urged his aquar to drift towards Osidian's. When he was close enough he waited until Osidian eventually looked up. Osidian was about to speak, but Carnelian gestured: *No words.* With his hands Carnelian explained some of his thinking. He told Osidian that he would return with him to Osrakum but, first, they would have to survive among the Marula. Osidian was watching his signs with half-lidded eyes. When Carnelian had finished, Osidian gave no indication he had even understood. Carnelian saw how listless he looked. Defeated, Osidian seemed to have lost the will to live. What little motivation he had left would, most likely, be focused on obtaining at least some measure of revenge against Aurum, the Wise, his mother and his brother. Carnelian recognized that, for whatever came next, he was on his own.

The sun was low when they began emerging from the shadow of the Pass. Surveying the emerald mottle of the swamps, the winking diamonds of water, Carnelian let it all flow over him and disperse the shadow from his heart. For a moment he even managed to forget his failures and the coming reckoning.

They wound through boulders, beneath stands of acacias, across ferny meadows until he saw, ahead, a cleavage in the earth. He took the Marula down into it, towards a watercourse nearly choked with white rocks through which myriad streams percolated. He chose a spot where jumbled slabs enclosed a honeycomb of caves and crannies. There among cascading rivulets he bade the Marula make a camp.

Poppy found them a cave: a wedge of cool shade that tapered into darkness. Here they laid Fern out on a slab, setting his puckered burns against the cold limestone. Soaking their ubas in a little stream-fed pool they applied them as poultices upon his angry, red skin.

Carnelian left Poppy and Krow nursing Fern, telling them he intended to beg help for him from the Lepers. Then he went in search of Morunasa.

The Marula inhabited all kinds of hollows, like nesting birds. The handful of sartlar had dug a hole in the earth to hide in. Morunasa and the other Oracles had taken up residence in a series of slots that lay up the slope of a vast, lichen-streaked slab. Two kneeling warriors were lighting a fire around which the Oracles were seated in a half-circle. All save Morunasa gave Carnelian a nod as he climbed up to them. Morunasa indicated a space for Carnelian to sit. He betrayed no reaction when Carnelian announced his intention to get aid from the Lepers, but first spoke to his people in their tongue, then fixed Carnelian with an enquiring look. 'To what end, Master?'

'We need to find another way to the land above. The Lepers are likely to know many.'

Morunasa gazed out over the watercourse. The black limbs and bodies of the Marula looked dismembered among the limestone boulders. Without looking at Carnelian he spoke. 'We have little belief left that getting there we'll achieve anything.'

Carnelian found it hard to push his claim further. He could see as well as Morunasa how bony were the arms of the men working on the fire. It was obvious to all how weakened the Marula had become, how dispirited. 'We all need time to heal our bodies and spirits.'

Morunasa gave a nod to this.

'We need options,' Carnelian said.

Morunasa regarded him.

Carnelian explained that he wanted to send as many of the

171

able men as they could to seek out Leper groups to negotiate for medicines, for food, for information.

'Why don't we all go east?' Morunasa asked.

Carnelian opened his hands. They were as empty as his strategy. 'There're many too wounded, too weary, to make a long march through the swamps.'

'The Ochre worst of all.'

Carnelian examined Morunasa's face. Was this mockery – or maybe even sympathy? He was sick of lying, but he dared not be frank. 'A camp so close to the Pass will more likely be safe from Leper marauders.'

'Who do you have in mind to head this expedition?' asked Morunasa.

'You?'

Morunasa shook his head. 'I'll remain here with the Master.'

Carnelian nodded. 'I'll have to remain here with Fern.'

'I alone among my people speak Vulgate.'

The fire between them began teasing up smoke. Flames crackled in the central nest of twigs. As the two warriors rose, Carnelian saw one of them was Sthax. The warriors bowed to the Oracles and padded off down the slab.

Carnelian feared drawing any attention to Sthax and so continued with what he had been going to say. 'Then we should send Krow and Poppy.'

'The girl?'

'As I've reason to know, the Lepers are frightened. Having a child speak for us will make us seem less threatening.'

In the morning, Carnelian stood with Morunasa watching Poppy and Krow ride away. Behind them rode most of the unwounded Marula warriors. Carnelian remained there until they disappeared. He feared he had lost them for ever.

Within a crevice, in shadow, Osidian lay like a corpse. Carnelian knelt beside him. It was hard to see in his face the boy from the Yden. The marble round the eyes had hairline cracks and not from laughing. The corners of the mouth drew down into the chin. The lips had thinned. It was a face that betrayed suffering. He regarded it, fighting sadness. Not just for the loss of what they had had, but also for what Osidian himself had lost and suffered.

Osidian's eyes opened and found Carnelian's face. For a moment he looked confused, vulnerable, but then his face set into its familiar, wilful mask. That mask drove compassion from Carnelian. The man lying there was the murderer of the Ochre. He focused on what he had come to say. 'Our greatest peril now is Morunasa.'

When Osidian said nothing Carnelian felt cheated and realized he had been hoping for one of Osidian's dismissive remarks. He continued. 'I find it hard to believe he does not suspect what we are up to. If we are to survive until Aurum comes for us you must strive to allay his fears.'

Osidian pursed his lips, shook his head. 'I can do nothing.'

'Cannot or will not?'

Osidian's eyebrows rose together. 'My god no longer speaks to me. I search for him in my dreams, but he is not there. He is gone so completely that I begin to doubt I ever heard his voice at all.' His gaze sharpened. 'Do you really believe that if I speak to Morunasa he would not see this?' He seemed to sink away as if his flesh were draining into the earth. 'You would be wise to keep him away from me.' His eyes closed and he seemed not even to be breathing.

Carnelian felt fury rising in him. He wanted to shout at him that he could not simply hide from the situation, but he sensed Osidian immovable and went to cool his anger by soaking cloths in the stream and then laying them on Fern's arm and shoulder to soothe the burns.

Old woman's face running with blood. Voice rustling leaves. Carnelian knows she is Poppy. Iron streams in her wrinkles pour down to the sea. Ravens kiting, scribing circles in the wind. Is

*that a body at the focus of their funnelling? No. Fresh uncurling
ferns, green foam on the waves. The tide is coming in. The tide
is coming in.*

Carnelian woke suddenly. Uneasy wisps of the dream unravelled, fading. He sat up and saw Fern lying near him, his
burns fiercely red against the brown-green of the fronds upon
which he lay. Outside their cave the sky was bright and vast
and clear.

As the days passed, Carnelian grew used to the routes between the rocks, to the murmur of the stream. He spent time
losing himself in the limitless sky or gazing at the white cliff of
the Guarded Land, imagining a return to his father, to Ebeny,
to his brothers in Osrakum. Much of every day he spent sitting
on a high rock gazing east across the valleys, searching for
Poppy's return. While the sun was up, it was possible to keep
fear and worry at bay. At night nightmares lay in wait for
him.

As for Morunasa and the Oracles, they rarely descended
from their lair among the rocks. The fear Carnelian had of
them abated. They seemed to have become no more menacing
than a flock of crows.

Though Carnelian had been watching them for a while, it
took some time for him to be certain that the distant figures
were the returning Marula warriors. They had been gone for
more than four days. Straining his eyes, he could still not see
Poppy or Krow among them. Neither was there any sign they
had brought any Lepers with them.

He became aware of movement nearby. It was Morunasa
and the Oracles descending their slab. He cursed. Morunasa
called up to him and he clambered down to meet them.
Together they watched the riders winding towards them
through the boulder field. Carnelian knew that as soon as
Morunasa and the Oracles were reunited with their people
the rest of them would be once more within their power. He

was relieved to discern Poppy and Krow riding at the head of the returning Marula. She waved and Carnelian waved back. As she came closer he unwound his uba so that she would be reassured by his smile. Though she returned it he could see the worry in her eyes. He stepped forward as her aquar sank to the ground and he helped her out of her saddle-chair. The Oracles clustered round them.

Carnelian saw how the returning warriors were making straight for the stream and turned enquiringly to Poppy. 'Are you thirsty?'

She looked at him, unsure what answer he wanted.

'There'll be time enough to drink,' said Morunasa. 'Tell us everything, child.'

Uneasily she looked round the circle of the ashen faces, her gaze coming finally back to Carnelian. He gave her a nod. It seemed futile to attempt to keep anything from Morunasa.

'For the first couple of days we saw hardly anyone. Those we did ran off and we couldn't catch up with them. On the third day, we left the Marula in camp and Krow and I went off on our own.'

Carnelian glanced at Krow, who had come to stand protectively behind Poppy, then returned his attention to her. She looked at him intensely. 'We found several who talked to us. We begged them for help.' She pointed at her saddle-chair. 'They gave us some salve that is good for wounds, but said they could do nothing more for us.'

Carnelian tried to hide his disappointment behind a smile. 'You did well.'

Morunasa turned a jaundiced gaze on Carnelian. 'Did she?'

Carnelian was sure he could hear an edge of menace in the man's voice. Confrontation could no longer be avoided. 'Shall we meet in council?'

Morunasa gave a solemn nod without taking his eyes off Carnelian. He spoke to the other Oracles in their own tongue. They too looked at Carnelian as they gave their assent. He could see they were waiting for him, but he needed time to think. 'Let's meet at nightfall.'

Morunasa gazed out over their encampment, now full of Marula warriors. 'You'll bring the Master?'

When Carnelian agreed, Morunasa began addressing the other Oracles. Carnelian slipped his arms around Poppy and Krow and led them towards their cave. Behind them the Oracles began moving off in pairs across the camp, to speak to their warriors.

Hunched together, they gazed down at Fern. Poppy knelt and pulled a jar from her bag. 'Let's put some of this stuff on his wounds.'

As she pulled the cloth cap back from the jar it exhaled an odour that overcame Carnelian with a memory. He asked her for it and Poppy put it in his hand. He raised the jar to his nose and inhaled. He recalled the sartlar woman applying her burning ointment to the wounds the slaver ropes had cut into his neck and ankles. It was the same smell.

Poppy looked alarmed. 'What's the matter?'

'Nothing,' he said. He returned the jar. 'It has a very characteristic smell.'

'And it burns in your wounds,' Krow said. 'But, soon after, it leaves them soothed.'

Carnelian nodded and Poppy, kneeling, began to apply it to Fern's arm. Carnelian knelt beside her and, taking some of the salve on his finger, bent to anoint Fern's shoulder. 'So they refused to help us?'

Poppy looked at him. 'They threatened us at first, but we could see they were terrified of Sthax.'

'Sthax?'

She nodded. 'I lied to Morunasa when I said we went alone. Sthax asked to go with us. I didn't mention it because I didn't want to get him in any trouble.'

'He asked?'

'Sort of. We made conditions.'

176

'He understood you?' he said, incredulous.

Poppy shrugged. 'Well enough.'

Carnelian frowned. 'You were right to lie about him.' Poppy was gazing at him, curious about his reaction. 'Please continue with your story.'

Poppy let it go. 'The Lepers became friendly enough when Krow showed them his burns. It was only then they believed we'd suffered from the dragons.'

Krow nodded. 'They said we could return with them to some cave, that they would hide us, even share their food with us.'

'Did they?' Carnelian sat back, thinking.

Poppy knew him well enough to be able to read something of his thoughts in his face. 'You want to leave us here with them, don't you?'

Carnelian grimaced. 'There's nowhere else.'

He looked to Krow for support. The youth put his hand on Poppy's shoulder and began to speak, but she jerked her shoulder free. 'What about you?'

Carnelian grew annoyed. 'Look, didn't you see the way Morunasa and the others behaved with me? We're in their power. Even if we manage to survive, I intend to leave with the Master.'

'Leave?' asked Krow, frowning.

Poppy half turned to him. 'Back to the Mountain with Hookfork.'

'Hookfork?' exclaimed Krow.

Poppy ignored him. 'And what about us?'

Carnelian shook his head. 'You two could still slip away, and take Fern with you.' He watched as their gaze shifted to their injured hearthmate. 'Please try to understand. You must know that the last thing I want is to leave you behind, but it's simply madness to imagine I could get you safely to the Mountain. Hookfork's a monster. He already hates me and would gladly use you against me. Eventually, he would make sure you both died, horribly.'

177

He waited, wanting it to sink in. 'Even if that wasn't a factor, we can't trust the Master. He's lost what heart he had. All that's left in him is bitterness and a reflex instinct for revenge.'

Poppy was still staring at Fern, battling tears. Carnelian leaned forward to kiss her head. 'You three will find yourselves a new life here among the Lepers. The one I met was not so different from a woman of your people.'

Poppy was shaking her head. He reached down to catch her chin and brought her eyes up to look into his. 'Poppy, this is the only hope for any happiness I have left.'

As she gazed at him the fierceness leached away. She ducked the slightest of nods into his hand. He let her go.

'What about the Marula?' asked Krow.

Carnelian raised his hand to his brow. 'I don't know.'

Carnelian was setting off to talk to Osidian in preparation for the meeting with Morunasa when a commotion broke out. From all across the camp Marula were converging on its eastern edge. Anxious, Carnelian was drawn to find out the cause. As he pushed through the crowding Marula he heard Morunasa's voice rise in anger. He broke through to find him confronting some shrouded figures. His heart leapt. Lepers.

Seeing Carnelian they surged towards him. The Marula drew back like crabs from a rising tide. Keeping his distance from the Lepers, Morunasa too approached him. 'They say they've come with a warning, but that they'll speak only to the Master.'

Carnelian did not flinch when one of the Lepers stepped forward. Their sudden appearance seemed a gift from the gods. He tried desperately to think of how he might best use this good fortune to save his loved ones.

'We came to warn you, Master.'

'Of what?'

'The Master who is your enemy and ours intends to fall on you with a numerous host.'

'Aurum?'

The Leper nodded and raised a bandaged arm to point towards the Pass. 'Even now he approaches.'

Carnelian was stunned. If this was true everything was suddenly overturned.

'You've little time if you're to escape.'

'What's this?'

Everyone turned to look at Osidian. While Morunasa explained, Carnelian tried to find a way out of the trap they were now in. Though he had achieved the contact with the Lepers he had been working for, their announcement of Aurum's imminent arrival had ruined everything. Morunasa was hardly going to let Poppy and the others go off to safety with the Lepers while he and his warriors remained behind to be destroyed.

The Lepers drew back as Osidian advanced on them. 'How could you possibly know that a force is coming down the Pass?'

'Information's come down to us from the Landabove.'

'Impossible. The Ringwall's closed.'

'It came by a route the Masters don't control. A route we could show you. A route that could bring you, Master, and these Marula up to the Landabove unseen.'

'Unseen?'

'It's a secret way, unprotected.'

Osidian stared at the Leper.

'We'll show you this secret way, but at a price.'

Carnelian had a feeling there was something going on he should understand. 'A price?'

Another Leper stepped forward. 'Au-rum. You must give the Master Au-rum to us.'

Carnelian's heart stopped as he recognized Lily's husky voice and her peculiar pronunciation of the Quyan name.

Osidian laughed. 'Madness, sheer madness.' His face became as forbidding as the cliff of the Guarded Land. 'Do you really imagine I would hand over one of my own

179

kind to you?' His lips curled with disgust. 'To a rabble of filthy lepers?'

Carnelian addressed himself to the Leper he now was certain was Lily. 'Even if we were to agree to this how do you think we could bring such a thing about?'

'What if we brought you up into a city of the Landabove, within its walls, unseen? Would this make any difference?' she said.

'Even so such a city would be well defended by its legion.'

'What if the city of which I speak had been stripped of its auxiliaries?'

Carnelian turned his head enough to see Osidian's eyes. As he expected, they were brightening with greed. Such a city would be vulnerable. What the Lepers were offering was a chance to acquire a legion of dragons.

Morunasa leaned forward, glaring. 'You were rash, Leper, to put yourselves in our power. We can take from you what you know.'

Lily moved to confront the Oracle. 'You could certainly force from us the knowledge of where it lies, Maruli, but it's far away and you can only hope to reach it with the help of many of my kind – you won't get that unless you promise to pay our price.'

This show of defiance to their Oracle was making the Marula bristle and growl. It was a most unexpected sound that silenced them: Osidian laughing. Morunasa looked at him in surprise. Fire had returned to Osidian's eyes. 'You're a fool, Morunasa. Can't you see that these lepers have been sent to me by the Darkness-under-the-Trees?'

As the sun was westering the Lepers led them up into the mouth of the Pass, so that it seemed they were riding towards the very thing they were trying to escape. Then the Lepers turned east towards the cliff of the Guarded Land. The ground began rising, becoming encumbered with boulders, earth turning to chalk that floated in veils around their march.

Though they seemed to be riding towards the cliff they were not following a direct route. The Lepers led them up winding watercourses that followed narrow and tortuous tributaries. The aquar were finding it hard going. As Carnelian watched the shadows lengthen, he wondered how he might find a way to talk to Lily alone.

The sky was striped with ochre as, dismounted, they began to clamber up scree. Behind him Carnelian could see the mouth of the Pass already in twilight. Above them the cliff rose so high it was almost impossible to see its crest.

Dusk climbed the slope after them. It overtook them even as a cave mouth came into view. Near-darkness forced them to slow their climb. At last, Carnelian saw the Lepers ahead begin to be swallowed by the cave. When its arch was over his head, he looked back, then flinched: a glimmering tide was pouring out from the black throat of the Pass. Countless torches and, in among them, clots of darkness that must be dragons. As the Lepers had warned, Aurum had come.

A columned cavern opened before them, haunted by the echoes of their arrival. Smoke hung like mist above fires whose light revealed the trunks of stalagmites. Pools cast spangles up onto the rough arches between the stalactites. Though this place bore a resemblance to the Labyrinth, its far humbler proportions made it seem a wood they were entering, a living place.

Krow and Poppy led the aquar that carried Fern. They chose a spot between a fire and a pool to coax the creature to kneel. Carnelian helped them lift Fern out and lay him on a shelf of rock. As they tended to him they became aware of shades crowding the edge of the firelight.

'Lepers,' Carnelian said in a low voice. 'They won't hurt us.'

Some of the shrouded figures edged closer. They huddled, peering at Carnelian, pulling away when he looked at them.

181

'They'll not have seen the face of one of the Standing Dead before,' whispered Poppy.

Carnelian nodded, then noticed one Leper approaching boldly. He rose to meet it.

'We need to talk, Carnie.' It was Lily, as he had hoped. 'You and us, the other Master, the Marula leader.'

He glanced at Poppy. 'You'll stay with Fern?'

When she nodded, Carnelian followed Lily off into the limestone forest.

When they reached a secluded spot Carnelian reached out to touch Lily's shoulder. 'Why are you helping us?'

The figure in front of him could have been a shrouded post. 'You must realize that Aurum would've easily destroyed the Marula and then left for the Mountain, taking me and the other Master with him.'

Lily turned and her bandaged hands went up to her brow to push back her cowl. The snow of her face and hair, her ruby eyes, were almost as much of a surprise to Carnelian as they had been the first time he had seen them. 'We know that, in searching for you, Au-rum will wreak more destruction upon us. We fear this more than words can describe. We're a traumatized people, terrified, but I believe and have persuaded others to believe that the only hope for us is resistance; that we must seek to restore the dignity we have lost.'

'You seek this through vengeance?'

Lily's eyes darkened. 'Through justice.'

Having his words thrown back at him made Carnelian pause.

Lily grimaced and her face lost its fierceness. 'Most of my people will pursue this as vengeance though, in time, this may change. What I've come to believe, however, is that this hope of justice alone can unite my people, can give them back strength enough to save them from being broken. This is the only way I can see to heal them, to heal our land.'

Carnelian's heart responded to her plea. He wanted to give

her his support, but there was a part of him that feared how much it might cost her people, cost her in the end. 'Even with dragons we might not be able to overcome Aurum. Even if we do, even if we give him to you, our rebellion will be put down by the Masters. Once they restore their dominion they'll pursue everyone they consider responsible. It's unlikely they won't discover the part you and your people have played.'

Lily's eyes, for a moment, seemed to become colourless. 'That is a risk we must be prepared to take. Will we not be in much the same position as your Plainsmen?' She put on a smile, affecting confidence. 'Besides, what more can they do to us?'

Carnelian gazed at her long enough to allow his silence to answer that. She reached out and took his hand. 'Nevertheless, I believe we've no other choice.' She frowned. 'Besides, my heart tells me you were sent to us.'

They both watched the reflections of the Marula dance in a pool like black flames. Carnelian felt dread threatening to overcome him. Her faith was too close to that Akaisha and so many others of the Ochre had put in him. The faith his weakness had betrayed. Still, he could not dash her hope. He believed what she said, that her people needed hope. Perhaps they needed *her* hope.

He put his free hand over hers. 'Lily, you must not trust Osidian.'

'The other Master?'

'It's doubtful he'd give you Aurum even were he in his power.'

Lily shrugged. 'I'm not sure that matters. For now it's enough that my people can play a part in bringing our enemy down. As for the other Master, it is not him I trust, but you.'

Osidian stood before a tapering pillar of limestone, Morunasa at his side, Lepers keeping their distance. He was asking them something about plague.

'Carnelian, they seem to know nothing of the Lord of

Plagues,' he said, his Quya populating the cavern with ghostly Masters. 'Though I should wonder at my own surprise. Still, it has struck me that the ability to spread leprosy by touch is an attribute of that avatar. He in turn is, I believe, merely an aspect of the Black God. Of whom,' he said, shifting into Vulgate and nodding towards Morunasa, 'the Darkness-under-the-Trees is another aspect.'

Morunasa turned away to stare into the shadows. Carnelian could sense by the cast of his shoulders how affronted the man was. He gazed at Osidian, hoping his own contempt was not soaking through into his face. Osidian's need for divine sanction seemed at that moment the most pathetic superstition. Carnelian wondered how Osidian might respond to discovering that, perhaps, every one of the Lepers before him was free of the disease.

'Now that you're here . . .' Osidian turned on the Lepers, among whom Lily was now lost. 'Describe to me this secret way.'

It was her voice that answered him. 'There's a city east of here built upon the very edge of the Landabove. This city controls seven ladders—'

'Qunoth,' Osidian said, a fierce hunger brightening in his eyes.

' – steep ways up to gates in the Ringwall, but there's an eighth ladder known only to the Lep—'

Osidian interrupted again. 'This ladder, this Lepers' Ladder, it comes up into Qunoth?'

'It does, Master.'

'And you say that only your kind know of its existence?'

'We're certain of this, Master.'

'How would we get there?'

'With Au-rum hunting you, we dare not take a route across the Valleys. Instead we must follow trails that run along the foot of the Landabove.'

Morunasa spoke for the first time. 'Can we ride along these trails?'

'No. They're difficult enough even on foot.'

Morunasa shook his head. 'This will take too long.'

Lily's shrouded figure emerged from the others. 'We'll have reason to count the days more than you, Maruli, for it's upon my people that Au-rum will prey as he searches for you.'

'How can we hope to remain supplied during such a journey?' asked Osidian.

Lily shrugged. 'My people have sought refuge in caves all along the margin of the Landabove. I believe they'll share what they have with you and your men.'

Osidian frowned. 'This has been arranged?'

'No, Master, but I believe they will help anyone who has promised to deliver our enemy to our justice.'

Carnelian sensed how distasteful Osidian considered the notion of handing one of the Great over to such vermin. 'Do you swear you'll give him up, Osidian? Will you swear it upon your blood, upon your faith in your god?'

The eyes Osidian turned on him were those of an eagle.

'Unless you do, Master, we'll not help you,' said Lily.

Carnelian could see that Osidian was calculating how he might achieve what he wanted without the Lepers' willing help. 'My Lord, forget not how Aurum has treated you. To save himself he seeks to take you back to Osrakum to your death. Why forgo the chance these people offer you, in order to save such a one?'

Osidian looked down for some moments, then, raising his head, he swore the oath.

'Master . . .' said Morunasa to get Osidian's attention. 'You know what we've suffered pursuing your ends. We've been so close to failure that, in spite of the proofs of favour our Lord has shown you, we're close to abandoning you and returning to the Lower Reach to salvage what we can from its ruin. I share your faith, my Master, but I dare not hazard my people's last chance of survival on anything less than certainty.

'Will you swear as you have done for these – ' Morunasa indicated the Lepers with a stab of his chin – 'that once you

185

come into your own you'll provide us with the means to bind bronze rings to the Upper Reach from which new ladders may be hung?'

Carnelian stared at the Oracle, wondering at his forbearance that he should be prepared to wait until they had conquered Osrakum. Why was he putting faith in such an unlikely outcome? Osidian too was surveying Morunasa with frowning suspicion, but nevertheless he swore the oath and the Oracle pronounced himself satisfied.

Carnelian had his own request to make, one that he wished all those present to witness. He addressed his comments to the Lepers. 'The wounded Plainsman we've brought here can go no further in his condition. I judge he and the other two of his kind are of no further use to us. However, they've served us well enough and I'd like to leave them where they might have a decent life. Would you make a place for them among yourselves?'

Carnelian kept his attention fixed on the Lepers, though really his speech was meant as much for Osidian as it was for them.

Lily spoke for the Lepers. 'Outcasts have always found refuge in our valleys.'

Carnelian nodded his thanks, then turned to Osidian. Their eyes met. Osidian seemed puzzled, but also pleased as he raised his hand to add his gesture of assent.

As Carnelian made his way back through the cavern, he prepared himself for the coming confrontation with Poppy. This time she would have no choice. He drew what thin comfort he could from having found his friends some kind of refuge. As for his own pain at the separation, that would have to wait for when he had the luxury to indulge it.

He reached the place where Fern was lying. Krow was there, resting against a stalagmite. Poppy was nowhere to be seen. The youth looked up at him. It must have been the expression on Carnelian's face that made him jump up. 'Carnie?'

Carnelian saw the youth's alarm, but could only manage a slight smile of reassurance. 'We're going east from here following a route to the Guarded Land.'

'And we're staying behind,' said Krow.

Carnelian nodded. He looked down at Fern. 'He certainly can't come with us.'

'And Poppy?'

Carnelian raised his head and saw how sick Krow looked. 'Where I'm going there's no place for her. You must see that's true.'

Krow nodded.

'And you must stay with her. I sense that that's what your heart wants too.'

Krow looked very young, his face expressing his feelings even as he strove to hide them.

'I've found a place for you among these people. They're not so different from Plainsmen. They're clean. Their leprosy is mostly a disguise they wear to protect themselves from others.'

Carnelian was not sure Krow was taking all of this in. He wanted to do what he could to give the youth back his pride. 'You know I love her too. I'm not allowing myself to feel how much it'll hurt me never to see her again, but it'll lessen my pain to know that you'll be here to take care of her.'

Krow surfaced from his confusion to gaze at Carnelian, checking to make sure he meant it. Then his face crumpled, close to tears. 'She'll never forgive me,' he whispered. 'Never.'

Carnelian moved to him and took his face in both his hands so that Krow was forced to look him in the eyes. 'That's not true, Krow. She's loyal to the memory of the Ochre, but growing in her heart is the knowledge that, whatever part you played, you did so unwillingly.'

Krow was looking at him through tears. He began mumbling, but Carnelian hushed him. He let go of him and stood back. 'I don't need to know anything. I don't want to. I have my own guilt to atone for.'

He looked down at Fern. 'Even he'll forgive you in time.'

Carnelian felt suddenly weary. The pain was beginning to leak through his control and there was still worse to go. 'Tell me where she went, Krow.'

'She wandered off towards the cave entrance.'

With a heart that seemed crumbling stone Carnelian went to find her.

Light from the fires did not reach the entrance and so Carnelian had to feel his way. The rock was cold under his hands, smooth as bone, but wet. The floor was ridged and whorled, so that he almost felt as if he were creeping across some vast Plainsman Ancestor House. Curves and surfaces became visible ahead, gradually, as if rising from the bottom of the sea. Then he saw a luminous aura whose stone-toothed edge made him realize it was the entrance. It grew brighter with each step. Reaching the opening he could feel the moth-wing touch of the night air upon his face. Stars were the source of all the light. Dark walls funnelled into the Pass. Down on its floor he spotted the tiny jewel. A phosphorescent mote in the deep: Aurum's camp.

'You're leaving us behind.'

Carnelian jumped. 'By the horns.'

He searched for Poppy and saw her face against the rock as if it had been carved there.

'Where we're going, even I might not survive. If I do I'll be returning to the Mountain.' Carnelian thought of making some vague promise that, once there, he would send agents to seek her out and bring her to him, but that was a commitment so threadbare it was indistinguishable from a lie. He wanted her to say something, anything. Silence was unbearable. 'You know I'd stay if I could, but if I've learned nothing else I've learned there's no place for any of the Standing Dead out here.'

A silence fell in which he could hear the beating of his heart.

'Aren't you going to tell me, Carnie, that I need to stay here to look after Fern?'

The coldness in her voice chilled him. Almost he told her all about Lily so that Poppy might understand the Lepers were not monsters. Almost he spun for her a vision of what her life might become. Almost, but the silence had grown so deep he knew his words would drown. So instead he sat down to watch the night with her.

They watched until a full moon appeared above the black wall of the Guarded Land. So cold and bright its stare, it was easy to believe it was blinding them.

LEPERS' LADDER

The population of a city can be considered to be composed of three categories: the administrative, the productive and the verminous. The latter two categories form a naturally fluid category and thus should not be considered as distinctive, but rather as polar. The verminous consists of beggars, thieves, lepers and other unproductive elements. Elimination of this category, while theoretically possible, would be inimical to the efficient operation of a city. Not only does control of the verminous provide a visible function for the administrative, but also its existence provides a salutary reminder to the productive of the depths to which it can fall. Additionally, the verminous, being parasitic on the productive, weakens it. Thus, the administrative must suppress the verminous only as far as is necessary to maintain the required level of urban order. This level shall be set dynamically by the local quaestor though subject to this Domain, particularly whenever it is necessary to coordinate suppression across a number of cities.

(*extract from a codicil compiled in beadcord by the Wise of the Domain Cities*)

Carnelian was shaken awake by a shadow looming over him. 'We're leaving.'

It was Osidian. Carnelian realized he was lying against one wall of the cave mouth. He must have fallen asleep there. Dark shapes were shuffling past. The characteristic silhouettes of the Marula: round heads followed by the spike of their corselets. Lances shook above them like a thicket of reeds. Beyond them indigo sky announced the near expiry of the night.

Osidian's shadow shifted and offered him a lance. Carnelian took it and pulled on it to help him stand, groaning at his stiff back. He looked for Poppy, but could see no sign of her in the darkness at their feet.

'The girl's not here,' said Osidian.

'I must say goodbye to her.'

Osidian pointed down into the Pass. 'There's no time.'

Carnelian looked and saw the glimmer of Aurum's camp stirring. Osidian took hold of his arm. 'We must be far from here before the day lights these cliffs and betrays us.'

Carnelian twisted free and went into the cave. He walked back along the file of the Marula as they exited the cave. What little light was filtering past them from the cave mouth soon gave out. For a while he was a blind man feeling his way with the haft of his lance. Then his eyes adjusted to the gloom and he found he could move more quickly. Fern was lying where he expected. A figure rose to meet him. Krow.

'Where's Poppy?'

'I thought she was with you.'

Carnelian could hear the anxiety in the youth's voice. He shared it. He cried out her name. Echoes boomed and faded. There was no answer. 'She couldn't be so stupid as to try to follow me.'

The silence that fell between them gave a lie to such certainty. Carnelian's anxiety flared into anger. The sight of Fern lying as if dead steadied him. He knelt and gazed at him. There was not enough light to see his face, but Carnelian knew well enough what it looked like. Stooping over Fern he found his lips and kissed them. He pulled away and, for a moment, listened to the rhythm of Fern's breathing. He rose.

'What shall I tell him when he wakes?' Krow asked.

Words flitted through Carnelian's mind. Clenching his teeth he silenced them.

A shape materializing near them made Krow jump. It was a Leper, perhaps Lily. 'Master, you're about to be left behind.'

A man's voice. Carnelian's heart rose in him. He turned to Krow. 'Tell him I . . . that I . . .'

He felt the youth's grip on his arm. 'I know.'

Carnelian realized it was time to say goodbye to Krow. He sensed the youth feeling awkward and caught a glimmer in his eyes. He pulled him into a hug. They clung to each other. Gently Carnelian disengaged. 'Take care of Poppy and of yourself.'

'I will, Carnie.'

Carnelian left him and made for the faint glow of arriving day. The cave was filled with the mounds of hobbled aquar. Lepers had gathered at the entrance. They parted as he approached them. Then he was through and jogging along the path they pointed out.

Clambering over rock-falls. Struggling over chalky scree. Sometimes the Lepers would lead them into galleries where massive columns held a skyful of limestone above their heads. Streams had to be forded. As the sun approached the earth Lily assured Osidian they would before nightfall reach a Leper settlement that had been told to expect their arrival.

The dying sun turned the water gushing from the ravine into frothing gold. Lily led them in single file along a ledge above the torrent. Squeezed between mountainous walls the river was deafening. They came into a hidden valley where the water roar quietened to a hiss. Three shrouded figures came to meet them. As they drew nearer, Lily turned to Carnelian and Osidian. 'I must display you to them.'

Carnelian glanced round to see Osidian's reaction. It was no worse than an irritated frown.

Lily saw this. 'If you expect them to feed your men they must believe what they've been told about you.'

She went ahead to meet their hosts and soon returned with them. The shrouded figures approached the Masters and peered up at them. One turned back to Lily. 'You're going to take them all the way to Qunoth?'

'If other caves be as generous as yours.'

The Leper nodded, examining Osidian. He turned again. 'And you say they've promised to give him to us?' The tone was incredulous.

Lily assured him they had.

The Leper came closer to Osidian. 'Why would you give us one of your own?'

Carnelian answered for him. 'He's as much our enemy as he's yours.'

The Leper's cowl shook from side to side. 'Oh no. I don't believe he can have hurt you as badly as he's hurt us.'

Carnelian realized his mistake too late. The Leper came close enough that he could smell the staleness of his shrouds. 'Why should we not hate you as much as we hate him?'

'You should hate us.'

The Leper seemed taken aback, but nodded. 'We shall feed you.'

They were led onto a rock that overhung the torrent. Carnelian followed its white thresh upstream to where it issued from a cave mouth. He leaned down to Lily and pointed. 'Do you know how deep that cave goes?'

She shrugged. 'It's said some wend their way through the blackness even to the very heart of the Landabove. A dark world none dare enter.' She indicated the river below. 'Sometimes strange creatures are washed out. So colourless you can see their blood running under their skin, their organs. Huge eyes or none at all. Sartlar have appeared out of such places claiming they've come from the far interior.'

Carnelian shuddered, imagining the creatures crawling through the endless dark. A world beneath the Guarded

Land, rotten with pits and channels through which sartlar and worse monsters slithered like maggots. He shook himself free of this dark vision. 'Do sartlar live among you?'

'All outcasts are welcome.' His face must have shown his disbelief for she added: 'Are sartlar so different from other people?'

Carnelian did not have time to argue with her. More Lepers were appearing from cave mouths that opened all along the back wall of the ledge. The smell of the food they brought made him aware of how ravenous he was. Soon he was digging into a bowl of fernroot gruel, its bitterness sweetened by his hunger. His gaze kept returning to the source of the river. He imagined Kor crawling out from it. He forgot to chew as he contemplated the horror of that journey. How terrible the lot of the sartlar must be that they should seek an escape through that underworld.

His hunger sated, he became aware of an ache in his heart for his friends. It seemed strange he had shed no tears. Perhaps it was because a part of him did not yet believe he would never see them again.

Two more days of following Lily and her Lepers along the margin of the Guarded Land. Two more difficult meetings with settlements of Leper refugees. The third day brought them to another system of caverns threaded by a river. The Lepers here were more timid. They left food, but Carnelian caught hardly a glimpse of them. Settling down to sleep he was haunted by the roar and echoes reverberating through the caverns.

He woke frightened, but not from a dream. Something needled a trajectory near his face. The sound of its passing was a scratch in his ear. A fly. Carnelian sat up. Another so close it made his skin itch. Sweat chilled him. All round him the buzz of flies. The menace of the Darkness-under-the-Trees tainted the air like rot. A murmur from the Marula warriors. He shared their fear. A commotion came from where the Oracles had lain to sleep, Osidian among them. The stutter of flesh being ripped by flint. Again. Again. The iron scent of blood. The Oracles subsided. He could hear them lying down. The dance of the flies thinned, then ceased. Staring at the dark, he made sure to breathe only through his nose. He swatted at itches he imagined crawling over him and prayed no wounds on his body were open.

He woke still feeling tired. As he made his way with others to greet the morning he considered the horror of the night and decided it must have been a dream, but as he looked around him at Marula faces emerging from the cavern gloom, he saw how weary they were, how red their eyes. In contrast, the Oracles when they appeared seemed radiant. Among them only Osidian looked grim. Morunasa even acknowledged Carnelian with his ravener grin. It was then that he noticed that the robes of the Oracles were streaked with blood.

For many long, weary days they continued eastwards. The Oracles grew increasingly irritable. They scratched constantly at their wounds. Eventually, fever began to glaze their skins with sweat. A twitching at the corners of their mouths showed the pain they suffered as the maggots in them fed. They stared as if their god was gazing back at them. At night they murmured, they cried out. The Marula would not look them in the face. When an Oracle passed by, the warriors would lower their heads almost into the dust. Even their Leper hosts shunned them, though they did not know what contagion it was they carried. Osidian walked among them, seeming the sum of their ashen paleness. Now more than ever they deferred to him as they came seeking his interpretation of their dreams. Morunasa kept his to himself. Sometimes Carnelian would see him squatting by a torrent, his eyes rolled yellow up into his head, his lips quivering in ecstasy.

*   *   *

195

Setting off one morning, they saw, through the mists below, the valleys narrowing towards a gap where the cliff of the Guarded Land approached the escarpment of the Earthsky. Carnelian recognized this as the mouth of the gorge he had seen the day Lily had freed him from captivity. All day it yawned wider as it vomited out the torrent that fed the swamps and river courses. In the late afternoon he became certain they must be making for the caves in which he had been held captive. As dusk fell, he saw the entrance to the caves. For a while now, memories of the dreams he had had there had been seeping unease into his mind.

The caves were smaller than he remembered. Smoke, the smell of food, the musk of people made them seem homely. He chose a place near the cooking fires. Hunched down in his robes and uba he hoped he might pass for one of the Lepers. He watched them roasting fernroot, stirring stews of meat and dried fruit. Steam curling up into the cavern vault caught his eye. The shapes were suggestive, unsettling. They seemed to be showing him things he had dreamed here, though he could not grasp at any clearly. He went for a walk. Passing among the Marula he avoided the Oracles and found that his feet were taking him to the cave in which he had been held captive. The sounds of the encampment were soon erased by the rushing of the stream. This cave too was smaller than he remembered it. He entered, slowly approaching the spot where he had lain. Images began forming in his mind. The water outside had acquired the hissing rhythms of the sea. He turned to face the sound, uncomfortable to have it at his back. He dared to close his eyes. Undulating red, its breath moist and carrying the tang of iron. He opened his eyes and left, desperate to be with people.

The odour of the stews dispelled that of blood. He had left the dream back there in the cave, but still it whispered to him. He moved into the encampment to drown the whisper in the bustle and domestic din. He glanced to the centre of the mass of Marula. The Oracles were lying there with Morunasa, communing with their god. Carnelian could not see Osidian among them and went searching for him.

A shadow appeared in front of him. It touched its chest. 'Sthax.'

Carnelian edged round until light caught the man's face. It was indeed Sthax.

'Where we goes?'

Even though Poppy had told him about Sthax, Carnelian was stunned. He crouched, pulling the man down beside him. 'You speak Vulgate?'

Sthax touched his ear. 'I hear. I learn.'

Carnelian considered asking him whether the Oracles knew of this, but realized that, if they had, this man would not be here now talking to him. Sthax glanced round, then fixed him with eyes Carnelian could not see. 'Where we goes?'

Sthax gave a grunt. 'Where are we going?' Gesturing, Carnelian explained as simply as he could their mission to the Landabove and Sthax nodded, or waved his hand when he wanted something put another way.

'Master promise Oracle?'

Carnelian guessed Sthax must be referring to Morunasa. 'Yes, he made promise to the Oracle to make ladder' – he mimed the ladder with his hand – 'down to your people.' He made a gesture mimicking the winding course of the Lower Reach river, then touched Sthax on the chest of his corselet. The man ducked a bow, then rose and soon disappeared among the other Marula.

Carnelian got to his feet, wondering how this changed things. He remembered where he had been going. Even in the gloom at the back of the cavern, Osidian's towering, narrow form was unmistakable. The Lepers around him barely reached his chest. It looked like a conference. Carnelian became immediately alarmed. He moved towards them, needing to know what was going on. Before he reached Osidian the Lepers began moving away towards where the food was being prepared. Carnelian recognized Lily by her gait and fell in beside her.

'What were you talking about with the Master?'

'Nothing much,' she said, without turning her shrouded head.

Carnelian walked a little way with her, but when he realized she was not going to say anything more, he let her move off and was left feeling uneasy.

When he woke, his first thought was of Lily. The anxiety to find out what Osidian had said to her had long kept him from sleep. He rose and went to look for her. Across the cavern, people were packing up. Marula were filing down to the stream to fill waterskins. They had left the Oracles behind, still lost in their dreaming. Looking for the Lepers who were their guides, he saw a huddle of them by the cave entrance. They bowed slightly as he approached.

'Lily?'

'She's gone, Master.'

'Gone?'

'West.'

'When?'

'Before daybreak, Master.'

Carnelian stared at them, hardly believing them. As he returned to gather his things he was angry with himself that he had not forced her to speak when he could. It was a while later that he realized he had lost the last person he could call a friend.

The gorge swallowed them into a narrow, vertical world ruled by the vast serpent of water that coursed past them, scouring great bowls with its coils, displaying its turbulent scales at rapids, frothing a furious white as it leapt falls. They crept across the mouths of vast bays gouged from the limestone, dank with shadows, heaped with slabs and scree, infested with pockets and wells all skinned with moss and struggling trees;

but mostly the path wound beneath sheer cliffs from which a constant hail of stones kept them anxiously waiting for the next boulder that would fall like a skystone to smash the edge from the path then bound down to the river to be consumed. Much of the cliff was rotten with caverns and slits and cracks that gave into depths that spoke with strange echoes. Sometimes, to circumvent a buttress of the cliff, they were forced to follow their Leper guides into the noisome dark. Stumbling through malodorous dripping tunnels hand in hand, they welcomed the return to light as if it was a rebirth.

Every morning Lepers from the place where they had slept would take over, while those they replaced would be carried off by the flood in a flimsy coracle. Around dusk the new guides would bring them to the next staging post: another collection of caves and ledges within reach of the spray from the roaring water or having access to it down some rough-hewn, precipitous stair. By the river, in some natural pool, a few coracles would jiggle, just safe from its fury. In the caves the Oracles would occupy what space there was. The warriors would make do with any crannies they could find among the rocks. Whatever store of food was there would be distributed to all as a meagre meal.

Carnelian loathed the Oracles with their sweaty muttering, their blind white-in-white eyes as they listened to their Lord roaring to them from the midst of the flood. He was glad to leave them with Osidian as they babbled to him their dreams, though how could he possibly understand them when Morunasa, his sole interpreter, remained aloof keeping his nightmares to himself? Carnelian preferred to eat with Sthax and the other warriors. Covertly he taught Sthax more Vulgate while the other warriors, who deferred to him, kept watch. Carnelian took to sleeping among them in some spot as far away from the voice of the river as he could find. Dreams of bread awrithe with worms plagued his sleep. Often the bread was the world; sometimes his own body.

*　　　*　　　*

'Behold Qunoth,' said one of the Lepers.

The plain to whose edge their guides had led them terminated, at its further end, in a dark wall. Sheer, it butted on one side against the limestone cliff of the Guarded Land, was breached where the river poured in a foaming cataract, then rose lofty again on the other side, where it faded away into the Earthsky. It reminded Carnelian of the Backbone at the Upper Reach.

'Where?' said Osidian.

The Leper pointed to the top of the black wall. Squinting, Carnelian could see that the northern half of it had a pale upper edge.

'A city wall?' Morunasa said.

Gazing up at it Osidian shook his head. 'The Ringwall leftway.' He pointed to the southern half of the rock, which did not have the pale edge. 'That will be the fortress.'

He glanced at the Leper, who gave a nod of confirmation. 'And the Ladder?'

'It's further round. We can't see it from here.'

Carnelian saw that the limestone cliff curved away and that its meeting with the city rock was out of sight.

Osidian was gazing up at the city. 'It would be foolish to cross this plain in daylight.'

They returned to where they had left the Marula. Through Morunasa and the Oracles Osidian told the warriors to prepare for war. Carnelian and Sthax were careful to avoid each other's eyes. They had ignored each other since the Oracles had emerged from their dreams some days before.

Carnelian ate sparingly, brooding on what the night might bring. He tried to dissipate anxiety by busying himself with the honing of his spear. When it was sharp he put it down and went among the clumps of warriors, stopping here and there to pat his belly with a quivering hand to show he shared their fear, smiling when they smiled, laughing with them though he did not understand their jests. With Sthax he exchanged the merest glance.

The crescent moon had fallen behind the cliff when they began to creep across the plain after their Leper guide. Pinpricks of light could be seen along the outermost, upper edge of the city rock. Carnelian imagined Masters there, sleeping perhaps or indulging in some lordly pleasure. That world up there, nearer to the stars than to the earth, seemed at the same time alien and alluring.

Countless gullies gouging the plain made the going hard. Rounding the cliff they saw the city rock looming before them as an immensity of blackness. The Leper led them down a path into a gully. They crossed a stream by means of a plank bridge. As they drew ever nearer to the city rock, Carnelian became aware of a sickening odour. With each step it wafted stronger so that he became convinced they must be approaching some immense, rotting corpse. He tried to wind his uba more tightly over his face, but still the stench thickened until he could feel it rasping at his throat. Seeing the Leper begin climbing a steep slope, Carnelian came to a halt. The night was filled with the sound of retching. A hill rose before them from which the stench was emanating.

'What is this?' he called up to the Leper.

'The Heap,' said his voice, already somewhere above them.

'We have to climb it?' Carnelian did not want to believe it.

'The Ladder's up there.'

He could not see the Leper clearly. Pushing his head back he thought there might be a crack running up the rock all the way to the sky. It seemed to him he had seen this before. Then he realized how much it resembled the fissure in the Pillar of Heaven that the Rainbow Stair climbed. He saw how the crack disgorged onto the Heap. It seemed that the Lepers' Ladder was actually the sewer of Qunoth.

Grimacing, he approached the mound. He put a foot on it and felt it give. Up he went, feeling the mush through his shoes, slipping on slime, hearing the squelch and crunch. Each footfall punctured the outer crust of the mound, releasing fluids and fetid exhalations. He fell several times, knees first into the soft excretions. When he put his hands out to stop his fall, they sank in up to his wrists. Yanking them out, he smeared the filth down his robe. Nausea curdled his belly. Eventually he could control it no longer. Tearing the uba from his face he added his vomit to the hill.

At last they reached the fissure, from which the sewage spilled like guts from a slit belly. Their Leper guide stood in what appeared to be an opening. As he saw Carnelian approaching, he ducked in. Carnelian peered into the tunnel, glanced round to see the Marula crawling up the hill like cockroaches, then crept into the darkness.

The Leper led him deep into the fissure. In the blackness he had to feel his way with feet and hands. The wall on his right was rock, upon which he scraped his hands as clean as he could manage. On his left was a barrier webbed with struts like the wings of a sky saurian. Their smooth curves suggested they might be bone. A leather membrane stretched over this framework was greasy with the noisome liquids it was holding back. Warm to the touch, it seemed the hide of some living monster. One mercy was that, in the tunnel, the stench was less violent.

Fumbling his way Carnelian ran into something that clutched at him. He fought down his horror, knowing it was the Leper guide.

'Do we have to do this in the dark?'

'Flame here turns the air to fire, Master.'

When the tunnel reached the crease of the fissure, it turned up to climb the rock. Carnelian clambered after the Leper, clutching at handholds, hooking his toes into steps made for smaller feet than his. They reached a ledge beyond which was another slippery climb. The Leper scuffing above him was a beacon in the blackness. Sometimes the sound would stop as the Leper waited for him. The first time, Carnelian froze. From below came a rustling as if a swarm of immense insects were following him. Something touched his foot and he jerked it free and moved on. It grew hotter and the air so stinking that, with each breath, he felt he was accumulating a disgusting paste in his lungs. Up and up he climbed until, faint from nausea, dizzy, he started to imagine himself nothing more than a maggot crawling through the cavities of a corpse.

At last he began to be able to make out above him the shape of the climbing Leper. Then Carnelian was pushing his fingers up into light. His arm followed, streaked with filth. A final few rungs, then a ledge. Squinting, he emerged into the open on the Leper's heels.

He and the Leper were standing on a cascade of rubbish dammed by a wall pierced with arches. The lower ones were buried up to their keystones, but the ones above were free and open. Piled one upon the other they carried a parapet of stone upon their backs.

The Leper saw where he was looking. 'The leftway, Master.' He made a gesture to show how it ran over their heads. 'This way.'

He began to scale the slope. Carnelian followed him, climbing through the muck. Rinds of fruit, mouldering gourds, pumpkins, carcasses, down and feathers. Everything was smeared with excrement, clotted with pastes, dripping cloudy fluids. The whole mass shuddered under each footfall. He tried to hoist his robe up, but it was already soaked through. Flies gummed his eyes. The impact of their bodies was like hail. A mat of them swarming everything. The stench was choking him. He stumbled as his foot broke through a saurian ribcage that snapped like twigs. He retched as his hand slid down into soft manure. He rose sobbing with disgust, flinging the stuff off him in dollops. Then he was up again, slipping and sliding. The morning swelled brighter as he came up over the brow of the slope.

'The Midden,' the Leper announced.

Carnelian saw they were on the edge of a hillocked expanse of rubbish hemmed in on either side by mudbrick walls, and running off towards a road already crowded with people.

Osidian strode past him. 'Come on,' he bellowed. He broke into a run and Carnelian chased after him.

Osidian sped ahead along a gully. Carnelian was relieved to have a firm, dry footing. Hovels gouged into the rubbish lined their route. Screeching with alarm, Lepers sprang from their path. Other trails joined theirs as it widened. The hovels rose higher, pierced with windows. Mudbrick walls reared higher still on either side. The hubbub of the road ahead was swelling louder. Soon he could see its bristling multitude. Along its edge men were emptying baskets of rubbish into the Midden. Here and there a cart sagged under a mound of filth. Men wearing sacks over their heads were shovelling it down to where Lepers were waiting to receive it. Faces were turning to gape as Osidian ran towards them. People began pulling at each other and pointing. Close behind Osidian, Carnelian leapt onto the road. Smooth cobbles under his feet. The crowd recoiled from their filthiness as Carnelian and Osidian ran at them. Their height allowed them to see over the sea of heads to where the road ended at a watch-tower that seemed no bigger than their thumbs.

Screams and chaos greeted the Marula as they flooded up from the Midden. Carnelian surfed the wave of hysteria along the road, his gaze fixed on the watch-tower, looking for the flashes that would betray them to the Wise. He saw none, even as the tower lifted its crown of wooden ribs up to the sky. It stood guard upon a gateway murky in the shadows. Nearing this, he was dismayed to see it closed. Ramparts on either side were unscalable stone. He saw the lookout suspended above them in his deadman's chair and slowed. Osidian came to a halt, then turned; though his face was hidden, Carnelian could sense his incredulity. To have come so far and to be thwarted by a gate!

A grinding sound made Osidian spin round. Incredibly, the gate was opening; sliding up diagonally into the wall. Through the gap erupted riders. The gleam of brass at their throats showed them to be some kind of auxiliaries. Osidian and Carnelian leapt from their path. Swerving past them, the aquar crashed into the Marula, who were so densely packed they could not get out of the way. Some were hurled aside, one screamed as he was trampled, but those further back were spreading out. As they circled, something about their smell or their appearance spooked the aquar. Their riders were in confusion.

'The gate,' cried Osidian.

Morunasa was there and understood him. He barked commands and Oracles appeared, their indigo robes streaked with filth. Carnelian saw auxiliaries being pulled down from their aquar. Blood greased the cobbles as the Marula stabbed them. Then he was running after Osidian towards the gate as it began to close. They were soon inside the fortress. Carnelian spotted a monolith guarding the stables entrance to the watchtower that stood sentinel upon the gate. He caught Osidian's eye. 'I'll secure the tower.' Osidian jerked a nod.

Carnelian tried to detect any movement up among the wooden ribs of the watch-tower. Oracles and warriors were pouring past him, chasing after Osidian, who was running up a paved road between walls of jointed stone. Carnelian, grabbing at some Marula, saw Sthax and gestured towards the tower. They exchanged grins, then Sthax began issuing swift orders to the warriors.

Carnelian slipped round behind the monolith. The portcullis behind it was raised as he had expected. He crept in, waiting for his eyes to adapt to the gloom. The place stank of aquar and render. Movement. It was only stable hands, cowering. There was no time to save them. He rushed up the first ramp, feeling the grip of its ridges. Oily, sour smell of machinery. Another ramp. Up into a chamber rocking with ripple reflections. He was aware of a tank against the opposite wall, but his focus was on the wall upon which his right hand rested. He breathed a sigh of relief as he saw the first ladder was down. He crept towards it and peered up into the heart of the tower. No sign of life. He glanced round to see Sthax, grimly determined, and behind him the bright eyes of his warriors as they took in their surroundings. Carnelian pointed up the ladder and began to climb. When he emerged into the first barracks level, he scanned it quickly. Detecting neither sound nor movement he clambered rapidly to the next level. It too seemed empty and so, swiftly, he climbed up to the top storey.

He arrived in a chamber lit only by the light filtering up through the shafts that opened in the corners of the floor. Doors were set into the walls. It was all so familiar; he felt as if he had been there in a dream. He gazed at the door across the chamber with anxious longing, possessed by the belief that, should he open it, he would find his father lying wounded in the room beyond.

Sthax's anxious expression made him remember why he was there. Carnelian stepped onto a ladder bolted to the edge of one of the shafts. Reaching up he opened a hatch in the ceiling and squeezed through it out onto the roof. Sthax clambered out after him. Six ribs curved up to hold a platform over their heads. Carnelian found the one that was laddered with staples. He crossed to it, stepping over naphtha pipes. Climbing the curve of the rib took him out beyond the tower. Its stone walls fell sheer to the world below. A patchwork of flat roofs spread away from the fortress wall. He reached the platform. A heliograph was there at its centre. Purple-robed figures huddled around its brass were aligning its mirrors to the sun. One ammonite was directing the signal not outwards towards the Guarded Land, but inwards into the fortress.

Carnelian advanced on these ammonites, bellowing in Quya: 'Attend me.'

Their faces of silver, turning to him, showed grey reflections of the sky. Their hands clutched the machine. 'You cannot be Chosen,' said one in the same tongue.

Carnelian raised his hands to his cowl. 'Do you wish to look upon my face as proof of what I am?'

The ammonites lost hold of the machine and abased themselves before him in terror. Their pates, not covered by their masks, betrayed them to be nothing more than men. Carnelian commanded them to move away from the heliograph and motioned Sthax and his warriors to stand guard on them. The Marula stared nervously at the mirror faces of the ammonites, but did as they were told.

Carnelian turned to look out over the fortress, trying to locate the target of their communication. His gaze skimmed over its roofs to an open, green expanse, beyond which a wedge of masonry sprang up, narrowing to a tower at the very edge of the sky. Its top was flat and he could imagine a sister machine set there. He strained to see if there were figures on the summit, but could not be sure. The tower appeared to be more massive than the one he stood on. It must be the seat of the Legate of Qunoth.

He strode towards the heliograph. Sun flashed off the strips that made up its mirror. Dazzled, he stooped to take hold of one of its curving handles and swung the machine round to put it out of alignment. He crossed to the opposite edge of the platform to look down at the city. The riot they had caused was still eddying along the main street. He returned to gaze down into the fortress. Its dense symmetries and stillness presented a sobering contrast to the chaos of the city. It seemed a ship becalmed. He lifted his eyes towards the prow of the other tower. Beyond that was hazy space. Carnelian's heart stopped as he realized what he was seeing could be nothing other than the Earthsky. He tried to penetrate its far horizon, then cursed, angry with himself. Was he really hoping he might see as far as the Koppie? Even if he could, what would he see? A cemetery. The memory of the massacre ached in him.

Glancing round, he watched Sthax and his people trying not to catch their own reflections in the metal faces of the cowering ammonites. Grim, miserable, he gazed out over the fortress again. His eyes were drawn to its heart where an immense circular hole sank into its masonry. That had to be a dragon cothon. Tracing its spiked rim he brooded on what he and Osidian were attempting to do. He searched for him or any sign of his Marula, but the alleys were too deep to see into. The deathly stillness of the place made him despair. How could they ever have hoped to take this with their paltry force?

'Master?'

The voice had come from the tower roof below. Carnelian craned over the platform edge, knowing it was Morunasa.

'What news?'

Morunasa's eyes appeared to be bulging out of his face. 'The dragons are his.'

CHOSEN AGAIN

Blood of the Chosen
O fiery river
You will never run into the sea.

(Chosen rhyme)

Leaving Sthax and the other warriors to guard the ammonites Carnelian followed Morunasa down the ladders through the watch-tower. He was struggling to overcome shock. He was also angry with himself. He had known they were coming to Qunoth to take its dragons. Clearly, he had never really believed they would do it. He remembered the dragons advancing on the Koppie amidst their firestorm. The power of a legion was his and Osidian's to wield. He watched his pale hands gripping rungs and was filled with foreboding. He was deluding himself. They might have taken this power together, but it would be wielded by Osidian alone.

Walls on either side were pierced with doors to which ridged aquar ramps climbed. Rising before them, above the roofs, was a curving rampart whose upper rim was catching the sun. Deeply recessed into this was a gate banded with green bronze. From his survey aloft, Carnelian knew this must give access to the dragon cothon. A narrow blade of light running down the middle of the gate showed it was open. When he reached the gap he peered through, but inside it was too bright to see anything. The air was sharp with the tang of naphtha. Underlying this was a duller odour that he could not identify.

Hearing Morunasa coming up behind him, Carnelian slipped through. Four stone piers formed an avenue leading to open space ablaze with light. He gazed up at the piers. They carried beams and bore tall structures like upright fists, between the knuckles of which ran ropes. Some kind of framework was up there, machinery, tensioned ropes crisscrossing like rigging and an immense mast. As Morunasa strode past him, Carnelian turned. Vaults were cut deep into the cothon wall on either side of the gate. He walked back to investigate and saw more vaults piercing the wall all along its inner curve, as far round as he could see, like shiphouses around a harbour.

'Master?'

Carnelian looked round, saw Morunasa waiting and went to join him. Squinting against the glare, they passed the second set of piers. A cobbled expanse opened before them, at its hub what appeared to be a spiked tower of bronze. The open space was ringed about by some three dozen of the stone piers as regular as the spokes of a wheel. Between each pair stretched beams upon which sat an ivory pyramid from which there rose a mast. The last time he had seen such structures they had been on the backs of dragons.

'The Master,' said Morunasa, pointing.

Tiny figures stood beneath one of these dragon towers. As he and Morunasa crossed the cothon floor, Carnelian felt they were a sort of insect crawling across the face of some infernal mechanism that, should it grind into motion, would smear them over the cobbles.

Nearing the figures he grew increasingly alarmed at how precariously the pyramid hung above them. The sagging beams did not look strong enough to hold it, nor the cradle of ropes. The figures were now coming to meet him. Osidian was not among them and they were not Marula. These men were honey-skinned and encased in ribbed cuirasses of black leather. Their skin, and the glint of brass at their throats, showed them to be marumaga legionaries. Instinct made Carnelian shroud his face. When still at some distance they fell to their knees and touched their foreheads to the cobbles. 'Master.'

Carnelian hesitated. No one had made obeisance to him for years. It felt wrong, unnatural. Yet a second impression warred with the first. He became aware of how tall he was, how powerfully he stood upon the earth. Their abasement elevated him. Though he stank from the passage of the sewer, though he was clothed in rags, their posture seemed to demand from him elegant condescension, which found expression in his lifted hand: *Rise.*

They responded to the gesture as if the only life they possessed came from strings dangling from his fingers.

'The other Master?'

Rising, they backed away, keeping their eyes averted. Making a barrier gesture, Carnelian stopped Morunasa from accompanying him and set off after the legionaries. As he passed under the dragon tower he glanced up. Tubes and sockets issuing from its murky base oozed a stench of naphtha. He could not imagine how this device could sit comfortably upon a dragon's back. Emerging from its shadow, he saw his guides were moving under the second ring of piers, upon whose beams rested a squatter structure, like a table that was narrower at one end and had, at each corner, a stump foot. He realized this must be the base of the tower of which the pyramid was only the upper part.

As he passed under this second platform, a saurian musk began to overpower the naphtha reek. Wariness that he was approaching an earther, or even a heavener, made Carnelian slow. It was the hair rising on his neck that alerted him to this being a creature even more dangerous. Further, the air was tainted by something like the carrion stench that raveners gave off. He peered into the darkness that yawned before him. They were approaching one of the vaults cut into the cothon wall. Framed in its dark mouth was Osidian's slender figure in his Leper shrouds, but Carnelian only had time to glance at him before he froze. Something vast lurked in the gloom. He began to make out a beak hanging high above Osidian's head. From this, vast curves swept back to the swelling bows of a cranium that branched on either side into backward-curving sickle horns. There before him, vast as a baran, was a dragon.

'He sleeps,' murmured Osidian without turning.

Carnelian gaped at the monster. He could have believed it only a colossus carved from a cliff had it not been for the warm odour it was giving off.

'Do you hear his heart?'

Struggling with dark memories Carnelian sought some reassurance in Osidian's face, but could not see past his cowl. It was a tremor like distant thunder that made him gaze back at the monster. He waited. From deep in its flesh another tremor reverberated. It seemed less a heartbeat than how the pulse of sap might sound in a cedar. Deceptively peaceful that slow drumbeat, but he had seen what such a monster became when fully armed. Such stillness was the eerie calm before a storm.

Doubt gnawed at him. He leaned forward enough so that he could peer into Osidian's cowl. How greedily his eyes were fixed upon the dragon. How bright they were. The same intensity no doubt as when he had overseen the murder of the Ochre. Carnelian pulled back, fighting panic. What had he done? How could he have helped put this terror in the hands of a murderer? He counted out the familiar arguments like beads. His breathing slowed as, grimly, he remembered what the Lepers had chosen to endure a second time so as to give him and Osidian a chance to take these dragons. Even now Poppy, Fern and Krow as well as Lily could be fighting Aurum for their lives. He had had a choice then, but now had none. He had to play the game to the end.

'I am certain the tower had no chance to send a message

212

into the Guarded Land,' he said. 'But there is another tower here beyond this cothon.'

Osidian nodded. 'The tower of the Legate.'

'I suspect it has a heliograph of its own.'

As Osidian turned to him, the power lust dulled in his eyes. 'That we could keep the Wise blind to what we are doing was only ever a thin hope. Nevertheless, I still believe we have time enough.'

'Time enough for what?'

'To get these huimur ready,' Osidian said, a gleam coming back into his eyes as he glanced up at the monster, 'before Aurum arrives.'

Carnelian wondered at Osidian's confidence. If an alarm had been sent from the Legate's tower it would take at least a day to reach Osrakum. Much depended on the nature of that alarm. It was unlikely the Wise could be certain that it was indeed Osidian in Qunoth. Even if the Legate here had known that beyond doubt, which seemed improbable, why would the Wise believe him? By what miracle could Osidian have appeared in the Guarded Land without breaching the Ringwall?

'Are you so certain the Wise will resort to sending Aurum?'

Osidian nodded. 'Even if they dared dispatch one of the Lesser Chosen against me they would be reluctant to do so.'

'Because they still hope to conceal all of this from Ykoriana?'

Osidian frowned and nodded again.

'Most likely, Aurum is still in the Leper Valleys . . .' Carnelian said, imagining again the valleys burning. A determination surged in him to save his loved ones and the Lepers from Aurum. He calmed himself. He could not afford to have his mind dulled by emotion. 'Can we operate a legion without the Chosen commanders?'

One of Osidian's eyebrows rose. 'Why should we choose to do that?'

'Surely they will not agree to fight for us?'

'They are accustomed to obeying the House of the Masks.'

Carnelian bit back a comment that it was Osidian's brother Molochite to whom the commanders owed allegiance, and realized he did so because he was reluctant to test Osidian's confidence in case it should prove brittle. Things were already tenuous enough. 'Is it not rather the Wise they obey?'

Osidian's hand sketched a gesture of agreement. 'The Domain of Legions to be precise, but we shall make sure to cut their link to each other.'

Carnelian looked for the Legate's tower, but it was hidden by the cothon and its mechanisms. 'You intend that we should storm the other tower?'

'I do not think it will come to that.' Osidian was smiling. 'The Legate is the key that will open our way to that tower.' Carnelian must have betrayed disbelief, for Osidian continued: 'I shall summon him and he will attend me.'

Carnelian tried to see behind Osidian's certainty. 'What then?'

Osidian shrugged. 'I have not lost my power to command.'

Again, Carnelian chose not to challenge Osidian's apparent confidence. He eyed the legionaries standing in the shadow of a pier. 'And the legionaries?'

Osidian flung a dismissive gesture. 'They did not hesitate to open the cothon for me. Partly this was because they sensed I was unmasked, but even without their fear of my face they would have obeyed me. Generations of subservience have trained them to serve any and all of the Chosen. I doubt if even with express instructions from a Lord of higher rank they would dare raise a hand against one of the Chosen. Nevertheless, I have made sure to display enough hauteur that they can have no doubts I outrank the Lords they have been used to serve.'

Carnelian remained unconvinced, but time would tell. 'What now?'

Osidian raised his arms to display his filthy shrouds. 'Would my Lord not like to be cleaned?'

Carnelian agreed enthusiastically enough to that. Whatever might come to pass, there could be no advantage in confronting it smelling of the Midden.

Marumaga legionaries were closing the shutters of the windows that looked into the courtyard. Standing with Osidian in the shade Carnelian watched their jerky movements with uncomfortable fascination. Four others kneeling nearby, hunched as they buried their faces between their knees, displayed the terror all were feeling. With his fist Carnelian held his cowl closed against his mouth and nose. He was viscerally aware a glimpse of his face would be fatal to them.

The last shutters closed, all but the four men kneeling fled.

'What are your ranks?' Osidian asked, though he already knew the answer because he had summoned them.

Without looking up, one whose hair was grey leaned his head to expose his collar. He pulled his sliders round. Three broken rings. 'Quartermaster General, Master.'

'These others . . . ?'

There was a clinking as the younger men exposed their necks to present their service rings for inspection.

'. . . they are the Dragon Quartermaster, the Master of Beasts, the Master of Towers.'

Carnelian saw that each had two zero rings and a varying number of five-bar and single-stud rings.

'You are responsible for mobilization?'

'We are, Master,' said the Quartermaster.

'Since we have no slaves of our own you shall wash us.'

Carnelian watched the colour draining from their necks. Osidian made a barrier sign that forbade Carnelian from interfering, then he glanced over to where bowls of water were steaming beside a stack of carefully folded cloth. 'Why do you hesitate?'

215

The Quartermaster lifted his head a little. 'We have not the skill, Master.'

'Nevertheless, you will do it.'

'Your . . . your faces, Master.'

'Your closed eyes will be mask enough for us.'

Osidian turned his back on them and raised his arms from his sides for them to disrobe him. Carnelian hesitated a moment, then did the same. It had occurred to him to suggest to Osidian that they could wash themselves, each other even, but he had seen this was foolishness. He was now as subject to the Law as those poor creatures. Besides, he understood that this exercise was intended to cow them, to make these legionary officers malleable to Osidian's will.

The feeling of being undressed was to Carnelian at the same time strange and familiar. He could not help a sigh of relief as the shrouds slid off. A legionary crept round him, eyes wedged into the crook of his elbow, carefully removing Carnelian's loincloth. He watched, breathless with fear that the man might stumble and lose his blindfold.

When he was naked Carnelian looked down with embarrassment at how filthy he was. He was shocked at how tainted his skin had become. He had grown so accustomed to its ruddiness he had thought it white, but in this place his body seemed suddenly that of a barbarian. He glanced over at Osidian. It had been a while since he had seen him naked. His body had changed. The boy had become fully a man. Carnelian liked the barbarian tone of Osidian's skin though it was much disfigured by the weals where the maggots had exited.

It was as Carnelian realized he was staring that Osidian caught him and registered that he was being judged. He turned away, but not before Carnelian had seen the pain of humiliation in his face. Carnelian looked across the courtyard, overwhelmed by sadness, confused. Everything there was conspiring to take him back to the time before they had been cast out of Osrakum; to a time when they had been lovers,

216

when Carnelian had wanted nothing more than to protect Osidian. To a time before Osidian had become a monster.

The touch of wet cloth on his skin brought him out of his reverie and he realized with first surprise then horror how easily he had forgotten the legionaries. He looked down at the one cleaning him. Over forty, he had the solid face of a man used to giving orders. His eyes were scrunched tightly closed. Carnelian could smell his fear, could feel the trembling of his hand as it rubbed away the grime.

When they had finished cleaning them the legionaries retreated. Carnelian and Osidian stood naked with their backs to them, drying in the hot air.

'Summon ammonites of the highest ranking you can find. Have them bring parchment and ink,' Osidian said.

'Instantly, Master,' said one of the legionaries and then he could be heard running off.

Carnelian did not dare turn to look at Osidian lest his face be seen. 'It is a delight is it not, my Lord, to be clean?'

'It is,' said Osidian.

As they waited, Carnelian found the temptation to turn to see what was behind him almost overpowering. His skin had dried when he heard a scurry of footfalls approaching.

'Avert your eyes,' Osidian commanded when silence had fallen.

From the corner of his eye Carnelian saw him turn and followed his lead. All four legionaries were there. Arrayed beside them on the flagstones were the purple-shrouded forms of ammonites. All had their heads buried between their knees.

Osidian approached them and, crouching, he touched two of the yellow heads, causing each of their owners to give a violent start. 'Give me your masks.'

The creatures mumbled in confusion. Osidian waited, frowning. 'I will not ask again.'

The ammonites fumbled their masks loose and held them,

shaking, up to Osidian, who took them, then rose and offered one to Carnelian. He accepted the hollow face and cradled it in his hand. Though it was not the gold of a Master's mask it evoked strong memories of that other life where he had worn one every day. Slowly he leaned his face into it. Of course it was too small. With the eyeslits where he could see through them, the mask's lower edge barely covered his mouth. Still, he reached behind his head to tie it on. It was a prison for his face. He turned to look at Osidian, a hand covering his chin. The small silver face superimposed upon Osidian's gave him a sinister cast.

'Rise and behold us,' Osidian intoned.

Reluctantly, the legionaries and ammonites obeyed. Carnelian judged the legionaries the braver, for they were first to dare raise their eyes. The two unmasked ammonites were the last.

Osidian addressed them. 'You have the parchment and ink?'

'At your command, Seraph,' one said and they showed him some creamy sheets folded into panels, an ink jar, some styluses.

'You will write a letter for me.'

One of the unmasked men sank cross-legged while the other ammonites laid the parchment, ink and styluses on the stone before him. He inked a stylus and turned his tattooed face up expectantly. Osidian began to dictate a summons to the Legate. It was cordial enough though all the verbs were in the requisitive mode.

When the letter was finished the ammonite looked up. 'How shall your letter be sealed, Seraph?'

Osidian held up his hand. 'As you see, I seem to have mislaid my blood-ring. Perhaps you would be kind enough to seal it yourself.'

The ammonite looked uneasy. 'What name shall I write, Seraph, what House?'

'Osidian Nephron of the Masks.'

The heads of the ammonites jerked up.

'Would you like to verify my taint scars?'

The ammonites waved their hands in frantic protest. 'Not so, Seraph . . . Celestial . . . Your word is enough . . . of course . . .'

Osidian's small silver face thrust forward. 'But I insist.' He pointed at the second unmasked ammonite and gestured for him to approach. Examination tattoos were lost in his wrinkling brow as the man shuffled up. Osidian turned his back for him. The man reached up to touch his flesh as if it were ice. He felt his way down the taint scars running on the right side of Osidian's spine. It was obvious to everyone the left was smooth.

The ammonite's legs seemed to lose their strength as he fell prostrate to crack his forehead on the cobbles. 'Celestial,' he murmured.

His fellows copied his abject abasement. Seeing this the legionaries joined them. Carnelian and Osidian were left like the only trees strong enough to have survived a storm.

Osidian commanded the ammonites to take the letter and deliver it to the Legate. They complied, fleeing as fast as decorum would allow. Then Osidian came to loom over the Quartermaster. 'Rise.'

He had to say it again before the man obeyed. 'How long would it take for a legion to reach here from Makar?'

'Master?'

'How long?'

The man narrowed his eyes, thinking. 'Perhaps six days, Master.'

'How quickly can the dragons here be fully armed?'

The man shifted from one foot to the other. 'Ten days, Master, is the standard requirement.'

'You will do it in five.'

The man blinked up at him as if he was convinced he had misheard.

'Five. Go and wake them now.' Turning his back on the

legionary Osidian held his hand out in a gesture of dismissal.

Carnelian stepped into the barracks block Osidian had had the legionaries prepare for them. He removed the ammonite mask and rubbed at where it had impressed its rim into his face. He enjoyed the cool limestone, smooth beneath his feet. He ran his fingers along the hairline joints between the stones in the wall. He wondered at the perfect square angles of the chamber. The sleeping platforms were of finely jointed wood. Thick mattresses lay over them, each provided with a blanket of raven feathers. He plucked one up, brought it to his lips, breathed in its clean odour. A ewer was set into a niche, from which he poured a draught of clear water into a bowl. He drank and was surprised at the taste. So pure it seemed sweet. He regarded the chamber in wonder. He had forgotten that such order was possible.

Osidian was drawn back to the door by a man begging audience. He returned holding a letter. Carnelian watched him read it. Osidian passed the letter to him. Carnelian paused for a moment, startled by the beauty of the glyphs on the parchment. Then he turned them into sounds. When he was finished he looked up. 'He is not coming.'

Osidian smiled. 'Oh, he will.'

Carnelian woke on the floor of the chamber. He had started the night on the bed, but it had made his back ache. He became aware of Osidian gazing down at him.

'Why are you on the floor, my Lord? We no longer have need to live like barbarians.'

Carnelian rose and wrapped himself in his raven-feather blanket. He indicated the mattress with his chin. 'After so long sleeping on the earth that seems too soft. Did you manage to sleep comfortably on yours?'

Osidian frowned, but gave no answer. 'Tonight we shall have no need of these primitive arrangements.' He took in

220

the chamber with an elegant gesture. 'We shall resume our proper place among the Chosen.' His frown deepened. 'We must be ready.'

Breakfast was hri cakes and water. The delicate wafers crumbled as they bit into them. Carnelian was amazed at their flavour. In his memory they had been so bland. Now the hri seemed rich, with a nutty, lingering finish. The taste was, at the same time, familiar. Each mouthful brought back more memories of the life that had been his before exile. Disturbing images mixed with joyous ones. Osrakum still seemed a fairy-tale, but his father was becoming real again – and Ebeny and his brothers. Wounds of loss he had long ago thought cauter-ized were opening.

A Maruli coming into the chamber was a welcome distraction. In his hand the man had a folded parchment. Carnelian was struck by the man's odour and wondered that he had not noticed it before. Osidian seemed uncomfortable as he accepted the letter. Carnelian looked from him to the Maruli and saw, with a jolt, how the man's bloodshot eyes were gazing at Osidian's face. The Maruli's stare had already earned him a terrible death. When the man had left, Carnelian tried in vain to read Osidian's impassive expression, and decided he must confront the issue openly. 'We will have to do something about them.'

Osidian looked at him.

'The Law will take them all from us.'

Osidian frowned.

'Perhaps we should adopt them into our Houses.'

Still frowning, Osidian broke eye contact to concentrate on the letter. He unfolded it and read. The corners of his mouth rose perceptibly. 'It seems our dear Legate is deigning, after all, to pay us a visit.'

Carnelian nodded. He had had time to think about it and was not surprised. One of the Lesser Chosen, even a Legate, would find it impossible to ignore a summons from a Lord of the House of the Masks. He was trying to imagine the meeting between Osidian and the Legate when he realized something. 'What shall we wear?'

Osidian shrugged. Carnelian hunted around. The best he could find were some robes of coarse black cloth. He showed them to Osidian, who gave a grimace of distaste, but then flung out a gesture indicating he did not care. He smiled humourlessly. 'A difference in rank inhabits the mind more completely than does the impression of proper state.'

Wearing the black robes and ammonite masks they returned to the cothon. Osidian had decided it was there he would receive the Legate. Carnelian was content with this, being curious to watch the dragons being woken.

It was the Master of Beasts who guided them to one of the vaults in the cothon wall. 'The Legate's own dragon, Master, and our strongest.'

A vast presence filled the vault. Horns gleamed faintly. Stripes of sun sculpted the contours of its head. Its reek oppressed Carnelian with memories of the Earthsky and corpses. In the depths of the vault, brass toppled in massive links. Instinctively Carnelian took a step back. 'Is it already awake?'

'Not fully so, Master,' said the Master of Beasts. 'Normally the waking takes many days as we wait for the drugs to wear off, but—' He glanced at Osidian. 'The command for haste means we've had to resort to administering waking drugs.'

Carnelian wondered if he was detecting a tone of reproach, but decided the man was only expressing genuine concern for his dragon.

Osidian walked over to one side of the vault. Seeking distraction from his unease Carnelian followed him. There a spar rose, barbed like a tree amputated of its branches. It was held between the prongs of stone forks that were set up the wall. Its trunk was smooth, its upper part sheathed in a green bark of copper. Glyphed oblong plaques were riveted all the way up to where this standard blossomed into a pair of grimacing faces.

'He is ancient,' whispered Osidian, pointing upwards.

Carnelian strained to read the plaques through the narrow slits of his ammonite mask.

'He has held many positions in the line.' There was passion in Osidian's voice. 'He is a lord of battles. Behold, he is called Heart-of-Thunder.'

As if responding to his name, the dragon avalanched towards them. Sun-stripes climbed the flare of bone behind his head. His beak sliced the air. A putrid stench exuded from his maw. His horns flashed. His eye was a blind, milky moon. The Master of Beasts was bellowing, but before they were overwhelmed, chains clattered taut to hold the monster back. The head swayed a moment there on cables of sinew, then it swung back into the gloom. Shock juddered Carnelian's chest, a relic of the thunder of the monster's feet.

The Master of Beasts barked instructions into the vault. Carnelian saw figures scrambling up the walls. He heard a metallic crunching as some windlass pulled the brass chains taut.

'Was he in danger of coming free?' Carnelian asked.

The Master of Beasts glanced at Carnelian in surprise. 'Oh no, Master.' His eyes strayed back to the tightening chains. 'He still dreams. His chains were too loose. We let them out slowly to allow his muscles to regain strength enough to hold his head up on their own.' He pointed into the gloom and Carnelian saw more chains fixed to the monster's legs and abdomen.

'Without those he'd collapse. The waking is a delicate business. If he were to break a leg he might not survive.' That thought was enough to make the Master of Beasts pale. 'Many would die with him.'

Carnelian imagined that a reference to his keepers. 'How long before he can have a tower put upon his back?'

The Master of Beasts turned to him. 'A tower complete, Master?'

Carnelian nodded.

The man shrugged. 'We dare burden him only in accordance with his returning strength. Perhaps four days, Master.'

'They recover more slowly than do the Wise,' said Osidian in Quya.

Carnelian looked round. 'The Wise take the same drugs?'

'Something very like,' Osidian said.

As a child Carnelian had been told stories of how the Wise often sank into a magic sleep so as to extend their lives. This was one of the many things he had dismissed as fantasy.

Osidian took his shoulder and led him away. 'We must prepare to give audience to the Legate.'

'Do the Wise live as long as the huimur?' Carnelian asked.

Osidian made a gesture of uncertainty. 'It is rumoured that some Grand Sapients have ruled their Domains for generations.'

Carnelian considered this. It made the Wise seem even more alien.

Osidian glanced back at the huimur. 'Does his name not seem an omen to you?'

Carnelian grew wary. He had heard that tone before. 'It had not occurred to me . . .' He lied. He knew perfectly well that it was the heart of thunder that brought the Black God each year to Osrakum.

Standing in the long shadow of one of the cothon piers Carnelian watched the Masters approach, swinging censers. Amidst the smoke, each was a spire whose gleam was filtering through their escort of Marula. They detached from the escort and came shimmering across the cobbles. Carnelian gazed entranced. They were appallingly tall. Sun flashed from their horned helms, from their faces of gold. They seemed unearthly beings.

Carnelian stepped back into the deeper shadow cast by the dragon tower above him. As the Masters passed between the piers their jewels, their masks brought glimmers of the late afternoon light into the shadows. The clouds of incense they were weaving round them had for a moment the scent of cedar, but he quickly resolved it to be sweet myrrh. Removing his ammonite mask he stepped out to meet them. They overtopped him by a head. Glancing down, he saw they were wearing ranga. It made him aware his own feet were planted firmly on the ground in clear defiance of the Law. Myrrh was not only in the smoke rising from the censers they swung in pendular arcs, but emanated from the dense samite of their robes, from the carapaces of their iridescent armour. He looked at their hands which were spotted with symbols. These Masters were wearing the ritual protection the Wise claimed was proof against the plagues of the outer world. It made Carnelian realize he had forgotten how utterly exposed he and Osidian had been and for so long. He had lived among the Plainsmen, eaten their food, even kissed them. It would seem he was irremediably contaminated. He suppressed a smile. The masks of these Masters might be looking down on him with imperious contempt but, in his heart, he still felt cleaner than they.

'I am Suth Carnelian.'

Though he knew the Law demanded they could not remain masked in the presence of a Lord of the Great it also declared that no Master should breathe unhallowed air. He was not sure which law took precedence, but thought it likely this was the reason they had taken the precaution of bringing incense. One by one they released their masks to reveal faces that seemed made of chalk. Startled, he remembered that the Chosen were compelled to paint their skin against the sun. Strange he had forgotten that when once it had seemed as natural to him as breathing. He began to feel unease at their predatory beauty.

'We have come to speak with the Jade Lord,' one said.

Carnelian saw around his neck a torc of jade and iron that bore four broken rings. 'You are the Legate here?'

The man raised his hand in elegant affirmation.

Follow me, Carnelian gestured, which in its agreement and

requisitive mode made it clear it was only the Legate he was inviting. Walking back through the piers he was pleased to hear the clack of only one set of ranga.

Beneath the arch of Heart-of-Thunder's beak Osidian seemed a coalescing of the shadows. Carnelian stood aside to let the Legate approach. He watched with trepidation as the exquisitely armoured Master moved to loom over Osidian. Osidian seemed overmatched but, when he spoke, his voice was commanding. 'Kneel.'

For a moment it seemed as if the Legate might defy him but, after settling his censer before him, shimmering darkly, the Lesser Chosen Lord subsided, spreading his gorgeous train upon the cobbles. Carnelian watched the Master's grey eyes seeking to pierce the myrrh smoke to make out Osidian's face in the gloom. 'We heard, Celestial, you had disappeared.'

'It seems I have reappeared.'

The Legate began to say something else, but Osidian raised a pale hand that closed his mouth. 'Where are your auxiliaries, my Lord?'

The Legate raised hands encrusted in gems, fingers vaguely framing evasions. 'When the Great Lord came he was impossible to resist.'

'Did he have a mandate from the Wise?'

The Legate did not wholly manage to suppress a grimace. 'His House is very high, Celestial.'

Osidian's voice came forth from the abyss of darkness. 'Is it to House Aurum you owe allegiance, my Lord? I thought you had sworn it to the House of the Masks. Was it not my father who appointed you, my brother who ratified that appointment?' Then, more severely: 'How do you imagine They will react to this betrayal of Their trust?'

Suddenly, brass began clattering behind Osidian. He did not flinch as chains collapsed link on link. Even when the prow of Heart-of-Thunder's head shifted in the air above him Osidian remained motionless.

The Legate had bowed his horned military helm.

'I will need fitting accommodation.'

'You shall have my own chambers, Celestial. Though miserable, they are the best I have to offer.'

'Very well, my Lord, we shall return with you to the sanctum.'

The horned helm rose. 'Now, Celestial?'

'Why not?'

As the Legate swept past Carnelian Osidian approached and raised his hand. 'Come, my Lord.'

'I shall remain here.' Carnelian realized the Legate was within hearing and added: 'Celestial.'

Osidian hesitated. Watching his hand, Carnelian detected a firmness in it that suggested Osidian was about to issue a command. The hand softened. 'My Lord Legate.'

The Legate turned. 'Celestial?'

'Go on ahead, we shall join you presently.'

The man bowed. 'As you command.'

Carnelian watched the Legate move away, resigning himself to a confrontation with Osidian. He turned to him. 'Someone needs to keep an eye on things here,' he said in Vulgate.

'Morunasa can do that.'

'I don't imagine the marumaga would be happy to obey a Maruli.'

'They will do as they are told!'

Carnelian was shocked at Osidian's vehemence. He could not understand why this should be so important to him. 'Surely it is obvious that we must take all precautions? These huimur have been purchased at a heavy price.'

Osidian lowered his head as he crushed one hand with the other. 'I really want you to come with me, Carnelian.' His anger had gone. 'Please.'

Carnelian gazed at Osidian in disbelief, then turned to look at Heart-of-Thunder lurking in his vault. 'Very well.'

*　　*　　*

The Legate and his companions had journeyed to the cothon in palanquins. Osidian commandeered one for himself and another for Carnelian. Two of the Lesser Chosen commanders were going to have to walk. As Osidian replaced his bearers and Carnelian's with Marula, Carnelian looked among them for Sthax, but could not see him there. He dismissed anxiety: there were more immediate things to worry about. As he watched the changeover Carnelian was surprised how much the bearers appeared disfigured by their Masters' heraldic tattoos. He wondered that he had ever thought it natural that men should be thus marked to show to whom they belonged. Once it had even seemed elegant; now it appeared hardly different from the branding on a sartlar's face.

When the palanquin was ready he folded himself into it reluctantly. In contrast with the samite brocades, the inlays of tortoiseshell and pearl, his rough-woven marumaga robe appeared to be little more than sackcloth. An Oracle slid closed the lacquered door and the Marula lifted the palanquin. Inside, Carnelian felt imprisoned. Each breath he took was cloyed with the perfume of lilies, the taint of myrrh. Finding a grille he slid it back to let in some air. Framed by its gold filigree, the machines and geometries of the cothon appeared more brutal. The southern gates of the cothon gulped open. He glimpsed gate chains, toothed wheels, then he was being carried through a garden. Trunks showed they were passing down an avenue of gigantic trees. Framed between them, verdant vistas. Shield leaves thrust up fiery flower-spikes. Paths wound among rocks, quaintly carved, banded and spiralled with cultivated lichens. Here and there he managed to snatch glimpses of the sky, but these only served to make the palanquin feel more like a prison. He was uneasy. Perhaps the feeling had been caused by Osidian's uncharacteristic gentleness towards him back in the cothon. Carnelian hoped he would not regret having agreed to join him. Perhaps his anxiety was about returning to the world of the Masters.

Perhaps he was afraid he might be changed back into what he had been.

The palanquin was set down amidst muttering. Carnelian covered his lower face with a fold of his robe before carefully sliding open the door. He cried in Vulgate: 'Look away, we are unmasked.'

Climbing out he was confronted by a gate that glared at him with a single, tearful eye. Wrought in the bronze, it was surrounded by a silver frieze of ammonite shells. These wards proclaimed whatever lay beyond to be under the jurisdiction of the Wise. Unsanctioned entry was forbidden under penalty of the Law-that-must-be-obeyed.

The gate opened a little and, from behind it, a silver face emerged with solid spiral eyes. 'Please enter this purgatory, Seraphim. The procedures of purification await you.'

As Carnelian and Osidian approached, more ammonites appeared, hunched as each gripped with both hands the handle of a ladle in which blue fire burned. At a command it was poured over the ground before them. Flames ran across the earth. Carnelian and Osidian were urged forward onto the now purified ground. Fingers fumbled at their feet, trying to free them of their polluted footwear. A hissing made Carnelian turn to see more arcs of blue flame being ladled over the ground on which he and Osidian had walked. The palanquins they had come in were already aflame. The Marula were backing away, eyes bulging.

'Enough! I have no patience for this,' boomed Osidian, chasing ammonites from his path. 'Morunasa, come with me. Bring your people.'

The Oracle gathered up the Marula and they swarmed after him. Ammonites flung themselves in their way, screeching, forbidding entry, but the Marula beat them aside. Some of the ammonites lost their blinding-masks and fell, grovelling, on the still burning earth. Carnelian glanced at the Legate and his commanders, who were watching in stiff disbelief, then followed after the Marula, who were pouring through the gate Osidian had thrown open.

Drugged smoke unfurled like ferns in the gloomy halls beyond. Carnelian felt a languor settle about his shoulders. His face began to swell, his bones to liquefy. He recognized the feeling from his entry into Osrakum. The drug was meant to encourage their submission to intrusive cleansing. A deafening clatter brought his eyes back into focus. Swaying, the Marula were knocking smoking brass bowls from their tripods. Carnelian squinted against the undulating surface of a pool in which mouths and tongues of light were kissing, separating. Backing away into the shadows were metal faces distorting reflections of their whole drunken procession. He saw a rectangle of daylight opening far away and did what he could to herd the Marula towards it. At last he was stumbling out with them into eddying daylight.

He found himself with Morunasa and the Marula in a gully between limestone walls pierced with gates. The place was already in afternoon shadow. Only the crest of the eastern wall still caught the sun. Bronze hoops held poles whose banners were swimming in a breeze. Guardsman niches were empty. A gate opened a crack. For a moment he glimpsed an eye widening with horror. Then the gate slammed closed and a voice beyond it began keening an alarm. Bolts were shot home. Commotion spread beyond the walls and a scurrying, so that Carnelian felt he was invading a termite city. Faces peered down from the battlements above. Carnelian felt as shunned as a leper.

He located Osidian, a shadowy shape striding away along the gully towards where a tower rose, tier on sculptured tier. Morunasa asked for instructions, but Carnelian ignored him and set off after Osidian. The Marula opened a path through their midst to let him through. Carnelian was only vaguely aware of their faces. He was concentrating on putting one foot in front of the other. As the effect of the drug faded, each footfall felt more solid than the last. When he caught up with Osidian, he spoke: 'Why . . . why break through?'

'I had my reasons,' Osidian growled.

Carnelian saw no point in pressing him further and fell in step with him. Behind them came scuffling Marula.

The gully terminated at a gate from which the two faces of the Commonwealth sneered down. Carnelian and Osidian threw their weight against the bronze and the gate opened, exhaling a waft of lilies. Penetrating the gloomy hall beyond, Carnelian noticed figures flitting away through openings all along its rim. Members of the Legate's household, no doubt. He glanced round anxiously to make sure the Marula were keeping close; he did not want any massacres. Huddled hesitantly on the threshold, they came when he beckoned them.

They crossed the hall among the echoes of their creeping footfalls. Carnelian did not blame the Marula for their wariness. Even to him this place felt like a tomb. The pillars on either side seemed guardians. Figures writhing in the pavement beneath his feet might have been a view down into the Underworld.

Their route took them within sight of archways that opened into the gold of late afternoon. Carnelian longed to escape through them, but Osidian always turned away into the shadows. The cold grandeur seeped into Carnelian's heart until he began to shiver. The polished floor seemed frozen meat whose veins had turned to stone. Columns might have been the corpses of trees. As he walked he became aware he was clutching his marumaga robe. Its coarse but honest weave brought him some little comfort.

They skirted one last court by means of a cloister. Walking close to its edge Carnelian was able to see they were nearing the tower whose tiers were borne upon the curved backs of humbled men. The cloister curved to deliver them to a stair that they began ascending. They passed chambers panelled with malachite and purple porphyry whose sterile beauty Osidian declared to be that of reception chambers. 'It is the Legate's private halls we seek.'

Higher they climbed until they came to a landing where they were challenged by guardsmen bearing the Legate's cypher on their faces. Osidian stayed the Marula with a command then climbed the last few steps towards the guardsmen and their levelled spears. If his height had not been enough to alert them that he was a Master, his disregard for their weapons proved it. Their spear blades clattered to the floor as they knelt.

'Clear this level. These chambers I claim for my own. Any creature left behind shall be slain.'

Carnelian had reached Osidian's side and could now see the great door upon which the men had been standing guard. Abandoning their weapons they fled through it into the chambers beyond. He noticed that the stair continued climbing. 'The roof,' he said, remembering the heliograph he suspected to be up there. Osidian nodded and bade Morunasa approach him. He selected some of the Marula to stand guard upon the door. 'Take these others,' he said to the Oracle, 'and bring me anyone you find up there.'

The Oracle was about to scale the steps when Osidian stayed him. 'I want them alive.'

The Oracle darted a nod and soon he and most of the Marula had disappeared up the stairs. Carnelian waited with Osidian as the Legate's household cowered past to scurry down the steps. The guardsmen were the last to leave.

'Nothing living?' Osidian asked them.

'Nothing, Master.'

As they ducked past him and away down the stair after the others, Osidian indicated to the Marula the recesses flanking the door in which they were to stand guard. Then he and Carnelian passed into the chamber beyond.

*   *   *

They emerged into a suite of rooms more humanly proportioned, graced with gilded furniture, with hangings of featherwork, walls pierced by ivory doors. Wandering, they came into a chamber in which bronze lecterns shaped like hands cradled books. Osidian took one, opened its jewelled cover and read. He looked at Carnelian.

'An inferior edition,' he said, stroking the binding.

There were tears running down his face. This sadness, that was also joy, made Osidian look young again. As they explored further together Carnelian watched him sidelong. Osidian professed disdain for such provincial architecture, aloofness towards the minor treasures that were all about them, but when he turned his gaze from something his fingers would linger on it a while as if he feared that, should he lose touch of it, it might disappear. Indeed, the polished stone in which they moved as shadows, the hanging silks that floated on the breeze like smoke, the narrow views some windows gave down into the hazy infinities of the land below, all these things seemed unreal, so that it was as if they moved together through a dream.

At last they came to a chamber in which water ran in channels in the walls. Here Osidian let his marumaga robe crumple to the floor and soon was standing in an iris-scented waterfall. He beckoned for Carnelian to join him. The eyes looking at him had something of the boy in the Yden, but now they were set in a face that had been hardened by pain. The water was making Osidian's maggot wounds redder than his mouth. The mark of the rope was livid round his neck. His once flawless limbs had been weathered by the margins of garments into different shades so that he seemed assembled from unmatched pieces of ivory. Pity became an ache in Carnelian's chest. He felt anew the agony of loss for what Osidian had been and sadness for what he had become. Undressing, he joined him in the waterfall. They stood together, sheathed in its warm pulsating embrace. Osidian's eyes seemed emeralds lost in the sea. 'Forgive me.'

Carnelian's heart responded to the appeal. There was still a part of him that yearned for the way it had been between them, but he could not so easily forget the dead. 'Forgiveness is not in my gift,' he said and endured the hurt that came into Osidian's face.

'At least, stay with me.'

Compassion and the dregs of their love fought within Carnelian with what his heart felt he owed the dead. At last he yielded nothing more than a nod though even that felt like a betrayal.

A clanging brought them back to the outer door. Putting his ammonite mask over his face, Carnelian opened the door. Morunasa was on the landing. He moved aside to indicate a huddle of ammonites ringed by Marula. There was another ammonite laid out on the floor. Carnelian approached the prone figure, crouched, then, using one hand to hold his own mask, with the other he released the ammonite's. Beneath was a sallow face marred with examination tattoos. Carnelian leaned closer. 'He's dead.'

Osidian had followed him. 'It is the quaestor of this city.'

Carnelian turned to look up at him. 'How can you tell?'

Osidian interpreted for him some of the markings on the corpse's face. Then he turned on Morunasa. 'Did I not tell you to bring all of them to me alive?'

The Oracle presented a stiff face. 'We found him like that on the roof.'

Carnelian leaned closer to the corpse. 'Look at how his tongue is swollen.'

Osidian crouched to see for himself. 'Poison.'

Carnelian was about to ask how Osidian knew that, but then remembered that he had grown up at court where such things were not uncommon.

Osidian rose and stood statue still. Carnelian sensed he was pondering something and chose not to disturb him. Instead he addressed Morunasa. 'On the roof, you say?'

'Beside one of those sun machines.'

That was suggestive. Carnelian turned his mask on the huddle of ammonites. They drew away from him as he approached. 'Have any heliograph messages been sent or received from here today or yesterday?'

He saw himself reflected in the silver of their faces. He raised his hands and signed the command: *Unmask*. They did so, hesitantly, glancing round at the Marula, their sallow tattooed faces sweaty with fear.

'Answer me.'

One braver than the rest shook his head. 'We do not know, Seraph. We have been forbidden the roof.'

'By the quaestor?'

The ammonite's eyes flicked to the corpse and back again. 'That is so, Seraph.'

Without a word, Osidian turned to the stairs and began climbing them. Carnelian assured Morunasa that neither he nor his men had done any wrong, then, telling him to wait, Carnelian followed Osidian.

When they reached the roof the dizzying view drove everything else from Carnelian's mind. He approached the edge. Laid out at his feet was the Earthsky, turned to copper by the setting sun. Osidian was squinting into the west. Carnelian joined him. Against the liquid gold horizon the limestone margin of the Guarded Land, scored and gouged by gullies, seemed gnawed and incised bone. Away from its rim, the rock became stained with earth like a crust of dried blood. Further inland, his eyes found the knife slash of the Ringwall. He followed this until he came to a thorn. Another watch-tower. He glanced back at the heliograph and saw that it was to that tower it was aligned. He made the inevitable deduction. 'The quaestor sent a message to Osrakum, then killed himself.'

Osidian shook his head. 'It seems more likely that he received a command to kill himself.'

'From the Wise?'

Osidian turned to him. 'Who else?'

'But surely there wasn't enough time for the signal to get here—'

Osidian turned back to gaze at the watch-tower. 'No, there wasn't.'

Carnelian felt suddenly exposed, as if at that very moment the Wise had lifted the roof off the world and were peering in at them. 'How could they know we were coming?'

Osidian shook his head, a look of resignation on his face. 'It is a fool who underestimates the Wise.'

Carnelian contemplated their situation. 'But why would they want the quaestor dead?'

'Perhaps they feared he would fall into my hands.'

Carnelian could not work it out. 'What could he possibly reveal to us?'

Osidian shook his head again, dejection in his face and posture. 'Their strategy, or some trap they have set for us.'

Carnelian realized how much he feared Osidian would fail. 'What shall we do?'

Osidian gazed at him. 'We proceed as before. What else can we do?'

Carnelian could think of nothing. As Osidian made his way back to the steps, Carnelian remained behind a while, gazing at the watch-tower, almost hoping to see it flash. If the Wise had them defeated he would rather find out there and then. Bleakly, he turned towards the steps.

Carnelian woke lying beside Osidian. Though he had agreed to sleep at his side he had not allowed anything more. Asleep, Osidian regained enough of his unsullied youth for Carnelian to see in him the boy he had loved. His heart ached as he gave in to the seduction of imagining they were still in Osrakum, still lovers. He stared at the ceiling, watching its gilded vault pulse with the pounding of his heart. That was a dream; the massacres were not.

He had to get away from him. He slipped from under the

feather blankets. The floor seemed ice. The walls banded with dark stone oppressed him and made him shiver. He drew on his marumaga robe and went in search of light. The next chamber was lit by a faraway opening. Shafts of sunlight beckoned him onto a balcony. Blinded, he advanced into the morning not caring that the sun would taint his skin further. As he basked in its warmth, its wholesomeness, only slowly did his sight return and then he saw he was perched on the rim of the sky. Bleached green mottled with gold grew purple towards a far horizon. It seemed the whole Earthsky was there at his feet. He closed his eyes and breathed the scent that was on the wind. His heart jumped as the world he had known there came alive again. He was sure he could smell the musk of the fernland sweetened by magnolia. He felt in his heart how clean and simple his life had been there. He longed for the murmur of the mother trees. He ached for the touch of Akaisha's warm hand, for the wise laughter in her eyes.

'We must talk.'

Carnelian turned and saw Osidian the murderer. He watched him falter under his gaze and was glad of it. Osidian retreated into the shadows. Carnelian tried to return to his reverie, but Osidian had snuffed out the vision of the Earthsky. Only tragedy remained and a sickening regret. He leaned on the balustrade and looked down. Far below in the gorge the blue river frayed white as it tumbled over falls. He was sure he could hear a whisper of its roaring. He gazed downstream, where the gorge carved its curves west to the Leper Valleys. A yearning for Poppy and Fern flared in him, but he crushed it. Regret was an indulgence he could not afford. He straightened and returned to the cold grandeur of his new life.

It was Marula who brought them breakfast. Carnelian vaguely knew two of their faces but, again, there was no Sthax. Plates of white jade, bowls beaten from several colours of folded gold, all sat incongruously in their calloused hands. As they came nearer their stale sweat overpowered the perfume of the food.

It was only when Osidian dismissed them that Carnelian found it possible to appreciate the saffron pungency of the porridge, the rosewater sweetness of the hri cakes.

Osidian frowned, gazing at the faraway doors closing behind the Marula. 'They must be washed and those barbarian corselets disposed of. Their ebony necks would look handsome collared with gold; their limbs adorned with greens, with scarlets. At the very least they must be made to wear legionary cuirasses. If they are to join my household, they must look the part.'

Carnelian noticed that Osidian was studiously avoiding eye contact. He watched him begin to eat, then took a mouthful of the golden porridge. The flavour assaulted him. He ate more, greedily, but subsequent mouthfuls failed to match the first. Soon it seemed too rich. He thought of sharing what he was experiencing, but the distaste on Osidian's face made him pause. Sensing he was being watched Osidian masked his previous expression. Whatever he was feeling he was clearly determined not to communicate it.

Nibbling one of the cakes, Carnelian looked around him. The magnificence left him homesick. That feeling centred him. He had been afraid the Masterly pleasures would seduce him. Having justifiable hope they would not made it easier to contemplate continuing to play the game. 'What plans have you for the huimur, my Lord?'

Osidian looked at him coldly. Carnelian waited, then lost patience. 'Though we may not be lovers we can still be allies.'

Osidian frowned. 'Even granted the Wise may know we are here, I believe we still have time.'

'Because you are convinced the Wise will dare use no one but Aurum against us?'

Osidian gave a nod. 'If the Gods be with us, we shall be ready to deal with the Lord Aurum.'

There was something in his tone that made Carnelian realize Osidian still had hopes of bringing Aurum over to his side. This would be to renege on the promise he had made to the Lepers. Carnelian dismissed a build-up of outrage. Aurum's defection was unlikely. He became aware Osidian was watching him. 'And what then, my Lord? What do you envisage once we have defeated Aurum?'

Osidian scrutinized him a while before going on. 'We shall turn the Powers against each other. My appearance will weaken my mother and my brother. The revelation of the role Aurum has played will weaken the Wise. Many of the Great will take my part. The Wise will be forced to negotiate with me.'

Carnelian almost asked him, To what end? But he knew that the lust in Osidian's eyes could only be for the Masks. Carnelian focused on his own aims: the salvation of the Plainsmen, and of the Lepers too if that should prove possible. Even here at the periphery of the Commonwealth the Earthsky seemed already far away; the Plainsmen, inconsequential. There was hope in that, but it would be foolish to underestimate the appetite the Wise had for being thorough. Osidian's attempt to reclaim the Masks must surely fail. Once the eddies of his rebellion had dissipated, the Wise would turn their minds to the Plainsmen and then there would be a reckoning. He frowned. It always came back to the Wise. He shook himself free of these musings. Though in playing any game of strategy it was important to look many moves ahead, it was also crucial that, in doing so, one did not fail to make sure one's next move was sound. 'Assure me we can count upon the commanders.'

'Now that we have broken the link between them and the Wise what choice will they have but to obey me?'

Carnelian thought Osidian's certainty sounded hollow. He shook his head. 'This weapon we would wield does not yet feel firmly in our grasp. How might we be certain they would fight for us against Aurum?'

'What does my Lord suggest?' Osidian said, irritably.

Carnelian grasped at what he knew of the Masters. 'Can we not bribe them?'

'Iron? Access to impregnating women from my House?'

'That is a payment your brother could more convincingly offer than we in our present circumstances.'

'What then?' snapped Osidian.

Carnelian pondered. Something occurred to him. 'Why would they covet iron or access to the women of the House of the Masks?'

Osidian frowned to show that he was uninterested in playing this game.

'Is it not because they wish to rise to being of the Great?'

Osidian sneered. 'Shall I transfuse my blood into theirs to awake in them divine fire?'

Carnelian smiled. 'Offer to enfranchise them.'

'What?'

'Tell them that, once you have regained what is rightfully yours, you will give their Houses the right to vote in elections; to participate in the division of the flesh tithe.'

Osidian looked aghast. 'What you suggest threatens the Balance itself.'

Carnelian hardly heard him as the idea took flame within him. 'Why stop with them? Why not enfranchise all the Lesser Chosen?'

Osidian stared at Carnelian as if he were mad. 'So you would break the Balance altogether?'

'What of it?'

Carnelian watched as Osidian's eyes dulled. Was he considering the inconceivable?

'At one stroke you would undermine any confidence the Wise have in the legions. It might sow havoc among them. It must surely weaken Aurum's ability to resist you. Certainly it would give the commanders here a real reason to risk following you.'

He could feel Osidian's resistance weakening. 'This one act could bring the Masks within your grasp, without need of the Wise, or the Great. You would tear her most powerful weapon from your mother's hand. You might even be able to wield all the power of the Chosen your-self.'

Osidian looked at him. 'Except the Ichorian Legion.'

What of it? Carnelian signed. He made a gesture of encompassment. 'In the last resort, you could lay siege to Osrakum herself.'

The moment he said that he realized he had gone too far. Osidian's disbelief returned. Carnelian tried to retrieve the initiative. 'It will not come to that, Osidian. The Wise will negotiate with you, but with their power diminished.'

Uncertainty returned to Osidian's face. 'Once broken the Balance might be impossible to rebuild.'

'Why would you wish to resume the chains that have bound your House for millennia?'

Osidian spoke distractedly: 'Not millennia. It has been only seven hundred years since my House lost the Civil War . . .'

Carnelian had only a vague awareness of this. It had happened so long ago.

Osidian began shaking his head. 'Your scheme is flawed, Carnelian. The Lesser Chosen that are not beyond my reach within Osrakum are scattered among the cities of the Guarded Land.'

'Surely you can get messages to them by heliograph or by sending couriers along the leftways?'

Osidian shook his head. 'Even if I had a seal, the watch-towers would not relay a message from me unless it was vouched for by the Wise.'

Carnelian sank into disappointment. It had all seemed so easy. He had made the mistake of underestimating the systems of the Wise.

'The Lesser Chosen know their place. They shall bow down to me,' Osidian said, frowning. 'You and I must return to all the traditional usages. We must resume the wearing of masks. The more we run our power along the usual channels the stronger the grip we will maintain upon their loyalty.'

He looked around him at the chamber, at its furnishings,

and seemed saddened by what he saw. 'There is nothing to be gained by remaining here.' His gaze fell on Carnelian. 'It would be best if we were to relocate to somewhere closer to the cothon; that has now become the heart of our venture.' He looked away. 'We must begin to adhere to the Laws of Purity.'

Carnelian felt as if he was being threatened with imprisonment. 'Do you mean the full ritual protection?'

'I do, my Lord.'

'I have experienced it and it was extremely uncomfortable.'

'Nevertheless.'

'But what is the point in it? For years we have been exposed to the outer world and we are still intact.'

Osidian scowled and touched the scar about his neck. 'I do not think, my Lord, that we are wholly untouched by its filth and humiliations.'

Carnelian was in no mood to back down. 'If you felt like this why then did you pollute the purity of this place?'

'I desired to make the commanders share something of our degradation. There, does that please you, Carnelian?'

It was the pain in his eyes that made Carnelian falter. When he opened his mouth to say something more, Osidian chopped: *Enough!* 'We are returned to the Commonwealth. Here none dare disobey her Laws.'

Twelve masks looked back at Carnelian and Osidian. They had been donated, at Osidian's demand, by the Legate and his commanders. He picked one up and turned it into the light. His lips curled. 'Surely this is the work of an apprentice maskmaker. Look how thick the bridge of the nose is, how crude the nostril flare. And as for the eyes . . .' He shook his head and picked up another.

Carnelian's fingers strayed to one that was reminding him of someone. He lifted it. It took him a while to see who it was. The mask had something about the mouth that made it resemble Fern's. Carnelian was about to put it down, not wanting such a painful reminder; instead he placed it over

242

his face. It seemed to fit well enough, though he knew that wearing it for any length of time would soon reveal where it did not perfectly fit his face. He turned to regard the ammonites kneeling, waiting with the strips of linen, the unguents and all the apparatus they had brought from the purgatory at Osidian's command. The masks they wore had solid spirals for eyes. They had tried pleading excuses: that only the quaestor was qualified to administer the ritual protection; that the purity of everything in the sanctum had been contaminated when it had been breached by the black barbarians. Osidian had dismissed all their objections with contempt.

Carnelian approached the prostrate men. 'Here, I have chosen.' He offered the mask and one of the ammonites reached out blindly. He put the mask with Fern's lips into the trembling hands.

When Osidian had selected a mask he commanded the ammonites to begin the procedure. Reluctantly, one of them rose to his feet, a length of beadcord in his hand. Reading it with his fingers he began to intone in Quya: 'You who are Chosen shall now make ready to leave this place. You who are Chosen must take all precaution before leaving the sanctity of this place.'

As the blind spiral eyes regarded him Carnelian recalled the time so long ago when he had endured this ritual in the Tower in the Sea. 'We are supposed to give a response.'

'A response?' Osidian said.

'Something about the obeying of the Law.'

Osidian threw his hand up in irritation. 'Ammonite, dispense with the catechism. Limit yourself to what is essential.'

'Essential, Celestial?'

'The practical elements,' Osidian said, his voice rising dangerously.

As the ammonite fell to the ground the forehead of his mask struck a dull clang on the floor.

'The ranga, Celestial, the filtered mask, the embalming.'

'Well, get on with it.'

243

Carnelian glanced at Osidian, unsure why he was so angry. With surprise, he sensed Osidian was apprehensive. He had to admit he felt the same.

Under the direction of the ammonite, the others began the procedure. Ranga shoes were produced, raised upon a green, a black and a red support. Osidian refused to anoint them himself and so it was the ammonites who applied the unguent. They stripped them and cleansed them with chill menthol. Climbing onto the ranga, Carnelian bore the tickle of their styluses as they painted warding symbols and designs upon his skin. When they had wafted the ink dry they submerged its itch beneath a glaze of myrrh. The odour reminded him first of Aurum, then of his wounded father, then once again, unexpectedly, of the scent of the mother trees. That brought tears.

They began winding him in linen, the first layer sticking to the glaze. As more and more strips wound round him they tightened as they dried. The feeling of being trapped swelled in him almost to panic. He felt they were preparing him for his tomb. At last they brought the mask they had prepared. He regarded the hollow thing with horror. He shuddered as they fitted it to his face. His breathing hard and fast was restricted by the gold. It became a roaring in his ears as he forced the air in through the narrow mouth of the mask. The nostril pads smothered his nose. Ill-fitting, the mask squeezed out some liquid from the pads that dribbled down his lip into his mouth. Bitter, bitter taste and its numbing reek pushing cold needles up into the root of his nose to sting his eyes. Forced tears blinded him to what little he could see through the eyeslits.

'We hide our faces from the world like lepers,' Osidian was saying, but Carnelian barely registered the words as he struggled to choke back the horror that he was buried alive.

MOBILIZATION

A legion is maintained as an unassembled weapon not
only by necessity, but also by design. Its assembly requires
procedures subject to Chosen authorization as well as a
properly maintained cothon mechanism. Naturally, we
mediate all such authorization. Further, in operation
a legion is wholly dependent on the logistics of
render and naphtha supply.

(extract from a beadcord manual of the Wise of the Domain Legions)

As Carnelian and Osidian appeared from the Legate's
chambers, the Marula guarding the door fell back, gaping.
Carnelian almost stumbled on his ranga. In their stares he saw
too clearly what he had once more become. It sickened him
to be back behind a mask looking down on fearful men. He
wanted to cry out that he was still the same man they knew,
but he had chosen his path. At least the Marula were on
their feet. Something pale moved in the corner of his vision:
Osidian's hand shaping a command. Carnelian half turned,
hearing the ammonites behind him settling to the ground.
Glancing at each other, the warriors, reluctantly, began falling
to their knees.

In obedience to Osidian's summons, the Legate and the
other Lesser Chosen commanders were waiting for him by

the door to the purgatory. A pall of myrrh smoke was rising from a ring of censers set around them. Only the Legate, and those subordinates who earlier had accompanied him to the cothon, stood outside the curtain of smoke, safe in their ritual protection. All knelt as Osidian approached. Carnelian noted that these Masters abased themselves more quickly than had the Marula. Osidian beckoned the Legate to approach him. Though his mask gave the man an air of imperious indifference, Carnelian detected anxiety in his gait and in the way he sank before Osidian.

Osidian pointed to the collar at the Legate's throat. 'Surrender that to me, my Lord.'

The Legate's hand went up to the jade and iron. 'Celestial, this was put about my neck by the hands of the God Emperor Themselves.'

'The might of the Commonwealth properly belongs to the House of the Masks. It is in the name of that House I take back from you the legion you were lent.'

As the Legate hesitated, Osidian turned his mask just enough to allow the Legate to see the Marula reflected in it. The man must have understood the warning, for he turned to the other Lesser Chosen. 'You are my witnesses. I have no choice but to yield my command to the Lord Nephron.'

This said, the Legate reached behind his neck, released the collar and offered it to Osidian, who coiled it around his fist. He stepped past the Master who had been Legate and addressed the other commanders. 'I am now acting Legate. Serve me well, my Lords, and I shall reward you with blood and iron. Fail me and be assured that, if I do not destroy you, you will surely suffer the vengeance of the House of the Masks.'

Osidian's gold face regarded them a while, then he indicated the ammonites who had followed him from the tower. 'These shall prepare you for the outer world. I do not know how long it will be before any of us shall walk again upon sanctified ground.'

Even through the closed gates of the cothon, Carnelian could hear the squealing of brass. As they began to open they belched a reek of naphtha and dragons. The view widening between the parting portals was of a vast and complex machine come to life.

Morunasa and his Oracles, coming to greet them, faltered. Dazzled by Carnelian's and Osidian's masks they were forced to squint. Morunasa found enough composure to address Osidian, but was ignored as the Master half turned to Carnelian. 'Behold, my Lord, the sinews and technology of our power.'

Carnelian could see the cothon in motion, shrunk and twisted in the gold of Osidian's mask. Osidian slid forward, forcing the Oracles to move from his path. Carnelian followed, onto the road that curved off between the piers and the stable vaults. Hawsers now ran out from each vault, which they had to step over. Up on the piers men were greasing stone trackways and the bone-lined channels in which ropes ran as taut as bowstrings.

Osidian came to a halt at the edge of a stable entrance. He turned to say something, but his words were lost amidst the rattle and groaning of counterweights falling in their niches. He pointed up. Carnelian saw above them the base of a dragon tower being hoisted, ponderously, off its supporting beams. When these were winched back, the tower base was left hanging, black against the sky. Along the curving run of piers, more were rising, creaking like the hulls of ships at sea.

Movement just in front of Carnelian caused him to step back. The hawsers lying across his path were rising, curving ever more steeply up into the mouth of the nearest vault. As they lost their slack, it became clear they were pulling on something within the shadows. A dragon was being dragged out. Carnelian glanced between the piers towards the bright heart of the cothon. Rows of men, yoked to the hawsers, swayed in rhythm to a chant as they heaved. Other men appeared, carrying cruelly spiked billhooks. Seeing the Masters, they hesitated, but Osidian waved them on and they rushed into the stable. As their billhooks clawed at the monster, it let forth a terrible cry. The last time Carnelian had heard that sound was amidst fire and rolling sulphurous clouds. The cobbles under his feet gave a shudder. Another. Like the prow of a baran sliding out from its boathouse, the monster's head began emerging from the gloom. The hawsers were attached to rings gripping its horns. Sun splashed up the hill of its forehead. He saw its white eye larger than a shield. Rusty tattoos coating its head seemed the dried encrustings left by a wash of blood.

'Five, three, four twenties and one,' Carnelian read. The glyph 'Battle' appeared in several places. 'Bending River' and 'I cast down' he saw, surrounded by other glyphs that folded illegibly into its hide as it flexed. The inscriptions ran up the slope of its crest, sweeping in complex interweaving streams of signs, lapping the rugged cuticle of a horn, enringing its milky eye. Then its shoulder was dragged into the daylight. A cliff monumentally inscribed, spotted with the cartouches of the Lords who had ridden it, dates, paeans to its lineage as ancient as a House of the Chosen. At last Carnelian's gaze was led to the 'Nu' roundel that rouged its forehead: a glyph, one of whose readings was 'Annihilation'. Circling that was its battle name, pricked into its hide with raised scars. This was Heart-of-Thunder.

'I must go and talk to the Quartermaster,' cried Osidian over the tumult, 'and then I will give the commanders an audience. Will you, my Lord, oversee the re-equipping of the Marula from the legionary stores?'

Carnelian, unable to take his eyes off the vast monster as it was urged past, raised his hand in the affirmative. Each footfall shook the earth. Majestic, vast, Heart-of-Thunder slid between the piers and under the suspended tower base like a finger into a ring. When he next looked, Osidian was gone. He moved round behind the pier so he could gaze up at the monster's head. Men were lifting bronze rings set into the cothon floor. Heart-of-Thunder shook his head. One of the hawsers whipped loose. Its yoke, yanking back, threw the men who had borne it onto their backs. They lost hold of it. Their cries of alarm mixed with the clatter the yoke made scraping across the cobbles. Other men pounced on it and, with the help of the bearers, they managed to bring the monster back under control.

Carnelian continued to watch as the hawsers were made fast about the bronze rings. Thrice the monster, jerking back, threatened to tear the rings from the ground, but each time, unable to budge them, he subsided. Throughout, he rumbled a growl that reverberated through the cothon floor and off the piers, seeming to threaten a storm.

A man Carnelian had not noticed before, who was sitting astride one of the monster's lower horns, shuffled along it as if it were a log. When he reached the beast's head he leaned against it just behind the moon of its lidless eye. Stroking Heart-of-Thunder's hide, he seemed to be talking to him. Unbelievably, the monster stopped his growling and had soon become as motionless as stone. A barked command, then ropes snaked down the mountainous flanks. Men rushed into the squeeze between the dragon and the pier. Grabbing the ropes, they hung on them. Two massive counterweights began rising in their niches. Glancing up, Carnelian saw the four-prowed tower base descending. Its feet came to rest upon Heart-of-Thunder's haunches and shoulders. As the feet pressed into his hide, the monster let forth a bellow that rattled the piers. While the keeper calmed him again, others were circling him, peering up at his muscles, tapping them with the curve of their billhooks. When they were satisfied, they waved a signal and men leaping up into the niches took hold of the counter-weights and began swinging them in and out like bells. At last, with one coordinated action, the counterweights were swung back onto shelves. Their ropes sagged, as Heart-of-Thunder's back took the full weight of the tower base.

More men appeared, lugging steaming pails, into which others dipped poles that they lifted, dripping, to begin greasing the belly of the monster.

Voices above him made Carnelian look up to see figures swarming onto Heart-of-Thunder from the pier. He noticed a pole running the length of the tower base onto which one man was working a hook. Carnelian gasped as, gripping a rope attached to the hook, the man leapt into space. He slid to the ground, then pulled the rope after him under the ceiling of the monster's belly. Another man appeared, coming the other way. Rope in hand, he scrambled up footholds in the pier, back to the tower base. More men descended, more ascended as rope after rope sank into the layer of smeared fat, weaving a tight girdle to fix the tower in place.

Carnelian found Morunasa watching his Marula warriors being cut out of their beaded corselets. To his relief he spotted Sthax among them. Morunasa was frowning. Carnelian shared his unease at seeing the warriors being shelled like oysters, their corselets discarded as rubbish. In lines, the now naked men were being fitted for armour. The leather was more flattering to their long-limbed beauty than their corselets had been, but they were left looking more like slaves.

On the other side of the courtyard, grooms were bringing aquar down ramps. These were not the dun creatures of the Plainsmen, but the larger ones of the Commonwealth, silver as fish. There was no doubt the elegant curves of their saddle-chairs accommodated the lanky Marula better than the cramped wicker of the Plainsman chairs, but Carnelian could see how uncomfortable the warriors were with the stirrups and their frustration at how these new aquar did not respond to the touch of their feet. How long would it take them to adapt to using reins? Just before setting off on a dangerous campaign seemed a bad time to exchange the familiar for the strange. Osidian did not make that sort of mistake. No doubt this change had less to do with efficiency and more with discomfiting the Marula. Osidian wanted to break these proud men into auxiliaries obedient to his commands.

A desire to see Heart-of-Thunder once more drew him back to the cothon. Light from torches set into the piers gleamed off machines and towers. Commanding his escort to wait for him, Carnelian slipped into the shadows. He wandered under piers, passing dragons each bearing a tower base, each being crawled over by men still hard at work.

When he reached Heart-of-Thunder, Carnelian saw the immense girdle was complete. Clambering over it, men were working toggles larger than their hands into its ropes. Carnelian watched one being twisted into a rope a turn at a time, tightening it. When the toggle could be turned no further, it was tucked under the next rope to hold it fast. The rigger drew a fresh toggle from a pouch slung at his hip and with it struck the rope he had just tightened, feeling its tone with his cheek. Satisfied, he moved on to the next.

Watching the men work, Carnelian grew aware of a sound like distant drumming. Aurum must have arrived even earlier than they had feared. In alarm he sought the direction from which the drumming was coming. Then he realized it was only the beating of the dragon's heart.

Figures were hunched round fires lit directly on the cobbles of the marumaga barracks. From their slimness, and the ash coating their skin, Carnelian knew they were Oracles. His escort brought him to a door before which a curtain of myrrh smoke was rising. Passing through it, he found a gold-faced apparition waiting for him. Wrapped in linen, it made Carnelian recall the term the Plainsmen used for the Masters. The apparition unmasked to reveal Osidian's face, his eyes seeming murky emeralds. He must have misunderstood Carnelian's hesitation for he said: 'These chambers have been ritually cleansed, my Lord.'

Carnelian removed his mask and stripped down to his

second skin of bandages. Osidian indicated a mat upon which lay some dishes of food. Realizing how hungry he was, Carnelian sat down and began eating.

Osidian was watching him. 'Tomorrow I shall leave with the Marula to seek signs of the Lord Aurum.'

Carnelian frowned. 'Have you reason to expect him to be close?'

'I would like you to remain behind.'

Osidian's face was as unreadable as a mask, but Carnelian sensed he was up to something. 'Will you take all the Marula, my Lord?'

'I shall leave you some; though I do not think it likely you will have problems with the marumaga. You will be the only Chosen here.'

Carnelian thought that strange. 'My Lord is taking all the commanders with him?'

Osidian made a sign of affirmation.

'The Legate too?'

'He is no longer that but, yes, he will come with me.'

Carnelian returned to his meal. Perhaps Osidian intended nothing more than to humble the Lesser Chosen. Forcing them to endure the discomfort of riding aquar in the world beyond the city could only serve, as in the case of the Marula warriors, to reinforce Osidian's dominion over them. Something occurred to him. 'And Morunasa?'

'He shall remain here as your lieutenant.'

'To keep an eye on me?'

Osidian did not reply, but sat down to eat.

Before the outer gates of the cothon were fully open, Osidian and the Lesser Chosen commanders sped through the gap, their black cloaks fluttering like wings. Watching the Marula pour after them Carnelian frowned, remembering other Chosen riders in black cloaks, with other Marula. When all were through, the gates slowly closed. He turned back to the cothon. With their masts and rigging, the dragon towers had a look of the barans in the Tower in the Sea. Seeking distraction, he set off across the cobbles towards Heart-of-Thunder.

The piers dwarfed the pack huimur, each under a pitched frame studded with sacs. These sacs, once unhitched from the frames, were being lugged towards Heart-of-Thunder. As each arrived under the prow of his beak, a keeper would tear it open with his billhook, snag the sac, then raise it to tip the render into the dragon's maw.

When he tired of watching this feeding, Carnelian wandered down the monster's flank, staying in his shadow, curious to find out what the other keepers were up to, whom he could see prodding mushroom-headed poles into the dragon's hide. He deduced they must be testing the strength of the monster's massive muscles. When the beastmaster came, he pronounced himself satisfied. Heart-of-Thunder's lower horns were roped to yokes. Keepers pricked his legs as teams of men pulled on the ropes. With a shudder, the monster came to life. One massive leg rose, swung forward, then dropped to the ground with an impact that shook Carnelian's bones. More quakes followed as the monster moved from the first set of piers towards the second, finally slipping beneath the beams that held aloft the pyramid-shaped upper half of a dragon tower.

After Heart-of-Thunder had been tethered in place by his horns, more huimur approached bearing sacs. Carnelian wondered if the keepers were going to resume feeding the dragon, but this time the sacs were being lugged to the piers, then hoisted to their summits. These new sacs were being carried with some care. Also, they were not brown, but black. Curiosity drew Carnelian to investigate.

As he emerged from the shadows, everyone within sight fell to their knees. He peered at one of the black sacs. His ranga would not allow him to reach down to it. 'Hold it up to me.'

As a keeper lifted it, Carnelian could smell its reek even through the nosepads of his mask. 'Naphtha.'

He let the men resume their work and stood where he could watch them ferrying the sacs over to the tower base roped to the dragon's back. After a while a reek of naphtha began wafting down from the tower base and he realized they must be filling its tanks.

The empty sacs were piled on the cothon floor away from the dragons. No doubt as a precaution against accidental fire. Near sunset the legionaries began clearing the cothon. Carnelian had been watching the mobilization for so long, his legs had begun to ache. A lone legionary dared approach to tell him that the gates would soon be locked. Carnelian followed the man across the cothon. The rest of his comrades were already beginning to huddle around fires they had lit upon the cobbles away from the dragons. As Carnelian passed through the gate it was locked behind him.

Alone in the marumaga barracks, Carnelian could hear the murmur of the Marula in the courtyard outside. How he longed to go and join them round their campfires. Twice now he had summoned someone to attend him but, when they had knelt before him, he had stood silent. What communication could there be between them? All they could see was a Master. He had had to be content with asking them to bring food and water.

He lay on the floor without a blanket, wanting the stone to spread its coldness up to numb his heart. What would he not have given for a glimpse of Fern or Poppy or Krow, or even just to hear their voices?

Beneath one of Heart-of-Thunder's piers, Carnelian was waiting for the Quartermaster. Though, by waking, he had escaped his nightmares, his mind was still stained with dread. The cothon and its activity no longer held a promise of power, but only of destruction. This great mechanism, so nearly wound up to readiness, was a weapon he knew Osidian would not hesitate to use. His heart told him they were close to the point of no return if, indeed, they had not already passed it. The immediate consequences of the events they were about to set in motion he could barely see; the ultimate consequences he could not see at all; but, though he was blind to the future, his heart was populating it with vague, terrible shapes.

'My Master, you summoned me?'

It was like being shocked awake. The Quartermaster was there, kneeling. Carnelian gestured him to rise. 'What remains to be done?'

'Some of the dragons have not yet recovered their strength, Master, and this is causing us delays. We dare not burden them until they're ready.'

Instinctively, Carnelian reached out to reassure the man, but let his hand fall when he saw him flinch. 'I'm not accusing you, but seek only your best estimate of when the legion will be ready.'

'Before nightfall most of the ranks should be full, Master.'

'And then?'

'For those dragons strong enough, we can attempt to seal their towers.'

Carnelian glanced at Heart-of-Thunder. 'Is he strong enough?'

'He is, Master.'

'What happens after his tower is sealed?'

'We shall connect up the pipes.'

'The flame-pipes?'

'Just so, Master.' The man raised a hand to point towards the centre of the cothon.

Carnelian gazed off to what he had thought a brass wall. The Quartermaster said something else, but Carnelian was not listening. He had not noticed before how much that wall resembled the bronze forest surrounding the Chamber of the Three Lands in Osrakum.

*   *   *

Mast and tower shadows were reaching across the cothon when the Quartermaster came to tell him Heart-of-Thunder's tanks were full and that his tower would now be sealed. Carnelian followed him back and found a place near the dragon where he could watch everything. Slaves greased the piers, counterweights were released, the upper, pyramid-shaped part of the tower rose from its supporting beams. When these were slid away the pyramid was left swinging gently like some vast but silent bell, men clinging to its sides. Chanting to keep their rhythm, gangs pulled the pyramid down, even as the counterweights rose in their niches in the piers. As the two parts of the tower came together, the men on its sides began threading ropes through blocks and rings. When the pyramid and base were sewn together, one by one the counterweights were coaxed onto holding shelves. Heart-of-Thunder groaned as his shoulders bulged under the increasing burden of the completed tower. Men ran around him, gazing up anxiously, testing his sinews with poles. Slowly smiles lit faces, eyes brightened, as they grew confident he was strong enough. At the Quartermaster's command they unhitched the cradle ropes. The tower was now completely free of the piers. It and Heart-of-Thunder were one.

Legionaries escorted two flame-pipes across the cothon: each a trumpet as massive as a fallen tree. Setting guards on the piers, one of the legionaries first sent his fellows clambering up, then gave a command to the beastmaster sitting astride one of Heart-of-Thunder's lower horns. Carnelian took a step back as the tower rocked. Under instruction, the dragon was shuffling sideways towards the pier. Legionaries began crossing to his tower. Clambering around on its sides, they threw down ropes to be hitched to one of the flame-pipes. Slowly it was hoisted towards the tower.

A commotion across the cothon made Carnelian turn to see that riders were pouring in through the outer gate. Osidian and the Marula had returned.

Carnelian waited for Osidian by Heart-of-Thunder's pier. He watched him consult the Quartermaster and then approach, accompanied by another Master. 'It seems, my Lord,' Osidian called out, 'it will be at least another day before we can leave. Some of the huimur are not yet strong enough to bear their towers.'

Carnelian tried to deduce something of Osidian's mood from his tone, from the set of his shoulders. He sensed Osidian was putting on a show for the other Master. They all turned to gaze up at Heart-of-Thunder. The first flame-pipe was already attached. Legionaries were working on the second. Osidian was nodding. 'I shall command the first cohort from his tower.'

He turned to Carnelian. 'I hope that you, my Lord Suth, shall condescend to command the second.'

Carnelian had not thought about it, but raised his hand in affirmation.

'The third we shall leave in your hands, my Lord.' Osidian indicated the other Master, who bowed.

'As you command, Celestial.'

Something about this man disturbed Carnelian, but he could not work out what it was. Then it occurred to him. His voice was not that of the ex-Legate. As the most senior of the Lesser Chosen it should have been he who took next place after Osidian and himself.

Later, as he followed Osidian to where the other Lesser Chosen were waiting, Carnelian searched among them for one who might be behaving differently from the others, perhaps showing some resentment. It was then he noticed ammonites unloading a body from a saddle-chair. He glimpsed an arm that was wrapped in ritual bindings.

'You murdered him, didn't you?' Carnelian asked, the moment they were alone and unmasked.

Osidian gazed at him. 'He defied me.'

257

'You needed to kill him as an object lesson to the other commanders.'

Osidian held Carnelian's glare for a while before turning away as he divested himself of his military cloak. 'We shadowed the road far to the west and saw no sign of Aurum.'

Carnelian was remembering how Osidian had killed Ranegale so as to take control of the Ochre raiding party. He focused his attention on what Osidian had said. 'What if he does not come by road?'

'He must if he is to have any hope of getting here before we complete our mobilization.'

Carnelian realized something. 'If you could see the road, then the watch-towers must have seen you.'

Osidian threw his hand up in a gesture of dismissal. 'The time for hiding has passed.'

For a moment Carnelian became lost in a maelstrom of anxiety. So they had finally passed the point of no return. He marshalled his thoughts. 'You have a plan?'

'We penetrate deep into the hinterland beyond the seeing of the Wise. Then we shall turn towards Makar.'

Carnelian saw it in his mind. 'You wish to outflank him.'

'And snatch his base from him.'

To capture Makar would put them astride the South Road that ran north to Osrakum.

Osidian's eyes went opaque. 'That should get the attention of my Lords the Wise.'

Even though he did not believe they would give Osidian anything, Carnelian felt uneasy.

Osidian's eyes brightened. 'Aurum will be forced to come to me.'

Could it be he still hoped the old Master would join him? Carnelian felt a need to put a crack in Osidian's certainty. 'How can you be so certain of that?'

'How else is he going to keep his legion supplied?'

Carnelian paused. 'Surely he will find all he needs here.'

When Osidian smiled, Carnelian could already see Qunoth burning.

Carnelian stood upon a low dais within a raised ring of stone. The curved alabaster wall suffused the chamber with soft white light. An ammonite entered, bearing a casket of ribbed ivory. He put this on the floor, broke its seals and opened it. Pulling back layers of parchment, he reached in and drew forth a pale garment. The torso was of a piece with the legs that followed, which another ammonite swept into the crook of his arm so that the suit would not touch the floor. Together they carried it towards Carnelian, climbed up onto the stone ring then let the suit fall, dangling its toed feet and fingered hands. It opened up the middle, inner edges fringed with ties and hooks. It seemed the skin flayed whole from a man. The ammonites asked him to raise his arms, then they fed them into those of the suit. The soft leather poured like silk, rucking at Carnelian's elbows. The gloves that formed the extremity of the arms were slipped over his hands. He helped the ammonites by worming his fingers into each pocket. They tightened the gloves along their outer edges with delicate ties like tendons. They did up the paired green and black buttons on the back of each wrist. Flexing his hands Carnelian was hardly aware of their covering. The ammonites smoothed the leather up his arms, fitting his elbows into the ridged joints, slicking it over the muscles of his upper arms and easing the shoulders of the suit over his own. As they pulled the leather over his chest, the dangling, empty head flopped down under his throat. The legs of the suit hung nudging at his shins. The ammonites lifted his left leg and fed it into the suit. His foot slipped into the leather foot as easily as had his hands into the gloves. They squeezed his big toe into one pocket and the other toes into another wide enough to accommodate them all. When he put his foot down he could feel soft calluses under his toes, the ball and ridge of his foot, his heel. Once his other leg was clothed he raised it, turning his foot up to see the sole. The heel was red, the ball and ridge black, the toes green. It was a ranga shoe integral to the suit. He felt the leather slide and grip his body as the ammonites began to engage the ties and hooks up his back.

As the suit moulded itself to his body Carnelian raised his arms, surprised at how it flexed at the gathering ridges of wrists, elbows and shoulders. He did not like the paleness of the leather which reminded him of the bleached faces of the Wise. In its sickly, greasy pallor it also bore a resemblance to the maggots of the Oracles.

He dropped his arms and practised breathing against the embrace of the suit. It was restrictive, but not so much that he felt trapped. He became aware of the way the suit was padded to accentuate the musculature of his body that the ritual bandages obscured.

When the ammonites asked him to climb down and walk around the chamber, he was pleased to find the legs of the suit articulating as comfortably as the arms. As he bent and twisted and crouched, the suit clung to him like a second skin. The ammonites asked him to stand still, then, after some adjustments, all left save one who, removing his silver mask, replaced it with one whose eyes were solid spirals. Begging his permission, the ammonite reached up and released Carnelian's mask. He took hold of the flaccid head of the suit, smoothed it over Carnelian's chin, then up and over his head. Carnelian pulled its opening around the contours of his face. He felt buttons being secured at the nape of his neck. Then the ammonite came round and bound his mask back on. Finally, the others returned with a great, black, hooded military cloak that they threw about his shoulders and bound across his chest with a clasp that, in jet and jade, showed the faces of the Twin Gods.

Carnelian followed Osidian onto the summit of the pier. There before them was a dragon tower: a pallid, three-tiered pyramid from which a mast rose, supported by rigging. In front, one

260

flame-pipe pointed towards the heart of the cothon; the other was just being raised. From the rear of the tower two thicker brass chimneys emerged with sooty swollen mouths.

Even as he was taking in these details, Carnelian became increasingly disturbed. He realized the tower was reminding him of a Plainsman Ancestor House, and of the boats of the ferrymen of Osrakum. Though smoother, it too seemed made of bone. Those other structures people had fashioned from their own dead, with reverence and as memorials. The dragon tower, though more finely wrought, was an instrument of war and thus seemed gruesome.

Osidian was facing a diagonal brass cross set against the tower flank. As Carnelian approached him, he saw it was no cross, but a gigantic woman wrought from brass. Her back to them, she was spreadeagled on a mesh as if crucified. Between her splayed legs he could see a portion of an opening that gave into the dark interior of the tower.

As she began to fall back towards them, Carnelian realized she was a drawbridge with ropes tied to her wrists. As her knuckles and the back of her head clinked against the pier, two legionaries emerged from the tower and ran out over her. When they reached Osidian, they unclasped his cloak, folded it carefully, then stood aside. The brass woman shuddered as Osidian's foot struck her in the face. His next step fell between her legs. A third took him into the dragon tower through its oval portal. As the legionaries removed Carnelian's cloak, he turned his head to see her face the right way up. Though it was worn almost smooth, he could still make out a noseless, eyeless grinning skull trapped within the circle of the deeply cut earth glyph. It must surely represent the branded face of a dead sartlar of the Guarded Land. He did not want to tread on that face and so he put his ranga down on the mesh between her head and an arm. Long, empty breasts sagged down the sides of her body. She was almost a skeleton. He stepped over her bony arm. Her vulva looked like a scooped out pomegranate. He stepped over her leg. It disturbed him that she was there to be walked on. He turned to the legionaries, now kneeling on the pier. 'Who is this woman?'

One of them mumbled something and Carnelian asked him to speak more clearly.

'Brassman,' the legionary said.

Carnelian frowned behind his mask but, seeing the man's discomfort, he stooped and entered the tower.

The ceiling of the cabin forced him to remain stooped. Just enough light squeezed past him to allow him to make out the organs and entrails of sinister machinery. When a voice behind him begged leave, Carnelian shuffled aside to let the two legionaries past. A porthole grated open in the opposite wall. More followed, letting in daylight. The rimless wheel of a capstan filled the rear of the cabin. In front of this a ladder led up to a trap set into the ceiling. The front of the cabin was dominated by a convoluted arrangement of tubes, vessels and other structures.

As Osidian gave commands, Carnelian was drawn to peer at these contraptions. Hanging in the air, a mass of leather strips wove around some metal ribs. Stepping round it, he saw this was a chair floating in mid air upon a limb of brass that came into the cabin like an oar into a baran. He could imagine the rest of it projecting out from the tower and knew it must be the end of the flame-pipe. He peered at some handles set upon its barrel. Taking hold of one, he found the pipe so finely counterbalanced he could swing it easily. Sliding his hand along the barrel, he touched the tube that curved from it down to a vessel of copper as large as a pumpkin. From the rear of this vessel a brass tube ran up to and back along the ceiling and out, presumably to emerge from the tower as one of the chimneys.

'My Lord, please move away from the furnace. It is about to be lit.'

Osidian was waiting for him by the ladder. Carnelian watched him climb it even as legionaries were opening hatches in the copper vessels and striking flints. As he followed him up, one of the furnaces roared into life.

He emerged into a second cabin partially filled with trumpets the size of canoes. Climbing further he came up into the brightness of a third cabin. He clambered up onto the deck. He was pleased to find he did not need to stoop. The front wall was a delicately pierced screen that curved round to open up the front half of each side wall. A single chair faced this screen, upon which sat Osidian. Carnelian had to avoid some contraptions lying on the floor to the side of the chair as he approached the screen. His eyes adjusted to the glare enough for him to be able to see out through the web of fine rods.

Below him the two flame-pipes pointed forwards. Beyond was the open cothon, piles of empty render sacs forming a ring around its hub. The hub itself was now only a scaffolding rack almost entirely denuded of the flame-pipes it had held. He could smell something burning. Gazing back into the cabin he almost expected to see it smouldering. A legionary had come after them and crept forward to kneel on one side of the chair. Another appeared through the floor and hesitated, a look of agony on his face. Carnelian realized he must be standing in the man's place. He moved back to stand behind Osidian and the legionary rushed forward to kneel beside the chair, then lifted a tube from the floor and connected it to his helmet.

'The pipes are ready for testing, Master,' the other legionary announced. Tubes snaked from his helmet also.

Carnelian noticed both legionaries were crouched over a kind of fork they held before them and from each of which two tubes hung. Osidian's gloved hands closed on the armrests of the chair. 'Target the render sacs.'

The legionary at his right hand leaned down and murmured into one prong of his voice fork. Carnelian heard a sound and looked up to see the flame-pipes lifting.

'Flame,' said Osidian.

The legionary spoke again into his voice fork. From the

263

bowels of the tower there rose a choking and gurgling. Then a high whine that made Carnelian grit his teeth. Screaming arcs of sunlight erupted from the mouths of the flame-pipes. A mist of smoke. Then the sacs began detonating. Their fiery brilliance was almost immediately concealed behind a mass of black smoke that boiled into the sky. A wall of heat struck the cabin, carrying a stench as if from a funeral pyre.

Night had fallen when Carnelian accompanied Osidian on a final inspection of all twenty-four dragons. Smoke obscured the stars. The incessant testing of flame-pipes had hung a pall over the fortress that had turned day to murky twilight. The fires of the Marula camp guttered across the cothon floor, where Osidian had insisted they must all spend the night. Carnelian had agreed to stay with him. He shared Osidian's anxiety. Now the dragons were fully armed, he did not want them out of his sight. Lit by the torches attached to the piers, the bellies and legs of the monsters formed a continuous portico that could have been the edge of the Isle of Flies. Carnelian shuddered. He gazed up at one of the monsters. Though its upper horns were now bound to its tower with a hawser, its lower horns were still tethered to the cothon floor. The sickly pale tower with its pipes, chimneys, mast and rigging seemed a sinister ship in a fog. For some reason he was recalling the fear Ebeny had felt on that night, long ago in the Plain of Thrones, when she had been chosen from the flesh tithe.

Carnelian awoke on Heart-of-Thunder's pier. He and Osidian had slept there so that they could be free of their masks. Dawn was running blood down the mast of the monster's tower. Osidian was gone. Carnelian put his mask on and rose to face the day.

He found Osidian down on the cothon cobbles talking to Morunasa. Osidian was instructing the Oracle on how he and the Marula were to seed the fortress with naphtha sacs.

Listening, Carnelian was struck by how thoroughly Osidian was planning his act of sabotage. He could not keep silent once Morunasa had gone. 'Is it necessary to destroy this place so utterly?'

Osidian's mask turned its imperious glance on him. 'This fortress must provide no succour to my Lord Aurum.'

'Is it not rather that you wish to send a message to the Wise?'

'My Lord, you will take your grand-cohort out immediately.' Osidian indicated the dozens of lesser huimur chained one to the other, each bearing a fully laden render frame. 'Take our supplies with you to safeguard them. When you reach open ground, deploy your huimur to cover my exit from the city. Do you understand?'

Carnelian frowned behind his mask, angry at Osidian's tone. 'No news of Aurum?'

Osidian made a gesture of negation, then indicated the brightening sky. 'The smoke we have been releasing will be visible from a great distance.'

'As far as Osrakum,' Carnelian said, knowing it must be clearly visible to the nearest watch-towers.

Indeed, signed Osidian.

'And while I am screening the city, you will be here incinerating this place?'

'I shall do nothing myself.'

Carnelian could hear the smile in Osidian's voice. 'You will make the Lesser Chosen commanders do it so as to fully implicate them.'

'There are more ways to bind others to one's cause than love.'

Carnelian would not allow himself to be stung by Osidian's bitterness. 'Which huimur is to be mine?'

Osidian made a summoning gesture and two legionaries rose from among the rest. 'These are your Righthand and Lefthand. They will guide you to your command, my Lord.'

'Until later then.' Carnelian indicated to his officers that they should lead and he set off with them across the cothon floor.

As he approached the dragon Carnelian judged that, if it was less massive than Heart-of-Thunder, it could not be by much. Gazing up between the swelling arches of its eye-ridges, he found the scar glyphs of its name: Earth-is-Strong.

Carnelian turned to his Lefthand. 'Have you ridden him long?'

'She, Master,' the man said, then shrank away at his presumption.

'You were right to correct me, legionary,' Carnelian said, gazing back at the dragon. He had not thought they could be female.

'Nine years,' the man was saying when Carnelian's chuckle interrupted him. He was amused to find he was detecting feminine curves in the monster's horns, her beak, the sweep of her crest. Her lower right horn was just a stump, so she really only had three.

Carnelian became aware of the legionaries' confusion. 'Come, let's take her out.'

He followed them to the rear of a pier, where they opened a door for him. He dismissed them and began to climb the stair alone. No doubt its form was intended to remind a commander of the Law. He used its spiralling path to compose his mind. He must be careful how he managed those under his command. When he reached the summit, he saw before him the bone pyramid of her tower upon her massive back. He could not help feeling a stab of elation that she was his.

His officers were waiting, kneeling. He passed between them, then crossed the brassman into the tower. He surveyed the gloom through the slits of his mask. Men were kneeling before the furnaces, beside the flame-pipe counterweight chairs, between the spokes of the capstan. Carnelian noted the hawser that emerged from a hole in the deck, wound itself round the spindle of the capstan, then disappeared through another hole on the other side of the cabin. It was this hawser, attached to the upper horns of the dragon, that allowed her to be steered.

He climbed to the next deck. Framed by the brass of the huge trumpets, this cabin had been turned into a storeroom and barracks. He continued up to the command deck, where he took his place upon its chair. His officers came up behind him, then knelt to either side and began connecting tubes to their helmets. His arms rested naturally along those of the chair. Its bone seemed polished ivory. He raised his gaze to look out through the latticework screen at the cothon. Below him were the gleaming spars of his flame-pipes. Further down still the slope of Earth-is-Strong's head sweeping out into the scythe and stump of her lower horns, into the hook of her beak.

He realized he did not know what to do next. He considered asking one of his officers, but decided it could not be that difficult. 'Take her out.'

His Lefthand put his mouth to his tubed voice fork and murmured something, then lifted his head. Nothing happened. Carnelian was beginning to feel they were waiting for him to give another command, when he noticed some movement down on the dragon's lower horns. Men were now sitting astride the brass cuffs, to which were lashed the tether ropes. Responding to some signal, both simultaneously leaned over and released the ropes. Earth-is-Strong's head came loose. Carnelian flinched as she swung it up. For a moment he imagined her bony frill would shatter the tower he was in to shards. She let forth a cry like tearing metal. The tower shuddered. Then it heeled over to one side, causing Carnelian to grip the arms of the chair. The tower surged forward. The impact of the monster's footfall jarred up into Carnelian's head. The tower began another surge, toppling in the opposite direction. To his relief, as Earth-is-Strong got into her stride, the movement gradually smoothed like a ship riding a swell.

267

They were heading straight for the centre of the cothon. 'The outer gate,' he said, quickly.

The Lefthand jerked a nod and muttered into his voice fork: 'Starboard for two counts.'

Carnelian felt the turn in his stomach. Ahead, the cothon was slipping right to left.

'Shall I give the signal for the others to follow us, Master?' the Lefthand asked.

Carnelian managed only a nod.

The legionary leaned to his voice fork and began murmuring instructions. Carnelian's curiosity was piqued. 'Who're you talking to?'

The Lefthand looked up, startled. When he saw it was a question and not a complaint, he pointed up. 'Our mirrorman on the roof, Master.'

Carnelian nodded, imagining something like a small heliograph up there. Earth-is-Strong was now pounding directly towards the outer gate of the cothon. As they approached, it opened before them. Soon its brass was glimmering past on either side. Then they began moving through the fortress towards the watch-tower that guarded its gate. Edifices slid past. Men scurried from their path. The fortress gate grated as it lifted into the retaining wall. Soon the shadow of the watch-tower fell over them.

'Master, shall we give warning of our coming?' said the Righthand.

Carnelian released the arm of the chair and raised his hand in affirmation. They were exiting the fortress. He could see the mosaic of squares and lozenges made up by the roofs of the mudbrick tenements. A trumpet roared beneath Carnelian's feet. He could feel its vibration through the deck. It blared again, its harsh, ragged voice echoing back off the buildings as Earth-is-Strong slid between them.

Carnelian had grown tired of watching the city slip by. His focus was turned inwards as he brooded on what was to come.

He was startled by a rumbling like thunder that came from somewhere far behind him. For a while he heard its echoes getting lost among the alleys below.

'What was that?' he asked his Lefthand.

Staring, the man shook his head. Carnelian rose, swaying with the deck, searching the rear wall of the cabin for windows. There were portholes to either side of the mast. Finding his sea legs, he strode to one. Another explosion sounded as he fumbled at the bolt securing its cover. Then he had it open and was looking back along the road. Beyond the long line of dragons following his, a frowning black cloud was rising as it fed on wavering tentacles of smoke. As he watched, there was a flash as if the sun had been caught suddenly upon some vast mirror. Moments later he was hit by a detonation that made him recoil from the porthole. He returned to it and watched the smoke rising. Suddenly, the branches of the watch-tower were wreathed in flames. It looked like one of the mother trees in the Koppie burning.

As Earth-is-Strong took them through the gate of Qunoth out onto the blinding expanse of the raised road, Carnelian brought her to a halt. Beyond the road there spread what appeared to be a vast midden. Carnelian leaned forward on his command chair. He could not imagine where so much rubbish could have come from. Then he noticed movement, as if the whole mouldering mass were writhing with maggots, and realized what he was looking at must be a suburb outside the city walls. Beyond these shanties he was sure he could see where their brown shaded into the red of the Guarded Land.

'Take us west along the road.'

The Lefthand murmured into his voice fork. Then the cabin lurched into movement as Earth-is-Strong swung westwards.

They pounded along the road that poured its limestone west to vanish in the haze. The road was so wide it easily accommodated Earth-is-Strong without blocking the flow of other traffic. Having made sure that Aurum was nowhere in sight, Carnelian distracted himself by peering down at the patchwork of the crowds. Here and there it was dense, but mostly it barely skinned the stone. Many faces turned up in wonder to watch the dragons go by. Others were looking south to where black clouds were rising from the tip of Qunoth. Though he had been hoping to recapture something of the excitement he had felt on the Great Sea Road, it was hopeless. During that journey he had been down there among the bustle and the stench. He had been one of them. Now it took effort to see it as anything other than a roughly patterned tapestry.

After they had left the shanties behind, he kept a look-out for a ramp. When they came to one, he ordered Earth-is-Strong off the road and had commands sent to the rest of his grand-cohort to follow. Descending the ramp, the dragon sat back a little on her haunches, so that, on the whole, the cabin remained level. Soon after she reached the earth, it seemed she was wading into a red sea. The billows of dust she churned up soon rose high enough to submerge her head.

When a message was received that the last dragon had left the road, Carnelian sent one back commanding that each should heave to, facing west in line abreast. When Earth-is-Strong had completed her turn, the cabin stilled. He could hear the creaking of the tower, of its rigging, of its flexing mast. As the dust settled, her head emerged like a reef from an ebbing tide. Soon it was quiet enough for Carnelian to hear the breathing of his officers.

Carnelian was drowsing when a remote murmuring brought him fully awake. The sound was coming from his Lefthand's helmet.

'What is it?' Carnelian demanded.

'A message from Heart-of-Thunder, Master.'

'What does it say?'

270

The man looked disconcerted. 'Join me.'

Carnelian returned to the porthole in the rear wall of the cabin. He had to move round to another to gain a view of the city they had left behind. Smoke, rooted in the fortress of Qunoth, had grown into a black tree under whose branches the city and the adjoining land lay in shadow. He searched for Osidian and his dragons upon the road, but could not find them. Then movement at the corner of his eye made him turn his mask slits away from the city. There they were, beneath the smoke, like a flotilla of ships ploughing a course directly through the midst of the shanties.

HINTERLAND

For more than one thousand years the Land has been
dying. Decline began eight hundred years before that, when
population pressure led to the Great Famine. At that time,
forced to abandon fallowing, we began the development of
irrigation. Consequently, most of the Land has come to yield
two crops a year. However, the soil is subject to an ever-
declining fertility. We have been able to compensate for this
by a variety of methods. With the ongoing refinement of our
systems we are confident we can postpone collapse
for an indeterminate time.

(extract from a beadcord manual of the Wise of the Domain Lands)

Red land gave way to green. Through the bone screen
Carnelian watched the rolling dust break upon the hri field,
then Earth-is-Strong emerged as if they were coming ashore.
Ahead of him the line of Osidian's dragons stretched away into
the monotonous grey-green distance patterned to the horizon
with sartlar kraals. Several times he detected movement in
their overseer towers. The sartlar themselves, who worked
the Guarded Land in vast numbers, crawled everywhere like
fleas.

As they penetrated ever deeper into the hinterland his command chair rocked Carnelian in and out of sleep. Half awake,
he imagined he was coasting along a shore. The pounding

272

rhythm of the dragon's footfalls seemed the sound of breakers.

A voice woke him. Lifting his masked face, he saw his Lefthand raising his hands to him almost in prayer. 'Master, a signal's been passed down the line from Heart-of-Thunder commanding that we should form a laager for the night.'

Outside, the long shadows cast by the overseer towers showed how late it was. 'Give the commands.'

The Lefthand touched his forehead to the deck before speaking into his voice fork. 'Hard to port.'

Earth-is-Strong began veering left. Gazing out through the port edge of the screen Carnelian watched the line of dragons sweeping round towards the sun. Far away the massive shape of Heart-of-Thunder was beginning to eclipse it. For moments his tower was a silhouette haloed with gold, then the sun slipped free, so bright Carnelian was forced to squint. Another dragon moved to obscure it. He watched the mesmerizing pulse of dragons passing until his own was moving into that part of the arc in which the sun was permanently obscured. He settled back into his chair feeling the slow pound of Earth-is-Strong's footfalls as if it were his own heartbeat. Then, suddenly, the cabin was facing due west and he was blind in its radiance. Through his eyelids, he saw only red. Slowly the sun moved to his right until they were moving south and it was possible to reopen his eyes.

At last the constant swaying of the cabin slowed but, at the end of each swing, the deck leaned at a more extreme angle than before, so that Carnelian had to grip the arms of his chair. A couple more swings and then the cabin settled upright.

The Lefthand spoke into his voice fork. 'Hard to starboard.'

The tower rattled and shook as Earth-is-Strong turned into the sun, flooding the cabin with incandescent gold. The Righthand put his mouth to his voice fork and murmured something. Squinting, Carnelian noticed movement down at the dragon's horns. Ropes were being cast to the ground. Men grabbing these ran with them to where others were hammering spikes into the earth. Earth-is-Strong's head was being tethered.

At last the Righthand raised his eyes to Carnelian's mask. 'Master, it is now possible to disembark.'

Carnelian gave a nod and both of his officers bent to their voice forks and issued commands into them. He felt more than heard the crew moving about the tower, but he remained in his chair, feeling it was his right to quit the tower last. He heard a creaking sound to port that he guessed was the brass-man being lowered. As it came fully down he felt its pull upon the tower. Then there was a jerking vibration as men moved along it. This went on for some time, then, heads bowed, his officers rose from their positions and retreated towards the ladder. Carnelian waited to hear them descend before he himself rose. He climbed down through the empty trumpet deck, glad of the respite its closed ports gave him from the sun. Reaching the lower deck he was forced to stoop. Through the portal he could see the brassman stretched out into space, hanging from its chains. As Carnelian walked out onto it his mask protected him from the glare. The distance to the ground was alarming. Ahead was another dragon tower, half in shadow. He glanced further round and saw he was on the edge of an expanse walled by the ring of dragons. Within this milled the Marula on their aquar and the pack huimur with their frames.

He used the rope ladder that fell from the brassman's hands to climb down to the ground. His officers and crew were kneeling all around him. Hunched sartlar were jogging towards him in pairs. Between each sagged a pole from which hung a leather box that spilled water with every bounce. He gazed back down the line of these water carriers to the black hole in the earth from which they were emerging burdened. The odour of render released into the air was managing to pierce the nosepads of his mask. At that moment the dragons began a moaning as if they were mourning the dying of the day. Their haunches and the pillared halls beneath their bellies already wallowed in night. Their horns against the purpling sky were crescent moons. Only their towers still held the guttering embers of the sun. He watched as the last gleam of day faded into indigo.

Within one of the pavilions erected for the Masters, Carnelian sat opposite Osidian on the thick mattresses that made a floor. A brazier was pumping myrrh smoke. Though overpowering, it allowed them to be free of their masks. He glanced at its hated shell, face down on a pad of silk. Through the haze he could see the stains Osidian had sweated into his bandages. He too had had his leathers removed. He fingered the mattress, which was thick enough to lift them the prescribed distance from the polluting earth.

Osidian was eating voraciously from the ceramic boxes filled with delicate wafers of hri, saffroned meats, dried fruit like dull, wrinkled jewels. Carnelian nibbled at a wafer; the whiff of render had turned his stomach.

Osidian looked up. 'Tomorrow we must carry out some manoeuvres.'

'I thought we had to make for Makar without delay.'

Osidian nodded. 'But I must get a feeling for coordinating our line.'

Carnelian bit into an apricot as Osidian began sculpting tactical dispositions in the air. 'You will take the left, I the right.'

Osidian woke Carnelian. Once their Hands had eased them back into their leathers, they emerged from their pavilion. Within the laager, preparations were already being made to leave. Carnelian followed Osidian past Marula saddling their aquar to where the Lesser Chosen commanders were gathered. After Osidian had explained to them what he intended to do he sent them to their towers. As he turned to Carnelian his mask caught some of the pink dawn. 'Let us see what power there is in these beasts.'

Carnelian could not help feeling a thrill of excitement as he approached Earth-is-Strong. The rising sun was sheathing her rump in copper. Her head and the hills of her shoulders were carved from shadow, but her tower seemed aflame. Men crawled up in the rigging like flies. He felt a momentary unsteadiness as she shifted. He saw a man sitting astride one of her horns ready to release the tether. He mounted the ladder. The brassman was grimacing as Carnelian came up onto it. Entering the tower he was struck by the already familiar mix of naphtha, sweat and leather. Climbing to the upper deck he slipped into his command chair. His Hands came to kneel beside him. He listened out for the commands they were murmuring into their voice forks. He felt the juddering as the rest of the crew scrambled up into the tower. At last his Lefthand raised his eyes. 'Everyone's aboard, Master. Everything's stowed.'

'Take her into the west,' Carnelian said. 'Order the rest of the cohort to follow.'

The man gave a nod and began issuing instructions into his voice fork. The cabin lurched as Earth-is-Strong's head came free. The capstan brought her head under control. The tower tilted right then left as she began to move forward. Soon it levelled as Earth-is-Strong found her pace. Through the bone screen Carnelian could see other dragons following as he had commanded. He gave his Lefthand further instructions and, as these were relayed down below, they began veering south-west. When messages arrived that convinced him he had reached the leftmost position in Osidian's line he had his dragon turn due west.

Sartlar scurried among the hri-spikes like ants fleeing a flood. In his command chair Carnelian was elated by the rushing speed, by the majesty of the dragon line half-masked by dust.

The sartlar in flight had, at first, evoked dark memories of the time he and Osidian had been slaves among them. Remembering Kor he had felt pity, but the subtle way in which he and Osidian, though so far apart, could manage to control the horizon-spanning line of dragons was intoxicating.

Something flickering in the corner of his eye made Carnelian turn to see a flashing from the furthest end of the line. His Lefthand frowned, hearing the signal decoded in the earpiece in his helmet.

'Sickle,' he said and looked up for confirmation from Carnelian.

At his nod, the legionary grunted a command into his voice fork. The swaying motion of the tower smoothed further as they picked up even more speed. Earth-is-Strong began to outdistance the other dragons in their cohort. Glancing round, Carnelian saw those in the centre had slowed, hanging back so that the whole line was becoming a crescent with its horns thrust forward. He craned to peer ahead into the murk that hid his dragon's lumbering gait. Down on the plain the sartlar were tiring; the dragons in the horns of the crescent were overtaking them.

Another flash came down the line from Osidian. An order to close the trap. At Carnelian's command Earth-is-Strong began veering to starboard, pulling the left half of the line round with her. For a while he watched his dragons curving in towards the sartlar. Then he saw another tide of dust coming straight towards them. Heart-of-Thunder emerged from it, horns spread like wings, tower gleaming, leading the other arm of their envelopment to close with his. The sartlar slowed to a stumble, began milling, as the encirclement grew ever tighter. More flashing that his Lefthand received through his helmet. The legionary turned to Carnelian. 'Light the furnaces.'

Carnelian regarded the man, a look of horror hidden behind his mask. Osidian was intending to unleash fire upon the sartlar.

'Master?'

Carnelian shook his head. Heart-of-Thunder and Earth-is-Strong had swung round to move in parallel as they closed upon the sartlar. He lunged forward to grab his Lefthand's shoulder. 'Send a signal along the line in both directions: desist!'

The man looked at him, his face stiffening with panic.

'Send it,' Carnelian roared.

The man's mouth approached his voice fork, muttered the commands. Carnelian peered out of the port screen, straining to make out Osidian's tower in the eddying dust-clouds. He waited for some response. Then he noticed smoke beginning to wisp from Osidian's chimneys. To starboard, more was hazing up from every tower within eyeshot. The ring of dragons tightened, training the spikes of its flame-pipes on the sartlar mass, which was darkening as they huddled closer. Without taking his eyes off them, Carnelian leaned to his Lefthand. 'No signal?'

'None, Master,' the man replied, his voice breaking.

Black smoke was pumping up all around the ring. Carnelian felt numb. Already it was too late. Nauseated, he gazed down upon the cowering, waiting sartlar. A command flickered round the ring. A sound like coughing issued from Heart-of-Thunder's flame-pipes. Then a whining that rose to a screaming. The sunlight made the fire arcs invisible until they hit the sartlar. Smoke erupted in their midst. Fire was there, incandescent in the darkness overwhelming them. More pipes were screaming. The blackness oozed out, feathering skywards. At its heart, man-shaped flames cavorted as they burned.

Leaden with horror, choking on a rage he did not want to vent on those around him, Carnelian sat frozen as they moved away from the pyre. All the rest of that day he remained thus, speaking only to give his Lefthand the minimum instructions to keep their place in the line as Osidian took them ever further westwards. A voice spoke within him that he could not shut out. It accused him of once again having become

Osidian's fool. That it was only sartlar who had been destroyed did not make him feel better. The only thin comfort came from his father's voice, speaking quietly within him, telling him he must play the long game.

The sun was low when they spiralled the dragons into another laager. Carnelian descended from his tower feeling brittle but determined. As legionaries erected pavilions, he stood aloof, watching the dragons being fed. He noticed Osidian talking to Morunasa. His gold face remained serene as Morunasa's folded into a frown. The Oracle glanced over to his fellows then, turning back, he gave a nod. Carnelian was curious, but had other priorities. Osidian was heading towards the pavilion that had been set up at the centre of the camp. Carnelian followed, told their Hands to remain outside, then entered.

A shape in the gloom greeted him. He was in no mood for pleasantries. Unmasking, he waited until Osidian did the same. 'Why was it necessary, my Lord, to torch the sartlar?'

Osidian frowned. 'I would have thought that obvious enough.'

'The flame-pipes could have been tested as effectively on empty ground.'

Osidian's frown deepened. 'It was more the commanders' willingness to obey me that I wished to test.'

Carnelian stared. 'You really believe their willingness to cremate sartlar proves they would make war upon the forces of the Commonwealth?'

Osidian's face hardened.

'Was this test worth betraying our position to the Wise? At least one of their watch-towers must have seen the smoke.'

Carnelian was undaunted by Osidian's glare.

'Examine your heart, Osidian. Look there for your hidden purpose. Are you sure you were not merely seeking to burn yourself clean of the taint of slavery?'

Osidian's eyes flashed. 'How dare—'

'Have you forgotten I shared it? No amount of killing will

ever remove the humiliation. Your failure to deal with how you feel endangers the very goals you claim you seek.'

The contempt Carnelian felt for Osidian's self-deception made it easy to withstand the wrath burning in his eyes. Still, when Osidian disengaged, Carnelian was left feeling sick to his stomach. The nausea warred with an unfamiliar triumph. As their Hands were called in and began undoing their suits, Carnelian wrestled with his emotions. Triumph was the one he distrusted: it was altogether too Masterly. Still, he must seek victory wherever it might be found.

'I leave tomorrow,' Osidian said, suddenly.

Carnelian looked up. 'Leave?'

Osidian's eyes were focused on some inner vision. 'I need to know what our enemies are up to. I need to gaze upon Makar.'

Carnelian felt uneasy. 'But you might be seen, perhaps captured.'

Osidian shook his head, slowly, still lost in his vision. 'I shall travel with but one companion, humbly, upon the road.'

'Morunasa?'

Osidian nodded. 'With him at my side, my height will not mark me as more than just another Marula.'

Carnelian could see Osidian would not be dissuaded. 'And the huimur?'

'You will take them west until you come within sight of the towers of the Great South Road. There you will await my return.'

Carnelian considered the power Osidian was putting in his hands. How easy it would be to betray him. That thought was bittersweet, but he decided he must hold to his strategy: Osidian's rebellion must be big enough that, in contrast, the part the Plainsmen and the Lepers had played in it would appear diminished. He raised his hand in assent.

When Carnelian woke, Osidian was gone. He rose and the legion came awake with him in the dawn. He could read the

Lesser Chosen commanders' uncertainty in the cast of their bodies, but chose to ignore it and banished them to their towers with a gesture. He sought out his officers and told them they would guide Earth-is-Strong as if he were sitting in her command chair. He assured them they would suffer no punishment for this infringement of legionary law, then he dismissed them, insisting that, throughout the day, they should stay within direct signal range of Heart-of-Thunder. Soon he was mounting the ladder up into Osidian's tower. Once seated in Osidian's chair, he sent commands flashing round the ring of dragons. Turning Heart-of-Thunder into his own shadow, Carnelian led them west.

It became hard to believe they were moving at all. Certainly, the grid of trackways gave an impression of forward movement but, every time they reached an intersection, with its identical overseer tower and the ring of the kraal behind it, it seemed they had merely returned to the same spot they had been in before. Dusty hri fields formed dun rectangles edged by the trackways. Sartlar laboured beneath the withering sun. Sometimes he would watch a gang of them jogging along the thread of a track. That would stir harsh memories of slavery and loss. He would turn away, letting the land blur, allowing the sway of the cabin to seduce him into thinking he was bobbing on a gentle swell. The sartlar became invisible to him, merging into the dull monotony of the land. Space lost its meaning. Time alone was perceptible. An eternity of it ruled by the tyrannous sun that made each overseer tower shrink and grow its arm of shadow.

In the evenings the meaningless vastness of the world contracted to the space within the laager. With darkness his world shrank to the smoky interior of his pavilion. Harried by doubt he would seek escape in sleep, but when this came at last he would be drawn down dark paths into the underworld of dream.

*   *   *

On the afternoon of the fourth day since Osidian had left with Morunasa, Carnelian was woken from a nodding half-slumber by his Lefthand. 'I dared to think the Master would wish to be woken.' The man glanced at the Righthand. 'We risked bringing the dragon to a halt.'

'Why?'

'Master, our lookout claims to have glimpsed a watch-tower.'

'Ahead of us?'

'And to the south, Master.'

Carnelian gazed out through the bone screen. Gridded land stretched to the same hazy horizon he had been seeing for days.

He rose from his chair. 'Signal the others to fall back.'

'Master.' The Lefthand punched the deck with his forehead even as he shuffled aside to allow Carnelian to pass round the back of his chair.

The Righthand scurried to attend him. 'Master?'

'I wish to see for myself.'

The legionary looked horrified. 'Climb the mast?'

Carnelian chopped an affirmative. 'Bring the lookout down.'

The man hesitated, squinting up at Carnelian as if he feared he might have misunderstood.

'Go on,' Carnelian said, softening his tone.

The legionary ducked a bow, then scampered to the staples set into the mast. Climbing them, he opened a hatch and slipped up onto the roof. Carnelian could hear his footfalls above his head. Heard him shouting something. At last, a face appeared in the hatch. 'He's down, Master.'

Carnelian left his cloak on his command chair, then climbed the staples. It was a squeeze to get through the hatch. The land spread vast and dusty beneath an immense, colourless sky. For a moment he was lost in all that airy space. Then he looked down; the ground was far away. The wedge of Heart-of-Thunder's head seemed like a prow. Carnelian focused on the men prostrate on the roof. The Righthand and two others. One was gripping a mechanism Carnelian recognized as a tiny version of a watch-tower heliograph. The other must be the lookout.

He gazed up the mast with its glyph plaques. It tapered upwards like a knotted rope hanging from the sky. Far above was the swelling of the standard. At that height the mast did not look strong enough to bear his weight. Nevertheless, he was determined to go up.

As he climbed the staples running up the back of the mast the breeze was causing it to shudder. Each plaque he passed was larger than a shield. Soon the men looked tiny on the roof below. He could see not only Heart-of-Thunder's head, but his rump and tail. Glancing up, he saw the standard was hanging huge above him. Soon he had reached it and found there, just beneath the grimacing paired faces of the Commonwealth, something very like a deadman's chair. He took a firm grip of its hoop with first one hand then the other. Then he swung himself astride the central drum. It threatened to rotate under him forcing a spasm as he thought he might fall. He righted himself, waited for his heart to calm, then gazed out over the land. Wind roaring in his right ear, he located what he sought. The prongs of a watch-tower due west. It had to be on the Great South Road. Two more watch-towers lay to the south, no doubt part of the Ringwall. Makar had to be nearby. Suddenly he felt utterly exposed. It seemed as if the Wise were gazing directly at him. He slid off the chair onto the first staple and began the descent.

The sun was low when a voice like a gull's caused Carnelian to push past his Hands and hurry out of his pavilion. The cry coming again from the sky made him glance up. The lookout clinging to Heart-of-Thunder's mast was pointing back the way they had come. It took Carnelian a while to notice anything in the long shadows the dragons were casting, but then he saw two riders approaching.

283

*　　*　　*

'There is no time for discussion, my Lords,' said Osidian. He glanced around at the makeshift camp Carnelian had made. He had not bothered with a laager, but had stopped the dragons where they stood in their ragged line of march. His pavilion and the others for the commanders seemed coalescing pinnacles of the deepening shadows. The commanders had gathered with Carnelian to welcome Osidian's return. Morunasa wore his ashen frown like a mask.

Osidian sent the commanders away to get everything ready for an immediate departure, then turned to Carnelian. 'We must reach Makar before dawn.' His mask was reddened by the sun. 'And I do not know how long it will take us to get there.'

Carnelian could hear tightness in Osidian's voice.

'We will advance in single file with Marula thrown out in front of us to check the ground.'

Carnelian remembered his experience fleeing with the Ochre raiders near Makar. 'The ground there is dangerously fissured?'

Osidian turned to look at him and gave a nod, then glanced up to the nearest dragon. 'We must do what we can to ensure they have solid footing.'

'We need to talk, Osidian. I want to know what you have seen and what it is you intend to do.'

'There is no time, I tell you!'

Carnelian could see the crews were already swarming up into their towers. 'I could ride with you inside Heart-of-Thunder's cabin.'

'Who then would command Earth-is-Strong?'

'My Hands have been doing that for days.'

'But they are marumaga!'

'Did you expect me to be in both towers at the same time?'

Carnelian was a little surprised at this prejudice, but then realized that, while his own experience with that caste had

284

been with his brothers, Osidian's was certain not to have been anything like as intimate.

Osidian made a gesture of exasperation. 'Oh, very well!'

They rode Heart-of-Thunder directly towards the flaming sunset. Below, the Marula spread before them in a fan, aquar and riders almost invisible because they seemed beaten from the same copper as the land. It was the shadows they trailed that allowed Carnelian to make out where they were.

He looked around him. The cabin seemed soaked in blood. Every surface glistened and glowed. An apparition, Osidian, stood gazing out, steadying himself against the dragon's gait by gripping the right arm of his command chair. Carnelian was holding onto the left. The two officers had to manage kneeling behind them.

'What did you see, Osidian?'

The apparition turned to Carnelian and began speaking, but he heard nothing. All he could do was stare at the reflection of his own mask in Osidian's. It seemed the same lurid red face that had been haunting his dreams. To the drone of Osidian's voice the red face thinned and twisted like a slow flame. It resembled Akaisha's face warning him, but Carnelian also recognized it as his own. He turned away, nursing his beating heart.

'What ails you, Carnelian?'

Carnelian breathed deep and hard, still haunted. As his heart slowed, he felt as if he was coming awake. Osidian's hand was on his shoulder. 'Just a momentary dizziness.'

'Sit in the chair.'

Carnelian glanced at it reddening further in the deepening dusk and shook his head. 'I am recovering; please begin again with what you were saying. Tell me everything.'

Osidian paused a moment. 'Very well. All day and all night we rode west then, before dawn, we found an abandoned kraal. We slept in its tower until dusk and then set off again, but this time turning south towards the Ringwall. We crept into a stopping place and as the sun rose we hid ourselves among the rabble. All day we endured moving among them on the road.'

'No one wondered at your height?'

Osidian made a gesture of annoyance. 'I hunched . . . Morunasa made sure they saw his face while I was careful to hide mine. They thought me one of his kind.'

Carnelian nodded, then motioned him to continue.

'We approached the city in late afternoon. When we reached a market outside its walls we found a place to hide until nightfall. Before the moon rose we passed through the city and found what we needed. That was last night. Before dawn we slipped away into the open fields. East we rode, then north, searching for your trail. Finding it, we rode along it until we reached you.'

'And?'

'We learned much from overhearing travellers talking. Morunasa got more from questioning others.'

'Is Aurum there?'

Osidian shook his head. 'I believe he is down in the Leper Valleys.'

'What?' Carnelian said. His shocked tone awoke concern in the officers. He calmed himself.

'He must be searching for me,' Osidian said. 'Though rumour suggests he is even now on his way back to the Guarded Land.'

Carnelian heard the glee in his voice and understood. 'You believe we shall arrive in Makar before him and trap him in the Valleys.'

Osidian was nodding. 'Put in such an untenable position, I have hopes my Lord Aurum will realize he has no choice but to negotiate with me.'

Carnelian could not deny the nausea he felt. He slipped round and slumped into the chair. He had thought he was leaving Poppy and Fern in relative safety. His mind was lit by nightmarish dragonfire. He lifted his head and let the darkness that was falling outside quench the flames. To save whatever

286

remained of the Leper Valleys, Aurum must be drawn back to the Guarded Land. Carnelian turned to look up at Osidian, in whose metal face lurked disturbing, murky reflections. 'We must make a plan to take Makar.'

They halted so that Carnelian could transfer to Earth-is-Strong. Standing astride the head of Heart-of-Thunder's brassman, Carnelian paused, stunned by the immensity of the night sky. The earth's lightless sea snuffed out the stars along the southern horizon. He noticed two burning on the boundary between earth and sky. He scanned east. There, though much fainter, was a third. Each beacon marked the presence of a watch-tower on the Ringwall. He gazed into the south-west and for a moment thought he could see the dull glow of Makar. His certainty wavered. He gazed further west, in the direction they were heading. He searched the horizon there for more fallen stars, but could find none. His vantage point was too low. He began the descent to the ground.

Reaching the earth he was struck by how separated he was from it by the ranga calluses of his suit and felt a powerful urge to stand upon it barefoot. Heart-of-Thunder was a cliff of blackness. His mast speared the infinite sky.

Escorted by Osidian's Lefthand, Carnelian made his way back along the dragon line. It was a long way. The monsters snuffled. Their rich musk permeated the night. Glancing up he caught a gleam running along a flame-pipe. Then the faint glow of a Master enthroned in his tower. He wondered if it came to battle whether the commanders would really obey Osidian. Would they really be prepared to make war upon the Commonwealth?

When they reached Earth-is-Strong the Lefthand cried up to her tower. The brassman was lowered, then a ladder rustled down to meet him. He climbed it, feeling he was ascending to the stars. One of his crew was waiting on the brassman to guide him in. Entering the tower Carnelian was cheered by its warmth, by the now familiar smell. He ascended to the upper deck. As he sat down in the command chair, he glanced to either side. His Lefthand and Righthand were there, kneeling in their places. 'Tell Heart-of-Thunder we're ready to go.'

His Lefthand gave a nod and bent to mutter into his voice fork. While Carnelian waited, he peered out through his bone screen. Directly ahead a dragon and its tower formed an indivisible shadow mass. He stroked the smooth arms of his chair as he considered the plan he and Osidian had come up with.

A sudden spark hovering in the night made him start. It was a signal coming back down the line. The dragon in front lurched into movement. Carnelian felt the tremors it was sending into the earth. He had no need to have the signal deciphered. He whispered his command to his Lefthand. The familiar rocking of the cabin once Earth-is-Strong had found her gait soon lulled him to sleep.

Some time later he woke and, peering, noticed two lights twinkling on the western horizon. He knew they must be the southernmost watch-towers on the Great South Road. Osidian had set them on a course that led directly between them as they had planned.

A whisper made Carnelian sit up. It was his Lefthand. 'Master, a signal—'

'From Heart-of-Thunder?'

'Yes, Master.'

'A command?'

The Lefthand shook his shadowy head. 'Wishing you good luck, Master.'

'Bring the dragon to a halt.'

The man did as he was told. Carnelian watched the mountainous shadow of the dragon in front slowly merge with the night. Osidian was making for the southernmost tower. Carnelian raised his hand to indicate the tiny beacon of its neighbour to the north and his Lefthand set a course for it. As they began to move, he could just make out the small body of

Marula below that had been assigned to him to make sure the ground before him could hold Earth-is-Strong's weight.

Carnelian had hoped for steady progress. It was essential to their plan that he should reach his tower before Osidian reached his. His recollections of the land around Makar had made him confident it was Osidian who would have to navigate around the most ravines and fissures, but this was the second massive sinkhole his Marula had had to lead him round. Carnelian could smell the fear from his men as they waited for the next thump to vibrate the cabin and show that Earth-is-Strong had made another solid footfall.

The moon was rising behind them when Carnelian sent his dragon crashing through the stopping place. He had done what he could to align her on the track that led from the fields directly towards the watch-tower and its gate in the hope it would give her a clear passage. He could not risk giving any overt warning of his coming lest he should alert the tower. He had hoped there would be enough people awake in the stopping place to feel the thunder of his approach, to see Earth-is-Strong's monstrous shape looming up out of the night towards them and then sound a general alarm that would send people fleeing from her path. Even so, he could hear screaming thinned by the cold air. The command chair transferred a judder up his spine each time Earth-is-Strong crushed something beneath one of her massive feet. However hard he focused on his objective, he could not stop imagining what it was he was leaving flattened behind him.

The cabin angled back as his dragon climbed a ramp towards the leftway wall. The tower loomed up, its rib arms held aloft as if in shock or surrender. The gate upon which it stood sentinel was closed. Osidian and he had expected this. He had his Lefthand slow Earth-is-Strong until she was edging towards the gate. Another command made her lower her head. The

289

point of her crest moved forward as she tipped her anvil head to target the gate with her flat crown. His whole body felt her making contact. His Lefthand was muttering commands. Carnelian had to put his feet out to stop sliding off his chair as she leaned into the wood. It groaned like the bow of a baran striking a massive wave, then it detonated once, twice more, and exploded, spitting splinters. Released, Earth-is-Strong stumbled forward. The cabin lurched, shaking everything, as the dragon lumbered through the ragged gap.

He moved her out onto the road. The glitter of campfires on the far side slid to the right as he turned her south. He could hear the rush and clatter of Marula riders as they surged up the ramp onto the road behind him. They had their commands. They would swarm the watch-tower and try to take it intact. Failing that, he would have to turn his flame-pipes on it. He trusted his lookout to warn him if any attempt was made to send a message north. He had instructed him to look for any signal.

Carnelian leaned forward, peering down the road. There it was, the next watch-tower, its twinned flares just above the straight black edge of the leftway. Heart racing, he looked for the telltale flicker that would show any attempt to betray them to the Wise. As far as he could tell, those flares were twinkling as innocuously as stars. He squinted, trying to see any sign of Osidian. He sat back, relieved. Everything suggested he had made it on time. A sudden wavering in the flares jerked him forward again. They steadied. There it was again. The rhythm seemed to him too slow to be a message. He gazed away from the far-off tower, west into the murky land. In a layer, a hazing was hugging the ground. It was barely perceptible, but it was there. Mist? He scanned further west and saw that there the night was clear. He squinted at the haze. Could it be smoke? But what could make smoke rise in such a neat band?

His heart leapt, forcing him to recoil back into his chair. 'Send her forward.'

He felt his Lefthand stirring. 'Master?'

'South along the road!' he barked. 'Fast as she can go.'

Down the road thundered Earth-is-Strong. High in her tower sat Carnelian, unable to take his eyes from the ragged wave of dust rolling south away from him and that the low moon was lighting into a silver swell. That dust had risen only a few moments before and confirmed what he had feared. A battleline of dragons advancing southwards. His reaction had been to instruct his Righthand to have the flame-pipes lit. Even now the clink of the furnace men at work was being transmitted up to his cabin through the bone fabric of the tower.

'Master?'

Carnelian resented the intrusion by his Lefthand. 'Well?'

'Master, the lookout reports a message being sent from the tower we just passed.'

Carnelian had forgotten his mission. 'North,' he said, resignedly. 'North to Osrakum.'

'South, my Master.'

'Are you sure?' Carnelian asked, incredulous. He craned round to peer through one of the rear portholes, but could see no light. He straightened. 'Check it was definitely south.'

'Master,' the Lefthand said and, leaning into his voice fork, began muttering. The man soon had a reply. 'South, Master.'

Carnelian fixed the dust wave with a baleful eye. Was the tower sending some prearranged signal to whoever it was commanding those dragons? He tried to work out what infernal trap he and Osidian had fallen into, but could form no shape of it in his mind.

He was weary from anxiety. Three more times his Lefthand had informed him their lookout had seen the watch-tower behind them attempt to send a message south. All that time Carnelian had kept the tower ahead under his scrutiny. The orbits of his eyes ached, but he was certain it had signalled

291

no acknowledgement. At least that part of their plan seemed to have succeeded. Osidian must have gained control of his tower.

The dust wave he was pursuing had, for a moment, submerged the watch-tower up to its waist. As the dust subsided the watch-tower seemed to have swollen larger. Periodically, he wrenched his gaze from the wave to the tower, measuring his progress by its increasing size. He feared he was only imagining he was closing on the enemy dragons. He would have urged Earth-is-Strong to even greater speed, but a peculiar irregularity in the shuddering of the command chair betrayed her fatigue. He did not know how much more the monster had in her, but he dare not let her slacken her pace.

Sniffing the air as best he could through the nosepads of his mask he became aware of a stronger reek of naphtha in the rush of air that was pouring into the cabin. The moon was finding dark shapes lumbering in the veiling dust. Dragons. If their pipes were lit they must indeed be pursuing some quarry.

The cabin came abreast of the watch-tower and still the enemy line seemed far away, but, gripping the arms of his chair, he was finding it easier to convince himself he was closing on them.

'The pipes are ready?' he said, above the clatter of the cabin.

'Yes, Master,' his Righthand replied.

Carnelian gazed along the mounding dust and saw how far it extended into the hinterland. His heart sank. What could they hope to do against such a preponderance of force?

Suddenly he became aware the dust ahead was subsiding. At first he feared that somehow the dragon line was speeding away from him, but the creatures were looming larger, not smaller, their towers emerging frosty in the moonlight, trailing pale banners of smoke.

'They're slowing,' he muttered. Then he understood. Fear gripped him. Osidian had been run down. Soon the line would open fire on him. Carnelian's instinct was to order his own pipes to fire. Even though the flame was not likely to reach his enemy it might distract him. He held back, knowing he probably had but one chance. Also, he could see that the line ahead had slowed so much that, with every passing moment, they were catching up. 'How long before we are in range?'

'Moments, Master,' replied his Righthand.

'Tell me when.'

'Yes, Master.'

Carnelian waited and with every heartbeat he could make out more of the dragon they were now bearing down on. First the berg of its tower. Then the rump of the dragon upon which it sat. Until even the rigging became distinct, iced by the moon.

'Now, Master,' said his Righthand.

Carnelian paused a moment, hardly breathing, one last time seeking to understand. Reluctantly he gave the command. 'Flame.'

In the corner of his eye he saw his Righthand put his mouth to his voice fork. The device swallowed his command. Then, nothing. Carnelian was disappointed. Then he felt under his feet a gurgling stutter. Then the rush of fluid through the pipes that could have been his rising blood. Shrieking incandescence spat from the flame-pipes. Fire jetted an arc through the night. That narrow lightning was all he could see. Splashing upon the dragon tower, causing a molten flower to bloom in the night. Flame devoured the charring ivory. Rigging snapped into fiery whiplash. The mast toppled, burning. Fire poured down the dragon's rump, curling crisping hide, cooking the livid flesh beneath. The monster, shuddering, let forth a scream like scraping brass. It veered away, its tower a bonfire on its back even as Carnelian's own jets spluttered dry, their brightness dying. His eyes took a moment to see beyond the ghosts he was printing on the night with each blink. Around him the cabin juddered as Earth-is-Strong turned away, stumbling, slowing. He let her go, tracking the other dragon as it burned, trailing sparks and smoke across his vision. Suddenly a flash stabbed him blind. Even as his hands flew up to his eyes a detonation rattled the cabin. He felt heat on his hands and coming through the gold of his mask to his face. A dull, thunderous thud reverberated in his bones. A stench was breaking over him of naphtha and charring flesh. For a moment he feared his hands were on fire, but the heat quickly abated and, when he clasped one with the other, the leather gloves were smooth and there was no pain. He tried peering through the eyeslits of his mask. At first he could make no sense of what he saw. Shadowy miasmas, shifting, gave vague glimpses into a fiery world. Patches of smoulder spotted with fire. At the heart of this a mound veined with melting gold. The dragon, ruptured, fallen, burning.

MAKAR

The more intimately one knows a creature,
the more perfectly one can design a snare to trap it.
(a precept of the Wise)

The enemy dragons fled into the north-west. Carnelian watched Osidian's approaching in a ragged line, signals blinking between them, their chimneys beginning to smoke. He was trying to identify which one was Heart-of-Thunder when his Lefthand spoke.

'Master, our lookout claims the third tower to the north has sent an acknowledgement signal.'

For a moment Carnelian was distracted by the strange quality of the man's voice. He realized every sound was coming to him as if he had his fingers in his ears. He focused on what the man had said. 'Which tower?' he asked, his voice sounding muffled so that it did not seem his own.

The legionary explained he had been referring to the tower to the north of the one whose gate they had broken down. Carnelian realized the implication. Only a signal it was sending south would have been visible to the lookout. Thus it was an acknowledgement to the tower to its south. The watchtower he had failed to make secure had finally sent a message northwards. Already it was speeding towards Osrakum faster than an aquar could run and so beyond all catching. Before the end of that day the Wise would know everything that had happened.

One of Osidian's dragons was heading straight for Earth-is-Strong. He was certain it was Heart-of-Thunder. He was composing a confession of his failure for transmission when Osidian's tower began to wink. Carnelian stared at his Lefthand, impatient for the mirrorman above to relay his interpretation of the message. At last his Lefthand spoke. 'From Heart-of-Thunder, Master. The Legate would like you to meet him for a conference on the ground.'

Carnelian had Earth-is-Strong brought to a halt. For some moments he watched Heart-of-Thunder easing towards them like a baran. Then, with a glance past the burning dragon to assure himself the enemy was still moving away, Carnelian bade his Righthand dowse the flame-pipes, then he rose and moved towards the ladder.

A dark figure appeared beneath the arch of Heart-of-Thunder's belly accompanied by two men who seemed, by comparison, to be children. Carnelian recognized Osidian's gait. 'Are we safe from those huimur, my Lord?'

Osidian came closer before he answered. 'I believe our friend the Great Lord is in full retreat.'

Carnelian knew to whom he referred and realized Osidian did not want to use his name. Their marumaga officers might not understand Quya, but the name Aurum was the same in both their languages.

'Are you sure it is he?'

Osidian gestured for his officers to wait for him, then indicated the smouldering mound of the fallen dragon to Carnelian and, together, they walked towards it. 'Who else could it be?' he said, not turning his head.

Carnelian had no alternative to offer, but he found this flight untypical of the Lord he knew. 'Why does he retreat?'

Osidian swirled his hand. 'Possibly he seeks to regroup. Your attack must have come as a nasty surprise to him.'

Carnelian was unconvinced. 'Still, he had your whole line at the mercy of his pipes.'

Osidian half turned to him, then away. 'A reaction to the shock of the explosion, perhaps . . .'

Carnelian eyed the dragon corpse. The smell of its charring flesh was drifting on the air. 'Perhaps . . .' Doubt nagged him.

'You failed to take your tower.'

'I saw Aurum bearing down on you. Would you rather I had let him torch you?'

Osidian turned, lifting his hands in a gesture of appeasement. 'I am not accusing you, Carnelian. Even with your intervention, I had only just managed to turn my huimur. Less than half had managed to light their pipes. Even those were not ready to fire.' He paused and his head sank a little. 'Had you not slowed him with your attack, I would have been overwhelmed . . .'

Carnelian sensed how hard it had been for Osidian to admit his debt to him. It was as close as Osidian would come to saying thank you. The nagging doubt emerged into Carnelian's mind as a clear realization. 'He was slowing before he knew I was there.'

Osidian stopped in mid stride. 'You cannot be sure he did not see you.'

'His whole line stopped.'

Osidian began a protest, but then understood. 'He sent no signals.'

'Though he may have seen me approaching, do you believe it possible his whole line should have done so and at one and the same time?'

'What other explanation do you have?'

'It was prearranged.'

'To what end?'

Carnelian squinted at the burning dragon. He was shaking his head. It came to him. 'He wished to give you time to light your pipes. So that—'

297

'So that I could repulse him! But why? Why set an ambush, then allow yourself to be defeated?'

Carnelian tried, but failed to work it out. This behaviour, though still uncharacteristic of Aurum, was now more believable. 'The trap he has set for us must be more subtle.'

Both pondered this further as they came as close as they could bear to the dragon corpse. That burning hill seemed too vast to have ever been a living being. Rather it seemed an outgrowing of the earth itself, an abscess ripe to bursting. Carnelian was not sure whether it was this sight, the stench of cooking meat and blood, or unease that was making him queasy. 'There is something else I do not understand.'

Osidian turned to him, his mask reflecting the gory mess. For a moment Carnelian was mesmerized by that strange and lurid face that once again seemed to have come from his dreams.

'What?' the apparition said.

The sound of Osidian's voice jolted Carnelian. He marshalled his thoughts. 'Before sending a message north the tower made several attempts to communicate south.'

'You are certain it did not first send one to Osrakum?'

Carnelian could hear the unease in Osidian's voice. 'Quite certain.'

Both turned to look at where Makar was an encrustation on the edge of the land.

'What could be there?' muttered Osidian almost inaudibly.

'Or who?' said Carnelian.

Osidian dismissed the city with a gesture as if he was trying to wipe it from the earth. 'Perhaps the tower was responding to some earlier command of Aurum's.' He indicated the nearest tower with a contemptuous hand. 'The creatures who operate these are slavish to their instructions.'

Carnelian sensed Osidian's conviction was hollow. A drumming in the ground alerted them to a rider approaching. An Oracle, by his robes. The man pulled the aquar up and quickly dismounted. By his movements it was recognizably Morunasa.

'Why have you come?' Osidian demanded. 'I commanded you to hold the tower.'

'I thought my Master would want to know that the tower further to the north—' Morunasa glanced at Carnelian as if to accuse him. 'It sent an alert to us, not once, but four times.'

'We knew this,' Osidian said in a cold voice. 'I hope you have come to tell me what the message said.'

Morunasa frowned. 'There were none in the tower who could tell me.'

Osidian angled his head in irritation.

'When we arrived there we found all the silver masks already dead.'

'Dead?' Osidian sounded increasingly exasperated.

'How did they die, Morunasa?' Carnelian asked.

The Oracle turned on him his baleful eyes. 'I don't know, Master.'

'Were their bodies marked?'

Morunasa glared at him, then, slowly, shook his head. Carnelian and Osidian turned to each other. Carnelian knew they were both thinking of the quaestor in Qunoth. For some reason, rather than be captured, it seemed probable the ammonites had taken their own lives with poison. Both turned the sequence of events over in their minds. At last Carnelian admitted he was at a loss. Osidian did not seem any more enlightened.

'What now?' Carnelian asked.

'With him out there we dare not leave ourselves unprotected. I shall have to remain here with the legion.'

Carnelian noticed Osidian glancing towards the nearest tower. 'I will help you find out what has been going on in the towers.'

Osidian shook his head. 'I need you to secure the city.' He must have sensed Carnelian's reluctance because he added: 'We need its fortress as a base.'

'What force shall I take with me?'

'Your own huimur and as many Marula as I can spare.'

Carnelian considered protesting that they did not know what awaited him in Makar, but realized they dare not further diminish Osidian's strength in case Aurum should return.

'Take Morunasa,' Osidian said. He turned to the Oracle. 'Obey Master Carnelian as you do me.'

The black man glared at him.

'Do you understand?' Osidian said, an edge in his voice.

Morunasa gave a reluctant nod. 'As you command.'

Carnelian gazed in the direction of the city, then back at Osidian. 'What shall I do once I have the fortress?'

'Send me enough render to feed my huimur.'

'Very well,' Carnelian said. He began walking back towards Earth-is-Strong. He stopped and turned. 'Be careful.'

Osidian gave a nod. Carnelian resumed his journey towards his dragon and could hear Morunasa's footfalls following him.

An umber stain on the horizon, Makar lay at the convergence of many gullies as if a fist, punching down from the sky, had shattered the land around it as if it were glass. In Earth-is-Strong's tower Carnelian felt that, vast as she was, even she was too small a thing to take on such a city. From his vantage point he was able to see the cobbles of the leftway slipping by and kept expecting to see a courier flash past to warn the city. Earlier he had stood looking back through the smoke his chimneys were trailing. He had quickly lost sight of Osidian and their legion. Only a haze indicated where the fallen dragon still smouldered. Of Aurum there was no sign. He was Osidian's problem now. In his bones Carnelian had a feeling he would soon have problems of his own to deal with.

From where the road crossed the outer ditch of the city, flat roofs of beaten mud spread away on either side like scales. Those close enough for him to see were crowded with jars and earthenware pots planted with small trees and shrubs. Washing fluttering on lines seemed drab flags. Crude tables and chests sat upon burnished earth floors spread with rugs woven from rushes. Each roof was a small world, giving down into chambers where people lived. He tried to imagine what those lives were like. Simple, no doubt, but though he would not pretend to know anything about such people, a part of him envied them.

The empty road before him was headache bright. Dry, pale, peeling walls banked its gleaming river, pierced here and there by the tributaries of alleyways. Doors and windows were shuttered closed as if against a storm. He searched away from the road across the rooftops and there, at last, he saw some people. They were peering at him over wicker partitions, round urns and leather curtains. Seeing those few enabled him to spot more. Everywhere there were small dark heads. Shocked, he became aware a multitude was watching him pass. He felt an urge to wave, to show he meant them no harm. He could see himself doing that. He imagined them coming into the open and waving back. Foolishness. He was a Master concealed within a dragon tower. The naphtha smoke twisting its black banners into the breeze was a sign of the fiery holocaust at his command. Any glimpse of him could bring only terror. He gave a snort that caused his officers' faces to turn up to him. Waiting for his commands they did not blink. What did he want? For all of these poor creatures to like him? For them to be warmed by his condescension?

They came to where the road forked around a watch-tower. One tine continued on through the city, the other passed through the open gate the watch-tower guarded. Carnelian knew they must have reached the Ringwall, the border of the Guarded Land. Staying on the main road they came into a narrow marketplace that ran off a great distance south-west. At its other end stood a second watch-tower guarding a huge closed gate. Something about its size and the way the worn stone sloped a little down to it made Carnelian believe this must be the head of the Pass. The same Pass Makar guarded and that they had tried to climb, only to be driven back by Aurum's fire.

As he turned Earth-is-Strong into the market his spirits sank further. Stalls in rows, water troughs. Cobbles, though smeared and caked with filth trodden into mush, had cleaner patches where normally a multitude laid out their wares. His arrival had caused all to flee. Emptied of its throngs, its hawkers, the place was dead.

Halfway across the marketplace, a crumbly worn pair of stumpy towers pushed their way through the leftway wall. Between them ragged gates patched with bronze gave the impression something ancient lay behind them.

They left the marketplace by means of a stone span across a gully choked with filth and entered another, smaller square where a third watch-tower stood guard upon a military gate. As they approached this it began to open. Carnelian regarded it with suspicion, feeling he was being welcomed into a trap. Still, he had his flame-pipes and so he murmured a command to his Lefthand and Earth-is-Strong turned to enter.

As they moved into the fortress he was surprised. No stables or barracks for auxiliaries confronted him, but only squat buildings. To starboard the curving wall of a cothon. To port the ground fell into a ravine whose other side rose as a cliff. Steps and terraces scaled this to towers crenellating its edge. Bone-white that cliff, striated, rotten with age, perforated with windows. Alleys squeezed out through gaps from which staining spilled down into the ravine. It seemed a half-ruined anthill, but also an ancient city, gently sculpted, smiling, delicate. This was a living cousin to the dead ruins Carnelian had seen on his way to the election. A Quyan city, then. Southwards the low buildings of the fortress curved away, following the bend of the ravine. There at the very tip rose a tower. He squinted. It had the look of a watch-tower.

'The gate, Master,' said his Lefthand. The man was pointing to where there was an opening in the cothon wall.

'It seems we are expected,' Carnelian said, to cover the return of his anxiety that they were entering a trap. He was determined to face it head on. He gave the command and Earth-is-Strong approached the gateway. As they passed through it, he glanced at his Righthand to make sure the man was ready to relay a command to fire their pipes. They came into the immense circular space all hedged about with piers. Carnelian sent his Lefthand round the portholes to look for dragons.

'Nothing but a few towers, Master. Spares, I think.'

Carnelian could see the tiny figures waiting for him in the open centre of the cothon. He leaned forward in his chair. They did not look threatening. He rose and peered through the bone screen. The cothon did indeed seem empty, innocuous. He returned to his chair to ponder, while Earth-is-Strong continued advancing on the welcoming committee, Marula pouring past on either side. At last he commanded his dragon to come to a halt. He glanced round one last time, then gave his Righthand the command to dowse the furnaces. He did not want any accidents.

Soon Carnelian was on the ground. Marula riders were swirling round to envelop the marumaga, who were wearing the cyphers of Aurum's legion. Carnelian bade his officers accompany him and went to meet the legionaries. As he walked he surveyed the cothon. The piers were almost entirely empty. The flame-pipe racks held but two of the weapons. Once far enough away from Earth-is-Strong, he snuffled the air. It was hard to be certain through the nostril pads of his mask and so he asked his officers. They confirmed that the air seemed free of naphtha and the musk of dragons.

As he approached the legionaries they fell prostrate before

him. He bade them rise even as he scrutinized their collars for their ranks. As he had hoped, one was the Quartermaster General. He began questioning him. Soon he had discovered that their Legate, the Master Aurum, had returned the previous day from the lands below, but he had passed through the city, marching north. He judged the man was hiding nothing from him. 'And the quaestor of this city?'

'He's in the Legate's tower, Master.' The man half turned, his hand rising tentatively to point southwards.

Carnelian gazed in that direction, but could see nothing over the cothon wall. 'The watch-tower at the edge of the city?'

'Just so, Master,' the man said, looking at the ground.

Carnelian was aware Morunasa had dismounted and was approaching. He focused on the Quartermaster. 'My dragon is to be fed, as are these men, who are my auxiliaries.' He indicated the Marula.

The legionary bent almost double. 'As the Master commands.'

Carnelian was distracted by spotting Sthax among the Marula. Could he get close enough to talk to him? He was a little startled to find Morunasa nearly upon him. He refocused on the Quartermaster. 'Also, you will gather render sufficient to feed a legion of dragons for three days and you will send this out of the city and north along the Great South Road.'

The man bent again. 'If it please the Master, to whom shall we deliver it?'

Carnelian saw an opportunity in this. He waved the Quartermaster and the other legionaries away and, when he judged them beyond hearing distance, he turned to Morunasa. 'I shall take twenty of your men. While you wait, form the rest in a cordon round my dragon. Let no one approach other than to feed and water her.' He indicated the Quartermaster. 'When that man has gathered the supplies, take enough of your people to control the entrance-gate watch-tower and to form a decent escort, then guide the supplies to the Master.

Tell him the fortress has been abandoned. Tell him that Aurum—'

Morunasa was frowning. 'The Master commanded me to remain with you.'

'Well, I am commanding you to return to him.' Carnelian examined Morunasa's face, unsure he would obey him. 'Tell the Master that Aurum returned yesterday from the Leper Valleys and that he's not had the time to replenish his naphtha tanks. You understand?'

Morunasa glared at the ground. 'Yes, Master.'

'Then go.'

Carnelian had two of his twenty Marula give up their mounts. One aquar went to the local legionary he had chosen to act as guide. Then he approached the other empty saddle-chair. He removed his cloak and gave it to Sthax, who was holding the aquar's reins. As Carnelian had hoped, the Maruli had managed to include himself in the twenty Morunasa had left behind. He thanked him, then clambered aboard.

After a Plainsman chair this one felt too loose. There was a problem with his feet. Instinctively, he had been trying to get them in contact with the aquar's back, but the shape of the chair would not allow this. Besides, he could feel nothing through his ranga soles. He was growing increasingly irritated. He recalled that auxiliaries used stirrups and he managed to find them, then slip his leathered toes into them. It felt unnatural. As he tried to make the aquar rise all that happened was that his feet pushed ineffectually into the stirrups. Then he remembered the reins, which he found wrapped around the pommel of the saddle-chair. He unwound them, then pulled. Startled, the aquar threw back its head, flaring its eye-plumes. Cursing under his breath, Carnelian pulled more gently and the creature finally lifted him into the air. He checked to see Sthax was mounted, then he gave the command for the legionary guide to ride ahead.

As they left the cothon, Carnelian glanced back at

Earth-is-Strong. He was reluctant to leave her, but had confidence in his Hands. On reaching the road their legionary guide turned right and Carnelian sped after him. His exhilaration at feeling the familiar rhythm of an aquar's gait was diminished only by the difficulty of directing the creature with the reins. He worried that the bit in its mouth was hurting it. He disliked not having his feet on its pulsing warmth. He realized with surprise how much he had relied on this contact to sense how the creature was feeling.

Passing through a gateway they came upon the barracks and stables of auxiliaries. Everything looked in order, but empty. The men who had been lodged here he had left as carrion in the Earthsky.

Soon they were leaving the buildings behind. Loping along the edge of the ravine they came to where a branch of it was crossed by a bridge to a wall pierced by a single bronze door that was studded with silver ammonite shells. As he brought his aquar to a halt, he regarded the door, knowing it was the entry to a sanctum. It would probably be as empty as the rest of the fortress save, perhaps, for the households of Aurum and his commanders. Over the sanctum wall he could see, rising in the distance, the tower of the Legate of Makar and, thus, Aurum's tower. No doubt it had a heliograph on its roof and he could not rid himself of the nagging worry that it was to this tower that the watch-towers on the road had sent a message. He dismounted and, reluctantly, crossed the bridge.

The bronze gate opened before he reached it and a figure appeared in its shadow. It performed a prostration as Carnelian approached. Its head, rising, revealed the silver mirror of an ammonite blinding mask with its solid spiral eyes.

'Welcome, Seraph,' the dead silver lips said in pure Quya.

'On whose behalf do you welcome me, ammonite?' Carnelian replied, in the same tongue.

The man made an expansive gesture cramped by

uncertainty. 'Makar, the fortress, Seraph . . . my Lord the Legate is not in residence.'

Carnelian had an intuition. 'You are the quaestor here?'

'Just so, Seraph.'

Carnelian wondered that the man had come himself, but then he considered that this quaestor might well suspect something of what had transpired to the north. Perhaps he had even observed it from the Legate's tower. Carnelian gazed down at the quaestor. The man would have as many questions as he did. Carnelian corrected himself. Not curiosity, but necessity had brought the quaestor here. His duty was to be the eyes and ears for his masters, the Wise. He had much to gain from any information he could send to them; everything to lose if he failed them in any way. Carnelian felt a stab of sympathy for him. 'How many Chosen lie within this sanctum?'

The blinding mask cocking to one side seemed a pantomime of surprise. 'Why, none, Seraph. All left some time ago with my Lord Aurum. None have returned.'

'What instructions did he leave you?'

'None, Seraph, save that we should await his return.'

Carnelian considered his next question carefully. 'And you have received none from your masters in Osrakum?'

The mask retreated a little as if Carnelian had threatened him. 'As the Seraph must know, such information is vouched inviolable by the Protocol of the Three Powers.'

'I was merely wondering why a watch-tower would seek to send an alert here before even considering sending one to Osrakum.'

The quaestor retracted his hands into the sleeves of his robe as if he feared they were about to betray him. In reply all he managed was an uneven shrug. Carnelian saw in this behaviour confirmation of his suspicions. He peered over his head into the dark recesses beyond. There was a suggestion of lazy curlings in the air. He could smell the narcotic smoke. 'I will enter.'

'As the Seraph wishes,' said the quaestor. He rose to his feet, stooping as he moved aside.

Carnelian beckoned the Marula, who held back, snatching furtive glances into the dark opening. Even Sthax seemed reluctant to obey him. Carnelian had to motion more insistently before he and the other Marula began to approach. He had taken one step towards the threshold of the sanctum when the quaestor's hand jerked up to loosen his mask. One eye was revealed and a sliver of his sallow, tattooed face. He fixed the Marula with a glare that stopped them in mid stride. They regarded him as if he were a serpent who had sprung up in their path.

Slipping the mask back over his face, he turned to Carnelian. 'These unclean animals cannot enter here.'

'I intend that they should,' said Carnelian.

The quaestor pointed vaguely to where Carnelian could see some steps cut up the sanctum wall. 'They must first pass through the quarantine.'

'Nevertheless, I am determined they will enter with me.'

The quaestor raised his hands as clutching claws. 'This cannot be, Seraph, the Law forbids it!'

Carnelian sensed the man's distress was genuine enough. 'This place is destitute of Seraphim. I myself have no time to be cleansed and no wish to suffer the delay of subjecting myself to fresh ritual protection when I leave. I shall keep the one I wear. If by thus entering the sanctum it shall become polluted, then so be it.'

The quaestor was shaking his head erratically, his hands trembling as if he were having a fit. Carnelian reached out to calm him. At his touch the man jerked back, colliding with the jamb. He wrapped his arms around his chest. 'At least, Seraph, I beg you, allow yourself . . . and these others . . .' His hand trembled out, then quickly returned to grip his shoulder. 'To be purified as best we can with smoke.'

Carnelian could see no harm in that. 'Very well.'

*   *   *

As Carnelian edged into the gloom, Sthax and the other Marula followed. Smoke curled thick tendrils round them. The quaestor fussed, muttering instructions. Carnelian felt his face swelling into his mask as if it were the shell of a sprouting seed. Sweet myrrh crept into him with every breath, jellying his bones. When his legs faltered, hands appeared from the darkness to steady him. Censers, swinging, layered the air with thicker smoke that had a peculiar, stale odour he had not smelled before. Needles pierced his temples. He heard his voice far away cry out as he spun down into darkness.

His father in a chair, his back to him, while their hands down his spine find him wanting. He calls out, but his voice is the cry of a gull. Carnelian feels thunder coming. Through the window a cliff of water rolls black towards them. Seaweed smell, so like blood. Dripping red from his father's fist as it opens offering twin pearls to a charnel mouth. Angling hand, they begin to roll. Carnelian screams: don't let them go! It is his hand, he tries to close it, but the pearls melt into tears that dribble between his fingers. Watering a hole in the ground. Two pits side by side. His father gazes at him, eyeless.

Carnelian came awake struggling against the undertow of his dreams. He saw a young boy with a face halved by a thread tattoo. On either side an amethyst almond for an eye, a blushing cheek. Split by the tattoo, the boy's lips were moving. A grim tide was sucking Carnelian back into sleep. He heard the words 'quaestor' . . . 'letter'. He tried to move to break his nightmare's hold on him. The hollow stone of his head surged with pain. The spasm subsided enough for him to open his eyes. The boy was gone. Carnelian tried to make sense of where he was; to resolve the fractured symmetries of the chamber. Guttering flambeaux gave twisting life to peculiar machines of brass and ivory and glass. Floors and walls meeting at strange angles seemed covered with tapestries and carpets of crusted blood. The boy returned holding a vessel of white jade so thin it looked like ice. Within its milky membrane water swayed. Drinking it quenched the fire in Carnelian's head and lungs. Straining to resolve the impossible symmetries of the chamber, he realized it was full of mirrors. Contorted surfaces of silver, of gold polished to the consistency of torrid air. Slopes of glass that gave reflections so perfect he could only discern them by their frames. There were far fewer machines than he had imagined. Frameworks of bone slid and turned in subtle, repetitive movement. Discs and pivots. Brass and copper twitching. Liquid silver pouring with a strange inner radiance. He could not understand what anything was.

The blinded boy spoke again. 'Master, the quaestor is without. He bears a letter addressed to you.'

Carnelian recognized something about the boy's face. The blue filament that divided his face in two split near his hairline into the broken circle of a horned-ring. A horned-ring staff. Aurum's cypher. Carnelian gazed around the chamber. The red samite hangings were flecked with the same forked-needle cypher. He glanced down. His eyes confirmed what his skin felt: his body had been freed from the bindings of the ritual protection. His skin felt so clean he imagined he could breathe through it if he chose. 'This is the tower of the Legate of Makar?'

'It is, my Master,' the boy said.

'How long have I been here?'

'Less than a day, Master.'

'And how did I get here?'

The boy hesitated and Carnelian noticed his shivering, which was not from cold. He realized he could smell the boy, smell his fear. There was another odour so pervasive Carnelian had been breathing it in unnoticed. Attar of lilies. A sharp heavy blanketing of it that he was only aware of through its contrast with the odour from the boy.

'I have no memory of coming here,' he said as gently as he could, but this only served to terrify the boy more. 'Whatever you tell me,' Carnelian said, 'no harm will come to you.'

310

The boy was struggling for composure. 'The quaestor brought you, Master. His ammonites bore you here on a litter.'

Carnelian remembered entering the purgatory. The smoke was still so heavy in his lungs he was momentarily surprised it did not curl out on his breath. 'And he is here with a letter for me?'

'He is, Master.'

The boy took some steps back as Carnelian, gingerly, swung his legs out from under the feather blanket. The boy stooped to slipper his feet before they settled on the stone floor. Carnelian considered sending him to fetch the letter, but decided he would like to talk to the quaestor. 'I must dress.'

'How does my Master wish to be adorned?'

Carnelian could see how the prospect of fulfilling what was clearly one of his functions calmed the boy. He looked for his cloak and robe, but could see nothing as drab as those among the fleshy tones that Aurum favoured, the glowing golds. 'Something plain?'

The boy frowned a little, then edged away. As he did so, other boys appeared, each moving to one of a row of lapis lazuli chests the colour of predawn sky. Lifting the lids with willowy arms they drew up robes and turned to display them: thickly embossed samite encrusted with jewels, mosaicked with iridescent feathers. Carnelian rose to his feet swaying, even as the pain abated in his head. He walked among them and they bowed a little, turning their heads as if they were detecting his movement from eddies in the air. Appalled by the awful magnificence of the garments, he settled for a relatively sombre robe that glimmered with rubies so dark they seemed almost jet and that, more importantly, seemed to be the least impregnated with Aurum's odour.

The boys guided him to a place encompassed by mirrors of gold. There they worked on him, their amethyst eyes turning black, pulling strigils from racks, wielding brushes and pads, glazing his skin with pigments, floating undergarments over him that might have been stitched together from the wings of dragonflies. He submitted to them and was several times fooled into thinking they could see him when their stone eyes caught a flake of light. He disliked how tall he looked among them when reflected in the mirrors, above which rose the quivering limbs of the machines.

Finally they masked him, then slipped away. Startled, Carnelian glanced round, but was too slow to see them disappear. He was alone, but for the other sinister versions of himself inhabiting all those other mirror worlds. He was wondering why it was Aurum had so much need to see himself, when there was a rapping at a distant door.

'Enter,' he said, echoes rippling some of the mirror worlds.

The door gasped open and guardsmen entered with the faces he remembered, round and yellow and bisected by Aurum's tattoo. So familiar were they that, when a dark figure approached, he drew back, alarmed, certain it must be Aurum himself. Then he saw the figure was far too diminutive and, as its mask caught the light, its metal was too wintry to be gold. The guardsmen knelt to form an avenue flanked by their forked spears, down which the quaestor approached him. The man came close enough for Carnelian to smell the myrrh that wafted off his dark brocades as he knelt and bowed his head. 'Seraph,' he breathed, offering up a folded parchment.

Carnelian took the letter and turned its seal to the light. It was not bright enough for him to read the impressions in the purple wax. Besides, at that moment, he was anxious to find out what had happened to him. A sudden thought caused him to glance up at Aurum's guardsmen. 'Where are my Marula?'

The quaestor curled so tight the forehead of his mask clinked against the floor. 'They were sent back to the cothon, Seraph. It is not permitted that they should enter here save through quarantine.'

Carnelian was trying to remember what he could about the moment he had entered the purgatory with them, but he could recall almost nothing. He sensed the quaestor's unease. 'Unmask.'

The man lifted his head from the floor, but not enough for the light to reveal his metal face. 'Seraph?'

'Remove your mask.'

Another clink as the man abased himself. He reached behind his head and fumbled his mask loose, then laid it upon the floor as if it were made of the thinnest glass.

'Look at me, ammonite.'

The quaestor hesitated, but then his pale face came up all written over with numbers. His eyes were still cast down.

'How did I end up here?'

The quaestor suppressed a shrug, licked his lips. 'My Lord the Seraph reacted badly to one of the purifying drugs. We are mortified, but—'

'I have been through many such purifications and never before have been affected thus . . .'

Numbers folded into the wrinkles of his grimace. 'The creatures that entered the purgatory on the insistence of the Seraph panicked like animals. They overthrew censers. They spilled fluids. Because of this, prodigious quantities of the drugs were released . . .' The quaestor cracked his forehead against the stone floor. 'Your servants did what they could for the Seraph. Forgive them for what they could not do.'

Carnelian did not feel it likely he would get much more out of him. It could wait. Curiosity over the letter now took precedence in his mind. He felt the seal. The wax was smooth. At first he did not understand, but then it occurred to him. It must be from Osidian, who had no seal to use. He broke it open and saw with some excitement that the glyphs were indeed drawn in Osidian's hand. He read it.

Expect visitors in the cothon. Equip them
as best you can.

Carnelian turned the parchment, looking for more, but

313

the rest of it was blank. Osidian had written nothing that could not be read by anyone. Carnelian read the letter again. Visitors? The quaestor, fidgeting, drew his eyes. Carnelian's mask hid a bitter smile. It was fully possible the wax had been broken, the letter read, then resealed. What did it matter? Its import seemed innocuous enough. His mind turned again to what had happened when he had entered the purgatory. The quaestor's explanation did not ring true. Carnelian regarded the letter. Visitors? What visitors? Obliqueness from Osidian was always a reason to worry. Carnelian tried to gather his thoughts. How could he think with all these people grovelling before him? His gaze fell on the face of one of the guardsmen. Aurum's mark there on that round face filled him with disgust. He shaped a gesture of dismissal and turned his back on them. As he waited, listening to them creep away, he became aware that, at the far end of the chamber, there was the merest diamond-bright crack. The promise of clean daylight drew him and a lust for unperfumed air to breathe. To his delight, as he approached, a waft sliced fresh through the stale lily odour of the chamber. He had to squint against the glare leaking through the crack like first light on a horizon. Shadows appeared; their litheness suggested they were the amethyst-eyed boys.

'I wish to gaze upon the day,' he rumbled.

They released a blinding flood of light that brought back his headache. He paused until the spasm had subsided, then strode into the blaze. He turned his face up towards the sun, waiting until he could feel its heat seeping through the gold of his mask. The scene began emerging round him. More of Aurum's guards kneeling. Stretching away behind them, a garden. Commanding the guardsmen to remain where they were, he wandered out along a path, delighting in the open space, in the dappled shade. Magnolia perfume soaking the air for a moment took him back to the Koppie. Disturbed, he pushed on. At last he reached a ragged wall, broken down here and there by dragon-blood trees. Moving into the shade of one he gripped its trunk. At his feet yawned a canyon. This could be nothing else than the same Pass they had tried to fight their way up, only to be repulsed by Aurum's fire. He pondered this, feeling again the agony of separation from his friends. So much had happened since, it seemed an age ago. He peered down that chasm, his heart yearning to carry him on wings down to the green land below. In his melancholy, it was some time before he noticed the dust hazing up from the canyon. At first he thought it smoke until he saw its pallidness was mixed with rust. He had seen enough such clouds to know that only a saurian herd could lift so much, or dragons, or perhaps a great body of riders. He tensed. Osidian had told him to expect visitors. Visitors! His eyes tried to pierce the hazy canyon below. He fought down panic. He had suspected Osidian had some hidden reason to take Makar. Those he had believed safe were now returning into the very heart of danger. A seedling of joy grew up through the dread. He turned his back on the canyon and returned to the tower. He must go to the cothon to see what could be done to avoid what he now most feared.

The outer doors opened as he approached them, revealing a staircase descending into gloom and shadows. As he reached the top of the stair, a rushing sound rose up from the vast hall so that he imagined some waterfall had been released, perhaps to cool the air, but then the disturbance ceased as quickly as it had begun. When he searched the gloom on either side of the steps, he could just make out figures in serried ranks. What he had heard was their obeisance. Another figure was ascending the steps towards him. As it looked up at him its mask caught the light and he knew it must be the quaestor. He descended to meet him.

The quaestor knelt on the steps. 'What is the Seraph's desire?'

Carnelian looked over the edge of the stair to the floor with its retainers. They must all be of Aurum's household.

315

He spotted some distant doors. 'Is that the way out of the sanctum?'

The quaestor's mask came up. 'It is, Seraph.'

Continuing his descent, Carnelian heard the quaestor creeping after him. When he reached the ground, he moved off along an avenue flanked by kneeling guardsmen. Beyond them he glimpsed small shapes in the shadows. He was half-way to the door when he realized they must all be children. He became uneasy, feeling as if half the flesh tithe was prostrate around him. Was it possible Aurum's household consisted almost entirely of children?

As he reached the doors, they clanked apart. Through them he saw the structures of the fortress wavering in the haze. He could make out the high wall of the cothon and the city itself, looking as if it were made of sand, verminous with windows, spired, tottering-towered. A hot breeze bore upon it scents, none of which lingered long enough for him to identify. A smell of life, though, that he longed to breathe free of the prison of his mask.

A shrill cry made him turn. The quaestor came scurrying towards him. 'The Seraph cannot mean to walk?'

'Can I not?'

Carnelian followed a paved gully. Ribbed limestone rose up on either side, pierced with gates and slits. The echoes of his footsteps combined with those of the quaestor's. No tyadra stood guard upon the gates. The rings on either side held no heraldic banner poles. The place felt desolate, abandoned, but he was certain that beyond those pale walls must lurk the households the Masters had left behind when they went on campaign with Aurum. He had the uncanny feeling that, through each slit, eyes were watching his progress.

The quaestor several times attempted to lecture him about the Law and its demands. Carnelian knew that, however much he resented these, it had too often been others who had had to pay for his defiance. Moreover, it would be foolish to ignore its edicts, however distasteful, where doing so might diminish his status and thus weaken what little power he had. So, by the time they reached the purgatory door, he was ready to submit to the full ritual protection. As ammonites disrobed him and began inscribing his skin, he told himself that whosoever the visitors might turn out to be, he was determined he would not return to Aurum's tower with its household of children. If there were no alternative, he would quit the fortress and return to the dragons and Osidian.

He had agreed to be carried to the cothon in a palanquin. First the quaestor had told him that there were no aquar for him to ride, then he had pointed out that it was too far to go wearing ranga. He wished he had not given in. The palanquin was turning out to be no faster than walking. All he had done was trade the exhaustion of tottering along on his ranga for imprisonment in this box, where there was nothing to do but fret about who the visitors might be, and why they had come. From time to time he peered out through a grille in the hope of seeing that they had arrived but each time he was presented with what seemed an identical view of the crumbling city. Attempts to resolve its pale intricacies wearied his eyes. Depressingly, the only difference between one scene and the next was the shadows, which had lengthened so that he became anxious that it would be nightfall before he reached the cothon.

At last he began hearing a sound like distant sea. Straining, he managed to distinguish in the hubbub countless voices ghosted by echoes. As a hush descended he was able to hear the snuffling of aquar. His heart pounding, he put an eye to the grille. All there was to see was a wall of bronze that had to be one leaf of an open cothon gate. He could no longer bear to travel blind and tapped on the palanquin wall. As it settled to the ground he put on his mask and readied himself to confront whatever might lie outside.

Sliding open the door, he saw his bearers kneeling. Two ammonites placed his ranga on the cobbles, then, gathering his robe, he climbed out onto them. Cries shrilled around him as the ammonites gave commands. Rising to his full height, he turned. A shrouded crowd confronted him. Lepers. Though these were the visitors he had expected, he was still shocked. He had been so convinced he would never see them again. A forbidding bulk looming behind their tide turned his shock to alarm. A dragon, the bright, uneven cross of her horns turned on the Lepers. Earth-is-Strong, like a ship upon a grey sea. Almost he surged forward, shouting frantic commands to her crew that they must not open fire. The realization that her pipes were unlit brought a debilitating relief. The ammonites were still shrilling, motioning marumaga to advance on the Lepers. Tentatively, the legionaries approached the crowd who were, it seemed, determined to stand their ground.

'They *must* abase themselves before the Master,' one of the ammonites called out.

The legionaries menaced the Lepers, but their shrouded mass seemed uncowed. Fearing bloodshed Carnelian strode forward, commanding the legionaries to desist, making gestures towards the ammonites that silenced their haranguing. As the legionaries retreated, he saw it was only the first few ranks of the Lepers that had confronted them; the rest and major part of the crowd were mostly turned to face Earth-is-Strong – many of them still mounted. He glanced up to make sure the dragon's pipes were still not lit. Then he noticed, with pleasure and relief, Sthax and the rest of his Marula to one side. He decided it was better not to get them involved, so located among the legionaries those whose stance emanated authority. 'Attend me,' he said, motioning them to approach. He scanned their collars and found the one he had hoped among them. 'Quartermaster, send a command to that dragon that she is to withdraw to the other side of the cothon.'

'As you command, Master.' The Quartermaster bowed and sent one of his men hurrying away to do Carnelian's bidding, then approached him, eyes cast down. Carnelian sensed he was about to be petitioned to make a decision as to what to do with this invasion. Uncertain, he turned away from the man and approached the Lepers, who recoiled from him. He put his hands up to stay them. 'I would speak with your leaders.'

He could see no faces in their cowls, but sensed their fear. A few glanced back towards Earth-is-Strong. 'I've given instructions that the dragon is to retreat. She'll not harm you.'

The people before him stayed as they were, uneasy, afraid of the dragon, afraid of him. He wished he could remove his mask, climb down from his ranga, walk among them. There must be some there who would know him. Of course, such actions would be madness. Any who saw his naked face the Law would have destroyed.

It was only once Earth-is-Strong started moving away that the whole crowd began turning towards him. He noticed an eddying in their midst as someone came through them. The front ranks parted and two figures emerged. Carnelian's heart leapt into his throat. Even shrouded as a Leper, he could tell by her size, by her gait, that one of them was Poppy. Both seemed very small as they came to stand before him. Carnelian gazed down at Poppy. When she looked up, her face appeared in the shadow of her cowl. He yearned for a smile of recognition, but her mouth was a line in a face tight with fear. It took a moment for him to realize it was not his face she was seeing, but an unhuman one wrought from gold. He felt trapped behind it. Everyone was waiting for him but, anxious about what effect his voice might have on Poppy, he was reluctant to speak. He turned his mask enough to see, on either side, ammonites, keepers of a merciless Law, as well as marumaga legionaries with cruelly hooked poles. The Lepers greatly outnumbered them, but they were, effectively, unarmed. Besides, if there were a riot, he might lose control of Earth-is-Strong. Still, he had to say something. 'Why have you come?'

319

Poppy's eyes widened as she stared up at him but, thankfully, she showed no other sign that she had recognized his voice.

It was the shrouded figure beside her who spoke. 'We've come to honour the agreement we made with the Master Osidian.' It was Lily.

'I had understood that agreement fulfilled.'

'There are things you don't know.'

Her tone convinced Carnelian she knew to whom she was talking. Its lack of reverence was causing agitation among the legionaries. Carnelian glanced round and saw, anxiously, how closely the silver masks of the ammonites were watching Lily and Poppy.

'You must leave the way you came.'

'We must honour our agreement.'

Even through her shroud Carnelian could see the stubborn angle of Lily's head and it made him angry. He had trusted her to protect Poppy. 'What possessed you to agree to anything that would bring you and all these others into the jaws of your enemies?'

When Poppy took a step forward and fixed burning eyes on his mask, marumaga moved to intercept her, but Carnelian jerked his hand in a gesture of command that made them retreat.

'We're free people,' said Poppy. 'Free to decide what risks we take.'

Lily's bandaged hand clasped Poppy's shoulder. Carnelian was glad when he saw Poppy accepting its restraint.

'Everyone here' – Lily swept her free hand round to take in the crowd – 'has suffered terrible loss. All are here moved by an implacable hatred of the one who has inflicted those losses upon us.'

Carnelian saw how resolutely the Lepers stood, while the legionaries, who had less to fear from him, cowered in his presence. He could not help feeling proud of these outcasts. If there were to be any hope of reversing this disaster he must

320

know what further agreement they had made with Osidian, but this was neither the time nor the place to ask such questions. There was one question, however, his heart would not be denied. 'And the Ochre?'

Carnelian followed Poppy's gaze back into the crowd to where a Leper stood taller than the rest. Seeing him, Carnelian's heart beat faster.

'He's become a commander among us,' said Lily.

Carnelian regarded Fern's shrouded form, rejoicing, though wondering how he had so quickly recovered from his burns. Poppy was looking away, a frown on her face. He knew her well enough to tell what passion and anger that bland expression concealed. Had he really believed he could persuade them to merely ride away? How could he have imagined Osidian had not bound them to him with chains not easily broken? He calmed himself. They were here now and if there was nothing else left to him he must do what he could to keep them safe. He thrust from his mind any consideration of the immensity of the forces ranged against them all. He knew there was no place for him here, though he yearned to be with them. To return to Osidian's side would be to abandon them to the ammonites and the Law. His heart sank as he faced up to his only option. He must return to Aurum's tower, for it was from there that he could best protect them.

Having made his decision he wanted to tell Poppy and Lily about it. He glanced up, his gaze lingering on Fern's form among the Lepers. How deeply he desired to approach him. Instead, he raised a hand and summoned the Quartermaster. The man came to kneel before him. 'Take these people into the barracks of the auxiliaries. Settle them there. Give them food and water.'

Carnelian saw dusk was encroaching. 'In the morning, equip them with armour, arm them, mount them.'

The legionary glanced round as if counting the Lepers. 'We have nothing like enough, Master, for all of these.'

'Then give them everything you have,' Carnelian said, his voice edged with irritation.

The man punched the cobbles with his forehead. 'As you command, Master.'

Carnelian turned to leave.

'Carnie.'

He froze. It was Poppy addressing him. It was unthinkable to address a Master by name and such an intimate contraction betrayed a fatal familiarity. He looked to the ammonites and convinced himself they could not have heard her clearly. Weighing his words he addressed one of them. 'Make these creatures join the others, silently. Any harm that comes to them shall be visited on you all.'

The ammonites touched their foreheads to the cobbles. Carnelian did not wait to see his commands obeyed lest Poppy attempt to speak to him again. He strode back towards the palanquin. Only when he reached it did he dare to turn. The legionaries had closed ranks behind him and the Lepers were already being herded away. He looked for Poppy, for anyone he knew, but they were an unindividuated mass. The dregs of his hope draining away allowed his fears, his agony of doubt to sicken him so that he felt unable even to lift his head. He glimpsed the palanquin out of the corner of his eye and felt a sudden revulsion at the thought of climbing into its prison. He returned to the legionaries and demanded they bring him an aquar. While he waited he beckoned Sthax and the Marula to approach him and made them understand, remembering to use only gestures, that he wanted them to accompany him. When he was brought a mount, he climbed into its saddle-chair, then, glancing back only to make sure Sthax was following him, he tore out of the cothon with furious speed.

It seemed no time at all before they reached the sanctum bridge. In the failing sun, the gate into the sanctum seemed painted with blood. Carnelian was determined to take Sthax and his Marula through with him. Motioning them to follow,

322

he rode his aquar across the bridge. Loosing a lance from its scabbard, he hefted it and struck against the bronze. As the door opened a crack he urged his aquar forward. It coiled its head back and its delicate hands retracted as if in surprise as its chest shoved the door open. He was forced to duck as they passed into the purgatory. Shrill cries issued from mirror faces that were reflecting the hazy light of flames. Carnelian held his breath against the wreathing smoke. A sinuous lash in his aquar's neck, a shudder running through its body, made him fear that the narcotic smoke might make it collapse.

'Open the inner doors,' he bellowed.

Cries warned that that would breach the purity of the sanctum.

His head was already swimming, but anger kept his focus sharp. 'Obey me!'

A paler rectangle opened ahead and he urged his aquar towards it. She stumbled, sending censers clattering across the floor, then they erupted into the light. Glancing round to make sure Sthax was still following him, he let his aquar carry him none too steadily down the limestone gully, across the second bridge and up the steps to Aurum's tower. He felt her tread stabilizing even as his head cleared.

At the tower gate he had no need to issue commands for it opened before him as he approached. He sent his aquar through the gap and, soon, they were loping down the spine of Aurum's hall of audience. Lanterns were lit here and there like stars. Their glow revealed guardsmen rushing to attend him. In the shadows, figures were rising, approaching him. He felt only loathing for their tattooed faces. He advanced on them and they fell prostrate so that there was a danger they would be trampled by his aquar. Rage rose in him and overflowed. 'Get you from my sight!'

The way they tried to crawl away disgusted him. An instinct to send his Marula against them rose in his throat like vomit. Then one painted face caught the light and he saw it was only a child. A child in terror. He saw others: girls leading amethyst-eyed boys stumbling from his path. Appalled, he watched them fleeing.

He reined back his mount, ashamed that he was inflicting such terror on slaves. He made the aquar sink and stepped out onto the floor. 'Stay where you are.'

Everyone fell as if scythed at the knees.

'There will be no punishment. My wrath is done. You were not the cause of it, merely its victims.'

He approached a guardsman. 'Are there any chambers here I could use other than those of your Master?'

The man mumbled something. Carnelian urged him to speak more clearly. The man dared to glance up, squinting against the glare of Carnelian's mask. Carnelian turned his head so that the reflected light moved away from the man's face.

'There are none, Master.'

Carnelian nodded and glanced up the steps, resigned. He looked back at the guardsmen, then round at the cowering children. It was clear this was not the first time they had known terror. 'Send to the purgatory for myrrh and censers. The sanctity of this place is breached. I must purify the chambers above.'

The guardsman punched his forehead into the floor. 'As the Master commands.'

Carnelian gave a nod, then advanced towards the stairs, morose.

A wheel divided in two by a horizontal russet bar. Wide-rimmed, its ratcheted hub meshed with a long brass pawl that was rooted in a float within a vessel of jade carved in the form of meshing chameleons. As a child, he had discovered a water clock like this discarded, and had tried to make it work. He slid a finger lightly around the wheel rim, of gold with a delicately chased arabesque of flames. His had been gilded copper. He touched the rays of the sun-eye showing above the russet bar, which was a solid piece of precious iron, unoiled so that it would rust to the colour of earth. On his clock the land had been merely carnelian. The sun on Aurum's clock had fallen beneath the iron horizon. The arc of rim following it represented the firmament of night. Squatting above this was a figure wrought from obsidian: the Black God, Lord of Mirrors. Carnelian reached up and caressed each of His four horns in turn, remembering Osidian and the legion they had stolen and the war they were making upon the Masters. His own clock had been crowned merely with a crude turtle shell. The God's empty eyepits glared down at him. He sought distraction in the finer points of the mechanism. The reservoir of such thin jade made the liquid it held seem blood in a bruise. A scale ran up its side, numbered from zero to nineteen. The liquid was above fifteen. He glanced up at the hidden sun-eye. This clock seemed to be keeping time, but there was no sound of water dripping. Peering above the jade, he saw a siphon. No drops were falling from it, but there was a glint like spider thread stretching between the siphon and the jade. He put his finger out to break it and was amazed when dribbles of light flashed across his skin. Upon his finger pad there rested a tiny bead. He touched his fingernail to the lip of the jade and let the bead roll off. Standing back he admired the clock. The liquid silver made it seem sorcerous, as if it were measuring time with moonbeams. He had always assumed the clock he had found at home had once been his father's. That was why he had repaired it, then taken it to him. Now he realized it had been no Master's device. In comparison with Aurum's it was less than a crude toy. His father had dismissed the gift saying he had no desire to measure time; it passed slowly enough already.

Anger rose in Carnelian, the same he had unleashed in the hall below. Almost he smashed Aurum's clock, but he knew that destroying its beauty would achieve nothing. His anger had its roots in fear: fear for Poppy, for Fern, for Lily, for all those innocents he and Osidian had brought into danger. He feared for Sthax, whom he had left outside, without a word, when the Maruli had risen with his fellows, clearly hoping for some reassurance Carnelian had not felt he could give them. His fear was like the first twinges of a recurring fever made worse because he had let himself believe he was cured of it. As it burned more strongly it was heating to panic. It was actually worse here in Makar. At least in the lands below it had been Osidian who had made the Law, who, though monstrous, was a man – and a man could be pleaded with, persuaded, killed even. Here, though he might defy ammonites, he knew that, ultimately, the Law was unassailable. He coughed a laugh. Had it come to this? That he was nostalgic for Osidian's murderous tyranny?

He grew more morose. What hope was there for his friends, his loved ones? He turned away from the liquid-silver clock. As he passed a mirror of polished gold he gazed sidelong at himself. All he could see was a shadowy Master. A fabulous creature: beautiful, but deadly. He stroked his hand down a pyramid of crystal standing on its point upon the point of another. Through the narrow waist of their meeting poured green sand. Powdered jade, no doubt. Perhaps malachite. Tiny emeralds, even. One emptying slowly into the other a few grains at a time. To contemplate this was to slow time. For a moment he fantasized that, should he invert them, he might be able to make time run backwards. Reaching back he might seek to unmake the past.

'Pathetic,' he said. Today they had been within reach, but he had not dared touch them. A wall stood between them, more impenetrable than bronze: his mask, his caste and the Law-that-must-be-obeyed. It was a barrier he could not breach.

A tiny hope flickered. Surely a door could be opened through which they could come to him. He could adopt them into his House. Poppy would come, even Fern. He imagined their faces disfigured by his chameleon tattoo. Poppy perhaps might accept it, but would Fern welcome becoming his servant, his slave? Carnelian's anger flared again as he felt trapped. His hands, reaching up, found the hard metal of his face. Even were he to manage somehow to bring them into his House, would he be achieving anything other than assuaging his loneliness at the cost of bringing others in to share his prison?

He glared at a copper disc on spindly ivory legs. An arc of numbers seemed to be grinning at him in derision. It had delicate arms holding sighting lenses, a fin. Some kind of sundial, no doubt.

Even his House was not a certain refuge against what might come. Besides, there was no assurance he would survive. Nor that, whether he did or not, the Wise would sanctify any adoptions he made. Nor, for that matter, even that his father would. Would his father see them as anything but barbarians?

Carnelian wrung his hands. What he really wanted was for them never to have come at all. There must be some way to persuade them to return to the Leper Valleys. He let out a grunt. To hope for this was foolish. Osidian had bound them to him with some accursed agreement. Carnelian tried to imagine what this could be. Promises of wealth? Power? Perhaps it was nothing more than revenge that brought them up to fight against Aurum, whom they hated. So was there anything he could do to save them?

He had been noticing a clicking sound for quite a while. Something was swinging, glinting back and forth in an arc. A stone chameleon swinging by its tail from a hive of wheels. Of brass and gold and silver. Toothed and meshing with each other, in convoluted, furtive movement. This mechanism had a face very like the liquid-silver clock, and had not only a sun-wheel but also another wheel for the moon, whose tearful eye hung just above the last rays of the westering sun. And there were other rings. One for the morning star and many more, concentric, stars and planets revolving round a silver ammonite shell. If this was a clock, it was surely one that had been made for the Wise. Carnelian backed away from it, glancing round the chamber. Why was this place filled with clocks? Unease descended upon him. He

327

felt like a child lost in a place where there was nothing he could understand.

Then he saw the pool. It seemed water except that it was set vertically up a wall. A miraculous thing. As he came before it, he saw a Master in its depths. His heart jumped a beat. It was a doorway through which another Master was gazing at him. Then he moved and the other Master mimicked him. The illusion was broken. He approached his reflection, amazed. When close enough, he reached out to touch his reflection's fingers. It was cold. Glass perhaps. He pulled his fingers from its surface and watched the ghost of his touch slowly disappear. It was a mirror, but one more perfect than water. He leaned closer, seeing his eyes behind the mask. He seemed a man peering through a prison window. The longing to escape from that hated shell suddenly overwhelmed him. Glancing round to make certain he was alone, he freed his face. It appeared like the moon from behind a cloud. He jumped. It seemed he was seeing Osidian. He cursed softly. It was clearly not Osidian's face, but it had the same green eyes. Uncannily the same. The face frowned and that too seemed Osidian, though there was no birthmark folding into the wrinkles. The eyes again. That same intense look. He looked at himself in a new way. Why was it always Osidian who led and he who followed?

'I can play the game as well as he,' he said, though he only half believed it.

He turned his head from side to side. How unwhite he had become. He decided that he liked it. It made him look a little bit more like a Plainsman. The face in the mirror smiled. He looked into its eyes and felt as if he was understanding something for the first time. He leaned closer still, fascinated by his face. He realized he had never really seen it properly before. There were wrinkles in his skin, especially around his eyes. He looked older than he remembered. Not as old as his father. Nothing like as old as Lord Aurum. Lord Aurum. He looked round the room, then back at the mirror. Why did the Master surround himself with mirrors, clocks? And children?

Carnelian felt repulsed by what these things suggested about the man, but at the same time he began feeling something else. This was surely a man who feared death. Carnelian regarded his face in the mirror. Though he had every reason to fear death himself, he realized he did not. He feared it more for others than himself. Lord Aurum was old even when he came to their island. Carnelian remembered how much Aurum had appeared to want a son. He remembered how much he himself had grown to despise the secondary lineage in his own House. Who knew what it was that Aurum feared? What would exile from Osrakum be like for such a man?

A scratching at the outer door made him jerk his mask up so fast he grazed his nose and chin. Quickly he secured it and approached the door. He gave leave to enter and ammonites appeared bearing censers that they began setting up around the chamber. Soon they were lighting them. Smoke began uncurling into the air. The odour of myrrh made Carnelian notice again the stale tang of attar of lilies that pervaded the room. Aurum's smell. He reminded himself this was the man who had had his uncle killed, who had inflicted atrocities upon the Lepers. Whatever his suffering, Aurum was a monster.

When Carnelian had dismissed the ammonites he began to feel drowsy. It had been a difficult day. He could do nothing more. He would resume the fight in the morning. He removed his robes until he was standing in nothing but the cocoon of the ritual protection. Weary beyond measure he slipped under the feather blankets and was instantly asleep.

Keeping the spider in a crystal box. Its legs moving, like hair in his eyes. He wants to look away, but fears if he does it will escape. Creeping, creeping, always creeping, seeking a way out. The horror of its thought as it watches him through the obscene cluster of its eyes.

Carnelian came awake, gasping. A child at the foot of his bed was looking at him. Not a child, but the metal facsimile of a child's face. A homunculus. The eyes, ears and voice of a Sapient of the Wise. Carnelian stared, petrified. Fading into the darkness, its child smile became the moon's crescent gleaming in a pond. Then it was not there.

When an amethyst-eyed boy woke him, Carnelian frowned, remembering the same thing happening before. His nightmares clung to him like a wet cloak. He closed his eyes. Pain was curled dormant in his head and he did not want to move lest he should wake it. He squinted at the ceiling.

'Would you break your fast, Master?' said the boy. His stone eyes seemed bruises.

'Please,' Carnelian said and was relieved when the face went away. He moved an arm and felt the bandages that clung to his skin like scabs. He had not imagined the previous day, then. His dreams would not let go of him. He shuddered, remembering the spider's eyes, then recalled the homunculus with its borrowed face. That part of his dreams had seemed so real.

As he sat up, the pain stirring in his head sent needles into the bones of his face. He wondered at that pain, but his eyes were already seeking the corner where the homunculus had disappeared. Try as he might, he could not pierce the shadows there.

More amethyst-eyed boys brought him food and served him as he ate. Taste seemed remote, as if he were reading about someone eating. He was aware he was sitting with his back to the corner. At last he could bear it no longer. He told them to take the plates away and disappear. Thankfully, the headache was fading. He rose, gazing into the corner. An inner voice was telling him it was just a dark corner, that it was dangerous to blur the boundary between dreams and waking life. Still he went in search of a lamp, but all he could find were the bronze flambeaux and they were too heavy. He edged towards the corner. It seemed to grow brighter as he came closer. Bright enough for him to see the tapestry of featherwork that

330

hung there upon the wall. He could make out something of its writhing designs, but nothing of its colours. When he was close enough he put out his hand. It was silky smooth beneath his touch. So fine he could feel the texture of the wall beneath. A crack. A vertical groove running up the stone. He stroked the tapestry aside. A door. He ran his hand over it and found a catch. It clicked. The door sighed open. The air beyond was cold and laced with a strong, disturbing odour. The spider in his dreams touched his face and he recoiled and the door clicked closed. He stood with his fingers on it, listening with his fingers for vibrations. He pulled away, allowing the tapestry to fall back, and retreated to the centre of the chamber, but kept glancing back at the corner. He summoned the boys and, when they came, he bade them bring him a lamp. When they had returned with it he lit it, but approached the corner only when they were gone.

Figures danced in the tapestry. Feathers that were green and black and red, so tiny they could have been brushstrokes. Once again he stroked the tapestry aside, saw the door, located the catch, opened it. Beyond, steps curved down into darkness. He put his head in, lifted the lamp and spilled light down a few more steps. Desiring to see more of them, he began descending. Round and round, spiralling down into the darkness.

He emerged into a pillared vault. Lifting the lamp, he saw, leaning against pillars, two cocoons, each taller than a man. He regarded them with horror, expecting at any moment to see within them some jerking, unhuman movement. What monsters could such things pupate? Once certain that nothing within them lived, he dared to approach. Ivory as translucent as wet parchment. Their narrow height had a suggestion of sarcophagi. Within, some darker masses that might have been bodies. He reached out and touched one. It had a skin-smooth surface, though he could feel swirls under his fingers. He lifted the lantern and peered close, but could not make out what lay inside. In the corner of his vision, he saw something that almost made him drop his lantern. A third cocoon not far away, but this one was open. In it he could see four feet side by side. He raised the light, trembling, up the legs. The outermost and larger pair were bound with pale leather bands. Between the legs, a smaller figure. He moved the edge of light up to see its face. It dazzled him. He angled the lamp and the dazzle abated to reveal a face like the moon. The face of a child near slumber. Carnelian gaped at the homunculus. Then he noticed what it was holding before it. A staff topped by a cross or what might have been a spider. This cypher was crowned by a crescent moon. His eyes darted to the creature's throat, where long fingers meshed around it in a stranglehold. He played the light up above the homunculus' head and found shadow welling in the hollows of a living skull face.

LEGIONS

Each Domain corresponds to a lunar month. Each takes the
form of a tree with a Grand Sapient as its root. Each has two
direct subordinates; each in turn has two more and so on.
The number of Sapients in a major Domain is sixty-three;
in a minor Domain, thirty-one. Only the Grand Sapients
of the major Domains have Seconds as their immediate
subordinates; all other Grand Sapients have Thirds. The
major Domains are Legions, Lands, Tribute and Cities; the
minor are Mentor, Roads, Law, Immortality, Labyrinth,
Gates, Rain and Blood.

(extract from a beadcord manual of the Wise of the Domain Mentor)

'Suth Carnelian,' said the Homunculus in a high, unhuman
voice that made Carnelian's scalp crawl. In shock, he stared
up at the Sapient. Skin, sallow leather. A cavity gaping where
there should have been a nose. Eyepits, empty. Except for the
straps that held him upright within the hollow of the capsule,
the Sapient appeared to be entirely naked. He seemed to
be strangling the homunculus that stood between his legs.
Carnelian's focus snapped back to the finial of the staff the
homunculus was holding. Its lurid red stone was in form
something like the horned head of a dragon. Though he had
never seen the cypher before, he could guess what it indicated.
'You are of the Domain Legions?'

'I *am* Legions.'

Carnelian froze with terror. Standing before him was one of the twelve Grand Sapients and master of by far the greater part of the Commonwealth's might. 'What are you doing here . . . my Lord?'

Behind its silver mask, the homunculus murmured an echo to Carnelian's words. A coiling around its neck drew Carnelian's eyes. The corpse fingers came alive like worms. Their fretting at the homunculus' throat made it speak again. 'It is you, my Lord, who have need to answer that question. What do you intend to do with the forces you have stolen from the Commonwealth?'

The authority in those words compelled Carnelian to explain himself. The reason Osidian would have given seemed too absurd to voice. How could they hope to remove Molochite, now God Emperor, and set Osidian up in his place? From Carnelian's heart came what mattered to him: to save his loved ones, the Plainsmen and the Lepers who even now were not far away in direct defiance of the Law-that-must-be-obeyed. Gazing up, he struggled to marshal enough belief to answer the Grand Sapient.

'You may have managed to defeat that fool Aurum with the rabble of barbarians you conquered with the Ochre tribe, but can it really be that you intend to challenge us directly?'

The mention of the murdered tribe snatched the breath from Carnelian's lips. How much did the Wise know? Though it felt like a betrayal, he must not hesitate to use the massacre of the Tribe in whatever way he could to save others. As for Osidian, he owed him nothing. 'Osidian destroyed the Ochre to the last child. It was through this that he terrorized the other tribes into obeying him, but their fear of the Commonwealth turned out greater and they soon deserted him rather than follow him to the Guarded Land.'

'But not before my Lord Nephron used them to annihilate an entire legion's auxiliaries.'

Beneath his bandages, sweat ran down Carnelian's back.

The looming Grand Sapient was standing in judgement upon the Plainsmen. Carnelian grasped at various retorts. All seemed dangerous, but silence most dangerous of all. The Grand Sapient's line of argument must be challenged. 'Still, they abandoned him as soon as they could.'

As the homunculus echoed Carnelian's words, the leathery face rose out of the hollow in which it lay. 'Does my Lord imagine we do not know it is Marula who do my Lord Nephron's bidding now?'

Carnelian felt panic rising.

'Not only they, but the vermin recently come up from the land below . . .'

Carnelian felt as if he were only now becoming aware of the web in which he was caught. He fought to calm himself. To struggle would only ensnare him more completely.

The Grand Sapient creased the horned-ring branded into his forehead. 'Though we have not yet determined why they would seek such futile and self-destructive defiance.'

This doubt was the first vulnerability Carnelian had detected in his inquisitor. 'Perhaps they seek revenge against the atrocities recently visited upon them by my Lord Aurum.'

'So in this case you admit they defy us of their own will?'

Carnelian recoiled. His resistance had served only to condemn the Lepers further. It seemed the ground around him was scattered with broken glass.

More movement at the homunculus' throat. 'Though you may have found a way up into the Guarded Land unknown to us, be certain we shall find it, plug it and chastise those who showed it to you.

'You may have obtained control of one of our legions, but do you imagine it will be enough to defeat us, who have more than forty we can wield against you? Do you really hope to prevail with your one where even Kakanxahe, with all the legions at his back, failed? Have no doubt, Suth Carnelian: your rebellion will end in failure. We seek merely to limit unnecessary destruction and bloodshed.'

335

The Grand Sapient leaned forward enough that light welled into his eyepits, which were revealed to have a reddish hue. 'Help me put this madness to an end, child.'

Carnelian stared at the red pits.

'Though Nephron has been wronged, what has been done cannot be undone. For him there is no hope. The moment his brother donned the Masks, Nephron's life was forfeit. You, however, can still be saved. Though you have transgressed against the Law, there are loopholes in it that I could help you exploit.'

Carnelian shook his head, mesmerized by the mummy face. He would not save himself if that meant leaving all those he loved to perish.

Though eyeless, the Grand Sapient seemed to gaze at him. 'The God Emperor might be grateful enough to gift you a bloodpure bride.'

Carnelian's expression must have been relayed to the Grand Sapient, for it receded up into the shadows of the capsule hollow. 'I could see to it that you were given the ruling of your House.'

Those words struck at Carnelian's heart. 'Would you have me supplant my own father?'

'No need for that, he has been deposed.'

'Deposed?' Carnelian said, feeling pressure in his chest.

'Ykoriana had the Clave depose him.'

'In revenge for his opposing her—' For a moment Carnelian felt relief, thinking that of all possible punishments, deposal was the lightest. Then he realized that, without him there, Spinel and the Second Lineage would have become masters of House Suth. Ykoriana's revenge was typically cruel.

'We know you have other reasons to hate the Empress.'

Carnelian stared up at the shadowy mummy.

'We know, though have been unable to prove, she was behind your kidnapping. She and the Brotherhood of the Wheel who captured you in the Yden.'

The pain of the news about his father was combining in

Carnelian with the anguish of that night that seemed now so long ago. Rage rose in him against the agent of all their woes. 'The Hanuses admitted they were her instrument?'

The Grand Sapient gave a slight nod. 'There have been reasons to suspect their involvement. How did the Brotherhood remove you from Osrakum?'

'In funerary urns.'

The Grand Sapient released his hold on the homunculus, who half-turned, perhaps startled at the separation. Watching the pale hands return to coil about the creature's throat Carnelian realized this was something the Grand Sapient had not known. Again the feeling of being ensnared. What else had he given away?

The homunculus began to speak again. 'You have good reason to feel grievance against her. She has taken much from you.'

Carnelian gazed at the Grand Sapient, who presently became aware of his wariness. 'It is she who has coarsened your skin, child. She who has given it the taint of the impure. You will never be free of that scar about your neck.'

Instinctively, Carnelian's hand rose to touch the scar, but his fingers struck bandages. His scar was concealed. Of course the ammonites of the purgatory had witnessed him naked. His unease flared to horror as he remembered the homunculus at the foot of his bed. Had the Grand Sapient examined him? That thought left him feeling violated.

'Even now she swells powerful on your suffering. We too have cause to hate her, child. Though it is her son who wears the Masks, it is she who rules. This is why we have sought to bring Nephron to Osrakum alive. If he accuses her, we can pull her down.'

'And then you would have him slain and use his blood to anoint his brother's Masks.'

'That is the Law.'

'The Law.'

'Without it, there would be chaos.'

337

Carnelian sensed how the Grand Sapient lusted to have Osidian in his power. Though his heart misgave at what he must do, he could not pass up this chance to negotiate while he still could. 'I will give him to you, but I have a price . . .'

'Name it.'

'Your vow that the Wise will take no vengeance on the barbarians who have been involved in this affair; not one of them is to be harmed.'

The Grand Sapient leaned forward again as if peering at Carnelian, who endured the regard of those eyepits. The Grand Sapient's silence was more terrible than his borrowed voice. He remained motionless for so long, hope began to well up in Carnelian that was almost enough to eclipse his ache at the thought of betraying Osidian.

At last the fingers started moving at the homunculus' throat. 'You ask nothing for yourself?'

Almost Carnelian answered: This *is* for myself, but his heart warned him against it. Instead he considered what might happen to him once he had given them Osidian. In the Three Lands, there was only one place he could live. He imagined returning to Osrakum. Hope lit in him that he could save his father. Mentally, he shook his head. It was already too complicated. Ykoriana's fall would have to be enough upon which to build his father's return to supremacy in their coomb.

'Nothing,' he said.

The Grand Sapient seemed to regard him for an age. Carnelian felt that he could almost see the thoughts flitting through that mutilated head.

'Of course I cannot accede to your request. The Commonwealth depends for her existence on terror. Without this, her fabric would unravel. Her subjects must know the Law to be absolute. They must have no doubt whatever that their transgressions will be punished mercilessly. To pardon even one of these barbarians their sins would be to put the Commonwealth into greater peril than that which you and the Lord Nephron pose.'

Carnelian's hope was quenched by flooding disappointment, but he felt also relief. 'Then you leave me no choice, my Lord.' He could not pretend to play the game further. 'I will fight you, though I do not know how or to what end it will bring me.'

The Grand Sapient's fingers kneaded instructions into the homunculus' neck. 'Then Nephron's fall shall encompass your own.' The pale hands let go the creature's throat and the Grand Sapient folded them over his chest.

Carnelian stared. The Grand Sapient resembled nothing as much as he did a huskman. Certainly, he seemed no more alive. Carnelian backed away, then turned and made his way back to the stair. He was relieved that he did not have to betray Osidian, but the greatest comfort was the removal of doubt. At least now he knew exactly who to fight.

'He has to come,' Carnelian muttered to himself. He had persuaded Sthax to go and fetch Fern from the cothon. The Maruli had wanted to know what was going on, but Carnelian could not even begin to explain. In the end he had told him that he did not know. He had not lied. The only thing he was certain of was that he could not handle Legions on his own. Osidian must be informed of his discovery. Carnelian had considered making the journey to see him, but he did not dare leave the Grand Sapient unattended. Were Legions to emerge from the vault Carnelian was not confident he could stop Aurum's household obeying him. He could not trust the quaestor, who was the Grand Sapient's creature, and to send Sthax with a letter would be to expose him to the scrutiny of Morunasa.

He gazed anxiously towards the outer door. Fern had to come. There was no one else he could trust, no one who had such a good chance to get through to Osidian.

He peered through the haze of myrrh smoke rising from censers into the corner of the chamber. Several times already he thought he had seen movement there. A smothered gleam that might have been a homunculus mask or the shadows coalescing into the sinister form of the Grand Sapient. Carnelian was frantic that Legions would escape. He wished he had had the presence of mind to look for other exits from the vault. He could go down there now, but he feared the Grand Sapient's voice, his logic, his power of command. He had no illusions. He had managed to withstand the Grand Sapient's arguments only because his mask of reasonableness had slipped momentarily to reveal the bleak mercilessness behind.

He glanced again towards the outer door. What was taking Fern so long? His gaze was drawn, unwillingly, back to the dark corner. He remembered the capsules. Those could not be native to this fortress. A creeping horror rose in him as he contemplated how the Grand Sapient might have travelled here in one. And who were his two companions? And was it a coincidence that he should have ended up occupying a chamber directly above the vault? He shuddered as again he imagined the Grand Sapient standing over him as he slept. Shuddered as he imagined those pale fingers touching him while he dreamed dark dreams.

When Fern entered, Carnelian could only stare. He seemed smaller than Carnelian remembered. A little older? He reminded himself that it was amazing Fern was there at all. The scars the fire had left on the side of his neck were like the baroquing on Ichorian armour. Carnelian wondered if it was the sartlar salve that had healed them so well. Though he could not see his shoulder and arm, Fern did not seem to him disfigured. Indeed, Carnelian was only too aware of how even the Leper shrouds could not conceal how well made he was.

'Kneel, barbarian,' an ammonite hissed.

Carnelian had forgotten the ammonites who had entered before Fern. He must remember where he was; who he was. He dismissed them with a harsh hand. They turned their masks to him, hesitated, but then retreated, bowing. He held his breath until they had left and closed the doors behind them. It was only then he became aware Fern was staring at him. He felt his gaze like a blow. His entire body reacted. He wanted so much to approach him, to touch him. The grim intensity in Fern's eyes would have been enough to stay him even had he not proceeded to reinforce the difference in their rank. 'Master.'

He did not even bow his head, so that the word had not a hint of subservience, but only a defiance that filled Carnelian with a wrenching fear for him. Brass glimmering at his throat was even worse. That collar proved Fern a deserter from the legions, which on its own rendered his life forfeit. Carnelian breathed deep, centring himself. The business he had summoned him for must be transacted as briskly as possible. 'I need you to go to the Master and take him a message.'

Grateful for Fern's tiny nod, Carnelian found he was re-membering how much Osidian hated him. Then there was the second agreement the Lepers had made with Osidian of which Carnelian knew nothing at all. 'Do you know of any new reason why it might be dangerous for you to go and see the Master?'

Fern's expression did not change. 'Should there be?'

'You know perfectly well how he feels about you!'

Fern scowled. 'He and I are certainly not the best of friends.'

Carnelian used the fear he felt for him to dowse his anger. He glanced into the dark corner, then, turning back, removed his mask. It was a risk, but he felt that if they did not talk man to man, they risked much more. 'Tell me what you know about this second agreement the Lepers have made with the Master.'

Fern's defiance softened and that, for some reason, relit Carnelian's anger. 'How can I help them unless I know what's going on?'

'They've come up to fight Aurum.'

341

'But the Master had already promised to give him to them.'

The corners of Fern's mouth tightened. 'He persuaded them that he could not succeed without their help.'

Carnelian felt there was more to it than that. 'He promised them something else, didn't he?'

Fern's gaze fell. 'He's promised them this city.'

'Makar?'

Fern looked at him again. 'He intends to let them sack it. They need some compensation for their losses,' Fern said, without much conviction.

'Surely they can see that will only make matters worse.' Carnelian was only too aware of the doom Legions had pronounced upon the Lepers.

'They made an agreement and mean to honour it.'

Carnelian recalled a meeting in one of the Leper caves between Osidian and Lily; how she had behaved at the time; her sudden disappearance.

'Honour is one of the few things they have left.' Fern must have sensed something of what Carnelian was feeling for he added: 'I tried to explain to her what had happened to the Tribe, but it was already too late, they had already made the agreement.'

Carnelian saw in Fern's face something of the hurt he must have felt when he had awoken to find himself abandoned. 'Are you fully healed?'

'Well enough.'

Silence fell between them as they shared understanding and sadness and, perhaps, some hopelessness too. Carnelian was reluctant to end that moment, which was the closest they had been for such a long time, but he knew he had to.

He began describing the threat he had discovered in the vault.

Fern's forehead creased. 'Legions?'

'That is his title, his name.'

Fern's eyebrows rose. 'And you say he's more dangerous than Aurum?'

As Carnelian nodded, Fern looked over to the dark corner of the chamber. He turned back. 'And this is the message you want me to take to the Master?'

Carnelian nodded and told him where Osidian was and how he could get there.

'All right.'

Carnelian felt pain that Fern asked nothing further. As Fern turned to leave, Carnelian moved forward, awkwardly, and touched his shoulder. 'I chose you because there's no one else I trust as much and no one else Osidian would believe.'

Without turning, Fern gave the merest nod and then began the journey back to the outer doors. Carnelian bound on his mask and through its eyeslits he watched him moving away, creating eddies in the myrrh smoke. His heart felt as if it was growing colder. The door opened. Fern went through. The door closed. Carnelian tried to convince himself it was better this way. Whatever was going to happen, they could never again be close. The greater the distance he maintained between them, the safer Fern would be.

He gazed back towards the corner with its tapestry and its secret stair down to the vault. It was hard to believe he would ever be able to prove the defiance he had thrown in the Grand Sapient's face to be anything more than empty bravado.

Carnelian came awake. His dream was a thorn. He shook his head, trying to dislodge it. He had only meant to lie down for a moment while he waited. Balancing on the edge of shadowy dream and waking, images from his nightmare uncurled in his memory as slowly as smoke. For some reason he was remembering the Marula in the Qunoth purgatory. Had he and Osidian not been there to calm them, they would have slain the ammonites.

He sat up suddenly. The quaestor had claimed that on that first day in Makar the Marula had apparently returned tamely to the cothon leaving him in the hands of the ammonites. Carnelian realized he had never fully determined what had happened then. Why had he not asked Sthax? Almost he rushed off to ask him there and then, but he sensed he knew everything he needed to already. He could remember entering the purgatory. Then he had woken here, late the next day, with the same headache he had now. Unease rose in him like nausea. Here, above the Grand Sapient's vault. Unease flared into a shocking realization. He had been entirely in Legions' power. A shudder went down his spine. With his own hand, the Grand Sapient had read the taint scars on his back. Carnelian saw it all. Aurum's ineffectual attack. The watch-towers signalling back to the city. He had been drugged. When Legions had discovered that it was not Osidian he had captured, he had made sure Carnelian would find him in the vault, calculating that he must then send for Osidian.

Legions wanted Osidian to come so that he could capture him. Blind with panic, Carnelian fumbled for his mask and ran for the outer door.

When, at last, he reached the gates of the purgatory, Carnelian asked Sthax to wait for him with the rest of the Marula they had brought with them from Aurum's halls. As Sthax talked to his people, Carnelian pulled the doors open. Smoke belched out from the darkness. Cries assailed him. Warnings. Threats. Paying them no heed, he plunged into the gloom. Light streaming in from the gaping doorway behind him found the silver faces of ammonites, the legs of tripods, the curving brass of censers. He kept going, aware of ammonites flitting round him. A glance back showed him the Marula as silhouettes in the doorway. His vision gradually returning, he saw smoke forming blue scythes in the air. He could feel the drug seep into him. His vision was swimming. Was that a huge shrouded body stretched out upon the floor? Ammonites were huddled over it like crows over a corpse. As Carnelian lurched towards it, their masks came up and they backed away, shrilling. It *was* a body on the floor; a body swathed in Leper shrouds. At first Carnelian thought it must be Fern, but then

344

he saw a sliver of a Master's mask in the half-closed cowl. It had to be Osidian. Carnelian could feel the drug creeping into his mind. Soon it would overcome him. The smell of blood. A dark shape lay beached on the floor some distance away. What little light there was caught on the long-limbed form of a Marula warrior; a dark pool spreading over the floor from under him. Ammonites were forming a barrier between Carnelian and Osidian, swinging thick strokes of poisoned smoke towards him.

'Murderers!' he cried, shoving into their midst, hurling them aside like dolls. Censers clattered to the floor. He reached the shrouded body, reeling. Stooping, he dug his arms under it and, with a groan, swung it up and over his shoulder. Then he staggered towards the wavering incandescence of the door. Ammonites moved to stand in his path. Hysterical with alarm, they wove drugged smoke around him. With his free hand he scooped up a tripod and, swinging it, struck. A clang as a mask flew off. That cleared a path to the open air. Loping, now, he reached it. Light engulfed him. He managed several more steps then stumbled, crying out for fear of hurting Osidian. As he fell onto one knee, he felt the burden lifting off him. He was choking. The mask would not let him breathe. He had good reason to know the risk, but feared he might lose consciousness. So he tore his mask off and gulped fresh air.

As his mind began to clear, he rose, turning. Ammonites streaming out from the purgatory collided with those who were standing motionless. Though they were masked, the stiffness of their poses betrayed their terror. Some had stains darkening the skirts of their robes. Through the eyeslits of their masks they were gazing upon his naked face. Sthax and his Marula too were in breach of the Law. It was a choice between the ammonites and the warriors. He was struck momentarily by pity, but then he remembered the Maruli lying in his own blood. Frowning, he made a sign to Sthax and his men, one they could not help but understand, then pointed at the ammonites. As the Marula advanced on them with lowered lances, the ammonites began keening. Carnelian forced himself to watch their massacre.

Osidian came awake, frowning.

'Where's Fern?' Carnelian demanded. Waiting for Osidian to recover he, Sthax and the other Marula had had time to drag all the bodies they could find in the purgatory out into the open air. There had been more than twenty Marula with their throats cut, but no sign of Fern.

Osidian's frown deepened as he focused on Carnelian's face. His eyes widened. 'We're unmasked!'

'There are none left alive to see our faces save for the Marula and to them our faces are nothing new.'

Osidian glowered. 'Blood and iron, what is going on?'

'Fern?' Carnelian almost barked at him.

As Osidian regarded him, Carnelian saw in his face that old familiar pain. 'He is safe enough, Carnelian. I left him commanding Heart-of-Thunder in my place.' He lifted his arms to show the dirty Leper shroud. 'While I came here in his.'

Carnelian found this news alarming. 'Do the other commanders know you have left?'

Osidian shrugged. 'If things go badly they might find out.'

Carnelian saw how precarious things were, but then what had he expected when he had sent his message to Osidian?

'Tell me what has happened. Why am I lying here?'

Carnelian told him about the drugged smoke; the destruction of the ammonites; Legions' plot against them.

'You are sure it is Legions himself?'

Carnelian described the finial on his domain staff and Osidian's face went pale, his eyes blinded by thought. He shook his head in wonder. 'Only this morning I chose to reveal myself to the Wise by heliograph. I was awaiting their reply when Fern came with your message.' He shook his head again. 'It was hard to believe.'

'But still you came.'

346

Osidian focused on Carnelian. 'So it is to you, once again, that I owe my salvation.'

Carnelian spoke quickly to quench the light of love that was stirring in Osidian's eyes. 'The Grand Sapient tried to buy me. Had he promised to spare the barbarians, I would have given you to him.'

Sadness returned to Osidian's face. He lowered his gaze. 'He would never promise you that. He could not.' He looked up. 'So you continue to fight at my side?'

'As you said, did I not just save you from falling into his power?'

'Don't expect me to make war, Carnelian, without your precious barbarians suffering casualties.'

'As long as you don't deliberately cause them to be hurt.'

Osidian held Carnelian's gaze. 'We understand each other?'

Carnelian gave him a nod. 'Release the Lepers from their agreement.'

Osidian made a gesture of negation. 'I cannot. We need them.'

Carnelian saw there was no moving him. He had not expected to, but had had to try.

'What did you tell him?' Osidian said.

Carnelian related what he could remember of his conversation with Legions.

'Nothing more?'

'I wasn't feeling very chatty.'

Osidian seemed blind again. Carnelian watched the muscles working in his jaw as he rehearsed what he would say to the Grand Sapient.

The Grand Sapient was in the vault. In the lamplight he appeared to Carnelian exactly as he had before. Displayed upright in his capsule, seemingly no more alive than a mummy, his homunculus between his legs. As Osidian unmasked Carnelian did the same. Revealed, Osidian's rapt expression was difficult to read. Wonder tinged with awe, but there was something else. Carnelian nursed an emerging impression, then realized, with shock, what it must be. Love.

'It *is* you, Legions,' said Osidian.

The homunculus murmured behind its blinding mask. Legions' fingers worked its neck and throat. 'It is, Celestial.'

'I feared we would never meet again, my Lord.'

'We shared your fear.'

Osidian gazed up at the Grand Sapient. 'You searched for me with your childgatherers, but I made sure to remain well hidden, never guessing you would send a legion. That I had not imagined possible.'

'We have often had to transcend the possible.'

'But to send the Lord Aurum, surely that was a terrible risk?'

They waited for Legions to take the sounds from the homunculus' throat.

'To use one of the Lesser Chosen would have been no less a risk, Celestial. Besides, we had used him before. He was an instrument who came easily to hand.'

Carnelian wondered if he meant that it was the Wise who had been behind sending Aurum to fetch his father from exile.

'My brother knows nothing of this?' Osidian said.

'Nothing.'

'That you have come yourself, my Lord, suggests your mind was primary in this affair. It suggests also the Wise are desperate.'

'It was Suth who kept from us the knowledge of your disappearance until it was too late. Our trust in him led us into error and left us exposed to your mother.'

Though the voice of the homunculus was free from emotion, Carnelian sensed the menace in Legions' words. So it was not only Ykoriana who had been his father's enemy. Carnelian would have challenged the Grand Sapient, but Osidian, sensing this, stayed him by touching his arm. As the homunculus continued, Osidian gave Carnelian a look of reassurance.

'She forced us to gift the City at the Gates to the Brotherhood of the Wheel.'

'She dared parade her guilt before you thus?'

Once he had understood that, Legions turned his eyepits on Carnelian. 'Without evidence, we could not touch her. Suth's sin had made her invulnerable. Though that brought him no gratitude from her.'

Carnelian would no longer be restrained. 'So you aided her against him?'

'It was she who had the Clave impeach him. We merely did not raise a finger to defend him.'

'Aurum was as much her enemy,' said Osidian.

'She commuted his deposal to exile, Celestial.'

'Why, my Lord?'

'Our thought combined has not yet been able to deduce a reason.'

'My mother is given neither to whim nor mercy.'

'Some factor is missing from our computations.'

Osidian frowned at this. Either he was disturbed by this failing of the Wise, or else he sensed the Grand Sapient was keeping something from him. 'And how did you persuade Aurum to do your bidding?'

'It has been our experience' – the eyepits glanced towards Carnelian again – 'that those of the Great will do almost anything to regain entrance to Osrakum.'

Osidian regarded Legions with a fixed concentration. 'It seems, my Lord, we have the same enemies, the same goals.'

Once the homunculus had echoed these words, they waited, but Legions' fingers remained so still that the homunculus could have been wearing a collar carved from alabaster.

Osidian looked up at Legions, uncertain. 'Join with me, my Lord, give me back the Masks. Once I am They, I will rid you of my mother . . . and make you other concessions besides . . .'

The alabaster fingers came alive. 'Surely, child, you know that what you ask is beyond our power to grant. You have been too long in the wilderness, too long free. Even I am a slave to the Law-that-must-be-obeyed and what you ask you must surely know the Law forbids.'

'But now that your scheme to take me captive has failed you cannot hope to keep your plotting concealed from her and, once she and Osrakum know of that, the power the Wise have to counter hers will be seriously diminished.'

'I am curious: what caused my scheme to fail?'

'Carnelian . . .' Osidian turned, puzzled, to Carnelian. 'How did you know . . . ?'

Carnelian shrugged. 'I was warned of it in a dream.'

Osidian looked incredulous. 'A dream?'

'A dream?' echoed the homunculus.

Carnelian and Osidian turned back to the Grand Sapient. 'Have there been other dreams of warning, Suth Carnelian?'

Carnelian felt uneasy at having become the object of the Grand Sapient's interest. His thought became tangled as he tried to work out what to say. In the end it seemed easier to simply state the truth. 'There have been others.'

'What does it matter? It did fail!' cried Osidian. 'And without me you are exposed to my mother.'

The Grand Sapient seemed to have withered back to a corpse. Carnelian's unease grew. He turned to Osidian for help, but was shaken by how young he looked, how helpless. Osidian's face sagged into anguish. 'It was I, not my brother, who was elected to wear the Masks. Surely my mother's plot cannot be allowed to overturn the expressed will of the Chosen?'

As the homunculus echoed Osidian's words, Carnelian regarded Osidian with increasing horror. After everything he had done, after all his claims, he appeared now to be merely a child demanding fairness.

'Once made, the Gods cannot be unmade,' said the homunculus.

Osidian seemed close to tears, exhausted. 'I too was anointed with blood. The God came to me not once, but many times. He spoke to me. He acted through me. I am His instrument.'

Carnelian felt his horror turning to contempt. He expected the Grand Sapient to swat Osidian with more relentless logic, but was disappointed when, instead, the homunculus began to question him, probing his claims. He watched the interrogation, incredulous that the Grand Sapient could be finding anything of interest in Osidian's deranged beliefs. Then, as Osidian unwound their story, Carnelian became mesmerized with fear that Osidian was betraying the Plainsmen, then the Marula. Carnelian reassured himself, first that Legions knew most of this already, then that the Marula were most likely already lost and, finally that, come what may, the Grand Sapient was in their power; that whatever Legions was learning from Osidian they would make sure he would remain unable to communicate it back to his brethren in Osrakum.

Osidian was done. He gazed up expectantly at the Grand Sapient. The homunculus spoke. 'I do not deny the signs, the portents, but they change nothing, Celestial.'

The change that came upon Osidian's face Carnelian had had reason many times to fear. 'We shall see if the rest of the Twelve shall be as intransigent as you, my Lord.'

'How do you imagine, Celestial, that you will fare better with them who are free, than you have with me, who am your prisoner?'

Osidian's eyes burned. 'Then I shall march upon Osrakum.'

Legions lowered his head, causing his eyepits to flood with shadow that poured down to his lipless mouth. 'You hope to overthrow the Commonwealth with a single legion?'

Osidian looked round as if for allies, but Carnelian was in no mood to give him support. Osidian looked up into the dark curves of the ceiling as if searching for something. Then his gaze returned to the Grand Sapient. 'I will enfranchise the Lesser Chosen and they will follow me to the Three Gates.'

The leather of Legions' face formed into an expression that might have been contempt. 'And how do you imagine you will communicate with them?'

Osidian's face reddened. 'No doubt, my Lord, you did not come here without reconfiguring the watch-towers to your needs. It would profit you nothing to be here more blind, more mute than if you had remained in Osrakum.'

The horned-ring was lost in Legions' frown. 'After your message reached the first few legions, we would lock down the system. Isolated, the commanders would not dare rise.'

Legions loomed forward, his fingers digging instructions into the neck of the homunculus. 'Do you really believe, child, that even with a dozen legions you could overcome our systems? You would dash yourself ineffectually upon the cliff of our defence. Why do you think we have named this the Guarded Land? However many legions you might gather to your rebellion, we would have more. The web of roads has been constructed to our specifications. Their walls dissect the Land and bind it. Our towers give us the vision of the Gods Themselves. Through them we speak with light, faster than the wind.

'And even should you break through the host that we would muster against you, have you forgotten the Three Gates? A thousand years have we had to perfect them. No force in the Three Lands could hope to breach them.'

The evident truth of this overwhelmed Carnelian, who had seen the Gates with his own eyes. He had watched Osidian bend beneath the weight of the Grand Sapient's statements. It seemed incredible that Osidian should find any more resistance, but he did. He looked up. 'I could rule at my brother's side.'

The Grand Sapient regarded them with his dead face, his fingers mute. Osidian's gaze clung to that face. 'Are we not twins like the Gods? Was I not marked for the Black God as Molochite was for the Green?'

The silence stretched, then, at last, the homunculus spoke.

'Long ago were the Two made One. It is upon this foundation that the Balance of the Powers stands. You know this.'

Seeing Osidian defeated, so drained, Carnelian felt almost unable to breathe. So much death, so much pain; for what? So that their rebellion should simply run dry? He had to release some of his bile. 'And what of you, my Lord Legions? Why should we not slay you?'

A languor came over the Grand Sapient that, strangely, made him seem more alive. 'It would profit you nothing. My brethren would simply elect another to stand in my place.'

As Osidian began to move away, Carnelian stood for some moments gazing at the Grand Sapient. At that moment, Legions did not seem a monster, but only a mutilated man. Carnelian knew what tyranny the Wise were responsible for but, seeing Legions powerless, he could not help feeling pity, though even that seeped away. Empty of all feeling, he turned and, taking the light away with him, followed Osidian.

Behind him an unhuman voice spoke. 'Ultimately, only the Commonwealth is immortal.'

Carnelian caught up with Osidian in Aurum's bedchamber. Seeing his dull eyes, his face still flushed, Carnelian's heart sank. If Osidian had lost his will to fight, it was all over. In spite of Sthax, Morunasa and the Marula were sure to become unmanageable. Worse, the Lesser Chosen commanders would desert. Poppy, Fern, Lily and the Lepers, all would be left exposed to the full wrath of the Masters. He could see the fire, could smell the blood and crucifixions. He stared at Osidian, realizing with shocked amazement how much he had come to rely on his relentless drive for revenge. It had become such a solid part of his world that, without knowing it, he had built all his strategies on it.

'Things are not hopeless,' his voice said.

Osidian's eyes remained dull. Carnelian had to lead them back to solid ground. 'We still have a legion. A city. In spite of anything the Grand Sapient said, it is we who have him in our power.'

Life came back into Osidian's face, then an expression of exasperation. 'Have you still not understood? This chamber, this fortress, the whole of the Guarded Land, all have been fashioned by the sort of mind down there.' He began wringing his hands. 'They were the basis of all my hope. They ratified my election.' He glanced at Carnelian, looking child-like, frightened. 'And it was obvious how much they were prepared to risk to unseat my mother.'

Carnelian searched around for something he could say that would reassure Osidian, but Legions' logic seemed inescapable. That made him boil. 'For all his wisdom, the Grand Sapient is still a man and, like all other men, he is prey to fear. He knows we have the power to do what we will with him. Cornered, is it any surprise he should have said the things he did?'

Osidian frowned, but gazed at Carnelian, hungry for more.

'You left the watch-tower, my Lord, before receiving a reply from Osrakum. Surely the rest of the Twelve will be nervous. At any moment the other two Powers could discover what they have been up to. At this moment of crisis they can have, at the very best, an imperfect idea of what is going on here. They probably know they have lost a legion. Perhaps they know we hold Makar. But, worst of all, they will have lost contact with he who among them is the master of their defence. Perhaps they already fear we have him in our power. If they do not, you could confirm this.'

'Wouldn't they just elect a replacement?' said Osidian, shifting into Vulgate.

'Perhaps, but consider how reluctant they might be to do that. The Gods know how long he's been the mind that's shaped the defences of the Commonwealth, but I warrant it must have been a considerable time. Is it likely that in such a crisis they'd wish to put their trust in someone less experienced? For the moment at least they're likely to hesitate and, surely, such hesitation is a weakness we can exploit?'

Carnelian could see the embers of belief he had rekindled in Osidian's eyes. 'With less leverage your mother managed to bend them to her will.'

Osidian observed him. 'But dare I go to the watch-tower leaving Legions unwatched?'

Carnelian felt trapped. Every moment that passed exposed Fern to discovery by the Lesser Chosen commanders. Never mind the disaster that would ensue should Aurum return. Osidian had to return to the dragons immediately. Carnelian knew what this was going to take. He tried to keep dismay from his face and voice as he said: 'I'll deal with Legions.'

Osidian looked uncertain. 'How?' He gazed at the floor as if he were trying to see through it. 'I know more about them than perhaps they suspect, but I'm not fool enough to imagine I know a fraction of their secrets. Who knows what powers Legions may have to wield against us?'

Carnelian put on a smile. 'Much of the power of the Wise comes from the awe in which they are held. Can you think of anyone in the Three Lands who's less likely to be impressed than I?'

Osidian regarded him with a frown, thin hope warring with doubt. At last he shook his head. 'Have it your own way.'

As he masked, Carnelian copied him with relief. Behind his mask he could release his face into what he knew must be an expression of near despair.

As he opened the door leading to the vault, Carnelian was overwhelmed by an odour that, for some reason, made him recall his wounded father. It was only myrrh. He could see its smoke creeping up the steps. He listened out for what might be happening below. Though he feared it might be sorcery he dared not give in to that fear. If anything, it was even more reason for him to confront it. He began a careful descent of the stair.

Smoke hung like mist in the vault, pierced by rays emanating from some lamp. Creeping towards the light he began to see a small figure hunched before Legions' open capsule. Within its hollow stood the Grand Sapient, arms folded across his chest, ribbed bands across his abdomen, thighs and shins holding him fast. His face seemed a skull set above his cadaverous frame. Carnelian dared go no further. As he watched, the homunculus raised a bowl to the Grand Sapient's groin from which liquid began emanating in a stream. For a moment Carnelian was startled by the thought that Legions was a woman. Then, with disgusted fascination, he recalled that the Wise were castrated. It had not occurred to him the mutilation might be so complete. Feeling he was observing something shameful and forbidden, he wished to retreat. Such delicacy was inappropriate. When the Grand Sapient ceased urinating the homunculus stooped to put the bowl down. One of his master's arms unfolded and its four-fingered hand reached out, questing. Seeing it, the homunculus clambered up into the capsule, raising its chin to facilitate the coiling of its master's fingers around its throat. Its gaze found Carnelian and it began murmuring. A shiver went up his spine as he felt that Legions was looking at him through the creature's eyes. The murmuring ceased. The pale fingers moved. The homunculus spoke. 'I have already been too long awake.'

Carnelian stared, not knowing what to say. The fingers released the homunculus and the arm folded back across the Grand Sapient's chest. With a gloved hand, the homunculus reached into an array of amber beads set into the rim of the capsule. It plucked one out and, clambering up the capsule, it touched the bead to Legions' lipless mouth, which opened to receive it.

As the homunculus climbed back down to the floor, Carnelian crept to its side. 'How often does that drug need to be administered?'

Stooping to retrieve something from the shadows, the homunculus rose to regard him with its old man's eyes. 'Every day, Seraph.' It raised the thing it had in its hands. A silver mask from whose single eye gleaming tears ran down the long tapering cheek. As the homunculus adjusted the mechanisms on its reverse, Carnelian peered at the creature, reassuring himself it was fully detached from its master. It seemed unnatural that it should be speaking on its own behalf. 'You will do this every day for him?'

The homunculus shook its head and indicated the triangular space between the Grand Sapient's legs. 'Normally I sleep there, with my master. Ammonites administer the elixir, overseen by a Sapient of Immortality.' The homunculus regarded the chamber with hooded eyes. 'We dare not entrust my masters to the ammonites here.' He made a gesture asking Carnelian for permission to disengage from their conversation. At Carnelian's nod, the creature scaled the capsule again. He leaned in to peer at his master's face. 'He sleeps.' He placed the mask carefully over the skull face, fitting the mechanisms into the cavities. He pressed the mask back, and its crowning lunar crescent gripped the central sphere of three that were set beneath the upper rim of the capsule and hung above Legions' brow like planets.

Back on the floor, the homunculus closed the lid of the capsule. Legions formed a dark core in the ivory vessel. The homunculus raised a stick of wax and melted some to fall into a circular recess on the edge of the lid. Then he pressed a seal into it. Carnelian craned over the creature and saw the impression of a cross that had been left in the wax. The nearer of the other two capsules was similarly sealed. 'Is that to protect him?'

The homunculus jumped, startled, and did not calm down until Carnelian had backed away. 'It shows who was responsible for the last feeding, Seraph.'

'You have sole responsibility for the Grand Sapient?'

'And for his servants, Seraph.'

'Who are they?'

'His Seconds, Seraph.'

Carnelian did not understand what the creature meant. Something else sprang to mind. 'Will they wake?'

'Only when the effect of the elixir wears off, Seraph.'

'How long will that be?'

The little man frowned. 'Around midday tomorrow. I shall have to feed them then.'

Carnelian could not believe his luck. It seemed his problem of overseeing the Grand Sapient had solved itself. 'You will come with me.'

The homunculus paled and his eyes widened. 'Seraph, my master has bidden me guard his sleep.'

'You can stand guard upstairs, but, henceforth, you will remain always at my side.'

Carnelian saw how fearful the creature was. He began walking back towards the stair. Not hearing footfalls following him he turned. 'Obey me,' he said, putting an edge into his voice that all not Chosen were right to fear. Reluctantly, the homunculus obeyed.

In the bedchamber, head bowed, its mask hanging from its hand, the homunculus seemed so like a child Carnelian found he was beginning to feel paternal towards it, but then it looked up. That wizened face was not a child's, nor its ancient, rheumy eyes.

Carnelian looked away. Finally, he had time to think. His mind blanked. He tried to focus on the issues, but his attention kept slipping from them. Exhaustion washed over him. Feeling under observation by the homunculus, he yearned to be alone. He glanced towards the outer door. Dare he trust the creature to the care of Aurum's household? He preferred to keep it where he could see it: the homunculus was the key that kept the Sapients locked in sleep, safe within their capsules.

He longed for the oblivion of sleep, but once he was asleep who was there to stop the creature creeping back to its master's side? He imagined the Grand Sapient, woken, coming up the stairs to loom over him as he dreamed. He shuddered and looked around for some solution to the problem. In the end he dragged some feather blankets into the corner and made himself a bed in front of the door to the vault. He told the homunculus that it would have to find itself a place to sleep. The creature bowed low, then crept away into the gloomiest part of the chamber. Standing over his makeshift bed Carnelian watched it make a nest. This arrangement would have to do.

'I am about to unmask,' he announced. The homunculus immediately put on its blinding mask. Carnelian hesitated. The silver child face was staring at him across the room more intently than had the homunculus' own. He turned his back on the creature and released his mask with a sigh of relief. It was a struggle to free himself from his robes. He did this all as quietly as he could. At one stage, he realized how ridiculous he must look and could not help laughing. The sound echoed around the chamber. When he was free he slipped under a blanket, his heart beating as he listened for any furtive sounds the homunculus might be making.

As silence settled he fell victim to misery. He was playing a game he did not believe he could win, for stakes he could not bear to lose. The Grand Sapient had made it clear what would happen should he and Osidian admit defeat. Only an outright victory over the Commonwealth would give him any chance of stopping the Wise meting out retribution upon his loved ones, upon all those others who were already victims of what he and Osidian had brought about – but could he hope for such an implausible outcome when even Osidian no longer believed it possible? And even were they to continue doing what they could to widen their rebellion, would this not serve only to bring more innocents under the shadow of inevitable punishment?

These arguments swung back and forth in his mind like the pendulums of Aurum's clocks. Back and forth. Back and forth. Until he became a slave to the click of the escapements and, weary to his bones, he hung suspended in despair, denied the comfort of sleep.

*   *   *

Akaisha, bloated, her dear face ochred for burial. Earth, or is it dried blood, on his hands? 'Eat me,' she sighs, fire peeling her skin. Carnelian breaks off a charred curl and puts it into his mouth. Too salty. Tears, perhaps? Flames in a black mirror find the contours of a face. A mask with green eyes. He fits his face into the hollow. Sees an emerald lagoon. Breathes with rapture its mossy air. Green water laps at white feet. He looks up. Osidian sitting on a throne. A black living face in his left hand, a green in his right. Osidian's own, lifeless, eyeless. The pits well tears. Wet on his lips. Tasting the sea. Liquid-iron blood running down white legs into the ebb. Roaring makes him turn to see a cliff of it avalanching to drown them all.

Carnelian came awake, gulping, tasting iron in his mouth. He sat up, choking, and spat blood into his hands. He rolled his tongue, making sure he had not bitten it through, swallowed it.

'Seraph?' The homunculus was there with its metal child's face. It called again from the other side of its blinding mask as if it were a door.

Carnelian reassured the creature. 'Bit my tongue in my sleep.' His voice was distorted by his swollen tongue.

In his mind's eye, Osidian sat eyeless on a throne, the Masks of the God Emperor in his hands. Carnelian could not rid himself of the conviction that he had had such dreams before and had always ignored their warnings. Why were his dreams always awash with blood? He could still taste its metal in his mouth. Osidian enthroned, but eyeless like the Wise. Why had Akaisha wanted him to eat her? He had to think clearly. At any time, Osidian might lose his grip on the Lesser Chosen commanders. The memory of what had happened to the Ochre unmanned him. He could not bear making such a mistake again. He dared not act until he was certain.

He sought distraction in some books he found. The titles were uninspiring. It seemed that Aurum was interested in nothing but war and intrigue. Dry treatises on strategy and manuals written for the Lesser Chosen by the Wise on correct legionary operation were only marginally alleviated by memoirs of Lords of the Great that were all about the minutiae of Clave politics, blood-trading and the elegant exercise of power over minions.

Abandoning these, he fell back into turmoil. At one point he determined to quit Makar and go to meet Osidian, but immediately his mind began listing the difficulties in getting there and the vital reasons why he should not go. Besides, what would he say to Osidian once he reached him? He feared sharing his dreams with him.

Then he remembered the interest Legions had shown in his dreams. If anyone could interpret them it would be the Grand Sapient. Madness. Any such consultation would lead only to manipulation. Legions would tell him what he wanted to hear.

Back and forth the battle raged in him, between doubt and hope. As he grew weary almost to tears, the vision of Osidian eyeless, enthroned, hung in his mind like an ache.

When the homunculus came to ask if he might go down to minister to his masters and their homunculi, Carnelian saw from one of Aurum's clocks that it was long past nightfall. The sun-eye hidden beneath the iron earth seemed a defeat. A whole day had passed and still he was as trapped in indecision as a fly in amber. The opportunity to accompany the homunculus was a blessed relief. At least it gave him something to do. Something real.

In the vault, the first lid they opened was Legions'. When the homunculus climbed up to remove his mask, Carnelian saw the faint misting in the mirrored hollow above the mouth spike. His gaze fell on the Grand Sapient's skull face. He wondered at the mind behind such hideousness and was tortured by the temptation that it might make the solution to his problems clear, shedding upon his dilemma the terrible, cool clarity of the Wise.

He was glad when he saw the elixir bead melt into the lipless mouth and was relieved when Legions' skull face was rehidden behind the shell of his mask. The homunculus closed and resealed the capsule. Each of the other two capsules contained not only a Sapient, but also a homunculus. Carnelian made sure to observe that all were fed an amber bead. He plucked a bead from its cavity on the capsule rim. When he brought it up to the nostrils of his mask, he could detect no odour. The eyes of the homunculus had grown round. Amused by the creature's alarm, Carnelian made a smiling gesture. 'I had no intention to eat it.' He replaced it where he had found it and the homunculus closed the capsule.

'What does it contain?'

'Mostly nectar, Seraph.'

'To mask the bitterness of the elixir?'

Busy sealing the lid, the homunculus shook its head. 'I do not imagine so, Seraph. My masters cannot taste sweetness. I believe its function is to supply the necessary sustenance.'

Leaving the Sapients and homunculi sleeping in their cocoons, they climbed the stair. As Carnelian came up into the chamber, he felt the vision of his dream coalescing around an interpretation he realized he had been resisting all day. Lying on his makeshift bed staring at the ceiling, he could no longer deny that, whatever else the dream might portend, one part of it seemed clear enough. Wading through blood, Osidian would win a throne, but how much blood and whose?

He came fully awake as if washing ashore. The ritual windings clung to him like flayed skin. He longed to escape their sickly embrace, to feel clean sun on his bare back, his face, to have the wind caress his skin. More, he wanted to be free of the dreams. Their omens oppressed him like the pressure of a coming storm. He had preferred hopelessness to a promise of a victory bought at the cost of the Gods only knew how much suffering.

He had crossed and recrossed this territory so many times

that it had become a churned sump. What chance was there to pick a single path through such a morass?

He needed to externalize it; to talk to someone. There was no one, except perhaps Osidian, and Carnelian knew, with a bleak certainty, that his dreams would almost certainly mesh with the bloody conviction Osidian drew from his dark god.

He rose from the bed, fumbled and found his mask, ignored the homunculus' questions and went in search of a window. Even the night sky might restore him to some balance.

When he found some shutters he drew them back and was blinded. Squinting, he went out into the light. The sun was risen. He could feel its touch beginning to warm the gold against his cheeks. The land's bony limestone blazed in the morning, but shades of night still haunted the Pass below.

Returning to the shadows, Carnelian considered what he could do. When he contemplated a visit to Osidian, anxiety pulled like a barb in his flesh. Dare he leave Legions unsupervised? A feeling of being trapped produced a surge of anger. Why not kill him and his staff and be done with it? Dread soaked into him. At first he thought it was horror at the idea of slaying even a Sapient in his sleep, but he decided it was something else. Some kind of superstitious fear. The kind that thrills a child at the unknown consequences of killing a sorcerer in a fairytale. There were good reasons against a meeting with Osidian, in any case. Not least how they affected each other. Besides, there were many practical difficulties.

A letter? It would not be difficult to obtain parchment, pen and ink, but once written, how could he convey it safely to Osidian? Sealed, even the quaestor might not dare open it, but he had no seal.

His cogitations were cut short by a rapping at the outer door. He put his mask to his face and bade the homunculus go and see who it was. The creature was soon back. 'The quaestor, Seraph. He claims to have a letter for you.'

Carnelian was startled by the coincidence. 'Let him come.'

363

The homunculus returned with the quaestor, who came forward, inscrutable. Carnelian took the parchment the man offered with both hands. Raising it, he saw it was unsealed. He turned his mask on the quaestor. 'You read this?'

The man fell to his knees, shaking his head. Carnelian opened the parchment. The glyphs were Osidian's. They read:

Send me that which will allow me to communicate with those who would follow me.

'Quaestor, who brought this?' Carnelian said.

The man did not raise his eyes, but said: 'A Maruli, Seraph.'

'He waits for a reply?'

'Just so, Seraph.'

Carnelian read the letter again and thought he understood: Osidian wanted Legions' seal. Using it might enable him to send messages along the roads to the Legates. After what the Grand Sapient had said, this seemed an act of desperation. Carnelian grew morose as what little faith he had in Osidian waned further. Not that he had an alternative strategy. All he had was dreams. He felt sick with self-disgust. He looked down at the quaestor. 'Go.'

The man turned up his number-spotted face. 'Your answer, Seraph?'

'I said, go.'

Carnelian felt drained. Since he could think of nothing better, he might as well do as Osidian asked. He decided against asking the homunculus for the ring. Once before he had asked someone for a seal and that had brought her a terrible death. He found a lamp and lit it. 'Stay here,' he said to the homunculus.

As the creature knelt, Carnelian headed towards the corner of the chamber.

'Seraph!' said the homunculus.

Turning, Carnelian saw how the colour had drained from its wizened face. 'I intend your masters no harm.'

He left the creature kneeling on the stone and descended to the vault. When he reached it, he made his way to Legions' capsule. Finding a grip on the lid, he pulled it back, breaking the wax seal. He raised the lantern so that its light crept up the Grand Sapient. He jumped when gleams in his silver mask made it seem as if Legions was waking. He searched every part of the capsule he could reach, but found nothing save for the cavities in which were stored the elixir.

'What do you seek, Seraph?'

Carnelian spun round and saw that, in defiance of his command, the homunculus had followed him. 'Your master's seal. Tell me where it is.'

Pale as alabaster, the homunculus climbed the capsule and, leaning across, he worked at opening one of his master's fists. When he had clambered back down, he offered Carnelian something that glimmered luridly upon his palm. Carnelian stared at the ring, reluctant to touch it.

'Take it, Seraph. My punishment is already unavoidable. My master appointed me guardian of his sleep.'

Carnelian saw the sharp determination in those ancient eyes and took the ring. As he watched the homunculus reseal the capsule, Carnelian wondered at the little man's motives for helping him.

Back in Aurum's chamber, Carnelian raised the ring and turned it in the light. An exquisitely carved ruby set in a bezel of precious iron. The head of the Horned God wrought as if into a large blood drop. Filigrees of rust bled from the fiery jewel.

Carnelian read his letter through one last time. It described his dream. He folded the parchment carefully. He placed a wax frame over the join and filled it with spluttering gobbets of molten wax. He thrust the Ring of Legions into the wax, then pulled it free. Lifting the letter, he saw that the seal looked like the arms of a crucifixion cross. The wax ridges had a look of branded flesh.

He closed the still warm ring in his fist and sent the homunculus to return with any Maruli who was not the first to approach him. When the man came Carnelian was relieved to see he was not Sthax. Sthax was, potentially, too valuable an ally to risk bringing to Osidian's or Morunasa's attention.

Carnelian gestured the Maruli to approach and offered him the letter. When the man reached out to take it, Carnelian caught hold of his hand and thrust into it Legions' ring. He forced the black fingers to close around it. The Maruli gazed up into Carnelian's mask, grimacing. Still holding the man's hand, Carnelian made him take the letter with his other hand.

'The Kissed,' he said, using the name they called Osidian. He would not let the Maruli go until he had repeated the name.

Carnelian had hoped that the sending of the letter and the ring would bring him peace of mind. Far from it. He fretted until it was time to accompany the homunculus down to the vault to administer the elixir. When they returned, he had something to eat. Upon a floor of mother of pearl he sat surrounded by the quivering of Aurum's clocks. The homunculus sat nearby with his silver child's face. Carnelian realized he was chewing carefully so that the creature would not hear him. He had tried to make conversation, but the silver mask had responded with single syllables.

Though wary of his dreams, he retired early. When he woke, he could recall nothing save perhaps for a lingering dread, like the taint blood left in the air even after it had been wiped away. The day stretched interminably. He tried to distract himself with books, with examining the treasures Aurum had left behind. Their beauty was cold and sterile. They seemed tomb goods which he fingered as if he were a soul denied rest. He was waiting for some communication from Osidian. His wanderings several times took him near the outer doors. He lingered in their vicinity, yearning for them to be struck from without.

That night he woke drenched in sweat. He had the impression he had been trying to climb up out of a pit. He lay trapped between the nightmare and waking as if between two walls of glass. When he could bear it no longer, he slid from the bed, then paced back and forth, harried by fear. A glint catching his eye drew him. It was the mask of the homunculus. The creature's child body lay slight and fragile on the floor. Dull in the dim light, its metal face seemed a device of torture. Carnelian tried to imagine what the creature's life had been like. Asleep, the homunculus appeared a child uncared for. Carnelian stooped and pulled a blanket over the blades of its shoulders.

A clanging echo made him lurch upright. He had been waiting for that sound, it seemed, for days. As the homunculus went off towards the outer doors, it was all Carnelian could do not to run after it. He waited, kneading his fingers. The homunculus seemed a long time returning. Then it appeared, bearing a letter. He waited for the creature to kneel and offer it to him. Taking it, he saw it was sealed with the curved crucifix of Legions' ring. He broke it open, unfolded the panels and read.

For days the Wise have refused to reply to my communications. Now they have closed down both the courier and the heliograph systems. They have left me no choice. Tomorrow I march against Aurum. Hold Makar for me. If your dream was true, you will have no need to fear for me.

Carnelian regarded the glyphs. Each face seemed Osidian's. A host of them, defiance in every eye. It seemed his letter had had a stronger effect even than he had hoped. Osidian sought to regain his certainty in the way he had done before: by making war. In battle there was no room for doubt, but only the struggle for victory. Carnelian felt no triumph. He did feel some relief but, mostly, exhaustion. While he waited, far from danger, those he loved would go to confront Aurum and his fire.

'Bad news, Seraph?'

Carnelian gazed down at the homunculus. His first impulse was to deny it any answer, but he could see no malice in its ancient eyes, only curiosity.

'The Lord Nephron marches forth to make war upon the Lord Aurum.'

'I see,' said the homunculus, leaving Carnelian with an uneasy impression it was playing a game of its own.

INCUBATING

Most things grow from the dark.
(from the 'Book of the Sorcerers')

'How did you come into the service of the Grand Sapient?' Carnelian asked.

The homunculus glanced at him with its ancient eyes. 'My master chose me, Seraph.'

'From the flesh tithe?'

The homunculus looked shocked. 'None of the Twelve would so demean himself, Seraph, least of all my master. A minor Sapient of the Domain of Tribute selected me with others for the training.'

The homunculus glanced up again at Carnelian, who said nothing, waiting for more. The creature continued. 'A candidate needs long training before he can become a homunculus.'

'How long?' Carnelian asked.

The homunculus made a non-committal gesture with its hands. 'It depends on the candidate. There are many skills to be learned, many procedures to be survived.'

'Procedures?'

Carnelian detected some memory of pain in its face.

'Each candidate, Seraph, must be fed the stunting drug.' It indicated its body, as diminutive as a child's. Wrinkles

369

gathered around its eyes. 'Many die from hearts that stop, from choking, from black swellings.'

Carnelian could hear an edge to the creature's voice. That time had left its scars. The creature focused on him again. 'Those that survive are castrated.'

'Like the Wise?'

The homunculus raised a hand that held negation, just. 'Not to keep us from distraction, Seraph, but because the onset of maleness would kill. The stunting drug makes a candidate like a seed coated in iron. To grow is to die suffocated.'

Carnelian felt he was trespassing on the creature's pain. 'It must be an exceptional candidate that is chosen by a Grand Sapient.'

'Such privilege, Seraph, comes only to those candidates who excel in the skills: sensitivity to touch; reading and writing in beadcord; reading of voices and faces.'

'Voices and faces?' The homunculus looked down at its hands. Carnelian felt its anxiety that it might already have said too much. 'Clearly you excel in all these skills.'

'Each of us is merely an instrument in our master's hands. An extension of his will.'

'Do you remember the place where you were born?'

The homunculus gazed at him, wide-eyed. Its head shook a little. Carnelian felt again he was intruding on private pain. He wanted to reduce the distance between them. 'I only ask because I witnessed for myself the coming of a childgatherer.'

'When you were captured by barbarians, Seraph?'

It had not occurred to Carnelian that the homunculus might know much of what its master knew. He wondered just how much. Would there be any point in asking? The homunculus was unlikely to reveal anything and would just be put on its guard. 'It is true they captured us, but then we stayed with them willingly.'

'Willingly, Seraph?'

'They were kind to us.'

The homunculus' face tensed as if it were having difficulty believing what Carnelian was saying.

'I saw the children being chosen for the flesh tithe. I saw them being torn from their kin and people.'

The homunculus looked up, eyes narrowed, mouth moving as if trying to make words. 'There was, perhaps, one child in particular . . . ?'

Carnelian regarded the little man through the eyeslits of his mask. It was a perceptive thing to ask, and brave. 'Poppy. She was chosen for the flesh tithe, but the Chosen will not get her.'

The homunculus frowned.

'She is like a little sister to me, a daughter, even.'

The homunculus gaped.

Carnelian's fear for her was sharpened by love. It made him see past what the homunculus had become to the child he had once been. 'Unlike her, you were taken from your kin.'

The body before him had not changed so much from that which his people had brought to pay their tithe to Osrakum, but the eyes revealed the man within. Carnelian wanted to reach out to that child. 'Do you remember them?'

'So long ago. I had almost forgotten.'

'What were you called?'

The homunculus shook his head, his eyes glistening. 'I can't remember.'

The sadness in that musical voice touched Carnelian's heart. He reached out to touch the homunculus' shoulder. The man drew back at first, but then let Carnelian touch him, a look of amazement lighting his face.

'Seraph.'

Carnelian woke, fleeing something terrible. He sat up, staring at the images already fading from his mind. He shrank back from the silver face hanging in the gloom. The homunculus. He was speaking from behind his eyeless mask. Carnelian made himself deaf, the better to reach back for his dream, though he feared it. It was a swelling mass like something vast emerging from the deep. Dread like a headache. Haunting clarion calls. Despair voiced in a language he had forgotten. He strained to remember the bleak sounds. He knew he had to hear it, to understand the warning.

'Seraph?'

Carnelian let go his dream and emerged into the chamber. The homunculus was still there. He was holding out a letter. The four-horned seal upon the pale parchment seemed a crusted clot of blood. Echoes of the terror snaked through the room at the sight of it. Reluctantly, he took it, broke it open and read.

All day I marched north as Aurum fell back before me.

Carnelian pulled the panels of the letter open. He examined both sides of the sheet. Only the seal and Osidian's glyphs marked the skin. He folded the letter and lay back, clutching it to his chest. He wanted to know more; needed to know more. Aurum would not fall back without reason. Carnelian tried to still the rising fear. A trap? Osidian was moving into a trap. He gazed up at the ceiling. The dregs of his nightmare seemed to be the shadows up there edging the gilding. Did his dreams prefigure some terrible defeat?

Powerlessness choked him into anger. What madness had possessed him to put his trust in dreams? Still, he could not deny his conviction that his dream had held a warning. Try as he might he could not grasp enough to make sense of it.

He sat up and saw the homunculus still there, waiting. 'Why was your master so interested in my dreams?'

'The Wise believe dreams to be echoes from the future, Seraph.'

'All dreams, all dreamers?'

The silver mask inclined a little. 'Some dreams the Gods put into those minds that are most closely aligned with the flow of events.'

372

'Such as the minds of Sapients?'

'More so those of the Grand Sapients, Seraph.'

'Is that why your master chooses to sleep here beneath our feet?'

'It is true, Seraph, my master seeks truth in dreams, but he sleeps also to keep his mind free of impure distraction. In any given year, he is rarely awake for more than twelve days.'

Carnelian was shocked. 'How can he hope to administer his Domain asleep?'

'A cascade of the lesser Sapients of his Domain do that. His thought is not to be wasted on minor matters. Once a year, at the Rebirth, he is woken and it is then that he transacts those matters that his staff have prepared for him.'

Carnelian pondered the strange life Legions must have lived. 'A living death.'

'Seraph?'

'He can have no grasp at all of reality, of life.'

'The opposite is true, Seraph. Remote from the world he gives thought only to that which is salient. His staff distill events finely and feed this distillation into his perfect mind.'

Try as he might, Carnelian could not see how such an existence could be other than the most terrible imprisonment.

Carnelian lay in his bed exhausted, trying to sleep. Though falling back into the well of dreams filled him with dread, he knew he must confront whatever was waiting for him there in the depths. He felt shame that this was now the only help he could give his loved ones, but even in this he felt undermined by his lack of skill. In any marketplace around the Commonwealth there were sure to be better interpreters of dreams plying their trade. Worse, a part of him rejected utterly such superstition. His only consolation was knowing how seriously the Wise took dreams.

*   *   *

Carnelian, swimming up to the light, came awake, spluttering. His confusion made a cavern of the chamber; monsters of the clepsydra and clocks. The face was there in his mind, fiery, the colour of blood. Akaisha's face, but not quite hers. Ebeny's? Thoughts of her penetrated to the child in him. How he longed for her warm embrace, for her hand stroking his head. Locked away in Osrakum she seemed more distant than the stars. He steeled himself. Such longings were weakness.

Blearily, Carnelian was making an effort to examine one of Aurum's clocks when he heard the sound he most hoped for and dreaded. A knock at the outer doors. Soon, the homunculus had returned with another letter from Osidian in his hand. Carnelian accepted it, his heart pounding. Almost he put it down unopened but, not allowing himself to weaken, he broke the seal and read.

He will not let me come to grips with him. I will pursue him all day and then through the night. He will not escape me.

Carnelian felt sick. He could hear Osidian's voice: the anger in it, the frustration. Such a reaction was predictable to anyone who knew him. He feared Aurum did. He could only hope the letter did not reflect all that Osidian was thinking. He had to believe Osidian was not so consumed by rage that he was blind to the possibility Aurum was leading him into a trap.

He paced up and down, desperate to do something, but what? He stopped and looked towards the homunculus. 'How does the elixir affect dreaming?'

Looking wary, the homunculus hesitated before answering. 'My masters believe it makes dreams lucid.'

'You have yourself experienced this?'

'I have, Seraph. The dreaming is intense, but I do not have the wisdom that makes their meaning clear.'

374

Carnelian frowned. What he most desired was clarity. He had to believe he would understand his dreams if he could see them clearly. 'I must take the elixir.'

The homunculus' eyes widened. 'You cannot, Seraph.'

'I have no choice.'

'But Seraph, it is forbidden.'

Carnelian laughed. 'It will be the least of my transgressions.'

'It is also dangerous, Seraph.'

'How so?'

The homunculus made vague gestures. 'Some who take it never wake.'

Carnelian considered this. 'Yet most do?'

'Most,' said the homunculus. He looked pained. 'Seraph, the initial doses, until the mind and body have become accustomed to its effect, produce unpredictable results.'

'Nevertheless.'

The homunculus' gaze fell.

'There is no need for your master ever to learn of this.'

The homunculus made no response.

'Fetch me a dose.'

The man bowed and had soon disappeared into the corner of the room. As Carnelian waited, he considered with a growing dread what he was planning to do. Something monstrous lurked in his dreams. By taking the elixir, was he going to trap himself in his dreams with it?

When the homunculus returned, Carnelian made him lie on the bed beside him. He took from him the amber bead. Holding it up to the light, he saw the spiral flows trapped in it. Strands more tenuous than spider silk.

'Close your eyes, for I am going to unmask.'

Glancing at him with anxiety, the homunculus obeyed him.

Carnelian bit the bead in half. Its fluids oozed sweet and bitter on his tongue. Swiftly he pressed the other half to the lips of the homunculus and made sure he swallowed it. Hopefully, they would both sleep for the same amount of time. Carnelian lay back. The room was already changing shape, as if it were breathing.

He feels the well behind him and the terror of its pull. He denies its whispering. His father offers him a cloak soaked with the wrath of the sky. Carnelian dons it like armour. It brings silence and stillness. It makes him taller. Ebeny offers a gleaming crescent in each hand. In his grip they are ivory ranga. Her feet bleed like crushed fruit. 'Take the spear.' He looks at his father, wanting it from his hands, but they are empty. He sees his mother impaled and does not recognize her raging face. Looking to his father for help he sees upon his face an expression he cannot read. Is his father to blame? His father shakes his head, sadly, holding his side, clearly wounded. Seeing the spike in his mother's belly, Carnelian curls his fingers round it, pulls and it comes free, releasing a flood of blood that soon runs clear. The blue spear is rusted iron. Blade soft as liver, riddled with worms.

Then he is lost and scared in a dark forest. It is raining cold, molten iron. A winking light draws him towards a burning tree. He touches its bark, smooth as bone. It is perfect and crystalline under his hand. Light is trapped in its glass, which looks so delicate he fears he must crack it. He becomes aware of the snake roof of branches shutting out the sky. Hears the sucking slurp as its roots leech blood from the flesh in which his feet are mired. Sickened by its feeding on the living and the dead, he raises his spear to strike, then sees the child trapped inside the chrysalis trunk. He knows it is himself, dreaming. He hesitates, fearing to wake the dreamer. The tree is the child's dream even though it imprisons him. To kill it, he must sacrifice the child, sacrifice himself. Aiming for the child's heart, he stabs. The spear comes out clean and sharp and well made. The child is birthed in a torrent of blood. Carnelian walks away, cradling him. They come to a river that he crosses dry-footed because of his ivory shoes. A woman waits for them on the other side. Ancient, vulnerable, he loves her. Her face is a skull. She is the mother of his mother. He offers up the child and she lets him pass. Barefoot on the fresh uncurling green, joyous in the sun, with his brothers and sisters, breathing the blue of the sky.

A wrinkled face. Crail? Carnelian strained to make sense of what he was seeing. The homunculus.

'The Two be praised.'

Carnelian reached his hand up to touch his own face and felt warm metal. He was masked.

'How do you feel, Seraph?'

Carnelian saw the homunculus' eager anxiety. When he tried to sit up, pain shot down his spine. His head seemed to have turned to stone. He fell back.

'The Seraph must rest, regain his strength. It always takes time to recover from such deep sleep. Much more so when one has been under for so long.'

Carnelian attempted to speak. Still half in the dream, his voice there was clear and strong.

'Seraph?'

Carnelian tried again and this time noticed the rasping in his throat. He realized that was the only sound he was making. He gathered his strength and pushed air out. 'How long?' he croaked.

'More than two days, Seraph.'

Shocked, Carnelian tried to rise again. The same shooting pain.

The homunculus dared to touch him. 'The elixir worked very potently in you, Seraph. There was not enough nectar in what you took to sustain you, but I dared not give you more.'

Through the eyeslits of his mask, Carnelian saw how scared the homunculus looked. Clearly he had been frantic. Two days! Something occurred to Carnelian. 'How long have you . . . ?'

'Been awake?' the homunculus asked. 'More than a day now, Seraph.'

377

Alarm flared in Carnelian. 'Legions?'

'My master sleeps undisturbed.'

Carnelian knew he dare not believe him. He struggled to roll over onto one side.

'Really, Seraph, you have not the strength to stand.'

'Legions,' Carnelian said, pushing himself up on one arm. He remained there, trembling, before the arm gave way and he fell back onto the bed.

'My master has not woken, Seraph. Truly he has not. Even if I had wanted to wake him, it would have been in defiance of his command.'

Carnelian rolled onto his back. 'What command?'

'When I asked him when he wanted to awake he told me I would know the time when it came.' The homunculus' face was sweaty with anxiety. 'I do not believe that time has yet come.' His eyes lit up. 'Another letter came for you, Seraph.' He disappeared from view, but was soon back, brandishing a parchment.

Carnelian stared at it as the homunculus showed him it carried Legions' seal. 'When?'

'Early this afternoon, Seraph. It is now well past nightfall.'

Carnelian gazed at the letter, wanting and not wanting to know its contents. 'Read it to me.'

The homunculus held the letter as though it had become dangerous.

'Please, read it to me.'

Grimacing, the man broke the seal as if he were tearing open a wound on his own body. Carefully, he opened its panels and began reading. '"It is dawn now. Though I have pursued him all night, he is still beyond my reach. Perhaps it is that I play into his hands, but I will not turn back now."'

The homunculus looked at Carnelian as if uncertain that he should continue.

'All of it,' Carnelian rasped.

The homunculus returned his gaze to the parchment. '"If he seeks to envelop me, I shall break through. If he offers me battle, then we shall decide this matter once and for all. If he continues to flee, I shall pursue him, if needs be to the gates of Osrakum herself. It is possible that he will evade me, that he will make for Makar. If he does, you must come to whatever accommodation you can with him. Save yourself."'

'Nothing else?'

'Nothing, Seraph.'

'Then please resume your mask so that I can remove mine.'

'At your command, Seraph.'

Carnelian heard the man pacing away. When the homunculus said it was safe, Carnelian peeled the mask from his face. Exposed, his skin was momentarily chilled. The pattern of his dream was clearer than the chamber around him. He closed his eyes and contemplated the shape of it. He tried to inhabit it, tease meaning out from it, but it yielded nothing definite. The memory of joy faded and the blue of that sky. He tried again to rise, but his body betrayed him. He felt he had washed up on some remote shore. He yearned for his friends, though they were far away with Osidian, in the Gods alone knew what danger.

With a crash the outer doors were flung open. Carnelian jumped to his feet. He heard cries of protest, quickly snuffed out. Heavy footfalls approached. He cast around for something he could use as a weapon. An immense shape appeared out of the shadows, of which its billowing cloak seemed a part. Pallid military leathers. The serenity of his gold mask belied the storm of this Master's entry.

Carnelian feared at first it must be Aurum, then recognized the features of the mask. 'Osidian,' he cried in relief.

Osidian glanced to either side and began unmasking.

Carnelian threw his hand up to stop him. 'We are not alone, my Lord.' He looked around and found the homunculus cowering behind a clock. 'Homunculus . . .'

The little man glanced up.

379

Be blind, Carnelian gestured with his hand. The homunculus put on its eyeless mask.

'Why do you keep the creature here?' Osidian said.

'There is no other place for him to go.'

'Very well. It makes no difference. I shall soon confront its master with everything I am about to say to you.'

Both unmasked. Carnelian did not expect the emerald fury in Osidian's eyes. 'Aurum?'

The emeralds narrowed. 'If he had known of your scheme, my Lord, even now I would be heading towards Osrakum his prisoner.'

Carnelian was startled. 'My scheme?'

'Spare me the pretence at innocence. How else could Legions have reached my commanders except through you who are his keeper?'

'The Lesser Chosen commanders?'

'Each had a letter delivered to him bearing the Grand Sapient's seal.'

'If they told you this, then surely they told you how they came by them?'

'Have you not even the courage to confront me, Carnelian?'

Osidian's look of contempt stung Carnelian to anger. 'I would if I knew what you were talking about!'

Doubt banked the fire in Osidian's eyes. 'You insist on maintaining this pretence?'

'It is no pretence. How did these letters come to them?'

Osidian's eyes narrowed further. 'None know from whence they came. They merely appeared.'

'When?'

'A couple of days after we arrived here.'

Carnelian gazed off into the corner, trying to imagine how Legions might have done it. Something occurred to him. He turned back to Osidian. 'The render I sent out to you, the letters must have gone out then. Homunculus, did your master send letters out of the fortress?'

380

Motionless, the little man made no answer.

'You will answer,' said Osidian, an edge to his voice.

The homunculus nodded.

'They were sent out of here on the same day that I arrived, were they not?'

'Yes, Seraph,' said the homunculus.

Osidian glanced into the corner with its hidden shadowy stair. 'He had the letters ready in the cothon, knowing I would have need of resupply.'

Carnelian saw how he would not meet his glance again. Osidian knew he had accused him unfairly. Carnelian, still angry, turned his attention on the homunculus. 'You knew this all the time, homunculus.'

The little man gave a reluctant nod.

'Why did you keep this from me?'

The eyeless mask looked up. 'My first loyalty is to my master, Seraph.'

'And you did not imagine that his plan would fail?'

'My masters rarely fail, Seraph.'

Still Carnelian felt betrayed. 'But you hate him?'

'Of what consequence, Seraph, the hatred of a slave?'

'Had you thought to confess this to me, I would have done all in my power to protect you from him.'

Carnelian saw the way the room was distorted in the homunculus' mirror face and remembered what he knew about the little man. His anger cooled. He gazed at Osidian. 'How did the commanders fail?'

Osidian's eyes met his. 'They were to take me alive. It seems they could not agree on how to do it, nor when. Then they saw a way out in delivering me to Aurum. The opportunity to hide their betrayal behind one of the Great was too tempting for them, but they left it too long. Eventually, fearing that another might betray him, one of their number revealed their plot to me.' His face seemed stone. 'Though that will not save him.'

'You blame them, even though it was a God Emperor who

381

appointed them, with the Wise that are Their mouthpiece? How did you expect them to react when they received a command directly from Legions?'

'Nevertheless, impaled upon my huimur's banner poles, they shall provide me with standards that will bring terror to all their kind.'

This threat was close enough to what had happened to the Ochre to sicken Carnelian. He felt only revulsion and contempt for Osidian, who once again was intending to use murder to assuage his own frustration and fear of failure. 'Do you really imagine that will bring you any closer to victory?'

Osidian flinched, his face darkening as he glared at Carnelian.

'Who is going to command your huimur now?'

Osidian's nose wrinkled. 'I shall promote marumaga legionaries. They at least will not dare betray me.'

'Are they ready to assume such responsibility?'

'Most have had long experience of watching their masters in command.'

'Assuming these promotions work, and you march out again, what will you do if Aurum once more chooses to fall back before you?'

'I will pursue him.'

'Even to the Gates of Osrakum?'

Osidian frowned.

'Could you breach the Gates with your legion?' Carnelian, who had seen them with his own eyes, knew how foolish such an attempt would be. Moreover it was clear to him that Osidian had not regained the confidence Legions had taken from him.

'I believe you know, Osidian, that the only way you will enter Osrakum is if the Gates are opened for you from within.'

'That will only happen if the political consensus among the Powers crumbles.'

'Surely knowledge of your reappearance will widen the rift between the Wise and your mother: just as the part Aurum has played will divide her from the Great? And news of your edict of enfranchisement must cleave the Great from the Lesser Chosen and could not help but weaken confidence in any plan to muster the legions against you.'

Osidian shook his head. 'The Wise control the means by which such news could reach Osrakum.'

'Then send your treacherous commanders back to Osrakum with that news.'

'The Wise have the means to stop them.'

Carnelian was taken aback. 'Would they dare to have them killed?'

'They would have no need to slay them, merely to delay them until the crisis has been resolved.'

Carnelian felt disappointed. He had been so certain he was following a thread out of this labyrinth. Then a way forward occurred to him. 'But why would they wish to stop them?'

Osidian gazed at him, waiting for more.

'Knowledge of your edict might very well serve the interests of the Wise . . .'

'Go on.'

'It would show the Great how you threaten the very foundations of their privilege . . .'

Carnelian could see his way clearly now. 'The Wise cannot hope to keep news of what has been happening from Osrakum for ever. Since this is so, it behoves them to manage its revelation themselves. Why not allow the commanders through? Surely the Great will see you as the paramount threat? Is it not the primary function of the Great Balance to keep the Imperial Power from escaping Osrakum and assuming control of the legions? How could your mother explain your presence in the outer world? It would be in all their interests to join together to destroy you.'

Osidian frowned. 'How would that help us?'

'How long do you imagine such unity would last?' Carnelian could not help a smile as Osidian began nodding. 'All we have to do is remain beyond their reach as long as we can.'

'And then what?'

Carnelian realized with surprise that at that moment, perhaps for the first time, he felt he and Osidian really were fighting for the same thing. Yet his confidence was already dimming. All the talk of grand politics had made him believe that they really might triumph. But on that issue Legions had spoken the clear truth. However fractured, the powers arrayed against them were unassailable. He tried coming at the problem from one direction after another, but always it was as if he were taking on a dragon with a spear.

'I don't know,' he said at last. 'We shall have to wait and see what opportunities arise. In the meantime you can weld our legion into a weapon that will be certain in your hand when we do choose to use it.'

Osidian gazed at him, clear-eyed, so that Carnelian felt he was seeing right through to his heart. 'Very well. We shall do it your way. I shall return to *our* legion.'

'I want to go with you.'

Osidian's face tightened as if he was feeling some old wound. He glanced down and saw the homunculus. Carnelian realized they had both forgotten the little man was there.

'What about Legions?' Osidian said.

Carnelian felt the Grand Sapient was a burden he had borne too long alone. 'Homunculus . . .'

'Seraph?' the little man said.

'Can the Grand Sapient be lodged in a watch-tower?'

'All the watch-towers of the Guarded Land are fully equipped with facilities designed to accommodate my masters.'

It was as Carnelian had guessed. Even sleeping in his capsule Legions must have needed to find accommodation on his journey from Osrakum.

Osidian was nodding. 'It would make sense to abandon this place.'

Carnelian felt a surge of relief.

'You can set off in the morning. Meanwhile, I will return to the watch-tower and make sure it is ready to receive them. The

Lesser Chosen traitors will begin their journey to Osrakum tomorrow.'

Osidian lifted his mask up to his face, then let it drop again. 'I will send you more Marula as an escort.'

Carnelian nodded. Then, after they had both remasked, he watched Osidian fade into the shadows.

TOWER SUN-NINETY-THREE

Hunger does not make bread bake faster.
(a proverb from the Ringwall cities)

Slack-mouthed, staring, the Marula crept across the marble floor of Aurum's chamber looking around them like children in a sorcerous cave. Among them, Sthax had become just another warrior the moment Morunasa had appeared. The Oracle glanced at the clocks as if he had seen such mechanical organisms every day of his life, but he jumped with the others when they saw themselves reflected in Aurum's mirrors. It took the Marula only a moment to realize they were seeing themselves, but that was enough time for their fists to tighten on their lances. For all their beauty, in that Chosen setting, in their leather armour they did look crude barbarians.

He had them wait while he and the homunculus descended into the vault. The capsules were there, pale in the gloom. Earlier, while the homunculus had helped him into his commander's leathers, they had discussed how his masters were to be moved. Carnelian set down his light and looked at him. 'Let us prepare the capsules for transport.'

The homunculus gave a nod and they broke open the lid of Legions' capsule. The Grand Sapient lay inside like a corpse. They administered the elixir through his mummified lips. The last thing they wanted was for him to wake in transit.

They checked his restraining straps then repeated the procedure with the other Sapients. When they were ready, the homunculus resealed the lids, even as Carnelian returned to the chamber above and brought Morunasa and the Marula down with him into the vault. They stared at the capsules with unconcealed horror.

'Corpses?' Morunasa asked.

'In a way,' Carnelian answered. 'We're taking them to the Master's watch-tower.'

Gazing at the capsules, Morunasa nodded. The homunculus located poles that Carnelian helped him slide into the carrying handles of Legions' capsule. Carnelian was aware of the Marula watching him as if he were preparing for them a poisoned meal. He was careful to ignore Sthax.

The homunculus checked the poles were secure, then announced: 'The capsule is ready, Seraph.'

Carnelian relayed this to Morunasa, who issued a command in his own tongue. When the Marula hesitated, Morunasa barked at them. Soon they had managed to slide the capsule horizontal, then, bending to the carrying poles, four on each side, they raised it into the air. As they began to climb the steps with it, the capsule started to tilt. Carnelian cried out in alarm.

The homunculus touched his arm. 'My masters are as safe as butterflies in their chrysalises, Seraph.'

More like pupating maggots, thought Carnelian as he followed the capsule up the stair.

They crossed the fortress like a funerary procession. When they reached the watch-tower at the outer gate the homunculus showed them strange, wheeled carriages stowed in its stables. They dragged these up onto the leftway with their aquar. From that vantage point, Carnelian became mesmerized by the market teeming below. After having been confined for so long in the Legate's tower it was a joy to see so much ordinary life. He raised his eyes to the horizon. Beyond the dun chaos of the earthbrick hovels of the city lay the rusty vastness of the land.

The homunculus showed the Marula how to secure each capsule to its carriage, in a near-vertical position. When all was ready, Carnelian climbed into his saddle-chair. He noticed the homunculus standing as awkwardly as an abandoned child. 'You do not know how to ride, do you?'

'No, Seraph.'

Carnelian beckoned him to approach, then helped him clamber into his saddle-chair, settling him between his legs. When he reckoned they were as comfortable as was possible, Carnelian made the aquar rise. He asked Morunasa to ride ahead with his men, leaving only three of them to lead the aquar hitched to the carriages. He eyed the maggot-pale capsules as they lurched into movement. The sun was bright enough to find the dark spindles at their core.

'The Standing Dead,' he murmured.

The homunculus stirred a little, tense as ice.

Soon they were loping along the leftway, Carnelian bringing up the rear of their cortege. They rode above the market, passed under two more watch-towers, then increased speed on the clear run north.

Even before they reached it, Carnelian could see the disc of Osidian's camp disfiguring the earth around the watch-tower. Ahead the leftway came to a sudden, ragged end. Some distance further on it rose again, continuing north. In between, it had been reduced to rubble. Surveying the land round about, he understood why Osidian had torn down the leftway: so that he could meet any attack, whether it came from the east or west, with his whole legion.

Morunasa and the Marula were dismounting. Carnelian made his own mount kneel. He helped the homunculus clamber out, then climbed out himself.

The little man looked around. 'Where are the ammonites of this tower, Seraph? They should be here to greet us.'

Carnelian gazed up into the watch-tower branches. It was Marula that sat as lookouts in the deadman's chairs. This tower was Osidian's and any ammonites could only compromise its security. 'The Celestial dismissed them.'

The homunculus' child mask glanced towards their Marula escort. 'Then, Seraph, we must make do with these creatures.'

Under his instructions the Marula unloaded the capsules and carried them into the tower. Inside, the homunculus climbed the ladder that was set against the back wall. As he disappeared up into the shadows, Carnelian and Sthax exchanged a glance. Carnelian was trying to work out a way to keep the Maruli close when the homunculus returned, pulling a rope from which hung a hook. Carnelian helped him remove the carrying poles from Legions' capsule and then watched him attach the hook to one of the freed rings. After the homunculus had fetched and attached a second hook, he showed the Marula some ropes and, at his command, they began to heave on them. As the capsule came slowly upright, the homunculus wrestled it against the wall, then clambered aboard. The Marula continued to pull upon the ropes and the capsule rose up into the gloom of the tower, with the homunculus clinging to it like a child to its mother.

Carnelian followed Legions' capsule up through the tower. When it reached the uppermost storey, he helped the homunculus drag it into one of the cells. The capsule was much lighter than he had expected. They propped it up against one wall. Carnelian looked around the chamber. It was so like the many he had seen on his journey to Osrakum that, for a moment, the time that had passed since then seemed an illusion.

'I shall descend for the others, Seraph,' said the homunculus.

Soon, he was out of sight, taking with him the hooks and ropes. While Carnelian waited, he opened the doors to the other chambers. All the cells save one looked as if they had not been used for a while. One smelled of sweat, but this odour was cut through by another, myrrh. The same smell that he was just aware of rising from his own, bandaged body. This must be Osidian's cell, then. He walked around it as if he expected Osidian to return at any moment. He felt that he was intruding; these cells were far more territorial than had ever been the hearth or the sleeping hollows. He backed out of the cell and closed its door. He really would prefer to sleep somewhere out in the open, but even if this had been advisable, he felt a need to stay close to the capsules. He chose the cell furthest from Osidian's, then returned to the landing to wait for the homunculus to appear with the next capsule.

After he had helped the homunculus stow the other two capsules, Carnelian climbed the ladder to the roof and had soon reached the platform, at the centre of which gleamed a heliograph. Movement drew his eyes to a Maruli spreadeagled in a deadman's chair. Carnelian looked west. Far away, red clouds hung like mist over the land. In their midst, he saw flashes. Motes moved, veiled by the rolling dust: Osidian's dragons on manoeuvres.

He let his gaze return to wander across the mottled semi-circle of the camp below. A glint caught his eye. There was a hole in the ground ringed with silver. Cisterns, perhaps, but it was the hole that drew his attention. It plunged into deep blackness. Pallid creatures were writhing up its sides. Sartlar, like maggots crawling out of a wound.

When he descended the tower, he took the homunculus with him, down through the stables to the bottom gate. As grooms raised this for him he became aware of the hubbub of the road. He slipped out behind the monolith that screened them from the traffic. He watched the multitude thronging past, and bathed in its ever-shifting odours. He feasted on the faces, the smiles and flashing eyes of so much raw humanity. The beasts, the heaped wagons with their slowly turning wheels.

'We must cross,' he said quietly to the homunculus.

He sensed the little man's fear and offered him his hand. Hesitantly, the homunculus took it and together they emerged onto the road. At first the shadow of the leftway wall concealed them, but then someone saw his mask, his looming height. Cries of 'Master' spread panic through the crowd. Pulling the homunculus after him, Carnelian began to cross the road. Everywhere people were falling to their knees. Carnelian did not turn his mask, for its gaze was terrifying to them, but restricted his attention to the bare stone before his feet. When they reached a ramp, they went down its slope to the red earth beyond. Each step thereafter, Carnelian made sure to scuff the earth to churn up dust to hide them.

He gave up counting the black hearths burnt into the land. Hazed with flies, hills of dragon dung gave off their stench. The glitter of the cisterns drew him and the promise of breathable air. Besides, he had a notion to take a look at the hole in the ground.

As they drew nearer, they saw the cistern was a trough, its lip gouged and cracked. Bright water rocked in its curve, which was the rim of an immense pit plunging down into blackness. The circling wall of the pit was pale limestone rotten with caves and rusted by the land's red earth. The closer he drew, the further he could peer down into the gloom. Sartlar infested the caves. Others were clambering up out of the blackness using handholds gouged into the soft walls. Each was burdened with a waterskin. As he watched, one of the creatures struggled up from the well and emptied its skin into the cistern. Free for a moment, it rested its gnarled hands on its knees, hacking breath. Suddenly, sensing him, it glanced up. It cowered as it caught sight of the mirror gold of his face. Disliking the creature's fear, Carnelian turned his back on it and, with the homunculus, he made his way back to the watch-tower. Weary of the world, he climbed to his cell and, as the homunculus hunched down against the wall, he lay down to await Osidian's return.

She is Akaisha and Ebeny, though looks like neither. Carnelian feels the itching of her wounds as if they are his own. Scratching, she picks out maggots that writhe over her fingers like drops of oil. She licks them off. Her nails return to dig the wounds. They widen like mouths to devour him. He loses hold and tumbles in and falls and falls and falls.

He came awake with Osidian standing over him. He had the uncomfortable impression that Osidian had been there for a while. When he sat up, Osidian did not back away enough to give him the space he felt he needed. Osidian seemed too large for the cell, which he filled with the odour of his leathers. Every part of him was reddened except for his face. It seemed he was wearing a mask of pallid alabaster. He frowned, but there was a shy tenderness in his eyes that flustered Carnelian further.

'Where are the commanders?' Carnelian said, to say something.

Osidian's frown deepened as he sensed Carnelian's unease. 'On their way to the Mountain as we agreed.'

In his military cloak, Osidian was filling the cell as Carnelian's father had filled the cabin on the baran. Carnelian wondered why he was making the comparison. He felt his face was burning.

Osidian took a step back, dismayed. 'I'll leave.'

Carnelian did not want to part like that. Though they were no longer lovers, they needed to be allies. He struggled to find a way through his feelings. 'Let's eat together tonight.'

Osidian glanced at the cell as if he was seeing it for the first time. 'Here?'

Carnelian grimaced. The cell would not do; it felt like a battlefield. He remembered a time long ago. 'Why not up on the platform, near the heliograph? It would be cool up there. Unrestricted.'

Osidian's eyes were flint. 'As you say, unrestricted.' He gave a weary nod and had to stoop to leave through the door. Carnelian watched it close, then was left with only his breathing and his beating heart.

Standing with his back to the heliograph mechanism, Osidian removed his mask and gazed north. Carnelian was reluctant to remove his own. 'There is no protection here, my Lord.'

Osidian turned to look at him. 'It was you who pointed out to me that we spent years unprotected among the barbarians.' He resumed his squinting at the northern blackness, which was relieved only by the naphtha flares of the next tower and the faint glimmer of the stopping place around its feet. 'Besides, up here we are as far from the contaminating earth as birds in flight.'

Carnelian glanced uneasily to where the homunculus was sitting astride the beam that ended in the hoop of a deadman's chair. The little man was wearing his blinding mask. Osidian had dismissed the Marula lookouts so that there would be no eyes to see them. As Carnelian unmasked, his face was chilled by the night air touching his sweat. He breathed deeply, enjoying not having to draw air through the mask filters.

'Will you take your place in Earth-is-Strong's tower and help me with the training of our legion?' Osidian said.

Carnelian regarded his back and sensed how tense he was. 'Who would guard the Grand Sapient?'

Osidian glanced round. 'You oversee the feeding of the elixir, do you not?'

Carnelian gave a nod and Osidian turned away again. 'The Marula will make sure no one enters the tower and they themselves would not dare.'

Carnelian remembered how Sthax and the other warriors had looked at the capsules. He considered whether to spend the next few days riding the dragon. No doubt it would be preferable to remaining cooped up in the watch-tower, but he was remembering Osidian torching the sartlar. He was not sure their brittle alliance could survive another such atrocity. He had fooled himself before that he could steer Osidian away from such behaviour. Of course, he might try imposing some conditions but, in the past, that had worked badly. Still, he could no longer pretend he was not committed to this war and he must be prepared to bear the consequences. 'I will join you.'

Osidian gave a couple of nods.

Carnelian turned his thoughts to what the coming war might involve. 'How long will it take the commanders to reach Osrakum?'

Osidian turned. 'You are likely to know that better than I. The Guarded Land is like a great wheel. The commanders are travelling along one spoke to its centre. You travelled along another when you came up from the sea. How long did that take?'

Carnelian cast his mind back to that journey. It stretched in his recollection to span scores of days, though he knew that it had really not taken so long. 'Five or six days, I think, but we were travelling at great speed.'

Osidian smiled coldly. 'The commanders will also be travelling at great speed.'

Carnelian thought about that. He could see how haste would benefit them. They might be hoping to be the first to arrive with the news of Osidian's revolt. It could seem to them that only thus might they avoid retribution. He felt a stab of anxiety. 'That is not going to leave us much time to get the legion ready.'

'Long enough,' Osidian said. 'Though Aurum is close, I do not imagine he will be sent against us alone.'

Carnelian nodded. 'It would be one legion against another.'

'The Wise prefer not to take risks. They will attempt to

muster overwhelming odds against us. Besides, Aurum's naphtha will be much depleted.'

Osidian gazed at him expectantly. Carnelian realized that Osidian was expecting him to ask just how bad it had been for the Lepers. If he was being tested, he would pass. 'What makes you think Aurum has not refuelled in the city to the north of here?'

Osidian regarded him, then allowed himself a smile. 'Perhaps. That is not important. What is, is that when the attack comes it will not be from a single legion.'

The certainty they would be outnumbered left Carnelian feeling bleak. He remembered the dragon tower exploding. Death in such circumstances would be quick, but his heart ached when he imagined how the Lepers and the Marula would suffer on the ground. 'How can we hope to prevail?'

Osidian's smile surprised him. 'I have a notion or two . . .'

Carnelian considered asking him what those might be, but suspected he would get no answer. He glanced down through the bars of the platform to the lights of the camp spread out below. Whatever Osidian's plan, it would be unlikely to spare the Lepers or the Marula.

Back in his cell, Carnelian was struck afresh by how identical it was to the others he had slept in before. He touched one of the walls, knowing that behind it Legions and the other Sapients lay dreaming in their capsules, but it could so easily be his father, wounded. This illusion was so great, he almost moved to the door, going to see if it was possible he had dreamed all that had happened since then.

A movement in the corner startled him. A small figure adjusting itself. For a moment he could believe it was Tain, his brother. Then, a flicker of the lamplight caught a surface of its metal face. Not his brother, but the homunculus in his blinding mask. Carnelian squinted and once again it could be Tain, whom Jaspar had threatened to blind. There was a strange parallelism in all this. A pattern that, should he be able to see enough of it, would make sense of everything.

He gave up the struggle, despairing, and went to one of the slits he knew must look down into the stopping place. The fires spangling the land below seemed, at first, very like all those other stopping places, but then he noticed the hills of blackness arrayed along the edge of the road. Dragons. Still, the flicker of the campfires seemed welcoming even from that distance. Poppy and Fern were there somewhere. How he yearned to join them.

The next morning he rose and put on his leathers again with the help of the homunculus. Then, after feeding the Sapients, they descended the tower with Osidian. To Carnelian's surprise, he did not go down into the stable levels, but walked out onto the leftway. As Carnelian followed him into the open, he was confronted by the flank of a dragon tower. Its brassman had the back of its head resting against the leftway where the crumbled edge had been hacked into rough steps.

Osidian's Hands were there. 'After I move Heart-of-Thunder away, they will bring up your huimur, my Lord. Follow me out.'

Carnelian lifted his hand in assent and Osidian descended the rough steps to the brassman. He crossed and entered the tower, his officers scrambling after him. The brassman was only half raised when Heart-of-Thunder began to move away. His footfalls sent tremors up through the leftway and caused more of its rubble to come loose and skitter over the edge. Carnelian watched the monster veer across the road, then saw below a dark mass of mounted Marula. Other dragons berthed all along the edge of the road, freed from their hawsers, were beginning to turn, their towers catching the morning sun. Beyond, spreading to the edges of the camp, was the paler multitude of the Lepers. He narrowed his eyes, searching among them for Poppy or Fern or even Krow, but it was impossible to make one figure out among so many.

More tremors in the ground alerted him to another dragon tower swaying towards the leftway. Taking a step forward he peered down and was sure he could see the distinctive configuration of Earth-is-Strong's horns. Soon her brassman was lowering. He had begun to descend the rough steps to it, when he remembered the homunculus. The little man stood petrified, but came when Carnelian called him. He took his hand to lead him into the tower.

Soon Carnelian was settling back into the familiar hollow of his command chair. He glanced round to check that the homunculus was braced against the bone wall, then gave the command to take her out. His Lefthand gave a nod of acknowledgement and Earth-is-Strong began lumbering out across the road. Carnelian peered down to see riders swirling below. Then the dragon was descending a ramp into a rolling mass of red dust into which she plunged on a westerly course. On either side other dragons seemed ships in a fog.

The dust-clouds subsided enough for him to be able to see that they were passing along a red road trampled through hri fields that stretched interminably to lilac horizons. He presumed the road had been made by Osidian's passage the day before. In the lazy heat he watched shadoofs like the necks of heaveners rising and falling as they poured water along ditches. The regular grid of kraals made the land look like some vast upholstery. Here and there dark lines of sartlar moved, hunched, across a field; he wondered that they did not lift their heads to watch the dragons pass.

At last they came into a region in which the tussocked hri fields were scorched and trampled. In places burnt kraals formed blackened craters. Osidian sent a signal from tower to tower, calling a halt. Carnelian saw other dragons turning and so gave the same command to his. Earth-is-Strong swung round and then the cabin stilled. For a moment rattles came from distant chains and mechanisms. Then all fell silent. The musk of hri rose up from the earth with the heat. Carnelian

397

felt the sweat soaking into the bandages binding his body. A muffled voice in the deck below was answered by another. Then he heard the Lepers coming in a rabble down the red road. Carnelian looked among the mounted and the walking, among the bristle of forks and scythes, but could find little point of reference among that shrouded mass, never mind the hoped-for sighting of anyone he knew. Marula came riding from the north where he knew Osidian and Heart-of-Thunder lay. Leading them, grey-faced Oracles. As they encircled the Lepers, Carnelian suffered acute anxiety that they were going to attack them. He relaxed as soon as he saw the Oracles were doing nothing more than separating off groups of several hundred Lepers who, with a single Oracle in command and some dozen Marula warriors in the vanguard, detached from the throng and set off along the dragon line.

When more signals came from Heart-of-Thunder, Carnelian listened to his Lefthand explaining what Osidian wanted done.

'This is what you did yesterday?'

'Just so, Master.'

'And no sartlar were harmed?'

'Inevitably, some were crushed . . .'

'But the pipes were not used?'

'Only against some empty kraals, Master.'

Carnelian nodded and relayed the commands to the other two dragons of his cohort. Soon they were pounding across some virgin fields, the Marula and Lepers assigned to them forming horns on either flank, pursuing hapless sartlar that they were trying to encircle.

From Earth-is-Strong's tower, Carnelian watched the Lepers pour back into the watch-tower camp. As they entered the stopping place they raised a great cloud that glowed in the light of the westering sun. He was troubled. All day he had worked with the Lepers assigned to him. All attempts to coordinate them with the advance of his dragons had led to a shambles. Some riding, others jogging, they had not even managed to keep together. The formations that the Oracles and Marula had attempted to marshal them into had ended up scattered all over the fields. The Marula had been difficult enough to manage from his high vantage point. He could hardly blame them for not understanding the signals flashed to them. Why should they? Even the other two dragons had made mistakes, though these were perhaps a consequence of the recent changes in their crew hierarchies. The dragons, Osidian could deal with. What was concerning Carnelian most was the Lepers. In any fight with auxiliaries, they would be annihilated.

As Earth-is-Strong cruised through the camp and up the ramp onto the road, Carnelian commanded his Lefthand to bring her to a halt short of the watch-tower. His Hands followed him as he descended to the ground. Heart-of-Thunder was sliding alongside the leftway. Marula were dismounting around him. A mass of dragons was moving along the road towards the breach in the leftway. The percussion of their footfalls was producing a constant thundering earthquake. Glancing up at the watch-tower, Carnelian was almost surprised it was not shaking to pieces. He turned west, angling the eyeslits of his mask against the liquid gold sun that was squeezing between the vast black shapes of the dragons as they were marshalled to form a rampart along the edge of the road. Through them he caught intermittent glimpses of the milling chaos of the Leper camp. He needed to talk to Lily.

'I am going down there,' he cried above the din.

His Hands grimaced, lifting the flaps of their helmets to hear him better.

'Down there,' he shouted, pointing towards the Lepers.

They made to come and stand behind him, but he waved them away. He pointed up to Earth-is-Strong, who seemed a cliff cast from gold, and, with his hands, he made them understand they were to return to her tower and take her to her berth alongside the watch-tower. He watched them begin

to ascend the rope ladder and then waited for the last dragon
to lumber past before setting off for the ramp.

As he stepped off the ramp, several legionaries rushed up.
Before they could kneel, he gestured them aside, declining their
obeisance and their offers to escort him. The odour of render
was tainting the musky breeze. Looking along the beaked
line of dragons, he saw they were being fed. Beneath their
prowed heads, marumaga were lighting fires and distributing
sacs for their dinner. Carnelian turned to contemplate the
Leper multitude, rosy in the sinking sun, and wondered how
he was going to find Lily. There was nothing for it but to go
and ask someone. He paced slowly towards the Lepers as if
they were a colony of seabirds he was anxious not to startle
into flight. When shrouded heads turned at his approach, he
expected panic, but they merely bent back towards their fires
as if he were a ghost they did not want to believe was really
there. He went right up to one cluster, coming close enough
that he could smell their sweat and the render that they were
eating. Towering over them, he asked to be directed to their
leaders: to Lily in particular. At first he thought they were
not going to answer, but then an arm rose that lacked fingers.
He moved off towards the cisterns, to which the stump was
pointing. Two legionaries came past, bearing a great waterskin
between them upon a sagging pole. He waved them on before
they could kneel and they loped past, spilling some water that
seemed to turn the earth to blood. Several times more Carnelian
asked directions and, each time, a spot near the cisterns was
indicated.

He was approaching one clump like any other, thinking he
must ask again, when he recognized the breadth of shoulders
beneath the shrouds of a hunched figure. One of the Lepers
nudged another and all who were round that fire stood up to
face him.

'Master,' said one with Lily's husky voice.

Carnelian saw the smoulder in their midst that turned it

into a hearth. It made him feel he was intruding. He touched the metal over his face and had a desperate urge to unmask.

'That's not the Master, it's Carnie.'

The voice came from a slim figure, Poppy. All of them save Lily pushed back their cowls: Poppy, Krow beside her, Fern. It was the latter who was regarding Carnelian as if he were an enemy. 'What do you want, Master?'

Shock made Carnelian unable to speak. Perhaps he should have anticipated Fern's reaction. What did he know of what his life had been since last he saw him? Raising his hands in appeasement, he was startled by how alien they seemed, sheathed in their pale leather. 'You're not warriors—' He sensed anger in a shifting of Lily's weight. 'I've come to offer my help to train you.'

Fern's eyes became a hawk's. 'Has the Master given you permission to make this offer?'

Carnelian was stung by that, but chose not to justify himself. 'I am here,' he said, simply.

Fern's contempt spread to his lips. 'So you want to help us so that we can fight for the Master . . . train us as you once trained the Marula . . . ?'

Carnelian felt anger burn his face.

Fern threw his hand out in dismissal. 'We don't need your help.'

'I think you do. If it comes to a battle with auxiliaries, you'll be annihilated and at no great cost to them.' Carnelian turned to Lily. 'Did you bring your people here to give your enemy more victims?'

'Are you sure it will come to a battle?'

Carnelian turned and saw the speaker was Krow. He paused for a moment, noticing Poppy's hand upon the youth's arm. 'I think it's likely.'

He turned back to Lily. 'If you are determined to fight, then I can help you.'

The Leper nodded. 'We are determined and so' – she turned towards Fern – 'we need all the help we can get, Ochre.'

Fern turned away, pulling his cowl back over his face, and returned to sit gazing at the fire.

Carnelian gave a nod of resignation. 'Tomorrow I'll ride with you.'

The murmur from the camp rose up with the campfire smoke to the watch-tower platform where Carnelian and Osidian were eating together. 'I'm going to take personal command of the Lepers,' Carnelian announced, in a tone that surprised him with its vehemence.

Osidian frowned. 'Why?'

Expecting a fight, Carnelian was for a moment put off-balance by Osidian's calm tone. 'They're a mess. If we take them out against trained auxiliaries, they'll be annihilated.' Osidian's expression had not changed. 'That would hardly be of much use to us . . .'

Osidian regarded him for a moment, then nodded, picked up a hri wafer and put it in his mouth. He chewed it for a while. 'That's why I put the Marula in charge of their training.'

'Today, I saw very little evidence that that's working.'

'Today was only the second day of their training.'

Carnelian felt the strength in his position deserting him. He imagined what Fern would think of him if he did not turn up the next morning as he had promised. That caused him to question whether Fern was the only reason he was doing it. His heart told him that Fern was *a* reason, but not the only one. 'They need more help than the Marula can provide.'

'Indeed?'

'They can't speak each other's tongue.'

'Morunasa's Vulgate is as good as yours.'

Carnelian almost reached for the justification that he was a Master, but his instincts were against this. It was a cowardly way out and not the truth. 'The Lepers will not easily take instructions from Morunasa.'

Osidian glanced up at him, but said nothing. He had no

402

need to. Among the Lepers it was only Fern who would not easily take instructions from Morunasa. Osidian looked back to his bowl and selected another wafer. 'Do as you will.'

Carnelian had no feeling of victory. He felt empty. A constant murmur was rising from the camp. Glancing down, he saw the twinkling campfires. He pulled his cloak about him. Up here the night was cold.

On the leftway with Osidian, Carnelian gazed past the dragons to the Leper multitude. 'I want to take them out by myself.'

'Without the huimur?'

Carnelian glanced at Osidian. 'They need to be forged before they can be used as a weapon. I am sure you have much work you can do with your huimur alone.'

Osidian gave a nod and Carnelian returned to the watch-tower on his way down to the road.

Carnelian gazed at the Lepers. It had been hard enough to get them here from the camp in anything approaching good order, but the sun had had time to climb the sky before Morunasa and the other Oracles had managed to marshal them into an approximation to a battleline.

As Carnelian turned to his companions, several threw their arms up against the dazzle reflecting off his mask. Lily was there with other Lepers, all shrouded. Bareheaded were Fern and Krow and Morunasa. Carnelian regarded the Oracle, wondering if he could work with him. He recalled how, when he had told him he was taking control of the Marula for the day, Morunasa had glanced up to where Osidian was standing on the leftway as if he doubted Carnelian's authority. Morunasa had obeyed him, had made the Marula do everything Carnelian asked of them, but with a visible reluctance.

'Ride with me,' Carnelian said to them all, then coaxed his aquar into a lope along the ragged Leper line. Only the detachments of Marula, each with an Oracle commander, formed a

403

regular pattern along the front. Behind them, the Lepers were a rabble. Fewer than half of them were mounted and, though here and there he could see clumps of auxiliary lances, the air above their heads was predominantly a confusion of hoes and hooks and stone-blade scythes.

He pulled his aquar up. The half-flare of her eye-plumes closing as he turned her. 'Lily, why are so few of your people mounted?'

'You've reason to know our valleys are more suited to boats than aquar. We mustered all we could find there and in the fortress.' She made a vague gesture in the direction of Makar.

Krow was nodding. 'The Master's been making us take all the aquar we can from the people on the road.' He scrunched up his nose. 'But they're generally rather weedy and there's not a lot of them and mostly they don't have saddle-chairs, but racks for carrying stuff—'

Carnelian nodded, noticing how Krow was at Fern's side, as he had been all day. He wondered how they had resolved their differences. 'What proportion of your Lepers are mounted?'

'Perhaps one in three,' said Lily.

'And are those good riders?'

Lily shrugged. Fern's face might have been wood. It was Krow who answered. 'Competent, Master.'

Carnelian glanced at the Lepers and wondered how long it would take for them to become good enough. He scanned those closest. They certainly did not look comfortable in their saddle-chairs. 'How are they commanded, Morunasa?'

'There are as many units as there are dragons, each commanded by one of my brethren. They answer to me.'

'Is each of these units organized as a single body?'

Morunasa shook his head. 'Under the Master's instruction, each Oracle chose three Lepers to directly command. Each of those chose three more. And those, three more and so on until they reached groups of three or four or five.'

'Does this work, Lily?'

The Leper glanced at Morunasa. 'No. Many have ended up

404

serving alongside those they don't know. Many have deserted to be with their friends.'

Morunasa's lips curled with disgust. 'It's been impossible to enforce the Master's scheme. These wretches all look alike.'

Lily turned on him. Though her shrouds hid her expression, Krow gave Morunasa a look of dislike strong enough for both of them. Fern, whom Carnelian would have expected to dislike Morunasa the most, remained impassive.

'Morunasa, how do your brethren give their commands to the Lepers?'

Morunasa raised his hands. 'With these.'

'What do you think, Fern?'

Fern did not look at him. 'What do you think I think?'

Carnelian wanted to break through Fern's impassivity to the anger he was impaled on. 'I don't know. Tell me. How were you organized as you came up the Pass?'

As Fern turned his dark eyes on him, Carnelian could see the hurt in them. In return, Fern could see only the gold of his mask. 'We were organized friend with friend, brother with brother.'

'No system?'

'Our settlements vary greatly in size,' said Lily.

Carnelian's gaze passed over the Leper crowd as he digested what he had been told. He came to a decision. 'Morunasa, gather your brethren and all your warriors and ride back to the watch-tower. Tell the Master I've no further need of you.'

The Oracle glared at him for a moment and it seemed he was going to say something, then his lips parted in a feral grin. 'As the Master wishes.'

He rode his aquar along the line crying out something in the Marula tongue. As the warriors began to detach themselves from the battleline, Carnelian turned back to Fern and Krow, to Lily and the other Leper commanders. 'Form them up as they were before. Friend with friend. Brother with brother.'

* * *

Carnelian swung from the ladder onto the landing. He was glad to see Osidian's door closed. He had reason to believe he was there in his cell. The dragons had been already in camp when he had returned with the Lepers. He was weary to his bones. His reorganization had not brought the fruits he had hoped. He did not want to have to deal with Osidian until he had had time to rebuild his faith in what he had chosen to take on. Opening the door to his cell, he was relieved to see that the homunculus was still there, sleeping under the effects of the elixir he had made him take. It was the only thing he could have done. It was not practical to take the little man with him and he did not want to run the risk of leaving him behind, awake, unsupervised.

He removed his cloak and reached up behind his head to release his mask. A movement in the corner of his eye made him freeze. There was someone gazing at him from the furthest corner of the cell.

'Poppy!'

The girl smiled at him.

'Great Father, what're you doing here?'

She raised her small hands in a gesture of appeasement. 'Now don't be angry.'

'Don't be angry?' he bellowed. Then winced, glancing at the door. The last thing he wanted to do was bring Osidian to find out what was going on. 'Do you know what could've happened if I'd removed my mask?'

'Nothing,' she said, grinning.

He raised his hands with fingers splayed, close to screaming at her. She came towards him and reached up to his right hand with both of hers and gently pulled it down, then the other, all the time talking. 'Now, Carnie, it makes no difference because I want to join your household and your household can look at you, can't they? You do remember telling me that, don't you?'

Carnelian grimaced behind his mask. 'Yes, but we don't know where all this will end. You'd be locked in.' His emotions were a mess. 'Besides, you'll have to wear my House mark.'

'I know, here, on my face.'

Her smile softened his heart. Calmed him.

A knock at the door made them both jerk round to stare at it.

'My Lord?'

It was Osidian's voice. Carnelian waved Poppy back into the corner, then opened the door and stood blocking the doorway. Osidian frowned. 'Why are you still masked?'

Carnelian pointed back into the cell with his head. 'The homunculus . . .'

Osidian pulled back into the shadows. 'How did it go today?'

'I'll tell you up by the heliograph over food.' Carnelian saw that Osidian had already removed his leathers. 'You go up and I'll be there shortly.'

Osidian's frown was deepening as Carnelian closed the door. He waited to hear him walk away, then confronted Poppy. 'You can slip out of here *now*.'

Poppy smiled at him. He knew only too well how stubborn she could be. 'Have it your own way. I don't have the time to deal with this now. You stay here, but make sure you don't make a sound.' He glanced at the homunculus. Hopefully he would sleep a little longer.

'Who's that? I took a peek under his mask. He looks very old.'

'Never mind him. Just help me change.'

'Where's the homunculus?' Osidian asked Carnelian as he appeared at the edge of the heliograph platform.

'In a drugged sleep. Did you expect me to ride around all day with him sitting on my lap?'

Osidian's eyebrows rose. 'I thought you said—'

Carnelian realized his mistake too late. 'Forget what I said. We've more important matters to deal with.' He sank to the platform so that the bowls of food lay between them. Then he began to describe the changes he had made to the way the Lepers were organized.

Osidian grew increasingly aghast. 'But without a deep command hierarchy they will lose all tactical flexibility.'

'Tactical flexibility? We'll be lucky if we even achieve a modicum of military capability. Have you seen how they're armed? And fewer than a third of them are mounted.'

As Carnelian saw Osidian's eyes dulling, he became concerned he might lose the Lepers to him. 'I have some notions as to how we might get round that problem, but I want to make sure we agree on this issue of tactical flexibility. You do not intend to use them interspersed among your huimur, do you?'

Osidian shook his head. 'They would be cremated.'

'As I thought. So you'll be using them on your wings?'

'Probably.'

'Well, I'll give you two independently controllable wings and, though they may not be up to any complicated manoeuvring, they should be able to stand up against Aurum's auxiliaries.'

Watching Osidian considering this, Carnelian wondered if he would be able to deliver on his promise. 'I've faith, Osidian, that you'll be able to come up with tactics that will accommodate these limitations.'

'Perhaps. What about the Marula?'

Carnelian smiled and shifted to Quya: 'I am sure my Lord can find a better use for them than to act as an impenetrable barrier between himself in his huimur tower and the Lepers on the ground.'

Osidian nodded, but he was already sinking into contemplation. Carnelian was initially glad of this, then found it only served to bring to the fore his rising anxiety about Poppy. Not only was the homunculus down there, but also Legions and the other Sapients. What was he going to do with her?

* * *

Poppy was waiting for him, smiling.

'Here,' he said, offering her some hri wafers that he had saved from his meal with Osidian. She put the food down without even glancing at it. Her eyes seemed to be trying to see past the mask as if it were mist.

'You must return to Fern and the others.'

Carnelian expected a protest, but Poppy's smile did not change. He began to list all the reasons why she must return. The disfigurement of the tattoo; the irreversibility of her joining his household; the unlikelihood that he would ever in fact return to the Mountain, never mind the difficulty of getting her there too; that even if they managed it, life there for her would be far from what she might imagine; that not only she, but he too would be severely restricted by the Law; that she had no appreciation of how truly vast was the difference between their ranks. He fell silent, unnerved by the fact that Poppy's smile seemed to have withstood his onslaught unchanged. 'You would end up separated from Fern . . . and Krow,' he added as an afterthought.

'Not if they were also to join your household,' she said.

That knocked Carnelian completely off-balance. Poppy seemed to have no doubt they would. He almost asked her what made her think that Fern would want to follow them to Osrakum, but something within him did not want to have that answered. 'Even if all of this were to work out, even if we were all to end up in the Mountain together, one day I would succeed my father and thereafter you would never see my face again . . .'

Poppy's smile thinned on her lips. Her eyes grew intense. 'Look, there's no point in going on about the things that could go wrong; I'm well experienced in how things can go wrong. What of it? At least we'd be able to spend what time there's left together. And if we get to the Mountain, I'll just have to learn to live with what we're allowed. Where do you think I'm going to have a better life?'

'Among the Lepers . . .'

She frowned and shook her head, tears in her eyes. 'I've tried that. I don't want to live there without my family.'

Carnelian felt his heart clench at that word.

'Besides,' she said, forcing her tears back with another smile, 'I want to do something now. Something useful. If a battle's coming, I don't want to watch everyone else getting ready for it and do nothing myself. I can at least look after you and, perhaps, I can act as a link between you and the Lepers. By being here I've proved how easy it is for me to pass through the Marula. They're used to me having access to you and so is everyone else. No one will notice me, either here or there.'

'The Master—'

Her eyes flashed. 'I'm beneath his notice. If you tell him I'm yours, he won't touch me.'

Carnelian considered that and thought she was probably right.

'I'm a woman now and can make my own decisions.'

He noticed how, indeed, she had grown taller; how her face was growing oval, her breasts swelling. If not a woman yet, she was also not a child. He wondered how this change had come upon her so young; then recalled that some orchids, threatened with death, flower early. It made him sad that it might be the pressures of her life that had snatched away what little childhood she might have had left. He had to ignore that, and the hope in her eyes, to focus instead on working out what he must do. His heart leapt at the thought that he might keep her with him. He regarded her. It felt right in his bones. He reached up and began to remove his mask. As it came off he breathed a sigh of relief.

'Carnie!'

She launched into him and he caught her, kneeling to embrace her. She pushed away and gazed at his face in wonder and her tears started his.

At last they disengaged, wiping tears, suddenly a little shy of each other.

'Who's that?' Poppy said, pointing at the homunculus.

Carnelian tried to explain.

'I thought he was a boy until I looked under his mask.'

'He's probably older than any Elder.'

Poppy gave him an anxious glance. 'Did you kill him?'

'Kill?' Carnelian laughed. 'He's not dead, merely sleeping.' Poppy gave him a look of disbelief. 'Really. I made him take a sleeping drug.'

Poppy's eyes grew sharp. 'He has something to do with those things next door?'

Carnelian saw she was pointing to the wall, beyond which lay the Sapients in their capsules. 'You didn't open them, did you?'

She shook her head quickly in a way that made her look very much like a little girl. 'I didn't dare . . .'

He tried to explain who was inside.

Poppy grew pale. 'Childgatherers.'

'Their masters.'

Seeing her fear, he felt a jab of panic. Poppy saw this and reached out to take his arm, smiling. 'Don't worry about me.'

He put his hand over hers and drew her towards the bed, where they sat side by side, with the homunculus behind them. He wanted to ask her so many things, but he needed time to marshal his feelings. 'Tell me about Krow.'

She turned to him, smiling. 'You've noticed how different he is.'

Carnelian nodded. 'I suppose I have.'

'He's a lot happier,' she said, with a warmth that Carnelian had never seen her show towards the youth. He asked her to tell him, from the beginning, what had happened between them.

'Well, when you left' – she gave him a sharp look that made him laugh, but then seized his hand and clung to it – 'we were forced into each other's company a lot. There was no one much else to talk to. I grew used to him, but there was always the . . .' She regarded Carnelian with haunted eyes.

411

'The massacre.'

She swallowed. 'Yes, that lay between us. However much I wanted to like him, it was there. Until one day I asked him about it.'

She frowned, unaware she was kneading his arm, staring at the ground as if seeing something far away. 'For days he stayed away from me, until one day he came and told me everything.'

'Confession can be unburdening,' Carnelian said.

'Yes, it was a confession of sorts. He *did* help the Master in the killing.' Poppy turned to look Carnelian in the eye. 'But only because Akaisha begged him to.'

'Akaisha . . . ?' Carnelian thought about it.

'I think she knew it was the only way to save him from the Master.'

'And she wanted him to carry a message to us.'

'And he did.'

'And we ignored him,' Carnelian said. He let out a groan. 'Why didn't he tell us?'

The sadness that came into Poppy's eyes was answer enough.

'He still did help.'

Poppy nodded. 'It took me a while to persuade him that he could have done nothing more than he did, that he was not responsible for the killing.'

Carnelian understood and smiled. 'No wonder he looks so different.'

'Yes, he is different,' Poppy said, her face suffused with a warmth that displayed how she now felt about Krow.

Carnelian was happy for them both, but this feeling faded as the pressure built up to ask another question. 'And Fern?'

'Oh, you can imagine that was hard. Though his body had recovered by then, his spirit seemed to have fled him, but I worked on him and, eventually, he came round to forgiving Krow. At least, he seems to have; it's difficult to say what he feels. He's so closed now.'

412

She had misunderstood his question. Carnelian tried again. 'You implied earlier that he might want to enter my household . . .'

She searched his eyes, then grimaced. 'I'm not really sure about that. But, surely, there's hope in him wanting to come up with the Lepers?'

Carnelian dropped his gaze, trying to hide his disappointment. He bit his tongue, which would have said: hatred could have motivated him to do that. 'What about Lily?' he asked, wanting to talk about something else.

'What about her?'

It was no good, he could not drag his thoughts away from Fern. He rose. 'It's time to sleep.' He looked around the cell and then back at the bed.

'Let me stay here with you,' Poppy said.

Carnelian nodded. She would be safer. He glanced again at the bed with the homunculus lying on it. In the past he and Poppy would have shared it, but she was getting too old for that. He thought of giving her the bed and making another for himself on the floor, but this was to set a precedent that could only lead to trouble. He found a cupboard that had some blankets in it. He threw these to her and smiled, indicating the floor. 'Wherever you want.'

She glanced at the bed, then gave him a nod. As she made herself comfortable, Carnelian lifted the homunculus and transferred him to his nest of blankets. He kissed Poppy good night, then dowsed the lamp and lay back on his bed. The murmur of the camp rose through the night. He wondered if he had done the right thing by letting her join him. He listened for her breathing. When he heard it, it soothed him. It was the most at home he had felt for a long time.

When he set off the next morning, he left the homunculus in Poppy's care. She had insisted that she could do it. When the little man had woken, they had gazed at each other warily. Carnelian had told the homunculus he had a choice.

413

Either he agreed to her supervision, or else he would have to be drugged. Clearly perplexed by the relationship the Master had with this strange girl, the homunculus elected to remain awake.

As Carnelian led the Lepers out, his body ached all over from the riding on the previous day. He nominated Krow to be his liaison with Lily and Fern. As he gave the youth instructions, he took time to reassure him that Poppy was safe with him. Krow was clearly relieved. 'I wasn't sure it was a good idea, but you know what she's like.'

Carnelian wished his mask did not stop Krow seeing that he too was grinning. 'Yes, I know what she's like.'

After that, in spite of being on either side of the mask, they were easy with each other. With the help of Krow, Fern and Lily, Carnelian divided the Lepers into two wings. Fern was to command one, Lily the other. Riding with a wing on either hand, Carnelian began the weary process of making them battle-ready.

He had to be content with slow progress. He came to understand that, even had he been able to find an aquar for every one of them, they would never become an effective mounted force. Not enough of them were natural riders. One day, in discussion with Fern and Lily, it occurred to him that perhaps their focus was all wrong. He asked the others if they felt that the Lepers would be happier fighting on foot. Lily said, with some emotion, that her people would be much happier. That evening Carnelian explained his idea to Osidian, who reluctantly agreed. The following day he had the Lepers modify their saddle-chairs so that they were more like those of the Plainsmen. The most important addition was a crossbar, but longer than a Plainsman one. As well as its rider, each aquar could now carry two more Lepers, hanging from either end of its crossbar. These pairs were matched closely in weight so that they would not unbalance their aquar. It took some practice, but soon, for the first time, the Leper force was able to move in a body without leaving stragglers. It was only then that Carnelian began to train them to fight in hornwalls. They improvised spears and shields by tearing apart abandoned sartlar kraals. To his satisfaction, the Lepers took to the new training well. Soon they were forming solid, bristling walls.

One afternoon he returned to the watch-tower well satisfied. That day the Lepers had swept forward in their two wings; at his signal, they had dismounted and, with almost no problems, had formed up into hornwall rings. These were not perfect and were of different sizes as each contained a single settlement contingent, but their shields had locked in an overlapping wall over which their rough spears had bristled, a hedge of fire-hardened points.

Poppy was waiting for him with a smile. These days even the homunculus smiled. Gradually, he and Poppy had lost their wariness of each other. Sometimes, they seemed almost to be friends. With his help, Poppy had transformed their cell. It smelled sweeter. Each day she and the homunculus brought up water with which they could wash a little. She prepared food for them both. Sometimes she would spend the night with Fern and Krow, and Carnelian would miss her. The homunculus perhaps did too. Certainly, one time, he had asked Carnelian when the 'mistress' was going to return. Often Carnelian found himself smiling at his strange new 'family'.

That night when, as usual, he ate with Osidian beside the heliograph, Carnelian told him he thought the Lepers ready to be combined with his huimur. Osidian raised a brow. Carnelian had been resisting his urging for this for quite some time. Osidian gave a nod. Carnelian had some idea of how the training of the dragons had been going. The crews and the new commanders had settled in well enough for Osidian to begin exploring ways in which he could combine the flame-pipes. Carnelian was not certain what it was Osidian was attempting to achieve, but he seemed focused on some particular goal. Sometimes, while with the Lepers, he had noticed some smoke smearing against the heat-white sky. Osidian had been sparing with his naphtha and had made sure to use different dragons for his experiments. It was unlikely that they would have enough time to take them back to Makar to replenish their tanks.

So it was that Carnelian brought the Lepers to join Osidian's dragons. The Lepers formed in their wings on either end of the dragon line. Day after day he and Osidian laboured to coordinate them, the Lepers learning to respond to simple mirror signals from the towers. Each night the Lepers returned coated red with dust. The dragons too, so that sometimes they seemed carved from sandstone, only their towers remaining pale upon their backs.

One day Carnelian noticed that Morunasa and the Oracles had all disappeared. That night, frowning, Osidian confessed they had retired into the stables to birth their maggots. With a shudder, Carnelian remembered them emerging from Osidian's wounds. Even high in his cell, Carnelian felt too close to the filthy thing that was going on down in the bowels of the watch-tower.

The manoeuvres had long ago driven the sartlar from a great swathe of land to the west of the watch-tower. Without their labour, the fields were not watered. The hri had yellowed, then dried brown. The constant passage of aquar and dragons had broken its dead grip on the land. Every movement churned up great choking clouds of dust. At first these had drifted slowly into the south-west, but more recently the breeze had failed. After that every day was spent navigating through red mist. From the watch-tower each morning, the land looked like a sea. Carnelian tried not to see in this the sea of blood that inundated his dreams.

*   *   *

416

Craning forward in his command chair, Carnelian was watching with pride as the Lepers' line kept pace with Earth-is-Strong. Through the murk he could see its blade curving away with only some nicks along its edge.

His Lefthand spoke. 'From Heart-of-Thunder. Now.'

At Carnelian's nod, the man spoke through his voice fork to the mirrorman on the roof. Carnelian imagined how, to Fern down on the ground, the flashing must appear like a star. The blade began dissolving, frothing like a wave reaching a shore. Carnelian watched breathlessly as the Lepers coalesced into rings around their aquar. His cheeks pushed up into his mask as he smiled. The pattern of rings held neatly to the same curve as before. Then they slipped out of view as Earth-is-Strong continued her inexorable advance. Carnelian was about to give the command to bring her to a halt, when his Lefthand spoke again. 'An urgent message, Master.'

'From Heart-of-Thunder?'

The man shook his head. 'The watch-tower, Master.' He paused, staring.

'Well?' Carnelian demanded.

'Dragons have been sighted, Master, advancing from the north.'

Carnelian's first thought was of Poppy. She was there, defenceless. 'Are you sure that's what it said?'

The Lefthand was half listening to him, half listening to some voice in his helmet. 'That's what our mirrorman says.'

'Send a message to—'

Carnelian broke off, seeing the Lefthand pressing his ear-piece into his ear. 'Battleline.'

Carnelian did not need to ask if that was from Heart-of-Thunder. He had been hearing that command from Osidian for so many days that, whenever it came, it was as if Osidian himself were in the cabin issuing the order. Automatically, he sent his instructions to Fern and was soon receiving more from Osidian as they slowed the dragon line to give the Lepers time to mount up and catch them. He was so busy with this it was a while before the realization dawned. They were actually going into battle. Though they had been practising for this for more than a month, it still came as a shock. It was as if he had never really believed there was going to be a battle. He could no longer hide from the reality of what might happen to Fern and the others on the ground.

The road was there in front of them, the wall carrying the leftway forming a pale foundation to the heat-grey sky. Upon that road dragons were marching in a column three abreast. A mass of saurian flesh bearing at least two dozen towers. The monsters filled the road, driving the travellers with their wagons and chariots off into the fields. Carnelian felt a twinge of pity that those innocents were now likely to find themselves in the middle of fire and carnage. His pounding heart seemed to be shaking him. He glanced to starboard to make sure Fern and his Lepers were maintaining their position. The enemy flank was still exposed to them. Carnelian's anxiety became exasperation. What were they doing? The battleline was churning up a duststorm that must for some while have been visible from the road, never mind from the dragon towers, but the monsters were marching on as if crewed by the blind. More incongruities forced their way through his confusion. If they did not find a ramp soon to get off the road, he and Osidian would catch them, unable to manoeuvre. Their pipes did not even appear to be lit.

He turned to his Lefthand. 'Ask the lookout if he can see their auxiliaries.'

As the man muttered into his voice fork, Carnelian returned to his staring. An abrupt silence brought his attention back. 'What is it?'

The Lefthand pointed towards the head of the dragon column. Carnelian grew angry, not knowing what he was supposed to be looking at. Then he spotted a twinkling on the summit of one of the foremost dragon towers. They were being sent some message. Carnelian waited impatiently for it to be relayed down by the mirrorman. At last, the Lefthand glanced up. 'I have come to join my strength to yours – Orum.'

'Aurum!' Carnelian stared at the dragons. Whose could they be but Aurum's? What did the message mean? Carnelian waited for Osidian's commands while, all the time, they drew closer to the road.

A movement from his Lefthand made him aware they were receiving another message.

'From Heart-of-Thunder, Master. Stand down.'

Carnelian began composing a reply. He had to know what Osidian's intentions were. A glittering made him look up. Aurum was transmitting again. He glanced down at his Lefthand. The man's lips mouthed some syllables, then he looked up at Carnelian. '"I will speak to you alone."'

On the ground, Carnelian watched the escort of auxiliaries approaching. He glanced back at his dragon line. The dust had settled, revealing its massive, unbroken wall. There at its furthest end was Heart-of-Thunder, still in his position in the battleline. That Osidian had chosen to remain there made it clear he believed Aurum capable of treachery. Though he no doubt was itching to come himself to meet the old Master, Osidian had delegated the task to him.

Carnelian looked around at Fern, dismounted behind him, holding the reins of both their aquar. Ranged around him was a detachment of mounted Lepers: squalid mounds of rags filling saddle-chairs of all kinds that had been brutalized by the crossbars which now projected on either side. The Lepers who had arrived clinging to those crossbars had unhitched their makeshift spears and were forming up into a hornwall. He wished he could see their faces to know what they were feeling. Surely they must know this legion to be the one that had devastated their land.

Drumming footfalls heralded a group of Marula coming to join them. Carnelian was glad of them and turned to face the auxiliaries, who were now near enough for the dust they raised

419

to be falling upon him like hail. They halted and a single rider rode through. Carnelian stiffened. Though swathed in black robes, there was no doubting this was a Master. The apparition pulled on his reins and his aquar settled to the ground. Servants who had dismounted sped forward and plunged knees first into the dust. They placed ranga ready and then the Master swung his legs out from the saddle-chair, put his feet into them, lifted out a staff and, leaning on it, levered himself erect. Rising to his full height he dwarfed his servants utterly. His black robe fell to the dust so that he seemed to have no legs. The Master stirred a rusty miasma from the earth as he came forward, using the staff as a walking aid.

Carnelian advanced to meet him with trepidation. He knew this Lord. As he neared he caught glimpses of an exquisite face of gold. The Master loomed before him. 'Celestial.'

'It is Suth Carnelian you address, my Lord Aurum.'

The gloved hand of the old Lord jerked a sign of irritation. 'It was Nephron I asked to speak with, my Lord.'

The voice stirred in Carnelian a visceral loathing. 'Nevertheless it was his wish – and mine – that you should speak to me.'

He regarded the towering shape, possessed by hatred. There before him was the murderer of the Lepers, the murderer of his uncle Crail. Carnelian heard the Lepers stirring behind him. He no longer cared how they might react. He welcomed their hatred to swell his own. They were there at his back like raveners he had trained himself and leashed. It would take only a word from him and they would fall on the monster that had inflicted indescribable suffering on their people. The Lepers would have their payment and Carnelian would have his revenge.

'Very well,' said the monster, his tones of condescension sweetening the lust Carnelian had for his destruction. 'I have come to join my legion to the Celestial's.'

'You wish to take arms against his brother, my Lord?' Carnelian said, his voice a knife.

A gloved hand rose and made an elegant gesture of negation. 'Against the Ichorian Legion that is only a few days behind me and that has been sent to destroy him.'

AURUM

Not everything, once broken, can be mended.
(a proverb from the City at the Gates)

'What?' Carnelian said, exasperated. He heard the Lepers behind him reacting to the tone of his voice.

'I will say nothing further except directly to the Lord Nephron.'

Aurum, the very image of unbending arrogance, stoked the fires of revenge in Carnelian's heart. He imagined turning to address the Lepers. Announcing to them that he whom they most hated stood there before them, within their power. They would seize him. He would watch as the Unclean put their hands upon a Ruling Lord of the Great. Perhaps they would tear his black cloak from him, his mask. Stripping the monster of his terrible, unholy power. Exposing him to their pitiless stares. For a moment Carnelian savoured it. The humiliation of the old Master he loathed; but then Aurum's words began to soak through his fantasy. Could it really be possible that the Ichorian Legion was bearing down on them? If so it presaged immense political upheaval in Osrakum. He tried to get hold of the politics, but his mind glanced off the complexities. He could not resolve how such a thing could have come to pass. This failure further weakened his confidence. Aurum's capture by the Lepers might lead to chaos. What if his legion reacted to defend him? Osidian would launch the attack. Lily and her people on the other flank could have no idea what had happened. The situation would ignite into a fiery holocaust. Even if Osidian were victorious, they would be maimed – and then have to deal with the Ichorian. If, that was, Aurum spoke the truth; but if not, why was he here? What could he hope to achieve with such an implausible lie?

'Your silence, my Lord, does not impress me,' said Aurum, seeming to rise even taller, holding his staff as if he were wearing a court robe in the Halls of Thunder.

Carnelian regarded him, lusting to tear down this imperious presence. If he did not destroy him now, what would come of his decision? Thrice before he had spared those in his power: the Maruli on the road to Osrakum, Ravan, Osidian. The consequences had been death and massacre.

He glanced round at Fern, who had suffered the greatest loss from his decisions. A movement from Aurum made him turn back. The Master was already starting towards his aquar. 'My Lord.'

The Great Lord looked round, his mask catching fire from the sun down its right-hand side.

'Return with me to my huimur, my Lord. Do this as an act of good faith and Nephron will talk to you.'

Reluctance was written in the cast of Aurum's shoulders. Anger rose in Carnelian. Here at least he had a battle he could fight to win. 'Nephron suspects treachery or else he would be here himself. He has no reason to love you, my Lord. It might be better if you were to remember that neither have I.' There was a Master's authority in Carnelian's voice that surprised him. Nevertheless, he meant what he said.

For some time they faced each other in what he felt was a contending of wills. He had drawn his line and would not retreat. At last he noticed Aurum's shoulders relaxing a little. His mask scanned the ranks of Lepers behind Carnelian as if he were seeing them for the first time. 'What manner of creatures are those?'

'Inhabitants of the valleys below.' Carnelian took pleasure in telling Aurum this. He hoped it would stir fear in his black heart. Instead the Great Lord reacted with a gesture of disgust.

'I had hoped I had succeeded in destroying all the vermin.'

The rage boiling up in Carnelian overflowed. Almost he forgot his decision and threw the Master to his victims, but he mastered himself. 'My Lord should take care. These people have reason to hate him, bitterly.'

Aurum laughed. 'Since when do we who are Chosen concern ourselves with the feelings of inferiors?'

Carnelian smiled a cold smile behind his mask. Let the monster feel invulnerable, for the moment. 'My Lord is free to return to his host. We can settle this business with fire.'

Aurum's free hand rose in a half-formed gesture of appeasement whose speed belied its casual framing. 'I shall come with you, my Lord.' He summoned his aquar and his slaves. They brought the creature and made it sink to the red earth. As Aurum climbed back into his saddle-chair, Carnelian watched how heavily the old Lord leaned upon his staff.

'Who is this Master?' Carnelian turned to Fern, who it was had spoken, hearing the suspicion in his voice. 'Aurum,' he said, then had to endure the look Fern gave him of shocked disbelief.

Once more aboard Earth-is-Strong, Carnelian stood behind his command chair in which the Lord Aurum was sitting. He had offered it to him in pity for his condition. He resented feeling any sympathy for the old bastard but, after watching with what difficulty he had scaled the ladders up to the command deck, Carnelian could not bring himself to force the old man to stand leaning on his staff against the sway of the cabin. Besides, he preferred not to have the monster behind him.

He had had his Lefthand send a message to Heart-of-

Thunder telling Osidian he had Aurum in his cabin. Osidian's only reply had been: 'Stand fast in the battleline.'

Attar of lilies was rising from Aurum's black-shrouded form. As always, Carnelian's gorge rose at the smell. It brought forcibly to mind the days of his near imprisonment in the old man's chambers with their clocks and mirrors. Other, earlier memories seeped in unbidden, of his father, wounded, on their journey to Osrakum. Carnelian realized he was reminded of the sickening odour of rotting blood that had come off his father then. Though he could not consciously smell it now, he became convinced Aurum was using perfume to disguise some similar decay.

He had to stop being distracted. Quite apart from Aurum's news, they had a crisis threatening here. How long would it be before the Lepers demanded to have their enemy delivered to them? It seemed to him unlikely Osidian would comply.

A command came from Heart-of-Thunder, demanding Aurum send instructions to his huimur. For some moments the old Master sat motionless as if he had not heard the Lefthand but then, without turning, he began to speak. His commands were broadcast from the roof towards his dragons, bidding his commanders descend from their towers and, leaving their crews, take all further orders from the Lord Nephron. Aurum terminated his message with his command code. Carnelian felt a surge of relief.

Carnelian clambered up the brassman to the leftway, then walked along its ragged, crumbling edge to gaze north. Upon the road, Aurum's dragons came lumbering, three abreast, their towers bobbing gently like the pendulums of the old man's clocks. Keeping pace with them, on a parallel course, Osidian's dragons were shadows obscured by the russet murk they were churning up through the fields. Carnelian looked west, squinting against the low sun. The Leper tide was coming in past the cisterns. He regarded them, wondering what it must be like for them to watch the same dragons that

425

had brought destruction to their valleys now being invited into their camp. He imagined what Lily must be feeling. He would have to do something to keep them placated, at least until he had a chance to find out what was going on.

The clank of ranga striking brass made Carnelian turn. Aurum's looming bulk was crossing the brassman with the aid of his staff. Reaching the rough stair cut into the rubble of the leftway, the Master paused; his mask, gazing up at the steps, looked like a cold flame. Carnelian gestured to his Hands, standing behind Aurum. They understood him and, coming forward, they offered their assistance to the giant Master. Aurum's mask, glancing down, caused the men to cower. He floated his arms up and, taking them like the poles of a chariot, they helped him up onto the leftway.

Carnelian approached him, hearing the Master's breath loud behind his mask. Again he was struck by how weak Aurum had become. It made him angry. He did not want to feel sympathy for his enemy.

Aurum glanced up at the watch-tower. 'Let us meet down here.' He struck the cobbles with his staff. Carnelian reminded him that Osidian's command had been specific. 'He wants us to wait for him up there.' He pointed up at the heliograph platform. For a moment the Master seemed again granite, then his shoulders softened. He bowed his head, nodding, so that his cowl slid forward to quench the cold fire of his mask.

As they entered the watch-tower together, the roar of the camp faded, even as, in the confined space, Aurum's breathing grew louder. Its rasp marked the labour of each step. Carnelian's hands rose to give the old man support, but he pulled them back as if they had been about to betray him. He made himself recall Crail, whom this Lord had had maimed to death. The memory of that loss made Carnelian glance up the hollow core of the tower. Poppy was up there. Fear that she might fall foul of the Master possessed him.

'My Lord, I shall go ahead to make sure the way is clear.'

Aurum's gloved hands clung to his staff. He seemed too

busy struggling with his breathing to respond. Carnelian climbed the first ladder. When he reached its top he glanced down to make sure Aurum was following him. The Master was halfway up, each rung wringing a groan from him. Steeling himself against compassion, Carnelian began climbing the next ladder.

Entering their cell, Carnelian saw two small heads wedged into the slits that looked down onto the camp. The heads pulled back and turned. Carnelian was struck by the shocking contrast between Poppy's face and the wizened face of the homunculus. She plucked the little man's blinding mask up from the bed and handed it to him; he put it on. Carnelian could not help smiling; not only at how the homunculus obeyed her, but at how he himself would now follow her implied command. He released his mask.

The severe look in Poppy's eyes drove away all amusement. 'Whose are the new dragons?'

Recently her voice had become more womanly. At such forceful speech in the tongue of the Ochre, Carnelian felt as if Akaisha and the other Elders were in the cell, judging him.

'They're Hookfork's, aren't they?'

'Yes.'

Poppy's eyes narrowed. 'Is he here?'

'He is.'

'You're going to give him to Lily?'

'It's— There are—' Carnelian grew angry. 'There are things you don't understand.'

Her eyes were burning into him. He and she had been here before with horrific consequences. Her anger was justified. His was fired by guilt. 'Look, I don't understand what's happening myself. I need— We need to know more before we act and I'm scared of what the Lepers might do.'

'With good reason,' she said.

'I will talk to them, but not until I know more.'

427

Her expression softened. 'Do you want me to go and do what I can to keep them calm?'

Carnelian shook his head. 'It's not safe for you to move through the tower alone. Besides, you would have to go through the stables.'

She paled, for she knew what was down there.

'Can you please just stay here?'

When she nodded, he took his leave of them both and, making sure they could not be seen from the hallway, he slipped out. He stood for some moments, his back to the door, telling himself she would be safe, then he advanced on the ladder that led to the roof.

Aurum was seated with his back to the heliograph, recovering from the ordeal of his climb. Carnelian moved to the edge of the platform and gazed down into the mass of Marula camped at the foot of the tower. In their midst stood the twenty or so black-robed Masters: Aurum's Lesser Chosen commanders. Carnelian felt as if he had left his heart behind in the cell with Poppy. He feared he might stray into betraying not only her, but also the Lepers and the Plainsmen, by dealing with the monster, Aurum. And it would be not only the living he betrayed, but also the dead.

Below, Osidian's dragons were manoeuvring into their positions in the circular rampart they made every night, facing out towards the land. Beyond lay the grey mass of the Lepers huddling down, as the waves of dust beat upon them from the passage of Aurum's dragons on a course to somewhere beyond the cisterns.

When Osidian climbed onto the edge of the platform, he dismissed the lookouts from their deadman's chairs. As he advanced on Carnelian and Aurum, the lookouts clambered down out of sight.

Aurum, who had risen, bowed as deeply as he could, pulling himself back erect with the help of his staff. 'Celestial.'

428

Though the old man was the taller, it was Osidian who seemed to loom, a black tower crowned by the muted sun of his mask. He reached up and began unfastening it. Masking Law dictated Carnelian and Aurum must do the same. When Carnelian's face was naked, he watched Aurum attempting to remove his mask one-handed. The bony hand he had ungloved fumbled at the fastening. The joints of his fingers were swollen red. Watching the procedure, Carnelian had to resist an impulse to help him.

As the gold shell came away, Carnelian stared in horror at Aurum's face. For a moment it seemed that of one of the Wise was looking back at them. Aurum's wizened, sallow skin looked hardly thick enough to stop his skull tearing out. Cheekbones, chin, the rims of his eye sockets were all a geometry of blades. His lips revealed the pattern of the teeth behind. His eyes, blue ice sunk deep. Ice that had a blinding bloom of frost.

'Why, my Lord, do you defect to me?'

Carnelian did not turn to Osidian, but kept his gaze upon Aurum's withered face. He remembered how once it had been cracked like a fine porcelain glaze. Now the cracks had deepened, uniting around the mouth and eyes into fissures resembling those that cut into the margin of the Guarded Land.

'Celestial, I would speak to you alone.'

Rage rose in Carnelian. Once before he had been excluded from hearing what Aurum had come to say.

'Lord Suth will remain here,' said Osidian.

Aurum gave a muted shrug. 'I have come, Celestial, so that together we can defeat the Ichorian.'

Shock overturned Osidian's composure. 'The Ichorian?'

'Even now it is only days away from here under Imago's command.'

'Jaspar?' Carnelian said.

Osidian's head cocked to one side as he frowned. 'Osrakum is undefended?'

'Apparently, the Great have chosen to garrison the Gates with their tyadra.'

Carnelian imagined his brothers at the Gates with all the other guardsmen of the Great. What part had his father played in these events?

Osidian's face pulled back into the shadow of his cowl. 'How came the Clave to sanction this?'

Aurum began some vague gesture with his clawed hand. 'Of course, Celestial, I did not witness their deliberations, but I believe Imago had been urging them to send the Ichorian against you for some time. His thesis seems to have been that, the Lesser Chosen having witnessed your election, the Great dare not trust to them any force dispatched to defeat you.'

Osidian's frown deepened.

'It will not surprise you, Celestial, to hear that the Clave long resisted him. Until, that was, the commanders of Qunoth were brought before them with the forbearance of the Imperial Power. There they claimed you had issued an edict enfranchising all their kind.'

Carnelian went cold. Was it, then, the act of mercy he had urged upon Osidian that had brought this thing about? He glanced at him, expecting to be accused, but Osidian's eyes seemed more opaque than Aurum's. Carnelian felt a need to put fire into their discussion. 'I had believed Imago's faction to be weak in the Clave, but if I understand you rightly, my Lord, they have made him He-who-goes-before.'

Carnelian half expected the old Master to ignore him again, but Aurum turned and seemed almost eager to answer him. 'He had the support of Ykoriana.'

'He has had that before and it was not enough.'

'He did not before have use of her rings.'

Carnelian frowned, trying to make sense of this. Aurum was speaking of her voting rings. Surely these could not be used in the Clave?

'She married Imago?'

430

Carnelian heard the disbelief in Osidian's voice, but his face was lit by shock.

The membranes of Aurum's lips slid back over his yellowed teeth. 'Indeed, Celestial, after she had divorced the God Emperor.'

Carnelian looked from the old man to Osidian, but there were no answers there. He turned back to Aurum. 'Does she fear Osidian so much?'

Before Aurum could answer, Osidian spoke. 'Why would the Wise reveal that I had survived to my mother?'

The answer to this at first seemed clear to Carnelian: it was the arrival of the Qunoth commanders that had betrayed Osidian's existence. But then Carnelian recalled that Aurum had claimed the Clave had already been discussing the situation for some time. He followed Osidian's glare to Aurum's face. The flame of life in the old man seemed to gutter. For a moment he might have been a Sapient wearing eyes of unpolished sapphire.

'It was the God Emperor who informed her, but it was I who had sent Them a letter.'

Osidian snorted.

Aurum came back to life. 'I will make no apologies, Celestial. After Legions' schemes failed, I was left in an untenable position. The letter was the regrettable conclusion of calculation.'

Osidian's lips curled. 'I had not assumed you joined me from love. What further calculation is it that brings you here, my Lord? Is it possible you believe that I will triumph?'

Though Osidian's stance and tone were communicating contempt, Carnelian knew him well enough to feel certain there was something else underneath. It made him sad. His heart told him Osidian really was hoping the reasons the old monster had come were love and faith in him.

Aurum had a predatory gleam in his eyes. Detecting Osidian's weakness, he was devising a way to exploit it. Carnelian sought to cut him off. 'We know that cannot be

431

why you have come, my Lord. It is some far more squalid motive that impels you.'

Aurum looked as if he was about to spit venom, but then his face became again an icy mask. 'Suth Carnelian is correct. It is inconceivable you will triumph, Celestial.'

'So why have you come, Aurum?' Osidian said, rallying.

Aurum's free hand sketched an elegant gesture, but his face grew brittle with malice. 'I have harboured contempt for those of my peers who saw fit to bow to the Empress and the Wise and conspired with them to send me into exile, but that is nothing to the disgust I now feel that they have become so subservient as to send the Ichorian from the canyon. All my life I have striven to maintain our ancient privileges against the encroachment of the other Powers.' His hand curled into talons. 'But I have lost my faith in the Great and what I now do I do for my own advantage. I come here because I have made a compact with the Wise.'

Osidian sneered at the old man. 'Your speech is filled with patrician pride, my Lord Aurum, but your long service to the Wise makes it clear that your House would be more comfortable among the Lesser Chosen.'

Some colour oozed into Aurum's deathly face. 'I would have thought my Lord would understand how circumstances can conspire to force one into unwanted alliances. I can see in your face how low you have fallen and I already knew what squalid accommodations you have had to stomach.'

Carnelian stepped between them. 'My Lords, we have all suffered humiliations, but what shall it profit us to cast these in each other's faces?'

He was glad to see their composure returning. Aurum made a vague gesture of apology. 'The Lord Suth is not in error. We have the same enemies and have both been the playthings of the Wise. You have no doubt encountered Grand Sapient Legions?'

Carnelian sensed the old Master was returning to his sly game.

'It was he who forced me to make an appearance of defending Makar. He assured me it would bring you into his power.' Aurum's taloned fingers closed into a fist.

Osidian shrugged and, though he spoke offhandedly, Carnelian felt he was watching Aurum carefully. 'It was we who took him. Even now he dreams here beneath our feet.'

Though the old Master appeared uninterested in this, he could not help glancing down as if he might see the Grand Sapient through the watch-tower roof. 'When he sent me no signal, I guessed he had failed. It was that which made me reconsider my position. I decided it was perilous to continue my alliance with the Wise. In my dealings with them, I had come to suspect that, behind the adamantine unity they present to us, there lie fractures. Though Legions had been for a long time dominant among the Twelve, there were other factions. With him out of contact, who knew what would happen? Certainly, I did not wish to fall victim to their calculations. I risked everything in a direct appeal to the God Emperor.'

'You were a fool to put your trust in my brother. He has always been my mother's creature. Though I confess to some surprise that being made the Gods has not put iron in his backbone.'

Aurum nodded. 'We both have reasons to hate your mother, but not only her. You must be aware of the part Imago played in your abduction.' The Master glanced at Osidian, perhaps hoping that this was news to him. 'Though you suffered most from that, Celestial, I too suffered. When your brother cheated you of the Masks, I too was cheated who had risked so much in your cause. Remember, Celestial, that both of us have suffered exile.' He glanced at Osidian again, but he seemed impassive. 'So, Celestial, even if only for these reasons, we might both enjoy destroying Imago.'

Osidian smiled coldly. 'I can see, my Lord, why you have had need to once more become the tool of the Wise, but you have not yet explained to me why I should share that choice.'

Aurum grew very still, giving Carnelian the feeling that

they were finally coming to the core of his intention. 'Celestial, even if you did not wish to pull Imago down and, through him, your mother; even if you cared nothing for the way she is subverting the Balance; still you would have no choice.'

Osidian groaned. 'Was it the Wise who told you that?'

'Grand Sapient Lands who is now regnant among the Twelve has informed me of his conviction that we can defeat Imago. He bade me tell you that, for all its fearsome reputation, the Ichorian is more accustomed to ceremonial than it is to war. Our two legions of the line would already be more warlike than the Ichorian, but have, besides, the unique experience of having confronted huimur against huimur.'

'I deny none of this, my Lord, but why am I bound to fight?'

'Because, Celestial, it is the only chance you have. You have reached the zenith of your stolen power. If you retreat, your strength will ebb. Defeat will become inevitable.'

Carnelian looked to Osidian, willing him to deny this, but he seemed peculiarly inert. Carnelian turned his attention back to Aurum. He desired to dull the predacious gleam in his eyes. 'Why was it that you, my Lord, sharing all my father's crimes, should be merely exiled, while he was deposed?'

It took some moments for the Master to disengage his eyes from Osidian. When he turned to Carnelian he seemed to be thinking of something else. He frowned as if he was hearing Carnelian's question again, but could not understand it. Then, before he could mask it, a sly expression flitted across his skull face.

Osidian drew the Master's attention away. 'My Lord, how far is Imago from here?'

Aurum shrugged. 'Two days ago I received communication from him claiming he was in Magayon. I know his courier took two more days to locate me. All in all it would surprise me if he was here within anything less than seven days.'

'He could be here in half that if he marched night and day,' said Carnelian.

Aurum shook his head. 'I believe my Lord Imago will be feeling too confident to incommode himself with night marches.'

Nodding, Osidian withdrew into himself. Carnelian watched Aurum watching him. At last the old man spoke. 'I am weary, Celestial. With your leave . . . ?'

Osidian seemed to wake. 'I have had a cell prepared for you below.'

Aurum frowned. 'I would rather return to my huimur tower.' His free hand began to make a sign, then stopped. He looked anxious, worn out. 'I have had it modified for my use. It has been my home for so long.'

Osidian regarded him with a frown. 'Very well. We shall send a signal to your huimur and have it come here to berth alongside this watch-tower. I would not wish to submit my Lord to the inconvenience of having to cross the camp below. However, I will have to insist that once the creature arrives, all its crew should quit it.'

As Aurum and Osidian negotiated over how many of his household he would be allowed to retain, Carnelian sighed with relief that they were not going to have to share their watch-tower with the old monster.

Carnelian stood with Osidian at the edge of the platform watching Aurum's dragon lumbering towards them. They had summoned it with a signal from the heliograph, using the last rays of the sinking sun. Its lurid disc was forcing Carnelian to squint in spite of the mask he was holding up before his face. Aurum had already begun his painful descent to the leftway. Carnelian reassured himself that Poppy was safe in their cell, then he took a step away from the edge so that he could allow his mask to drop. For a while Osidian did not react. Something about his stillness made Carnelian uneasy. 'Osidian?'

He still did not move.

'We need to talk, my Lord.'

At last, he turned. As his mask fell away, his face was revealed. Carnelian's heart faltered. Such sadness. 'What ails you?'

'Have you not heard enough to know?'

'I thought you wanted this.'

Osidian gave a humourless chuckle. 'Oh, no, not this.'

'Can we even be sure he tells the truth? We only have his word that Jaspar is marching here. Perhaps it is another ruse to take you alive.'

Osidian shook his head slowly. Carnelian wondered at his fatalistic certainty. 'And you would trust him enough to have him fight at our side?'

'He is as trapped as are we.'

Carnelian gazed out over their camp, all washed with gold. Beyond their dragon wall, the Lepers. They would never accept fighting alongside their most hated enemy. 'How can we ally ourselves with him?'

'How can we not? Can you provide me with another legion, Carnelian? Shall we fight the more than fifty huimur of the Ichorian with but two dozen of our own?'

Carnelian struggled to find reasons other than the hatred of the Lepers or his own revulsion. 'If we must use his huimur, can we not strip him of his command?'

Osidian shook his head and seemed to be seeing someone else before him. 'There is no time to train their crews to operate without their commanders. We might be able to control the legion through them, but the last time we tried it, you may remember it was not a great success. They are accustomed to taking orders from Aurum. He has been their Legate for years and, as far as they know, has been appointed by the God Emperor.'

Such logic was unassailable. Carnelian felt cornered. 'Why fight the battle at all?'

Osidian frowning, staring blindly, gave Carnelian hope he was considering an alternative. 'We could retreat back to Qunoth, or down to the Leper Valleys. The longer we deny

Jaspar victory, the more time there is for the political situation in Osrakum to destabilize further.'

Light came back into Osidian's eyes, as if he had climbed up out of darkness. 'If Imago secures anything approaching a victory, then not only he but also my mother shall conquer . . . everything. What would remain to stop her pursuing the Wise for their plotting against her? What was left of the Balance would shatter in her hand. Her power would become absolute.'

'Only in Osrakum,' said Carnelian. 'It is the only world that she cares about.'

'Can you be sure of that?'

Carnelian realized he could not. Apart from himself, or his father perhaps, every Master he had met was so dazzled by Osrakum that, in comparison, the outer world appeared a colourless miasma. Nevertheless, it was likely he and Osidian had drawn Ykoriana's gaze out past the Sacred Wall. Even if they were delivered to her, could he be certain she would not vent her bile on the subject peoples? Though he might hate the world as it was, how could he be sure the world remade would not be worse?

Osidian interrupted his thoughts. 'Even were we to adopt this strategy, it could not hope to work. Wherever we went, the rope would tighten around our throats. We would quickly run out of supplies, without which the huimur would soon lose their strength, their fire. What other forces we had would melt away.'

Osidian shook his head, sadness ageing him. 'What power we have now, we must use or let it wither in our hand. The Wise have us in a trap I can see no way to escape.'

Desperation made Carnelian irritable. 'Surely it is the Empress who has ensnared us?'

Osidian shook his head again. 'It is possible she is as ensnared as we are.'

Carnelian frowned. 'Are you claiming that the Wise wanted the Clave to send the Ichorian?'

'It would seem so. Perhaps they did not wish to disrupt their military system. Perhaps my edict has reached more Legates than I imagined. It might even be that, without Legions, the rest of the Twelve are loath to operate his Domain. If, as Aurum claims, Lands is regnant, he might wish to keep that Domain weak. The flows of power among the Twelve are too subterranean to fathom.'

Carnelian had grown increasingly frustrated, as if the snares were catching at his limbs and mind. 'But what you are saying is that they have deliberately collaborated in the breaking of the Balance.'

'It was already broken. Aurum's letter to Molochite put the Wise in my mother's power. How would you seek to heal such a breakage?'

Carnelian imagined the tripod of the Commonwealth with only two legs. 'Break it further in the hope of putting it back together as it was before. But, then, why would they send Aurum—?' Carnelian gaped at Osidian. 'The Wise want us to defeat Jaspar. If we do, Ykoriana will fall.'

Osidian was staring into the ground. 'Not only she, but the Great would have failed, for they voted for Jaspar; voted to send the Ichorian.'

Carnelian understood. 'So each of the Powers would be seen to have played its part in undermining the Balance.'

'More than this, it would be evident that the House of the Masks was in conflict with itself. Threatening another civil war.'

'To which the Balance was the original solution . . .' said Carnelian, dazzled by the elegance of such a scheme.

'And would be so again.'

Carnelian saw a problem. 'But we would still be out here, and now victorious, with the Three Gates poorly defended against us.'

Osidian hunched over. 'Lands does not believe we will triumph.'

'But I thought—' Carnelian understood. 'We are equally matched.'

'Yes, we and the Ichorian will destroy each other. Even if we survive, we will be maimed, pitifully weak. None would dare give us aid. Some means will be found to stop me reaching Osrakum alive. The Wise will rebuild the Balance, mortaring it with blood from all three Powers: a three-way sacrifice.'

'You and Ykoriana; Jaspar . . . and me . . .'

'Do not forget our dear friend Aurum.'

'But of the Wise . . . ? Legions?'

'Did you not notice how Aurum reacted when I told him we had the Grand Sapient here?'

Carnelian slumped. 'So we have already lost.'

Osidian glared, nodding, frowning so hard his birthmark foundered among the creases. 'Unless I can devise a way to defeat Imago and emerge with our legions unscathed.'

Carnelian gazed at him in hope. 'Do you believe you can . . . ?'

'Not by myself.'

For a moment Carnelian thought Osidian was asking for his help, but then he saw Osidian was not looking at him, that he had once more retreated into some inner darkness. 'Who else . . . ?'

Osidian hung his head and Carnelian knew what he meant to do. He shook his head with horror. 'You cannot mean to submit yourself to the maggots again?'

Osidian lifted his head. 'Do you believe I want to do it? Only the God can help me now.'

'But you can't—'

Rage flashed in Osidian's eyes. 'Have you any other suggestion? Well, do you? I would be happy to entertain any alternative.'

Carnelian had none to offer. 'What am I supposed to do while I wait for you?'

Osidian shrugged. 'Maintain order?'

Fear and disgust flared to anger in Carnelian. 'By which

you mean, among other things, that I have to keep the Lepers from getting their hands on Aurum?'

'If we are victorious, there will be plenty of time after the battle to pay them what I owe.'

They climbed back down into the tower. Carnelian eyed the ladder that Osidian would soon descend. Emotions were twisting in him so fast he could not grab hold of what it was he felt. Unexpectedly, Osidian moved across the landing to open the door that gave into the cell in which the Sapients were lodged. Carnelian followed him in. Osidian unmasked. Carnelian anxiously closed the door before removing his own mask. As Osidian looked round at the capsules leaning against the walls, Carnelian watched his face. There was a sadness there, a quietness. He noted how Osidian held his mask against his body with both hands. Stooping, he laid it upon the floor with such care it seemed he feared to wake the Sapients. He approached the capsule containing Legions' vague shadow form. He grasped its lid. The seal shattered as he pulled it back to reveal the Grand Sapient standing strapped into the leather hollow, arms crossed over his chest. Osidian gave a nod that might have been a bow, then raised his eyes to the Grand Sapient's silver mask. Carnelian almost cried out when Osidian reached up. His pale fingers closed around its edges. Carefully he worked it off. Carnelian watched the breathing tube sliding out from the mouth. The mask came free. His earlier notion that Aurum looked like Legions had been wrong. This face was monstrous. A skull to which wet vellum had been plastered. The face of a corpse long dead.

He glanced at Osidian and was arrested by the look in his eyes. They were seeing no horror. Instead, Osidian was looking at Legions with love. Carnelian recalled he had seen that look before, but, with everything that had happened, he had forgotten how Osidian felt. He gazed again upon the object of that regard. He allowed himself to look with compassion. Legions was not a monster, only a mutilated man. Pain was written in his tight, leather skin. And he was ancient, like some wizened, lightning-shattered pine. What spirit lay within that shrivelled husk? What life had this man known? What suffering?

Carnelian turned again to Osidian and felt in his heart just how much he loved this old man. This old man who was losing his purpose, when that purpose was his life.

Osidian bowed again and then tenderly replaced the mask. He reached up and traced the sickle of its crescent horns. He closed the coffin and turned away.

Carnelian, moved, now yearned to save Osidian from his decision. 'Delay going down until the morning.'

Osidian turned sad eyes on him, but did not speak.

'Sleep on your decision. Perhaps, unforced, your dreams will gift you the tactics you desire.'

'Will you stay with me, Carnelian?'

Carnelian's heart was yielding to the entreaty in Osidian's eyes, but his memory recalled another time like this: in the Upper Reach before Osidian had gone to the Isle of Flies. Mercilessly, Carnelian quenched his desire and his compassion. There were others who had more call on those than did Osidian the murderer. 'Delay until morning for your own sake.'

As Carnelian saw Osidian's eyes harden, so that they seemed to have only the life of emeralds, a resolve arose in him. Once Osidian returned, he would most likely be changed, as he had been the last time. Anything that could be done to bind the monster he would become must be done now. 'It's not only the Lepers that have their price, Osidian. I've reason to fear the obscene thing you are going to submit to. You will swear to me an oath upon your blood or else I'll give Aurum up to the Lepers and disband them. Even, I might wake the Grand Sapient and give you to him. For there, perhaps, also lies a way in which I could achieve what I seek.'

'And what oath is that?' said Osidian.

Carnelian was taken aback by his sadness, by his mildness.

Almost, he would have preferred wrath. 'Upon your blood, swear that, should we take Osrakum, you shall make certain that neither you, nor any of your servants, nor the Commonwealth shall take any retribution upon the Plainsmen, the Lepers or any barbarian whatsoever, whether ally or enemy to us or to the Chosen.'

'I swear,' said Osidian.

'Upon your blood.'

'Upon my blood I swear it.'

Then Osidian left the cell and Carnelian followed, wishing he felt that he had actually gained anything. The oath had tamed none of his doubts. He expected Osidian to move to the ladder, but instead he disappeared into his cell. Carnelian watched the door close and stared at it for a moment, filled with painful memory and regrets. At last he turned to the door of his own cell in which, for company, he had only the homunculus and Poppy with her questions.

THE ICHORIAN

Deception *is* the art of war.
(a precept of the Wise of the Domain Legions)

Tears well from Osidian's eyes. Not tears, maggots. Carnelian feels their itch across the slab of limestone. A cliff verminous as cheese. Touching it, he finds it is warm flesh puckered with wounds. Mouths whispering, calling out for something. He tries to clap his hands over them to keep them quiet, but there are always more mouths in his flesh than he has hands to silence them. Thunder behind him under a forbidding sky. Turning, he sees the tide rippling in. He tries to flee to higher ground, but always, inexplicably, he runs back towards the waves. Spiral wormcasts everywhere in the sand. He can feel the tickle of their heads nuzzling up into holes rotten in the soles of his feet. He clasps a ladder, desperate to escape, but he cannot move his legs, now one with the earth. Unbearable itch as the maggots invade his flesh. They reach his knees. The itching rises in pitch until it becomes cutting blades so sharp they scream.

Carnelian jerked awake. The cessation of pain was so instant he was sure he must be a corpse. Was he blind in a capsule? He lifted his hands and they found his face. The wonder of touch. Listening to his breathing anchored him to the edge of the nightmare that gaped behind him, hungry to swallow him back in. His feet touched the cold floor. He shambled towards the wall. As he searched it with his fingers, it seemed vast enough to encompass a city. Finding a slit, he pushed his face into it, seeking, then drinking the night air. Drunk with it he pulled back. He could not let Osidian endure that obscenity again. Trying not to wake Poppy and the homunculus, he found his door and slipped out onto the landing. The moment he entered Osidian's cell he knew it was empty. Nevertheless, he crossed the cell and ran his hands over the bed. Only the ghost of Osidian's warmth was still there. Carnelian returned to the landing, then moved towards the ladder and peered down into the watch-tower core. Utter blackness. He could hear nothing. It was too late. In the bowels of the tower, Osidian had already sacrificed himself to his filthy god.

Carnelian returned to his chamber to await the dawn. The whole burden of their rebellion was now his alone to carry. The last time Osidian had lain infested with maggots listening to Morunasa's god, Carnelian had not acted. When he had, it had already been too late. Horror of what had then happened tormented him. The accusing dead seemed to be standing all around him in the darkness. It was not enough to say to them that he had neither the strength nor the wisdom to work out what to do. Curled up, he rocked back and forth, fighting despair. The responsibility was his. He had in his hands the fate of those still left alive. He drew a little strength from that certainty. Slowly he assembled arguments; tried to work things out. The first light of dawn filtering into the cell brought with it some thin hope. He even managed to find a reassuring smile for Poppy and the homunculus as they woke.

In the watch-tower entry hall, Carnelian, Poppy and the homunculus peered down the ramp into the blackness of the stables. Carnelian knew he must go and talk to Lily and the Lepers, and he also wanted to get Poppy out of the tower, but he was afraid of what might lie below in that darkness; he had not forgotten the victims the Oracles had hung from the vast banyan of the Isle of Flies to be eaten alive by maggots.

Making sure Poppy was well wrapped up, he took her by the hand. Then, urging the homunculus to follow, Carnelian began descending the ramp. In his free hand he held a lantern. The edge of its light slid slowly down the ramp, a ridge at a time. With every step they took, the odour of dung and aquar grew stronger. When they reached the first level, he raised the lantern. The floor was strewn with chaff. Along the wall the stable doors were closed. Masked, cowled, gloved and cloaked, Carnelian could feel nothing directly, but he detected slight movements, as if the air was subtly tearing. He gave the lantern to the homunculus, then pulled his hand free from Poppy's insistent grip and drew back his hood to free one ear. He flinched as something sliced the air near his cheek. Back and forth, slashes in the air. He tugged the cowl back over his mask. The air was thick with flies.

He gave his hand again to Poppy. The lantern light wavered. The homunculus was clearly in some distress. Down more ramps they went, Carnelian itching with disgust at the delicate hail of flies striking against his mask. The gold was too thin a membrane between him and such vermin.

At last they reached the lowest level, where he found, to his relief, that the portcullis giving onto the road was raised. Eagerly he strode out, past the monolith, into the bright morning, where he and the homunculus sucked at the clean air as best they could through their masks. Poppy glanced back, pale with fright.

As they emerged from the rampart of the Qunoth dragons, the Lepers rose like an ocean swell. Carnelian glanced back to the road, where the Marula camp huddled right up against the doorway into the stables. He was trying to rid himself of his unease at the way they had cowered when he had appeared among them.

He turned and saw the Lepers surging towards him. Poppy

clenched his hand and the homunculus drew closer. The Lepers swarmed around them, murmuring, staring at them though keeping their distance. As he advanced a way opened up through their midst. Glancing from side to side, he could see he was surrounded and began to wonder if he had made a mistake in coming. There was nothing for it. To hesitate might be fatal.

Some figures stood their ground before him. With relief he saw a tall shrouded shape among them that could only be Fern. As Carnelian came to a halt the Lepers pressed in so close he was breathing their rankness. Their low menacing grumble beat around him.

'Make space,' cried a voice he recognized as Lily's. Fern strode in a circle round Carnelian, shoving the Lepers back. 'Give them space. Space, I say.'

As Poppy let go of his hand, Carnelian glanced down. Her face was set in an expression he could not read. He raised his eyes. For a moment he considered asking Lily for a private meeting, but he was only too aware of the dangerous temper of the crowd. What he had come to say he did not want to be heard by Aurum's Lesser Chosen commanders or, even worse, Aurum himself, but he calculated that his voice would most likely be smothered by the Leper mob. And he did not believe that the Lepers would betray him even to the auxiliaries, never mind the other Masters.

His silence seemed to be heating them into anger. Voices began shouting questions from the back of the crowd. Others took these up until the noise swelled into a baying in which he could detect, in many voices layered one upon the other, the demand: 'Give him to us.'

Carnelian raised his hands for silence, but their storm continued to build around him. The homunculus pushed against him. Carnelian too feared for their lives. For a moment he considered removing his mask whose cold, arrogant expression could not but be provoking them.

Then Poppy moved in front of him and her treble carried

above the hubbub. 'Let him speak.' First Lily's husky voice joined hers, then Fern's booming tones, and slowly the noise abated.

Carnelian turned in a circle so that they could see he was addressing them all. 'You shall have him.'

They answered him with thunderous cries and a stamping rhythm. He raised his hands again and this time they fell silent. 'But if I attempt to give him to you now, you will have to fight for him against the auxiliaries and the dragons.'

Spears sprang into the air about him as they roared their rage. Once again the homunculus pressed in close. Carnelian looked round, sure that at any moment they would fall on him. Beyond natural fear he felt the first stirrings of panic that he had misjudged the situation.

Fern came to his side, and Lily and a figure that had to be Krow. With Poppy, they formed a shield around him, facing the mob, bellowing at them until, raggedly, the Lepers again fell silent.

'Will you hear me out?' Carnelian said. He gazed out over their heads, anxious to gauge whether the auxiliaries or the Marula or, worse, the dragons were making any move to intervene, but the dust the Lepers were raising in their agitation had shut the rest of the world out behind a hazy wall. He focused his attention on the front rank of the crowd. 'Will you hear me out?' he repeated.

He waited until nods in the front ranks spread out into the crowd. 'Listen then,' he said, using the strength there was in his Master's voice. 'If what I am about to say fails to persuade you otherwise, I'll give your enemy to you now as was promised.'

Fern and the others moved away from him, turning to face him so that they could listen too. Carnelian gave Poppy a little shove. She glanced up angrily, but went to stand by Krow.

'As you now know, your enemy is here. He came to join his strength to the Master's. He came to fight with the Master against one more terrible even than either of them.'

A murmur soughed across the Lepers like a breeze over fernland.

'He who is your enemy is also mine, for he tortured my uncle to death.' He gave time for that to pass among them and registered Poppy's puzzlement. 'But he who comes against us is more dangerous still. He's the consort of the Master's mother and it is she whom you should fear more than any other. She it was who betrayed her own son and would have murdered him, as she did her daughter, if he hadn't escaped with me out of the Mountain. More than this, it is she who sent your enemy to your valleys.'

As this news passed back through the crowd, Carnelian felt unhappy that he was bending the truth. He had worked this out in his cell. Even when he had imagined he would be talking only to Lily and a few others, he had already half decided he would not attempt to explain who the Wise were, nor the part they had played. Neither was he minded to attempt an explanation of the politics of Osrakum. Gazing at his friends, he knew he was deceiving them. As the Lepers fell silent again, Carnelian drew strength from what he knew was no lie. Jaspar and Ykoriana were at least as dangerous as Aurum and Osidian; and to tip the balance there was the fact that, in the current circumstances, he had some power over the latter two.

'If you take your enemy now and return to your valleys, the Master's mother will not forget you. She'll not forget the secret way you showed us up to Qunoth.'

He glanced at Lily, fully aware that had been her gift to him. 'What she'll not forget nor forgive is that you've come up to the Guarded Land in arms. Worse, you've taken the part of the son she hates. Your enemy, Aurum, attacked you for his amusement; she'll do so seeking to exterminate you utterly.'

He waited for his words to reach them all and then waited even longer to allow their threat to penetrate each stomach.

'I didn't come here to frighten you, but to give you hope. I've

448

extracted from the Master an oath that, should you choose to help us fight his mother and her minion, and should we be victorious, you shall be pardoned.'

He looked at Fern, then Poppy, then Krow. 'As will be all those who've risen in rebellion.' He had hoped for more of a reaction, at least from his friends. The Lepers standing round him had their heads bowed and so he could not see their faces, but he felt that, there too, his words had awoken precious little hope. Almost he stumbled into making stronger promises – that the world would be changed; that they would play a part in freeing many others from the tyranny of the Masters – but he knew that would be going too far. Even what he had promised he could not be certain of delivering. 'Choose to fight with us and there is a good chance you will gain the peace to rebuild your lives.'

Still they besieged him with their silence. He wished Lily could see his face. 'You were prepared to fight for revenge against your enemy. Will you not fight to secure a future for yourselves?'

Lily freed her face with its blood-red eyes from its shrouds. 'You speak to us of Masters we do not know, of threats that lie beyond the horizon. You make promises we've no way of knowing you can fulfil. What do you expect, Master?'

Fern raised his head and fixed Carnelian with a baleful gaze. 'And are you so certain we can win this battle?'

Carnelian regarded him through the slits in his mask. It had come to the point when what he now had to reveal would fall upon Fern more heavily than any other. 'I'm less than certain.'

As din erupted around him, he kept his gaze on Fern, whose face was screwed up with incomprehension. Carnelian spoke knowing he had run out of options. 'Even now the Master communes with his god. He believes he'll be guided by him onto a path to victory. I'll not lie to you. I've no faith in his god and thus little hope he'll find what he seeks.'

Fern's look of pain threatened to break Carnelian's heart.

The wound the massacre had cut in Fern, so deeply it had almost destroyed him, was being reopened.

'And you expect us to put our trust in that!' Poppy glared at him, her face ashen.

Carnelian composed himself. This was no time for him to give way to their pain, nor his. 'I didn't come here expecting you to do this thing from faith nor out of trust. In surety of the risk you will take in waiting, I'll give you control of your enemy, of the Master and of myself.'

Lily grimaced, not understanding. 'How?'

Carnelian lifted his hand to point back at the watch-tower. 'Move your camp around the foot of the tower. We shall then all be your prisoners. I'll make it impossible for any of us to give commands save by your leave.'

He waited, keeping his mind and heart numb, feeling pain around his eyes, but seeing nothing but Lily's bowed head. At last she raised it. 'We'll discuss it and let you know. Now leave us.'

Carnelian felt a twinge of anger at being dismissed thus, but he gave her a nod, left the homunculus with Poppy, then began the journey back towards the watch-tower.

Up on the road, more and more Marula were rising to gaze in his direction. At first Carnelian felt, uncomfortably, that they were responding to his approach, but then he realized they were looking past him. Glancing round, he saw Lepers were pouring towards him through gaps in the dragon line. He turned back to the Marula with a sense of urgency. If he did not manage to make them quit their posts quickly there could well be bloodshed. Without help this might prove beyond him. They had been set to guard the watch-tower not only by their Oracles, but also Osidian. He searched along the ranks of faces, and breathed relief when he found the one he was looking for. He made straight for him.

'Sthax,' he called out.

The Maruli glanced nervously towards the watch-tower

foundation wall, behind which the Oracles lay communing with their god. As Carnelian climbed the ramp up to the road, the other Marula made space for him to approach Sthax. 'I feared you lost.'

Sthax regarded him with what seemed to be suspicion.

'You have to move your people away. I've given the tower to the Lepers.'

Sthax's face hardened and Carnelian felt the Marula round them sensing his anger. 'You have no choice.' Carnelian glanced round at the approaching Leper tide to reinforce his point. The light his mask was reflecting into Sthax's eyes was making him squint. Again Carnelian's instinct was to talk to him face to face, but what was the point in pretending he was other than he was? 'Tell the Oracles you were forced to obey my command.'

Sthax, unappeased, stood his ground. 'What happen?'

Carnelian felt rage rising in him against this man, but knew he was not being fair. His disgust at the Oracles and their god and his obsession with the Lepers had made him treat these people shabbily. They had every right to an explanation and so he began to give Sthax one.

'Battle?' Sthax said, nodding wearily. His eyes seemed to be seeking Carnelian's face through the mask. 'We wins?'

Carnelian felt drained at having to trot out the same fragile reasons he had had to give to the Lepers, but as he explained they were waiting for Osidian's dreams, Sthax's back stiffened. Of course, Osidian's god was the god of all the Marula.

Carnelian opened his arm to take in the warriors behind Sthax. 'In a battle, many will die.'

Sthax's smile was like unexpected sun. 'We warriors. We fears no die.' Light left his face. 'We fears for loves. We fears for homes.'

This man was no fool. Sthax knew how narrow was the hope upon which his land and people hung. Carnelian explained why he had given the tower to the Lepers. 'If they do not believe the Master will give them victory, there will be no battle. The Lepers will go home. The Marula will go home.'

He could tell from Sthax's face that he saw even less hope in that. Grimly, the Maruli took leave of him as he began the work of persuading his fellows to quit their posts.

The Marula yielded to the Lepers. Lily left Fern behind to organize a new camp and then picked some of her people to accompany her. With a glance back at Fern, Carnelian led her and her people into the watch-tower. He climbed the ramps, keeping his gaze fixed always ahead, and was relieved when they reached the cistern level without mishap. Lily's shrouded head turned as she surveyed the chamber with its shafts and ladder rising up into the tower. She gave a nod of acceptance, then assigned some of her people to stand guard upon the ladder, while to others she gave the duty of controlling the ramps they had just climbed.

As Carnelian walked out onto the leftway, he glanced over to where three of Aurum's guardsmen rose to deny him access to their master's dragon tower. Regarding their sallow, bisected faces, he judged they were unlikely to cause any trouble. It was not their job to react to changes in the camp, but only to protect their master. He busied himself with supervising the raising of the drawbridge that connected the watch-tower to the long run south to Makar. As the device was ratcheting up, he noticed anxiously that Lily had appeared and was gazing at the guardsmen and the dragon tower. As he approached her she turned. 'Is Au-rum in there?'

Carnelian admitted that he was, then thought it best to explain that, without its crew, the Master had no means of operating the dragon, nor any way to communicate with the rest of his forces. When he was certain she was not going to make an attempt to seize Aurum, a need arose in him to have her answer some questions. 'Do you really intend to sack Makar?'

'Do you think it selfish of us that, after what we've suffered, we should seek the means to rebuild our lives?'

'Would you heal your own wounds by wounding others?'

A furious glint came into her eyes. 'You forget how badly the Clean have always treated us.'

'They fear you . . . and it is, besides, a fear you've encouraged.'

Lily bowed her head. 'Even if I wanted to pull back from it,' she said, in a quiet voice, 'it's too late.'

Carnelian felt sympathy for her. He was certain she had used that promise to persuade her people to follow her here. 'You're not the first he's trapped by turning your desires against you.'

She nodded.

'If only you had come to me with this at the time . . .' He paused. 'Why didn't you?'

Lily shook her head, then moved away to the edge of the leftway and gazed down. Carnelian was aware of the barrier between them. He moved to her side. Her people were occupying the whole breadth of the road below and, spilling down the ramp, covered much of the ground there too. 'You have us all in your power, Lily.'

She did not turn. 'It would appear so.'

Lily permitted Carnelian to continue residing in his cell with Poppy and the homunculus. He encouraged her to place a guard upon the tower heliograph and her people replaced the Marula as lookouts in the deadman's chairs. He had discussed the situation with her and she had allowed Poppy to go down to see Fern and ask him if he would be prepared to go north to the watch-tower beyond the next and to remain there, keeping an eye out for Jaspar's approach. When Fern agreed to do this, Carnelian sent him a mirrorman as a heliograph operator.

Days passed during which the breeze from the north-east gradually became the merest breath before failing completely. Without it the heat rose so that, even though the nights were chill, the stone of the watch-tower stayed warm to the touch. Carnelian lingered in his cell with Poppy during the worst of it, then, under cover of night, they would climb to the high platform where beneath a star-studded sky they often sat, hardly saying a word.

Then one afternoon a servant emerged from Aurum's tower seeking Osidian. Lily allowed Carnelian to talk to the man. Cowering, sallow-faced, he was at first reluctant to divulge his message, but he could not long resist the imperious glare of Carnelian's mask. It seemed that Aurum wanted to know if the Ichorian had been sighted. As Carnelian watched the man skulk back to the tower with a negative answer, he felt an increased level of anxiety. Jaspar must be close. He spent the rest of the day upon the watch-tower summit gazing north.

The following morning, Carnelian came awake certain he could hear gulls screaming above a gale. Poppy was there, staring at him. 'Is this it?'

Carnelian sat up, hunched against the vast wave that was about to engulf them. The fear in Poppy's face freed him from his dream. A muffled cry was coming from somewhere above them.

'The lookouts,' he cried, jumping up. They stared at each other. It was what they had been waiting for for days. He pointed at the ceiling. 'I'll go up and find out what it is. Can you please go down and tell Lily I'll come to see her the moment I know?'

Poppy ducked a nod and made for the door. Carnelian put on his mask, took his leave of the homunculus, trusting him, then followed her out. As he scrambled up the ladder to the roof, the anticipation of what he would see up there was like lead in his stomach. He climbed the staples. Even as he crested the platform edge, he could see the Leper lookouts gathered, agitated, pointing. He clambered up onto the platform, blind to everything but the hazy north. A flash. He waited. A double flash. His heart, racing, measured the time to the next flashing. Three in a row. The prearranged signal. It meant Fern had sighted dragons coming along the road. Carnelian ignored the repeat as he peered into the vague north, straining to see the Ichorian. Dread arched over him like the wave in his dream: not just anticipation of the coming trial, but the acceptance that the time had come to wake Osidian.

Carnelian glanced back to where he had left Poppy with Lily and then he began the descent into the stables. He had had no need to go down there for days. The drain stench seemed worse, but he could detect no flies. He held a lantern out before him. He angled his mask so that its eyeslits would shield him from the glare. Reaching the first level, he saw the doors along one wall were all still closed. Transferring the lantern to his other hand, he reached out and touched the nearest. It gave under the pressure. Standing near its hinge, he pushed it open and swung the light in. A body came into view. It had the look of an Ochre corpse bitumened for sky burial. Leaning as close as he could stomach, and angling the light, he saw some twitching in the Oracle's face. Squinting, he could make out the pink wounds pocking his skin. He retreated. So many doors with more Oracles behind them and two more levels beneath this one. His heart quailed at the thought he might have to look in all of them before he found Osidian.

Something moving at the edge of his vision caused him to spin round, his heart in his throat. He could see nothing beyond the circle of his lantern light. He shuttered the light to a narrow beam. His hackles rose. Someone was there. A pair of eyes appearing suddenly made him gasp. A ravener grin curved into being beneath the eyes.

'The Master is startled,' rumbled a voice Carnelian knew.

'Morunasa.'

The grin whitened, feral in the darkness. Carnelian opened the shutter and flooded Morunasa with light. The man recoiled, an arm up before his face. He was naked, his skin free of its customary covering of ash so that Carnelian could detect the subtle curling currents of his tattoos. He kept a wary eye on Morunasa's teeth. He would not allow Morunasa to bite him as he had in the Isle of Flies. 'Where's the Master?'

'Why?'

Carnelian felt his fear turning to anger. 'I need to see him.'

'The cries?'

Carnelian knew Morunasa would find out everything soon enough. 'Dragons are coming here from the north.'

Morunasa's eyes narrowed to slits, then he passed close enough for Carnelian to be able to smell the blood oozing from his open sores. He followed him down a level, then into a stable wider than the others, in the back of which lurked counterweights and cables. There was a pale thing lying on the ground. For a moment he had the impression it was one of the Sapients, but the flesh, though starved, was firmer. He looked and recognized Osidian's face, as thin as it had been when he had had the fever. He stooped to touch him and recoiled from the marble cold of death.

'He lives,' slurred Morunasa. His eyes rolled up as if he had just been stabbed. The dark irises descended. 'He is with our Lord.'

Unmasked, Carnelian knew his face must be betraying what he thought of Morunasa's god. He reached out again and, taking Osidian's arm, shook him. Osidian released a groan, but did not wake. Carnelian felt the wetness on his fingers and turned to see them dark. He wiped the blood on his robe, fearing, irrationally, that he might have touched not only a wound, but also one of the maggots.

'He shouldn't be woken.'

Carnelian glanced up. 'I've no choice. Will you help me carry him up out of here?'

Morunasa regarded him with a glazed expression, so that Carnelian had to repeat his question. The second time, Morunasa nodded.

* * *

Carnelian watched Poppy as she gazed, frowning, on Osidian's skeletal face. He and Morunasa had laid him out upon the cobbles within the shelter of the leftway monolith, round to one side of the entrance so that his face could be seen neither from the leftway nor from within the watch-tower. Carnelian had left him unmasked because he feared his mask might smother him. For what Poppy was doing, the Law demanded death, but he imagined only Aurum would dare attempt to enforce it. If Aurum did, Carnelian would immediately hand him over to the justice of the Lepers.

Waiting for Osidian to wake, they had watched the shadows lengthen across the camp below. Now, beyond the monolith, everything was bathed in the reddening gold of the dying day. Carnelian had concealed Osidian's bony body and its wounds beneath a blanket. The mask he had used to hide Osidian's cadaverous face from Lily was lying on the ground beside him. The gold face seemed to have been flayed from what was little more than a skull. Seeing how Osidian had suffered stirred feelings in Carnelian of guilt, of loss, of rage. He glanced into the shadows of the cistern chamber where Lily was waiting with her Lepers. Against the objections of her people, she had given in to his plea that they should be patient at least until the morning. A tiny twitching in Osidian's thin lips gave the impression he might be talking to someone in his dreams. Carnelian had tried many times already to wake him, without success. This sleep was the brother of death.

Morunasa had reacted with anger when he discovered his Marula had abandoned their posts to the Lepers. Carnelian had told him that they had done so in obedience to his command and that, besides, the warriors could not have withstood the Leper numbers. He suspected that Morunasa was not appeased but had bade him return below to wake the Oracles. Both knew that they might well play some pivotal part in the next day's events.

Everyone was waiting for Osidian to wake, but there was

no certainty he would choose to climb up from the depths in which he wandered, lost. Even if he did, what hope was there he would have found what he sought?

Hearing voices, Carnelian started awake. Night had fallen. He must have dozed. A muttering was coming out from the cistern chamber that was punctuated now and then by a raised voice. Listening, he was sure he could hear the rumble of Fern's voice. Carnelian sat up and reached for his mask, instinctively knowing Fern must soon appear. He paused with it in his hand and glanced at Osidian's, smouldering darkly on the ground. He put his mask down and leaned back against the monolith. Fern had the right to see them both.

A dark shape appeared in the doorway beneath the toothed edge of the raised portcullis. Poppy rose and moved towards Fern as if to give him a hug of welcome, but she halted and let her arms fall. 'What news?'

Fern gave no answer and, though his face was in shadow, Carnelian sensed his gaze was on Osidian. 'Has he revealed how we might win the battle?'

'We've not yet been able to wake him,' Carnelian said.

'He has the worms in him?'

'He does.'

Silence.

'Will he wake in time?' Fern asked at last.

Carnelian was only too aware of what Osidian had done the last time he had awoken from such a sleep. 'I don't know.' He peered into Fern's shadow face, yearning to see him clearly. 'Tell us what you've seen.'

The shadowy figure shifted. 'Mid afternoon we saw dragons approaching from the north. After sending you word, we rode south to the next tower. We climbed it and waited there until nightfall. When I was certain they'd formed a camp around the forward tower, we returned here.'

'So it'll be tomorrow?'

'If we choose to fight.'

Carnelian's chin sank into his chest as he contemplated what the next day might bring. Perhaps a battle. Perhaps the Lepers would take Aurum and leave. Whatever was to come, there would be losses.

As Fern began turning away, Carnelian could not suppress panic that he might leave tomorrow, that he might go for ever. 'Please, Fern . . . please, stay here with us.'

The man became inanimate shadow. Then the shadow approached so that the light from within the tower found the contours of his form. Poppy moved aside, exposing a space beside Carnelian. 'I'll fetch you a blanket,' she said and darted into the tower.

Carnelian sensed Fern standing there, but did not want to look up in case their eyes should meet. Poppy was soon back. Fern accepted the blanket from her, wrapped it about his shoulders, then sank down beside Carnelian with his back against the monolith. Intensely aware of the warm pressure against his shoulder, Carnelian regarded the sky. The ribs of the watch-tower black against the stars seemed the branches of some massive baobab. His heart remembered the time so long ago when he and Fern had shared a blanket in the Upper Reach. He turned his head enough to see Fern's profile. He was gazing up at the night sky. Carnelian wondered if Fern too was remembering that night.

Carnelian jerked awake and saw an ice face pulled into a silent scream. Its eyes, fixed on something beyond, communicated their terror to him. Osidian, releasing a stuttering gasp, raised the gleaming bony shard of an arm to point at the sky. Carnelian gazed up, expecting some horror to fall on them. For a moment he saw only the black arms of the watch-tower ribs, but then he saw the moon. A diamond scythe so sharp it felt as if it might slice through his eyes. He looked back to Osidian, who had subsided, mumbling. Closed, his eyes seemed to have sunk back into the silver mask of his face. Carnelian became aware Poppy and Fern were staring at Osidian too.

Just then a hail of tiny flutters on his face made Carnelian throw up his hands in alarm. Masked by his fingers, he could feel the pinpricks on his skin. It was not, as he had feared, an assault of flies. With a delicate hiss, something blowing on the breeze was striking him. He was disturbed by the memory of the sporestorm he and Fern and Poppy had endured on their way to the Koppie. This was only blown dust. Squinting against the delicate hail, he saw his friends had covered their heads with their blankets. Osidian seemed dead again. Carnelian hunched his blanket up, pulled it over his head, then settled back to sleep.

Waking once more, Carnelian sat up. Osidian was standing there with the camp pouring its undulating dark reflection over his mask.

'It is an omen,' Osidian said, his Quya a whisper.

Carnelian glanced around; not only the leftway, but everything below was in strange shadow. On both sides of the monolith, the leftway was dusted red, the colour collecting in the cracks between the cobbles like dried blood. More of this rustiness clung to the folds of Poppy's blanket. He shook his own blanket and filled the air with it. 'The dust?'

Osidian turned his mirror face slowly towards Carnelian. 'The breeze,' he sighed.

Carnelian moved to stand beside him, squinting against the dusty air.

'It is my Father's breath urging me to Osrakum.'

Carnelian was lost for a moment, contemplating the pale tendons, the corded veins in the arm and hand with which Osidian was holding his mask before his face. He wondered at where Osidian was getting the strength to stand. He focused on what Osidian had said and understood. 'The rain wind.' It was true. The wind had shifted. It was coming from the south-west. He should have realized that when he had woken during the night.

'Why did you wake me?'

Carnelian regarded him. 'Jaspar is here.'

He expected some kind of agitation, but instead Osidian gave a languid nod as if his mask were too heavy for him. 'I saw him in my dreams.'

Carnelian indicated the dusty mass of the Lepers stirring below. 'I gave them control of this tower. I have put you, my Lord Aurum and myself in their power. If you cannot convince them we will be victorious . . .'

Osidian gave another, slow nod. 'Your precautions, Carnelian, were unnecessary.' He shifted into Vulgate. 'Today we'll annihilate our enemies.'

Carnelian was uneasy at his certainty. He glanced round and saw Fern was awake, angry and disbelieving. 'How will we do that, my Lord?'

'Summon the Lord Aurum and I shall tell you.'

Calculating that it could do no harm, Carnelian asked Fern if he would fetch the old Master. Unease was bright in Fern's eyes, but he went. Carnelian looked round for Poppy, but she was gone. He could not be sure how much she had heard, but he could hope she had gone to urge Lily and the Lepers to wait just a little longer.

Slaves struggled to help their master across the brassman up onto the leftway. As Aurum straightened, his slaves cowered away. He approached, hobbling. Watching him, Carnelian wondered again at his condition. Osidian sketched a gesture of concern. 'Is my Lord strong enough to command today?'

'Imago has come?'

'We shall engage him before midday.'

The old Master seemed to grow more massive in his black cloak. 'My will shall provide me with the strength my body lacks, Celestial.'

Carnelian thought that both his allies looked frail.

Gingerly, Osidian crouched and ran a thin finger through the red dust. 'This is Imago's line.' Facing its mid-point, he traced what seemed a smile and from its centre dragged two fingers back to make a double line. 'This is how we shall destroy the Ichorian.'

As he explained, Carnelian was noticing how the crescent matched the moon Osidian had pointed to during the night. Though the tactics were fascinating, he wondered whence they really had come.

Aurum's mask regarded them. 'And you are convinced, Celestial, this novel tactic will break Imago's line?'

Osidian gave a slight shrug. 'If it does not, then it is we who will be destroyed.'

Carnelian saw another objection. 'Will Jaspar not realize what we are preparing for him?'

Osidian made a smiling gesture with his hand and turned towards the camp. Dust blowing against his mask collected its red powder upon lip and brows. 'Behold my Father's breath.'

Carnelian nodded, understanding. 'You intend that we should come at him with the wind at our backs?'

'We shall raise a red twilight that shall conceal our storm from him until it is too late.'

Carnelian pondered the appearance of the rain wind that very morning, wondering if he dare believe it really was an omen. Ultimately it was not he but the Lepers who must believe. 'What about those who will fight upon the ground?'

Osidian winnowed the dusty air with a dismissive gesture. 'They merely have to withstand the Ichorian aquar until we have broken through.'

Aurum was nodding. 'If their huimur fail, the rest of the Ichorian will break.'

Osidian's 'merely' was making Carnelian fret, but he knew that quizzing him further would not help gauge the threat to the Lepers. Osidian's plan was akin to hazarding all on the flight of a single arrow.

'My huimur tower is not equipped for such a battle, Celestial.'

'That is why, my Lord Aurum, you shall be commanding your legion from my tower.'

Carnelian waited for Aurum to object to this. When he did not, Carnelian realized that, of course, the Master really had no choice. Though commands would be issued to his legion in his name, it was Osidian who would in truth command them. 'And you would have me command the Qunoth huimur, my Lord?'

Osidian turned to Carnelian. 'If my Lord would deign to do so?'

Carnelian considered that it was Lily and her Lepers who ultimately would have to make that decision. 'I shall go, my Lord, to begin the marshalling of our forces.'

Osidian's hand made a crisp affirmation. 'I shall remain here long enough to determine with my Lord Aurum how best we might communicate our tactics to his commanders.'

'Celestial,' Carnelian said and, bowing, turned towards the monolith.

When he entered the cistern chamber the Lepers rose to face him. He came to a halt between the first two pillars, wondering if it was because they knew him that they did not bow or kneel or whether they had come to a point where they would dare show such defiance to any Master. Lily was there, Poppy beside her and Fern. Knowing there was not much time, Carnelian launched immediately into an explanation of Osidian's proposed tactics. When he was done their shrouds did not allow him to see the reactions of the Lepers. Fern's eyes, however, seemed flint. Lily turned her hooded head to scan her peers as if she was hearing them speak. She turned back. 'And the Master believes this to be a revelation from his god?'

Carnelian felt uncomfortable discussing the source of Osidian's tactics, but he could tell from Lily's tone that what for him seemed a point of weakness seemed to her a source of strength.

'Do you believe truly his god speaks to him?'

Carnelian squirmed, then remembered. 'He claims it was

his god who told him how to lead us out of the swamps that the waters in your valleys feed.'

This information produced a muttering among the Lepers.

'I was there too,' said Fern, his mouth twisting with disgust. 'He led us, but who is to say we would not have found the way ourselves? Unless you're claiming that his filthy god has always led him infallibly.'

Carnelian withered. Osidian had claimed it was the Darkness-under-the-Trees that had led him to massacre the Tribe.

Fern shook his head as if trying to dislodge his anger. 'Talk not to me of gods. Instead tell me if you believe this tactic can bring us victory against the Bloodguard.'

Carnelian stood frozen, unhappy to have his opinion influence the decision upon which these people would risk their blood. His mask was casting glimmers over them. If he was going to tell them what he believed he did not want to do so wearing the imperious majesty conferred by that false face. They flinched as he reached to release it. Fern frowned as Carnelian exposed his face. Poppy was the only one to smile. 'Look into my eyes and see for yourselves what it is I feel about this. I don't know if this will work. I wouldn't have you believe that I do. What I do believe is that the Master has a genius for battle; that if any plan could work, his might. More than that, I will not say.'

He gazed round at them, enduring their scrutiny. 'Even if it works, it'll depend on you holding the mounted cohorts of the Bloodguard. Perhaps you know their reputation?'

He looked at Fern, whose father an Ichorian had wounded fatally, whose brother and uncle the same Ichorian had killed. 'I'm not the only one here who has seen them kill.'

He felt their doubt and saw it on Poppy's face; it was there too beneath Fern's coldness. A sound behind him made him jerk his mask up. He paused before it had wholly covered his face, feeling the heavy footfalls of Masters approaching,

464

hearing the scrape of Aurum's staff. He let his hand fall, the mask hanging from his fingers, and turned.

'Horns and fire,' cried Aurum. Carnelian sensed his Quya making the Lepers falter. 'Is it possible, boy, that you have not yet learned the lesson of the baran?'

Carnelian watched the old Master half turning, his hands rising to give the commands. He remembered how on the baran they had chopped gestures and how, in obedience to those, his guardsmen had massacred the crew.

'We're no longer on the ship,' Carnelian said, deliberately, in Vulgate. 'And you're here with none who'll heed your murderous commands.' Defiance was sweet.

Aurum turned to Osidian. 'Celestial, these creatures must all be put to death.'

Osidian's mask turned to Carnelian, who could see a glitter of eyes moving behind its slits. His hand rose, making a smile gesture that, though it carried appeasement, was also shaded by a dismissive amusement. 'It would seem, my Lord Aurum, impolitic for me to destroy the commanders of my auxiliaries.' He rolled an elegant hand. 'Let us say that these creatures are become members of House Suth.'

Confident his gambit had paid off, Carnelian glanced round. Fern was considering what he had said to them and, Carnelian was sure, Lily and the Lepers were too. The decision was theirs to make. Their enemy was there unarmed among them. They could take him now and return to their valleys and flee the coming battle. Fearing either outcome, he waited, not willing them to decide one way or the other.

It was Lily who first gave him a nod. Others followed. He turned last of all to Fern. As their eyes met, his heart gave a lurch. He dared not name what had passed between them lest he should destroy it. Fern broke the contact with a nod.

Carnelian turned back to the Masters. Their gold faces seemed to float disembodied above their black cloaks. 'My Lords had best go now down to the camp. It will take my Lord Aurum a while to negotiate the ramps and we must make haste lest our enemy be upon us before we have had time to prepare our battleline.'

Osidian gave him a nod, then advanced on the Lepers, who moved from his path. Aurum was forced to follow him, each punt of his staff gouging the floor. Carnelian watched them until they had disappeared down into the darkness of the stables. He wondered how Aurum, already discomfited, would react to the Oracles and their sacrament.

Lily speaking made him turn to her. 'Our enemy seems weakened.'

Carnelian was still savouring his victory over Aurum. 'Don't worry; he won't die before we give him to you. We Masters maintain a fierce grip on life.' Almost he added: and we are made of finer clay. That made him smile and ignited in him a fierce desire to destroy Jaspar. At that moment he felt he had the power to tear down the Commonwealth. Then he saw the people standing before him and his ardour cooled. A large part of the price for victory would most likely be the spilling of their blood. 'You will fight then?'

They answered him with a cry of assent that made the portcullis counterweights shiver. He felt moved and covered this by going over again the part they would play in the coming battle. When he was sure they understood, he told them they must go and make their people ready. 'While I'll do the same for my dragon commanders.'

'I'll go with Fern,' said Poppy.

'What do you mean?' Carnelian said, suspicious.

'I can't let Krow go into battle without saying goodbye to him.'

The frown Fern gave her showed he was sharing Carnelian's misgivings. 'You're *not* going to fight in the battle.' Carnelian pointed up into the tower. 'You can watch it from up there.'

Poppy's face hardened. 'What if Krow should die?'

Fern gripped her shoulder. 'I'll take care of him for you.'

Poppy wriggled free and glared at them both. 'I'm not going

to stay here when you're all out there. Besides, what makes you both think this tower's safe?'

Carnelian and Fern glanced at each other. She had a point. Carnelian thought about it. He hung his head. 'You can come with me.'

Poppy beamed. 'In the dragon?'

Carnelian looked to make sure Fern approved and then nodded heavily. The Lepers were already descending the ramp. Fern gave Carnelian a look he could not read. 'Take care.'

'Don't forget you promised to look after Krow,' Poppy said.

'I won't,' said Fern. He looked at Carnelian. 'Make sure we win.'

Carnelian gave a nod, his heart aching. As he and Poppy watched Fern disappear into the darkness, a nausea crept over him that he feared was a premonition of Fern's death. Poppy took hold of two of his fingers and squeezed them. 'Don't worry. While Fern's taking care of Krow, Krow will be taking care of Fern.'

Sitting in his command chair, Carnelian saw in front of him a long file of dragons trampling their shadows as they lumbered into the west. A cohort of his own Qunoth dragons was immediately in front. Beyond them Aurum's with the old Master and Osidian on Heart-of-Thunder at their head. Carnelian was confident the rest of his dragons were following him in single file. All along the starboard edge of their march the dragons were unfurling a vast red banner of dust that was drifting away into the north-east. Not only was it hiding the road, but everything that lay in that direction. More disconcertingly, it was proclaiming their position to Jaspar. Earlier, Carnelian had bidden his Lefthand to get their lookout to relate what he could see of the road. Word had returned that, even perched aloft, he could see nothing at all through the dust. This was exactly what Osidian had hoped for. If their lookouts could not see the road, then Jaspar should not be able to see their banner masts. Nevertheless, none of this stopped Carnelian feeling nervous that, at that very moment, the Ichorian could be bearing down upon their flank unseen. He fretted again over whether his commanders had fully understood his explanation of Osidian's tactics. He was also beset by doubt whether, when it came to it, they would follow him into a battle against the feared double legion of the Bloodguard.

He glanced round. Poppy was there sitting against the bone wall. The homunculus was hunched beside her, his head sunk between his knees so that he appeared to be nothing more than a boy. It was Poppy who had asked to have the little man along. Red dust in the folds of her Leper shrouds looked like dried blood. More carpeted the deck and formed drifts in the angles of the cabin. Had he been foolish to let Poppy come with him? Was she really safer here than back in the watch-tower?

To port, the cool blues of the morning were only lightly wisped with the dust the riders were churning up. The Marula rode nearest to the dragon line, two abreast. Beyond, ranks of auxiliaries faded into their own dust, their jiggling mass grotesquely animated by long shadows. He had divided the Lepers into two groups. The first under Lily rode up at the front of their column. The second under Fern brought up the rear. In the camp he had been glad Osidian's wish to have the auxiliaries fight next to the dragons had banished the Lepers to the extreme flanks. Now he was not so sure. Though the intention was to advance with both flanks re-fused so that they would be as far as they could be from the Ichorians' fire, what if Jaspar attempted to outflank them? Then the Lepers would bear the brunt of the fighting on the ground.

He gazed at the rump of the dragon in front. Each of its footfalls gouged up a red spiral of dust. Several of these intertwined, feathering diagonally up to feed the clouds rolling towards Jaspar. At least, Carnelian thought, by placing the aquar to port both they and their riders were being spared that choking fog.

At last Osidian veered them north-west. Carnelian gave the order to turn an eighth to starboard, then watched as the auxiliaries matched the new course and the hazy shadow of the duststorm oozed out over them. Then he gazed out to starboard. Though he knew they must now be marching parallel to the road, he could see no hint of it through the murk.

A muffled, deep-throated cry sounded from far ahead. This was taken up by another trumpet and another, in a cascading sequence that grew louder as it sped towards them. This was one of several prearranged signals. Even before it reached them, Carnelian gave an order to his Righthand. The man muttered into his voice fork and, a moment later, the cabin shook as a vast, nasal groan was released by Earth-is-Strong's trumpets. A movement in the corner of Carnelian's eye made him turn to see Poppy startled. He considered saying something to reassure her but in the end he stayed silent. He did not wish to diminish the martial atmosphere of the deck. Worse, he feared that one kind word might encourage Poppy to some action. It was better she should sit there quietly.

The trumpet blasts were fading away to the rear of the march. Carnelian gave the command that made Earth-is-Strong turn to starboard even as she slowed to a halt. He watched with some relief as the neighbouring dragons turned too. He had deliberately held his dragon back so that the rest of the line would advance a little in front of him. Leaning on the arm of his chair, he peered to port, down the forming line of dragons. At last he saw what he was looking for: a dragon half lost in the dust it was raising as it approached. It was Heart-of-Thunder coming to join him in the centre. He watched the monster slow, then turn, inserting himself into the line six dragons away: the six that would form the horns of the crescent.

Gazing to starboard, Carnelian watched a seethe of dust undulating down the line as his auxiliaries rode off to form the right wing. He screwed his eyes up, but could see no clear evidence of Fern's Lepers at its very end. Grimly, he gave a command, and slowly, with the cabin rocking from side to side, Earth-is-Strong edged into her place in the line. On either side, the dark shapes of Marula were pouring forwards to form their skirmish screen in front. The breeze was carrying the red dust wall away from them, sinking as it thinned. The glare of the sun was beginning to coalesce into a patch, then into an orb so bright he had to lower his head so that the slits of his mask would shield his eyes. His heart was pounding. At any moment he might see a wall of dragons thundering towards them. From violet, the north-eastern sky was turning blue. At last he realized he could see all the way across the plain to the horizon. No sign of movement, of the road, of anything.

He became aware of the tower settling around him, creaking, releasing tension. He heard and felt the tremor of Earth-is-Strong emitting a snort. Furtive sounds rose from the crew in the lower decks. He was conscious of his breath as it passed in and out through the nostrils of his mask. He leaned forward. In the far distance a long flat sliver of movement. A twitching, shifting strip that could have been the froth of a blood sea breaking its waves upon a shore.

A lurid twilight filled the cabin. Carnelian felt they had been pushing through its red fog for days. He had lost all sense of time. Anxiety that at any moment an enemy dragon would emerge from the murk had left him weary and irritable. Though he feared it, he also longed for the battle to begin.

Osidian had waited while the Ichorian formed its battleline. The froth of dust had widened along the horizon. That it thinned to the edges suggested Jaspar had matched his battleline to theirs as Osidian had prophesied. Dragon was matched to dragon; aquar to aquar. Why not? Jaspar knew he had the greater strength.

The mirror signal Osidian had sent flickering towards either flank consisted of a single command. 'Advance'. The dragons had lurched forward stirring red surf into life at their feet. Soon this had rolled over the cordon of Marula stretched across their front. Higher and higher it had boiled, tendrils smoking up to grip the blue morning. Soon, the red, rolling wall had risen to quench it altogether.

Carnelian leaned forward in his command chair, peering into the rolling cloud they were driving before them. He was sure he had seen something, but it was probably just another phantasm. He glimpsed three small dark solid things there on the ground. Marula labouring like ants through the sand-storm. It gave him stale satisfaction that this dust would be striking directly into the faces and towers of Jaspar's host.

'The signal, Master.'

Carnelian jumped, having almost forgotten his Lefthand was there. Instantly he looked to port, where the nearest dragon seemed a ship in a fog. A tiny glow like a marsh light upon its tower roof was moving from side to side. This was it. He gave the command for Earth-is-Strong to slow. As the cabin began to rock, he commanded her pipes lit. The dragon to starboard was keeping pace with her. Hopefully this was happening all the way down the line. To port, he saw the dragon there pulling ahead. The other five were surely advancing in line with it. He turned Earth-is-Strong an eighth to port. Slowly they began shearing in behind the six. Carnelian peered into the murk counting the shadows while at the same time looking out for Osidian. The horns and beak were the first to emerge, like a floating crucifixion. Then the massive bulk of Heart-of-Thunder with her tower solidified in the gloom.

'An eighth to starboard.'

Earth-is-Strong responded, wheeling away from Heart-of-Thunder though still closing, until the two monsters were lumbering forward side by side. Carnelian glanced over to Heart-of-Thunder's tower, but it was too murky to see Osidian. As they picked up speed Carnelian could make out ahead the six dividing into two cohorts with a gap between them. Carefully, he and Osidian guided their dragons into this gap until they were moving in line abreast with the six. Carnelian turned to look back, but could see nothing clearly. It was the intensifying reek of naphtha that confirmed that the rest of their dragons were feeding their lines in behind them. To starboard, the sandstorm was thinning as he expected. Soon, only the Marula churning the earth would sustain it along their original front. If the fog failed too soon, Jaspar might see there was no longer a battleline of dragons confronting him.

When his Lefthand made him aware Osidian was sending the second torch signal, Carnelian had this relayed to the three dragons on his starboard flank. He watched as the nearest advanced and imagined the other two doing the same, each further than its neighbour to form the right horn of Osidian's hollow crescent. They were ready for battle.

Lightning flashed to right and left in the murk. A shrill screaming was muffled by the dust-cloud.

'Dragonfire,' Carnelian muttered.

A throaty brass voice groaned. He was already giving the predetermined command even as the Marula rushed back towards him, like ants fleeing a forest fire. 'Ahead full.'

His Righthand had hardly finished muttering into his voice fork when Carnelian felt the change in Earth-is-Strong. The power of her sinews caused the tower to vibrate in a way that made him expect it to chime like a bell. Air wafted in against them. He felt dust scratching against his mask. Then all this was forgotten. A colonnade of shadows was solidifying ahead. For a moment Carnelian had the impression the fog would clear and he would see before him the Isle of Flies, or the edge of the Labyrinth. As each pillar grew more visible, his eyes widened behind his mask in disbelief. Dragons they were, but even more massive than the one he rode. A flash of flame seemed to oil the gold-sheathed curves of immense horns. A head that was a wedge of hide and bone weightier than the prow of a baran. The tower emerging from the gloom was four-tiered and had three flame-pipes pointing straight at him. He felt he was gazing down those barrels, waiting for fiery death to come searing out at him. An electric arc screamed into being so close he braced for the scorching of the fire upon his skin. He saw it was in reality a twin jet of flame pouring towards the oncoming monsters from Heart-of-Thunder.

'Flame,' he said.

He felt a rumble through his feet, a sighing almost too low to hear, a choke and splutter, then the screams vibrating their harmony against each other as liquid flame spat out. Its arches collided with Osidian's. More were coming in from around the curve of the crescent. Glaring light that made him jerk up an arm to shield his eyes. Heat upon heat building along the leather of his upheld forearm, beginning to seep through the gold cheek of his mask. Head averted, teeth clenched, he squinted, watching the sun they were rolling before them. Its white heart coruscating, pulsating in time with the spluttering gurgle of naphtha pumping out below his feet. He sensed, more than saw, the massive Ichorian monster veering away from the fireball. He was mesmerized by the carved complex geometries of its tower, stark in the blinding light. His starboard companion dragon was slowing, being left behind. The sun before them was flickering, dulling as the flame arcs of his horn of the crescent swung away. A jet of burning naphtha splashed against the flank of the Ichorian dragon. Carnelian leaned on the arm of his chair to watch the fire pouring off it, stunned.

Then he felt his own pipes shut off. The fire in front of them vanished into black smoke that, as it thinned, allowed him to see that the way ahead seemed clear. He gaped, incredulous, as the fog ahead paled from violet to blue. Sky and land stretched empty to the horizon.

The plan coming unbidden to his mind issued a command through his voice. 'Hard to starboard.'

As Earth-is-Strong wheeled, the rear of Jaspar's dragon line came into view. Rumps moving away from him partially veiled by the dust fog. Incredulous, he gave another command. 'Pipes to fire at will.'

The pipes beneath him began spitting long fiery jets feathered with black smoke that fell upon the dragons and their towers. As they thundered along behind that long line, raking it with fire, Carnelian rose to his feet and swayed over to grab hold of the screen and peer through. Osidian's plan was working. Carnelian could think of nothing else. The fearsome destruction his fire was wreaking upon the defenceless monsters was confounding his disbelief. As their towers began to smoulder, the creatures reacted by trying to turn away from the heat. Order soon turned to chaos. Their screeching was like tearing bronze as their hide blistered and ruptured. Maddened by pain, blindly they swerved and, here and there, were punching into each other. Towers crashed together, or began to heel over.

He felt a tiny grip and saw Poppy had joined him, wanting to hold his hand as she surveyed the carnage. For a moment he watched its effect upon her face. Watched her eyes twitch as they darted here and there. Watched her grimace as they passed through a pall of smoke that carried a pungent shock of charring flesh and bone.

At last, miraculously, they saw the end of Jaspar's dragon line coming into view. As Carnelian turned, he caught the incredulous glances of his Hands before they ducked their heads. He understood their consternation: they had seen a Master holding hands with a barbarian girl. He disengaged Poppy's grip and asked her to go back to sit beside the homunculus. She made her way past his Righthand, and Carnelian returned to his chair.

As they approached the last enemy dragon, he slowed Earth-is-Strong and turned her so that her pipes could play their fire upon the creature and its tower. As they circled round its flank, other arcs of flame, from the dragons following him, fell on the same target. The bone tower blackened, charred and fiery mouths began opening into the decks within. He grimaced, imagining the crew's fiery hell. Fire pouring down over its flanks and head, the enemy dragon screeched and tossed its head, yanking violently against the tyranny of its tower. With an audible crack its golden horn snapped, its tip flashing as it spun away upon its chain.

'Look,' cried Poppy.

Somehow she had crept back to the screen. The alarm on her face brought him quickly to her side. She pointed her thin arm through the screen. Peering at where she indicated, Carnelian could not at first see anything but smoke billows and dust rolling red over the land. But occasional ragged openings tore in the palls, through which Carnelian glimpsed masses, shapes that his mind resolved. Hornwalls, their circles squeezed out of shape by the pressure of attacks. He felt his blood draining to his feet. Unbelievable victory had made him forget their people on the ground. His first instinct was to take his dragons to their aid. Then at the edge of his vision he saw, to starboard, the vast movement of Jaspar's dragons in flight, aflame. They were heading straight for Fern's wing.

A thunderclap hurled Carnelian against the cabin wall. It was a moment before he could make sense of anything. A ragged hole had been torn in the starboard screen. Through it he saw an incandescent mass tumbling earthwards, streaming smoke. The enemy tower had exploded. Then he saw Poppy lying on the deck and surged forward, stooping to lift her. Stillness came upon him, deafness. She was dead, but then she stirred and the cacophony returned, though there was now a hissing in his ears. Poppy looked at him; she was only stunned. He gestured the homunculus to look after her, then threw himself into his command chair. He had his Lefthand flash a message to his dragons, commanding them to turn inwards towards the centre and herd Jaspar's fleeing dragons into the open space between their aquar wings.

LIKE A TREE

A passion for permanence
Is nothing more than a fear of death.
Everything changes.
The wise man lets go.

(a Quyan fragment)

Lurid fires smouldered in depressions in the ground. The earth was everywhere ploughed up. A drifting mist of smoke and dust tearing across his vision made Carnelian cough behind his mask. At least he had its filters. The dozen or so men he had brought with him were squinting, stumbling around him, wheezing, grimacing, their swords drooping from their hands. Ahead, through the miasma, Carnelian could make out a swathe running east to west that looked like a ridge of debris washed up by a tide of tar. Peering through the eyeslits of his mask, he could make out furtive movements suggesting something there was still alive. He regarded them with more horror than hope. How could anyone have survived that firestorm or the stampede of dragons enraged by their own flesh burning? Though he had managed to herd his half of Jaspar's dragons away from Fern's wing into the open space to the west, Osidian's attack had driven the other half directly into Lily's wing.

As Carnelian plodded closer each step was more reluctant

than the last. He did not want to see, but had no choice. Lily might be there somewhere, still alive. Looking west along the curve of carnage, it was obvious none of her wing had escaped the dragon tidal wave. Even the mounted auxiliaries of their left flank had been overwhelmed. An arc of smoke and dust running from the south round to the north-west showed where Osidian was still carrying on a relentless pursuit. With its flashes of dragonfire, its black angry clouds, it seemed a receding thunderstorm. Carnelian could still feel its tremor in the earth, but there was another, deeper thunder. A slow, rhythmic pounding. He glanced round and saw Earth-is-Strong following him, churning up spiralling tatters of dust, sheets of smoke tearing on her horns, her tower a pale slab upon her back. Her brassman, hanging open, was dangling the rope ladder that danced in time with the monster's tread. He had left his Hands in charge and told them to follow him at a distance, vigilant for any command he should send them by means of the mirrorman he had brought with him. Poppy was up there. He had had to forbid her to accompany him, putting her in the keeping of the homunculus, whom she had come to respect.

Behind the dragon, dust was fluttering off in russet banners from a ridge moving south-east towards their camp. No smoke there and it was closer to the ground, Fern's wing riding down the Ichorian aquar who had broken even as Carnelian turned their burning dragons away from them. Perhaps it had been the explosion of the tower, perhaps the flames and smoke and smoulder burning all along their line that had made the Ichorians flee. Carnelian suppressed a fear that Fern and his Lepers and auxiliaries might yet find the Bloodguard more than a match for them. Before he had had a chance to make a choice, they had already sped too far away for him to intervene. So he had detached Earth-is-Strong from the pursuit and turned her towards Lily and the left wing to see what he could do there.

A whiff of burnt flesh made him return his attention to

what lay ahead. How could anything in that black strand have survived?

As the miasma cleared, Carnelian saw he had reached the dead. His gaze flitted across the charred carpet of mangled men and aquar hoping not to see anything clearly, but so much blood and shit had soaked the earth it had become too wet to rise as dust. He looked back to where Earth-is-Strong loomed, wreathed in smoke. The rest of the world seemed insubstantial in comparison with the reality at his back. He turned slowly until the edge of the carnage came into view in the corner of his left eyeslit. Most likely, Lily would lie somewhere at the end of that forbidding curve. He began walking. He stopped. 'Too easy,' he muttered. He spied what seemed a rock rising from that dark surf. Pale it was, though blackened by the tide. Finding a dark path slicing away through the dead, he set off along it, hardly aware of his attendants lurching after him. He kept his head down, walking around the smoking boulders that were strewn all along the path. It intersected another. Lifting his head, he determined which seemed more likely to lead him to the rock. As he watched his feet, he became aware that the path he walked must be an arc branded into the earth by a scything flame-pipe. The organic shapes of the boulders were threatening to become limbs and torsos and heads. He pressed on, switching naphtha paths, his pale-leathered feet blackening.

He came to a depression filled with brown paste. Its rim of limbs made it seem the remains of some gigantic crab a vast footfall had crushed. Then he saw a torso rising from it: a bag whose contents had been squeezed out to add to the paste. The vomit rose and he struggled to release his mask. Too late. His stomach pumped acid against the barrier of his mask. Vomit thrust up into his nose and oozed out under the chin. Stinging, it choked him. The mask came loose and he almost flung it away. With his free hands he scraped the filth from his face, blew his nostrils clean and gulped at the air.

The noisome miasma was so thickened by the stench of decay his lungs clamped tight. Tears in his eyes, blinked clear. He was confronted by the crazed skull-grin of a face stripped by fire of its nose and lips. He doubled over and pumped more vomit out on the ground. His mask was digging into his hand. He glanced at it and saw its gold lips were rouged with filth. He pulled his cowl down over his face and cautiously looked round. The crewmen were all either being sick or reeling, sickly pale, staring blindly. He began to move on, and they staggered after him.

He walked through that realm of filth and death, his stomach clenching in dry heaves. His gaze darted from horror to horror, but there was always more. What steadied his steps was the discovery that some still lived among the dead. Of these, most had faces already greyed with death, but others looked as if they might survive. It gave him a focus: the hope of salvaging something from this atrocity.

At last he came to a region where the irregular contours of the dead gave way to rings. There the Lepers lay fallen in the hornwalls he had taught them to make. Rimmed by the ridged leather cuirasses of the half-tattooed Ichorians, the Leper formations were still unbroken. He felt a manic pride that they had withstood the Ichorian onslaught.

He reached his beacon rock and found it to be a ruined dragon tower heeled over on its roof. Its mast, now a splintered stump, propped it up. Charred and shattered, in places its bone walls had blistered, exposing its decks, spilling its entrails of pipes and ropes and furnaces. The wreck lay in an ooze of naphtha like black blood. Raising his eyes, Carnelian saw the trail of carnage the tower had made as it rolled to a halt and realized he had witnessed its meteor fall. As far as he could see, the earth was clothed by the dead and dying. A moaning exhaling from many throats stirred in him again the need to save those he could.

* * *

479

It was the pale corona of her hair that showed him where she lay. An Ichorian corpse half covering her had torn the shrouds from her head. Carnelian took hold of the man's black-tattooed arm, then rolled him off. He gaped at Lily. Between her legs a still wet welling of blood glued her shrouds to her thighs and oozed out to join the gore soaking the earth so that, for a moment, it seemed it was her menstruation that had flooded the battlefield. He crouched and, gingerly, pulled aside the cloth looking for a wound. The flesh below was rosy, but whole. The blood was not hers. He moved up her body, peering into her face, smearing red finger-marks on her white hair as he carefully turned her head. A bruise there was already blackening, but under it her skull seemed unbroken. He let go of her as she groaned, eyelids fluttering open. Her ruby eyes stared at him. She frowned in a way that suggested she was not sure what she was seeing.

'It's me, Lily.'

Her hands fumbled at him, pushing him away. She sat up, staring around her, confused. There was a lack of comprehension in her eyes as she gazed upon the blacks and scarlets of the Ichorians interleaved with the greys of her people patterning the earth as far as she could see.

A vibration was approaching like a downpour. Lifting his head, Carnelian saw a wall of dust sweeping towards them. He offered her his hand. She took it. Carefully he pulled her up. He watched with concern as she stood, shakily, then together they turned to meet the riders.

The wall of dust began collapsing as it scudded thinning away into the north-east. A mass of riders were revealed scraping to a halt. A few of them were still coming on. When they reached the edge of the fallen they dismounted. Carnelian recognized Fern by his height and gait. He looked for and found, with relief, Krow at his side. As Fern drew closer Carnelian began to notice how dark his hands were, how stained his sleeves. Brown swathes across his chest and his right shoulder. Across

480

his face. Dried blood – though, by the way he moved, not his own. His eyes seemed over-bright in his blood-crusted face as he took in the scale of the carnage. At last his gaze fell on Lily. 'Are you hurt?'

She did not answer, still blind with shock. Krow had thrown back his cowl. His shrouds too were bloodstained, but only as if he had been too close when Fern had dived into a lake of blood. The rest of their companions were the same; all were staring around them at the dead. Carnelian gazed at Fern. 'You've defeated the Bloodguard?'

Fern refused to look at him. Krow, gazing at him, had pity in his face, but also anger. 'We drove them onto the road and there, against its wall, we butchered them.'

The skin around the youth's eyes twitched as if he were seeing it again. Carnelian considered Fern's averted gaze, wondering what it was Krow was not saying; then Fern glanced up at him and Carnelian knew how it had been. Fern's shame connected with his own. He understood Krow's expression. What had just happened was bound up with the massacre of the Ochre. Carnelian knew that Fern had reason to hate the Bloodguard. One of them had killed his father. It was that death and the woundings suffered that day on the road that had led to Carnelian and Osidian being taken into the Earthsky and, ultimately, to the massacre of the Ochre. Still, what a lone Ichorian had done back then could not justify such merciless destruction of his fellows; Carnelian knew in his heart that the rage Fern had unleashed on them should have fallen on Osidian, perhaps even upon himself. And now Fern recognized that he had acted like Osidian: unable to take revenge on those he truly hated, he had vented his fury on those within reach. Almost Carnelian said: But it's different; Osidian acted in cold blood. He held his tongue. Even if he had wanted to condone massacre, Fern was in no way prepared to hear it condoned. He sought in vain for a way to offer comfort. Finally, it was his heart that spoke. 'Fern, among this mess many are still alive. Get your men to come and search with us for those we can take back to camp. As for the dying, we can at least release them from suffering.'

Fern and Carnelian connected, wordlessly, but in a way that threatened to overwhelm them with pain. The Plainsman turned and strode back towards his men. Krow jerked Carnelian a nod and a pale smile, then followed him.

Smoke from the burning Marula dead drifted above the camp, smearing out the stars. Their casualties had been relatively light, but Carnelian, sitting at Lily's side unmasked, was concerned Sthax's body might be in that pyre. Morunasa had survived; Carnelian had seen him moving among his people.

Consternation among Aurum's auxiliaries was now spreading to the Lepers. Carnelian glanced round, wearily. What he saw caused him to jump up and cover his face with his mask. Darkness was rolling towards them from the west. His heart pounded as he waited. Vast black shapes were looming up out of the night. If these were dragons the whole camp lay defenceless before them. As the campfire light found horns and bellies, their towers too became clearer. Carnelian counted their tiers, then released a sigh.

'They're ours,' said Krow.

Carnelian announced he must go and talk to the Master and would be back when he could, gave Lily one last look of concern, then made for the watch-tower.

When the two Masters walked out onto Heart-of-Thunder's brassman, Carnelian's immediate impression was that the one holding a staff must be Osidian. The weakness evident in the other's gait seemed more characteristic of Aurum, but as he watched them climb to the leftway, he realized the stronger of the two was Aurum.

Slightly hunched, Osidian raised his mask to Carnelian. 'You left your legion leaderless, my Lord.'

'Was I needed for what remained? I assumed you could handle the pursuit without my help. Is Jaspar dead?'

It was Aurum who answered. 'Whether he is or not makes no difference. Even if he has survived, the stump that is all he has left of the Ichorian poses little threat to us.'

Carnelian regarded the old Lord. Though he still walked with his staff, he no longer leaned on it. He seemed taller and much more like the man who had come to the island. Even his voice had regained its brazen resonance.

Osidian's hand flew up, shaping a ragged sign: *Silence!* 'You left your appointed place, my Lord.'

Carnelian was in no mood to apologize for anything. 'I sought to do what could be done for our left wing that you caused to be trampled and incinerated by the fleeing huimur.'

'The destruction of our enemy was my prime concern,' Osidian said, icily.

'As it was mine; however, I still managed to direct the flight away from my wing.' He extended his hand, inviting Osidian to gaze over the camp. It was clear just how many fewer camp-fires there were than there had been before the battle. It would have been still fewer had he not brought back the wounded. His heart lingered on how the life seemed to have gone out of Lily and sadness quenched his anger. He turned to Osidian. 'Was all this carnage worthwhile?'

'With Imago's failure, my mother will fall. The Great who supported her in this perilous adventure will be discredited. The Wise, already weakened, will be only too aware of what damage we could do to them should we reveal the part they played in this. This defeat is as much theirs as it is my mother's. The Powers have no choice but to negotiate with me. Even were they not in disarray, they cannot be unaware of how exposed they are to my threat.'

'You intend, then, that we shall march upon Osrakum?'

Osidian sketched a vague gesture. 'I do not believe it will come to that. Once they learn of my victory, they will be able to read the board as well as I.'

Carnelian pondered this. 'How do you intend to com-municate the news to them?'

For answer Osidian raised his arm, slowly. 'I shall send them this and its brothers.'

Hanging from his trembling fingers, a thick band of metal caught the light. It seemed a bracelet, but if so, for an arm of a girth greater even than a Master's. A waft of iron coming off it made Carnelian look closer. Surely it was gold? He noticed the rings threaded onto its curve. Sliders. A legionary collar, then, with three broken, zero rings.

Aurum's mask glinted in his cowl. 'It belonged to a huimur commander. Our commanders will bring us the rest. The Lesser Chosen have little love for the Ichorians.'

Carnelian regarded the trophy. Without the skills the Wise jealously guarded there was but one way it could have been removed from its wearer's neck.

As he followed Osidian and Aurum into the watch-tower, Carnelian glanced towards the stables ramp. It was the way back to his people and poor Lily. He yearned to be with them, but knew he was too conflicted. His confidence that the victory justified the blood price was ebbing. They would look after each other.

'Why do you linger, my Lord?'

Carnelian gazed at Osidian with Aurum beside him and wondered how it was he had come to have these two as allies.

'Has the Grand Sapient already been fed his elixir?'

It took a moment for Carnelian to make sense of the question. Then alarm sparked in him as he realized he had forgotten all about it. 'The homunculus is down in the camp.'

Osidian nodded. 'Good. I want him to wake.'

Carnelian was thrown further off-balance. 'The Grand Sapient? Will that not be dangerous?'

Osidian made a smiling gesture that seemed somehow too soft in his hand to be convincing. 'Have we not just broken the power of the Wise? I think we can handle one blind, old man.'

484

Carnelian regarded him. Could the maggots or the victory have made Osidian lose his awe of Legions? More likely this bravado was for Aurum's sake. 'Why do you want him awake?'

Osidian made another vague gesture. 'During the negotiations it might prove useful to have direct access to one of the Twelve.'

Weariness overcame any further attempt at opposition Carnelian might feel he ought to make. There were already enough battles to fight. Besides, in the morning things might appear clearer.

Roaring, the vast wave sweeps in. Hunched halfway out of his dream, he stands in the deepening shadow of the rising dark wall of water bracing for the unbearable weight of its impact.

Carnelian opened his eyes, desperate to escape. The familiar ceiling beam of the cell was an anchor against dread, but the roaring sound was still in his ears, reaching him from the nightmare's churning depths. He sat up, realizing the sound must be real. He peered out through a slit. Down on the road the Lepers were pouring north. At the margin of their tide, the mounted auxiliaries were herding them. Fear clutched him. It was but a matter of moments before he had put on his mask and pulled his cloak around him, then he left the cell.

Emerging from behind the monolith onto the road, he paused, blinded by the morning, feeling the din as if it were his nightmare wave rearing up before him. Regaining his sight, he saw a torrent of Lepers climbing the ramp onto the road, pouring along it and swirling through the gap in the leftway wall into the land beyond, but it was a gathering of the more than twenty Lesser Chosen commanders that compelled his attention. Forbidding beings, they stood at the centre of concentric rings of prostrate Marula, marumaga legionaries and, further out, auxiliaries. As he approached, an odour of fear wafted up from the abased as they crawled from his path. It gave him the impression he was approaching a pack of predators in possession of something they had brought down. The contrast of their stillness against the Lepers' storm of motion chilled him most.

Two of the Masters turned. Their gold faces glinting darkly in the shadow of their cowls made them seem to be peering into the world of the living from some remote, infernal realm. As the circle opened for him, he saw a mound of legionary collars piled in their midst.

'My Lord Suth,' said one, his deep voice Aurum's. 'Behold the evidence of our victory.'

Carnelian glanced at the service collars, the fire of their gold dulled and clotted with gore. He looked up, searching for Osidian. There was a slight inclination in the heads of those Lords that led his eye round to the one inspiring their deference. 'And Imago?'

'There are only fifty-two collars here and his body was not found,' said Osidian.

Carnelian knew there should be fifty-four.

'If he still lives, he will come to me.'

Carnelian tried to deduce the basis of this certainty. Jaspar had failed not only Ykoriana, but also the Great. He could hardly expect to find succour among the Wise. Thus, all he could hope for now was that he might come to some accommodation with Osidian.

Aurum gazed north. 'He will be in a nearby watch-tower. The only leverage left to him is controlling communications between ourselves and Osrakum.' The Master's tone of contempt was edged with glee.

Osidian shifted and all there turned to see him indicating the collars. 'My Lord Aurum, oversee the loading of these onto a beast and escort it to the nearest tower. There make arrangements for them to be couriered to the Clave.'

'Under whose seal, Celestial?'

Osidian removed Legions' ring from his finger and gave it

to Aurum. Carnelian could not see how this could work. 'Will Jaspar let them pass?'

Osidian made a smile gesture. 'We have to leave him something to bargain with. I expect we will, quite soon, manage to persuade him to send them along the road under the seal of He-who-goes-before. I shall now climb to the heliograph and attempt to open communications with him.'

'May I accompany you, Celestial?' Carnelian asked.

Osidian lifted his hand in assent. The other Lords bowed low as they let them through.

'What are you doing with the Lepers?'

In the shadow of the monolith, Osidian's mask had a sinister cast. 'I have no further need of them.'

Chilled by his tone, Carnelian, glancing out, saw some Leper stragglers moving off along the road and wondered if Lily was once more among them. He denied his dread its hold on him and mustered his strength for a fight. He turned back. 'You are going to honour the oath you swore to them?'

Disdain was frozen into the gold of Osidian's mask. 'The situation has changed. As soon as the supplies I have sent for arrive from Makar, we shall march upon Osrakum. Even if I wished it, there is no time to train Aurum's crews to replace their Chosen commanders.'

Carnelian understood then from where Aurum's renewed vigour had come. 'What have you promised him?'

Osidian made a gesture of dismissal. 'What is pertinent is that my imminent triumph in Osrakum has made him unconflicted in his support. With him come those he commands.'

'I did not think you would so easily betray your honour.'

Osidian's fingers began to curl, but then quickly straightened. 'There will be time enough to send him back once I have no further use for him.'

Carnelian felt icy fear at where his next question would

lead, but he knew he had no choice but to ask it. 'And what if the Lepers do not accept this?'

'Do you imagine they are in any position to defy me?' Osidian turned into the shadows of the stables. 'Persuade them to leave while they still can.'

Carnelian was left frozen where he stood, watching Osidian become one with the darkness. He could not rid himself of the conviction that the Master who had massacred the Ochre had returned. Were things sliding towards the abyss as they had done before? Osidian had had no further use for the Tribe; they had been in his power too. Lily and her Lepers had become at least as much of an affront to his vision of himself as had been the Ochre. Carnelian felt his fear fraying into panic. How much had this to do with him letting the Lepers take Osidian prisoner? Even without the maggots gnawing at his flesh, this was not the kind of humiliation Osidian left unrepaid. Suspicion arose in him. Had Osidian really lost control in the battle? Had he really been unable to steer Jaspar's rout away from their left wing? The wing commanded by the woman to whom he had sworn his oath.

Carnelian centred himself. Osidian had not yet moved against the Lepers, though he could have done so easily. There was some hope in that. It seemed his oath still bound him to some extent, but for how long? The Lepers must leave immediately.

The Marula had resumed their guarding of the watch-tower. As he moved through them, they abased themselves. He took his time and was rewarded by a black face momentarily glancing up at him: Sthax showing he had survived.

From the road, Carnelian descended a ramp made from compacted rubble. Larger fragments of the demolished section of leftway formed a boulder field on either side, from which he emerged on the edge of the new Leper camp. Their multitude seemed a colony of gulls. He lingered, gazing at them, wondering if Lily was there and, if she was, how he might find her without exciting a riot. Near the edge of the crowd, a figure rose and must have noticed him, for it came directly towards him. As he recognized it was Fern, Carnelian's heart misgave. He knew that what he had come to say could only serve to tear open yet again the wound of Fern's grief. However, it was Fern who would understand better than anyone else what terrible danger the Lepers were in and Carnelian needed all the help he could get to persuade them to leave.

'Is Lily there?' he said as Fern came near.

Fern nodded grimly, so that Carnelian became afraid for her. 'Has she recovered?'

'As much as can be expected. Wait here and I'll bring her to you.'

Carnelian watched Fern as he returned to the crowd. When he came back, there was a smaller shrouded figure with him. Carnelian led them both into the shadow of a boulder and there unmasked. The others responded by freeing their heads from their shrouds. Carnelian regarded Lily, saw how aged she looked, how fragile.

'You're going to have to leave now.'

Lily looked up at him, haunted. 'Give us Au-rum and we shall go.'

Carnelian regarded her bleakly. 'The Master's not ready to give him to you.'

'He's not going to keep his promise?'

'He'll send him to you once he has no further need of him.'

Lily, frowning, looked close to angry tears. 'When?'

He rejoiced at the return of some of her spirit. 'I don't know.'

Her frown deepened. 'He's not going to give him to us at all, is he?'

Carnelian wanted to contradict her pessimism, but when he imagined Osidian far away, imagined him having achieved his aims, then he could not see him sending Aurum back to the Lepers. 'You must leave while you still can.'

'Do as he says,' Fern said, the pain raw in his voice.

Lily looked at the Plainsman, bewildered. 'We can't return empty-handed, we simply can't . . .'

A look of shame came over Fern: 'We can still sack the city?'

Carnelian did not feel he was in any position to lecture them and was trying not to judge them. 'As long as you don't interfere with his supplies, I don't imagine the Master will care what happens to Makar.'

Lily was shaking her head, staring. 'This makes a mockery of all we've suffered. How can we add this defeat to that which destroyed so many of my people? If we return defeated, we will fade, slowly, broken. We may as well die here.' Her pale lips formed a thin smile. 'And wait here in hope that we'll remind you and the Master of your honour.'

Carnelian could think of nothing to say.

Lily set her face. 'Besides, too many of the wounded are not ready to be moved.'

Carnelian nodded, feeling hollow. 'Once he has his supplies we'll be marching north.'

Lily nodded absent-mindedly and, then, pulling her shrouds back over her head, began walking away. Carnelian and Fern caught each other's look of despair. Fern grunted something, then followed Lily.

Standing on the northern edge of the heliograph platform, Carnelian gazed down into the camp. On his right the chaos of the new Leper camp; on his left, the far greater expanse of the auxiliary camp that faced the Lepers through the gap in the leftway wall.

He glanced round to where Osidian was sitting in the shadow of the heliograph. Beside him was the homunculus, ready to operate the device. When Carnelian had come up onto the platform he had hidden nothing from Osidian. He had said that, justifiably, the Lepers were reluctant to leave without that which they had been promised. He had tried to make light of this, saying, What does it matter? Osidian had growled that he would starve them, refuse them water. Carnelian had pointed out that their wounded needed time to build up the strength to make the move. In a few days' time the supplies would have arrived from Makar and they would leave the Lepers behind, who would then have no choice but to return to their valleys. Osidian had made a loose gesture that Carnelian chose to see as agreement.

He focused on their camp. What would they be returning to? He could only hope Lily was wrong, that her people would manage to rebuild their lives even without Aurum as a symbol of justice. He grew grim at the thought that in a few days he would have to part from Fern once more, for ever. He wondered if he should attempt to send Poppy and Krow back to the Valleys with him.

He squinted north along the road, as if hoping to see the future and Osrakum. All there was to see was the road narrowing away to a thread from which, far away, there rose the peg of the next watch-tower. He willed it to begin flashing. His feelings were too much in turmoil for him to know how he would react to seeing Jaspar again, but at least he would provide some distraction, though not necessarily a pleasant one. Osidian seemed to be awaiting Jaspar's arrival with the predatory patience of a spider sitting at the heart of its web.

The Master approaching seemed enveloped in red flame. With his vast cloak he could have been the sandstorm made flesh. Two figures flanked him, glimmering as if they were clothed in sunlit water. Behind came slaves with dragonfly tattoos upon their faces. They had descended from a dragon, all sweeping slopes of rouged hide, sickle-horned, bearing upon its back a castle of bone from which rose a mast that held aloft a rayed sun gleaming in the dusty air. Behind the monster stretched a field of lances that flickered scarlet pennants north along the road as far as Carnelian could see. Drifts of aquar plumes, the

491

long volumes of their beaked heads, the casques of their riders, spired and feathered, gold collars at their necks, their half-black faces: everything combined to make an ever-varying tessellation that confused the eye. This spectacle was flanked by an avenue of Osidian's dragons that stretched down the side of the road to hazy distance.

Though Carnelian wanted to glance round to see the reassuring bulk of Earth-is-Strong and Heart-of-Thunder, he could not take his eyes from the advancing scarlet apparition. He had had a notion of remaining aloft in his command chair in case Jaspar should be planning some treachery, but Osidian had insisted they must confront their enemy together. The scarlet apparition raised its hand to show the emberous red jewel of the Pomegranate Ring like a wound through its palm. From the right eyeslit of its mask rays radiated across the golden skin. The last time he had seen that perfect face, it was his father who had been behind it. For a moment he expected it to be his father who spoke.

'I have come, Celestial, as we arranged. Are you prepared to make the same oath to me now that you made by means of the heliograph?'

Carnelian knew that voice, but it was not his father's.

'On my blood I swear I shall not harm you, Imago,' said Osidian.

Carnelian flinched, shocked, but said nothing.

'Honour now your part of our agreement, my Lord.'

Jaspar hesitated a moment, then glanced to one of his lictors and made an elegant sign with a gloved hand. The lictor bowed. 'As you command, my father.'

The lictor turned to the massed Ichorians and, raising his standard, he angled it down until it nearly touched the road. The nearest aquar ranks sank first, this movement sweeping back along the road. In their thousands they climbed out from their saddle-chairs. The striking of their feet upon the road was like a sudden hailstorm. Jaspar, who had turned to watch, waited until the sound was faint in the distance, then turned back. For moments that perfect face gazed imperiously upon them. The only sound a creaking as one of the monsters behind them caused the tower on its back to shift. Carnelian was trying to grasp what he was feeling when, suddenly, Jaspar fell to one knee. His cloak floated for a moment then settled. He offered up something that glimmered in his hand. 'I give the Ichorians to you, Celestial, with myself.'

Carnelian registered the look of horror on the half-black faces of the lictors. One took a step back, staring at their kneeling master. Carnelian was not sure whether it was the statement or the action of kneeling that had shocked them. For He-who-goes-before to offer himself to one of the House of the Masks was inconceivable. But then, so was such an act of abasement before one who was only a Jade Lord. After all, Jaspar had been elected to incarnate the majesty of the Great. Such a being should kneel before none but a fully consecrated God Emperor.

Movement made him glance round to see Osidian accepting from Jaspar what Carnelian saw was the Pomegranate Ring. Osidian seemed to be examining it even as he raised his hand. Carnelian was trying to read its shape when twined voices of brass from behind him blared so thunderously he was bent by their gale. Heart-of-Thunder's trumpets. A signal, then.

He sensed Osidian's expectation. His masked face was fixed towards the road before them. With increasing alarm, Carnelian followed its gaze and, at first, he could see nothing but a swirling consternation among the Ichorians. Then he saw the pall drifting up from the dragon towers all down the road. Their pipes were being lit. His gaze darted to the road, where men were running, trying to mount their aquar, crying out. He moaned with horror as a whining almost beyond hearing swelled into a choking scream and the first pipe spat fire. All down the line, flame jets ignited. He inclined his head so that the slits of his mask shielded his eyes from the glare. The space between the dragons and the leftway wall began to fill with rolling black smoke that, as it frothed and boiled, allowed glimpses of the furnace in which the Ichorians and their aquar were burning like tinder.

The flame-pipes guttered, spitting a few last gobbets of liquid flame, then, silence. Stunned, Carnelian watched the smoke lift from the road, ripping, thinning as it rose. The road was black, but covered with lumps, riddled with threads of smoke that unravelled into mist. Flames sprinted through the crusted mess. Red-rimmed gold fissures gaped, puffing steam sprinkled with sparks. The tar tide washed all the way up the leftway wall.

Redness swelling near him made him jerk round to see Jaspar rising. At the same time the lictors dropped, releasing their standards with a clatter onto the road. Tears and phlegm glazed the nearest half-black face. The man's mouth released a moan as if he were deflating. His unblinking stare of loss made revulsion rise in Carnelian like vomit. He turned on Osidian. 'Why?'

Osidian's hands framed appeasement. 'They would have harried us all the way to Osrakum. Besides, they had lost their use.'

'But we could have brought them over to our side,' Carnelian nearly screamed.

Osidian shook his head. 'They were the creatures of the Great, brought up since childhood to adore them. Nothing would have persuaded them to take up our cause.'

Jaspar's mask was gazing at the massacre impassively. Carnelian wanted to understand. 'You brought them here for this?'

Jaspar turned to him his rayed eye. His hand rolled an elegant gesture, as if he were about to pronounce on some dance he had just watched that was skilled, but not quite perfect. 'They failed me, cousin, neh?'

Staring at that hand, Carnelian became blind with rage.

'Carnelian. Carnelian?'

He turned to Osidian. 'I give Imago to you. Do with him as you will.'

Jaspar's voice: 'Surely you jest, Celestial . . . your oath . . .'

Osidian's voice: 'I swore an oath to you. The Lord Suth Carnelian did not. I am sure you have not forgotten the part you played in our fall. You did not realize we knew? As much as you have wronged me, my Lord, you have wronged him.'

Carnelian saw Jaspar haloed by blood. For a moment he savoured tearing that mask off like a shell, rending the face beneath. He feasted on fantasies of furious tortures. He felt his passion ebbing. It was not just Jaspar who was a monster, but all the Masters.

Carnelian extended his hand. 'Give me your mask, Jaspar.'

The sun-rayed gold face turned to Osidian, but there was no help there. It turned back to Carnelian. 'You cannot—'

'I will not ask again.'

Jaspar pushed back his hood, then fumbled behind his head. The mask came away to reveal a joweled, glistening, pasty face. He put his mask in Carnelian's hand then shrank away, fear putting a curve into his shoulders and back, his eyes fixed on Carnelian as a bird might regard a serpent arching above it.

Carnelian hardly recognized the man he had once known. He no longer felt rage, just contempt. 'You two, lictors, bind your betrayer.'

The two men looked up, blearily, their faces blank.

Carnelian was patient with their shock. 'He brought you all here to die . . .' He pointed at the smoking charnel field. 'To die like that. You no longer owe him service. Look into his face, see what kind of man he is.'

A hungry gleam came into the eyes of first one, then both as they fixed upon him whom they had so recently called father.

Jaspar, trying to stand his ground, shrieked: 'You shall not lay your unclean hands upon me!'

Everyone could smell his sweaty terror. Taking hold of

495

Jaspar's cloak Carnelian yanked at it, over and over, pulling the Master off-balance, until the silk came away in his hands. Finding an edge he began tearing it into strips. He gave these scarlet ribbons to the lictors. 'Bind him with these. For what he's done, we'll have to determine a fitting punishment.'

When they had finished, Carnelian forced the sun-rayed mask into the hand of one of the lictors. 'Use this to buy yourselves new lives.'

The last of the Red Ichorians glanced at the metal face they had spent so much of their lives in awe of, before gazing back at their dead with empty eyes.

'His consciousness rises,' said the homunculus.

He released his grip from behind the Grand Sapient's heel, rose from his knees, backed away. Strapped in, Legions stood in the open capsule that was propped up against the wall, his skeletal arms crossed over his chest, his skin like bleached leather, his face concealed behind his one-eyed mask.

Carnelian found it hard to believe this was anything more than a huskman. A tiny movement made him peer through the myrrh smoke uncurling in languid spirals. Legions' left fist was opening its pale flower a petal at a time. The four fingers splayed, then recurled. The right hand, blossoming, was joined by the first opening again. Soon both were opening and closing, opening and closing. Then the wrists slipped a twist into this motion, turning the hands into the wings of a bird in flight. Then the hinges of the elbow opened and closed, moving this flight away from, then towards, the chest. Crossing, recrossing the arms several times. The motion slowed and died. The arms crossed, the elbows began rising, falling. This turned into a sinuous opening of the arms as if they were seeking to embrace someone. Closing, opening, closing, opening like seaweed in a tide. At last the hands came to rest, open, slightly apart, their heels resting on the bands wrapping round the Grand Sapient's stomach.

Carnelian's trance was broken by the homunculus, now

wearing his blinding mask, backing towards the capsule. Reaching behind him to grip one of the bands, he raised his heel and placed it next to one of the Grand Sapient's cadaverous, yellow feet. With a grunt, the little man pulled himself back and up to stand within the capsule. As he nestled his neck into the waiting hands, the fingers meshed about his throat and immediately began to flex.

When they stopped, the child mask of the homunculus murmured: 'Lord Nephron has it.'

The fingers moved again.

'A cell, fourth storey, sun-ninety-three. Ten, ten, three.'

Osidian advanced, removing his mask, revealing a sweaty face and eyes bright with anticipation. Unsettled by that expression, Carnelian hesitated before he in turn unmasked.

Osidian addressed the capsule. 'Sapience, contrary to your expectations, I have won a great victory.'

The homunculus, repeating Osidian's words, was momentarily interrupted by a convulsion of the Grand Sapient's fingers that must have hurt the little man, for he flinched. 'Nephron,' he said, then resumed his echoing of Osidian's words.

'With two legions of the line I have annihilated the Ichorian.'

Carnelian was watching Osidian. He looked so strange: eyes open wide, mouth open too, lips holding a smile. He looked so young. Carnelian realized, with shock, that he had forgotten that Osidian really was not much more than a youth.

'Has Osrakum been informed?'

The new, strong voice made Carnelian jump. Almost he looked around for some being unexpectedly arrived within the cell. It was the homunculus who had spoken, now nothing but a conduit for his master.

Osidian answered that he had sent the collars of the Ichorian huimur commanders to Osrakum by courier.

'Has any heliograph been sent?'

Osidian replied it was possible that He-who-goes-before had sent a message, but he did not think it likely.

'You speak of Imago?'

Carnelian was stunned. How could the Grand Sapient possibly know about Jaspar? While still in Makar, if Legions had known about the Ichorian and Jaspar, surely he would have used that information to gain power over Osidian? And, since then, he had slept, oblivious of the turning of events. Carnelian's mind raced with superstitious conjectures of what powers this creature might possess. He calmed himself, strove to be rational; it was nothing more than deduction from what they had just told him. The Ichorian had been sent forth from Osrakam. Since it was likely Ykoriana was somehow behind its sending, it followed that whoever commanded it must be one of her allies, and Jaspar had been her chief ally among the Great.

Legions spoke again. 'It would be in Imago's interest to remain silent.'

Carnelian tried to work out why that might be the case, but his mind was simply not fast enough.

'You sent the collars under my seal?'

Osidian began a gesture that, if he had finished it, would have been an apology. 'Under that of He-who-goes-before.'

A momentary stiffening of the fingers seemed to Carnelian to betray the Grand Sapient's disappointment. 'Tell me how all this has come about.'

The verb used the requisitive mode but, to Carnelian's surprise and dismay, Osidian submitted to its command. As he began explaining, the Grand Sapient steered his narrative, until it seemed to Carnelian he was reading events as if they were beads on a cord.

'How was this victory achieved?'

Osidian's face lit up and, oozing pride, he began describing how the battle had proceeded according to his tactics. As he spoke, Carnelian watched the Grand Sapient's fingers. He detected a twinge when Aurum was mentioned; thereafter, nothing. It made him wonder if the Grand Sapient was divining the part his brethren must have played.

Osidian concluded by recounting how he had destroyed the survivors of the Ichorian, the glow of his achievement bright in his eyes.

'Your tactic was a commonplace in the early part of the Civil War,' said the Grand Sapient.

Osidian's cheeks coloured as if he had been slapped.

'Until it was rendered obsolete by a counter-tactic. Though you may not be aware of it, it would seem likely you picked this up from the reels you read in our Library.'

These words lit another light in Osidian's eyes. Beneath knitted brows they bored into the long silver mask. His lips thinned. 'Nevertheless, I won. There will not be another battle. My victory will lead to chaos in Osrakum. When I appear at the Gates with my legions, the Chosen will bow to me. If they do not, I will lay siege to the Hidden Land.'

'Your analysis, though sound, is incomplete. News of Imago's failure will break your mother's power and shatter the unity of the Clave. The Wise have played badly and their influence is weakened, but is there not a power you have forgotten?'

Osidian frowned, incredulous. 'My brother?'

'The God Emperor.'

Osidian looked exasperated. 'He is my mother's creature.'

'You have released her grip on him.'

'But he is spineless, incapable of independent action.'

Carnelian remembered his meeting with Molochite, relived the power of his presence, his malice, and fear crept into him that Osidian was wrong; that Osidian had miscalculated.

'He was capable enough to murder your sister and remain unpunished.'

Osidian paled. His eyes widened. 'My mother—'

'Was unable to protect her. As, no doubt, she has been unable to protect her new daughter, Ykorenthe, your sister-niece, whom your brother will take for wife.'

Osidian's face became weak with uncertainty.

'Child, there is a reason why we have laboured to keep the

499

Chosen locked inside Osrakum. Whenever they have been free to leave, it has led to this chaos.'

Carnelian, wanting to fight back, almost threw the example of the Lesser Chosen legates at the Grand Sapient, but then he recalled how encompassed about by the Law they were, spied upon by ammonites, the communications between them carefully filtered. Perhaps these, who were the least of the Chosen, might only be let out into the outer world, the better to keep the powerful imprisoned within.

'The Balance of the Powers was constructed to safeguard the Commonwealth from your meddling. It seeks to protect you from yourselves. Removing the Red Ichorians from Osrakum is like unstoppering a bottle.'

Osidian's face had grown paler than his leathers. 'The Sinistrals,' he sighed.

'You were raised among them; did they seem to you ineffectual?'

Carnelian saw in Osidian's face that he had never given them much thought. They had always been there, part of the ritual of his world. Carnelian remembered how confident the sybling Quenthas had been, with their swords, to challenge the Red Ichorians, who had come into the Sunhold to guard his father.

'Two of the Powers rely on the Sinistral Ichorians for protection from the third.'

Osidian rallied. 'We have the legions.'

'Child, you have not seen the Gates. The legions would never have been able to intervene in time to save the Isle from an assault by the flame-pipes of the Red Ichorians.'

Carnelian saw the truth of it. Only the strength of the Sinistral Ichorians had held the Great in check.

'The Sinistrals were in perfect balance with the Red Ichorians.'

Carnelian digested this, then grew cold, understanding Osidian's earlier shock. 'There's nothing to stop them taking the Three Gates.'

A jerking motion drew his eyes to the homunculus' throat.

'Suth Carnelian,' it muttered and he realized the Grand Sapient had not known he was there.

Osidian's face distorted with rage. 'He would not dare!'

'It is not too late,' said the homunculus.

'What?' Osidian looked in despair.

'Let me return to Osrakum.'

Osidian shook his head, looking drained.

'At least let me communicate with my brethren.'

Osidian threw his arm up in angry dismissal. 'You almost had me convinced. I should have known you would do anything, say anything, to escape with your miserable carcass.'

The voice of the homunculus cut through Osidian's display. 'Examine the logic, child. If you do not let me act, the Great Balance itself will fall. Your brother's power will become absolute.'

'I will listen to nothing more,' Osidian cried. He lunged forward, grabbed one of the homunculus' arms and tore him from the Grand Sapient's grasp. The little man fell to the floor, his arm twisting in Osidian's grip. He yanked him up onto his feet.

'This was a mistake,' he bellowed. 'A mistake!'

Carnelian raised his hands in appeasement, 'Osidian—'

Osidian raised a hand in a stark barrier gesture. 'Enough! Nothing has changed. The moment the supplies reach us, we march on Osrakum.'

As he stormed out of the cell dragging the homunculus after him, a piercing screech made the hackles rise on Carnelian's neck. It was a while before he realized it was coming from behind the one-eyed mask as the Grand Sapient clawed the air for his voice.

Dust hissed against his cloak. Standing on the edge of the heliograph platform, Carnelian was watching the cluster of black-shrouded forms down on the road inspect the latest caravan of pack huimur from Makar. For three days now they had been arriving, plodding beneath frames globed with render sacs. Soon it would be time to leave.

He could tell that one of the Masters was Osidian, because of the small figure of the homunculus that he now kept always at his side. Even when it was time to feed the Sapients their elixir, Osidian went with him. It spoke of his anxiety that the Grand Sapient might wake. With the homunculus, Osidian looked as if he was himself one of the Wise. Carnelian had come up to the platform to escape the fury of preparation. He wondered at how, through sheer will, Osidian daily overcame the debilitation of the maggots burrowing through his body. He was grateful for Osidian's determination to go on, for it prevented him from falling back into the embrace of the Darkness-under-the-Trees. Still, Carnelian kept up a constant vigilance, fearful that Osidian, desperate to expunge his doubts, might turn the Leper camp into a new Ochre Grove. Not that Osidian's feverish energy fooled Carnelian. He saw in it only ever more evidence of how shaken Osidian was by the Grand Sapient's analysis: that Molochite was now free to seize absolute power and, with it, Carnelian felt some grudging sympathy for him: having scaled so close to the pinnacle of victory, to be pulled down so suddenly into contemplating the trough of defeat. Worse, to know it was he who had brought this about.

What was torturing Carnelian was the conviction that all the suffering they had caused, all the carnage, had been for naught. His gaze fell upon that portion of the road caked with a greasy, rancid crust of melted, rotting flesh. High as his vantage point was, whenever the rain wind dropped, the stench rose up as from some gargantuan corpse.

Carnelian pulled his cloak about him. In his bones he felt a storm coming. As if responding to his thoughts, the wind picked up, lashing him with a rasping sand hail, causing him to turn his mask into its hissing, so that he saw a mass of it rising from the land like some immense humped beast crowned with snaking tendrils of spiralling red. Yes, a storm was coming and, when it came, much would be swept away. He veered away from contemplating just how much. Here was the danger of solitude. The danger Osidian hid from in ceaseless activity. Carnelian's thoughts resisted his attempts to quell them. He tried to draw some bleak comfort from his certainty that he would not survive. He dismissed that with a growl. There would be time enough to die, but he still had hope his loved ones might escape with the Lepers, though into what kind of life he tried not imagine.

He gazed on the Leper camp. He had given up any hope of persuading them to leave. They had rejected his arguments once and, after having witnessed the annihilation of the Ichorian survivors, would be unlikely to be frightened by some new threat of a vengeful god unleashed. What did they know about the Great Balance, about the Three Powers? How could he even begin to explain to them what he now believed was happening at the heart of the world? Besides, they could see Osidian acting as if nothing had changed. If things went well, in a day or two he would march north and Carnelian would go with him. Left without supplies, the Lepers would have no choice but to return to their valleys. He hoped he would find the courage to bid a final farewell to Fern, to Lily and Krow. He grew grimmer still. And Poppy too, for he was now determined she must go with them, by guile if possible, otherwise by force.

Osidian slumped against the heliograph, the homunculus beside him wearing its smiling blinding mask. Carnelian watched Osidian's face betray with each twitch around the corners of his mouth and eyes the agony he was enduring. It was only up here, in the cool, enfolding night, that he gave himself fully to the maggots. Sometimes, looking at him, Carnelian felt his own doubts and fear eating through him like those worms.

A voice came up from somewhere on the watch-tower roof. 'Master?'

Carnelian recognized the rumble of Morunasa's voice. 'Master, I have a letter here . . .'

Osidian groaned, lost in his pain. Carnelian peered down through the slats and called: 'What letter?'

There was a silence, during which Carnelian sensed Morunasa's resentment so clearly it almost gave him shape in the darkness below.

'A letter taken from a courier at the tower north of here.'

Carnelian rose, his heart beating, having a presentiment of disaster. He put on his mask, then crossed to Osidian, stooped to retrieve the mask from where Osidian had let it fall. He covered the face gleaming with sweat with the serene one of gold, bound it on, then he gave Morunasa leave to climb up.

He appeared like a black sun and seemed the very heart of the night. As he approached, Carnelian put out his hand and Morunasa, reluctantly, gave the letter to him. In his hand it felt as smooth as his own skin. Carnelian turned it and saw the large seal clinging to it. Two faces looking away from each other. His throat grew dry, even as his hands moistened. Though he had not seen this seal before, it clearly had something to do with the Imperial Power.

He looked at Morunasa. 'Do the other Masters know of this?'

'No.'

They both flinched as a paler shadow rose beside them. Osidian raised a ghostly hand. 'Give it to me.'

His voice was hollow, dull. Carnelian gave him the letter. A sense of crisis saturated the air like an anticipation of lightning. A pair of eyes that floated nearly disembodied in the dark reminded him of Morunasa's presence. The last thing they needed was another witness. 'You may leave, Morunasa.'

The man stood looking at Osidian as if he had not heard.

'Leave now,' Carnelian said. Stress suffused his voice with menace. Morunasa turned to him. For a moment it seemed he would defy him, but soon he had slipped out of sight.

Osidian sank to the platform and put the letter down

before him. He reached behind his head to release the bindings of his mask. Carnelian saw how the last living colour had drained from Osidian's face, how he was regarding the letter with the eyes of a corpse. Reaching out he took it, broke the seal, unfolded the parchment, turned it to the light and read. Carnelian watched his face harden until it was stone. He could bear to wait no longer. 'What is it?'

Osidian handed Carnelian the letter. The glyphs were exquisitely formed. For a moment Carnelian was confronted by the unblinking, probing eyes of its faces, then they began making sounds in his mind.

Following treasonous, rash actions by the Wise, We

Carnelian stared at the glyph: the divine, dual 'We' that only a God Emperor or the Twins Themselves could use. He grew cold. From Molochite, then. He continued reading.

We have been forced to act in haste to secure the defence of holy Osrakum left sinfully defenceless by the reckless sending forth of the Red Ichorians against a foul Rebel who has been allowed to rise against Us. Fear not for the immediate sanctity of the Hidden Land, for we have taken the precaution of securing the Gates. Neither should you fear this change. We intend to abolish the distinction between you and the unworthy Great. Henceforth shall you be entitled to vote in Holy Elections. Further, so that your House shall be suitably provided with slaves and riches, We shall double the flesh tithe and the taxes on the cities. To those of you who serve Us most ardently We shall not only gift you the daughters of the Great but, to the most deserving among you, We shall give access to the daughters of Our House that Our blood fire shall burn more brightly in the veins of your offspring.

Fear only the Rebel who treacherously destroyed the

Red Ichorians and, even now, advances upon Us with stolen legions and a plague of barbarians.

Hasten hither with all your strength that We might together destroy his pretensions and then wreak a terror of retribution against all who have dared rise against the Chosen and so restore harmonious peace to our Commonwealth.

Carnelian lost his focus on the glyphs. His worst fears had come to pass. Molochite had taken the Three Gates as Legions had prophesied. He had removed any possibility of the Lesser Chosen supporting Osidian by enfranchising them himself and had summoned them all to Osrakum with their legions, so as to use their overwhelming strength to crush Osidian's rebellion. Carnelian suppressed a sweating surge of panic. Most terrible of all, news of this disaster had reached Osidian while the Lepers were still here, within reach of his flame-pipes. Carnelian prepared himself, then looked round. So great was Osidian's wrath, it seemed to be streaming from his body as dark pinions. Carnelian feared that anything he might say could unleash a massacre. His first instinct sickened him. Murder. No. Osidian dead, Aurum would be unchained, Morunasa too. He could not hope to control them both. Somehow, Osidian had to be engaged, his black passions turned away from bloodshed. 'What are we going to do?'

Osidian spoke, staring blindly. 'He sent this to me.'

'Who?'

'It is in his own hand.'

Carnelian glanced at the glyphs then back at Osidian. His fear grew as he sensed the madness in him rising. 'Surely this was meant for a Legate?'

Osidian's eyes sharpened and fell ravenously upon Carnelian. 'Look at the seal!'

Carnelian disengaged from that glare with difficulty. He folded the parchment, bringing the two halves of the seal together. Each half of the seal bore a face. Carnelian looked up, agonized at not understanding him.

Osidian's face dissolved into an exasperation that seemed close to tears. 'It has been turned on its side, deliberately, so that the heads would be separated by the opening of the letter. His is the green head; mine the black. It is his declaration of war.'

Carnelian glanced back at the seal, certain of Osidian's madness. If anything it seemed a splitting in two of the Twins. Osidian mumbling made Carnelian look up again. Words were escaping from Osidian in a shapeless, meandering rant. Carnelian tried to make sense of it: claims that he had always bested his brother; resentment that Molochite had always been his mother's pet.

Osidian shook his head. 'This time will be no different. I shall overcome him.'

Relief released Carnelian. 'So we are still going to march on Osrakum?'

Osidian gave no sign that he had heard. 'He will have overwhelming force, but I shall have my Father with me.'

Carnelian's dread returned with redoubled strength. Osidian was nodding, leering. 'I shall feed Him and He will inhabit me.'

Carnelian felt he was drowning, flailing. 'We're tired,' he heard himself say, 'exhausted. We will see more clearly in the morning. Now we need sleep.'

His tone soothed them both and so he kept it up, smoothing his speech into a lullaby of persuasion. Slowly, the madness drained away from Osidian's eyes. His face softened until he looked more like himself. Carnelian helped him up, digging his shoulder into Osidian's armpit, maintaining a constant, droning flow of words as, with the homunculus' help, he began to half drag, half carry Osidian back to his cell.

Carnelian watched Osidian drift into a troubled sleep, thinking how easy it would be to kill him. The same logic as before would have been enough to stay his hand, but there was added poignancy in how much Osidian, glazed with sweat, twitching, resembled the fevered boy Carnelian and Fern had nursed down from the Guarded Land. Carnelian bore a share in all his crimes. He was glad he had that logic to lean on, to justify him avoiding an act he had no stomach for – not now, nor ever before when it might have saved the Tribe. He was glad he had not been lying to Osidian: it would be easier to face what had to be done in the morning. He had a focus. He had to nurse Osidian's rage against his brother enough to get them all – dragons, Masters, auxiliaries, Morunasa and Marula – north and safely away from the Lepers before anyone else learned what had happened in Osrakum.

He turned away from Osidian, exhausted. Something was crouching in a corner. The homunculus.

'Master, my masters have not yet been drugged.'

Carnelian hung his head and wondered if he cared. What if Legions and the other Sapients should awake? For a moment that thought brought hope. The Grand Sapient might know something that could be done. Had he not asked to return to Osrakum? At the very least he would be someone to whom he could talk, someone who would understand. He shook his head. This was not some friendly uncle. This was a creature soaked through with guile and unfathomable motives. Carnelian's only remaining hope was that he would be able to contain and guide Osidian. An intervention by the Grand Sapient could send the whole situation careering even further out of control.

Heavily, he rose. 'Let's do it, then.'

He took the homunculus' hand to guide him out of the cell. Once they came into that of the Sapients Carnelian masked, to allow the homunculus to see. He leaned against a wall watching the little man advance upon the Grand Sapient's capsule. He broke the seal and pulled the lid open. He reached up to coax a yellow bead into his hand and climbed up, reaching for the chin of the long silver mask.

Legions' hands struck like snakes. Carnelian let out a cry of shock even as the homunculus pulled himself free and fell to the floor. The pale, bony fingers combed the air and then, slowly, came back to settle their heels upon the Grand Sapient's ribs, open, facing each other.

The homunculus turned to stare at Carnelian, a rictus of horror fixed deep into the wrinkles of his face. 'Master?'

Carnelian willed his heart to slow, tried to list all the dangers, but it was a desire to talk to someone, anyone, that made him nod. The homunculus frowned, jerked a bow, then backed towards the capsule, clambered up and settled his neck into the waiting hands. Immediately they snapped closed around his throat with such force the homunculus let out a choked cry, his hands jumping up as if to tear the fingers away. The grip loosened and the homunculus relaxed and gave out a long gasp that did not seem his own. The sound a man might make reaching air after a desperate struggle in drowning depths.

'What has happened?' the homunculus said.

Still alarmed, Carnelian was trying to make sense of this. 'Have you just woken?'

Legions' hands jerked instructions. 'For three days I have been awake, listening for the vibration of your tread, Suth Carnelian.'

The homunculus' eyes had a spider gleam that seemed to belong to his master. Carnelian's mind raced, trying to understand. 'Homunculus, is it possible he could avoid swallowing the drug?'

The homunculus began an answer, but Legions strangled it. 'What has happened?' he demanded.

Carnelian tried to work out what to do, but his thoughts slipped and fell against each other. He was too tired to think properly. In the end, he began to relate the content of the letter. As he did so, he watched a tremor creep into Legions' pallid fingers. The homunculus' echoing murmur ceased and he looked confused. He raised a hand to ask Carnelian to wait. Then he lost focus as he listened to the play of fingers upon his neck. He began murmuring again, then indicated for Carnelian to continue.

When he reached the end of what he had to relate, he fell silent. The murmuring continued for a while, then abruptly ceased. The Grand Sapient's grip released. His hands and arms fell away, to dangle lifelessly.

The hopelessness in that gesture struck Carnelian in the chest. He had not realized until that moment how much his view of things depended upon the unshakeable certainties of the Wise. Without that it seemed the very foundations of the earth must soften and fail.

He clapped his hands to get the attention of the homunculus, who was craning round, slack-jawed, to gaze up at its master. As the little man looked at him, Carnelian instructed him with gestures. The homunculus gave a nod and then reached out to take first one of his master's hands, then the other, shaping the fingers around his neck.

'Can nothing be done?' Carnelian asked. As the homunculus murmured, Carnelian watched anxiously as if he were petitioning an oracle.

The homunculus fell silent and they both waited. Slowly, Legions' fingers began to work. 'Nothing,' said the homunculus.

It became important to Carnelian to do for the Grand Sapient's spirit what he had asked the homunculus to do for his hands. 'Surely Molochite can still be defeated?'

The pallid fingers did not move.

'What if you could have access to the heliograph here on the roof?'

No movement.

'What if I made arrangements for you to return to Osrakum tonight?'

The fingers came alive. 'So many legions could not be gathered effectively without the coordination of the Domain Legions and that is nothing more than an extension of the mind of its Grand Sapient. My brethren have had no choice but to elect a new Legions. I am dead. The living heed not the dead.'

Carnelian persisted, needing words to fill the void deepening within him. 'We could get there before most of the legions reach Osrakum. Use the hollow crescent.'

'Enough huimur would have reached there to confront you with a double line.' The homunculus continued to speak, cutting off any questions. 'Resign yourself. I have. Nothing can be done.'

A bleak silence fell.

'Even Kakanxahe with all his legions failed to take Osrakum. What I did then, none could do again.'

Carnelian frowned. 'What you did then?'

The fingers continued to work the throat of the homunculus. 'You fought for eighteen years and nearly brought the Three Lands to waste. If I had not acted, the Commonwealth could have fallen. It was I who bound your passions with the bonds of reason. It was I who wrought the Balance of the Powers and, in so doing, ended the Civil War.'

Carnelian felt giddy. 'But— What—? That is impossible. That would make you hundreds of years old.'

'Child, I was born in Osrakum more than thirteen hundred years ago.'

Carnelian gaped, wondering if the strain of defeat and catastrophe had broken the Grand Sapient's reason.

'I have witnessed time like a tree. How ephemeral have seemed me the lives of men. Almost forty Emperors I have made, have watched die, have buried in the Labyrinth and still have I endured.'

Carnelian's mind was reeling. Could this possibly be true? He felt he was losing his grasp on reality. 'How is it possible that the Chosen have forgotten who you are?'

The chin of the long silver mask began nodding as a choking sound came from behind it. Carnelian watched this new sign with a foreboding that turned to horror as he realized the

Grand Sapient was laughing. 'Do you imagine that mortals have the continuity of memory that do the Wise? Your short spans ensure that the passing down of the past is a fragile process, a process we have manipulated. It is the least of our skills. It is not difficult to encourage men to forget that which they would rather not know.'

Legions' fingers stilled. Then they began flexing again, though more languidly. 'But now that my great work is undone, was it worth the sacrifice I made? For my reward was to be put into lightless silence. A reward I bequeathed to all my kind. A gift that allowed our minds to span centuries.'

The homunculus paused, frowning.

'I was first to be put into the darkness and though, for you, it was so long ago, for me it seems not so very long. I have not forgotten the blueness of those skies. The sweetness of the pomegranates of the Yden. And now that death is close, I want more life. For my years seem short to me. Without my senses to anchor me in the now, I have moved swiftly through my own, inner time. A life measured by thought and not the senses is exceeding short. And yet, a paradox: with my death, the ancient world that lives now solely in my mind will perish utterly.'

Silence fell, a silence in which Carnelian could hear only the subtle pulsing of his blood, his mind ensnared in the wonder and the melancholy of this oldest of men. At last Carnelian could no longer bear his sadness, his heavy heart. He left, hardly aware what he was doing, finding himself in his cell, sinking into the longed-for oblivion of sleep.

THE DREAM

Some say dreams are sent by the Gods
Others that they arise from within.
But surely what matters is whether they are true?

(*a Quyan fragment*)

Red so dark it could be black. Tastes salt. Floats, anchored at the centre of the world. Its tiny sea pulsed by a slow, gentle drumbeat. Speeding up. The walls crush him. Impossible pressure. Squeezing, squeezing. Rolling out, gasping, into sudden lurid light. The world stoops beneath the glowering sky. Thunder's monstrous heartbeat. Lightning veins the tar-black clouds. Wet iron. Looking down he sees his hands gloved with sticky blood. Is he wounded? Guilty, the colour of slaughter itching his skin. The pallid land weeps blood. Ruby pebbles strew a plain that is matrixed bone. Blood dews into limbs. Limbs knit to form men. Not men, sartlar? Bestial brows conceal animal eyes. So numerous, their footfalls could be every wave detonating on every shore. A rumble swells to a thunderclap. Lightning flash. Two cedars, struck, burst into flames like banners in a gale. Fury high as mountains. Screaming incandescence connects earth and sky. It is possessed of sentience. Its face is brighter than the sun. Beauty so intense it impales his mind. Such power! God incarnate. Fearing blindness, his eyes veer away. They find a rim to that perfect face. Not a face, but a fiery mask that conceals a twisting face of smoke and rage. Revulsion boils his blood. The god, brow in the heavens, is drawing his spiralling substance from a pyre of burning men. Snapping like twigs, shrieking sparks, their suffering feeds the holy grandeur. Horror is pounding in his ears. Is it his own blood washing him away in its tide? He struggles to swim, but his body is a stone. To drink is to drown. His ears, trumpets, feed the roaring into him. The sea! The sea! From the oceanic red, an iron wall lofts high. Vast odour of liquid rust as it advances, combing the stars with its froth, to collapse its thunder into the pillar of fire and smoke. Reek of charring, screaming flesh. The pillared flame seems invincible, but there is too much blood. Light falters, gives way to black naphtha smoke, then is consumed in the tide. He sinks beneath the surface, too weary to fight any more. A warm hook of a hand pulls him out. He is in a pale boat that Fern is steering. Upon his face a smile that is all comfort, all peace, all love. They fish the clotting surge for Poppy and Krow and Lily and the Lepers and Sthax and his Marula and a multitude too numerous to count. Rowing the bone boat upon a red billow even as the sea hisses to dust; a sporestorm; a spitting plague of flies that wipe day to night, but seeing a narrow diamond light, he turns, pointing, then leads them up out of the blackness onto a fresh fernland. He gulps the perfumed breeze rippling through the spiralled green beneath a smiling sky.

Carnelian came awake, gasping, only slowly aware there were others in the cell with him. Three identical dolls were kneeling by the door: homunculi wearing blinding masks. He sat up, confused. 'What . . . ?'

The central figure came to life. 'Seraph, Legions, my master, bade me give three beads of the elixir to him and to each of his Seconds and two to each of us.'

The homunculus, by his voice the one Carnelian knew, gave a slight nod to either side. 'I chose to save myself and my brethren. Though my master considered the continuance of himself and his Seconds futile, I felt we three might still be of use to you, Seraph.'

Carnelian came fully awake. 'Grand Sapient Legions is dead?'

The homunculus gave a deep nod. Carnelian was stunned by the enormity of the news. That such an ancient being should have ceased to live. The extinction of a memory that reached back to a world now completely lost. Was it Legions whom, towering like a god, the wave had quenched? Was that wave then death? Carnelian did not believe his dream so simply read. Its threat seemed to be filling the cell, indeed the whole world. Its dread made the three homunculi appear sinister. Had they murdered Legions and their other masters, even as they slept? As if sensing his loathing, the homunculus fell forward so that his face clinked against the floor. 'We offer ourselves to you, Seraph.'

The emotion in that unhuman voice touched Carnelian's heart. He had come to know him; Poppy had grown to like him. Who was he to judge these men? What did he know of their lives?

'What normally happens to a homunculus when his master dies?' he asked, already certain of the answer.

'He is terminated, Seraph,' said the homunculus, his voice causing his mask to reverberate against the floor.

Carnelian sensed their terror. He recalled Legions declaring himself already dead. Why should his homunculus have to die with him? It counted in the little man's favour that he had chosen to save the other two of his kind. Now he had brought them to Carnelian knowing, truly, that he was their only hope. Compassion stirred in Carnelian. He could not deny them his help. Besides, he had a feeling that, in what was coming, they might prove useful. He wished to look upon the faces of these two strangers. As he reached for his mask, his fingers came to rest upon its gold forehead. His heart was urging him to an act he was not sure was rational. He attempted to work out where their best chances of survival lay, but soon gave up. There were too many unknowns. He decided to trust his feelings. 'You want to serve me?'

'We do, Seraph,' said his homunculus, not lifting his face from the floor.

'Will you then join my House?'

The homunculus raised his masked face a little. 'Your House, Seraph?'

'I am asking all three of you to enter my household.'

The other two heads came up even as his homunculus sat up completely. 'Your household, Seraph?'

Carnelian smiled at the tone of incredulity. 'Come. Decide now.'

The three of them drew together, muttering. When they fell silent, his homunculus turned to Carnelian. 'All three of us shall willingly become your slaves.'

'Well, then, look upon my face.'

Clumsily, they loosed their masks. They leaned forward to cradle their silver faces in their hands. His homunculus was the first to look up. As his eyes met Carnelian's, the little man flinched, but held his gaze. The other two lifted their heads only enough to glimpse him from under their brows. Wonder lit their wizened faces so brightly, they forgot their fear and squinted at him through tears as if he were dazzling them.

At first Carnelian thought them identical, but soon he saw they had faces of their own. He became uncomfortable with their gaze, but was reluctant to scold them.

'They have never beheld an angel,' said his homunculus. 'Compared to the scarred moon of the Wise, your beauty, Seraph, is the sun.'

Embarrassed, Carnelian told them to leave him for now. As they went out he turned in on himself. His dream was an ache he felt the need to nurse.

Osidian grabbed Carnelian's arm as he leant over him. 'I was foolish to imagine I could triumph on my own.'

Carnelian prised himself free, took some steps back, uneasy about Osidian's stare, his sweat-glazed face. 'You're not alone. I'm with you.'

Osidian looked somewhere else. He released a sigh, closed his eyes. 'All night I have felt him tearing at me.' His eyes snapped open. 'He has shown me the way before and will do so again, but first I must buy back his favour by feeding him.'

Carnelian had seen this before, in the Isle of Flies. It made him queasy. He knew only too well what Osidian's god liked to be fed. Carnelian's skin itched as if flies were crawling over him. In his gut he knew it was to the Lepers Osidian would turn for victims.

Osidian's eyes rolled up in his head. 'He has been here with us all along. I have been wilfully deaf to his whispering.'

Carnelian refused to believe in any malign presence in the dark corners of the cell. If Osidian was again possessed, it was his madness Carnelian must fight. 'Legions killed himself.'

Osidian stared at him. 'He is dead?'

Carnelian nodded, seeing how grief seemed to be making Osidian sane. 'All three Sapients are dead.'

Osidian's eyes clouded in a face bleak with misery as he fell into a nodding that could have been trembling. Carnelian could sense the madness returning. 'Use their corpses.'

Osidian shook his head. 'My Father prefers to sup upon the living, for in their agony does he find a voice.'

Carnelian cast around desperately for other victims. His mind fixed on some, though almost he turned away from such a solution. It was true they were dangerous and could easily become his enemies, but to deliver them to the Darkness-under-the-Trees? He hardened his heart. Was he not, after all, making war upon the Masters?

'The commanders.'

Osidian's reddened eyes looked up at him. 'Chosen?'

'Sooner or later they will learn about the edict. Do you imagine they would still obey you then?'

Osidian smiled predaciously. 'They would indeed make a rare offering.'

'Why not?' said Carnelian. 'Have you not offered up your own flesh?'

517

Osidian nodded and a wicked grin lit his face. 'And there are those higher still the Lord could feast on.'

'Jaspar?'

Osidian's grin widened. 'My Lord Aurum too.' He regarded Carnelian. 'You do not approve? Do you wish to save him, Carnelian? Do you? And here I was believing you hated him.'

Carnelian felt he was being toyed with and could not be sure that even he was entirely safe, but he had to have Aurum. 'I would prefer to deliver him to a different end.'

'To the Lepers, for example.' Osidian's face gave the impression he was amused, but his eyes were bright with cruelty. Carnelian hesitated, feeling that the slightest miscalculation could close the trap.

'Are you not going to lecture me about my oath, Carnelian? No oily flattery that I am an honourable man?'

'I want to save them from you.'

When the madness dulled in Osidian's eyes, Carnelian was as shocked as if, wandering lost in a dark and threatening wood, he had come suddenly upon a friend. Osidian lay back. 'Why not? Give them the old fool. I have no further use for him, nor them.'

Carnelian controlled his euphoria. Dare he hazard what he had won to get more? An understanding of what his dream must mean had risen in him. Disturbingly, he had a feeling he had long known what it had shown him. 'Whatever help your god will give you, it seems unlikely he will cause to rise up from the earth a host sufficient to overthrow the legions your brother is mustering against us.' Carnelian flinched, seeing in his mind the terrible fire and thunder of dragons in battle. The host Molochite was gathering was many times more vast than anything he had seen. Could his dream really be promising victory against such odds? He tried to grasp how it might be possible, but the more he thought about it, the more its reality eluded him. Faith would have to be enough.

Osidian glared at him. 'You doubt what you do not understand.'

Looking into that furious face, Carnelian's gut warned him against saying anything further about his dream. 'Can I leave Jaspar and the commanders to you?'

Osidian's face filled with such wide-eyed, gaping horror that Carnelian reached out to him, but retracted his hand when the expression dissolved into a leer. 'Yes, leave them to me.'

Carnelian became suddenly possessed by a desire to flee. The air in the cell felt saturated with a madness that was seeping into his skin. He abandoned Osidian to his dreams, to go and follow his. Though both were nightmares, they contained all the hope that was left.

Carnelian wiped the blood that had sprayed over one of his gloved hands onto his cloak. Aurum's guardsmen lay on the deck, butchered. Sthax and his Marula had slain them. Carnelian had gone down to the road to seek the Maruli out. He had explained to him his dream and its promise of victory. As he had hoped, it seemed to be enough for Sthax. Still, it had been a relief. He knew he needed him. Without Sthax, what hope would he have had of getting any of the warriors to follow him up through the stables, where their Oracles had returned to nurse their infestations?

Gazing at the guardsmen, Carnelian felt unhappy at how he had tricked them. When he had appeared, they had knelt. All he had had to do was raise his hand and the Marula had fallen on them like raveners. Aurum's poor creatures had not even had time to deploy their forked spears.

He took the deck in with a glance. The flame-pipes, the counterweights and the furnaces had all been removed. Only the steering capstan remained. Thin mattresses were rolled up all along the wall. Each with its own pathetic bundle: the dead men's personal possessions.

He stooped to pull a sword free from its scabbard, turned to Sthax and told him to remain below, but to come if he heard him cry out. When the Maruli nodded, Carnelian set his foot on the first rung of the ladder and began climbing.

As he came up onto the mid deck, it took a moment for his eyes to adjust to the gloom. Then he saw a clutter of chests and boxes; a glint of metals, the gleam of precious stone. It was a storeroom of sorts. Then he saw the figures grovelling, pressed into corners, gripping each other with trembling hands. Mostly painted children, their heads sculpted by mutilation. They dared not look at him. He thought to tell them he meant them no harm, but they had heard the slaughter below. It was perhaps kinder to ignore them and so he continued climbing.

Reaching the upper deck, he swung up onto its smooth floor. Movement caused him to hold the sword up before him. He breathed again. It was only a reflection in one of those mirrors clearer than water. The device was leaning up against one wall. The cabin was empty. At least, there was nothing living. He cursed, softly. Somehow Aurum had eluded him.

The command chair was there. Near it, something like a crab with spindly legs. Its clicking immobility betrayed it to be one of Aurum's clocks. Then he saw the capsule standing in the alcove to one side of the mast. Its colour had made it seem a part of the bone wall. He approached it, cautiously, a frown rucking his forehead against the warm gold of his mask. A Sapient capsule. A suspicion grew in him. His finger felt along the edge of the lid, but found no seal. He pulled the lid back. The old Master stood strapped into the capsule as if he were one of the Wise, though he wore no mask. Carnelian peered at the wizened face. Aurum could have been fashioned from wax. Stillness robbed him of even an approximation to life. Carnelian could see the skull beneath the porcelain skin. He wondered how long Aurum had been taking the elixir. What pact had he made with the Wise to obtain such a dispensation? What hold had the old fool given them over him? He seemed so frail. Carnelian felt pity stir in his heart. Then it occurred to him that, in this state, it would be much easier to deliver him to the Lepers. Imagining Aurum's horror at waking among his most bitter enemies, Carnelian felt a stab of sympathy. He hardened his heart. What pity had Aurum shown the Lepers? Or Crail?

He made sure to remove from their cavities all the beads of the elixir. When he was sure he had them all, he piled them on the deck, then crushed them beneath his foot. The Lepers must not be cheated of their revenge. Chewing his tongue against pity, he closed the lid and called down for Sthax to come up and aid him.

Carnelian walked ahead of the capsule as they penetrated the Leper camp. Commotion spread as people rose to watch him. By the time he reached the heart of the camp, their hubbub was deafening. Gazing over their multitude, he saw how filthy were their shrouds, how thin their limbs, how they stooped. He yearned to set them free.

He was glad when their leaders came to meet him, and bade Sthax ask the Marula to put down the capsule. He recognized Lily by her gait, Fern by his height. Poppy and Krow were beside him.

'Why have you come?' said Lily.

Carnelian did not blame her for her bitter tone. 'To fulfil the oath that was made to you.'

Lily came close enough that he could see her narrow face startled within her cowl. 'You're going to give him to us?'

He moved aside so she could see the capsule. Lily slipped past him and peered at its ivory shell. 'We were promised him alive.'

'He merely sleeps.'

A ripple of grumbling disbelief moved outward through the crowd.

'Show us.'

He realized he should have expected this. Even if Lily were prepared to believe him, the Lepers had suffered too much for their prize to be expected to leave without seeing him.

'You're still within the Guarded Land, Lily. It's forbidden to look upon a Master's face.'

521

'How often have I seen yours?' There was a hint of a weary smile. 'We won't tell if you won't.'

He turned to gaze at Fern. There was an intensity in the dark eyes that he did not feel confident he could read. 'Very well,' he said and asked Sthax to return to his post. The Maruli frowned, then said something in their tongue and he and the other warriors moved off through the Lepers, who healed the wound of their path so that Carnelian was entirely surrounded.

'Help me.' He reached down for the handles and, with the aid of other hands, swung the capsule up to stand upon its feet. He walked around it urging people to move back. Then, glancing at Lily and his friends, he pulled back the lid.

All eyes stared into the capsule. A hissing grumble rose from the crowd as those who could not see shoved through, trying to get a look. 'He's dead,' cried a voice. Others took up the cry.

Carnelian gazed into the capsule. Exposed to the harsh light, the thing standing in it did indeed appear to be a corpse already partially decayed. Skin thinned to a membrane revealed the bones and sinews lying beneath. The face could have been moist vellum moulded to a skull. Carnelian's heart misgave: perhaps Aurum really was dead. Freeing one hand from its glove, he stooped and sought a pulse behind the swelling of a bony ankle as he had seen the homunculus do. The crowd quietened. At first the cold flesh felt lifeless, but then he detected a tiny pulse. He waited as the silence round him deepened. Waited so long he began to feel he had imagined it. Another pulse.

'Lily, come . . .'

As the woman knelt beside him, Carnelian took her hand. She flinched, but did not pull away. He guided her fingers to the ankle.

'Lightly,' he murmured, 'for it's very faint.'

Lily nodded, her brow creased in concentration. A twitch

of a smile. The smile broadened. She rose, crying out: 'He lives, our enemy is ours and he lives.'

The crowd erupted into a storm of fury and rejoicing. Carnelian rose, his heart quickening as he faced their din. He heard their cries and moaning, glimpsed some tearful, bloodshot, staring eyes. Their rage coursed through him, but also their grief. And he could not hide from them so released his mask. Yielding himself to them, even if they should choose to tear him apart as they took their vengeance upon the monster. Ever louder they bayed as if they could not bear that their enemy should sleep in the face of their wrath.

Lily's voice shrilled above their roar, joined by the voices of others of their leaders. As the storm abated, Carnelian became aware Fern was gazing at him; Poppy and Krow likewise.

'Why doesn't he wake?' said Lily, anxiety sharpening her voice.

Carnelian turned to her. 'His sleep's drugged but, some time soon, the drug will wear off and then he'll wake.'

'I need him alive.' She faced her people and repeated to them what Carnelian had said.

Again he felt a twinge of horror imagining himself in Aurum's place, waking naked among such hatred. Lily was shouting commands into the crowd and he realized the Lepers were getting ready to leave. He felt panic as he glanced over at his friends. This was goodbye then.

The next few moments, he was distracted by having to help Lily close the capsule and show her how it should be carried. Their hands touched as they gripped the same handle. They pulled apart looking at each other. He felt he had to say something, felt he wanted to say something. 'Are you going to be all right?'

'I can't wait to get home, to get away from here.' Her face twisted as if she had a bad taste in her mouth.

Carnelian reached out and took her hand. 'I won't forget you.'

She smiled. 'Nor I you . . . Carnie.'

He liked her calling him that. He held onto her hand as she tried to pull away. He waited until her eyes met his. 'Don't sack Makar.' Rage and horror, but also pity were at war in her. 'Don't mar the justice you've achieved and paid for with so much blood, with the injustice of an attack on innocents.'

Her gaze fell, she twitched a smile, then gently she pulled her hand free. Carnelian felt a small grip on his arm and turned to see Poppy there. 'We're staying here with you.' She glanced at Krow who gave a solemn nod. Carnelian saw that Lily was already marshalling her people as they lifted the capsule into the air. In a turmoil, he turned back to Poppy and Krow, protest rising in him, but saw in their faces that this was a battle he had already lost. Defeat brought swelling joy. Then he remembered Fern and his joy dissipated like smoke. Fern stood very still against the chaos of the Lepers breaking camp. Carnelian approached him, accompanied by Poppy and Krow. Fern's eyes were preoccupied with some inner pain.

'Things have changed since the battle,' Carnelian said. He sketched out for them the contents of the edict. 'Utter defeat is likely.'

Poppy nodded, tears beginning to well. 'So? We'll die with you.'

'If it's hopeless, why do you go on?' said Fern.

Carnelian regarded him, considering what to say. Then he decided to discard all attempts at managing the situation. 'I've had a dream that I believe promises victory.'

Fern shrugged. 'Then I'll hazard what's left of my life on a dream.'

Carnelian had not expected that. 'You want to come with me?'

Fern glanced up into the sky, frowning. 'Though I'm not sure any longer what it is I'm fighting for, I want— I need to keep fighting the Masters.'

'Besides . . .' said Poppy and Carnelian was glad to turn to her, not wanting to see the agony and confusion that Fern was struggling with.

'. . . if your dream's wrong, the vengeance of the Masters will find us wherever we hide.'

Krow gave a solemn nod. 'I too would rather die fighting the Masters than hiding somewhere waiting for them to hunt us down.'

Poppy hugged Carnelian. Eyes lensed with tears, he sought for restraint, as he sensed the others were also doing, muttering all the time, 'I'm glad. I'm glad.'

With his friends, Carnelian watched Lily and her people march away. He could just make out their tiny forms amidst the red, sky-high banners of dust their column was raising. He was glad they had agreed to take a route to the east of the leftway wall. It was much harder going than it would have been upon the road, but he had not thought it wise for them to attempt to pass through the camp of Osidian's auxiliaries.

Amidst the relief of seeing them go was sadness that he would never see Lily again. His gloomy contemplation of that loss diminished the glow of having his friends with him, along with his worry that selfishness had stopped him from trying harder to get them to leave with the Lepers. There was something else, too, an irritation. Why could he feel no satisfaction at having got revenge on Aurum? It seemed a betrayal of his uncle Crail, whom Aurum had had murdered. Carnelian had sworn one day to avenge him and now he had. Once again he imagined Aurum waking among the Lepers. Perhaps outrage and anger would keep his terror at bay, but not for long. Soon he would discover he was alone. For the first time in his life he would be powerless. He might no more be able to comprehend this than a bird its inability to fly if its wings were shorn off. Nothing in the Lord's long life could have prepared him for the humiliation and agony. Carnelian shuddered. The Lepers would not let him die quickly.

Carnelian had come to the edge of the heliograph platform to watch the commotion below. Masters with a Marula escort, moving in convoy through the camp, were sending a bow wave of kneeling out through the auxiliaries. The Lesser Chosen commanders were heading towards him. They must be obeying a summons from Osidian. Carnelian shuddered, knowing none would leave the tower alive.

Hearing movement behind him, he glanced round. The homunculi were approaching. He had had them send heliograph signals south to the watch-towers of Makar commanding them to give free passage to the Lepers. Hoping to ensure obedience, they had used Legions' codes. While waiting for confirmation, Carnelian had asked them how he might summon sartlar and the little men had huddled down in earnest discussion.

It was Legions' homunculus who now addressed him. 'Seraph, though we are not of the Domains Roads or Lands, through our duties we have picked up some understanding of their systems. One protocol in particular might be appropriated to your purpose: that which is used to bring sartlar to the roads to repair them. Our judgement is that we are close enough in appearance to the ammonites who would normally convey such a summons that the overseers will heed us.'

Carnelian nodded. 'How many sartlar will come?'

'That is uncertain, Seraph. The overseers we directly communicate with will pass this on to others deeper into the hinterland; a process beyond our control.'

Carnelian nodded again, brooding.

'Seraph!'

He looked to where one of the homunculi was pointing. There, in the south, a mote of sun was flickering. They decrypted the message for him. '"A mass of the unclean have entered the Pass and are now marching down to the land below."'

Carnelian felt a shadow passing from him. Glancing back down at the procession of Masters he hardened his heart against them. Let them pay for the suffering they and their fathers had brought upon the barbarians.

*　　*　　*

The next morning, from the leftway, Carnelian watched the homunculi ride out, each with an escort of auxiliaries. East and west they went, seeking overseers in working kraals beyond the region Osidian had devastated with his manoeuvres. He had misgivings. Perhaps his mind was still in the shadow of his dreams. He had not slept well. Knowledge of what was happening in the bowels of the watch-tower had made him feel he was precariously balancing over a gaping cesspit. He was going to abandon the tower. Osidian could have it all to himself for his filthy maggot rituals.

Carnelian took Poppy with him on Earth-is-Strong and soon they were leading their forces out into the dust of the land. Aurum's dragons followed those from Qunoth, their Lefthands sitting for the first time in command chairs. Fern led the auxiliaries and Marula, with Krow as his lieutenant. That day would be the first of many spent on manoeuvres.

Later, their shadows reaching the camp before them, the army returned, weary, caked in the earth's rust. Carnelian descended to the road to find the homunculi waiting for him. They told him they had accomplished their mission. Even now his summons was spreading across the land.

Haunted by doubt, it was a joy for him to slump beside the fire Fern lit for them upon the road. After they had eaten, Carnelian lay down to sleep, free of his mask, trusting to the homunculi and his friends to keep unwanted eyes away.

In the days that followed, he constantly scanned the vague reaches of the haze wondering if any sartlar would obey his summons and, if they did, whether in sufficient numbers to fulfil the purpose he believed had been shown to him in his dream. Then they began arriving, hobbling under baskets of their rotten bread, trailing infants, coming to form pathetic cringing huddles near the edge of the camp beneath the blind stare of the dragons.

527

The days merged into a monotonous rhythm. Each morning Carnelian set off with their host. They made lines, they wheeled and charged, churning dust up into red veils. In the evening they would return to find the sartlar numbers swollen. Soon their multitude reached beyond the cisterns and, daily, crept further and further out into the desiccating land. He became aware that, every day, it was taking him longer and longer to reach open ground. At his manoeuvres, in whichever direction he looked into the murk he would see small groups of sartlar crawling towards the dark spire of the watch-tower.

At night he slipped through labyrinthine nightmares threatened always by a dark welling sea. Always the sea, the drowning sea. Waking, his eyes as bleary as the sun, he gazed out over the endless sartlar, hearing the swell in their ceaseless muttering.

Imperceptibly a blood-red sun came to hold sway in a bloody sky. Everything took on that hue; all shapes and outlines softened to ghosts. The only things that seemed truly real to Carnelian were his own hands and the people near him. Every face was bound up: not to breathe through cloth was to choke. The rain wind had picked up and lashed them with scratching sand so that, when he was not in his command chair, he would turn his back upon it and gaze listlessly north-east. Legions' homunculus told him that, as ever more sartlar left the land, it would turn to desert. It seemed too small an explanation in the face of this new world.

At first the sartlar, heads bowed, had waited around the cisterns patiently for men and beasts to drink their fill. Now, all such decorum had been abandoned. To slake the thirst of their limitless numbers, they now drew their water directly from the sinkhole. Night and day it brimmed with their frantic climbing. As Carnelian passed the sinkhole high in his dragon tower each morning, he would gaze down in a sort of horror at that entrance to some vast ant-nest from which the earth herself seemed to be giving birth to the brutes.

For as long as he could, he had fed the sartlar from his own supplies, sending auxiliaries to hurl scraps into their multitude. As food dwindled, he had sent to Makar for ever more. When the fortress quartermaster came himself to convince him his demands could no longer be met, Carnelian had sent Fern into the city with several squadrons of their auxiliaries. He returned with wagons, but with a grim face and furious eyes, and Carnelian saw the blood drying upon the lances of the men who rode behind him.

At last, one day, Carnelian returned to find the sartlar crawling like lice over the remains of the Ichorians. Disgusted, he almost sent men to drive them away but in the end he turned his back on their scavenging. That night he could not sleep for what he imagined was the sound of their feeding. In the blackness it was harder to feel confident in the rings of dragons and soldiers that lay between them and the sartlar.

Once the road had been picked clean, the brutes began to starve. The nights were now disturbed by an oceanic moaning that moved him with its anguish. Marching out he would look out over the sea of heads and spot clumps of smaller heads. Sartlar squatting, hugging swollen bellies. Not mothers-to-be, but starving children. He knew that, if they did not set off soon, the sartlar would begin to die in vast numbers. So it was with relief that he greeted Morunasa's news that, at last, Osidian had fallen into the birthing fever.

RED DUSK

What kind of society survives turning to cannibalism?
(a Quyan fragment)

Carnelian slumped beside the fire stirring the still warm ashes with his foot. He was weary of waiting. Morunasa had said Osidian would wake in five days. It had already been eight, perhaps nine: he had lost count. It seemed a long time since he had suspended manoeuvres. Neither he nor their host had left the camp for days. He had hardly ventured away from their fire. Poppy and Krow went to fetch food for them and water. Fern went out periodically to walk around the camp. Sometimes Krow went with him; sometimes he remained behind, his head hanging, as miserable and worn out as everyone else. No one wanted to look upon the famine stalking the land beyond the dragon wall. They could not avoid hearing the moaning. Night and day it lent a desolate, bleak voice to the choking wind that blew ever more fiercely from the red desert the land had become. Hearing that sound of suffering, Carnelian feared that, if they did not soon march, all that would be left of the sartlar was bones. He glanced up and saw the great crag of towered Heart-of-Thunder looming up in the gloom, against the leftway wall. He had had him moved there so that they could march north the moment Osidian awoke. A fantasy of green land

530

and clear air possessed him. There the sartlar would find food.

He trailed his gloved hand along a crack between two flag-stones, heaping red dust. He took some in his palm and prayed Osidian would soon wake.

'Master?'

The voice made him jump. It was Morunasa's gravel tone. 'He's woken.' The Oracle was there and gave him a grim nod.

Carnelian put on his mask and sprang to his feet. He gazed out over the auxiliaries huddling against the duststorm, their aquar like rocks in a bloody tide. He saw Fern coming towards him and cried out: 'Get the legions ready. Send messengers among the sartlar. We're marching north.'

Relief flooded into Fern's face even as the news began spreading through the camp, waking men from their lethargy so suddenly that, everywhere, aquar heads were popping up, eye-plume fans half opening. Carnelian lingered for a moment watching the camp come alive like the Earthsky after the rains. Then, as he saw Morunasa turn towards the base of the tower, he grew grim and prepared himself for what lay within.

The red light of the outer world snuffed out and the moans of the starving multitude faded as Carnelian followed Morunasa into the tower. As the portcullis was raised in the mouth of the stables a stench flowed out that made Carnelian flinch. Morunasa stooped and entered. Gathering his courage, Carnelian followed. Doughy shapes formed a pale frieze about the walls. Quick dusk as the portcullis fell, then darkness. He refused to give in to the fear that he was trapped. The sickening fetor thickened as he drew nearer to one of the pale shapes. It must once have been a man. A Master hung on hooks, his flesh sagging away from his bones. A beam of light sprang out to illuminate the corpse. Carnelian glimpsed Morunasa behind him holding aloft a narrowly shuttered lantern. He turned back to what it was the Oracle wanted him to see: a dead body not so unlike how his would be were it hanging there. A half-melted tallow doll. Sallow skin spotted with twisted black wounds like the eyeslits on a mask. Feet and hands dark bloated clubs. He had seen this kind of thing before. He looked up at a face frozen in pantomime surprise. He scanned along the walls and as he did so, the light followed his gaze. The commanders were all there, all surprised, all riddled with the Oracles' holy vermin. Carnelian steeled himself against guilt. Though he had offered up these Masters as victims, it had been to save the Lepers. Besides, it was Osidian who had carried out this abomination. He might claim his god demanded victims, but what had really killed these Masters was Osidian's injured pride.

Seeing the way Morunasa was gazing at him, Carnelian was overcome with revulsion. 'I'm not afraid of you, Oracle. Enjoy this, because you know you will never dare visit your vengeance on him.'

Snarling, Morunasa began climbing the ramp to the next level. When they reached the top level of the stables Morunasa halted outside a stall and cast his lantern light into it. Carnelian's head eclipsed the light as he peered in. He crouched, seeing two prone figures: another Master, this one laid out upon the floor, muttering, and beside him a skeleton. Carnelian gasped with horror and fell to his knees. 'Osidian,' he murmured, his voice breaking towards a sob. He gulped it back, knowing Morunasa was watching. He removed his mask and put it on the floor, then leaned close. The skeleton was indeed Osidian, all his flesh drained away, leaving only bones, and skin marred by many recent wounds. Carnelian grew angry that he should be seen like that. He unfastened his cloak and covered him. Blearily, this almost dead thing opened its eyes. Bright jewels among the ruins of his beauty. Carnelian's tears were blinding him. He leaned closer, whispering: 'What have you done to yourself? What have you done?'

Osidian began a smile that his lips were too tight to finish. He tried to raise one withered arm, but had not the strength.

He smiled again. 'I have been to the Shadow Isle and have returned.'

His breath was stale. His eyes seemed to sink back into his skull. Carnelian had no problem believing Osidian had returned from death.

Osidian's soul seemed to rise up again from the depths. 'I found peace there,' he sighed, but his eyes were haunted by some recollection. Then they ignited. 'I bring back a promise of victory.'

Carnelian drew back a little. Those eyes had in them the mercilessness of a raven's. The light subsided and Osidian stared madly as if he were seeing some horror. Carnelian reached under the cloak and found his hand. He winced at its frailty, like the remains of a bird's wing. He dared not squeeze it lest all its bones snap. 'Famine threatens to destroy our forces. We must move to where they can feed or else there will be nothing to follow you to victory except the dead.'

Osidian frowned, but showed no comprehension. His brow smoothed. 'My Father promised me victory and peace thereafter.'

Carnelian knew he would gain nothing by further speech and so he told him he was going to carry him up to Heart-of-Thunder.

'Jaspar too.'

On the point of asking what he meant, Carnelian became aware once more of the other body, and its muttering as constant as the babbling of a stream. He leaned over to see the face. A narrow face that at first he could not recognize as Jaspar's, so wasted it might rather have been Jaspar's aged father. His white flesh looked as if he had been the victim of a frenzied stabbing. Carnelian noticed some movement. A pale tongue was poking out from one of these wounds. Carnelian bent double, retching.

'The God has entered him and speaks to me through him.'

Carnelian glared at Osidian.

'He seeds my dreams.'

533

Carnelian regarded Jaspar with disgust. He was giving birth to his maggots. 'Will he die?'

'Oh no, he will suffer long.'

Carnelian turned back to Osidian.

'He shall be tended well so that I may use him as an instrument of divination.' Osidian must have misunderstood Carnelian's look of horror, for he added: 'Worry not, we shall make sure he shall be fully aware of the God devouring him.'

Carnelian rose, trying to overcome his disgust, his loathing for Osidian and his filthy obsessions by instructing Morunasa how the two Masters were to be carried up out of the stables.

Carnelian emerged from behind the monolith onto the leftway and gulped fresh air through his mask. Heart-of-Thunder seemed insubstantial against the vast world beyond, which Carnelian felt he was seeing through a film of blood. A sea of sartlar stretched away to a murky horizon. Shock made the moment silent and eternal: he had stepped into one of his dreams. He forced his head to move, his eyes to focus on something with a human scale. Osidian lying masked upon a bier borne by Oracles, Jaspar upon another. The Marula stared as if they were seeing their deaths rolling towards them. Carnelian could not resist the pressure of their gaze and once more turned to look upon the multitude.

'Millions . . .' he breathed. His feet carried him closer to the edge as he sought to take in the vastness of such numbers. A great disturbance struck the shoreline of that sea where it came close to the dragons. For a moment Carnelian feared the dragons were attacking them, but there was no smoke, no fire, and the monsters seemed as motionless as rocks. The disturbance surged out across the masses, rushing towards the horizon like some vast wave sucking back from the shore. As he watched it race away, Carnelian understood what it was he was seeing. They were kneeling. An oceanic act of abasement. Was he its cause?

'The brutes feel the presence of my Father.'

Carnelian turned and saw Morunasa had lifted Osidian's head enough so that he could look out. The dark hands reverentially let Osidian's head down. He was too weak to lift it himself, Carnelian could see that. Then Carnelian noticed Heart-of-Thunder's Hands kneeling a little way off along the leftway. He summoned them and they came. 'Dispatch a message to Earth-is-Strong. Her Lefthand is to command her until I return.'

The Hands touched their foreheads to the stone, so that when they came up they were bloodied by the dust. Carnelian gazed out once more and saw the wave of kneeling was still receding towards the horizon. He brought his gaze back to the edge of the camp. The dragons were beginning to swing round towards the ramp that would lead them up onto the road. Beneath him, the auxiliaries were already mounted. He gave the sartlar one more glance, then led the procession of Oracles and biers towards the dragon tower.

Moving along the open road, Heart-of-Thunder was easily outpacing the sartlar, who were pouring like oil across the murky land. Carnelian's heart leapt when he noticed the miasma ahead wavering. He held his breath as the haze slipped to the ground in undulating thinning veils to reveal a vision of clear air, of a land running green to a far horizon. He let out a sigh that mixed relief with wonder. He felt free and had to fight a desire to tear the mask from his face so that he could enjoy the clean air unfiltered. Even through its nosepads he could detect the rich pungency of hri. He scanned the land and saw its greens were duller than they had seemed at first. These fields were tinged with brown. The rising heat was already turning the morning sky to enamel. He scanned round to the west. There the red haze formed a vague cliff fading away into the south-west, from whose base shapes were emerging like ants. He watched them slowly darkening the earth, turning the fields a dunnish red.

'It is nearly harvest time,' said the homunculus.

Carnelian turned to the little man, a question on his lips, but he forgot this and everything else as a shadow rose up at the edge of his vision.

'Like locusts.'

Carnelian gazed at Osidian and wished he could see beneath his mask. Though his voice sounded sane enough, only looking into his eyes would make Carnelian certain. Still, he rose, steadied himself against the motion of the deck and offered the command chair to Osidian who, moving like an old man, slumped into it. For a long while he hung forward watching the sartlar devouring the land.

'Numberless,' he said, almost in a whisper.

He half turned so that Carnelian could see the gleam of an eye behind the mask. 'Why did you gather them?'

'I too was promised victory in a dream,' Carnelian answered. He expected more questions, a dismissal, but at that moment a long, vibrating stream of Quyan syllables began pouring out from behind them. Carnelian saw Jaspar's shadowy form laid out against the cabin wall.

'The Lord speaks,' said Osidian, in deep tones, as he nodded ponderously. He watched the sartlar stripping the land of its green to leave it red. 'They consume the land as the worms did my own flesh.'

As dragons pushed the sartlar back to make space for a camp, Carnelian descended to the road from Heart-of-Thunder, glad to escape Jaspar's incessant babbling. Auxiliaries were pouring off the road, fanning out over the cleared land. Their torrent veered away from him as he approached the ramp. Once he had reached the earth he set off in search of Fern. All around him men were choosing spots upon which to light fires, dismounting, unhitching packs from their saddle-chairs, sacs, waterskins that some were carrying off to fill at the stopping-place cisterns. Carnelian was glad of his mask that filtered the air. Even so, he realized he would be lucky to spot Fern through the churned-up dust. It occurred to him to ask one of the auxiliaries whether he knew Fern's whereabouts, but his instincts were against the abasement such an enquiry would produce. Already there was a region around him into which none dare stray.

At last his wanderings brought him to the margins of the camp, where the dragons rose as a forbidding rampart, black against the westering sun. As he came closer he noticed men scrabbling up a rope girdle and walked round to get a better view. One man had clambered onto the monster's haunch and was daubing something on what Carnelian saw was a wound that a leg of the tower had worn into its hide. That disturbed him; clearly the creature had already worn its tower too long.

Then he forgot everything else as he became aware he could hear the sea. At least it seemed the sea, though he knew it to be the murmuring of the sartlar multitude. He was drawn to gaze upon them and slipped into the shadow under the monster's belly. He saw the silhouette of a beastmaster hefting up a sac to feed the monster. Pulling his cowl over his head, he crept behind its right front leg, making sure the massive column was firmly tethered to the ground. He just wanted a peep, but feared his mask might reflect some ray of the sun. Imagining the panic of the sartlar, he removed it. The tumult swelled as he slipped out of the shadow. Their stench wafted like the miasma from a midden. Squinting against the sun's orb, at first he could see nothing but swirling currents. Then he began to make out the individual creatures on the margin of the host. Ragged, hunched, they crouched huddling in groups. Some limped among these clumps on stick legs. Everywhere his gaze snagged on filthy, bony limbs. Then he began noticing that some had stomachs swollen like render sacs, above legs that seemed far too brittle to bear them. Pregnant females? Difficult to tell, but then he saw some so small they had to be whelps. Children, he thought. Matted hair, hideous profiles. So many faces made monstrous by the earth glyph burned deep into nose and skin. He saw an old woman with one eye milky from a careless branding. He became aware of a pair of eyes gazing

537

towards him. One of their young. The face already melted by the brand, but such bright eyes. The realization sank in that he was being watched. It was the child who broke their link first. It ran, screeching, into the body of the multitude. Carnelian darted back behind the dragon's leg, fumbled his mask on even as he heard behind him the commotion building to a roar. Without glancing back he returned to the camp.

Later, when Osidian insisted they must sleep high in the watch-tower, Carnelian gave in, hardly heeding his arguments. Something about the need to maintain the awe with which their men regarded them; how else could they expect their obedience in a battle against his brother, the Gods on Earth?

Morose, Carnelian shared some render with him on the heliograph platform. There was nothing else left to eat. He hardly looked up at all at the dark mass of the sartlar clothing the land. He returned to his cell and gave one-word answers to Poppy's questions. As he lay trying to sleep all he could see was the sartlar child's bright, human eyes.

For the next two days they marched along the road. Carnelian was relieved to be back in the tower of Earth-is-Strong with Poppy near him and away from Jaspar. Always, as far north as he could see, sartlar were streaming from the west along the tracks between the hri fields towards the road, concentrating along its margin as if they were sightseers coming to watch a procession pass by. He could not understand how they found their way, for he had summoned them to come to a watch-tower now away in the south.

The hri in the fields ahead turned brown, then yellow, then white as if the land itself was ageing before his eyes. As the green in the world faded, the hope it had brought faded in his heart and memory. Everywhere water-wheels were still. The rain wind picked up steadily. Wafts of dust came dancing from the south-west, cavorting and gyrating in spirals that thinned as they reached for the dead white sky. Then, as they passed a watch-tower near the middle of the third day, the wind angered to a gale that made Earth-is-Strong's mast rattle in the cabin. A great front like a frothing wave came rolling towards them, eating up the sky.

'A sporestorm,' Poppy said, eyeing it with alarm.

'Just the earth turning to dust,' Carnelian said, but as it broke over them the day turned to red dusk.

Each day they woke to a thin violet light oozing from the east. The mosaic of the camp came apart even as the dragon rampart broke into its cohorts and loomed up towards the road to follow Heart-of-Thunder north. Dozing in his command chair, Carnelian rarely saw the auxiliaries pouring after them in their column. The nearest dragon seemed like some rock rising up out of the sea. The leftway, a seawall slipping slowly past, faded away into the murk ahead. All sound was muffled, only the nearest murmurous swell of sartlar noticeable.

As the midday sun diffused orange in the haze above, they could look forward to reaching another watch-tower. Like some vast and lonely tree it would loom ever more distinct until its grim bulk was threatening to topple onto them. There, upon the leftway, leading a squadron of riders, Fern would meet them and confirm the land ahead was clear. This done, he would hurtle off with his escort, heading for the tower beyond the next, which he would occupy, spying out the way ahead as best he could until their rendezvous at the same time the next day.

The march would leave the midday tower and soon they would once again be adrift in the ghostly land. Well before nightfall another tower would begin to solidify ahead. Though weary of sitting in his chair, Carnelian would still eye it with some dread. For there, just below its branches, he would have to spend another night of dreams.

When they reached it, while Earth-is-Strong and Heart-of-Thunder remained on the road beside the watch-tower, the other dragons would descend to the earth, fanning out across it to form the margin of a new camp, pushing deep enough into the sartlar to bring the stopping-place cisterns within their curve.

Krow was always there on the road to greet them, having set off at dawn to keep watch from that tower. Sometimes, he and Carnelian would exchange a few words but, mostly, he left Krow and Poppy to each other. He would climb to the summit of the tower as if ascending to his execution. Often he would reach the heliograph platform in time to watch the disturbance the dragons made ripple away to the vague margins of the sartlar multitude. Sometimes he would imagine the tower and camp had just that moment risen up from the depths of the sea. He would sit there watching the auxiliaries pouring off the road into the camp until the dusk bruised the murk purple. Only then would Osidian appear upon the platform and they would share some render. Carnelian loathed the stuff, but there was nothing else and so he ate just enough to sustain his strength.

At last, beneath a starless sky, the time would come he most dreaded. He would descend and the world would close around him to become nothing more than his cell. Every night it seemed to be the same cell. He had tried to catalogue their differences, but it was their similarity that dominated his mind. It was hard to believe he had ever left that cell. As if the journey of that day had been merely a recurring dream. When Poppy appeared he was pleasant enough, but always claimed exhaustion so that he would not have to talk to her. He feared he might pass on his misery to her and so lay down and faced the same stone wall and tried to stay awake until morning. He dreaded the ambiguities of his dreams for they cheated him of certainty about that which he had set in motion.

In the neighbouring cell the three homunculi slept together. He had long ago put aside his fear that they might betray them. The duststorms made it impossible to use the heliograph or the flares. Besides, what could they tell the Wise that they did not already know?

Through the other wall Osidian and Jaspar shared a cell. A near-dead thing, Jaspar was carried up and down each watchtower locked within a Sapient capsule that had belonged to one of Legions' Seconds. Sometimes, through its ivory skin, Carnelian could hear mumbling. The same mumbling he could hear now, though he pressed his hands against his ears. Those mumblings that fed not only Osidian's dreams, but his own. He pulled his hands free and tried to listen instead to the murmuring of the sartlar, or the squealing water-wheels with which they were drawing up water to quench their oceanic thirst. While at the same time he clung to the edge of his own black well into which he knew he must eventually fall.

Blearily, through his bone screen, Carnelian watched the tiny figure grow more distinct beneath the bulk of another midday tower. When that figure became two, he narrowed his eyes, thinking he was mistaken. Soon he saw it was not only Fern waiting for them, but, beside him, a smaller figure that seemed in comparison a child. It could only be Krow. What news had he brought from the next tower?

As Earth-is-Strong came to a halt behind Heart-of-Thunder, Carnelian could just make out Osidian's voice emanating from his dragon tower as he questioned Krow, who was on the leftway looking up at him. Strain as he might, Carnelian could make out nothing of the youth's answer. Osidian said something that caused Krow to bow and fall back. A while later, Heart-of-Thunder's mirrorman began signalling with his arms. Carnelian watched his Lefthand reading the signals. At last he turned. 'Master, you're to assume command of the host.'

Carnelian began relaying a reply, but then he saw Heart-of-Thunder's brassman falling and Osidian walking out upon it. Soon he had descended to the road. Frustrated, Carnelian waited. Osidian appeared from behind the monolith onto the leftway, a flood of Marula and aquar pouring out after him. Soon, riding away, they were fading into the haze.

Carnelian moved Earth-is-Strong past Heart-of-Thunder, then led their army along the road. All that long afternoon he kept his gaze fixed on the leftway, waiting for Osidian's return or, at least, some messenger, but all in vain. So it was that, when he saw the world ahead darkening, for a moment he thought it was approaching dusk. Except that the west was still glowing orange. As they drew nearer, he saw the earth crusted with shanties and realized they had reached the outskirts of some vast and gloomy city. The sartlar slowed as they poured into ditches and along alleys like a wave infiltrating a pebble beach. Carnelian searched for signs of anything living, but the hovels seemed abandoned. Even though they were now leaving the sartlar behind, he did not slow Earth-is-Strong and led the army deeper into the city. A region solidified ahead from which rose several spires. He shuddered, having the impression they were approaching the eaves of some murky forest. It occurred to him that, perhaps, he should order the flame-pipes of the leading dragons lit, but the city seemed dead. The two nearest spires grew branches and slowly resolved into watch-towers, one on either side of the road and each rising from a dark rampart. He detected movement there, upon the leftway, beneath the rightmost tower. He breathed a sigh of relief, certain they must be his people. He gained confidence in that feeling with each lumbering step his dragon took. At last they came close enough to see a figure waving.

'Krow,' said Poppy, and so it was. Carnelian gazed at the dead city and made his decision. He ordered the army to a halt, then, leaving Poppy in the care of his Righthand and Earth-is-Strong in the care of his Left, he bade the homunculus follow him and together they climbed down to the road. Before them the two watch-towers faced each other, each rising from a forbidding rampart, each standing guard upon a massive gate. His heart misgave. These were surely legionary fortresses. He listened for the enemy, but the only sound was thunder fading back along the road as his dragons drew to a standstill. He set off to meet Osidian.

Osidian was there on the edge of the heliograph platform with Morunasa. As Carnelian approached them he became aware of the city stretching off in all directions.

Osidian acknowledged him. 'Behold the city of Magayon.'

A charred, ruined labyrinth lay directly below, another on the other side of the road. At the heart of each the circles of cothon wells. Fortresses, then, torched by their legions before they left, no doubt to deny Osidian equipment and supplies. More watch-towers clustered where the road reached a junction with another running off into the west. Duststorms had already begun to bury Magayon. Carnelian recalled with melancholy the ruins he and his father had seen on their way to the election. He searched along the northern road for enemy legions or any other sign of life. The horizon there seemed to be sucking ink up from the land. 'Burn-off?' he said, wondering.

'If so, Seraph,' said the homunculus, in a low voice, 'it would be unusually early. Generally the stubble is not burned until the Rains approach for fear the earth, unfettered, will turn to dust.'

Carnelian glanced down at the little man, wondering if he was being ironic, but his face was grave. Carnelian returned his gaze to the north. There was an obvious conclusion. 'They intend to starve not only us, but our sartlar.'

Osidian came alive and half turned to him. 'A sign of weakness.'

Carnelian gazed at the profile of his mask. 'What do you mean?'

The mask turned to him. 'If my brother has commanded the earth be burned before us, does it not suggest he fears us? You should be happy, Carnelian. It seems your sartlar strategy has disconcerted him.'

Carnelian could see no cause for happiness. 'Whatever Molochite may be feeling, surely he has succeeded—?'

543

Osidian's mask jutted towards him. 'In what?'

Carnelian could hear in Osidian's voice the madness rising. 'How far are we from Osrakum, my Lord?'

Osidian's hands tensed. 'More than twenty days.'

'How do you imagine we could cross a charred wasteland for more than twenty days with millions?'

Osidian became a motionless doll. 'I've faith our Lord will provide,' he said in Vulgate.

Morose beside them, frowning as he gazed blindly out over the abandoned city, Morunasa gave a slow nod.

Carnelian lolled in his command chair. He had slept even worse than usual. Haunted by the dead city, he had wandered lost in nightmare labyrinths. Waking, he had led the army through a gate, past the junction with the western road and north between the mudbrick tenements with their blind windows and the alleys between them choked with the red dust that made them seem to be running with blood. The screams of Osidian's flame-pipes had echoed through Magayon. He had joined Poppy to watch the leftway wall crumble under the fiery onslaught. Like a collapsing seawall it had released a torrent of sartlar. They had watched them infest the city even as their flow caused the gap in the wall to widen.

Tenements gave way to hovels, then the whole termite architecture gave way to middens. Through the haze, the city boundary ditch was approaching. Beyond its neat edge the land ran charred and dismal as far as he could see.

It was Poppy who pointed out how the world seemed to have been turned upside down. Red sky above; black earth below. As the sartlar riptide crept across the land, their feet became blackened, then their legs right up to their bellies, so that they were transformed into creatures divided equally between the new earth and sky.

As the days passed, Carnelian watched the sartlar, waiting

for them to weaken, watching for those that would fall behind, searching for signs that famine was winnowing their millions, but each day they maintained their tidal surge.

At last he was driven to pay another visit to the dragon wall. Again he spied on them from the shelter of a dragon. Slumped on the ground, their heads hung weary, but he could see no stick-like limbs, no bellies pregnant with hunger. He retreated back into the camp and wondered if the blackened hri was still capable of providing sustenance. He found a bush and reached out a gloved hand to its fruiting head. At his touch it crumbled to a charred chaff that blew its powder away on the breeze. He tried to take hold of a leaf, a stalk, but, at his touch, each became just a brief stain upon the air. The hri was nothing more than a black ghost.

He returned to the watch-tower, brooding on the miracle of how the sartlar found food in a dead land. His mood darkened further as he passed through the Marula, at whose heart many Oracles lay in the fevered birthing sleep. At least upon the tower summit he could unmask, though he and Osidian had to turn their backs upon the west with its dust-pelting wind. Fishing within his render sac, he drew up a gobbet of meat. Reluctantly he put it in his mouth. Its saltiness stung his tongue. The gelatinous mass came apart under the pressure of his teeth. He jerked forward, spitting out the chewed meat. It was disgusting.

'You're right. This stuff is sickening,' grumbled Osidian, though he continued to eat. He needed to; he was still cadaverous.

Carnelian rose, putting his mask up as a barrier against the sandblast of the wind, and surveyed the scarlet multitude. 'They're consuming each other,' he said, the taste of the render still in his mouth.

'What?'

Carnelian turned to Osidian. He let the mask fall. 'That's how they're surviving. They're eating each other.'

Osidian frowned, then began nodding. 'The Lord provides.'

Carnelian was outraged. 'Doesn't it appall you?'

Osidian shrugged. 'They're beasts.'

Carnelian was feeling queasy and wanted to be alone. He began walking to the platform edge.

'You haven't eaten anything,' Osidian called after him.

Carnelian kept walking. He wondered if he would ever be able to eat render again.

Waking, it took him some moments to realize he was not in the cabin of the baran. The sound of the sea. The swaying. The sandy wind lashing the dragon tower like spray. Disappointment tore at him. His father was not there to make things right.

He cast a jaded eye out through the bone screen at the blood-red world. The sartlar swarmed the earth like cockroaches. He felt lightheaded. He had not eaten anything for days. Even the hunger pangs had faded. His body ached so that he wondered whether this was, at last, the burning in his blood that was proper to one of the Chosen. There was a dark pinnacle ahead, vague in the ruddy twilight. A watch-tower he would sleep in. He would be initially dizzy when he rose from his command chair. The climb up through a tower now exhausted him. His fear of nightmares was now balanced by a horror of lying awake. Sometimes, in the night, he was sure he could hear the wet sounds of the sartlar feeding.

In his cell, Carnelian woke sensing something had changed. The world seemed brighter so that, for a moment, he almost could believe the long days of red twilight and dust had been nothing more than a nightmare. He rose. A window in the stone wall gave out into clear blue. He was drawn to the freshness of that colour. Below, the camp was in the shadow of the watch-tower. Only the dragon towers reached high enough to catch the first gold of the sun. Beyond stretched the sartlar: an indigo sea. Their murmur reached him.

'The wind has fallen,' he muttered, lost in wonder.

'What is it?' said a voice.

He turned to see Poppy. 'Come and see for yourself.'

She rushed to the slit and pushed her head into it to breathe the cool, clear air. He left her there, put on his hooded cloak and picked up his mask.

'Where're you going?' she said.

Carnelian pointed upwards.

'I'll come with you.'

Together they left the cell, climbed the ladder to the tower roof, then the staples up onto the platform. As Carnelian stood up he gasped. His mask forgotten, he gaped, turning slowly on the spot to take it all in.

'So many!' Poppy exclaimed.

Carnelian's attention was drawn to the south-west. There, the hem of the sky was steeped in ink. At first he thought the darkness was because the sun was still low – so low it spilled the legs of their shadows over the platform edge – but though the indigo west was brightening fast, the stained horizon stayed obstinately black.

'The Rains,' said Poppy.

Her look of wonder suggested she had not imagined that rain ever fell upon the Guarded Land. In truth, he had forgotten how late it was in the year. He looked back at the angry horizon.

'Look there.' Poppy was pointing northwards. Another band, but this one was of gold. Carnelian forgot to breathe.

'What is it?' Poppy said.

The fear in her voice wrenched the answer from him, though he could not look away. 'Osrakum,' he said, in Quya, then, in Vulgate: 'the Mountain.'

He stared at the Heaven Wall. He could not quite believe he was seeing it. A part of him had been convinced he would never do so again. It was like the longed-for face of a lost lover but, if so, it was a lover who had betrayed him.

'Osrakum.' Voiced behind them almost as a groan of pain. They both turned to see Osidian there. Half his mask

547

blazing in the sun; the other half in murky, glimmering shadow. Carnelian felt compassion for him, but he could not long resist the siren fascination of Osrakum. He turned back to feast his eyes upon her wall.

It was a diamond flash somewhere near the earth that woke them from their trance. Another and another, pulsing in a repeating pattern. A heliograph.

Carnelian turned to Osidian, but realized he was equally unable to read the signal. So he sent Poppy to fetch one of the homunculi. Watching the diamond flicker, something occurred to him. 'If that's the next tower . . .' Fern was supposed to have been there. Carnelian's heart faltered from fear of what might have befallen him. Who could be operating the device there?

'Not the next one, but the one beyond it,' said Osidian.

Carnelian saw that, indeed, the spine of Fern's tower rose to the right of and slightly higher than the flashing. 'What does it mean? Are the Wise trying to contact us?'

Osidian's mirror face gleamed sinuously as he shook his head. 'The pattern is too repetitive to carry any complex communication.' He became stone. 'My brother is close.'

Carnelian shielded his eyes and scanned the northern horizon. With all the excitement he had forgotten Molochite must be nearby, waiting for them.

The sounds of someone climbing up onto the platform made him put his mask in front of his face before he turned, to see it was Poppy approaching followed by the homunculus. The little man stopped to peer at the flashing.

'Well?' barked Osidian at last.

The homunculus flinched and sketched a gesture of apology. 'I cannot read it, Celestial. The signal is faint, but I have the impression it carries no words.'

'What then?' Carnelian said.

The homunculus gestured again. 'Perhaps some diagnostic.'

'To check the integrity of the system?'

'The sandstorms have been blinding the mirrors, Seraph.'

Osidian shifted his weight. 'Perhaps it seeks to detect any discontinuity.'

Carnelian tensed. 'They are looking for us.'

'Homunculus, could we answer it from here?'

The little man knitted his brows. 'At this distance, Celestial, lucid communication might be difficult.'

Osidian gave a nod. 'As I thought.' He turned to Carnelian. 'My Lord, I will ride to the next tower. Will you bring the army there?'

'But it could be a trap.'

'If so then we must scout as far forward into the enemy position as we can. It is critical that it is we who decide when and where we are to give battle.'

Osidian's mask regarded Carnelian until, reluctantly, he agreed. He made a gesture of thanks and, then, taking the homunculus with him, left the platform. Carnelian lingered, brooding, until he saw, below, Osidian hurtling northwards along the leftway, a clot of Marula flying after him. Carnelian's heart was heavy with foreboding. He glanced round at the black smudge of the approaching Rains, the ocean of sartlar, and then fixed his gaze upon the glowing Heaven Wall, wondering if this was the calm before the storm.

Rolling with Earth-is-Strong's ponderous gait, Carnelian sat in his command chair, gazing at Osrakum. As the sun rose higher, it seemed to heat the Sacred Wall into a bar of white-hot gold that branded his vision so that he blinked its ghost whenever he turned away.

At some point the heliograph began to signal again, but this time its beat was complex. He watched the flickering, silent voice and knew Osidian must be holding a conversation, but with whom? The Wise? Molochite? Carnelian feared Osidian might make some mistake. There was even a part of him that feared he might be betraying them all.

*   *   *

'We shall go no further today, but make a camp here.'

Upon the leftway, Osidian was half in the shadow of a monolith. Dragon towers formed a battlement running back along the road. Carnelian had come up to meet him the moment he had arrived. He had climbed up through the stable levels frowning. This was watch-tower sun-nine. There were only eight more between them and Osrakum.

'What has happened?'

'Under my promise of safe passage, the Wise are coming here to conclave with us.'

THE COMING OF THE WISE

Each of the Chosen can be considered as a two-pronged
blood-fork lying in the flow of time. Upstream, the tines
connect to the blood-taint nodes of the parents. The
handle extends downstream the length of the lifespan and
terminates at the death node. Of the other temporal nodes,
the most significant are those of conception and birth. The
node of conception locates the meeting of the prongs and
handle. The birth node lies approximately nine months
further downstream. These five nodes constitute the
critical input into the astrological calculus.

(extract from a beadcord manual of the Wise of the Domain Blood)

Blots of shadow, their palanquins in the dusk. Along the
leftway they came in a sombre procession. Preceded by a
dense formation of guardsmen encased in articulated green
bronze; one side of whose faces appeared the crystallization
of the darkening east. Cruel billhooks and halberds in their
hands. Cloaks merging so that they seemed borne forward on
billows of tar smoke. The palanquins seemed to float upon the
silver stream of their ammonites' masks.

Carnelian had not seen Sinistral Ichorians since he had
quit the Halls of Thunder in Osrakum. As they filed past he
could smell the sweat that was causing the densely tattooed
half of their bodies to gleam like polished leather. The lead

551

palanquin swayed as it approached and he saw it was not black as he had imagined, but midnight purple. The front ranks of ammonites swinging censers wove thick garlands of myrrh into the air. Carnelian watched as the palanquin settled to the ground upon silver legs in the form of infants.

For two days he and Osidian had waited. They had decided Carnelian would greet their guests. A pair of ammonites now approached bearing a ladle in whose cup blue fire danced. Drawing the device back, they swung it forward to release its contents in a sheet. The fire spread its blue and violet flame across the stone, turning it black as it died. Through the myrrh smoke Carnelian saw a panel in the side of the palanquin sliding open just enough to allow a pale, gloved hand to put out two high ranga. The panel opened more and two childlike feet emerged seeking the shoes. A shape encrusted in purple brocade was soon standing there, its silver sleeping-child face allowing Carnelian to see a warped reflection of something else stirring within the palanquin. The homunculus reached in and fetched out two more ranga which were fully a third of its height. Once these were set up, the little man gave a nod. Two pairs of ammonites appeared, each bearing between them a staff that blossomed high above their heads into silver spirals like the croziers of some frozen fern. Two gloved hands emerged from the palanquin to take hold of these staves, then two long feet sheathed in ivory silk slipped into the high ranga. A vast rustling dark shape rose immense upon the ranga, its face the long, shield-like, single-eyed mask of one of the Wise. The ammonites knelt. The Sapient released his hold upon the croziers, extended a four-fingered hand to its homunculus and allowed himself to be guided forward like an aged grandfather by his grandson. As the Sapient loomed over him, Carnelian tried not to be awed. He saw the panels of beadwork that formed the slopes of the Sapient's robe. He could smell the dusty pungency of ancient myrrh.

'Are you a Grand Sapient?'

The homunculus removed its master's gloves and raised one

pale hand to its neck. The other hand rose on its own. Eight colourless fingers meshed around its throat. It murmured. The fingers flexed.

'I am only a Second of Lands,' the homunculus sang. 'You are not the Lord Nephron.'

'He awaits your masters upon the summit of this tower.'

'Prepare it,' intoned the homunculus.

Ammonites fluttered past like a flock of startled crows. Most disappeared behind the monolith into the tower. The Sapient began a stately progress in that direction and Carnelian made to follow. The Sapient halted and turned an eyeless profile. Carnelian felt the need to explain himself. 'I am to attend the meeting.'

The Sapient's blank face hung motionless for some moments, then with one hand he reached for the homunculus' neck and his fingers made a burst of frenzy. 'Then you will have to be cleansed, Seraph.'

Carnelian had a protest on his lips, but the Sapient was already slipping behind the monolith and so he followed him. The chamber within glowed violet as tiny flames scurried over every surface. Carnelian's cloak was pulled off him. Reacting to this, he was suddenly enveloped by smoke. The chamber reeled. More Sapients appeared through the doorway, overseeing the pale chrysalises of capsules being carried in. Carnelian observed with what quick hands the ammonites hitched these up to hooks. Soon the capsules were rising into the watch-tower.

The sky had darkened enough to reveal a moon that was the merest rind of ice. The fire that had rained violet sparks down through the grating had left only its shadow soot. Three capsules rose like pillars of salt. Before each stood two Sapients, their homunculi in front of them. Carnelian glanced at Osidian, who alone had refused the cleansing. Censers in a ring around them all were growing a hedge of myrrh smoke. Silently the Sapients raised pale hands to the capsules, whose

553

ivory made their skin seem whiter than the nearly eclipsed moon. The Sapients pulled the lids back and knelt before their masters within. Three Grand Sapients, masked, their arms crossed upon their chests, their homunculi, also masked, standing in place between their legs. One of each pair of Sapients rose to hold a staff up before his master. Carnelian started as the homunculi within the capsules took hold of these staves. Each held a finial of ruby fire before the chest of its Grand Sapient as if it were his heart freshly gouged out for display. The pale spiders of the Grand Sapients' fingers began to writhe. Pale petals opening and closing. Gestures that were bringing life back into sleep-frozen limbs. Until, at last, they reached down to sensuously strangle the throats of their homunculi.

'We are Law,' said the leftmost one.

'Tribute,' said the homunculus on the right.

'Lands,' sang the one in the centre.

'What do you hope to gain, Celestial, by taking up arms against the Commonwealth?' said Law, to which the other two Grand Sapient homunculi murmured an echo.

Osidian fixed the sightless masks of the Grand Sapients with an expression Carnelian could not read. 'To put right a wrong.'

'Though you have cause to be aggrieved, Celestial, what has been done cannot be undone. The moment the rituals were completed, your brother was made. They and your life became forfeit without hope of appeal. In your desperation to preserve yourself you have wilfully precipitated a calamity greatly disproportionate to your grievance. The Balance of the Powers is fractured. The Law so closely bound to it is in peril of dissolution. Have you forgotten that the Law is the foundation upon which stands the Commonwealth? Without Law, Chaos is lord. Your brother has escaped Osrakum. Even now, given time, we shall subdue Them with those pleasures that They have demonstrated They are slave to. Your apparent futile intention to challenge Them in battle will only serve to make Them more uncontrollable. All you will achieve is to further imperil the Balance.'

Osidian's eyes were eagle sharp. 'What do I care for your Balance? Do you imagine, my Lord, that I grieve with the jailors from whom my House has managed to break free? As for the foundation of the Commonwealth, that is terror. What we hold' – Osidian extended his hands as if he held the world in them – 'we hold through power and because to rule is our divine right. Raw power is the law that all must obey.' His hands came apart in a gesture of disdain. He half turned away, snarling, then fixed the Grand Sapients with a baleful eye. 'And I would advise my Lords not to make the error of assuming we are already defeated.'

The three homunculi mumbled on, then fell silent. Carnelian became aware of the oceanic murmur of the sartlar who inhabited the dark vastness of the land beneath.

'It is true, Celestial, the Commonwealth has also for foundations terror.' The homunculus who spoke was the one who had identified its master as Tribute. The Grand Sapient's fingers were working at its throat. 'But by your statement you must surely realize that the Commonwealth exists only in the minds of men. What power to coerce the Chosen possess is itself in the minds of their subjects. The Commonwealth is, in truth, only a dream given solidity by belief. We have made our dream the universal dream but, at the margins of the world, our dream competes with others. You must realize this who have dwelt among the barbarians. Did you not impose your dream upon those creatures, Celestial, in opposition to the Commonwealth?'

Carnelian saw the truth of it and, glancing round, saw Osidian's certainty weakening.

'Why do you think it is we bring them here to the centre of the world? Even now they are gathering in ever increasing numbers before the gates of Osrakum. Why do you think, Celestial, we seek to bring them into the very heart of the Hidden Land?'

The question hung bright in Carnelian's mind. He saw the answer. 'To show them the dream in all its terrible, beautiful reality.'

The homunculus continued as if Carnelian had not spoken. 'Because monolithic power seen close up will tower over them. Far away, its terror fades. In its presence, it saturates their minds. Witnessing our grandeur, they are reduced to nothing. How can their petty dreams hope to withstand such glory, such wonder?'

The vision in Carnelian's mind faded more slowly than the sonorous voice.

'And yet, Celestial, at this very time, you intend to show that power, that glory, divided against itself. At the very moment we have designed for them to see the Commonwealth as immutable as the stars in the heavens, you would show them contention.'

Carnelian felt like a child, made aware of how petty were his notions, how foolish. Osidian, too, looked crushed. Carnelian felt panic seeping into him. Had they fooled themselves? Had he led them both into error?

Osidian's voice shocked Carnelian. 'They shall see the Gods Themselves and the seraphim making war.' Osidian had returned from his depths possessed. 'By this display of power they will be more cowed than all your subtle theatre could hope to achieve.' Fury burned in his eyes. 'What have we to fear from being observed quarrelling? Do the sun and moon fear the vermin that crawl upon the earth as they contend for mastery of the sky?'

Carnelian looked to the Grand Sapients to see if Osidian's words had made any impact on them. Their three identical eyeless masks hung in the darkness, implacable, unyielding. Grand Sapient Lands' fingers began to move. 'You have interfered with my management of the Land. Because of you the harvests have not been gathered. The fields, unirrigated, turn to dust. Already it is too late to avoid a famine.'

'You hope to appeal to my compassion?' Osidian's tone was incredulous, his lips twisted into a sneer. 'What is it to me if a few barbarians starve?'

'Not a few, Celestial, but most of the Commonwealth will suffer hunger.'

Osidian swung his arm in an arc to take in the land below. 'Am I a child, Lands? Though the number of sartlar we have gathered is vast, I know that they are but a scoop from the ocean of those that remain upon the land.'

Once the murmuring of the homunculi ceased, Carnelian was aware of the Grand Sapient's fingers faltering. They came alive again. 'Even now the sartlar of several provinces are coming in response to your summons.'

The sneer grew thin on Osidian's lips. He frowned. 'Several provinces?' The homunculi gave his words a ghostly echo. Osidian looked at Carnelian, the question an accusation in his eyes. Carnelian could make no sense of it himself. 'I only put into action the same process that yearly brings sartlar to repair the roads.'

The murmurous homunculi became a background to Osidian's questions, to which Carnelian provided the best answers he could.

Lands' homunculus interrupted. 'The summons was yours, Suth Carnelian?'

Wrathful, Osidian replied. 'He told me he did it in response to a dream.' He seemed to draw strength from his own anger and perhaps, Carnelian thought, from the feeling that the Grand Sapients had lost their stranglehold on the discussion. 'A dream that promised me victory. The God has Himself promised me this.'

Lands choked his homunculus quiet before it had finished relaying Osidian's words. 'Do not delude yourself, Celestial: victory is impossible. Already twenty legions are ranged against you and more arrive each day. Return to the Southern Plain. There you can have a domain beyond the knowledge of the Chosen. If we have erred it is in having disrupted your

557

empire among the barbarians. Return. We shall send you any luxuries that you desire.'

Osidian's face was childish in its utter outrage. 'Do you imagine my ambition so small? That I would be satisfied being a sovereign among vermin?'

Carnelian gazed in wonder at Osidian. It seemed that at any moment he was going to break into tears. Then he saw the rage rising. Osidian's face hardened. 'I will take back what is mine.' His voice like extruding glass. 'Though I was cast out of Osrakum, I shall enter her by force if need be. However mighty the host my brother brings against me, I will vanquish him and then, my Lords, you shall kneel to me.'

The Grand Sapients seemed as unstung by the venom as if already dead.

'Then we have failed,' said Lands. 'You will be destroyed. In your fall will be encompassed much of what we have built, but we are patience incarnate. With time we shall rebuild everything as before.'

Rage was burning Osidian up. He bared his teeth. 'What if I was to slay you here, now? What then for your reconstruction?'

The Grand Sapient actually shrugged in his capsule. An incongruous sight. 'What you see before you is merely three branches. The tree remains beyond your reach. To stop us you would have to uproot us all.'

Osidian bowed his head and Carnelian watched the fight leach out of him.

'We shall depart immediately,' said the homunculus. 'It would be better if instructions be given below that none are to impede us.'

Carnelian glanced at Osidian. 'I will go, my Lord, and see to it.'

As he reached the edge of the platform, he looked back. Osidian was watching the Grand Sapients being sealed back into their capsules with an expression on his face of one betrayed.

*   *   *

Carnelian descended the tower against the flow of ammonites climbing it to begin the process of bringing down the Grand Sapients in their capsules. On the leftway, preparations were being made to leave. He saw that no Marula were entering the cordon of the Sinistral Ichorians and turned to gaze into the night, brooding over what Grand Sapient Lands had said. Light from the camp did not reach beyond the dragons to the sartlar, but their murmuring made him feel as if he stood upon a cliff looking out to sea. He tried to imagine the extent of several provinces of the Guarded Land. Could the sartlar over such a vast expanse really be moving in response to his summons? So much parched earth rising to clog the air. Hri yellowing, unwatered. The harvest meant to feed so many mouths left to rot in the Rains. Was he really responsible for bringing famine to the Commonwealth?

He became aware of a figure near him and turned to see an ammonite. The figure knelt. 'Master.'

Carnelian regarded the man uneasily. Uncharacteristically, the ammonite had addressed him in Vulgate. 'What do you want?' he said in Quya.

'Carnie, it's me,' the ammonite hissed.

Carnelian stepped back, alarmed, confused. He looked up and saw, close by, some Ichorians holding torches, but they were focused on the entrance to the tower. His Marula were within calling distance. Movement drew his attention back to the kneeling ammonite. There was a glint as it removed its silver mask and turned a little into the light. Expecting to see a face smothered in numerals, Carnelian began saying something. His tongue stilled. A chameleon tattoo. He stared at it, shocked. The cypher was achingly familiar and yet so very strange. It took him a while to notice the face smiling tentatively. His throat clenched as did his heart. 'Tain?'

The young man beamed. It was Tain. It was his brother Tain. The boy become a young man. He fitted his face back into the mask, became an ammonite again, so that Carnelian was left almost feeling he had imagined it. Tain rose and beckoned Carnelian to follow him, who did, his thoughts frozen. Then he had enough to do dealing with getting through the Ichorian cordon, through ammonites, as Tain led him towards the first palanquin. They passed that, passed the second, continuing on, moving away from the tower and towards the rear of the procession. Carnelian's mind thawed into an avalanche of speculation. He was reluctant to stop the purple-clad figure walking in front of him, though he wanted, needed answers.

At last they reached the seventh and final palanquin. It was quiet here, since most of the ammonites were clustering back near the tower, but one stood as if waiting for them. It indicated the palanquin with his head. 'You don't have much time.'

Carnelian stared. 'Keal?' It was the voice of his brother, whom he had not seen since he had left him on the coast so long ago.

The man gave a nod. 'Hurry.'

Carnelian managed to wrench his gaze from his disguised brother to the palanquin. As he did so his heart beat faster. It was more desire than expectation prompting his hope of who might be inside. Unmasking, he reached out to take the handle and slid the panel open.

Peering into the gloom, he withered with disappointment. The old, wizened man inside the palanquin was unknown to him. A Master, unmasked, pale eyes in a sunken face.

The face lit up. 'My son.' Carnelian saw with shock it was indeed his father. Horror overwhelmed him. 'What has happened to you, my Lord?'

Sardian was too preoccupied feasting his eyes on him to answer. He reached out to take Carnelian's hands. 'Son, it is a joy to see you.'

Carnelian glanced down at the bony hands gripping his, sapphire veins running over tendons and bones. He took hold of them, brought them up and bent to kiss them. 'Oh, my father, what has happened to you?' He looked up and, through tears, saw his father's eyes sadden. He shrugged in a manner that tore at Carnelian's heart for he had not seen that gesture for, it seemed, a lifetime. Sardian's right hand pulled free of Carnelian's grip and strayed back up his body to hover gingerly over his side.

'The wound has never healed.'

Carnelian remembered the night his father had been stabbed by Ykoriana's assassin.

'The drug the Wise gave me has preserved me in the exact state I was in when I arrived for the election.'

Carnelian gave a shudder as rage rose in him, but his father raised a hand so thin it seemed translucent. 'Immortality warned me what the drug would do, but I had no time to linger in a sick bed.' His father smiled and Carnelian was warmed to see something of his beauty still there, though most had now fallen into ruin.

'You must not grieve for me, Carnelian. On balance, I have had a fortunate life.' His hand returned to cover Carnelian's. 'For instance, I had no hope of seeing you again.'

Carnelian sank for a moment into comfort. He had not felt so safe since, well, he could not remember. A thought came to him that made him stiffen with alarm.

'What is it?' his father asked, eyes widening.

'Why are you here? The Wise . . . ?'

His father squeezed his hand. 'I have come here with their permission.' He frowned. 'We have scant time. Desiring to converse with the Lord Nephron, the Wise persuaded the God Emperor to let them come here. In exchange, they promised to bring Them you.'

Carnelian felt a chill of doubt in his chest. 'Me?'

His father's eyes flashed in reaction to something he thought he saw in Carnelian's face. 'Do you imagine I would betray you?'

Carnelian only half heard the words, contemplating, with

surprise, how his father's eyes had lost their power over him. Their gaze softened. 'Forgive me. I have no right to be angry. What do I know of what you have suffered?'

Carnelian tried to work out where to begin, but his father had moved on. He held up his right hand, which bore no Ruling Ring. 'I am no longer Suth.'

Carnelian's nod caused his father to raise the ghost of what had been an eyebrow. 'But I can see you knew that already.'

'Aurum told me.'

His father's face darkened. 'Did he?'

Carnelian focused his mind on the situation. 'The Wise have promised to reinstate you in exchange for you persuading me to return with you?'

His father nodded. 'Not only that. They have promised me you will be pardoned so that you can assume the rule of our House.'

Carnelian could see how much his father yearned for that and it filled him with confusion. First he was surprised how much he yearned for it too. Then, even more surprising, his gut reacted against the thought of deserting Osidian.

His father cut through his turmoil. 'But I have not come here to ask you to return.'

Carnelian looked a question at him.

'Rather I have come to bid you flee.'

Carnelian was lost. 'Flee?'

'You must abandon this ill-conceived venture. Return to anywhere you have hope of finding refuge. Otherwise you will be encompassed in Nephron's ruin.' His father paused, suddenly very weary, weak, old. 'I need to know that you are safe.'

Carnelian shook his head. 'I do not understand, Father.' He saw in his father's face something he had never thought to see there: fear.

'You know I have loved you since you were born?'

Uneasy, Carnelian gave a slow nod.

'Never forget that.'

Carnelian watched his father's face growing ashen and his heart began pounding. What was it that he wanted to say?

His father rallied his courage. 'The thing is this. Though in every way that matters to me you are my son, it is not my blood that runs in your veins.'

'What?' Carnelian said, half numb, half exasperated.

'Your mother came to me already carrying you.'

Carnelian felt his head was filled with ice. 'Why then did you accept me as yours?'

'I only discovered it much later.'

'Much later?' He groaned. 'When?'

'When I could no longer deny how much you look like your real father.'

Carnelian knuckled his forehead in a sort of agony. Then it all became clear. 'The God Emperor.'

Sardian nodded solemnly.

'That is why you took me to visit him.'

Sardian was nodding.

Carnelian was startled. 'I drank his blood.'

'We arranged it thus.'

For only the blood of his real father would ignite the ichor in his own. Carnelian stared at the man he had thought was his father. 'This is why you chose not to come back from exile for so many years.'

Sardian nodded.

Carnelian felt his heart was rattling in his empty chest. 'Then why did we return?' He knew the answer. 'Aurum!'

Sardian nodded. 'The moment he first saw you, he knew you were Kumatuya's son.'

Carnelian watched a dangerous light come into his father's eyes. 'To protect you, I would have slain him, all of them . . .'

Carnelian looked down at his hands, then he understood. He looked up. 'You wanted to bring me back to Osrakum and so you put yourself in his power.'

'He assured me your identity would be safe, for he alone was old enough to have seen Kumatuya's face before it was hidden for ever behind the Masks.'

Carnelian nodded. It was all so clear. 'In exchange you agreed to help him in the election . . .' He paused, feeling as if he was falling. 'He's my brother.'

'Will you forgive me?'

Carnelian glanced at his father, but barely registered his look of entreaty. 'Osidian, my brother?' Things fell into place and with each realization he released a groan. He became aware of his father's distress, but a wall of ice had risen up between them. 'There is nothing to forgive. You saved my life.'

Even to himself, his voice sounded cold. He watched his father withdraw behind his own defences, but something stopped him from reaching out to him.

'And I seek to do so again, my Lord.'

Carnelian felt they were trapped on either side of a barrier and could see no way to scale it. It was easier to slip back into the relationship they had once had: father and son. He focused on what his father had said, instead of the look of pain on his face. 'Only Aurum knew,' he said, half to himself. Then it became obvious. 'He told Ykoriana.'

His father nodded. 'I do not know that for certain, but I can find no other reason why she would have commuted his deposal to exile. She has as much bile for him as she does for me.'

Carnelian looked at his father. 'She fears I will accuse her of abduction?'

His father snapped a gesture of anger. 'To attempt your life before, it was enough for her that she blamed you for the death of her sister in childbirth. To protect herself, as well as out of hatred, this time she will make sure you die.'

Carnelian nodded. It made sense. 'If I do not return, what will happen to you, my Lord?'

His father shrugged. 'For the time I have left I can endure Spinel. Then, our— my lineage will die with me.'

Carnelian felt a stab in his chest. The hollows of his father's face already seemed to be cradling the shadow of death. He wanted to say something, but he was too numb to work out what.

'I brought your brothers so that you can say farewell to them.'

Carnelian rose, nodding, wanting to get away from this man, who was and was not his father. He turned his hooded face enough to make sure no one else could see him unmasked. He regarded his brothers, now both also unmasked. Their faces had changed, but in a way they were just the same. Suddenly he could not bear the tears in their eyes. He gave them a curt nod, pushed his face into his mask, then strode back towards the tower.

Carnelian stood on the heliograph platform almost unaware of how he had got there. Osidian was a hole cut in the shimmering band of the embassy of the Wise below as it moved off along the leftway. Osidian was his brother. So many things suddenly made sense.

The black shape turned its head as Carnelian approached. Standing beside him, Carnelian gazed down at the torches moving north. The man who had once been his father was down there and those he had once believed to be his brothers. Though they were no longer that, he still felt a tug at his heart to follow them. 'So what happens now?'

'Nothing has changed,' Osidian rumbled. 'We march against my brother and destroy him.'

Carnelian felt another shock. Molochite was his brother too. He focused on Osidian, struggling to grip this new world. 'Did nothing the Grand Sapients say affect you?'

Osidian cast an angry gesture into the night so that, for a moment, against the lights below, his hand seemed the wing of a crow. 'The Wise are desperate. They would do anything, say anything, to regain the power they have lost.'

Carnelian snatched at some hope. 'You think Lands was making up the threat of famine?'

'I imagine that is true enough.' Osidian shrugged. 'Should we care about some of our subjects perishing? That is their lot. Once I wear the Masks we will re-establish the food supply. Their numbers will soon be replenished. They breed like flies.'

Carnelian turned to see his profile. His brother. It was there clear to see in the face, but their hearts were nothing alike. Sadness soured to anger. 'Remind me, Osidian, why it is we deserve to defeat Molochite?'

Osidian began one of his interminable speeches about his rights, his god. Carnelian cut through it. 'This is hopeless. Every move we make only serves to bring more victims into our circle of destruction. And for what? Your childish need to undo something done to you that you consider unfair?'

Anger leached away leaving him feeling sickened. He was no better than Osidian. He had been driving himself on with the delusion he could save others. He was like a fish caught in a mesh whose ever more frantic struggling only served to draw others into the net. When had he come to believe that power would be safer in Osidian's hands than Molochite's? Had his confidence that he could influence him always come from a hidden understanding that they had a bond that could not be broken?

Osidian was looking at him, but his face was shadow. 'The Wise have frightened you. Have you forgotten the promise in your dreams?'

Carnelian burst into laughter that quickly gurgled away to self-disgust. He shifted into Vulgate. 'We really are so alike, both driven by dreams. By Earth and Sky, I can't deny I hate the Masters and I've supported you because I'd hoped that together we might destroy them, but now I find I can't go on. Can't you see that the Wise are right? Even at the price of letting the cancer that is the Masters suck away at the world, our order is better than chaos, than famine' – Carnelian swept his arm out to take in the sartlar below – 'better than letting those poor wretches be turned to charcoal by

Molochite's flame-pipes.' He brought his arm back and took Osidian by the shoulders. 'This madness has to end. Let's end it together.'

Osidian pulled himself free, snarling. 'What's happened to you?'

Carnelian felt suddenly almost too weary to stand. He knew nothing short of death would stop Osidian. He knew also that he would never be able to kill him. 'My father came with the Wise. We spoke.'

Osidian's hands came up to his head. 'Surely you can see they brought him here to trap you?'

'Nevertheless I'm going to join him.'

Osidian's hands fell to his sides and he grew very still. 'You intend to betray me?'

Carnelian shook his head, finding some comfort in understanding the true nature of the love he felt for Osidian. 'Not willingly.'

'Then you'll stay with me.'

Carnelian shook his head again. 'Not this time. I'm going to do what I should've done long ago and walk away.' Misery claimed him. 'I really don't know why I ever thought this was a good idea. It's all such a stinking mess.'

'I won't let you go,' Osidian said, his voice ice.

Carnelian heard in it the tones of an abandoned lover and wanted to tell him they were brothers, but even were Osidian to believe it, Carnelian could not see that it would change anything. 'Then, you'll have to kill me.'

They stood as shadows, confronting each other. Just then, Carnelian would have welcomed death at Osidian's hands. The moment passed. He turned and walked away.

By the time he reached the roadway, he was cold with fear. Not for himself, but of what Osidian might do to Fern and the others. He strode through the camp until he found them around a fire. Poppy and Krow looked up at him. Carnelian motioned and they made space for him to sit. He sank beside them, hunching, seeking not to draw too much attention from the auxiliaries around them. 'I'm leaving.'

Poppy's face lost colour. 'Where're you going?'

He nodded towards where the embassy was a faint gleam along the leftway.

'Why?'

Krow beside her seemed as anxious as she was, but Fern was staring into the fire as if it did not concern him. Carnelian focused on the youngsters. He tried to marshal his thoughts. 'I feel I've just woken from a strange dream. In the horror . . . the guilt following the massacre . . .' They all glanced at Fern, but he showed no reaction. 'I allowed myself to get drawn along the same sort of path the Master walks. Led by dreams; sacrificing people with a view of reaching some goal.'

Carnelian looked first into Poppy's eyes, then Krow's. 'Even if my motives are wholly different from his, my methods have been too similar. The people who've just left came to explain to both of us the stark realities. We can't hope to win and, even if we did, we'd gain nothing. Just in making the attempt, countless more people will die. Worse, what we've already done is going to bring famine to the Gods know how many.'

The fear in their young faces made him pause.

'For the Masters this is all a game and I believed I could beat them, but I was wrong. I've just made things worse.'

He saw how they would not look at him and felt a stab of shame that they were feeling let down. He wanted to take Poppy's hand, to tell her that her belief in him had been justified, but he had nothing with which to back that up. He glanced at Fern, who was still impassive. He resisted an urge to tell them that very likely he was going to his death. That seemed a poor way to restore their faith in him. Besides, it might only serve to have them attempt to persuade him not to go and that he did not want. His heart ached with the need to save them. That at least was something that might be in his power.

568

Poppy looked up at him, her lips pursed. 'Perhaps it's for the best.'

'Have you told the Master?' asked Krow.

At Carnelian's nod, the youth gazed up at the watch-tower with fearful eyes.

'I want you all to come with me,' Carnelian said.

Krow jerked back round to look at him. 'Won't he try to stop us?'

'He might. That is why we must go immediately.'

Poppy fixed Carnelian with a stare, glanced at Fern, then back with her fingers tracing a chameleon over her face. He understood and said it for her, but looking towards Fern. 'You'll all have to join my household. I'm not making any promises, but I believe there's a chance that you'll survive this.'

Fern showed no reaction – not then, nor after first Poppy, then Krow declared they would follow Carnelian. All of them were now looking at Fern, waiting.

'Fern,' said Carnelian at last, 'will you come with us?'

Fern only frowned and Carnelian felt for him. He was in an impossible position. Had he not already submitted to fighting under the command of the murderer of his people and this because he could at least tell himself he was fighting against the Masters who were the oppressors of all the world? Now he was being asked to abandon even that shaky cause, for what? To become, at best, a servant of the Masters in Osrakum?'

Poppy crouched at his side and, grasping his hand, begged him to come. 'Because we love you. We all do,' she said and turned round and got Krow and Carnelian's nod. 'We're the only family you've got left.'

Carnelian wanted to say that this was not true. That Fern had cousins where they were going, but he bit his tongue. Fern's head sank. 'I'll come.'

They crept up through the stables. Carnelian had decided they would attract less attention if they went on foot. He was sure they would soon catch up with the embassy. When they reached the cistern level, he remembered the homunculi. He had not seen them for days. He realized that, even if he could find them, they would hardly wish to return to their masters. They would just have to take their chances with Osidian.

As they came round the monolith onto the leftway, a shadow blocked their path. From his shape and sour odour, Carnelian knew it was Morunasa. Fearing the man had been sent by Osidian, he reached for his sword.

Morunasa's sharpened teeth appeared in a grin. 'And where would you all be going?'

Carnelian saw no point in lying. 'We're deserting.'

Morunasa's smile widened as he moved aside to let them pass. Uneasy, Carnelian led them off north along the leftway, unhappy that he was leaving Sthax and the rest of the Marula warriors at the mercy of Osidian and the Oracles.

As they walked they listened out for any pursuit. None came and soon the glimmer of the camp was too dim to see and only the pinpricks of the naphtha flares showed where the watch-tower lay. On they walked, nothing but their footfalls disturbing the eerie silence. The stars filled the heavens with their frost. All around, the land lay black. Hardly a breeze stirred the night air. Far ahead a star lower than all the others suggested the position of the next watch-tower. Of the Wise and their embassy there was no sign. As they continued it seemed that, for all their walking, they were always lost in the same place. Carnelian began to regret his decision not to bring aquar.

The hem of the eastern sky was sucking up the first paleness of the dawn when they saw a watch-tower stark against the indigo like some monstrous baobab. This was the third tower they had come to. They had been walking all night. Having come within sight of the radiance that the embassy were carrying along the road, they had followed it, keeping their distance. They were weary and it was with some relief Carnelian saw a flickering spilling out from the watch-tower onto the leftway over which it loomed. 'Thank the Mother, they're making camp at last.'

Striding towards the cordon of Ichorians, Carnelian was relieved when they fell to their knees. 'I have business with the Suth Lord who travels among you,' he said, affecting a Master's tone of command.

Though he had hoped they would obey him, he was made uneasy when their cordon opened without anyone even being sent back to get instructions. It gave him the unsettling impression he was expected. He hesitated only for a moment. There was no going back. Gesturing for the others to follow him, he moved into their camp.

The untattooed halves of Ichorian faces floated in the darkness like so many crescent moons, but Carnelian quickly lost interest in them. Just beyond the tower, the leftway disappeared. He could see the pale edge of the road catching the first light, but the leftway that should have flanked it was simply not there. He could see no disturbance in the earth, no rubble. It seemed just as if it had never existed. What he saw next made him forget everything else; halved by the road, a great disc lay to the north, spread out glimmering beneath the forbidding blackness of Osrakum's Sacred Wall. It could be nothing but a military camp, but in comparison with those Carnelian had seen before it was a pomegranate to one of its seeds.

His brothers glanced up at him nervously as he entered the watch-tower atrium. He bade them rise from their knees and their faces lit up, knowing his voice. Uncertainty returned as they saw Carnelian's companions walking in behind him.

'Father?'

'He sleeps,' said a familiar gruff voice. When the speaker appeared from behind a pillar, Carnelian did not at first recognize him. He had changed so much and yet Carnelian saw the man he had known in the ruin that remained. It was Grane, his eldest brother, his eyes put out and replaced with stones. Carnelian did not feel comfortable staring at him, even though Grane could not be aware of it. Shocked, angry, Carnelian wanted to know how Grane had come to be blinded. He became aware of the pain in his other brothers' eyes. 'I'll not disturb Father.'

Grane nodded, clearly relieved. Carnelian felt a pang of worry for his father's condition.

'Who're these others?' said Tain.

'Are these your brothers, Carnie?' Carnelian turned to Poppy. He could not help smiling behind his mask. She was standing her ground, stating her claim of intimacy with him by using his diminutive. Tain and Keal were staring at her, wondering who she was. Carnelian extended his arm to take in Fern and Krow as well as Poppy. 'These're as much my family as you are, Tain.'

Of his brothers, only Grane did not frown. Carnelian introduced Poppy and Krow. Then he indicated Fern. 'This is Fern, your cousin.'

At that, even Grane looked shocked.

'His mother was Ebeny's elder sister.'

Tain and Keal gaped at Fern. Carnelian saw that even Fern's moroseness was lightening a little with curiosity. He looked from one to the other, enjoying their interest in each other. He fancied he could even see a common resemblance. Then it occurred to him that Fern was more closely related to his brothers than was he. That made him feel sad, then angry.

'Seraph?'

An ammonite had appeared at the foot of the ladder that led up into the tower. 'My masters wish to converse with you, Seraph.'

Carnelian was about to object but twisting in the surface of the man's silver mask were shadowy greens and blacks. He glanced at the Ichorians who had escorted them into the tower. The last thing he wanted was any bloodshed. Besides, he knew he would have to confront the Wise. Now was as good a time as any.

He looked towards his brothers. 'Grane, please take care of my friends. I'll return as soon as I can.'

His brother gave a solemn nod. Carnelian noticed that Krow had extended a protective arm around Poppy. Fern had regained his grim demeanour. Carnelian felt content they would sort things out among themselves.

As he approached the ammonite, the man moved aside. Reaching the ladder Carnelian glanced up into the tower and saw a complex pattern of light seeping in from the various levels. Even through his nosepads he could smell burning and myrrh. His heart fluttered at what lay up there, but he began to climb.

'We have been expecting you, Suth Carnelian,' said the homunculus.

Four capsules stood open against the walls. One was empty and its occupant was looming behind the homunculus that had spoken. The horns of the Grand Sapient's silver mask were almost forking the ceiling. Carnelian recognized the emerald finial of the staff the homunculus was holding before him, which was carved into the form of a man.

'Immortality.'

The homunculus murmured and a little later its master inclined its almost featureless face. In their capsules, the other Grand Sapients remained as motionless as the dead.

The myrrh-thick air had already made Carnelian queasy with anxiety. The unexpected presence of another Grand Sapient quickened his heart to fear. He felt in his bones that Immortality was there because of him. 'My Lords, if you vow to reinstate my father in his House as you promised him, then—'

Another high homunculus voice broke in. 'That depends on what you have to tell us.'

The staff it held proclaimed its master to be Law. 'That was

573

not what I had— I shall tell you what I know, but it might be less than you had hoped for.'

'Perhaps you know more than you imagine.' This was Lands' homunculus.

'You will submit to an examination,' said Immortality.

Carnelian only became aware he was backing away when he felt the door of the cell against his back. 'Examination?'

'Disrobe.' The face of the homunculus was impassive, but a sharpness in its voice seemed to convey the menace that was in its master's mind.

Carnelian felt trapped. 'I don't understand. Why?'

'You will find it more comfortable if you submit willingly.'

The voice seemed to be dissecting him. He took in the four homunculi. He did not believe they could easily overpower him. Immortality's bones seemed as if they would snap under the merest impact. The other Grand Sapients did not appear to have enough strength even to leave their capsules. Carnelian felt the door at his back. He could turn, flee, except that the tower was filled with ammonites and surrounded by Ichorians. Besides, there was his father to think of, Fern and Poppy and Krow, his brothers.

He felt the thick silk of his military cloak, then pulled it off. It fell to the floor like a shadow. Carefully he released himself from his commander's leathers. They fell away like discarded skin. The ritual bindings were stained beneath his arms, down his chest, his crotch, his inner thighs, his feet. The cloth gave off an odour of stale sweat that even the myrrh could not conceal.

'Approach us.'

Carnelian gazed at Immortality's mirror mask and obeyed. As he came close, the Grand Sapient released his hold on his homunculus and his pale hands opened to receive Carnelian, who shuddered as they floated towards him like colourless moths. One finger then another settled upon his chest. Quick as a serpent, the other hand stung his neck. Carnelian reached up instinctively, then fire poured into the roots of his veins.

574

His flesh felt as if it was fraying apart; his bones melting to oil. He was on the floor. A tearing sound and the surface of his body seemed to be releasing its tension. Like a ripe fruit spilling its seeds.

'Why did you summon the sartlar?'

The words formed a perfect calligraphy like smoke and could not be denied, yet Carnelian struggled to fight against their compulsion. It was his own voice that betrayed him, though not completely. 'To use them against Molochite.'

In some remote chamber in his mind, Carnelian smiled. They would ask him about tactics, but he could give them only emptiness in reply.

'Where did the notion come from?'

Carnelian rushed away, closing doors behind him so they could not follow. An arch of pain formed inside his shell like a trumpet blast, forcing a groan out against his will.

'From where?'

He tried to hide, but then he was exposed naked in a coruscating flash of pain. His voice like an animal's. 'A dream.'

'Describe this dream.'

Carnelian tried to choke his throat, but the words poured out like water between his fingers. He relived the dream through his own voice. The blood tide was pulling him out to sea, but he was caught, like a jelly fish impaled upon a stick. Questions probing his soft, exposed, transparent innards.

'Calculation on the basis of the brothers' cusp birth remain stubbornly inconclusive.'

'Could this shed light?'

'Confirm his birth date.'

'No correlation.'

'Can it be incidental?'

'Something is missing.'

'Shall we terminate him?'

'Dare we? They will have Their price.'

'There I could examine him more minutely.'

'What could he reveal in Their hands?'

'Is it conceivable They could extract more than we?'

'Hatred blinds Them.'

'But if he dies?'

'Then he is not the missing factor.'

'Besides, by intervening we might have sundered his connection to the crisis thread.'

'Certainly perturbed its stream.'

'Perhaps he is, after all, irrelevant.'

THE IRON HOUSE

Run, run from Iron House
Though he'll always catch you
Turn him round and knock him down
You're all locked up.

(a Chosen nursery rhyme)

Cramp twisting in his thighs forced Carnelian conscious. He clamped his teeth against the pain. The spasm releasing allowed him to open his eyes. His chin dug into his chest which felt as heavy as a plate of lead. Struggling against the weight he managed one breath. Then another. A smell of blood, perhaps his own. He lifted his head to remove its added burden from his chest. The movement was arrested by a tearing, rending in his shoulders. Blearily, he saw a flickering filigree of light giving form to shapes vaguely human in the gloom. Brightness was glowing from below. Carnelian became aware of his own skin and followed it down to his distended belly, his genitals in the fork of his splayed legs, his feet spreading on ledges of red flecked black. Iron. Rusty, precious iron. His ankles bound to the sky-metal with leather thongs. The iron was draining the heat from his flesh. He heaved his chest up for another breath. He groaned as he forced his head round against the agony. His white arm ran up along more iron to a bound wrist. His body betrayed him and his head fell, punching into his

577

sternum. He struggled for more air even as his mind reeled, flailing as he tried to make sense of why he was bound naked upon an iron cross.

Myrrh and the fresh blood smell of the iron seeping with other rare scents in through his nostrils made him strive to lift again the boulder of his head. Balancing upon the blade of unbearable pain, his gaze flickered, searching for any understanding of where he was. In the gloom, a pattern of bright flecks spattering over human forms. In the corner of his eye he could see the screen through which the light was filtering. Achieving focus, he became able to distinguish the shapes of each face pushed up against it. Sinuous markings broke up their outlines, making it difficult to see where one ended and another began. Subtle jewel fire sparkled at ears, nostrils, glimmered around throats, over breasts. A woman eyed with stones that had dark fire at their cores had her ear turned, waiting, into the light. A beautiful boy, his head slick with feathers, regarded Carnelian with a smirk, eyes devouring him. Carnelian wanted to cross his arms over his body, hide, find shelter. All he could do was collapse his head, the first boulder in an avalanche. His knees seemed as soft as warmed wax. His legs trembled, threatening to buckle. His guts and organs were swelling his abdomen so that he felt he was ripe, that at any moment he would spill his innards out upon the floor. His arms, two leashes of sinew, snapped taut, stopped him falling. Hanging on them he was sure they must tear.

A voice cut through his collapse; mellifluous, a pouring of honeyed Quya syllables. The peculiar pronouns it was using forced themselves through his pulsing agony. In the first person, declined in the divine mode, dual. Only the Twin Gods spoke thus, or their incarnation on Earth. A God Emperor speaking? Molochite!

Carnelian focused his attention like a needle through the raw pain.

'. . . his rebellion pitiful. Though he managed to destroy the Red Ichorians, what does that demonstrate except the impiety of their sending? A folly in which the Wise and those of you who call yourselves the Great conspired, led by incompetent Imago, betrayed by perfidious Aurum, came inevitably to disaster. Are We surprised?'

As he listened, Carnelian's gaze had been crawling across the contorted, writhing surfaces of the floor. He frowned, unable to understand what it was he was seeing.

'So have We been forced to come out from the Hidden Land seeking with Our power to heal this wounded Commonwealth.'

Carnelian lost hold of the beautiful voice as his eyes tried to unravel the exquisite traceries of the pavement upon which his cross was set. He lifted his head enough to allow his gaze to scale the wall to where it emerged into the light. Ribbed stone? Through its peculiar, dark patina, he saw evidence it was assembled from fragments. Bonework? An Ancestor House? He squeezed the confusion drop by drop. This was no barbarian work. Besides, it was pocked all over with holes. The ribbing curved up from the floor. Was it possible he was in the hold of some immense bone boat?

The cross trembled under his skin to the rhythm of feet approaching. Shadowy forms swam into his vision, crablike, each with several arms and legs and double-headed. Hands, some pale, some so densely tattooed they seemed veined ebony, curled into the handles that grew from his cross. He knew these odd but graceful creatures. Syblings: the joined twins of the elite cohorts of the Sinistral Ichorians.

One pale woman's face arrested his gaze. Though she was not as she had been, he knew her. 'Quentha,' he sighed.

The sybling's eyes pierced him. 'Seraph?' An urgent whisper.

'Have you forgotten . . . ?' he managed.

Her sister turned the jet almonds of her stone eyes upon him, but then the sisters responded to a gesture of command from the other syblings. Together they took the strain. The cross rising into the air caused Carnelian's shoulders to threaten dislocation. He threw back his head, choking off a cry.

'Behold Suth Carnelian!' cried the beautiful voice.

Spreadeagled on the cross, as the syblings carried him into the light Carnelian was blinded by pain. The impact as they put him down sent through him a surge of nausea. He pushed his consciousness into the soles of his feet, clawing his toes, digging his heels into the ledges, finding just enough strength in his legs to push back, squeezing his stomach, drawing up his innards, adjusting his shoulders gingerly to relieve their tearing agony.

'Behold another of the Great who threw in his lot with Our rebel, apostate brother.'

Blearily Carnelian tried to locate the source of that pure voice. His racked body gave a shudder as he saw the towering horned shape that could only be the Darkness-under-the-Trees having assumed a near-human form. Then he saw this was just the shadow of the apparition sitting upon an iron throne. Jade its sublime face, its head encased within a four-horned helm that gave it the look of a spider. Behind rose a green man, above whom a black man loomed with vast glimmering obsidian mirror wings stretching like startled hands. All around the throne, children huddled naked, their Chosen skin a dazzling headache.

The apparition rose, its body clothed in a sinuous metal skin that might have been that of a fish, along the midline of which a lightning bolt jagged down. Taller by far than any mortal should be. Carnelian knew this was the God Emperor. Molochite extended Their hands, which were sheathed in what appeared to be shadowed, glimmering water. In obedience two of the children rose, extending trembling fingers. The God Emperor took their hands, then slid across a fur of blue fire towards Carnelian, whose attempt to recoil was thwarted by the cross. The apparition loomed over him, its horns like scorpion stings. He could not bear to look upon the jade of that perfect face. His gaze fell and was for a moment snared by the exquisite mail. Metal duller than silver, each link no larger than a fingernail. It chinked as They gestured. In response the syblings leaned against the cross and turned it.

Below, beneath the vaulted ribs of the ceiling, stretched an assemblage of Masters. A field of gold masks, gleaming. Squinting, Carnelian saw the white cross of his body reflected, melting, over noses and brows and lips; displayed for them like a whore.

Molochite drifted back into sight. 'Now suffers he the fate to which all shall be consigned who dare raise their hand against Us.' They offered Their left hand to one of the children. The Chosen girl looked up, her blue eyes frozen terror. Not only had the hair been shaved from her head, but even her eyebrows. The rims of her eyes were red from where the lashes had been plucked. Tiny fingers fumbled at the hand of the God Emperor and peeled off the glimmering glove. Molochite's hand was living porcelain as it floated towards Carnelian's throat. He turned his head away as far as he could. Molochite's touch settled finger by finger along his jaw line. He tried to shake it off, but this only caused the touch to slide down to his throat, where it lingered on the scar around his neck.

'You were his lover . . .' They murmured.

The fingers spread across the span of his collar bone, cupped his shoulder, slid down his chest so that Carnelian could feel the heel of Molochite's hand as it rubbed over his nipple. One finger tip, another, grazed it. Again, Carnelian tried to pull away, but the cross and its agony tamed him. As the hand pulled down over his stomach horror boiled into his head. He gazed down through tears at the Masters, but they only watched with cold indifference. He tensed his muscles against the pressure of Molochite's hand as if somehow that might stop it moving lower. His muscles began shuddering as the strength poured out of them like water. His bones felt as if they were coming out of joint. His heart melted like wax down into his bowels. He struggled against the shame, but his body no longer obeyed him. He threw back his head, wanting to die as his body relieved itself upon the floor.

The hand withdrew, suddenly. A hissing. 'Filthy animal!'

Molochite's shadow slipped off him. Sensing movement Carnelian lowered his head and saw the Quenthas stooping to clean the floor.

'Take him away,' said the beautiful voice, disgust clipping the syllables.

Carnelian gritted his teeth as the cross was lifted and glared defiance upon the gathered Masters as he was carried down steps towards them. At each shudder fighting the panic that his arms must tear out from their sockets.

'Behold how far from his Chosen nature this one has fallen,' the God Emperor announced.

The Masters drew back as Carnelian was set down in their midst. Pale as maggots they were, each clothed in commander's leathers.

'Examine him carefully. See how tainted he is in flesh and mind. However high, not even one of the Chosen can hope to endure an existence among the bestial creatures of the outer world without much of his angelic nature leaching away. As it is with this one, so it is with Our brother. Neither is now fully Chosen. What else could explain that one of Our own blood should stoop to recruit vermin to bring against Us? Not only has Our brother become hopelessly corrupted but, evidently, he has lost hold of that divine reason that once was his birthright.

'A host have We gathered here immeasurably more powerful than his rebellion. Though, insanely, he seeks to conceal his weakness within a deluge of bestial slaves, does he really imagine they can withstand Our flame? My Lords may demur that Our apostate brother has won a victory over the Ichorian, but this he did through no genius of his own, but by adopting a tactic common during the Civil War. Within the same books We have found described the technique that rendered that tactic obsolete. This is why We shall deploy Our huimur in two lines. Though the Apostate might pierce the first, Our second shall then be ready to annihilate him.'

Sinking in a mire of shame and agony, Carnelian closed his eyes.

'Now, my Lords, behold your enemy!'

The clattering awoke in Carnelian a little strength. Light struck the side of his head in bursts. He managed to grind his chin up his shoulder. Another sudden flood of light. Another. He opened his eyes to the merest slits and endured the slicing incandescence. One shutter at a time, a wall of the chamber was being opened up upon a lurid dawn. Beneath a sky clotted with fleshy cloud rose the towers of a leprous city with a pale road running through it like an exposed spine. Carnelian could make no sense of where he was. Then fear bleached the pain away. He stared, convinced he was in a dream. Beyond the city, beneath the clouds, a blood tide was coming in. This was a nightmare he would not wake from. Against the red, the leprous towers were spined with masts and billowing banners like sails. No city this, but rather a vast military camp upon which a wave of dust was bearing down, its surge churned up by Osidian's sartlar millions.

Though Carnelian had managed to straighten his legs, his balance on them was precarious. Each breath was a struggle against agony and exhaustion. As he sucked air into his lungs in a narrow, snagging thread, he doubted he would find the strength to do it again.

A stench of sulphur woke his senses. He ungummed his eyes. It was a shock to find the chamber before him empty. How long had he been sunk in the fight for breath? Blue fire, swimming below him, released wisps of smoke.

'Was it not gracious of Us to let you use this cross?'

Carnelian saw Molochite's dull silver mail, but was too weak to raise his head.

'We brought it with Us so that We might bear Our brother back to Osrakum upon it.'

Silence. Then Carnelian's jaw was caught by fingers and his head raised so that he was forced to gaze at the monster. The sublime face of jade seemed to have changed its expression to sneering amusement. 'We had planned to have you by Us so that you might observe your lover being humiliated.' The hands shaped airy gestures. *Never mind.* 'We shall not subject Ourselves to the odour. Even were you cleansed, how could We be certain you would not foul yourself again?'

A gloved hand melted into a vague gesture that had a nuance of unkind regret. 'We are sure you understand that nothing must be allowed to mar the pleasure of watching Our dear sibling being brought low at last.'

At that moment the wind gusting into the chamber whipped the God Emperor's cloak against Carnelian's thigh. For a moment he was certain he could smell the Rains. For some reason that kindled a spark of joy in him. He yearned for its waters to wash away the filth, the pain, his soul, even.

'You cry for him? Or is it for yourself?'

Carnelian wished the hand holding his chin would let go. Something cold pressed against his cheek. It was the God Emperor's mask.

'Why do you love him?' Molochite whispered through the jade. 'How does he draw love to him?' The mask jerked; one of the horns of his crown clinked against the cross. 'Always he vexed me, encompassed me, thwarted me. But now I will destroy him. Surely I must. How could I not? Have I not crushed them all? Even her.'

Molochite pulled away. 'We doubt you realize how complete will be Our triumph. At the moment of Nephron's destruction, We shall regain the absolute power Our ascendant lost to the Wise and you Great centuries ago.'

Carnelian stared at Molochite as he raised his arms, horror mixing with disgust, but there was also some pity.

'This armour of tempered iron was Theirs, this helm.' The jade mask gazed around the chamber. 'And we are here within Their Iron House that We brought out from Osrakum.

584

Today shall We undo the wrong done to Our blood. Undo all wrongs.'

As the jade face turned towards Carnelian, in its slits he was sure he could see the glimmering malice of Molochite's eyes. 'Be not worried, cousin, you will not miss the battle. We shall have you hoisted to the roof of this chariot and We are certain you shall live long enough to watch your lover die.'

The gloved hands shaped some signs. *Take him.*

As the syblings bent to lift the cross, Carnelian saw Molochite moving away, then tumbled helpless into a well of pain.

Raging agony was devouring his mind. Then, miraculously, its frenzy calmed. A breeze coolly caressing his skin. He heard the voice and felt something touch his lips. He threaded more air through his raw throat. He opened his eyes and saw the bladed black half-circle of iron, saw its rust-veined surface.

The voice again rose above the rasping of his breath. '. . . slit your throat.'

Carnelian drew his mind into his core. He managed to look up from the iron blade to find eyes filled with tears.

'Please . . . let us end this.'

Carnelian recognized Right-Quentha's face; her lips moving, tears in her eyes. 'Yes?'

Carnelian tried to nod, but once he lifted his head, it flipped back as if his neck were broken. Black wings blotting out the sky, as if a vast raven were descending to feed upon his eyes, but the wings were frozen and he saw they formed a wall that rose before him. Feathers wrought from iron, among which were bleak masks, whose eyes were windows, whose mouths gaped as must his, in agony. The whole mass floated above the ground with only a bronze staircase lolling like a tongue from a gate in the iron wall. As his mind tried to resolve how so much mass could rest upon such a narrow support, his gaze, wandering, found a great arch. Columns radiating from a common centre showed it to be a wheel, but one as high as the back of a huimur. This thing, then, was some kind of immense chariot.

Eyes closed, he struggled to lift his chest against the pain. He let his head sag back and opened his eyes again. A green face swam in his vision. Huge, it hung above the chariot, bearing the same four horns. Confused, he thought it must be Molochite grown as tall as the sky. Then he felt a difference in the way it looked at him. Was that a smile upon the gargantuan lips? It comforted him.

It was the plaintive desperate thinning in the voices of the Quenthas that made him find the strength to disengage his gaze from the God's face and bring his head forward. Their lips were moving, but he could not understand what they were saying, though he caught the panic in their eyes.

The Quenthas suddenly fell silent, turning fearfully. In a remote corner of his mind Carnelian understood his chance for release from agony had gone. A Master was approaching. The Quenthas bowed. Carnelian's gaze caught upon the stranger's mask and was confused when he recognized it. His heart exploded. It was his father's. Something was wrong. Suddenly, he knew it was not his father who wore it, for this Master was not tall enough, his shoulders not wide enough beneath his black military cloak.

The imposter lifted a thickly painted hand and said something that at first Carnelian did not understand because he was expecting Quya. In Vulgate the words were: 'Free him.'

The Quenthas swung the blade towards the stranger's throat even as Carnelian recognized his voice. 'No,' he barked, then choked as he lost the rhythm of his breathing. When he regained it, he saw the Quenthas were gazing at him.

'My . . .' he said and took another, rasping breath. 'Friend . . .'

Both Quenthas frowned, then they turned to each other; a pale face facing one dark with tattoos. Though neither spoke it was as if they were exchanging thoughts. They nodded even as all four arms swung the fanblade halberd. As the first blow

586

fell, Carnelian was certain his left hand had been sliced off.
The arm slumped, slapping his thigh like a hunk of dead meat.
The ribs on his left side seemed to snap like a rotten ladder.
He slumped forward and was only caught by his other arm,
wrenching the shoulder.

'Help him!'

As his second arm came free, Carnelian crashed forwards
into an embrace. The body beneath him reeled, but managed
to catch his weight. Smell of leather. Feeling the rumble in
Fern's chest as he spoke. The relief of his spine curving the
other way. The joy of taking a deep, deep breath. He felt Fern
stagger back as his right leg came free, stubbing his toes. When
the left was released, Fern leaned back so that Carnelian was
fully off the ground. Carnelian felt a cloak settling over him.
Felt its grip as it was tucked over him and a hood was pulled
over his head.

'Flee,' two throats said in Quya, 'while you still can.'

'Can you stand?' rumbled Fern almost in his ear.

Carnelian just wanted to hang there, draped over him,
loving him. He edged his weight back and felt his toes touching
stone, his heels, his feet spreading as they took his weight. As
his legs buckled, Fern leaned back to take his weight again.

'Flee,' hissed the Quenthas.

Fern began to drag him away and as he did so Carnelian's
feet found passing purchase on the stone. He felt the strain in
Fern's body and tried to walk, as best he could, hanging off
him. His mind lived for each step, willing the strength back
into his legs, counting the joins between the paving stones
of the road pass, each one a victory. When he felt Fern tense
up, he managed to lift his head, clamping his teeth against
the strain. He peered through the slit of the collapsed hood.
A watch-tower rose from the side of the road, stripped of its
leftway. Around the monolith protecting its stable door stood
syblings and ammonites. Surely, at any moment they must
come to question him and Fern, but when they did not budge,
he dropped his head to concentrate on walking.

Then a ditch opened up before their feet. The usual mess from the road was overlaid with rubble and stone dust. Fern manoeuvred him to where a slab had been thrown over the ditch. As they hobbled across, Carnelian's nostrils caught a fragrance. Attar of lilies suffused with rare musks. Glancing up, he saw a path running between pavilions that fluttered with the colours of butterflies, their silk walls thick with the cyphers of the Chosen. He dragged his heel to bring Fern to a halt.

'What is it?'

Carnelian used him as a support upon which to turn and gaze back the way they had come. Between its wheels, the Iron House swelled up from the stem of the bronze stair into a baroque black tulip. In the air above it, supported on a mast, the green face. Then he became aware of a mountain of darkness looming up behind it.

'What is it?' cried Fern again, in response to Carnelian's violent shudder.

Too weak to raise his arm, Carnelian pointed with his chin. 'The Horned God.'

He felt Fern shaking his head. 'Just a thundercloud.'

Gazing up, Carnelian saw Fern was right. An immense tower uncannily like a baobab grew up from the dark layer of cloud roofing the sky. It was its smoky branches he had taken for horns. He regarded it uneasily. Its faceless immensity seemed to be gazing down on them with the malice of the Darkness-under-the-Trees.

Fern tensed. 'They hunt us!'

Carnelian could see, beyond the Iron House, a dragon, and the traces, the hawsers and hooks with which an ant crowd of men were hitching the monster to the chariot. Then he saw upon the road a posse of syblings coming their way. Leaning upon Fern, he allowed himself to be half dragged into the encampment of the Masters.

*   *   *

They had passed perhaps a dozen pavilions when cries broke out behind them and they knew they were being pursued. Carnelian had been managing to keep up a reasonable pace, though only by leaning on Fern, whose breathing had grown more and more laboured behind his mask. Carnelian knew they would be chased down unless he could move on his own. He disengaged from Fern, batting away his protests and his arms even as he tottered forward and found his legs just strong enough to bear him. Balance was another thing altogether and, as he broke into a clumsy lope, Fern often had to reach out to steady him. The sound of pursuit grew louder. Focusing on each stride, half lost in the aching of his abused body, Carnelian did not dare to look back. The cries of their pursuers were drawing curious retainers out from the pavilions. The tattooed faces of guardsmen and other servants grew wide-eyed as they saw Carnelian and Fern bearing down on them. Reacting to Fern's mask, these retainers fell to their knees, imagining they were two Masters. In places there were so many of them they blocked their path and Fern was forced to pull them off to right or left, along another alley.

At last he came to a halt at one of the crossroads. Carnelian fell to one knee, his head swimming. Glancing up, he saw his father's mask turning as Fern tried to spy out the way. 'I don't know where we are. I can't see anything through this thing.' He gave out a growl of frustration and reached back to loose the bindings of his mask. Carnelian glanced round and saw faces giving them frightened looks, expecting at any moment some syblings to come careering into sight.

Fern sighed his relief as the mask came away. Carnelian was glad to see his dear face. Fern looked at the mask.

'Throw it away,' Carnelian said.

Fern hesitated, then threw the thing down, grimacing. He pointed. 'I think it's this way.'

Soon they were up and stumbling along. A clump of guardsmen appeared before them. Fern was about to turn away at a junction when Carnelian, with a grim laugh, threw back his cowl to expose his face. The guardsmen's faces suddenly sickened and they ducked back from where they had come and he and Fern moved on.

Suddenly, they found themselves on the edge of a ditch whose depths were lost in shadow. Along its further edge a road ran, dense with dragons and squadrons of riders. They had worked at digging ditches long enough to be shocked by the vast labour this represented. The ditch curved round and out of sight: a stupendous work that seemed beyond the power of men. Again Carnelian gazed across to the other side and saw, beyond the vast melee of the camp, the wall of red dust full of a slow, blossoming life and his heart raced.

'I've no idea where your father's tent lies.'

Fern stood at bay regarding the route they had come, his head turning slightly from side to side as he listened out for the cries of their pursuers. Carnelian wanted to ask about his father, about Poppy, about how Fern had come to save him disguised as a Master, but that Fern was here was answer enough. To ask for more was to risk the decision he felt stirring in him. He tried to clear his mind enough to work things out. Notions of finding his father, his brothers, rolled together with other, inchoate feelings. One thing he knew: as things stood, in joining them he could only bring them more suffering. He focused on Fern, trying to think of a way to save him. He shook his head, letting out a growl that caused Fern to turn to him. It was those dark eyes that seemed the only solid thing in the world. 'I'm going to cross this ditch.'

Fern scowled. 'What about your father?'

'You go and find him, but I'm going to cross this ditch.'

Fern looked surprised. 'You want to fight in the battle?'

Carnelian had not thought that far ahead.

'Is it because you want to help defeat the Master?'

Carnelian shook his head. 'I don't care about him.'

'But is he going to lose?'

It was a strain for Carnelian to give any thought to that. He regarded the vast turmoil of the camp. 'He has all that ranged against him.'

'But you still believe he will win?'

Eyeing the red dust, Carnelian nodded.

'So you want to fight on the losing side?'

He regarded Fern, feeling sadness welling up in him. 'I no longer care who wins.' He felt doubt fall from him; a burden he had been carrying for so long, he had forgotten how much it weighed. 'I just want to be free.'

'So do I,' Fern whispered. He raised his hand tenderly to Carnelian, but his fingers hesitated short of touching him. 'Are you strong enough?'

Carnelian caught his hand and pulled it to him. 'I will be.'

Fern began to cry, but also to laugh. Carnelian let his tears join Fern's and the laughter came bubbling out of him. Like sun after a storm, Fern's smile stirred Carnelian to joy. 'It's a good day to die.'

Together, like children, they slid down the earthy wall into the ditch, leaning back against the slope, using clawed fingers and heels as anchors to try to control their descent. Soon they had plunged into a region in which night yet dwelt. Here the earth gave way to a stinking mulch that sucked at their limbs. The stench intensified until they felt their feet sinking into some noisome pool. Carnelian tried to gather up his cloak, but its edge was already heavy and dripping. He peered across, but could see nothing. They could easily have been on the edge of some filthy swamp. Carnelian raised his gaze to the black sky and saw the upper edge of the further wall of the ditch rising like a cliff into the morning light. He searched along the rim until he saw a gully leading up from the darkness. He reached out and found Fern's arm and lifted it to point at the gully. 'We can climb that.'

'Unless we drown in this filth,' came back Fern, his tone enough for Carnelian to imagine his face twisted with disgust.

Together they began to wade through the sewage. It climbed up to their knees, but no further. Carnelian made sure to breathe through his mouth, giving a shudder every time he put his foot back into the sludge.

At last they reached the other side and, moving sideways, found the mouth of the gully. Then they began the long, careful clamber up its slippy, slimy course, clawing at clods of sewage-sodden soil. As they climbed, Carnelian began to feel a tremor in the earth. Glancing up, he wondered if it was thunder, but the higher they went, the more the tremor resolved into an arrhythmic pounding he recognized.

As they emerged into the light, they saw their limbs were sheathed with dark slime. Carnelian's cloak dragged and he wanted to discard it, but it was all he had to wear. The pounding intensified so that it seemed the earth itself was alive. A fine red dust settled upon them and rouged their filthy skin. The closer they came to the rim of the ditch, the louder grew the din. At last they pushed their heads up over the edge and their ears were assaulted by a roar. They gaped. Dragons were thundering past, the leprous pyramids of their towers scratching the stormy sky. Their horns were huge bone scythes. Their heavy heads were rising and falling like beaked ships upon a swell. Walls of hide stretching, rucking, flexing as massive muscles pistoned beneath. Tree legs lifting improbably, swinging forward, settling with a thump that sent a rumble and shudder through the earth. Among this heaving tide of hide and flesh and bone, squadrons of aquar cantered past, their riders watching the monsters nervously. As the vast procession slid from left to right across their vision, Carnelian peered among the reed legs of the aquar and the forest of the passing giants and caught glimpses of the camp beyond, from which an inexhaustible torrent was pouring out to join them. In this distant melee, a few twinkling flashes made him look round and see the watch-tower rising behind him, from whose summit a constant stream of instructions was being transmitted. This seeming chaos was being directed by the Wise, perhaps relaying instructions from Molochite.

He turned to Fern. 'The battle will soon be upon us. We need some beasts to ride.'

Grimly, his friend nodded. Carnelian saw in Fern's face that he was still determined to fight.

'Let's do it.'

Pulling his cowl over his head, Carnelian clambered up onto the road, a rough mosaic of blocks and fractured stone probably cannibalized from the demolished leftway. Glancing round to make sure Fern was close, he made his way along the edge of the road, all the while keeping a wary eye on the massive lumbering dragons, until he saw a squadron of auxiliaries approaching. When he stepped out in front of them, they came straight at him. He raised his arms aggressively. As they slowed he thought they were responding to him, but then he saw they were gazing past him. The object of their scrutiny was Fern. Though spattered with filth, encrusted to knees and elbows, the paleness of his commanders' leathers was still unmistakable. One of the auxiliaries cried out a challenge, his face distorting with anger and confusion. Perhaps the man could see that, in spite of his costume, Fern was not a Master. Carnelian sensed that the man was about to order his squadron to resume their march and he strode towards him. The man regarded Carnelian with some uncertainty.

'Give us two of your aquar,' he said, in a ringing tone of command.

The man hesitated. Carnelian realized that all the man was seeing was a tall figure in a filthy cloak. He became aware that the auxiliaries were impeding the flow of traffic along the road. Voices were rising in angry consternation. He drew back his cowl to expose his face and continued to advance towards the auxiliary. The man grew sickly pale as if his face was seeking to mirror the whiteness of Carnelian's own. Faces everywhere were averting their gaze with such violence that this communicated to their aquar, whose plumes raised in alarm. Carnelian had nearly reached the man who was bent forward in his saddle-chair moaning, when he felt a vast shadow looming up and saw the great horned head of a dragon above him. The monster's reek oppressed the air. Suddenly a screaming roar tore the air, making Carnelian's teeth rattle. Its commander was sounding his trumpets to clear the road, or perhaps he had seen the Master below. Carnelian did not care. He clasped the auxiliary's thigh. 'Down!'

The man was not so lost in terror that he dared disobey. His hand pulled the reins and the aquar sank to the road.

'All of you down!' Carnelian bellowed.

As the whole squadron sank, he grasped the auxiliary's arm and pulled him out of his chair. Looking round, he saw Fern. 'Take this one.'

Fern jerked a nod. Carnelian went down the line and pulled another auxiliary from his saddle-chair. Taking the man's lance, Carnelian clambered into his place, feeling the warmth still in the leather as he adjusted himself into a cramped sitting position. He recalled how to control an aquar with reins and made her rise. Fern was already mounted. Again the air was rent by trumpet blasts. Carnelian glanced up, but could not see past the head of the dragon to its tower. He pulled his cowl once more over his head and then sent his aquar loping along the road, glanced round to make sure Fern was following and had soon insinuated them into the traffic up ahead.

Carnelian and Fern became lost in the march. The smell of fear accentuated the malty musk of beasts and men. Its light in every eye ran like hairline cracks through that monumental procession of military power. Both could sense it lurking behind the grim expressions on every face. Shuddered by the constant thunder of dragon footfalls, their own hearts were quick, uncertain. Watching more and more of the monsters heaving onto the road, and trapped in the narrow canyons walled by their flexing hide, neither could imagine how such might could be withstood.

At last they neared a junction. Ahead dragons were turning left into a road running away to the east, but to the right a massive earthbridge crossed the ditch back into the Masters' camp, from which there was coming a strange and relentless grinding. As they came abreast of this bridge, they saw, beyond the cordon of Ichorian bridge guards, that the Iron House was in motion. Two massive dragons pulled it that were the colour of dried blood. Carnelian sought out the standard high above the chariot, but it was side-on. His gaze fell to the chariot wheel, its rim taller than the sybling Ichorians that clustered beside it. Ponderously that verdigrised circle turned, impaled by red spokes that emanated from a dark hub. A map, then, of the Commonwealth: Osrakum at the centre, the barbarian lands at the rim taking turns to bear her crushing weight.

Carnelian was allowed to see no more, for, at that moment, his aquar made the turn into the east and he and Fern began moving along the road towards the edge of the camp. They made slow progress. As before, dragons drifted slowly onto the road from the left, seeming to be afloat upon the torrent of riders eddying around their feet. To the right a vast field over-brimming with aquar was pouring more squadrons onto the road. Over their heads Carnelian could see the dragons that had been moored within that quadrant of the camp drifting away towards its southern edge in a stately armada.

The outer ditch approached. Then Carnelian and Fern were crossing it upon another earthbridge. Riding into open ground made them feel as if they were being released from the neck of a bottle. The dragons were sailing in columns southeastward, up to their haunches in billows of dust. Auxiliaries were coalescing into rhomboids already vague in the haze their aquar were stirring up. Looking south, Carnelian lost hold of that human scale and even the dragons appeared small. For the red plain stretched away to a boiling cliff of dust, churned up by the approaching sartlar, that rose towards the frowning clouds. Black with rain, these seemed the Sky Lord's wrathful brow. A subtle light played behind that might have been the

God seeing in His mind the coming flame. In his bones, Carnelian felt the sky's growling was warming to thunderous rage.

Harsh trumpets sounding caused him to turn back towards the camp. Through tearing red miasmas, a dense press of dragon towers was pouring out through the southern gate. Above them hung an apparition that chilled Carnelian's marrow: the infernal face of the Iron House standard, black and leering, sprouting four horns like scorpion stings. It was only a representation of the Twins, whose other face had given him comfort.

'We're getting left behind,' cried Fern, pointing with his lance to where the auxiliary squadrons were moving towards the blinking eye of the sun. As they caught up with them, the sun climbed behind the clouds, instantly plunging the world into a lurid twilight.

THE MIRROR BREAKS

Even a hairline crack can shatter a mountain.

(a Quyan proverb)

Carnelian gazed at the cliff of dust that countless Sartlar feet were driving towards him and the rest of Molochite's host. The half-light was giving it a darker, bloodier hue. In its rolling depths growled nearing thunder. Sometimes faint lightning, like a twinge of toothache, made him remember his dreams and, for some reason, his voyage to the Three Lands. He gazed up into the leaden heavens dreading the weight of rain above them. Fern was watching the sartlar approach. Before them both stretched more than a dozen ranks of heads and banners, of backs of saddle-chairs, of lances that combed the gale the mountainous wave was hurling at them. Carnelian opened his cowl to sample the air, almost expecting the tang of the sea, the iron of blood, but there was nothing save the smell of aquar, of men and their sweat and, perhaps, the dry musk of the land.

Left was the vast sweep of auxiliary squadrons bristling all the way towards the pale thread of the Great Eastern Road. Right, a dragon loomed that was the nearest bastion in the wall of monsters that ran unbroken into the west as far as Carnelian could see. Their flame-pipes gave them the appearance of some vast hornwall. Chimneys lit, this whole first line was streaming banners of black smoke back over the second: another rampart that would stand should the first fail, and Molochite's ancient tactic to counter Osidian's hollow crescent. Not that such a precaution seemed necessary. Regarding such a concentration of raw power, it seemed ridiculous to imagine that Osidian could triumph. A bleakness at the thought of his defeat alerted Carnelian to what he had not known he felt: that he still yearned for Osidian's victory. Willing his gaze to penetrate the gloom behind Molochite's second line, he was sure he could see the demonic face hanging leering above the Iron House. It was a perfect representation of the mind that moved that vast host. Adjusting his position in the saddle-chair made him aware his torn muscles were beginning to seize up. His joints ached where they had almost come apart. His skin shivered, remembering the brutal touch of the cross. He relived his pain, his shame, but also the naked children and Molochite's bitter malice. Was it strange, then, that he did not wish that monster to triumph?

Resuming his survey over the heads of the auxiliaries, he watched again the sartlar advance rearing its wall of curling dust. Though it looked solid, it was not. This was no wave of blood that would drown Molochite's power, merely a mirage behind which lay nothing more terrible than a multitude of starved, poorly armed brutes. Would their flesh resist Molochite's fire? Would their bones withstand the trampling thunder of his dragons? Carnelian chuckled mirthlessly. Still he could not let go hope of Osidian's victory. Scanning the dust wall, he searched for any sign of him. A light flickered, there towards the far end of Osidian's right flank. It flared again. A tiny flicker too close to the ground to be lightning. Dragonfire, then. Carnelian's heart leapt as he had a thought. Could it be a feint to draw Molochite's strength from his centre, weakening it perhaps enough to land a fatal blow? He looked back towards the Iron House and watched it for a signal. Nothing. The two lines might have been granite walls upon whose ramparts fires smoked.

Suddenly the air was rent by a ragged, shrill chorus pumped out by many brass throats. The blasts reverberated beneath the heavens. Again the fanfare sounded, so harsh it seemed as if it might pare flesh from bones. Their commander, in the front rank, jabbed his lance as if he sought to spear the clouds. The men behind him answered him with a roar that seemed mild in comparison with the trumpets. Carnelian and Fern could feel the excitement around them heating. The battle-cries rushed away along the line, turning distantly to a hiss that set the lances vibrating like a wind through ferns. Fern bared his teeth and nodded.

Then Carnelian became aware the front ranks of their squadron were sliding forward in a packed mass of flesh and hide, of bronze and wood. He did not even need to signal his aquar. Her head dropped and she sprang forward. He was thrown from side to side. Faster and faster until the rocking smoothed and she was leaning into her run as her feet reached forward, clutched the ground with their claws, then whipped back. Carnelian adjusted his position, wound his wrist into the reins and clutched his lance in both hands. Its grip was greasy, but firm. Around him other riders were hazy jiggling shadows. Only glimpses of Fern's pale leathers allowed him to know his friend was close.

Peering ahead Carnelian could see little through the dust their aquar were scratching up from the ground. He lowered his head against the pelting sand, deafened by the furious drum and rush of their charge. From up ahead came muffled, crashing sounds. His aquar rocked him as she slowed, her head rising a little with her plumes. Then the ground became rough, uneven. He was jerked this way and that as her footfalls landed on things that collapsed suddenly like eggs beneath her weight. One of her legs snagging threw him forward. As she yanked her foot free he was punched back into his saddle-chair. Her head was high now, crowned with startled plumes, and she had slowed to a jerky stride. A shudder. Another as her footing slipped and she fought for balance. Carnelian clung to the saddle-chair, his lance lying flat across his knees, and he peered down to see the field of rocks or whatever it was they were fighting through. At any moment she might lose her footing and he would be thrown.

The ground seemed for a moment to be meshed in the roots and stems of dark ferns. Then he saw a thick hand, limbs contorted into loops and hooks. Boulders resolved into heads furred with hair. Some staved in, crushed and leaking moist pulp. Bestial faces torn and bloating, lips drawn back revealing black peg-encrusted maws. A stench rose up of shit and blood as his aquar stumbled forward through that quagmire of mangled flesh.

Seeing the dust thinning, he pulled her up. Around him other riders were struggling through the carnage, fanning out. Less than ten ranks ahead they met the edge of a sea. He gaped at that milling ocean of heads. Cries and screams were coming from where the auxiliaries met the sartlar in a frothing boundary. Arms rose and fell wielding blades of gleaming, dripping bronze. He felt a horror greater even than his disgust of the slaughter. Clearly, the beastmen were unarmed. Then there was a small but sudden change in the scene. A man and rider toppled, and disappeared. At a different point along the boundary, another vanished. An aquar that had been screeching fell abruptly silent. His scalp began to crawl. He glanced round and saw Fern's pallid shape hunched in a saddle-chair some distance away.

'Fern,' he cried, but his voice was lost in the tumult. He wanted to work a path to his side, but there were too many auxiliaries in the way. He became aware of how desperately they were eyeing the fighting up ahead. He and Fern were being fed into that front with everyone else. He glanced back, contemplating retreat, some attempt at regrouping. Carnage carpeted the land to their rear, but this mess was slowly being overrun by an eddying tide of sartlar creeping around their flank. Ahead, he saw how much the line of auxiliaries had thinned. A surf of hands grasped at man and beast, which the auxiliaries hewed at with their blades, but as a hand was cut away, more replaced it. He saw one aquar struggling to stand as a skirt of sartlar clung to it. The creature flailed its neck as it toppled, spilling its rider into the waiting grasp of dozens.

His sympathy for the sartlar had all dried up. His fingers fumbled the toggle that closed a scabbard. Slipping his fingers around the handle of a sword gave him a thrill of relief. He pulled its fanblade free and glanced round. Their way back was now closed. He focused his gaze on Fern and urged his aquar towards him. In pushing past another rider, their saddle-chairs scraped against each other. Carnelian had no time for the man's gaping panic. Fern glanced round and their eyes met. The next moment he looked away and Carnelian saw the man before him being pulled down, adding his cries to the pandemonium.

Then, suddenly, at the edge of his vision, an auxiliary disappeared. He spun round and they were upon him. He saw first their filthy mouths. Then their monstrously branded faces. Then the animal gleam of their eyes. He swung the fanblade, pruning off a couple of hands. Twisting, he swung it back, feeling it snag as it bit into bone. It caught, the blade turned transverse and the central ball cracked a skull. Even as his wrist got control of it, he felt the tethers of their fingers hooking his saddle-chair. He dashed the flat along a knobbled run of knuckles and was jerked back by their release, but other hands came and a face slavering for his arm. He sliced the blade into that mouth, clinking against rotten teeth, widening the grin, then the blade struck bone and stuck. Grinning impossibly wide, the corpse fell back, yanking the sword from his grip. He laid about him with his fists as hands and arms hooked over his aquar's neck. She screeched as they gouged her with their claws, then worked their fingers into her wounds to widen them. More hands were reaching ever higher up her neck as they bent her head down towards them. Her plumes snapped like twigs when a sartlar grabbed her skull and swung up to tear at her throat with its teeth.

She convulsed. Her legs buckled. Carnelian was tumbled out. His head cracked against another, even as his elbow dug into flesh. Stunned, he watched the world whip past as he plunged in among their legs.

Then he was lying on the earth, gazing up at an angry sky. A livid crack opened it for a moment. A booming, slow, stuttering voice sounded. He turned into the earth, gouging dust as he sought to stand. His feet under him, pushing up, unbending his spine. He was startled by his whiteness. He was puzzled to be naked under the cloak. Corpses seemed stones scattered over the earth. An aquar, one clawed foot twitching, her belly torn and spilling entrails. Carnelian became aware of the circle round him. At first he could make no sense of it, then he saw they were sartlar kneeling, their heads bowed into the dust. A movement of his head was enough to make them shudder. He regarded them, feeling eerily calm. Then he became aware of a pale figure being pulled down. As he remembered Osidian and the slavers, anger rose. Sartlar were bending to their victim like raveners. Then he knew what it was he was seeing and roared, 'Fern!'

He ran towards his friend, ready to rend any who opposed him, but the sartlar sprang from his path. Fern was now invisible beneath their frenzy. Carnelian grabbed hair and the dark, coarse stuff of their clothing and pulled two off. Faces came up, snarling, but their maws snapped closed as they ducked away, whimpering, abandoning their victim prostrate upon the earth. Carnelian fell to his knees at Fern's side, and had eyes for nothing but the blood smearing him. The sartlar assault had been so violent they had torn him almost wholly free of his commander's leathers. Carnelian felt Fern's body for wounds. Though his skin was striped with gashes, none seemed deep. Fern groaned. Carnelian was transfixed by the overwhelming relief he was alive. The bloody face opened an eye that stared in wonder.

'Are you hurt?'

Fern frowned, clearly dazed. Carnelian spat on his fingers and gently began to wipe Fern's face clean. A metallic screaming echoing beneath the rumbling sky made Carnelian rise and look in the direction from where the sound had come. There the sartlar envelopment was thinning. Through the gaps he could see that, in the centre, unopposed by aquar, the sartlar had continued to advance to well behind his current position. Beyond them dragon towers rose as a crenellated rampart. Another blast sounded even as, beyond the sartlar, a violent dawn erupted that caused him to shield his eyes. Feeling the coruscation dim, he peered over his arms. Thick sooty smoke had risen like a fog. Flashes sliced through the writhing billows. He froze with horror. Molochite's first line was advancing, vomiting fire. Oceanic surges of terror were rippling back through the sartlar mass as the creatures tried to escape the holocaust. Their numbers choked their flight. He thought it was their shrieks he was hearing, then he recognized the whine and scream of the fire jets as they scythed through their ranks.

As he watched, he saw their flank shivering, vibrating. With each moment, a tremor in the ground was growing stronger. He realized the creatures were fleeing in the only direction they could: towards the flanks. He and Fern were right in the path of their stampede.

That brought him back to life. He spun round. Fern was still lying prone upon the ground. Carnelian cast around for even a single aquar, but all those he could see were dead or dying. The sartlar rout was almost upon them. He stooped, thrusting an arm under Fern's right shoulder and head, pulling with his other hand on Fern's left. He managed to sit him up. Still frowning, Fern's gaze strayed to meet Carnelian's.

'You've got to get up!' Carnelian shouted in his face.

Fern's brow creased deeper as if he did not understand but, clutching at Carnelian, he scrabbled up onto his feet, the tatters of pale leather falling from him. Carnelian dug his shoulder under Fern's arm, pulling it like a yoke over his neck, then grabbed hold of the hand on the other side. They stood unsteadily for a moment. He could make out bestial shapes hobbling and stumbling towards them. He manoeuvred Fern round and began striding, half carrying, half dragging him. When the sartlar flood smacked into them, it almost lifted them off their feet. Saturated with the odour of fear, the stench of the sartlar further quickened Carnelian's heart so that he became too frantic to think. Constantly buffeted, he threw everything he had into keeping his footing and steadying Fern. He was slow to become aware of a deeper thunder in the earth. The shrieking of the flame-pipes was now sliding in pitch like a blade whipping past his ear. Ahead the sartlar flood was mounding as it flowed over some obstruction. Then the flow grew turbid; heads were dropping suddenly, arms flung up were then sucked down. He tried desperately to slow down, but the rout swept him and Fern inexorably towards the pile-up.

Closer and closer they were driven towards that bank of threshing limbs. Then his feet were catching in the mesh of bodies. Bones cracked under his heels, flesh slipped under his toes, warm wetness mouthed his bruised feet. He was stumbling, lowering his head, ramming through hard and soft obstructions, screams and yells, elbows arcing into him like pick-axes, thuds and shudders as bodies crashed into him, his arm yanked nearly from its socket as he pulled Fern towards him and, together, on all fours they scrabbled up a writhing slope of struggling flesh. Torrid breath wafted over him, laced with naphtha, thick with the stench of cooking meat. Desperation gave him new strength, but they were hopelessly enmeshed in flailing limbs and maned heads. The whole mound of bodies was quaking. He was engulfed in the aura of the monster. It avalanched towards them, red up to its knees. A footfall like a meteor strike. Another sent a concussion into the earth that shunted Carnelian hard against the sartlar among whom he was embedded; his bones jellied, his brain rattled in his skull. He had an overwhelming impression the Horned God was lunging to crunch them in His maw.

Then an arch of sun erupted so that he was blind to everything save its coruscating arc. Vibrating incandescence forced through his slitted eyes. Its odour a pure, bitter promise of death. His mind, like crystal, resonated to its shrill, terrifying song. He clung to Fern, wanting that they should die together. Among the shrieks of those set alight, he could hear the crackle of their flesh crisping. A bonfire whoosh. The heat intensified and he screwed his eyes closed, waiting for the unbearable touch of fire on his naked skin. Then its scream changed pitch and he opened his eyes and saw it pass, dancing over the arms and legs above him, skin peeling back from chests and faces, hair igniting in quick bushes of flame, all suddenly lost among thick black blossoms. Tar smoke rolled hot over him, oozing an acrid burn into his lungs. Then he was drowning, choking, coughing so hard he could taste blood. Iron in his mouth; iron infusing into his being. Stretching his neck up until he was sure his throat would tear, straining for breathable air. Then a sweet draught, another, another, until he surfaced, eyes raw, blinking, feeling the thunder almost upon them, saw the dim lantern of the high cabin in which a Master sat and, beneath him, the swelling monstrous dragon. Hawsers pulling on its horns caused it to drop its head, so that it was the flat of its skull that rammed the sartlar pyre. Carnelian was aware of the corpses rising round him in a bow wave. He was rolled in tumbling bodies, heavy blows from heads like clubs, a mass sharp with knees and elbows, lubricated with blood, reeking from smouldering flesh and sinew.

Buried alive. Terror consumed him as he lay there, smothered. Bodies sheathed him. Writhing in gore and shit and piss. He was one worm among many. He managed to turn his head to find a pocket of air to suck at. Among the moaning, the rustle, the gasping, he found the sound of his own breath. He listened to it, slowed it, deepened it, fighting for calm. Fern's warm body under his arm. He managed to work this up his chest. He squeezed his hand up to the side of Fern's neck, his jaw. A finger pressed up over the angle of his lips. Moist breath against his skin. Carnelian let out a sob of relief. For a moment all he could think about was how to save Fern. Eventually he realized that, to help him, he must first free himself. Focusing on his body, he became aware his left hand was cooler than the rest of him. He lay for a moment gathering his strength, then pushed towards that coolness through the press, wriggling like a maggot in flesh. His arm came out into space, he worked his shoulder free, then his face. He gasped at the air as if he had swum up out of the deep. He used his free arm to lever himself out, sliding more skin out with each try. When his right arm came free, he shoved down with both hands and slid out in a rush. Then he was tumbling and hit the ground with a stunning thud.

He came to feeling the good earth cradling him. He rose, groaning at the ache that was his whole body. A ridge of limbs and bodies and lolling heads rose up before him that twitched and slid against itself. The ridge ended abruptly at a gaping wound as if it were a gum from which a tooth had been torn. On the other side of the gap, the ridge continued. The edges of the gap were ripped and bloodied, but its floor was raw with a dark paste squeezed from sartlar bodies by the dragon's feet. Carnelian stared in horror and the horror stared back: eyes gaping at him from a mangled, branded sartlar face. A mane clotted with gore. The creature propped up on a crooked arm. Her breasts sagging gourds. Her body squeezing to gore and skin merging into the quagmire of blood.

'Is this the Land of the Dead?' she rasped, with her thick sartlar voice.

Carnelian managed to free his gaze from her and saw around him a landscape ridged and rutted by corpses. Perhaps she was right. His finger remembered Fern's warm, living breath. Soon he was scrambling up the slope, clasping at the fleshy flowers of hands and feet, treading on thighs and heads. He heard a moaning rising from his chest and knew it was fear he would not find Fern. He clambered, peering, into the nest of bodies, interspersing his moans with barks of 'Fern, Fern.'

And then he saw a brown leg. He slid his fingers between its warm skin and the matted hair of a head that lay upon it like a boulder, past the ear to the stomach underneath, shoving his hand up then over, following the ridge of the rib cage until he had a good grip of him. Then, digging his feet in, he leaned back and tugged and slowly, one heave at a time, the body came out and then the face. Fern, eyes filled with wonder, as if he were being born. His brows contracted, his lips opened in a circle. 'What . . . ?'

Carnelian ignored the question, putting his strength into freeing him completely, then propping him up upon the slope.

'What . . . ?' Fern said again, but Carnelian hardly heard him, his gaze snared by another in the heap. The small, bright eyes of a child. Its little hand reached out for him. He avoided the grip, caught the tiny wrist, slid his other hand in seeking an armpit, aware of nothing but the desperation in those eyes. He managed to work the morsel of a body free, but it was still attached by a thin arm. He reached in to prise its grip loose, but it shook its head in violent distress repeating a sound, a word, over and over: 'Mya, mya . . .' And feeling along that bony sliver, Carnelian found the tiny fist held fast in a larger one and soon he was working to free their owner and was struggling to loose her, when two strong brown arms came to help him: Fern was there beside him. Together they fought to free the child's mother.

A remote detonation brought Carnelian's head up. As the sound reverberated under the sky, he and Fern looked at each other. After freeing the sartlar mother, they had gone back for more. Even though she had been dead, there were many still alive among the corpses. Carnelian had become hardened to their fear of him and blind to their deformities. All he had been able to think of was that they were trapped as he had been. He had laboured ceaselessly, ignoring the pain in his muscles, finding in the work a way to avoid looking into that dark place deep inside in which lurked the conviction that all this carnage was, in great measure, his doing.

A harsh trumpet blast shocked him to stillness. His arms hung, his grip on a sartlar leg slackening. He bent his strength once more to pulling out the creature. He registered its wide-eyed horror as it saw him. He could feel the creature's muscles knotting under his touch. Only when he knew the sartlar had no more need of his help did he finally gaze in the direction from which the trumpet call had come. His view was blocked by another ridge of corpses. He turned back to the slope and began to clamber up, trying not to tread on any moving limbs, his feet remembering the rootstairs of the Koppie.

When he reached the summit, he saw the dragon that had trampled them was, with the rest of Molochite's first line, spreading a sickle of fire through the sartlar into the east. He followed the flickering round to the south, where it thinned with distance. All along its curve the blade of fire was going out. Only at its most southern extremity did it burn brightly. He squinted at the conflagration that seemed a star fallen to earth and realized it marked the intersection of the sickle curve with the Great South Road. He swung round. Molochite's second line, still in position, though now exposed, was folding like jaws towards its centre from behind which rose the standard of the Iron House. He was certain it was from there the trumpet signal had come. As he watched, the two halves of the line of dragons continued to close as if seeking to devour some morsel. It was while searching for what this might be that he became aware of the lurid, churned landscape that lay between Molochite's two, separated lines. The air was too hazy with smoke, the black ceiling of the sky too dark to allow him to see clearly, but fires burning all across the land hinted at how it had been transformed. He had the impression of ridges, of snaking curves as if a labyrinth had been ploughed into the earth. Then he knew that what he was seeing was a vast tract of land patterned by the mounds and ridges of the piled-up sartlar dead.

Fern came scrambling up the corpse logjam to join him. He cursed, stumbling, and they grabbed each other for support. Carnelian watched him gazing out as he had done and saw the unbelieving horror come into his face.

Fern raised a finger pointing. 'Look there.'

Where the faint thread of the road disappeared into the maw of Molochite's second line, there was a bristling movement.

Then a sun ignited in the heart of Molochite's second line.

'Osidian,' Carnelian breathed, entranced.

Though the curving wall of Molochite's dragons hid the fire, its glare was flung up stark into their towers. One at the centre flared into flames. Another joined it. Another two. They burned like torches as they veered away from each other. He and Fern watched, mesmerized, as more towers ignited, one after the other, outward from the centre as Osidian's dragons incinerated Molochite's line. Then the Black Face standard was lit up from below. The sun of Osidian's attack had penetrated all the way to the Iron House. Its standard shivered like a thing alive, turned towards them, grimacing as it caught fire. Carnelian watched, stunned. The Iron House itself must be alight. Relief that Molochite would die was choked by a memory of the children he had with him. The standard fell like sputtering wax. As if this were a signal, the sky flickered, then released a booming roar. Instinct jerked Carnelian's head back as the air above hissed. Then he had to close his eyes against the needle rain. A cool sheath slipped down over his skin. He gasped with delight as it scoured him clean of gore, then he was drinking the gift of the sky. He dropped his head, rubbed the water from his eyes and saw Fern gazing at him in wonder. For a moment they gaped at each other, then gave themselves over to laughter, that was not joy, but perhaps a release of terror.

The downpour diminished. The towers of Molochite's second line had ignited like marsh lights as Osidian's flame-pipes burned their way from its centre towards both flanks. Flying from the inferno, the monsters streaked the guttering torches of their towers through the gloom, but were soon enmeshed in the labyrinth of the sartlar dead. Here and there the burning towers lit the folds and creases of the corpse mounds. Sometimes one would detonate, its explosion dulled by the hissing rain. A flash, then gobbets of liquid fire would spill, strike the ridges with sparks, smear bright-backed smoulder over sinuous, crumbling contours, that would dull to pulsating scars, then nothing. Fallen dragons were left nestled among the dead as smoking boulders.

Though it was all happening some distance away, Carnelian and Fern eyed the path of Osidian's fiery destruction as it burned nearer, glancing at each other, feeling exposed on their corpse hill. A dragon emerged from behind the last of Molochite's line. It swept round the exposed flank belching flame. Its victim was soon alight and picking up speed as it fled with a ravening conflagration on its back. The ground quaked as the monster veered towards them. Carnelian felt Fern's hand on his shoulder and put his own up to hold the arm there, for he judged they were safe. They watched as the monster lumbered south trailing flames and smoke. Its pursuer sailed after it, first one pipe then another snuffing out. The monsters disappeared into the labyrinth, then the pipes screeched back to life so that Carnelian and Fern could follow their progress by the smoke.

To the west the haze tore, thinning enough for them to be able to see, in the distance, something tilted burning among the smouldering mounds of the dragons that had pulled it half off the road. The Iron House seemed a child's toy with a broken wheel, but Carnelian knew the truth of what he was seeing. 'An oven,' he muttered, imagining the fury of heat within its iron walls.

'What?' cried Fern above the rain.

Carnelian stared. Within that wreck people were being cooked alive. Not only Molochite, but the children of the Chosen; no doubt also the Quenthas and many of their brethren and who knew what others.

Then a harsh brazen cry echoed across the battlefield. Twice more it sounded, with an urgency that made Carnelian's heart beat even faster. He glanced at Fern for some explanation, but he clearly had no idea what new horror this might presage. A rumble in the earth was causing the corpses upon which they stood to tremble. Casting around, Carnelian saw a boiling in the east like the rough edge of an oncoming flood. Molochite's first line was returning. He swung his arm out, blindly feeling for Fern, even as he saw the horned heads rising and falling in time with the shaking earth. His hand finding nothing, he turned and saw Fern was staring in the same direction. Soon they were scrambling down to the ground as fast as they could.

They crept along a valley. Mounds of corpses rose up on either side, striped black by the passage of dragonfire. The rain had quenched most of the burning, but furtive, lurid flames still flickered in the depths of the piled-up dead. The rain pummelled their backs, forcing them to bow their heads, though they still had to blink away drops to see. Horror would have been enough to stoop them and they would rather have walked blind were it not that they feared snagging their feet upon an arm, a leg, a crushed head, then falling into the foul mud. Earth mixed with rain and gore and shit, churned by panicked sartlar, formed a treacherous, sucking mire. Everywhere streams ran like arteries exposed to the air. Everywhere sartlar like crushed shellfish were extruding pastes, leaking fluids. Wounded sartlar crawled over the slopes and dragged themselves in clumps through the marshy flats, unsteady on their bony legs, sliding, slipping, holding on to each other with desperate knobbed hands. Even at this extreme, they found the strength to pull themselves from Carnelian's path. He regretted adding to their agony as they scrabbled to avoid him but, try as he might to keep his distance from them, there was no other way through. Most cowered as he passed, but some sneaked glances, squinting at him as if he were a dazzling flame.

Raw wounds gaping in the corpse ridges showed where Molochite's first dragon line had crushed through. Carnelian and Fern had already crossed swathes of fiery destruction that might have been left by meteors crashing from the sky, when they came across the pitiful sight of a dragon of the second line run aground upon a reef of bodies. Exploding, its tower had scattered around it a pale field of bone splinters, at the centre of which the hump of the dragon's back formed a halo of pulverized meat around the black crater of its body cavity. As they crept past, Carnelian regarded the concentric rings of destruction and saw in it a sinister representation of a wheel-map.

Further on, another dragon, front legs buckled, had plunged its head into a corpse mound as far as its upper horns. Its beak had gouged a bow wave of earth and carcasses. The ruin of its tower, still restrained by some girdle ropes, leaned over the mound like a half-fallen tree, its flame-pipes snapped like branches against the sartlar dead. The monster's flanks and rear had been burned through to the bone by the conflagration that had spilled down from its tanks. The tower, eaten away by fire, exposed a blackened interior where the stump of its capstan was still manned by its charcoaled crew. Sitting like a shadow high in his command chair, the remains of a Master.

On they walked, clambering where they could through gaps in the mounds, shutting their hearts to the horrors to which they could not shut their eyes, each imprisoned in his own mind. Carnelian was remembering their flight through the limestone runnels on their way down from the Guarded Land, but was haunted too by memories of the Isle of Flies, of the Labyrinth.

The clump of sartlar seemed like others they had seen, except that they stood so still. Above them loomed a broken dragon tower that had been hurled some distance from where the monster that had borne it lay fallen. Carnelian and Fern were forced to draw nearer to the sartlar because they and the tower almost blocked the way. When one of the creatures turned its gore-encrusted head, Carnelian expected it to cower away, taking its fellows, trembling, with it, but the head turned back and the sartlar remained where they were. Carnelian and Fern glanced at each other, sharing their unease. As they edged round the sartlar, they became aware the creatures were in a ring looking down at something in their midst. Though Fern signed against it, Carnelian was drawn to look. Something pale but smeared with black lay upon the ground. The sartlar seemed to sense his interest and several heads came up. They regarded him with their dark eyes. For some reason he felt they wanted him to look. As he stepped forward, they moved aside. It was a Master on the ground, his body twisted into an unnatural shape. He stared, feeling how incongruous the expression of terror and surprise seemed upon that beautiful pale face, upon those pale, dead Chosen eyes. He saw the mask that had come loose and saw himself reflected in it like a crack of light in a winter dawn. The sartlar were gazing at him. Steadily they gazed at him and he grew afraid. He tried to rationalize his fear away, reminding himself of how much they had suffered and that they were victims. He told himself it was suffering he was seeing in their eyes, but he knew it was something different. At the very least, a lack of fear. At worst, a slow-burning, cold hatred.

It was Fern who pulled him away. Carnelian managed one last glance back before Fern drew him out of sight behind a buttress of sartlar dead.

Beyond a gateway framed by corpses, the open plain seemed the land of the living. As they moved through, nervous of the tottering walls on either side, Carnelian relived the passage through the gutter of the purple factory. Though then he had been riding an aquar. Still, it was easier to pretend he was wading through crushed shellfish than acknowledge what it actually was.

Reaching the edge of the red pools, they clambered out onto clean, solid ground, their toes gouging into the good earth. They took several half-running strides and then Carnelian bent to scoop mud, using it to rub his legs clean, to scrape the muck from between his toes. Glancing up he saw, through tears, Fern was doing the same, his face a mask of disgust. When they had done what they could, they turned their faces up to the heavens, letting the rain wash their tears away. Carnelian lowered his head, rubbing water from his eyes, and looked back the way they had come. Gory footprints led to the carnage in the gateway through which they had escaped the corpse labyrinth.

He saw how the ridge of bodies resembled some vast breaker. 'So many dead,' he muttered.

He was possessed by the act of imagining how that great ridge had come about. The panic of the sartlar as the earth shook beneath their feet. Their terror as they saw the wall of dragons lumbering towards them. The animal imperative to flee. The front ranks pushing back into the unyielding mass of those behind. Stumbling, people were shoved down, trampled, tripping those that had pushed them, falling, crushing those beneath who continued to struggle for air, for life, but the receding tide of flesh could not be denied. At these obstacles, the fleeing fell and those behind scrabbled over them, in wave upon wave, building the ridge of the fallen ever higher, burying alive those beneath, until the screaming fire gushed and trickled down to light infernos among the matrix of the struggling. Carnelian closed his eyes, remembering being trapped; living their dying.

A firm grip upon his shoulder made him open his eyes with a gasp. He saw Fern's concern for him, but also that he was pointing at the ridge. Carnelian looked up at it, at first aware only of the dead, but then realizing that the crest was lined with sartlar, like citizens manning a city wall. Turning, he saw what it was they all were watching: the Iron House smouldering.

Across the mud-glazed plain a dragon lay collapsed, its tower heeling over so that it seemed a ship left stranded on the mud by a receding tide. Then they heard paired trumpet screams, scratching from the south. As the sound repeated, Carnelian and Fern lurched into a lope, breathing hard against the strain of running through the mud. They reached the island of the fallen dragon. Dangling above were the brass mouths of its flame-pipes. They walked round the monster, keeping an eye on the tower leaning towards them. Up past the boulders of the dragon's knees and thighs, the brassman had fallen onto the rear haunch, one of its chains broken, dangling from one ankle. Carnelian was the first to advance under the shadow of the tower. He halted at the back knee, glancing up warily. He reached out to touch the hide. It was still warm. He scrambled up onto the monster's shin, then scrabbled up its rain-slicked thigh, grabbed hold of the edge of the brassman. It rattled as he pulled himself up onto it. He smelled the burnt thing before he saw it. The charred remains of a man cooked to the brass. Fern was waiting to come up. Carnelian eyed the gaping maw of the tower entrance, then climbed towards it. The brassman gave a shudder as Fern came up onto it. Carnelian approached the doorway, wrinkling his nose against its charcoal breath. He reached up, caught hold of some of the rigging, then pulled himself up to stand to one side of the doorway. The brassman juddered with each step as Fern climbed it to take a place on the other side of the door. They both leaned in.

A black cavity sloped down into a pit where the deck should have been. At first they could make no sense of it but then Fern pointed and Carnelian saw the arch in the bottom of the pit with its individual stones and knew it was the exposed backbone of the monster. How fierce had been the inferno that had eaten its way down through decks and tank and flesh? The tower rose black and hollow like a chimney to the sky. Everything inside had been consumed.

Another doubled trumpet blast made them look south, but they could not see over the corpse ridge. Using the rigging, they clambered up the remains of the tower. As he pulled himself up onto the ledge around the topmost tier, Carnelian peered through a porthole. The command chair and the Master who had sat in it had fallen into the conflagration below. Using a guy rope, he pulled himself up the mast onto the narrow ledge that was the remains of the roof. There was just enough space for Fern to join him. It was only then they gazed out over the land. Dark ripples stretched away behind the first corpse ridge like those a tide leaves in sand. Here and there tiny dragons with their towers gave scale. Both stared, appalled, unable to comprehend how many dead there must be to make up such a landscape. A flashing in the midst of this carnage drew Carnelian's eye. There upon the thread of road, a fire was burning. It died. Its smoke spiralled up, thinning into a haze, and he saw the dragon on the road and more behind it in a long column. The flame-pipes spoke again, the fire igniting against the road just before everything was obscured by naphtha smoke. At the root of that boiling black column, fire pulsed.

'A signal,' Carnelian and Fern said together. Carnelian looked further south and saw the ripples of the dead growing fainter and a scattering of ruined dragons like pebbles. He glanced east and saw a line of dragons there. There was another in the west. The two flanks of Molochite's first line turned inwards, facing each other across the labyrinthine ripples of the dead and at its heart those flame-pipes signalling.

Sitting with their backs against the mast, Carnelian and Fern were frozen together like two blocks of ice. The rain pouring over them had drained their flesh of life, their minds of thought. Their eyes might have been glass as they gazed towards Heart-of-Thunder and Osidian. Who else could it be? In response to his signals, the two surviving wings of Molochite's first line had exchanged communications by means of torches. As a result of all those firefly signals, a dragon from each wing had wound its way through the corpse labyrinth to meet Osidian on the road. By means of the torches their attendants lit, Carnelian and Fern had watched the commanders descend to the road and, there, in the shelter of Heart-of-Thunder's belly, they had spent a long time, no doubt negotiating terms. After this the emissaries had returned each to his wing, where, after more torch signals, they had all moved south and had, a long while past, disappeared into the rain haze.

A light came suddenly from the west, shocking Carnelian and Fern to life. The curves and windings of the corpse labyrinth were thrown into sharp relief with a texture of piled-up fishbones.

A growl emitted from Fern's throat brought Carnelian's head up to see Heart-of-Thunder was turning. Shadows moved and melted upon his tower, and soon Osidian and his dragons were marching south along the road. Watching this, Carnelian felt a yearning to follow him, but as quickly as he felt this, he rejected it. He looked at Fern. For a moment his face seemed that of a stranger, but when Fern's eyes came alive surveying the scene Carnelian's heart jumped. It was then he determined that, come what may, he would share Fern's destiny.

A bleak warmth upon his cheek made him turn to see the sun fallen beneath the ceiling of black cloud, already westering. Beneath its orb, the wheeled box of the Iron House was all burnt out. Imagining its oven horrors was not enough to deter his need to go there. He lingered for a while, examining without success the motives of his heart before he turned to Fern. 'We must find shelter for the night.' The words seemed spoken by a stranger. Fern was looking back at him, a question in his eyes. Then he must have seen Carnelian had no answers, for he shrugged. They broke their immobility with difficulty. Their limbs and backs felt stiff enough to snap off at the joints. Like old men, they began the descent to the earth.

The wreck loomed black against purple sky. Above hung the gory clot of the sun. They were weary from the long slog through the mud. Chilled to the bone by the rain, at first they welcomed the warm aura of the ruined Iron House. Until, that is, they began to smell its funeral-pyre reek. Half off the road it lay, like a ship run aground upon a reef. Carnelian imagined how it had happened. In pain and panic, the two blind draught dragons had pulled it off the road so that one side had tipped, a wheel rolling for a moment in the air before landing heavily enough on the earth below to buckle. In all, three dragons were piled up against the wreck like foothills. The nearest, having lumbered completely off the road, had avalanched down, shattering its forelimbs, plunging its massive head into the rubble of the demolished leftway. One of its lower horns had snapped off at the skull, from which a pool of blood had oozed. Its beak had buckled as it punched into the ground. Its rump and back formed a fleshy buttress crushed beneath the toppling mass of the Iron House. The second dragon had crashed down into bloody ruin and now lay slumped half on, half off the road. The third was one of Osidian's that had been caught up in the disaster. Its head lay hidden, but by the way the body lay, it must somehow be wedged between the wheel still on the road and the further wall of the Iron House. The monster sloped up from its collapsed haunches, suggesting its head was lying upon the axle. Its tower, angled back, was blackened but had not burned, so that perhaps its crew had been able to abandon it. The same fire that had licked the tower had burned furiously upon the backs of the two draught dragons. The summits of their backs were black craters ringed about by ashen flesh. Charcoaled gashes and clefts cutting deep into the meat showed where the wooden housings and the yokes as large as bridges had been consumed in the holocaust.

It was the wall of the Iron House, sheer and forbidding, that showed the greatest damage. The same long line of windows through which Carnelian, crucified, had seen the sartlar approaching that morning – had it really only been that morning? – those windows were now nothing more than a ragged slit from whose fissured upper lip wisps of smoke were still hazing up. Above, the wall had blackened and thinned. Through the surviving sooty filigree, Carnelian and Fern could glimpse hideous cavities the colour of charcoal. The whole smouldering mass rose mountainously before them, its cliffs and clefts, its mounds and gullies running with sheets and streams and rivulets from the rain that glazed it.

Overwhelmed, they almost fell to their knees, overcome by weariness and horror, weighed down by the immensity of death they had already witnessed that day.

Carnelian took Fern's shoulder and drew him away to where something lay embedded in the mud. A black bowl that either of them could have lain outstretched in, strangely contoured, filled up with water. Carnelian bent to touch it and brought his fingers to his nose. Iron. He unbent and regarded it, thinking it had a look of Osrakum with its lake. Then he realized it was Osrakum, or at least a representation of it. The iron hollow was, in form, a turtle. Looking round, he saw the wheel from which this hub cap had fallen. They approached it together, gazing up to see where the green arch of its bronze tyre had come loose. The ruin of the Iron House loomed over them. Their eyes fixed on the wheel. The end of the axle showed the cracks and rings of the vast tree it had once been. The red spokes radiating up from it were whole, but many of those below had shattered. The massive rim had cracked in two places so that it now folded in like lips of a mouth in which the spoke stumps were uneven teeth. Gold discs studded the rim, which Carnelian knew must represent the cities of the Ringwall. Gazing at this immense, broken wheelmap, then glancing back at the Osrakum hub thrown away, half-buried in the red mud, he could not help feeling this was some kind of omen for the Commonwealth.

As if speaking to him, another of the spokes snapped, causing the wheel to fold in on itself a little more. Fern pulled him away as, with a hideous grating, the chariot slid towards them, shedding panels of iron. Stumbling, Fern fell with Carnelian almost on top of him. They gaped up. They flinched as panels clattered to the ground, right and left. Then the sombre stillness of the scene returned and the rain hiss. They rose, still gazing up uncertainly at the Iron House.

Fern was the first to walk away. Carnelian followed him, glancing at the bloody sky over the pale horizon formed by the edge of the road. Night was nearing: they needed to find a place to sleep. Fern was heading towards a strangely textured green ramp leaning up against the road. As Carnelian neared it, he became aware of the huge upside-down face embossed into the verdigrised slope of copper. The face smiled up at the black sky, surrounded by a halo of curls and spirals. He knew this thing. It was the Twins' fallen standard. He remembered the hope it had given him that morning. He watched Fern reach up to touch its spiralled edge and, though he could not see his face, Carnelian saw the slump in the shoulders and dread rose in him that Fern was remembering the ferngardens of the Koppie. Fern ducked under the standard and disappeared into the gloom beneath it. Carnelian stood for a while, unable to focus his emotions. He glanced west, where the sun was making a bloody end to a bloody day, then he followed his friend.

In the cavern beneath the standard, Carnelian could hear Fern struggling for breath. Rain drummed upon the copper roof and some dim red light oozed in, but they were in a place separate from the world; safe from it. Listening to Fern's struggle for air, Carnelian at first chose to believe it a reaction to all the death outside. He told himself he was too numb to care, but the sound was stirring up panic in him. He moved towards Fern's barely defined shape, wanting, fearing to touch him. As he came closer, the sound Fern was making was like a cough, as if he were trying to rid his lungs of smoke. The strained wheezing was pulling Carnelian apart. He reached out. At his touch, Fern began sobbing. The grief in that sound sent cracks through Carnelian's frozen heart. Each shudder in Fern's body brought them closer. Carnelian felt his own grief spilling out, racking his whole frame. They collided and clung to each other as the grief overflowed. They sobbed for all their mothers, for all their fathers, for the children, for the Tribe and for love lost and the suffering of the world that was their own and for the dead forming the hills of the earth. Clutching each other so hard helped to squeeze out the poison and the tears. In the pressure of Fern's arms, Carnelian felt he was being forgiven and he abandoned himself to forgiveness; forgiving all those others, forgiving himself. He was not the sky, nor the earth. He was nothing more consequential than a blown leaf. He was too small a thing to be responsible for all the suffering, to be the reason for it. The forces of the world shaped him; were not shaped by him. Carnelian drew Fern against him, wanting him to feel that too; feel the pain drain away. The heat in their bodies awoke a fire in them. Amidst so much death there was a need to assert the flame of their lives. For them both, it was a miracle to explore each other's body by touch. The warmed brass around Fern's neck. The scar about Carnelian's. Fern's fire scars. His four-fingered hands upon Carnelian. Warm tears on cheeks lubricated the turning of their faces to each other. Lips guiding them to that first kiss. The world forgotten. Breathing love names. Though Carnelian was the younger, it was Fern who was like a boy. They fell into their own joined flesh, both lost and found.

MURDEROUS GRIEF

Which mother can forgive the killing of her children?
(Quyan fragment)

Carnelian woke suddenly and, for a moment, struggled in the riptide of the wave that was about to engulf him. Breath in his ear made him aware of Fern, warm in his arms. Thin grey light leaking in under the eaves of the fallen standard allowed Carnelian to see him. He gazed in wonder, remembering the night's frantic lovemaking. With his eyes closed, Fern was as beautiful as a child and Carnelian was loath to wake him. He lay back, adjusting his spine, feeling the ache from having lain all night upon the unforgiving earth, his shoulder numb under Fern, but he did not care about the discomfort, only the delicious weight pressing down on him.

He became aware of the barrelling python of the Black God's lower lip curving its grimace away off towards the eaves. He could see the curling rim of the upper lip, the nostrils, a suggestion of the glaring eyes. On the outer surface of the roof, rain was drumming on the Green God's copper face. Carnelian reached his hand up to touch the metal. Its delicate vibrations transferred through his arm to his back, setting off the first shivers of the feeling from the sound of rain.

Reality seeped into his thoughts. A harsh reality. Osidian had survived the battle. Such a victory could only serve to engorge his mad devotion to his god. There was no hiding from him, nor could he hope to hide from him what Fern and he had become. Not that he would have tried to do so. The rippling shivering down his back became trembling for a moment as he feared what Osidian might do to his beloved. Carnelian wished he was confident he could protect him. Crazed notions of flight flitted through his mind. He dismissed them all as fantasy. In all the wide world, there was no place he and Fern could hide. Osidian would have to be confronted. Carnelian ground his teeth, feeling how deeply anchored in him was his determination to protect his lover, or die trying.

He tensed. The rain had stopped and he was certain he could hear the scrabble of aquar claws on stone. Already? Of course it was obvious Osidian must pass here on his way to Osrakum. Fern was still asleep. It would be better not to wake him until he knew what was going on. Gently, Carnelian pulled his arm free. Fern sighed, but did not wake. Carnelian sat up, grimacing at the ache in his back, pulling his arm across his chest, rubbing some feeling into it. His legs ached too and barely supported him as he rose, then tottered towards the triangle of light. Nearing this, his skin became so bright it forced him to squint. He glanced back and saw Fern lying brown in the shadow of the eaves. There was nothing with which to cover their nakedness. Carnelian cocked an ear to listen. The sound of claws had ceased. Was that a mutter of voices? He wished he had had the foresight to bring some weapon. If the Law still held sway, his face unmasked might be weapon enough. He dismissed a pang of guilt at the deaths he might cause. So many had died already, what were a few more? Was he becoming callous? He quenched his doubt by telling himself that none now could claim to be innocent of killing.

Keeping close to the side of the road, which rose like a wall, he edged out into the rain. He was already drenched by the time he reached the ramp that climbed to the road. He paused to listen again. He could definitely hear voices speaking with the lilt of Vulgate. By their tone they could not be Masters.

Auxiliaries, perhaps? Whoever they were, it was likely they would be terrified by the sudden appearance of a Master. He could not imagine they would dare disobey him. He could get an aquar from them, perhaps two, and something for him and Fern to wear.

Vaulting onto the ramp, he began climbing it. As he came up onto the road, he saw three aquar turned away from him, their riders gazing up at the Iron House. For a moment he too was lost regarding its vast bulk, black and ominous against a grey sky. Then he raised his voice. 'Attend me.'

The aquar whirled round, but it was Carnelian who was surprised: the riders showed no fear, but simply stared at him. He resolved one face and was shocked to recognize his House tattoo. Before he could see anything more, the aquar began folding their legs. Their riders sprang out even before the creatures had fully sunk to the road. One of the saddle-chairs had two riders, the smaller of which came running towards him.

His heart leapt. 'Poppy!'

She stopped short, in some confusion, no doubt because he was naked. Two men with chameleons across their faces approached. He spoke their names: 'Tain, Keal.' Looking at the three of them, he acknowledged to himself that there was more to family than blood.

His brothers were unfastening their cloaks and, as they neared him, held them up. He allowed them to wrap him in one, while all the time they talked excitedly, Carnie this and Carnie that, but he was too stunned by their sudden appearance to be able to listen to what they were saying. When he was clothed, Poppy ran at him and he embraced her, laughing as joy came upon him that he was indeed among family. All of them were talking at once. They were asking him if the plan they had kludged together with Fern had actually worked; describing how frantic they had been when he too had disappeared; telling Carnelian what they had witnessed of the terrible battle; of the shock of seeing the God's chariot burn; about the desperate hope that had brought them out from the camp that morning to seek for him and Fern among the wounded and the dead. Unable to respond to this flood, Carnelian beamed at them, until his smile caught on their faces and they were all grinning at each other like idiots.

He noticed a figure standing outside their group. It was Krow, gazing at him with an uncertain smile on his face, wanting to come forward, but unsure if it was his place.

'It's good to see you, Krow.'

The lad beamed and Poppy turned to him, grinning. She offered him her hand. 'What're you doing over there?'

Krow allowed himself to be drawn towards Carnelian. 'You're family too,' he said and smiled when Krow sank his head.

'And Fern?' said Poppy, anxiously.

Carnelian glanced down at the green roof of the fallen standard, for a moment mesmerized by the oblique grin of the God, then saw a figure coming up the ramp. Poppy had spotted him already and went to meet him, taking Tain's cloak. Fern was glad to throw it round himself, then stooped to kiss her. When he straightened, his eyes found Carnelian's and they grinned at each other, shyly, embarrassed by their arousal. Becoming aware the others were staring at them, Carnelian broke the link with Fern and laughed, and they all laughed with him.

The questioning resumed and Carnelian allowed Fern to answer them so that he could feast on their faces, his heart overbrimming with love for them all. Keal, who had wandered back to his aquar, was now returning with something glinting in his hand. He offered Carnelian the thing he was carrying. 'Father thought you might need this.'

Carnelian took the mask, turning it to see its face. He frowned. It was with a strange sense of dislocation he recognized it as the face his father had worn during their exile. Though, of course, his father was not really his father. Anger rose in him. Such thoughts were a betrayal. He lifted the hollow face up. Out of loyalty and with a desire to prove

625

his love for his father, almost he put it on, but then he let his hand fall. 'I will not wear this.'

He saw with what sombre faces they were watching him. 'I've no need of it. We're all family here.'

His smile and words lit them all up. At that moment the rain, which had slackened to a drizzle, turned heavy once more. Carnelian became aware of a dull rumble of thunder, then realized he was feeling it through his feet and saw that the others could feel it too.

The monster appeared from behind the Iron House, Marula riders eddying around its feet. Even with rain driving into their eyes, Carnelian and Fern both recognized Heart-of-Thunder, his chimneys sputtering smoke.

'Stand your ground,' Carnelian said to his family as the monster came closer, its flame-pipes swinging towards them so they could look up into their throats. Each thunderous footfall rattled their teeth.

There was a determined look in Fern's face. Carnelian knew Fern would not part from him, even if it cost him his life. Carnelian felt a fierce pride in him. When he grinned, Fern grinned back and they turned to face Osidian together.

One last shudder as the monster dropped a leg. Then the hawsers tightened on its upper horns and the monster lifted the prow of its beak and came to a halt, leaving them in its rain shadow. Carnelian looked up at the topmost tier of its tower. He was certain it was Osidian sitting there gazing down at them, but he was as hidden by the ivory screen as if masked.

'His fires are out,' said Fern.

Carnelian saw that smoke had stopped rising from Heart-of-Thunder's chimneys. A familiar rattle made him glance round to see the brassman being lowered. A figure scurrying out to its end released the rope ladder. Even as this unwound, a larger shape was crossing the brassman and soon descending. As this

Master reached the road, he raised his hand in a command and Carnelian saw the Marula around the trunks of Heart-of-Thunder's legs retiring. He was glad so many had survived the battle. As the Master approached, Carnelian could feel his father's mask in his hand. He resisted a compulsion to put it on, determined he would confront Osidian barefaced. 'I shall try to talk to him in Vulgate, Fern.'

Osidian came so close Carnelian felt certain he was going to touch him. The desire seemed there in Osidian's gloved hands. 'I thought I'd lost you.'

'You have,' said Carnelian, still finding it hard to believe Osidian was his brother.

Osidian's mask turned to Fern standing beside him. As it lingered, the menace of its imperious face seemed to intensify. Glancing at Fern, Carnelian saw his rising anger.

'You've won, then,' he said to Osidian.

The mask stayed fixed on Fern a moment longer, then turned to Carnelian. 'You have no mask, my Lord?'

Carnelian felt the Quya like a threat. He raised his father's mask so that Osidian could see it. 'I no longer feel I want to hide behind a mask,' he said in Vulgate.

'But the Law . . .' Osidian's voice sounded softer in Vulgate so that Carnelian was certain he could hear some doubt in it.

'You— we shattered the Law there upon that battlefield.'

Osidian half glanced round as if he could only bear to look upon it with a single eye.

'Did you cause that carnage merely to restore things to the way they were?'

Osidian's mask turned back, but he gave no answer.

'You must make a new Law.'

Osidian regarded the Iron House. 'I must know beyond doubt my victory is complete.'

'Do you seek your brother's body?'

'We must recover all our Chosen dead.'

Carnelian remembered the Master he and Fern had seen

627

lying dead on the battlefield, unmasked, sartlar staring down at him. 'The commanders too?'

'I have already set the Lesser Chosen that task.'

Carnelian glanced towards the battlefield, where he could see the ridges of the dead and, for a moment, he imagined the Lesser Chosen commanders seeking the Lords, dead in their towers. Gathering those bodies was not a task they could delegate to their minions.

Osidian was beckoning the Marula. Carnelian watched him. There was a disturbing stillness about him and no sign of the elation he had expected. 'You wish to bind the Lesser Chosen to your cause by miring them with the blood of your victory?' he said, wishing to probe behind Osidian's impassive exterior.

'And to keep them occupied while I negotiate with the Wise and the Great,' said Osidian, who was gazing off towards the Iron House.

Carnelian could see the strategic sense of it. 'What did you offer them yesterday to have them stand down?'

'Blood from my own House.'

'And they are to bring the dead they salvage here?'

Osidian gave a distracted nod. Carnelian saw his intention: Osidian would gather all the Powers here, so that he might negotiate terms with them within sight of his victory over them. Carnelian was reminded of Osidian standing astride the ravener he had slain and of the power that had given him over the Ochre – and how, ultimately, he had used that power.

Carnelian's stream of thought was muddied by the approach of the summoned Marula. They were Oracles, among whom was Morunasa. There was malice in the glance the man gave him, but also fear. Clearly, Morunasa had never imagined he would see Carnelian again. Did he fear that Carnelian had told Osidian that it was Morunasa who had let them go? Osidian was telling Morunasa and the other Oracles that they must find a way into the Iron House. He was indicating where the drawbridge stair was slightly ajar and how they might enter that way.

'Bring me all the bodies you find in there.'

As they watched Morunasa and the other Oracles moving away, Carnelian was frowning. 'There will be a lot of bodies.'

Osidian turned on him. 'How could you know that?'

'Before the battle I was there with Molochite.'

Carnelian sensed Osidian wanted to know more. He frowned, haunted, imagining the interior of the Iron House. 'All the children.'

'Children?' Osidian's voice betrayed the first colourings of emotion.

Carnelian explained how Molochite had with him the children of the Great, presumably as hostages for the good behaviour of their fathers commanding in the battle. As he did so he saw a rigor taking over Osidian's body.

'You did not know?'

Osidian seemed lifeless.

While they brought Heart-of-Thunder up towards the door of the Iron House, Carnelian described to Osidian something of his time there. He was not sure Osidian was listening and it seemed he was not, for he said nothing when Carnelian fell silent. As its keeper kept the dragon still, Marula scrambled up its horns and onto its head, and from there managed to clamber up into the open gap of the drawbridge stair and so gain entry into the Iron House. Some time later, the chains began to be paid out and the stair, jerkily, fell, until one corner of it clanged into the stone of the road.

The first corpse to be brought out from the black maw of the Iron House was that of a sybling pair. The Marula carrying the dead twins leaned away from them, as if they feared some contamination. Though blackened, it was clear the syblings were male. Carnelian was relieved it was not the Quenthas. When a second sybling pair was carried down, Morunasa came ahead, to report the stairs within the Iron House choked with bodies. Carnelian and Osidian hardly heard him, focused as they were on the dead syblings. Curling in on each other, they held within their embrace the body of the Chosen infant they had been trying to protect. Soon more small bodies were being brought out and laid upon the stone. Once beautiful children, blackened, but unburnt, faces scrunched up, eyes slivers, mouths opened as if singing. Some of the small bodies clung to each other so desperately they were brought out by the Marula as knots of limbs. The warriors frowned carrying them, putting them down as if they were glass.

Carnelian became trapped in looking from face to face. When he tore his eyes away, he saw Poppy gazing at the dead children with a rapt expression, as if she was listening to something they were saying. He became aware Osidian was unmasking. His face, revealed, seemed weathered marble in the rain. He was muttering something.

'What?' Carnelian asked.

'I thought I had already paid the price for victory.'

This stung Carnelian to anger. 'What exactly did you pay?'

Osidian gazed at him, pale, wild-eyed. 'They will blame this on me.'

'And why should they not?' Carnelian said and his anger turned to despair. His own hands were not clean of this.

The flow of children ceased at the same time as the rain. As the Marula penetrated the upper levels of the Iron House, Carnelian and the others were left to stand guard upon the dead. Then the Iron House began to disgorge more corpses. Chosen and syblings, their gorgeous armour and robes stained black with their faces and limbs, some clutching at their throats as if seeking to strangle themselves. Their jewels now seemed tainted tomb goods.

Then Carnelian saw them bringing out a body sheathed in dull silver. As he approached it, he saw Osidian was already there watching it being put down. Molochite's beautiful, cruel face was distorted by a grimace that combined horror and surprise. Osidian gazed down upon his brother, eyes wide and bleak. Carnelian looked from one face to the other, marvelling at how alike they were. He recalled how much his own features resembled theirs, and why. He too looked down at a dead brother, but was glad to find he felt nothing but disgust. Turning back to Osidian, he saw his gaze transforming to a staring panic. He tried in vain to gauge the cause in the sight before him, then realized it was not what Osidian was seeing, but what he was not seeing. The face that had been hidden behind the Masks during the Apotheosis emitted no light. It was the face of a dead man, not a dead god.

Osidian pulled away and clutched hold of a Maruli whom Carnelian recognized, with shock and distracted relief, as Sthax. Osidian shook him. 'Where is it? Tell me now!'

Sthax tried to shake his head and opened his mouth, so that Carnelian feared the Maruli might be about to give himself away by speaking in Vulgate, but suddenly Osidian cast him aside. Morunasa was there, trying to calm Osidian, who began rattling out some command. Morunasa listened to him for a while, nodding, then barked an order to one of his men. Carnelian saw his family witnessing how close Osidian seemed to madness. At last two Marula warriors approached him opening their hands. He looked down with horror at what they were offering him. Shards of what appeared to be green ice. Pieces of jade. Osidian plucked these from the black hands and frantically seemed to be attempting to join them together. Then with an eruption of rage, he cast the pieces to the ground. Some shattered into smaller fragments, or skittered over the paving. A single piece came to rest near Carnelian's foot. He stooped to pick it up. Its translucence was like the sun through leaves. His finger felt its sinuous curve. It was the bridge of a nose and twin prongs of cheek and brow that had enclosed the hollow of an eyeslit. A piece of the Jade Mask. Through that gap, God Emperors had looked out upon their perfect world for a thousand years.

Carnelian glanced up as if woken. Fern was looking away from the Iron House towards Osrakum. There, coming along the road, were mirrored palanquins. The Wise. Osidian was tying on his mask with clumsy fingers, like a child hoping to conceal from a returning parent something he had broken.

Three Grand Sapients emerged from the mirror palanquins. Upon high ranga they stood, forbidding, their long faces of silver crowned with crescent moons. Each had a homunculus before him holding the staff of his Domain.

'We greet you, Lord of the Three Lands,' the homunculi chorused.

Osidian inclined his head a little to each in turn. 'My Lord Tribute, my Lord Cities, my Lord Law.'

'We would speak to you privately,' said Law, through his homunculus.

'None here can comprehend our tongue, save for the Lord Suth, and I would have him by my side, for this victory is as much his doing as mine.'

Carnelian glanced at Osidian, unsure if he was being given a share in the glory or the blame.

'Suth Carnelian is unmasked,' shrilled the homunculus.

'Recently the Law has been much disobeyed,' said Osidian with something of his old defiance.

The homunculi muttered an echo. Then Cities' fingers began to flex around his voice's throat. 'And for that very reason does the Commonwealth stand in peril of dissolution.'

'My Lords are as guilty of this as any here.'

'We do not deny it, Celestial,' said Tribute. 'We come not to make recriminations, but to help you restore the Commonwealth.'

'The legions that survive must return to their fortresses,' said Cities.

'The Seraphim must return to within the sanctity of the Sacred Wall,' said Tribute.

'You must resume your place at the centre of the world,' said Law.

Osidian stood very still. 'It is not for the conquered to dictate terms to their conqueror.'

'Celestial,' said Tribute, 'we do not deny your right to rule, but if you are to have anything to rule over, then you must allow us to re-establish order.'

Osidian's hands crushed to fists. 'I will not submit to the Balance.'

'And yet, a balance there must be,' said Law.

Osidian's hands opened. 'Yes.'

'We must recover the dead.'

Osidian nodded.

'Has the God Emperor been found?' asked Law.

As Osidian indicated where his brother lay, Law freed one of his cloven hands and gestured some quick commands. Ammonites poured forward so that, very quickly, Carnelian could no longer see Molochite at all as they wound him into a cocoon of green silk.

Law's hand returned to move at the throat of his homunculus. 'Even if we are to consider the Law suspended for the moment, to have any of the Seraphim exposed thus to animal eyes is folly; to have a consecrated God Emperor thus displayed is madness.' The homunculus swept a hand to take in the people round about. 'All these should be destroyed.'

Carnelian tensed, careful to avoid glancing in the direction in which he had sent his family off the road for fear of the Wise. He relaxed a little when he saw Osidian making a clear gesture of negation. 'All here are of my household or of that of the Lord Suth. I will allow none to be executed.'

'Is it possible, Celestial, you do not realize how much this diminishes you?'

Osidian chopped an angry gesture: *Enough!*

Silence fell, then Tribute's fingers came alive again. 'Have measures been taken to recover the dead from the battle-field?'

Osidian's head had sunk so that his mask seemed to be contemplating the crack where two slabs in the road met. Seeing he was not going to answer, Carnelian spoke for him. 'The legionary commanders have been instructed to bring them here.'

'Who else has been recovered from the Iron House?' said Cities' homunculus.

'The children of the Great, syblings and others of the court.'

'No sign then of our colleagues who counselled the God Emperor?'

Carnelian shook his head.

'Perhaps you will help me search, Suth Carnelian?' said the homunculus.

Carnelian glanced at Osidian, still staring at the ground, then up at Cities' blank silver face. He was not going to be able to stop the Wise conversing with Osidian alone. 'As my Lord wishes.'

The Grand Sapient released the neck of his homunculus, who turned to place the Domain staff in his master's left hand, then clasped the right. Together, Carnelian, Cities and the homunculus began moving towards where the bodies were laid out on the road. Looking again upon the faces of the dead children, Carnelian forgot everything else and was only woken from his sombre survey by the homunculus crying out. As it pulled its master off along the line of dead, Carnelian followed them. The corpse of the Grand Sapient lying on the road might have been long-withered. There was another beside it and, further along the line, beyond some ammonites, a third.

Standing before the first, Cities knelt, using his staff as a support. His homunculus guided his fingers to the corpse. The cloven hand touched the skull head, then rose, hesitating. The hand presented itself to the homunculus, who also hesitated. It shaped a command and the homunculus peeled off the glove. The hand, naked, seemed opaque glass. It fell gently upon the

634

face of the dead Grand Sapient, moving with painful delicacy down to feel the glyphs tattooed in a ring around the root of the missing ear. Cities gave the slightest nod, then rose and allowed himself to be guided to the next corpse. There he knelt again, to repeat the procedure. Another nod. This time he had to have help to rise, and leaned upon his homunculus as they moved to the final corpse. Cities knelt for a third time. His fingers tracing down the rucked skin around the eyepit with its jade stone began to tremble as they reached the ear root. There, they shook so much, the Grand Sapient was unable to read the tattoos. He released his hold on his staff, removed the glove from his left hand, then brought them both back to the skull head. Steadying his right hand with his left, he felt the side of the head, then collapsed onto the body.

The homunculus turned to Carnelian, stiff with panic. A hissing was coming from the prostrate Grand Sapient. A hissing that swelled into a harsh, tearing sound. The homunculus ran back to where the other two Grand Sapients were still standing before Osidian. Carnelian's gaze returned to Cities who, back rounded and convulsing, seemed to be choking. Carnelian knelt beside him, tears starting in his eyes at the man's grief. He looked in wonder at the Grand Sapient's body being racked by the strange sobbing. At first he thought the mourning was for the passing of what were perhaps the most ancient creatures in the world, but then he realized it was this corpse alone that had provoked Cities' prostration and he wondered whether, despite the detachment cultivated by the Wise, this was perhaps some kind of love. Through shared fate, their passing together through the ages, was it not possible some Sapients became like brothers? Or perhaps this was a father with his son, or a son mourning the death of his father? And moved by the thought, Carnelian stretched out to touch the grieving man.

Cities' homunculus returned with ammonites and they drove Carnelian away from their master. He walked back towards

Osidian, brooding over loss. As he came closer, he saw him watching the ammonites tending to Cities.

'He mourns his fallen colleague,' Carnelian said and was aware of Tribute's and Law's homunculi murmuring so that he knew their masters heard his words.

Some moments later Osidian gave a slight nod, as if he had only just registered what Carnelian had said. 'We have been negotiating my Apotheosis. It shall be held in seven days' time. They have kept the tributaries waiting in the City at the Gates. Tribute's primary concern is that the awe of witnessing my ascension should replace what they have seen of our disunity and strife. He hopes that thus, at least for the moment, the outer ring of the Commonwealth will hold without need of further intervention.'

The murmuring of the homunculi continued a while and then fell suddenly silent.

'Celestial, the sartlar must be sent back to the Land,' said Tribute.

Osidian turned to the Grand Sapients. 'Will this avoid the cities being visited by famine?'

'With rationing it can be hoped they will suffer little degradation.'

'And the sartlar?' Carnelian asked.

The two Grand Sapients stood motionless long after their homunculi had completed their echoing of Carnelian. Then Law's fingers stirred, causing his homunculus to sing out: 'They will starve in vast numbers.'

Carnelian frowned, trying to accustom himself to the weight of responsibility he would bear for that. He glanced towards the battlefield. At least those had died quickly. Hunger was a cruel killer.

'The legions must return to their fortresses, Celestial. They will be needed to quell disturbances among the sartlar.'

Carnelian felt crushed by this new prophecy of disaster.

Osidian was nodding. He raised his head. 'Six legions shall remain here to herd them away from Osrakum.'

'As you wish, Celestial,' said Tribute.

Law's homunculus gazed at them. 'And now we must haste back to Osrakum. We have all been too long exposed to the pollution out here.'

Carnelian looked around him, weak with relief at the thought of fleeing all this destruction and death. In his mind's eye he saw the ordered perfection of Osrakum and yearned for it. At the same time he was ashamed of these feelings. How easily he was allowing himself to think like a Master. How easy it would be to wash his hands of the holocaust he had helped to bring about, then go safely behind Osrakum's mountain wall, where the disaster that was to come would be hidden from his eyes.

Following the direction of his thoughts, his gaze had drifted north towards Osrakum. He became aware of a darkness creeping towards them along the road. Palanquins. Hundreds and hundreds of them. The Chosen were coming to gather their dead.

The first ranks of palanquins disgorged Masters the colours of butterflies. Their iridescent robes and the sunlight hue of their masks spilled glorious summer out over the grey, puddled road. Carnelian pulled the hood of his brother's cloak further over his face, peering down its tunnel at this alien spectacle as their bright flood left the palanquins behind and approached, Masters towering above their tyadra. Osidian was lifting his hand, holding it aloft to form gestures of command. *Come alone.*

The Masters left their guardsmen behind and continued to advance on their ranga, their gait measured as they passed along the rows of children, their masks glancing at the dead faces, the sight of which only seemed to quicken their approach.

Carnelian dropped his head as they drew closer, for a moment seeing nothing but the shimmer of their silks, the glitter of their jewels. They slowed as they neared Osidian, trailing their sleeves in the filth of the road as they made obeisance, their greetings of 'Celestial' like a whisper of breeze. And in the midst of their pomp Osidian was a spindle of shadow, seeming more a part of the angry sky than anything to do with the mundanity below.

He addressed them, his Quya ringing through their ranks, telling them that, of their Ruling Lords, perhaps only eighty had perished, but that the rest lived still and had accepted him as their master and, further, that he had confirmed the new rights his brother had gifted them. Even if Carnelian had not given half his attention to this speech, he would have known these were only the Lesser Chosen, for he was now watching the approach of a more sombre procession. In more autumnal splendour, the Great were filing out of the raft of palanquins and coming on in stately gravity. Slowly they approached the dead laid out upon the road and, though Carnelian watched for a change in their demeanour as they realized these were their children, they did not flinch, but moved along the rows, searching, with as much decorum as if they were appreciating a display of lilies. Suddenly, one raised a hand, throwing a gesture back towards the waiting guardsmen that stirred up a commotion among them. Other hands began rising, their fine bones obscured by the linen of the ritual wrappings, some seeming to tremble a little, perhaps, so that Carnelian felt a tightening around his eyes, recognizing in that little sign what grief was tearing at their hearts. They might be Masters and of the Great, but they were fathers too and these stiff and sodden corpses on the stone were their children.

Servants filtering through the guardsmen were creeping towards their Masters, their steps slowing, faltering as they drew closer to them. Falling at last to the wet road upon their knees so gingerly it seemed they feared to bruise its stone. Cowering at their Masters' feet, they received instructions. Some produced blades with which they made cuts beneath their eyes so that down their cheeks began to trickle blood tears. Their Masters allowed their cloaks and outer robes to be removed. The servants bore these to where their Masters pointed and the servants began wrapping the dead children in these borrowed shrouds. Watching this, Osidian and the Lesser Chosen Lords had fallen silent. Only when the servants were carrying the shrouded children back to the palanquins did the Great turn towards Osidian and, slowly, they advanced on him. As they drew nearer, the Lesser Chosen Lords, bowing their heads, moved aside and the Great came on like ships under sail. Among the palanquins, Carnelian could see the dead children in their silk cocoons being stowed away.

When the Great were close enough for Carnelian to see the glimmer of their eyes behind the perfect gold faces of their masks, they came to a halt, and for a moment they regarded Osidian with serene malice before one, then all, bowed before him.

'Great Lords,' Osidian said, his voice lacking its customary power, 'those of your Houses that served under my brother are most likely also perished. Even now the commanders from the Lesser Chosen seek their bodily remains.' Osidian made an unnecessary gesture indicating the battlefield behind him. 'When they bring them here, we shall all return to Osrakum.'

Carnelian's attention was pulled in the direction of the palanquins by a commotion there among the guardsmen. As he watched, a fanblade rose, then fell. All the way along their line, weapons were being used. Carnelian became aware of things rolling, of dark stains swelling, joining into streams that swirled into the rain-puddles, reddening them. He grew cold with anger. The slaves who had carried the dead to the palanquins were being slaughtered. One knelt, then his head, severed, rolled; his trunk, collapsing, sprayed blood upon the feet and legs of the guardsmen round him. The slaves had looked upon the faces of the children of the Great. Though their crime merited only blinding, their Masters were not feeling merciful.

Carnelian gazed upon the Great, who seemed impassive

even though their people were butchering each other. This was how they had chosen to show their grief. Further, he realized, this was how they had chosen to display their displeasure to Osidian even as they paid him homage.

'My Apotheosis shall be held in seven days' time,' Osidian said.

As the Great again bowed to him, Carnelian felt in his marrow that it was Osidian who was the true author of this theatre. Had he displayed the dead children deliberately so as to give the Great an easy opportunity to vent their grief upon their slaves, in the hope of turning their rage away from him?

Carnelian pulled his cowl down further over his face as one of the Great approached him.

'You are Suth Carnelian returned?' the Master said.

Carnelian raised his hand in a gesture of affirmation.

'I am Opalid, of your House.'

Carnelian remembered meeting this Lord a few times. He recalled also that he was the son of Spinel, who had recently usurped Sardian's place in House Suth. Opalid's serene, forbidding face of gold turned to the dead children. 'My own son lies there.'

The gold mask then surveyed the battlefield. 'I wait for them to bring me my father's corpse.' The golden lips and dark eye slits swung back towards Carnelian. 'The same price have I paid as the others of the Great, but yet, unlike them, I am not to have the compensation of rising to the ruling of my House.'

His bitter tone stung Carnelian, who wished to find words to deflect the man's grief, to tell him he did not wish to assume the power Opalid felt was his due, to confess the possibility that he would soon die in Osrakum, but he was trapped in a maze of guilt, anger and confusion. 'I am sorry you are in pain, Opalid.'

The Master seemed to pull back. 'Spare me your pity, my

Lord. You are like your father. Do you think your blood justifies your absence any more than it did his? Your lineage is either in exile or else you seek to rule from a sickbed. For a generation you have permitted the power of our House to wane in the councils of the Great.'

He snapped his fingers in a gesture of contempt. 'But why should that surprise me when this weakness saps even our coomb. If I had risen to rule, I would quickly beat the ancient discipline into our slaves; cease this disgusting consorting with them that makes us an object of ridicule among those of our peers who should fear us. How shall you rule, my Lord?'

The Master's rant had freed Carnelian. 'You seem to forget, my Lord, our Ruling Lord still lives.'

'No doubt as the . . . the favourite of the new Gods you expect to bring great power to our House?'

'Enough,' snapped Carnelian. He sensed Opalid resisting an instinct to bow. 'Is my father here?'

'So that he might savour my grief?'

Carnelian grew weary of the confrontation. 'You little know him if you imagine he would delight in your pain. Please, just tell me if you know if he is here.'

'Not as far as I am aware, my Lord.'

'Perhaps he was too weak to make the journey,' Carnelian muttered, his heart growing heavy with concern.

'Yes, my Lord, it shall not be long before you wear the Ruling Ring.'

Carnelian stared at the Master, amazed, wondering if it were possible that he really believed what he was implying. It seemed Opalid's grief might be more for himself than for his fallen father, perhaps even than for his child. 'I wish to be alone, my Lord.'

Opalid hesitated, then began a bow, terminated it abruptly and, off-balance, moved away. As he watched him, Carnelian froze. He was all that stood between Opalid and the ruling of House Suth. He could not bear the thought of his family at the mercy of such a man, but, as things were, Carnelian knew his chances of surviving long enough to thwart Opalid were slim.

Carnelian found Osidian with Morunasa and several syblings watching some dragons on the road approaching from the south. No doubt they were bringing the corpses of the Ruling Lords they had salvaged from the battlefield. He felt a pang of urgency. 'I am going to return to Molochite's camp, my Lord.'

Osidian's mask turned to regard him.

'To seek my father.'

'Take Earth-is-Strong.'

'What danger could the camp hold?'

'None if you take the huimur.'

Carnelian realized there would be other advantages to complying. 'Is she close by?'

'Not very far. I kept her close to me during the battle.' He indicated the gutted mass of the Iron House. 'In the attack on that, her pipes were second only to mine.'

Carnelian wondered why Osidian had told him that. He disliked being reminded of the way the children had died. Was his real reason for seeking his father to escape the scene of so much death?

'Take the Quenthas with you.'

Carnelian looked round and saw, with relief and joy, that among the syblings nearby were the sisters who had been his companions at court. Their heads came up, grief hardening their faces. There was shock in Right-Quentha's eyes at seeing his naked face. He needed to know Osidian's intentions. 'What is it that you fear, Celestial?'

Osidian laughed in a way that to Carnelian sounded un-natural. 'What have I to fear now? Take them. I give them to you. They themselves confessed to me how they disobeyed my brother.'

Carnelian had to defend them. 'To save me.'

'And for that I am grateful but, having once betrayed the

trust of one God Emperor, how can I be certain they will not betray another?'

Carnelian glanced at the sisters and saw how pale Right-Quentha looked, how both sisters lowered their heads, inclining them towards each other.

'If you do not take them, they shall have to be destroyed.'

Carnelian saw that the sisters did not flinch at this threat. 'I shall be glad to have them with me if that is their wish.'

Right-Quentha glanced up at him, in her sad eyes acceptance of their fate. He felt their shame and wished he could tell them that, in truth, he too was of the House of the Masks, so that there was no dishonour in serving him, but he could not speak and, as he walked away, the sisters followed him.

'How was Grane blinded?'

His brothers, Poppy and Krow stared past him. Carnelian glanced round at the syblings. Right-Quentha was countering their stares with proud aloofness. Her sister's tattooed face bore an uncertain frown. Carnelian turned back to his family. 'These are the Quenthas, right and left. They saved my life' – he glanced at Fern, who was nodding – 'and, henceforth, are part of our household.'

He looked into every face to make certain everyone understood he wanted the sisters welcomed. All concurred. Only Fern's gaze did not soften, disturbed beneath his troubled brow; he was concerned not at all with the syblings, but only with Carnelian. They needed to talk, but this was not the time.

'Grane's eyes?' he said to Keal.

His brother began a shrug. 'While Father still ruled, Grane was his steward.' His mouth tightened. 'When they stole the power away from Father, the new master had Grane flogged, then blinded.'

Tain's eyes flashed. 'Spinel removed his mask in front of him!'

Carnelian caught his meaning. Spinel had done the same to Grane as had Jaspar to Tain on the road to Osrakum. Grane had been used to make clear to Sardian and the rest of the House exactly who was now master. Carnelian could see in his brothers' faces something of what they had had to endure in the subsequent years of Spinel's rule.

Tain's smile startled Carnelian. 'But everything will change, now you're back, Carnie.'

Carnelian's first reaction was anger. Almost he reprimanded him for his dangerous familiarity. But, realizing his anger was really fear, he let it go. He could not bear their hope, for it was sure to founder in bitter disappointment. Desperation rose at the thought they might spend the rest of their lives under Opalid's tyranny.

A tremor in the ground steadied him. Another. Up on the road a dragon was approaching. With relief he recognized Earth-is-Strong and he threw himself into getting his family up into the safety of her tower.

Carnelian ran his hands down the smooth arms of the command chair. He found some reassurance in its familiar feel, in having his Left and Right in their places awaiting his commands. He glanced round and saw his family crammed against the cabin walls, safe for the moment. Poppy and Krow leaning together, his brothers staring blindly, Fern with his knees drawn up to his chest, head lolling. Carnelian's gaze lingered on his lover, recalling the feel of that wiry head, tasting again the sweetness of their lovemaking. This was too soon soured by confusion, anger, fear. Why had he been so weak as to start a relationship that he knew was certain to end in loss?

Carnelian turned back to look through the screen out over the abandoned Twenty-Legion Camp. He remembered its roar and power, but now only rain knifed across its bleak, littered, empty spaces. Nothing of the host of beasts and men was left but their tracks in the churned-up mud.

He could not help still thinking of this man lying upon silk and leathers, like something assembled from bird bones, as his father. Carnelian saw him through tears. A commotion out in the camp made him turn away, worried about his people. He focused on what he was there for. In the light of the single lamp, it was clear how much Grane had changed, yet Carnelian could see the brother he remembered in the ruin that remained. Grane's ravaged face seemed a warning of what could happen if Carnelian should be unable to become the Ruling Lord of their House.

'He must be woken, Grane.'

His brother's mouth twisted, lips thin like an old man's. 'We've been unable to wake him since he collapsed.'

Carnelian heard the tone of bitter accusation. Collapsed when, for a second time in his life, searchers had come back to him with news that they could not find his son. Carnelian corrected himself: adopted son. 'I know that his care for me has so often brought disaster for others.'

'You're his son,' Grane said with bleak finality.

Carnelian almost laughed at the irony. Should he tell his brother that they were not brothers at all? Tell him that, of the two of them, it was only in his veins that any of their father's blood ran? Not a drop of it was pulsing in Carnelian's. He said nothing. At that moment it could only deepen Grane's pain at being deprived of a father's love.

Carnelian looked at their father. Even if he were awake, could he help them? Carnelian realized it was up to him to find a way to save his people. His gaze followed the blue-veined bones of his father's hand to the jewelled swelling on the smallest finger. The Ruling Ring of House Suth where it belonged. Once before when his father had been near death Carnelian had taken it from him. Then he had not known how to wield its power. His aunt had died.

'I must take his ring, Grane.'

Grane frowned. 'Why?'

645

'I must control our coomb.'

Grane's face softened to putty. His head wilted. 'Can't you wait, Master, until he's dead?'

Instinctively, Carnelian reached out to this broken man, but his brother flinched at his touch. Carnelian considered confessing his fears, but they were his burden to carry. He must not risk fear spreading among his people. If even a rumour reached Opalid's ear, the last chance to do something might well be lost. Instead he must play the Master. 'From your own experience, Grane, you know what can happen when our House is not ruled well.'

Carnelian watched how his assumption of authority put iron back in his brother's bones. Grane gave a nod. 'As you will, Master.'

He moved aside, allowing Carnelian to lift his father's hand. It seemed as light as a child's. He slipped the ring off as easily as if it had been strung on a cord. He turned it in the light, then put it on. 'Prepare Father, we're taking him home.'

Carnelian stood by his father's palanquin, wearing the mask his father had sent him, one of his robes and a black military cloak he had found in his pavilion. He was all the time aware of the unfamiliar weight of the Ruling Ring upon his hand. He had had the bearers set the palanquin down by the northern gate of the Masters' Camp. Grane stood beside its sombre bulk, his head hanging, rain running down his face, dewing like tears upon the polished surfaces of his stone eyes. House Suth tyadra formed a cordon separating them from the rest of the camp. Carnelian was watching the funeral procession of the Masters coming down the road. On either side their slaves lay prostrate in the mud, their backs sodden, in terror of their Masters returned grief-stricken and murderous.

Carnelian lingered long enough to make sure the Masters were giving commands to disassemble their pavilions for immediate departure to Osrakum. Then he raised his arm in a signal he had prearranged with his Lefthand. Earth-is-Strong lurched into life, her footfalls causing the nearby gates to shudder and rattle. He gestured a command and the palanquin rose into the air and, swaying gently, began following the dragon. Carnelian was only too happy to accompany it; he had no wish to witness any atrocities the Masters might visit upon their cowering slaves.

The watch-tower loomed up out of the rain-fogged air. It was the second tower they had seen since leaving the camp. Carnelian was no less sodden than his guardsmen. His robe and cloak clung to his back like flayed skin. As they drew closer he peered up, his mask keeping the rain from his eyes. Sun three. There were only two more watch-towers before the road terminated in the Wheel. Time was running out. What land he could see on either side was drear grey marshland. Osrakum filled the eastern horizon with its leaden rampart. The road curved away across a flinty mere towards an island, upon which, through the murk, he could just make out the huddle of the first tenements of the City at the Gates.

When he reached the monolith standing guard upon the road gate of the watch-tower, Carnelian found Fern, Poppy and the others waiting for him, having just climbed down from Earth-is-Strong's tower. He motioned them into cover and soon was following the palanquin into the shelter of the tower stables. He wanted to get them all as far away as he could from the road and the vengeful Masters.

Up on the leftway, he leaned upon the parapet. Below, all across the stopping place, slaves with tattooed faces were raising tents and pavilions under the gaze of their Masters, whose gold faces were watching them from their palanquins with icy malice. Dragons were churning through the mud outwards from the road in an arc to form a protective rampart. Only Heart-of-Thunder was heading for the watch-tower, behind a procession of palanquins: the Wise, amid the sombre purple of their ammonites and the greens and blacks of their Sinistral guards.

Night seemed to be seeping up from the Sacred Wall. On the leftway, Carnelian fixed his gaze on the monolith that stood before the watch-tower. He had pulled his guardsmen back from the tower so that they would not become involved with ammonites or Sinistrals. He had watched the Wise enter from the road below; had watched Osidian set Marula to guard the lower gate, after which he had entered escorted by syblings.

A bluish light began flickering on the inner face of the monolith. Ammonites were purifying the interior of the tower with fire. Carnelian waited. The reflected radiance died and no one appeared. He looked up the trunk of the tower to the branches that held up the heliograph platform. Clearly, the Wise were already up there and, it seemed, Osidian with them. Carnelian turned the Suth Ruling Ring upon his finger, reluctant to join him, but knowing he had no other option. He approached his father's palanquin and saw Fern watching him, his brothers, the Quenthas.

'I must climb to talk to the Master – to Osidian,' he added for his brothers, for whom 'the Master' was their father.

The Quenthas stepped forward, their hands upon the hilts of their swords. Carnelian's hand shaped a gesture of negation. *Remain here*, he signed; *protect my people*.

Frowning, Right-Quentha muttered his command to her sister. Carnelian took his leave of them and turned towards the monolith. He felt it was safer to go alone. Besides, he did not wish to force upon the sisters the humiliation of appearing before their fellow syblings.

Climbing out onto the roof of the tower, Carnelian was first aware of the bright air, free of the odours of sorcerous burning and myrrh. Then he noticed the silence and knew it had stopped raining. Between the ribs, he caught glimpses of a world bloodied by sunset. The roof with its snaking pipes was still slick and

648

slippery. He found the staples and climbed. When he reached the platform, he gazed out. Below was a red lake from which crusts and scars of land arose and the towers of the City at the Gates. Curdled, fleshy clouds formed a ceiling to this wounded world. Osrakum's rampart was an ever-cresting wave of yet more blood, at which Carnelian stared in tense horror, waiting for it to break. He felt he was back among the corpse mounds, or witnessing one of his nightmares with waking eyes.

At some point he became aware of Osidian, black against the gory sun. Carnelian found the will to move. Osidian turned as he approached, the last rays revealing the sadness in his unmasked face. Osidian turned back and Carnelian stood by his side, watching the sun being consumed by the earth. The lake was darkening to a mirror of obsidian whose reflections seemed so real, Carnelian felt for a moment it was the world they inhabited that was the illusion. 'Tomorrow when we enter Osrakum, I shall accompany my father to our coomb.'

Beside him, Osidian remained as still as a Sapient in his capsule.

'There are matters there I need to settle. I will return in time for your Apotheosis.'

'What can be so urgent it cannot wait?'

Carnelian could glean nothing of how Osidian was feeling from his neutral tone. For a moment he considered telling him the secret of his birth. He yearned to reveal his fears, to ask for help, even to be held. But he could not predict Osidian's reaction and could not risk interference. There was little enough time already in which to make his coomb safe for his people. 'My father is dying.'

'If you were any other, I would assume you sought to ensure your smooth succession. Is it that you wish to be there when he dies?'

Carnelian frowned against the thought of his father dying. 'I want to make my coomb safe for my people.'

Osidian's head dipped, then turned a little towards

Carnelian. 'I would like you to come into the Labyrinth with me.'

Defiance rose in Carnelian as he anticipated a command.

'I need you with me when I confront my mother,' Osidian said, his voice taut, as if at any moment it might snap.

Carnelian's anger receded. For Osidian to admit need, he must be fragile indeed.

'You have as much right to be there as I.'

'Is she not in Jaspar's coomb?'

'The Wise tell me she has returned to the Labyrinth.'

Carnelian regarded the filigree of twinkling lights tracing the arms of the City at the Gates and coalescing at its pulsing heart. The Sacred Wall was now a rampart blacker than the night. Beyond it lay Ykoriana and – what? His death? Was that really so certain? A vague, disturbing hope rose in him. It was at the meeting between mother and son that his own fate would be decided. If he was to survive it could only be because Osidian submitted to having his mother put a collar around his neck. To save him, Osidian would have to swallow his bile, become his mother's creature, probably take her for his wife. Anger stirred in Carnelian. Even if Osidian were prepared to make that sacrifice, could he allow him to do so? For all Osidian's crimes, Carnelian did not want him to become again a slave. Weariness washed over him. It seemed he had spent more than half his life caught upon a web from which every attempt to break free brought only disaster to others. By living he might achieve uncertain gains, but more solid ones might be purchased with his death. Another pang of hope cheated him of what comfort there was in that acceptance. Becoming confused, he took hold of one grim certainty: the meeting with Ykoriana was where his fate would be decided.

He looked into Osidian's eyes, all the time fighting down strange, disturbing presentiments. The longing to save his people was something to cling to. 'Swear upon your blood that if I come with you, you shall do all in your power to facilitate my visit to my coomb before the Apotheosis.'

Osidian made the oath without hesitation. 'In place of the Ichorians I intend to take our legions into Osrakum. Six others I left behind to herd the surviving sartlar back to the land. The rest of my legions will march with us to the City at the Gates, from where they will return to their fortresses; save only their commanders, who shall remain behind to attend my Apotheosis.'

In the silence that followed, Carnelian was left feeling he should say something. 'It is good they should be there . . . all the Chosen must witness it as an act of unity . . . the better to restore order . . .'

Osidian gave a ragged nod. Carnelian took his leave of him and made for the edge of the platform, seeking to spend what certain time he had left with those he thought of as his family.

Picking his way across the pipes and tubes upon the watch-tower roof, Carnelian stubbed his toe, cursed, slowed, heading for the faint light of the trap that led down into the tower interior. Around him the ribs rose like the trunks of trees, between which stretched the indigo of the darkening sky. One of the ribs gave birth to a form. Carnelian tensed, but it was upon him. He was struck, then he was falling. The odour of the assassin was obscured by the iron welling of his own blood.

INTO THE BLACK LAND

If night is the hidden face of day
What then is the hidden face of Paradise?

(a Quyan riddle)

Blades sliced in from the darkness. More shadow heads. A burst of foul breath as a cry was cut off. Carnelian swung his arm and hammered bone. A groan of pain in a lighter voice. 'Seraph, it is us.' A woman's voice. Carnelian saw a two-headed silhouette against the night sky. 'The Quenthas,' he said, shocked to his core that they had turned on him.

The sisters crouched. 'The assassin is dead.'

One of the ribs was shuddering as someone heavy was coming rapidly down its staples. A thump as that someone jumped down to the roof. The Quenthas had already turned to meet this new threat, swords slanting back ready.

'Out of my way, fools.' Osidian's voice. The sisters moved aside and he came to kneel at Carnelian's side. 'Are you hurt?'

'I'm not sure,' Carnelian said, pressing his hand against his thigh, the palm sliding on a slick of blood.

Osidian and the sisters helped move him into the light of the naphtha flares. Osidian snatched Carnelian's hand away from his wound and peered at it. 'It doesn't look deep.'

'I feel fine,' Carnelian said, stunned at how close he had

652

come again to failing those depending on him. All he could focus on was how his life was the thread upon which hung their fates.

Osidian pulled away, seeming to grow larger. 'I shall have them flayed.'

'Who?' said Carnelian, still confused.

'The Marula I set to guard this tower.'

'Celestial, we are certain the assassin was already here.'

Osidian turned on the sisters, who were kneeling, heads bowed. Carnelian realized how close they had come to cutting Osidian down. 'They saved my life.'

Osidian glanced round at him.

'We came up after the Seraph,' said Left-Quentha; her sister indicated Carnelian.

'No one could have passed us coming up from below.'

'Fetch some light,' Osidian growled.

The sisters rose and soon returned, carrying something aflame. Osidian directed them to cast the flickering light over the body of the assassin. One cruel gash through his nose had opened his temple to the skull. Another had sliced down through his shoulder, so that his arm hung at a strange angle. He wore a dark spiralled robe and a silver mask at his belt but, with his stubbled, thin, swarthy face, he was clearly no ammonite.

It was instinct that made Carnelian stoop to pull the purple robe down from the man's neck. With his other hand he rolled the man's head away. There it was. The tattoo of a six-spoked wheel.

'My mother,' Osidian breathed, sounding surprised.

It was the obvious conclusion, so Carnelian was puzzled at feeling doubt. Osidian was staring at the assassin as if he were a window he could look through. 'I was the target of this attack, not you.'

'How could she know you were to spend the night here?'

Osidian threw his hand up in a gesture of irritation. 'For all we know she may have infested every tower between the battlefield and Osrakum with her assassins.' The fury in his eyes dimmed. 'Though it amazes me she would be so inept as to use these scum a third time.'

He turned to squint between two of the watch-tower ribs towards the black abyss of the Sacred Wall. 'Perhaps desperation forced her to risk one last throw.'

'Why could it not have been the work of the Wise?'

Osidian turned crazed eyes on him. 'However much they may fear me, they fear and hate her more. Besides, they would have as much reason to fear the ensuing interregnum as have the Great. With no candidate of pure blood left, one would have to be chosen from among the Houses.' Osidian's lips curled. 'In terror for their lives, the Great would be unable to muster a common front against her. Enough of them would scramble to fall at her feet.' Osidian's eyes cooled with hatred. 'Imagine their terror as she lingered over her choice. The more impure the candidate, the deeper into the Great would be cast his shadow of death. The new God Emperor alone would survive from his own kin, his peers and superiors. A single tree left standing after the forest all around was blasted by the storm. The Great cowed, the Wise naked before her, she would have absolute power in her grasp.'

Osidian's expression was bilious, but yet Carnelian could see something else in his eyes. Was it avarice?

Osidian was nodding, on his face a look of understanding, of admiration. 'For such gains who would not risk everything?'

Carnelian was overcome with horror, of Osidian and of the thought of Ykoriana triumphant. Though, after everything he had experienced, why was he still surprised? Were they not mother and son?

Carnelian sagged. And yet, he was Osidian's brother. A thought crept into his mind: Osidian had been incorrect when he said there would have been no pure-blood candidate left. If Osidian were dead, then the path to the Masks would surely be open to his only surviving brother. Carnelian saw how he could present himself to the Great and Wise as a saviour; the more so because he would come unlooked-for. Ykoriana might oppose him, but even she could not impose her will if the Great and Wise stood behind him. He could discard her as she deserved, take her daughter for a wife. In the time before Ykorenthe became capable of bearing children, he would rule protected by the fear of the chaos that would ensue should he die without pure-blood issue. With such power he would be able to keep his loved ones safe. More, what could he not do to heal the wounds of the world once he became God Emperor?

Osidian came alive. 'Come, we must get your wound tended. Then we must wait for dawn, so that we can get this business over.' He let forth a sigh. 'How weary I am of this outer world.' A childlike look of hope came into his eyes. 'Tomorrow, Osrakum.'

Carnelian gave a solemn nod. 'Yes, tomorrow.'

Carnelian sat hunched in Earth-is-Strong's command chair, listening to the rain drumming on the bone roof above his head. It had been falling incessantly since they set off. Ahead, through its mist, he could just see, across the moat bridge, the mass of the gatehouses. He was not sure, but it seemed that the great brass gate between them was closed, barring access to the Wheel: the heart of the City at the Gates.

He glanced round at Fern and the others. It was too gloomy back there to see their faces. He looked forward again, watching the rain-stained tenement walls slide slowly past on either side. Perforated with unnumbered windows shuttered against the rain – or perhaps it was that none dared look upon this sodden procession of the Masters.

Some steps squeezed down to a mess of boats, many half capsized, lifted by the rising waters of the lake, tethered to mooring posts already submerged. The road was flooding, filthy with scum, the run-off foaming into alleyways, fed from above by spouts vomiting from the roofs as if the sky was trying to scour the city clean. It had been like that all the way. Carnelian had expected, perhaps even hoped for the termite frenzy of the crowds, the views into rooms and lives, even the mouldering stench of the metropolis he had entered as a boy, but he had not seen a soul.

When they had set off along the causeway towards the city, the flinty lake had been unscratched by the ripples of a single boat. True, in many places on either side he had seen wheel ruts in the mud, the churn left behind by feet, but these had held glimmers of reflected sky; had looked as if they had been left there in some ancient time and that nothing but this funeral procession had passed there for long ages of the world.

When they reached the first towers, these had seemed almost ruined, decayed. Above the slurp of the water lapping tunnels and alleys, steps and quays, Carnelian was sure he had heard a child crying, some vague voices, the screeches of an animal being killed, but these could have been the ghosts of the city's dead inhabitants and were soon lost in the noise of the thunder and the falling rain.

As they slipped through the twilight beneath the crowding tenements, Carnelian felt a lament rising in him and was not sure whether he grieved for the lost city, for the dead, or for himself.

After Osidian and the Quenthas had helped him descend from the watch-tower roof, he had not slept. All night, deprived of Fern, he had struggled alone with his fears and choices. When morning came, he had found that, though his leg ached, it bore his weight easily enough. The sisters had accompanied him down to the road. He had sent them to fetch Fern and his brothers. While he waited, the Wise had given him instructions on how to negotiate the Three Gates.

A grinding sound snatched his attention. Ahead, between the gatehouses, something massive was twisting, changing form. It was just reflections in the brass gates as they opened for him. He realized they must already be on one of the bridges that spanned the Wheel moat. Glancing to starboard, he looked down into the great curving trench and saw how much higher the water was than it had been the last time he had crossed it. Through the opening gates, he glimpsed what seemed the cobbles of the marketplace, but then these began to rise in a surge that faded away in the veiling rain. A dense throng. Earth-is-Strong pounded closer, and ripples of panic moved through the multitude as they struggled to get out of her way. In the milling pattern of heads, Carnelian detected many smaller than the rest. Children. Filling the Wheel as far as he could see were the tributaries and the flesh tithe.

It was Poppy who first moved to peer through the screen at the tributaries. Krow went with her, then Fern. Carnelian watched them for a while then rose and joined them. The crowd below had opened an avenue down which Earth-is-Strong was pounding. Carnelian regarded the sea of humanity, saddened by how different this was from the tumultuous marketplace he had once crossed. How quietly the people below watched their progress. He remembered that Fern had once been among just such a throng with his father and brother. He glanced round and saw Fern braced against the sway of the deck, his face grim as he gazed out.

'How long have they been here?' Poppy asked, softly. She had poked her fingers through the bony lattice and clung to it.

Krow put an arm around her. 'Probably quite a while.'

Carnelian recalled that he too had been with Fern and the tithe children of both their tribes.

'They will be starving by now,' growled Fern.

So many children. That such numbers should be given up to the Masters each and every year. The way they watched the Masters pass in such perfect silence. Contempt rose in Carnelian at their docility. Where was their rage?

'Master?'

Carnelian turned on his Lefthand, making the man start. He calmed himself. 'What is it?'

'If it please you, Master, which way shall we turn?'

657

Carnelian glanced back down to the Wheel; they had reached the ring of black stone inlaid into the Wheel that was called the Dragonway. 'The shortest way.'

His Lefthand muttered into his voice fork and the hawsers on Earth-is-Strong's horns pulled her head round and she began to turn east.

'The Standing Dead,' exclaimed Poppy, pointing.

A vast gash seemed to be opening in Osrakum's mountain wall that was guarded on either side by figures that might have been men except that those of flesh and blood were mere dust at their feet. Even through the rain Carnelian could see the brooding stare that those giants cast down upon the tributaries. Between them more and more of the Canyon they guarded was coming into view. The deeper he could see into that dark mouth, the greater grew his dread. After everything that had happened, it was miraculous that he should be here again, but it did not feel like any kind of homecoming. He glanced round, seeking some distraction. Perhaps he had hoped to see wonder in the faces of those he loved, at least for a moment, but there was only fear, as if they were looking upon the very gateway to the land of the dead. And why not? Once they went in, what hope had any of them of ever returning?

The ankle of one of the colossi slid past the starboard screen as an immense column of scabrous rock. They heard more than saw the walls of the Canyon funnelling together as the thunder of Earth-is-Strong's footfalls reverberated, the judder of her tower and harness shivered and echoed. The scuffle of the palanquins following them was a constant scratching on their hearing. More disconcerting than this was a swelling roar. He had started to hear it when they were crossing the bridge over the Wheel moat into the Canyon mouth. The last time he had heard the Cloaca, it had been a murmur. It had been tame then; now it was carrying the run-off from the Skymere swollen by the Rains. The bass rumble reminded him of the Blackwater Falls in the Upper Reach. No doubt Morunasa would hear in that roar his god speaking.

Then he became aware of the twilight illuminating the turn up ahead. He knew what he would see when they rounded it, but even so, as it came into sight it shocked him. The vast hedge of bronze that filled the Canyon from side to side was holding back a glow of morning light but, in one place, this sombre dam was breached. Perhaps as much as a third of it had been torn down.

When Earth-is-Strong moved into the breach in the Green Gate there was more than enough space to spare. The ripped edges of the bronze thicket loomed, its blades and thorns like frayed threads. On their passage through what had been the first of three gates, chambers were exposed on either side like the hollows of a crushed snail shell. Torn floors hung in shreds. Doorways opening like wounds at various heights funnelled away into dark, still-secret recesses of the fortress. Propped up against these ruins were the gates themselves, two slabs of bronze rising higher than they could see. Carnelian had been told to expect this, but still he was appalled that Molochite had been prepared to demolish a part of Osrakum's defences merely to indulge his whim to go to battle in the ancient relic of the Iron House. Was it his certainty of victory or, perhaps, his concern to maintain his majesty in comfort that had led him to this vandalism?

Once they were through the Gate, the Canyon opened up before them, its smooth floor running off towards the next turn. Carnelian looked for and found the Lords' Way running in its groove in the cliff along which he had travelled in a chariot with his father. The roar of the Cloaca had become more remote as it had widened into a black chasm. He knew the shelves of the quarantine were down there somewhere. Remembering Tain's description of his ordeal in that darkness, Carnelian resisted turning to look at him. Each day being moved to the next shelf down the Canyon before passing under the Blood Gate. His brother had thought the chasm a way down to the Underworld. At least, this time, neither Tain nor the rest of his people were going to have to endure that. Molochite's breach in the Green Gate had already allowed the pollution of the outer world to reach deep into the Canyon. It was strange they had him to thank for their deliverance. Carnelian watched the next turn approaching and longed to reach the light flooding from it. What he really wanted was to save his people from quarantine altogether. He desired them to go immediately to their coomb with his father. He wanted to have them all as far away as possible from what was going to happen.

With each sway of the cabin, a tower had been solidifying in the twilight ahead, like the blade of some immense axe half embedded in the Canyon floor and splitting the Cloaca in two. The closer they came, the deeper Carnelian could see the roots of the tower going down into the fork of the chasm. As the tower reared above them, the spikes in its crown which he had taken for the ends of joists glimmered. He saw they were brass, these structures, shaped like the calyxes of lilies swelling their trumpet mouths down towards him. They were the throats of massive flame-pipes; passing under their gape, Carnelian imagined with horror what would happen to them should these weapons begin vomiting fire.

A lurching shift in the monster's gait made him drop his gaze and see her turning to move onto a slab that spanned the nearest branch of the forking chasm. Under the looming flame-pipe tower, they crossed to the great oval space that lay within the embrace of the chasm branches and that was in the deep shadow of a vast rampart rising at its further end. A massive fortress, gloomy against the morning. Carnelian felt the hackles rising on his neck. He had seen this place before, though then, so close up, he had not fully appreciated its scale. This was the Blood Gate whose portals, he judged, would overtop a watch-tower of the Guarded Land as much as a Master did a sartlar. Gate-towers on either side rose loftier still. Disturbed, he remembered the instructions the Wise had given him before setting off. 'Is there enough light?'

His Lefthand murmured into his voice fork, then, nodding a few times, turned to Carnelian. 'Just enough, apparently, Seraph.'

'Send the signal.'

As the man relayed the command to the mirrorman on the roof, Carnelian became aware of a glimmering coming as if from the sky. He rose from his chair and advanced towards the screen. Gripping it against the cabin sway he looked up. The towers swooped so high, he could not see their summits, but he saw they grew gills in which clusters of flame-pipes nested like worms. Together with the pipes on the tower behind them, the space upon which Earth-is-Strong was walking was a plain of death. Molochite had not, after all, left Osrakum undefended. In comparison to these structures, the Green Gate was nothing but a flimsy fence. Legions' boast had not been vainglorious. Had Molochite chosen to remain behind these defences, he would have been invulnerable. Had Osidian dared bring his dragons in so far, they would have been incinerated.

Carnelian fought vertigo as, with a dull shudder, the gates began to open, making it seem the whole world was collapsing. Soon they were moving in between the receding cliffs of bronze. A spindle of grey light widened up ahead as the second pair of portals began to open. The walls of the fortress, its doors and tiers, grew increasingly substantial as their edges caught the light. Rows of tiny figures lined the avenue between the gates. Half-black they were, but not girded with the blood-red cloaks of the Ichorians who had once manned these gates. Instead their garments were green and black and their collars wintry in the gloom.

Carnelian had agreed to lead the funerary procession.

Osidian wanted to bring up the rear in case he should have need to linger at the Blood Gate to ensure the Ichorians there swore fealty to him. He had no wish to become imprisoned in Osrakum as had been his fathers for centuries.

The second set of portals parting gave them access to the Canyon beyond. Its walls had been reddened up to a great height as if by a tide of blood. As Earth-is-Strong crossed over the lefthand chasm branch on another span, Carnelian's gaze descended the barracks' galleries to the colonnades below, with their machines and piers and counterweights. When he, long ago, had seen these structures, he had not known what they were. Now he recognized them as the mechanisms of a cothon. Arches and berths upon which the Red Ichorian dragon towers had rested disassembled. Racks where their flame-pipes had been stowed. Behind, the shadows must conceal the openings to the stable caves in which the dragons of the Red Legion had slept. All empty now, all smashed and broken and dead at Makar. He brooded over this as they continued down the Canyon; how much had already been lost, how much destroyed.

Ahead, running from cliff to cliff, the final fortress reared its sombre wall. Behind was the Hidden Land of Osrakum. Carnelian's heart began to beat so loudly he was amazed none in the cabin seemed to hear it. Even as they moved into the shadow of the Black Gate, the leftmost of two portals began to open. Poppy and Krow were standing against the screen, though Carnelian had not noticed them moving forward. He rose, a childlike enthusiasm rising in him to watch the wonder on their faces. Bells began bruising the air. Not a single bell to announce his blood-rank as had happened when he last entered, but a multitude of them, their pealing building echo upon echo until he became sure the Black Gate and the walls of the Canyon must shatter from the reverberation. He did not care, for he had reached the screen and, with a quick glance at Poppy and Krow, he fixed his gaze upon the opening gate.

A landscape wrought from flint. Not blue and smiling, the Skymere, but dark, opaque. Certainly no mirror to heaven. Carnelian looked for the Yden, but its emerald had lost its fire. Dull, it looked, lifeless, its once verdant riot seeming to have been smothered by mould. From its faded heart the Pillar of Heaven rose, a black thorn that seemed to be pricking the brooding sky. The Labyrinth mound seemed no less forbidding than the Isle of Flies. Osrakum's sacred mountain wall, the curving grin of a greying corpse. The coombs, rotted pockets in which palaces lodged their grey moraine.

Carnelian's elation drained away. His memory of Osrakum's beauty died. He was reluctant to look at Poppy's face, but he could not help himself. It reflected the grey crater. Her expression was very far from wonder. Krow had his arm around her and together they looked, stone-faced, upon what was to be their home. Almost Carnelian said to them that it could be glorious in the sun, but he remembered how dangerous a place this was. Could any amount of beauty compensate for such danger? As he gazed upon the Hidden Land, it occurred to him, grimly, that the face she was showing them now might be her true one.

Down through the Valley of the Gate they went, between the thickets of polygonal columns whose tips bore the shape of men. Not angels, as they had appeared to him the previous time he had seen them; instead a miserable near-faceless multitude, seeming to watch them pass. He brooded on the accepted belief that they were the Quyan host turned to stone.

As a more human assemblage came into sight, at first he felt relief. A rising pyramid of gilded, perfect Masters that enringed the bowl in which the Great were wont to hold their Clave. When last he had gazed upon them, he had been wandering at their feet. From this height, however finely wrought, they seemed mere carvings. The furious fire the sun had lent them then had died. As they slipped past, he watched the bulk of Earth-is-Strong reflected in their gold, fragmented into a many-scaled shadow. It made him shudder. He could not help feeling it was a glimpse of the Darkness-under-the-Trees creeping into Osrakum.

The Valley columns bristled to a sudden end where they reached the Skymere shore. To either side, as far as Carnelian could see, flights of steps cascaded down to the water. Only the road they were on continued, borne out over the lake on the back of a vast causeway. Sartlar numberless as sand grains had built it and mortared it with their blood. For a moment, Carnelian brooded on the mounds of their dead he and Fern had wandered among upon the battlefield. It seemed that, whatever happened, it was the flesh of the brutes, their blood, that was the matter from which all else was built.

He was woken from his musings by noticing what appeared to be leaden blocks forming a neat barricade across the mouth of the Great Causeway. Not of lead, but silver: the many-wheeled chariots of the Wise. Cordons of dark figures formed a barrier before the steps from amongst whom tendrils of smoke were beginning to rise. Here and there along their line, some furtive glimmers. He leaned forward, squinting through the slits of his mask. Ammonites, crowds of them spilling down the steps, amongst them all manner of structures.

He sat back, thinking. What had to be said would be better said unmasked, even though his face might betray his doubts. 'Be blind.'

Immediately his Left and Right clasped their hands to their faces and bent forward to touch the backs of their hands to the deck. Carnelian removed his mask and looked at Fern, then Poppy, then Krow. 'You must leave me and accompany my father and brothers to our . . .' He tried to find an Ochre word for coomb, but failed. He half pointed in the direction where he knew Coomb Suth lay. 'Across the water.'

'Why can't we stay with you, Carnie?'

'I need to go on alone, Poppy. Where I'm going, you'd only get in the way. I need to know you're all safe. And I want you to take care of my father.'

'What is it you need to do?' asked Fern, sensing his fear.

'It's something dangerous, but something I have to do. Do you trust me?'

Fern, slowly, gave a nod.

'When will we see you again?'

Carnelian saw how scared Poppy was. 'Whatever happens, in a day, two at the most, I'll cross the water to you.' He buried deep his dread that, on that day, he might be coming to say goodbye to them for ever. He saw Fern's misery. As their eyes met, Carnelian was sure Fern guessed something of what he was trying to hide.

'We need to descend to the ground now,' he said, hoping Fern would accept this. When his lover gave an imperceptible nod, Carnelian felt a lightening of his burden. Whatever happened, he convinced himself that Fern would survive and would take care of Poppy and Krow. He managed a smile for the two youngsters. 'You must take as much care as if the people on the ground were raveners.' He was glad to see the colour draining from their faces. He remasked and bade his officers see again. The marumaga sneaked glances at Fern and the others. Carnelian could see their shock and appreciated how strange it must seem to them, in spite of not understanding a word, the intimate way he talked to his people.

As he rose painfully from the command chair, he raised his hand to stop Fern coming to help him. Putting weight on his wounded leg, he was sure it would carry him. He pulled the Suth Ruling Ring from his finger and thrust it into Fern's hand. 'Give it to the eldest of my brothers.' He considered urging all kinds of advice on him, but the handing over of the ring would have to be enough to show his brothers how important Fern was to him. 'Tell my father everything that you know.'

Fern raised his eyebrows, but then nodded and closed his hand around the ring. Carnelian sent him ahead, then Poppy and Krow after him. When they had disappeared through the hole in the deck, he turned to his officers. 'Hold her here until I return. You will take commands from none but me.'

The two men jerked their heads. 'As you command, Master.'

Satisfied, Carnelian turned to the ladder.

Leaning a little on Fern, Carnelian watched ammonites swarming the palanquins. Masters emerging from them were coaxed by the silver-masked ammonites towards the ragged wall of smoke that was rising at the head of the Turtle Steps. There, from among the ranks of purple figures, rose the taller shapes of their masters the Wise, who, though motionless, seemed to be overseeing the reception of the Chosen. Like ants the ammonites clipped the finery from the Masters. Robes as bright as butterfly wings were cast into braziers, where their iridescent colours soon turned black. Divested of their gorgeous carapaces, the Masters grew thinner, paler. Stripped of their distinguishing heraldry, they were revealed as being very much alike as they approached the wall of smoke. Next they were flayed of their ritual protection. The windings came away like dead skin, revealing the white beneath. Painfully thin they seemed, in their icicle nakedness. Vulnerable. Wearing nothing but their masks they disappeared into the smoke.

The ache in Carnelian's leg stung him into motion towards a nearby clump of Sapients. Closer, he became aware of the figure at the heart of their conclave. The stone surmounting his staff was emberous whilst all the rest were emerald. The murmuring of the homunculi faltered. Carnelian recognized the red finial with a sinking heart. It was too late to retreat. The eyes of the homunculi indicated the awareness of their masters to his approach.

'My Lord Law,' he said, dismayed that the Grand Sapient

had reached the cleansing cordon before him. It was going to be harder to get what he wanted.

'Suth Carnelian,' said Law's homunculus. Neither had turned towards him.

Before Carnelian had time to marshal his thoughts, the eyes of the homunculi released him to fix upon another Sapient approaching. The staff with which he walked gave off a ruby glint above his pale fist. A homunculus was holding his other hand. When close, the little man took the staff with one hand, while guiding his master's fingers to his throat. 'Greater Third of Gates,' he announced.

The other homunculi murmured an echo. The Third's homunculus locked his gaze to that of Law's. 'Does my Lord wish to pass through the cleansing system now?'

'I shall be cleansed in Thrones,' said Law's homunculus. 'Another system is being prepared at the Forbidden.'

'And my Lord's ammonites?'

'Through the cages.'

'I too wish to pass my servants through the cleansing,' said Carnelian. He could not help glancing back to where he had left Fern and the others with his father's palanquin. His brothers were there. The Quenthas. He was relieved to see they were all still kneeling with their heads bowed. He had asked them to do that so as to make them invisible to the Masters processing past them. He fingered the roughness of the military cloak he was wearing, that he had found in his father's tent. Certain he had heard his name in the muttering of the Third's homunculus, he turned back.

'. . . come to petition me,' Law was saying. His homunculus turned on Carnelian. 'Why do you want this, Suth Carnelian?'

The Sapients crowded round him like crows, but he sensed their wariness. It occurred to him they might think he spoke on Osidian's behalf. His mind focused on his need to get his people through this safely. It could be dangerous to show any concern for them. 'My father ails.'

'And would have died long ago were it not for our ministra-tions.'

Anger rose in Carnelian. Rather than saving him, just then he felt they had poisoned him. There was also the part they had played in his deposal and the recent use they had made of him. He felt no gratitude. 'Still, I fear for him should he be long delayed here.'

'The Ruling Lord Suth is high among the Great and so will naturally be among the first to be processed.'

Carnelian clenched his teeth. He had played badly and was now trapped. He could see no way except the truth. 'My Lord, I want our servants to be processed with him because they know how to tend to his needs.'

'Is House Suth possessed of no other servants?'

Carnelian felt the trap pressing in on him. He had already all but confessed he had some special interest in these servants. Fear rose in him lest he had made them pieces the Wise could use in their struggle against Osidian. If so, that was too late to undo. Now even less did he dare trust them to the quarantine. 'Nevertheless, I wish it.'

'What you ask directly contravenes the Law.'

'Much is already out of balance,' Carnelian said, with stress. 'This does not seem to me a great sin.'

The homunculi muttered an echo of his words then fell silent. Carnelian became aware of the bustle all around him. He resisted an urge to turn and look at his people again.

'We shall grant you this boon, Suth Carnelian,' said Law's homunculus. The little man turned his gaze on the homunculus of the Third. 'Process not only the Ruling Lord Suth, but also his slaves, though only after all the Great. We do not wish to needlessly provoke their ire.'

Carnelian had got what he wanted, but at what cost?

Standing against the cabin screen, Carnelian watched his people embarking onto a bone boat. After taking his leave of Grand Sapient Law, he had summoned the Quenthas and asked them to shepherd his people through the cleansing. Then he had climbed back to his dragon tower, from where he could see down to the water's edge.

He sighed with relief when the bone boat pulled away from the steps. The mirror of the lake was being opaqued by the wakes of dozens of the pale boats rowing the Great back to their coombs all along the outer shore. He limped back and sank heavily into the command chair. While he waited for the chariots of the Wise to move aside, he gazed down the causeway towards the brooding Yden. At last the way was clear. When his Lefthand confirmed that the funerary procession was ready, Carnelian gave the command to begin the crossing.

Thunder reverberated around the crater. The rain was giving the Skymere the look of knapped obsidian. It was drumming on the roof above his head. The mirrorman up there was surely nearly drowned, but still Carnelian could almost envy him and, even more, the lookout, exposed to the raw energies of the sky, washed by the elemental downpour. Osrakum could be seen only dimly through the rain. He could just make out the looming shadow of the Pillar of Heaven. At its feet, the lagoons of the Yden had swollen into a single, murky mere. Its verdant glories lived only in his heart, illuminated by the summer light of childhood. The actual world was dark and forbidding.

Even above the hissing rain he could hear the Yden's black water roaring under the road to gush out, furious, down the channels to froth the edge of the Skymere below. Paths of marble wound down beside the streams; flights of pale steps and landings cascaded down to quays. Carnelian imagined the Masters would soon be disembarking there from bone boats, climbing up to the road on their way to the Plain of Thrones and the Labyrinth. Then he noticed the narrow house, end on to the Skymere shore. A kharon boathouse like the one in which he and Osidian had been kept prisoners after their kidnapping. He remembered again the sybling Hanuses, minions of their mistress Ykoriana. The woman who, after everything that had happened, still had the power over him of life or death.

It seemed an age since they had reached the hill that held within its summit the Plain of Thrones. Gradually the road had been winding up its flank. Hunched in his chair, Carnelian was shivering, listening to the rain. The rough stuff of his father's cloak was in his grip. Lifting his head he peered westwards seeking to glimpse Coomb Suth but, through the rain, he could see nothing except for the shadowy Sacred Wall, which seemed a far, leaden horizon.

His Left muttered something at Carnelian's feet, then Earth-is-Strong began to turn. Sliding off towards his left, steps swooped down in many flights. He recognized them as the same he and Jaspar had climbed from the Quays of the Dead. Then the view of the rain-filled void was snuffed out by a wall of stone. The command chair pushed hard into his back even as the deck tilted up. They were climbing into a ravine by means of long shallow steps. Everything shuddered and rattled as the tower began to swing heavily first to one side, then the other. His grip tight on the arms of the chair, he watched with alarm as a ravine wall would lurch towards them, then away. After a while, he relaxed his grip, reassured that Earth-is-Strong's gait would not dash her tower to pieces against the rock.

As they climbed, Carnelian fell to wondering what had happened to Jaspar. He hoped the man was dead: even considering his sins, he had suffered enough.

At last the deck tilted forward, even as the ravine gave them up into the vast and airy cliff-walled Plain of Thrones. Carnelian had eyes for nothing except the black trunk that rose from behind that wall. The Pillar of Heaven was a tree whose storm-sky canopy cast all the world beneath into shadow.

They were approaching the centre of the plain when the rain stopped, suddenly. The sky gave one last shudder, then eerie silence reigned. Before them lay a ring within a ring. Carnelian had seen this thing before, but not from above. The outer ring swept round like a cothon. From this a mosaic of ridges of fiendish complexity converged on the inner ring. His gaze became enmeshed in the radial branching tendrils that seemed like the iris of some vast eye. Escape lay only in the double inner ring that enclosed the dark pupil. For a moment he was possessed by an uneasy conviction this was an opening to a well, a smooth sinkhole into which he might tumble.

It began to drizzle. Drawing back into himself, he gazed at the Stone Dance of the Chameleon, ostensibly a calendrical device. At its centre, the twelve month stones. Eight red, two black, two green. Upon these twelve was carved the Law-that-must-be-obeyed. The stones had a round-shouldered look as if they were hunched against the rain, or against the too-vast sky. Still square and young, another twelve stood behind like ghosts. It was from these that ridges flowed, branching, meshing, intertwining to connect with the outer ring of, as he recalled, commentary stones. The twelve innermost stones were the least imposing of the Dance and yet they were clearly the jewel for which all the others were nothing more than a setting. He could see how time had softened them. His gut told him that even when Legions had been a child, these had been ancient and once had stood there on their own.

As Earth-is-Strong carried him round the rings of stones, Carnelian gazed for a moment, sombrely, upon the road running off south-west, along which the funerary procession would soon go. At the end of that road were the caves in the wall of the plain, where the Wise embalmed the dead. As the wall continued to slide past, he discerned, in a long row with their backs to it, a line of what seemed pale homunculi. Except that he knew these were not tiny men, but the colossi who stood each astride the entrance to a tomb. These it was who, gazing down upon the Plainsmen tributaries, had given them the name for the Chosen, 'the Standing Dead'. The view continued to swing round and he saw the terraces and galleries of the lower palace carved into the cliff above those tomb guardians. He frowned, desolate. There, penetrating deep into the cliff like a nasal cavity into a skull, was the hollow pyramid in which the Masters would stand in tiers as bright as angels as they gazed down upon their tributaries. Earth-is-Strong was heading straight towards this now. Before her a black rectangle stretched out over the floor of the Plain. Upon this tens of thousands would cower. Soon they would be there, gazing up to watch Osidian made God. Perhaps they would see Carnelian sacrificed.

His Left gave the command to turn the dragon onto the road that skirted the black field.

'Belay that order,' Carnelian said. 'Steady as she goes.'

On the ground, his back to the Forbidden Door, Carnelian looked back the way they had come. Grand Sapient Labyrinth was there behind him with one of his Thirds and a gang of their ammonites. They had offered him an immediate cleansing so that he might enter the Labyrinth, but when Grand Sapient Law on arrival had declared he would wait for Osidian, Carnelian had said he would wait with him.

The funerary procession had already reached the caves of the embalmers. There the palanquins seemed a nest of tiny beetles. He could just make out a thread of people returning along the road towards the standing stones. He guessed these must be the bearers being driven to the cages of the quarantine.

He squinted back towards the ravine through which he had entered the Plain. Watching the minuscule movement on the floor of the slot in the cliff, he became certain it was a towered dragon entering the Plain. It had to be Heart-of-Thunder. Grumbling, the sky was beginning to blacken in the east. Carnelian's spirits sank even further. Night would fall before Osidian reached him. He had hoped they would confront Ykoriana in the light. He gazed up at the galleries scaling the cliff like some vast ladder to the sky. Rock everywhere riddled with holes. From any one of those myriad cavities she could be scrutinizing him with borrowed eyes.

Starless night. A tremor in the ground made Carnelian relive the horrors of the battle. Many dragons were approaching. The massing shadow of the leading monster was growing larger, carrying the lantern of its tower. The world quaked as light filtering down from the honeycombed cliff began to sketch Heart-of-Thunder's mountainous form.

Carnelian met Osidian as he descended from his tower. 'I had expected you sooner.'

There was only shadow in the loop of Osidian's cowl. 'I had to take the submission of the Sinistrals at the Blood Gate then wait while they gathered supplies.'

Render, thought Carnelian, almost tasting it. Then he gave a start as the night dewed into flesh: the ash-misted faces of the Oracles. Their grim expressions could have been fear. Whatever they were feeling, Carnelian was filled with unease. At that moment Osidian angled his head back. Some of the light coming from the terraces above found the sinister mirror of his mask. 'Come.'

Together they advanced upon the Wise, who were framed by the pale silver faces of their ammonites. They halted beneath the jewelled gaze of the two Grand Sapients.

'Welcome, Celestial,' said Labyrinth's homunculus. 'We have brought the means by which you shall be cleansed of the taint of the outer world.'

It seemed to Carnelian it would take more than unguents to do that.

'I shall submit to the cleansing, my Lords,' said Osidian, 'but I give warning I intend to bring these barbarians in with me.' He turned enough to take in the Oracles and the Marula warriors behind them.

As soon as the homunculi finished repeating his words, Labyrinth's homunculus began to speak, but was interrupted by Law's. 'We cannot allow this, Celestial. The Law-that-must-be-obeyed is unequivocal. These barbarians may be infested with corruption that external examination will not reveal. To bring them onto holy ground is to endanger its very sanctity.'

'Whatever danger they pose, my Lord, I am no less a threat. You will clean them as you clean me.'

'It is perilous, Celestial, to let these animals pass through the Forbidden Door untamed,' said Labyrinth. 'You may have fought your way back into Paradise, but you must not force your way into Heaven.'

'Lecture me not, my Lords, about peril. Only last night was my own life endangered. I will not leave myself thus exposed again.'

'Celestial, the Sinistral Ichorians are the proper guardians of your life.'

'Who then will guard the Gates?'

The Grand Sapients absorbed his words through the throats of their homunculi. For a moment, it seemed they would respond, but their fingers faltered.

'I intend to breed from these creatures a new caste of Ichorians that shall be in their person a joining of the two previous castes. Their skin shall symbolize the unity of my rule.'

Carnelian's unease rose in unspoken protest: Have you forgotten the promise you made to save their Lower Reach? He found among the Oracles Morunasa's sombre face. Was he aware of Osidian's plans for them? He bit his tongue when it would have warned that the wealth of Osrakum would corrupt these barbarians. He had enough problems of his own. Behind the Grand Sapients, he could see the Forbidden

Door. What dangers might lie beyond that portal? If he were to be slain before he had a chance to put in place the necessary arrangements, his people would suffer. He focused upon the long, blind masks floating above. The fingers of the Grand Sapients formed collars of ice around the throats of their homunculi. Carnelian wondered what thoughts, what calculations were flashing through their masters' minds.

It was Osidian's voice that broke his reverie. 'If needs be I will blast my way through to the Labyrinth.'

Carnelian remembered the thunder in the ground. He knew what power Osidian had brought with him and was not surprised when the Wise capitulated.

IN THE UNDERWORLD

Does a dreamer walk in the Underworld?
(Quyan fragment)

Arrayed in a robe of vibrant green, Osidian reminded
Carnelian of Jaspar's father on his bier of ice. Save for the
lances they had had returned to them after purification, the
Marula warriors were naked. Morunasa had commanded
them to submit to the ammonites as he and the Oracles
were doing. Enraged with fear, the Marula had nevertheless
allowed their leather armour to be cut from them and burned.
Lotus smoke relaxed them enough to allow the ammonites
to wash them, to rasp the curls from their heads. Even their
mouths were invaded. Every part of them strigils could reach
was scraped until, in places, they bled. The ammonites had
been more gentle with Carnelian and Osidian, but no less
thorough. Something had been put on Carnelian's wound
so that now he hardly felt it. He had insisted on keeping his
father's cloak, but it had had to be thoroughly cleansed before
he was allowed to wrap it over the green robe provided by
the ammonites. As they were ushered into the tunnel that lay
behind the Forbidden Door, the familiar drugged remoteness
gave way to dread.

*   *   *

Tomb shelves on either side cramped their stumbling march. The lanterns the ammonites carried lit their masks from beneath, making them seem to be the vengeful dead. Carnelian tried to find Sthax among the warriors, but they could all have passed for shadows were it not for their staring eyes. The fear in the Marula soon took root in Carnelian as they crept down into the Underworld.

Around him the Marula collapsed suddenly to the ground. Shocked, Carnelian came to a halt. The tunnel walls had disappeared. Unawares, he had strayed into a vast forest of the night. The girth of the trunks implied monstrous height. He focused on the green flame he had been following: Osidian once again leading them to the hoped-for light of the Earthsky. Carnelian's eyes filled with tears of longing to look upon those he loved among the Tribe. Only his breath separated him from the dead. He reached out and touched one of the trunks. Cold stone, not bark. This was the Labyrinth. He gazed up and saw the stone, baroqued with glyphs, rising up beyond the reach of the lantern light and knew it to be a sarcophagus whose pith was the mummy of a God Emperor long deceased. For a moment he was haunted by a memory of the pygmies buried in their baobabs. Then he was gazing about him. Dimly, he could see more of the columns marching off in every direction.

A whimpering around his feet made him look down and see the Marula warriors curled up, cowering, their hands clasped over their smooth heads, their quivering shoulders, muffling their ears. Perhaps they believed they had been brought to the Isle of Flies. Were they wrong? Panic rising, Carnelian glanced up, feeling hunted. The Oracles gaped, staring with wonder. Among them Morunasa, a stranger without his ashen pallor, in whose yellow eyes Carnelian saw what he most feared. Morunasa knew his god was here. Carnelian did not care whether the Darkness-under-the-Trees had come in with them, or if he had always dwelled here. Morunasa cocked his head, his eyes closed. Carnelian listened too. A strange rumbling was pounding the air. His breath caught in his throat. It was so like the sound the Blackwater made as it forked round the Isle of Flies to tumble, roaring, into the Lower Reach. The sound the Oracles maintained was the voice of their god.

Monsters surrounded them. Sybling Ichorians, two-headed, many-limbed like crabs. Carapaced with bronze, cloaked with darkness. Osidian barked a command that confirmed Carnelian's fear this was an ambush. Morunasa and the other Oracles reacted by shouting at the Marula, rushing back among them, kicking them, so that the warriors scrambled to their feet, scrabbling for their lances. Beyond this chaos, the sybling Sinistrals fell some on one knee, some on two, lowering their casqued heads, both tattooed and not, their cloaks subsiding like billows of tar smoke. 'Celestial,' they murmured.

Osidian was still tense as he surveyed the guardsmen. The Marula warriors had formed up with their lances. Carnelian saw their eyes and knew that, at a word, they would fall upon the syblings, releasing their fear as bloody rage.

It was Osidian relaxing a little that calmed everyone. 'Have the Halls of Rebirth been made ready to receive me?'

The syblings kneeling in front of Osidian bowed their two heads further. 'As much as could be done in the time available, Celestial.'

Osidian extended a hand to raise the guardsmen from their knees. 'Lead on.'

The commander of the Sinistral Ichorians looked uncertainly at the Marula. It seemed to Carnelian the syblings were reluctant to cede their place at the Jade Lord's side to these barbarians, but when Osidian gestured more insistently, they obeyed. At Osidian's command Morunasa and some of his Oracles put themselves between him and the Sinistrals, then they all set off.

As he walked, Carnelian listened again for that distant

roar. It had to be rain being drained by gutters from the vast canopy of stone above their heads. Still, glancing into the crowding blackness all around, he felt a creeping unease that, in such a place, Osidian should choose to put so much faith in the Oracles of the Darkness-under-the-Trees.

Then, through the columns, Carnelian glimpsed a trembling spire of light. They moved towards its beacon. With every step it widened, but also it grew taller until it seemed to him the path of the sun lay twinkling across a brooding sea. They were entering a world that appeared lit by the melancholy, slanting amber of a northern late afternoon. The columns of the sarcophagi soared in the reflected glow, until the soft wavering light had reached up to reveal the faces surmounting them and the lofty arches that flew from one to the other upon which sat the distant ceiling. He realized that the reason everything was bathed in glimmering light was because the columns and vaults were all skinned with gold.

'The Shimmering Stair,' Osidian breathed and Carnelian saw the source of light was a flight of steps of mirror gold climbing a hill flanked by sarcophagus columns and banistered by walls in which fluttered countless flames. Dark mouths, in pairs, opened all the way up the stair, culminating in a single gape.

As they continued to advance, a vast moat opened up before their feet whose mirror doubled the glowing golden vision. Crossing this on a causeway, squinting against the coruscating air, Carnelian only slowly became aware of a dark figure standing at the foot of the stair, haloed by its shimmer. The hackles rose on his neck. Was this Morunasa's god in human form? The closer they approached this apparition, the more mortal it appeared to be. It had a strange globular head, a crown, perhaps, except that Carnelian had a nagging feeling he had seen it before. A few more steps and he knew who it was. He looked for and found upon its dark head the glimmer of its double mask: two gold Master's faces set side by side.

'You!' Osidian exclaimed.

Carnelian had good reason to remember the sybling Hanuses: Ykoriana's lackeys who had overseen him and Osidian being forced, drugged, into funeral urns to meet a certain and terrible death.

The syblings bent forward, leaning to one side and reaching for the ground with a thin arm. Thus supported, they folded into a prostration so painfully that Carnelian felt they must be wounded. Osidian waved the Sinistrals and Marula out of his path and went forward, Carnelian at his side. They both gazed down at the double-lobed head. It had changed. One side of it was smaller, wrinkled.

'Rise,' Osidian said, his voice tight.

Carnelian observed with what difficulty the syblings came to their feet. The twin faces of gold, though imperious and beautiful, hung at an angle that cheated them of their power.

'Unmask,' Osidian commanded and Carnelian could hear how dangerous he was.

A single, tremulous voice sounded from behind the double mask. 'Celestial . . . the barbarians . . .' The syblings lifted a hand to indicate the Marula.

Coldly, Osidian informed them that, since he had taken the barbarians into his service, they were now a part of the household of the House of the Masks. The syblings bent their head to comply. Their right hand struggled up to worry at the bindings behind the misshapen head. Carnelian looked for and found the left arm hanging withered, useless at the syblings' side. Then their faces were revealed. The left was unlike Carnelian's memory of it, but he could adjust to how much it had aged, to the folds in the putty flesh, and in its pitted eyes it had the same black diamonds. The right shocked him. Shrunken, wizened like a dried fig. Where it met the living face, it dragged down the corner of its mouth, the empty cheek, the right eye so that it seemed that, at any moment, the black jewel might be squeezed out like a pip, might run down the cheek like an oily, black tear. Clearly, it was Left-Hanus alone who stood before them. His brother had died. Carnelian gazed with horror at the shrivelled remains of Right-Hanus. In his bones he knew this was Ykoriana's handiwork.

'What made you dare appear before me?' Osidian said.

The sybling's face grew moist. 'Your mother, Celestial, bade me come and bring you to her.' The sybling's speech was slurred by him being forced to speak out of the left corner of his mouth. 'To bring you both to her.'

It was as much the sound of that voice as the words it had spoken that chilled Carnelian. The moment was upon him. That Ykoriana had sent the sybling must be a sign that she felt no remorse for what she had done to them. On the contrary, she was clearly determined to brazen it out. Carnelian grew grim. She had reason to be so confident.

'Take us to her then,' said Osidian, a weariness in his voice that suggested he was thinking similar thoughts.

Left-Hanus ducked a bow, then motioned with his good hand. A child rose from the shadow at his feet and nestled its head under his hand. Then, hobbling, the sybling turned to the steps and began a slow ascent. Carnelian watched the man as they followed him. He felt no rage, not even anger, but only pity. He could imagine what it was to lose a brother, but even then he could claim none as close to him as the sybling's. For Carnelian, if one of his brothers were to die he would bury him; he would not have to carry the corpse as part of him all the remaining days of his life.

They climbed the central, raised stair of the Shimmering, passing several of the immense portals that penetrated the slope in pairs. At last they came to the final gateway that gaped at the summit of the steps. Two colossi flanked it, one of jade, the other of mirror obsidian. Osidian came to a halt gazing up to either side. Carnelian could not see what he was looking at, but then noticed the hinges twisting out of the rock from which massive gates had been wrenched. This made him recall the gap torn in the fabric of the Green Gate. Most likely this desecration had the same cause. Portals of iron had stood here, that Molochite had melted down to sheath his chariot. Brooding on this, Carnelian looked through the gateway. His eyes found it hard to grasp the strange geometries of the spaces beyond.

'The Halls of Rebirth,' Osidian said, sounding surprised, as if he had never again expected to see them.

They entered a realm of dream. Vast halls they crossed, giving onto perspectives apparently infinite. Forests of gleaming stone. Cliffs of filigreed marble liked bleached bone. Walls of translucent alabaster hung like mist. Pools bisected landscapes of stone polished to a sheen like oiled skin, that was veined with fiery filaments. Chambers echoed to falls of water. Hanus led them through sequences of spaces like the hollows of a seashell, all hung with lamps like clouded stars. Up flights of steps they followed, each stair bringing them into some new world of form, of shimmering colour, of sound. Every surface was slick with subtle reflections. Gargoyles pushed out through membranes of coral, of lapis lazuli. Faces everywhere vanished when you looked at them directly. Feeling eyes upon him, Carnelian, turning, saw only jewel mosaics so fiendish they mesmerized him. Shadows flitted at the edge of vision but, when he looked round, there was nothing there.

Among these wonders the Marula stumbled, their thick feet leaving trails across the mirrored stone which blushed then faded like breath on glass. Some of the Oracles looked around them wild-eyed, their mouths hanging open. The rest hung their heads, gripping each other, like children skulking through a haunted wood.

Rising into open air was like coming awake. Glancing back the way they had come, Carnelian could see nothing but shadow. The splendour of the palace was already fading. They were on the roof. Terraces spilled their cataracts into the immense pit of the Plain of Thrones. He felt a vast presence behind him so menacing it took courage to turn. As the towering blackness came into sight he stopped breathing, certain it was the Darkness-under-the-Trees rearing to engulf him. He gasped back to life as he recognized the Pillar of Heaven: a black shaft plunging down from the light-veined clouds to impale the earth way off down the broad belly of the Labyrinth.

A distorting shadow, Hanus guided them across the Labyrinth roof. When he came to a halt, at his command the Ichorians lit lamps. Carnelian followed Osidian to stand beside the sybling on the brink of a well, still partially covered by an immense slab. Osidian snatched a lamp from one of the guardsmen and held it aloft. Its light found steps spiralling down into blackness.

'The Path of Blood,' Osidian muttered and his words seemed to find an echo in the rumbling sky. He turned to the sybling. 'My mother went this way?'

'She did, Celestial.'

'It is forbidden.'

'She waits for you, Celestial, alone.'

'Without attendants?' Osidian's tone was incredulous.

'I myself watched her descend, Celestial. None followed her.'

'Only a candidate may walk this path, accompanied by the primary sacrifice.'

Carnelian's heart misgave at that word.

'She asked that you should bring the Lord Suth with you.'

'She expects us to walk defenceless into her trap?'

The sybling bowed his misshapen head. Carnelian saw a trail of spots leading down the first few steps. He crouched and reached out to touch one. He expected it to be wet and was surprised when it felt like skin. He pinched the thing up, brought it to the nose holes of his mask. Inhaled. Rose. He extended his hand into the light. The petal sat in his palm like a wound. He looked again at the petals on the steps that still seemed like a trail of blood. The well was exuding from its black throat the odour of blood. The hackles rose on his neck. Was this the well that had so often haunted his dreams? He glanced back at the Pillar of Heaven remembering the stair that had taken him to his first meeting with Osidian. In his gut he knew it was his fate to descend into its depths. Even though what lay down there might be his mortal enemy and his own certain death. 'I think we should go.'

Osidian's mask turned to him, imperious. 'Even after what happened last night?'

'I am certain she will be alone.' Carnelian was. Ykoriana would want no witnesses for what she was going to say.

'You saw this in a dream?'

In so many dreams, Carnelian thought, but said: 'Trust me.'

Osidian's gold face regarded him impassively. 'Very well.' He raised the lantern, perhaps to check it had enough oil.

'Light is forbidden—' the sybling began, but Osidian cut him off with a harsh gesture. He passed the lantern to Carnelian, then commanded two of the Sinistrals to give him their swords. Taking them, he offered one to Carnelian, who shook his head. Osidian handed back the unwanted sword, then muttered some instructions to Morunasa. Carnelian set his foot on the top of the stair and, holding the lantern out so that its light fell on the next few steps, he began the descent. As he followed the wall of the well round, he glanced back to make sure Osidian was following him. A grating sound made him aware the slab was being pulled over the opening.

'We will not be coming back this way,' Osidian said.

Carnelian suppressed a thrill of panic as the last rind of the dark sky was eclipsed by the stone. Then he resumed the descent, their footfalls having acquired a disturbing echo.

* * *

The steps spiralled them down, down into the blackness. Fearing his sight dangerously impaired by the eyeslits through which he was peering, Carnelian removed his mask and hung it at his waist. A moist exhalation rising up from the depths made his skin clammy. The air was thick with the odour of spilled blood. Carnelian put his hand out to touch the wall. It was gritty, slimy. He brought his fingers to his nose.

'Rust,' said Osidian.

Carnelian glanced up and saw he too had unmasked. He watched Osidian squinting into the blackness below.

'If you were going to your Apotheosis, I would be going to my death.'

Osidian focused on Carnelian's face and he frowned. 'Go on.'

Carnelian resumed the descent, each step taking him closer to his doom. Notions flitted through his head: of murder and becoming a god; of despair and a striving for absolution.

Down and further down they went. The breeze from below slowly died. It grew hotter until their robes were clinging to their skin. It became harder to breathe. The lantern flame was guttering.

At last they reached the ground and saw a tunnel leading off into blackness. As they moved into it, their hackles rose: shapes were following them. Carnelian convinced himself they were only reflections given feverish life by the pulsing flame. Then the light died and they were in blackness. They came to a halt. The only sounds in the world were their breathing and his own heartbeat. The blackness was smothering. A touch on his hand made him recoil.

'Just me,' Osidian whispered.

Carnelian let his hand fall, questing in the darkness for Osidian's. Their fingers found each other. They crept forward, hand in hand.

*   *   *

Ahead, beyond the end of the tunnel, was what appeared to be a clot of blood glowing. Carnelian and Osidian slowed, unsure of what it was they were approaching. Osidian slipped his hand free of Carnelian's as they advanced. He raised his mask to set it before his face. Reluctantly, Carnelian copied him and was glad when its slits subdued the glare.

They emerged into open space, both still mesmerized by the mass of redness. This was surmounted by a halo of darker red. Crusted and ridged, like a dried puddle of blood, at whose centre was a face of gold, so beautiful it stopped Carnelian's breath.

'Mother,' said Osidian, coming to a halt at the entrance to the tunnel, half emerging into the light, half remaining in shadow. His mask fell with his hand, exposing his pallid face. Carnelian registered the movement, but his attention could not long be diverted from the scarlet apparition. She was clothed in rose petals. A countless number of them sewn together in drifts, each like a tiny gouge of bloodied skin. The whole robe seemed almost to bleed, in contrast to the deathly, perfect mask that sat above it.

'My son,' the mask said, in a rich, melodious voice. The jewelled halo flashed and coruscated as Ykoriana gave Osidian a nod. 'Carnelian,' she said, giving another nod.

The rose robe whispered, tore red, shedding petals as she raised an arm. A porcelain hand emerged and formed a gesture of invitation. Drawn by its command they both stepped further into the light. Carnelian raised his mask as a screen, breaking the compulsion of fascination long enough to be able to look up and round. They were emerging from an opening set into a staircase that rose precipitously, lit with lamps, to a great height. On either side tiers shelved off into the gloom. He was becoming aware of the vastness of the cavern they were entering when a flash of light momentarily illuminated its entirety for a moment. An immense space backed with a ladder of tiers set with stone seats. A dull rumble caused the world to quiver as he looked down. He waited until another flash revealed the Plain of Thrones below. They were standing in the Pyramid Hollow. When the darkness returned, the only thing he could see out there was, far away, something like a star fallen burning to the earth.

'On your head is all the destruction, all the deaths, even among the Chosen,' Osidian said, pointing to the fallen star. Carnelian regarded the point of light. It was located near the rim of the Plain of Thrones, where the Chosen dead had been carried. That light was likely a pyre made from the palanquins that had brought them there. He remembered other pyres.

He dropped his mask and gazed once more upon Ykoriana. She towered above them; no doubt she stood on ranga. Her robe gave off an intoxicating perfume.

'I played my part in the destruction of the Balance, but let us not pretend, my Lord, I brought it down alone.'

'My part in it was also your doing, Madam,' snarled Osidian, his sword rising in his hand so that Carnelian feared he might impale his mother. 'You snatched from me what was rightly mine.'

'I too have lost much, had much taken away from me,' said Ykoriana, oblivious to the blade aimed at her. Carnelian remembered that she was blind.

'The Chosen chose me to become the Gods. What you did was a crime, a sin.'

The jewelled halo winked and ran with light as it jerked back. Ykoriana laughed. 'A sin? You turn the world upside down to right a wrong committed against you and that is perfectly justifiable but, when I act against the wrongs done to me, you name that a sin.'

The point of Osidian's sword slowly fell. Carnelian was relieved. He gazed up at Ykoriana's face of gold trying to work out what it was he felt. Whatever it was, he did not want her slain there, now, in cold blood.

Osidian's face saddened. 'Years I endured living among filthy barbarians.' Tears lensed his eyes. Carnelian felt that sight awakening his own grief.

'I was a slave,' Osidian said, bleakly, gazing up at his mother through tears. 'A slave.' Horror paled his face. 'It was a living death within the funeral urn.'

The halo dulled as the gold face inclined towards them. 'You forget, Nephron, to whom you speak. All my life I have been confined, much of it in darkness.'

Osidian grimaced. 'But it was not I who did that to you,' he pleaded.

Ykoriana straightened. 'That hardly matters. What I did to you was not out of hatred. It was simply a tactic in the slow, cold war that has been fought within the House of the Masks for centuries. We are all casualties of that war.'

But not the only ones, thought Carnelian. He flinched when he saw Osidian's face changing. So would Ykoriana had she been able to see his barely contained fury. Many who had seen it had died. 'Unnatural mother,' he hissed.

The gold mask above them moved a little to gaze down on them with imperious scorn. 'I deny your right to make a claim on me. I know you not who hardly ever saw your face, who never felt your mouth upon my breast. Even your voice is a stranger's. You were taken from me at birth so that I did not even have a touch of you to salve the pain of your release.'

Her head fell. 'But you cannot know what it is to carry a child within you, to have it torn bleeding from your womb, knowing it is born to die in sacrifice, to be imprisoned, to be used as I have been used. Yet I have done what I could to protect those of my children that I love.' She raised her head. 'You know, Carnelian, how far your father was prepared to go to protect you.'

Carnelian, even while he wondered at the softness of her voice, felt a barb in those words that tore at him.

She pulled herself up and became imperial again. 'A mother's love is stronger by far than a father's. To save her child, she would destroy the world.'

There was a terrible edge to her voice that shook Carnelian, not only with fear, but also with a twinge of desire to be that child.

'And, yet, you gave yourself and the Masks to the murderer of your daughter.'

Carnelian looked at Osidian, stung by the venom in those words, but saw no rage burning in his eyes, only . . . was it hope?

The petal robe, shivering, gave off a wall of perfume. 'Would seeking revenge against her murderer have brought my daughter back from her tomb?' Her voice was as cold as the metal of her mask. 'Women are forced to see life as it is. In contrast, you men are so ready to believe in your fantasies, to have your every expectation confirmed. In spite of hating your brother for what he had done, I protected him because he was my path to power. You prefer to believe women victims to their passions, but we can be at least as calculating as you. Love does not make us weak, but strong. Do you remember, Carnelian, when your father brought you to see me? He did so hoping that, through love of my sister, I would stay my hand against you and, even, against him.' She laughed. 'Why do men prefer to make themselves blind to who we really are? Perhaps this is why you use us as you do, but be certain I will not let it happen again.'

Carnelian, who had felt he was being reduced to a stupid child, could not follow her. 'Let what happen again?'

Her mask seemed to regard him for a while. 'Molochite, I lost control of; you, Nephron, I will not.'

There was doubt and confusion in Osidian's face. Carnelian felt no doubt, only fear, but also a longing for the relief of at last confronting what he knew was coming.

'I shall wield not only the power I once had but, now the Balance is broken, vastly more; not only here in Osrakum, but in the world beyond.'

'What are you talking about?' Osidian said, anger and anxiety warring in his face.

'About the power I will have after your Apotheosis, once you wed me.'

Osidian gaped at her, incredulous. 'Wed you?'

'I shall be your wife, as I was your brother's and your father's before him.'

Osidian stared at her, shaking his head as if he could not believe what he had heard. He looked at Carnelian, seeking confirmation of her madness, but Carnelian only managed a shrug. Osidian swung back towards his mother, grimacing. 'Recent events must have unwitted you, my Lady.'

In response, her hands emerged from her robe. The sleeves tore, revealing inner layers of sewn petals more intensely red that released an overpowering odour of roses. The porcelain fingers reached behind her head and her mask came loose. Carnelian flinched as her naked face was revealed.

At first he was aware of nothing but her eyes: tapering, oval peridots as limpid as dew caught in the calyx of a flower. Her pale skin reddened where it met the stones so that they seemed to have been forced into wounds. The lips were thin and pursed as if from the strain of biting back too many bitter words. It was a beautiful face, but one that betrayed suffering impatiently borne.

Osidian was gazing at his mother, seeming to seek someone he knew, or thought he knew, or remembered and had lost. 'I shall lock you away. No one will ever see you again.'

Ykoriana smiled. Though it seemed that tears might at any time squeeze from under her stone eyes, those lips bore the certainty of victory.

Osidian rubbed his face, blinking, as if wiping cobwebs from it. 'I have no need of your blood, mother. To produce an heir, I shall mate with my sister-niece, Ykorenthe.'

Ykoriana's face hardened to ice. Her eyes flashed as she pointed over their heads to the steps that rose behind them. 'We watched your father's Apotheosis from up there, your grandmothers, your great-aunts and I.'

Carnelian had a feeling Ykoriana was addressing him as

much as she was her son. They were his grandmothers, his great-aunts too.

'All the women of our House watched. We had all taken leave of our brothers, our cousins, our sons. Since the election of your father, they had been held as captives. For days, they had been starved so that they would not pollute the rituals. Even as the Chosen took their places . . .' She swept her arms up, taking in the tiers that rose in a cliff behind them. Carnelian looked up and, even though they were in darkness, he imagined the Masters in their glory taking their places on their thrones. '. . . our kin had already been placed within the torsion devices.'

She pointed to the nearest of several peculiar contraptions that hung from posts up both sides of the stair. In the lamplight they looked like the dried carcasses of huge squid, their heads hanging from the posts on hooks, their tentacles dangling almost to the ground.

'You have not seen these in operation,' she said, 'but you will. An ingenious invention of the Wise.' She raised her left hand with the long fingers drooping. 'The man or boy is strapped inside.' She formed her right hand into a beak as if she held a plum stone between the tips of her fingers. She moved this up into the cage of her left hand and withdrew it, closing the cage as if she had left the stone within it. 'The thongs are all pulled together.' She drew imaginary threads from the ends of her left fingers. 'And tied to a capstan.' Carnelian glanced and saw a capstan beneath the nearest device. 'Then it is turned, twisting the thongs.' She spiralled her fingers. 'Turn after turn, the tentacles above tightening, digging the barbs that line their inner surface deeper and deeper into flesh.'

Carnelian grimaced, glancing at the device. He saw the barbs like fish teeth.

'When they can twist it no further, the capstan is locked. Then, at the right time during the ritual . . .' The silence made him turn to see Ykoriana frowning. Her hands formed two cones touching at their points. '. . . they are released.' Her

691

hands spiralled apart in opposite directions so violently her sleeves shed a mass of scarlet petals into the air. 'The bodies within them, ripped apart. Their flesh sieved through an obsidian-bladed mesh. Scattering blood across the Chosen. Creation through blood sacrifice.'

Carnelian remembered his father speaking those very words when they had sighted a turtle, as they stood together in the prow of the baran on the approach to Thuyakalrul. Right after the massacre he had sparked off by appearing on deck unmasked.

'Kumatuya, your father . . .' Ykoriana lingered, gazing down with her fiery green eyes upon neither of them, but both. '. . . stood there.' She pointed at the plinth that rose between them to their waists. 'The Twelve about him, bearing the Masks and the Crowns and all the other divine insignia. As this chariot rose to the apex of the pyramid and they transformed him into the Gods . . .'

Carnelian could not see why this was a chariot, but he noted for the first time the cables that ran up the steps.

Her rose-petal robe sighing, she moved to one side, revealing a slab of iron rising at an angle behind her in which there was the impression of a man spreadeagled. 'In which procedure my other brother played the Turtle.'

Her hand lingered for a moment, tracing the edge of the man-shaped hollow in which some petals lodged like spots of blood. Her brow knitted and the lids narrowed her stone eyes. 'The Wise gouge out his eyes to be the sun and moon. They take his tongue, his hands, his feet. Each portion plays a role in the ritual. Finally, as your father watches . . .' Carnelian was as close to the hollow now as Kumatuya had been. '. . . the closed doors of his ribs are broken open one at a time.' She spread her fingers. 'His still beating heart is torn out and held above him. The warm blood gushes, from which your father drinks, so that as he takes the life of his brother, two become one. From death, divine life risen.'

She regarded them both, her face blank with horror. She

had seen this with her own eyes before they were taken from her.

'My uncle was drugged,' Osidian declared. He swung his arm round to take in the torsion devices. 'They were all drugged. They felt nothing.'

Ykoriana frowned. 'That certainly is what the Wise claim. It is true my brother made no movement; he did not cry out.' She leaned towards them. 'But your father, who witnessed his mutilation at close hand, told me afterwards he had seen in our brother's eyes, before they were plucked out, a terrible, animal fear. It haunted him.' She grew aged beyond her years. 'It haunted me.'

Her hand strayed back to the hollow in the iron, caressing its edge as if the fingers wished to reach inside but dared not for fear of what they might touch. 'It was I who had to make the choice between them. It was I who chose who would lie here . . . and who would stand there.' She pointed towards them. 'Suth Sardian with his exile saved your father from lying here.' She tapped the iron. Her brows knit again. 'I demanded this proof of love from your father, Nephron. I loved him, though I had reason to hate all men. I submitted myself to his touch, though it brought me little joy.' Her face grew sour with remembered pain. 'For an unripe fruit will carry any early touch as rot when it ripens. And though Sardian was no longer there between us, your father hated me for it.' She clinked one of her stone eyes. 'And he took my sight.' She frowned. 'Once I thought it was in revenge for depriving him of his lover; now I am not so sure. Perhaps it was vengeance for what he was forced to witness.' Her face darkened. 'Though it was the Wise he should hate, and the Great who cast their votes but hazard nothing.'

She put on a smile. 'Still, that is politics.' She raised her head and her green eyes glittered as if she was seeing something far away. 'But then Sardian chose to stay away.'

Carnelian tensed.

'Year after year when he could have returned, he chose

not to. Almost I had forgotten him when that fool, Aurum, had the Clave elect him He-who-goes-before. I was confident Sardian would not return; but then he did and the minion I sent to find out why now, why not before, came back to me with nothing.'

'What has this to do with anything?' Osidian said, looking weary, upset. Carnelian gazed at him, wondering if it could possibly be the description of the blood rituals that had penetrated to his heart. He had looked on massacres unmoved, but this was bloodshed and torture among his own.

'It has everything to do with your Apotheosis. To save himself, Aurum told me at last. For he had seen it when he arrived on Suth's island.'

'Seen what?' Osidian cried, exasperated.

Almost Carnelian answered him, but felt a need to hear it told by Ykoriana. 'Aurum was intimate with that old monster, my father. He was often at court.'

'Please, tell me what you are talking about.'

Carnelian saw the weariness in Osidian's face, but saw also how he had to listen, because this woman was still his mother.

'That Carnelian here is the living image of your father.'

Osidian's face folded in confusion.

'The living image of his father.'

Carnelian watched the realization smooth Osidian's face. For a moment, shocked, he looked like a stupid child. Then he gazed at Carnelian as if he were seeing him for the first time. His eyes narrowed. 'You knew this already.' His face darkened. 'How long have you known?'

Carnelian explained how his father had told him when he came secretly to their camp.

'Why didn't you tell—?'

Carnelian watched the realization dawn.

'That's why you deserted me.' The blood left Osidian's face and he looked at his mother, then beyond her to the hollow man, in horror.

Ykoriana smiled. 'That you ignored Sardian's warning, that you are here, proves, Carnelian, does it not, that you know to what lengths my son will be prepared to go to save you.'

'On the contrary, my Lady, it proves only that I came here knowing what you would threaten and to make sure Osidian does not submit to you.' Carnelian turned to find Osidian staring at him and smiled at what was left in him of the boy in the Yden. 'For I would not wish him enslaved again.'

Osidian's lips seemed to be trying to return the smile, tears starting, but then his chin fell and there was a twitching at the corners of his eyes, his mouth, as if he were seeing scenes in rapid succession, or having fleeting conversations. Almost imperceptibly, his head sank further, his shoulders rounded, so that instinctively Carnelian glanced at Ykoriana, fearing that, by not even trying to mask his feelings of defeat, Osidian was making her victory over him, over them both, more complete.

But then Carnelian remembered that her eyes were stones and saw, besides, no trace of victory in her face, but only confusion and a pale fear. In his bones he felt it was not for herself she feared. 'So as you see, Celestial' – he paused, ready to gauge every nuance in her face – 'your son will have no need to wed you. I will die at his Apotheosis and, afterwards, he will take Ykorenthe to be his empress.'

There! At the mention of her daughter's name, he had seen the blade of fear cut deeper into her heart. It was the girl she sought to protect. Carnelian regarded Ykoriana afresh. Perhaps she had wed her other son for power, but what she sought now was to put her body between Osidian and her daughter. She was trying to protect the girl in the way no one had protected her. He no longer saw a terrible empress in her bitter pomp, but only a woman, aged by suffering beyond her years, who had dressed herself in a robe of rose petals in her attempt to seduce her own son, to protect a child; to protect what was left of the child that she had been.

Carnelian blinked back tears and looked from mother to son and back again. How defeated they looked. Both trapped and he along with them. Rage rose in him, as his heart sought to free itself from this ensnarement. 'It is the Wise who bind us,' he cried.

They both turned their green eyes upon him, stone and living, both needing, demanding more. Carnelian tried to think it through, but the pressure rising in him was beyond analysis. 'We came here believing you had sought your son's life.' He described the assassination attempt and believed the shock in Ykoriana's face was real, knew he had expected it. 'It makes no sense now that you would do this, but the use of the Brotherhood of the Wheel must be intended to implicate you. So if not you, my Lady, who?'

Osidian's eyes widened in disbelief. 'The Wise?'

'Why not the Wise?' Carnelian said. 'Would the Brotherhood attempt such a thing on their own? Or the Great, who could only expect to be decimated by it?' He frowned, considering what his heart was urging him to. Feeling it was a kind of madness, but unwilling to dam its flow. 'We are all three here of the House of the Masks.'

There, he had said it. It was the first time he had felt it.

'Instead of fighting each other, we should unite against our common foe.' Carnelian paused and saw in their faces they were waiting for his words. He glanced into the hollow man. 'I do not want to die here, nor do I want to live under a perpetually deferred sentence of death.'

Ykoriana lowered her head a little. 'Does Aurum still live?'

'I believe that unlikely.'

'Well, then, assuming Sardian will not betray you, if I choose not to speak of it, I doubt if any could discover your secret.'

'And the reason we cannot announce the truth of my birth openly is what?'

'The Law-that-must-be-obeyed,' she said.

'And yet have we not all three defied it?'

Osidian frowned. 'The blood rituals are essential for Rebirth, for Apotheosis.'

'Are they?' Carnelian could not shape in his mind what was coming; the words would have to find their own shape. 'It seems to me these blood rituals have been conceived to set the House of the Masks against the Great. Further, to divide our House against itself. Are these mutilations, this massacre of our own, necessary? Can we not invoke the Creation without reproducing it? Or is it, perhaps, that the Wise wish to bring the candidate face to face with his own mortality? Even as they give him the symbols of power, even as they transform him into the Gods, they show him the flesh of which he is made, how easily his blood flows. Even if they can give you divinity, Osidian, you know they cannot give you immortality.'

'Nevertheless, the Chosen will not accept my Godhead unless it is consecrated with ichorous blood.'

Carnelian saw in Osidian's face that, on this issue, he was immovable. He feared losing impetus and so he turned to Ykoriana, the mother. 'What if you were given your daughter to raise until she was of age to become empress and wife?'

Carnelian watched Ykoriana grow younger with hope.

'That would destabilize my throne,' Osidian said. 'To rule without possibility of an heir for so long.'

Carnelian turned to him. 'If you were to die this instant, who would most likely become the next God Emperor?'

Almost imperceptibly, Osidian's eyes narrowed. 'You would.'

'Ever since my father came to speak to me, I could have sought the Masks, but, clearly, I have not.'

Osidian nodded.

'Do you really believe I covet such power?'

Osidian's face became brittle. 'To save your beloved barbarians, perhaps.'

Carnelian saw the truth in this. It seemed for a moment as if everything would founder on that doubt. 'Well, then,

697

let me rule the outer world as your viceroy. Anyone who moved against either of us would have to fear the vengeance of the other. Until either of us produces an heir, the Great will live in fear that we should both die, for then one among them would have to be chosen to wear the Masks and the Law would force many of his peers to be slaughtered at his Apotheosis.'

Carnelian could see Osidian was still not entirely convinced. 'For years you will be needed here to hold Osrakum together. How much energy would you have left to rebuild and safeguard the Commonwealth?'

'You want to save your barbarians.'

'I will not deny it, but also, and more pressing, there is the need to work against the famine that is coming.'

'And when Ykorenthe comes of age and we produce an heir?'

'I will retire to my coomb, to Coomb Suth.'

'You will no longer be Suth.'

'The Great will be unable to defy you when you give me the coomb as a gift.'

Osidian regarded him, weighing his judgement of this new brother. Carnelian knew there were several political attractions in such a scheme, but he wished to remove the last vestiges of doubt. 'By then I will have done enough to appease my conscience.'

Osidian nodded.

'And in the meantime you can keep an eye on me through the Wise and their watch-towers.'

Ykoriana stirred. 'There is hope in this.'

As they both turned to regard her, it seemed she was holding her breath, waiting for Osidian's response. He gazed at Carnelian, then sank his head. The wind soughed in the vast space above them. At last Osidian raised his eyes to Carnelian and smiled, grimly. 'Let it be as my brother says.'

*　　　*　　　*

All three touched hands and swore oaths upon their blood.

Even if they had wished it, they knew they could not return by the Path of Blood, so it was necessary to climb the stair to the apex of the Pyramid Hollow where portals gave into the imperial strata of the Halls of Rebirth. Ykoriana removed her ranga and they began the climb, Osidian on her right hand, Carnelian on her left. The steps were steep so they supported her. Her robe tore upon the steps leaving a trail of petals. Glancing down it seemed to Carnelian to be the blood that had been shed there, but sweet and fluttering away on the wind.

TRIBUTARIES

Truth is written in the fabric of the world
If only one has the eyes to read it.
(Quyan fragment)

A vast bloated corpse floats on a dark sea. Flesh awrithe with maggots. Sartlar consuming each other? Blood and render licking up his body. Sucking at his armpits so that he is forced to raise his arms as branches. His hands and face are dry, caked earth. Dry earth everywhere. Catching in his throat so that he is racked by coughing. Carnelian scratches at his eyes so as to see her clearly. A woman clothed in plates and clods of blood-red earth, shedding it in flakes and dust away on the wind. He grips her hand as a child would his mother's. Smug, he gazes up at her, but the face she turns down to him is a grinning skull.

Carnelian jerked awake, hugging the black cloak around him. It was a while before he fully surfaced from the dream. Morning was slipping in through high windows. He sat up, swinging his legs out so he could perch on the edge of the niche he had slept in. Lifted the pits of his knees away from the chill stone lip. He saw the wound in his thigh and was surprised how little he felt it. He looked towards the vast bed, bare of its silk and feather coverlets. Even from this distance he could smell its aura of lilies. Away across the chamber the

700

hearth was now grey and cold because he had forbidden any-one to come to tend it while he slept.

He stared blindly, filled with dread. Was the dream a foretelling of the famine that was coming? A flash of anger. He had felt so certain he could work against it, but was it already too late? Was he fated to return to the outer world to do nothing more than witness the sartlar, driven by unbearable hunger, devouring each other? Fear rose in him. Was Ykoriana the woman with the skull face? In trusting her, had he committed a fatal error?

Submerged in a deluge, he stood trying to wash away the taint of the dream. The warm water was caressing life back into his body. He raised his arm against the pressure into the air space in the shelter of his bowed head. He looked at his hand as if he hoped to see some mark left by the dream woman's clasp. Thinking of her brought Ebeny into his mind, made him yearn like a child to go to her. There was another press-ing reason he must cross the Skymere: he needed to talk to his father before the revelation of his birth became common knowledge throughout Osrakum.

He emerged from the waterfall, dripping, onto the icy jade floor. The whole chamber was carved from the mossy stone into the appearance of rushes. The fall frothed into a pool, that cascaded into another into which more water poured. By means of steps, he ascended to a chamber of mirrors. Obsidian polished to the consistency of a midnight pool. Panels of silver and of gold. All held his ghosts as if in other places, other seasons. Ridges of white jade around the walls supported jars hollowed from jewels, vessels carved from stone like swirling smoke, racks of strigils and brushes made of feather filaments.

Unnerved by the crowd of himself, he left. Back in the bedchamber he moved towards the outer portals. There, on the floor, were the robes Marula had brought in when he had forbidden entry to the slaves sent to tend him. The folded bundles had in places come apart. Exquisite fabrics interwoven with metal threads, subtly patterned like lichens, like ripples on water, like high, feathery clouds. He stooped because his fingers were drawn to touch them. As smooth as lips or the moist-skin texture of petals. Then he saw the parchment sitting incongruously on a boulder of cloth. He plucked the letter up and turned it into the light. It had been sealed with a blood-ring. The double face of the House of the Masks. He peered at the name glyph. 'Nephron,' he said, surprised. He counted the blood-taint zeros. 'Four.' He frowned, remembering the last time he had seen a letter sealed thus. That ill-fated day when he had persuaded Osidian to go down into the Yden. It made him suspicious. Osidian's blood-ring had been taken from him during the kidnapping. Could there have been time to make another? It was more likely to be one of Ykoriana's tricks. Still. He broke open the letter and read.

Come, break your fast with me on sweet pomegranates as we did long ago.

Surely only Osidian possessed that knowledge? Carnelian turned the parchment to look upon the broken seal. It was Osidian's ring so perhaps Ykoriana had sent it to him. Carnelian pondered the import of this. Surely such an act was to invite incrimination? So, done deliberately, it could be a sign of peace. There was hope in Ykoriana making herself so vulnerable. He sank his head, wondering if he dared believe in the proposals he had made the night before in the Pyramid Hollow, but still he could not wholly rid himself of the omen of his dream. He read the letter again, becoming uneasy at what expectations Osidian might be nurturing with that reference to their lovemaking in the Forbidden Garden.

Carnelian glanced at the seductive beauty of the robes. His skin longed for their touch, but he turned his back on them. Even if they had not been too complicated to put on without servants, they would encumber him on his journey. He wandered back to where he had left the green spiralled robe the ammonites had dressed him in. He slipped it on, put on his father's mask and military cloak.

When he emerged from his chambers, his Marula guards rose, discarding the resplendent covers he had given them from his bed. Seeing him, their faces lit up as if he were come to save them. Their red eyes spoke of a fearful night. He saw one among them who had not been there the night before. Though he looked different with his head shaved, it was unmistakably Sthax. Carnelian was about to address him when a voice came rumbling from various directions at once. The Marula all jerked round to search the cavernous hall spreading off behind them. As the rumbling died away, though Carnelian knew it must be thunder sounding through the palace from the sky, he could not help fearing that the source of that voice was lurking somewhere close by. He was sure the Marula must feel – as he did – that they were intruders deep in the lair of some monstrosity that might at any time return.

He refocused on Sthax and was going to speak when the Maruli indicated a man half black, half white, kneeling, waiting. Carnelian approached him. 'Have you come to guide me to the Jade Lord Nephron?'

'I have, my Lord,' said the Ichorian.

Carnelian saw that the questions he had for Sthax were going to have to wait. 'Then lead on.'

Through immense spaces they wound their way. Rustling echoes made it seem they were being followed. Movements glimpsed from the corner of his eye, when looked at, revealed nothing but shadows looming in the penumbral gloom. Ghostly reflections accompanied them. Strange odours moistened the air. In some places they had to pass beneath the gaze of giants, whose faces could only be guessed at in the overarching darkness. Every surface was pierced with openings that gave shifting views of other, eerily lit worlds. Carnelian began to feel they were creeping through the carcass of some vast being that had been gnawed by the passage of massive worms.

At first, when he saw the procession approaching, he thought it nothing more than his own party reflected. But the Master who processed amidst a naked escort rose taller than did he. Besides, his robes were so massive they threatened to eclipse his mask of gold. Even as this apparition approached him, Carnelian knew by the heraldry of its crowns this must be Osidian.

The apparition brandished a pair of pale hands. 'Ravenous, despairing that you would ever appear, my Lord, I came to meet you. I would eat before attending what is bound to be a dreary conclave with the Wise.'

Carnelian had to look up at him. Osidian's new mask was the face of a beautiful boy, entranced. He wore ranga beneath his robes, the outer one of which seemed flowing naphtha. As he half turned away, its lustrous black sheened with iridescence. 'I have brought a feast with me,' Osidian said, pointing to the tail of his procession, where syblings bore a great variety of burdens. He made a vague gesture. 'There is a spot not far from here where we might consume it in some comfort and seclusion.'

Carnelian regarded Osidian's towering form with misgivings. He seemed a puppet being worked from a distance. Laughter coming from behind the puppet's mask sounded forced. 'Really, my Lord, you will have to get used to being Chosen again.' He took in Carnelian's green robe and rough military cloak with a mocking hand. 'Why did you choose these rags in place of the gorgeous robes I sent you?'

Watching this performance, Carnelian became increasingly glad of the decision he had made. 'Though you are kind to have thought of bringing breakfast, Celestial, time is pressing. The sooner I reach Coomb Suth, the sooner I can return.'

'That would be inadvisable,' said Osidian.

Carnelian could hear the tightness of anger in his voice.

Almost he reminded Osidian of the oath he had sworn upon his blood, but first chose to give thought to what reasons Osidian might have for feeling angry. Beyond the emotional ones, Carnelian saw others more politic. 'You fear my crossing the Skymere could antagonize the Great?'

'Considering the coming revelations, it would be better, my Lord, were we to observe the accepted forms at least until I am invested with divine authority.'

With a sinking heart, Carnelian saw the logic in that. Nevertheless, he had to find a secure way to contact his father and was, besides, desperate to escape the Halls of Rebirth. He focused his mind on the politics and thought he could see a way out. 'Be that as it may, Celestial, for reasons of safety it is incumbent upon us that we should maintain a separation between us.'

Osidian took some moments to answer. 'I take your point, my Lord.'

'Perhaps I could assume command of the huimur as they perform the functions that once were the Red Ichorians'.' Carnelian paused here, realizing he was not entirely sure what those functions might be.

'You are not even painted.'

Carnelian glanced at his hands. 'I shall be careful to stay out of the sun.' A solution to his other problem suggested itself. He took in Sthax and his escort. 'With your leave, Celestial, I shall take these for my protection until some of my household tyadra have time to reach me from my coomb.'

'You are now of the Masks, Carnelian.'

Carnelian thought it best to say nothing to that.

'Where will you sleep?'

Carnelian shrugged. 'Somewhere in the Plain of Thrones, I imagine.'

There was a long pause. 'You will attend my Apotheosis?'

'Of course.'

'I will send you notification of the day on which the ceremony shall be held.' Osidian extended an open hand.

Upon his palm lay an iron ring. 'You may as well have this.'

Carnelian took the ring, noticing that Osidian wore one on his own hand. 'Your mother sent them both to you?'

Osidian made a gesture of affirmation. 'It seems she really does intend to keep our bargain.'

Carnelian examined the edge of his ring. It was indeed his, the same Aurum had brought to their island.

'Of course, that ring is a lie. We shall have to get a new one made.'

Carnelian considered that. 'But, for the moment, I shall wear this one.' He put it on. Its weight upon his little finger brought back a time long past.

At the edge of some immense hall, where their shuffling produced the faintest echoes, Carnelian called a halt and drew Sthax into some shadows to talk to him. 'Why did you appear this morning?'

'Oracle trust I.'

'Morunasa?'

Sthax nodded.

'Why?'

Sthax opened his mouth to speak, changed his mind, looked to the floor as if he might find the words there. His face came up bright-eyed. He brandished his spear. 'We is this for Oracle.'

Carnelian thought he understood. Like the Masters, the Oracles did not really see their subjects, did not imagine they had any volition of their own. He regarded Sthax. Of course, he could be playing some cunning double game of his own but, in his heart, Carnelian trusted him and believed Sthax sought nothing but the salvation of his people.

Carnelian removed his mask, then, a phrase at a time, he explained how he was to be given power over the outer world and, with some difficulty, about the Apotheosis that was its only precondition. This last concept caused them both a lot of difficulty, for Sthax knew nothing of the Rebirth, never mind the politics of the Masters.

When Carnelian was done, he gave Sthax time to digest it all, then asked him: 'Will you do something for me?'

For some moments, Sthax examined Carnelian's eyes, then gave a nod of agreement, and Carnelian began to coach him in the message he wanted him to carry.

Gazing down into the Labyrinth, Carnelian's heart misgave. With the Shimmering Stair unlit, the columned cavern of the Labyrinth had become a haunt for shadows. The Marula were huddling together, averting their eyes from the view. Carnelian asked Sthax to reassure them he was going to lead them back to the light. The hope Sthax gave them unbowed their backs. Carnelian nodded in satisfaction, then began the descent into the gloom.

After an interminable shuffling through the tunnel, Carnelian's lantern light found some feet in the darkness ahead. Jerking its beam up, he saw a Sapient waiting with his homunculus. Behind them he could see the closed portals of the Forbidden Door.

'I am Carnelian—' It was unlikely the Wise knew about his true birth yet. He must avoid causing unnecessary confusion. 'Suth Carnelian . . . and you, Sapient?'

'A Fifth of Labyrinth, Seraph,' sang the homunculus in such an unhuman voice that the Marula around Carnelian began to tremble. 'We were not informed of your coming,' said the little man, as he cast sharp eyes upon the black men.

'The Lord Nephron has sent me to oversee the preparations for receiving those who must attend his Apotheosis.'

'Still, it is my masters who have set me to guard this portal, Seraph. They must be consulted.' Though the Fifth's fingers continued to work at the neck of the homunculus, he said no more. Disengaging from his master, he disappeared into an opening in the wall.

As Carnelian waited, he gazed past the Sapient at the Forbidden Door, hungry for the daylight that lay beyond. When the homunculus returned, he drew his master's hands up to his throat, murmured something, then fell silent. Carnelian waited for the little man to speak, but he stood, eyes downcast, as still as his master. At last Carnelian could bear it no longer. 'Well, what are we waiting for?'

The homunculus echoed him, then the Fifth's fingers began to flex. 'Instructions from my masters, Seraph.'

Carnelian felt choked with frustration. No doubt the Grand Sapients were already deep in conclave with Osidian. 'Open the door or else I shall have it opened myself.'

The homunculus was soon voicing his master's protests, but Carnelian made it clear he would not be defied. Eventually, the Sapient bowed to his will, and stepped aside as the doors opened, releasing a flood of light. Blind, Carnelian walked out into the day, the Marula stumbling in their eagerness to follow him.

Carnelian sat upon rugs that ammonites had rolled out on ground first purified with their blue fire. He had chosen to wait there because he did not wish to subject himself or the Marula to another cleansing when they returned to the Labyrinth. He was watching more ammonites laving Earth-is-Strong. The dragon rose from their midst like a sea stack. She was being prepared to purify a path all the way to the Great Causeway with her flame-pipes. Carnelian had decided not to command her himself. Instead he had summoned his Lefthand and instructed him to do so.

When the sun burned its way through the clouds, in spite of the assurances he had given Osidian Carnelian was glad to feel its warmth upon his skin. The shadows cast by the flesh-tithe cages had almost entirely shrunk away. Dragons formed lines down either side of the Black Field, which now looked like just another military camp, but it was to the centre of the plain beyond that his eyes kept being drawn.

He gazed between the gate stones, through the outer fence of commentary stones, across the inlaid, cobbled floor to the inner, double ring of the Dance. There, almost completely hidden by the outer stones, he could just glimpse the edge of one of the green stones of the innermost ring.

He had approached the Stone Dance of the Chameleon along a road burnt black by Earth-is-Strong's flame-pipes and still warm beneath his feet. The Fifth had been scandalized at his insistence on proceeding barefoot, but had failed to persuade him to use a palanquin. When he had reached the place where the road divided around the Dance, he had waited for the dragon's thunder to fade away and for the boiling clouds of naphtha smoke to subside. The rings of stones had emerged as if from a mist. Fascinated, he had approached the pair that stood guard upon the road running from the Forbidden Door into the Dance. He had seen that, there, entry to its heart was between a red and a black stone. For some reason he had felt he did not want to enter that way. Instead he had led Sthax and the other Marula round until they had arrived at where the road spoked off towards the House of Immortality.

He glanced in that direction, straining to make out any details that might show where it lay in the cliff wall of the Plain of Thrones. He could see nothing. To the north-east, the pall of smoke being produced by Earth-is-Strong's pipes was trailing its fraying banner round the outer edge of the Dance. Sthax's tiny figure was following the dragon and her fire. Carnelian frowned, feeling the message Sthax was carrying was a poor substitution for a visit. Among other things, he had sent for some of his people. While he waited for them he wanted to explore. Motioning the Marula to stand guard upon the gate stones, he passed between them and entered the Dance.

Between two commentary stones, Carnelian stood gazing across the cobbled ground to the inner rings. The pale mosaic confused his eyes. He was reminded of the bone traceries of an Ancestor House, but this work was more subtle. Tendrils of stone snaked across the floor, crossing and recrossing each other like seaweed abandoned by a tide. Nodules studded the design and it was embedded with rings of smoothed stone and small panels. At first he had taken it all to be marble, but he began to see the grain and shades of different stones and how portions and paths were tinted variously by lichens.

He stepped onto the design. It felt subtly textured. Closing his eyes, he could feel his feet on a path that he followed. Opening them, he looked back at the meandering trail his sooty feet had left. Not a path he could have easily located by sight. He remembered how the Wise used such paths in their library in the Halls of Thunder.

He became aware of the beautiful and complex inner faces of the commentary stones. Returning to them he reached up to touch one. Its swirling patterns were bewildering, but under his fingers they seemed a pebbled beach. Again he closed his eyes. As he glided his fingers slowly across the surface the nodules seemed to whisper in his mind. He reopened his eyes. 'Like beadcord,' he muttered. He noted how tendrils of the floor mosaic lapped at the stone. The nodules were divided into registers, the higher of which could be reached by climbing up onto taller cobbles. Glancing round the whole curve of commentary stones, he saw how, with the floor, they formed a delicate web of meaning emanating from the double ring.

As he approached the inner stones, he saw that their outer faces were patterned in the same way as the commentary stones. Then he became aware that these stones stood each like a ghost behind what appeared to be huge figures. Cracked and round-shouldered, hunching now, but once they had been tall and straight. Entering between a pair of ghost stones, he was confronted by two immense slabs of jade, fissured and veined by pale lichens. As he passed between these, he noticed their inner edges were spotted with round projections. Reaching out to touch one, his finger found its spiralling groove. The same ammonite shells were embroidered into his green robe. Turning, he saw the clear path leading back across the mosaic, through the commentary stones, between the gate stones and on towards the House of Immortality.

He entered the heart of the Dance. Round the mossy space stood the coven of twelve worn stones: two green, two black, eight red. He sensed he was in the presence of something ancient and holy. The inner face of each stone had been cut into. Moving to stand in front of one of these depressions, he realized it was a hollow man, arms and legs outstretched. The hollow was just large enough that he could have climbed into it. From each foot, each hand, a channel ran down to the earth. The channels made the hollow man seem a puppet with rods to move his arms and legs. It did not seem likely their purpose was to drain the hollow of rain water. He sought distraction in the columns of glyphs, worn almost smooth, that covered the surface of the stone. This must be the Law-that-must-be-obeyed. He frowned. Why did it feel like a disfigurement? The glyphs followed the contours of the stone as if they were tattoos or brandings. The Law had been carved into the stone when it was already ancient.

He walked slowly round the Dance, withershins, giving in to his need to understand it. The two green stones led him to the two black. Then began the sequence of eight red stones. Where the black met the red, their inner flanks were carved with circular motifs now almost flush with the stone. Gazing out between these stones, he was looking directly towards the Forbidden Door. The Pillar of Heaven lifted its tornado of stone into a frowning sky. Carnelian looked again at the flank of the black stone, certain the circular carvings had been sky glyphs. Starting with this stone which lay to the sunward of the Rain Axis, the Dance followed the sequence of the months so that the red stone ended the year.

He followed the Dance further round, caressing the

711

time-worn porphyry of the red stones, but when he came to a pair between which Earth-is-Strong's column of smoke was visible, moving away towards the entrance to the Plain of Thrones, he saw their inner flanks bore more of the faint discs. He ran his fingers over them and found one that had within its slightly raised edge a number of pips. His fingers remembered the red stone coin he had received the first time he had passed through the Blood Gate. That had borne a pomegranate. He saw how the gateway formed by the red stones would give direct access to the Dance to anyone entering the Plain of Thrones. He surveyed the Dance, now certain it must be far more ancient than anything else in Osrakum. More ancient even than the Law. More ancient by far than Grand Sapient Legions had been or his Great Balance. Thinking of that ancient, now dead, Carnelian gazed across the Dance at the black stone opposite. Twelve in all. It was as if the Grand Sapients were the living embodiment of these ancient stones.

At that moment the clouds parted, slanting a ray of light into the centre of the Dance. He was drawn to stand in it, turning his face up to allow the sun to bleach the unease from his heart. He sank to the mossy earth and stretched himself out as he gazed through the opening in the stormclouds into perfect, blue heaven.

Swaying beneath a vast, smiling sky. Memories of his mother, of her smell, of the comfort in her hands. Cedars net the blue in their branches. Clean, resinous perfume of her mother tree. Sifting sand, his hand dries up like a fig. Not the breath of the mother trees, but myrrh. Breathing out and out and out as he wizens into a huskman. He is Legions turning to stone. Trapped in an ivory sarcophagus like a brain in a skull. Seed in a pod. A tickle in him, an itch; the heartbeat of the baby inside him. Carried, sleeping, into the ring of twelve. Entering through the still weeping edges of a freshly cut wound. Singing, so mournful. Then swaying out of the clearing watching clouds streak the sky. Out of the clearing into the ferns. Their croziers knock, knock, knocking their heads

together. To whose rhythm the sun bleeds away into the earth.
Away, into the earth. Absorbed into it with the blood and the dying
light. Something's burning. He has to become the worm eating his
escape through the bread, but then, confused, he is scrabbling into
a cradle of bones. His hand drags the nets of his fingers. Dragged
down by the weight of fish in his net. Rope burning his hands,
running deep in a channel of flesh, as it pulls free of the hooks of
his hands, but he holds on, the waters rising.

Carnelian came awake, disorientated. The silhouettes of
heads moving back. He rose, aware of giants standing round.
It was night. Human-scale figures near him were partially lit.
Others were holding the dim stars of lanterns. He recognized
the giants behind them as the monoliths of the Dance, their
looming shadows the incarnation of the foreboding he had
brought with him out of his dream.

'Master?'

It was Tain offering him a sinister face. Carnelian took the
mask. 'I must've fallen asleep.'

Sthax, a shadow with human eyes. Beside him a shrouded
figure whose dear face grounded Carnelian. He approached
him, embraced him. 'I'm so glad you're here, Fern.' He turned
to Tain, to Sthax. 'So glad you're all here.'

Still haunted, Carnelian stared deep into the fire. He was
reluctant to sleep. One dream and all his hope had turned to
despair. He turned the Ruling Ring of House Suth upon his
finger. Fern had brought it for him from his father. A proof, if
he needed one, that his father still considered him his son.

He turned, sensing someone behind him. Rising above the
sentinel monoliths, higher than the glimmering gashes the
terraces of the Halls of Rebirth made in the wall of the plain,
the Pillar of Heaven loomed a deeper black against the blackness.

He returned his gaze to the flames. Why had he not allowed
his people to erect the pavilion they had brought for him? He

hungered for the oblivion that, in its privacy, he could have found in Fern's arms.

He sat up, woken by something. Bells were beating out a funereal dirge. Light throbbed, filtering through the three rings of the Dance. A procession of the Chosen making their way to the Forbidden Door. He recalled the time he had seen another such moving distantly upon the Ydenrim. Then he had been in the Yden with Osidian.

'What is it?' whispered a voice in Ochre.

In the faint light oozing from the embers of their fire, Carnelian could just make out Fern's shape.

'Some Standing Dead,' he replied in Ochre, feeling a furtive delight in uttering that barbarian tongue in that place. Then a rumble ponderously shook the sky. A sudden breeze set him shivering. 'I'm cold.' Fern opened his blanket. Carnelian crept in beside him. They snuggled together. Comfort quickly gave way to passion.

He woke into a world suffused by a faint dawn light, feeling groggy. The sound of bells seemed to have followed him out of his dreams. Sitting up, he saw, to the east and south-east, movement in the gaps between the monoliths. Fern stirring against his belly made him glance down. He watched him come awake and smiled. Fern grimaced and took some moments to register him.

'You didn't sleep well either?'

Fern shook his head. He propped himself up on his elbow, watching the procession of the Masters. 'It's been going on all night?'

Carnelian nodded, remembering snatches of dream in which the world was carried away in a terrible and irresistible flood.

Sitting with Fern and Tain, Carnelian watched servants with chameleon-tattooed faces laying dishes of jade and silver upon a rug. He offered Tain some food. 'How're things with Father?'

His brother dipped his head to one side and looked down, then glanced up at Carnelian. 'Well enough to send you that,' he said, indicating with his chin the Ruling Ring on Carnelian's finger.

Carnelian saw a grimmer truth in his brother's eyes, but he kept silent. What use was it to know more? He could not go to his father's side. He glanced at the Ruling Ring. That was its own message. His father expected soon to die. Carnelian was not sure his father had believed the assurances in his message that his adopted son would, in time, rule House Suth. He might only have sent him the ring in the hope that it would give him enough power to affect the succession in their coomb. Certainly it should make it possible for him to get his people out of there, but bring them where? Into safekeeping in the House of the Masks? Glancing at Tain's face tattoo, he wondered how people wearing that could possibly reside in the Labyrinth. For a moment he became possessed by a fantasy of taking them all with him into the outer world. That possibility seemed even more unreal. He became aware Fern was watching him. He smiled, but only the corners of Fern's lips twitched in response.

'What about Poppy and Krow?'

Fern grimaced. 'You can imagine how she reacted when I told her she would have to stay behind.'

Carnelian smiled grimly. 'We can't have her here.' Fern and Tain's faces stiffened, as they sensed the threat underlying his words. Carnelian wanted to lighten things a little. 'Even now she's probably trying to swim the lake to get here.'

Fern smiled and even Tain who, in his short acquaintance with Poppy, already had some notion of what she was like.

After they had finished eating, he took Fern and Tain with him out through the two inner rings and across the mosaicked stone to the outermost ring. There, with Carnelian in his mask and military cloak, they watched the Masters pass by. Their palanquins were carried by slaves whose faces bore the same heraldry as the standards that glowed like jewels under the sombre skies. Banners streamed rainbows. Feathered parasols fluttered like birds. Bells rang, of dull stone or sharp bright silver. Chariots were pulled among the processions by pale aquar, each led by a Sinistral Ichorian.

Carnelian retired with Fern into the pavilion his people had erected. In the gloom they fed off each other's bodies. They slept, they woke to more passion and drowsed afterwards, exhausted. They were vaguely aware of the day fading. They lit no lamps. Dawn found them drugged by ecstasy and joy, Carnelian's tainted by the dregs of dreams.

Carnelian lay half wake, waiting for Fern to return with some food. The pavilion smelled of sex. A movement in a dark corner brought him fully awake. A shadowy form was looming there. He sat up with a jerk, fearing this to be something supernatural, but still casting round for some weapon. A beautiful voice stilled a cry of alarm in his throat. 'Calm yourself, Seraph.'

Carnelian's gaze found a child's face frozen in the shadows. Above floated the murky mirror of its master's mask. Carnelian saw the emberous finial the homunculus held before it, but could not make out its cypher. 'Who are you?' he said, shocked that his people had given him no warning of this visitor.

'Tribute,' sang the exquisite voice. 'I am come to bid you give entry tomorrow to the tributaries.'

Carnelian nodded as the homunculus relayed to him details of how it should be done. Only vaguely did he note the instructions, unease worrying at his concentration. At last, when the homunculus fell silent, Carnelian spoke. 'Why had you need to come yourself, my Lord? Could you not as easily have sent a letter, or one of your Sapients?'

716

Tribute's fingers were a furtive movement at the throat of his homunculus. 'I have come as the voice of the Twelve.'

'Does my Lord Nephron know of this?'

'It is unlikely, Carnelian . . . of the Masks.'

Carnelian tensed. 'He has told you then.'

'The Law demands you be slain at his Apotheosis.'

Carnelian heard the finality of those words reverberate long after silence had returned. 'And yet the Lord Nephron has seen fit to defy the Law.'

In the further silence that fell after the homunculus finished echoing his words, Carnelian's heart misgave. He listened out for any evidence of slaughter going on beyond the silken walls of the pavilion. Perhaps Osidian had betrayed him. Perhaps this Grand Sapient had come with Ichorians to take Carnelian captive.

'He did so even when we told him his transformation into the Gods could not be complete without your blood.'

The homunculus put on those last words an edge that he might, inadvertently, have picked up from some change in pressure in his master's fingers. Carnelian's instinct told him that, whatever they might claim, what the Wise sought most of all was his death. He recalled the trap they had set for him that they had baited with his father. With a shudder he remembered their inquisition. The pieces of the mosaic fell into place. 'It was I whom you tried to assassinate.'

'We were desperate.'

Carnelian became aware how he was naked, exposed to this cold apparition. 'Have you come to kill me?'

'That route is now closed to us, child. Even to you it must by now be clear that you are the agent of a god.'

Carnelian's mind tried to deflect that, but his heart was ready to believe it. 'The dreams.'

'It is through dreams the Gods choose to guide us. Believing you the agent of a god, it would be foolish for us to attempt to slay you, especially in this holy place in which you have taken refuge.'

Carnelian almost protested that he had sought no refuge and yet he wondered if some part of him had.

'To slay you might precipitate the very cataclysm we dread.'

Carnelian felt that dread soaking into his bones. 'What, then, do you want from me?'

'That you should submit yourself, willingly, to sacrifice.'

Stripped of any requisitive or necessitive modes, the words were all the more chilling. 'Why should I do that?'

'Because you are possessed of that quality that we have lost and have for so long striven to drive from the hearts of the Chosen: compassion.'

The homunculus must have communicated Carnelian's shaking head to its master for he had it say: 'If you do not, the world may die.'

'Die?' Carnelian said, feeling defenceless against the Grand Sapient's bleak certainty.

'Consider, child, how inconsequential, how fleeting a thing you appear to be and yet how great is the destruction you have already wrought. For too long we had no clear understanding from whence this disruption was emanating. In you we have found its source.'

Carnelian shook his head again, as if these accusations were clogging his mind. He struggled to understand. 'My birth?'

'When the Lord Nephron informed us of it, we were certain, without need of computation, that this was the missing factor we have sought so desperately. Subsequent calculations have confirmed it absolutely.

'When the birth of Nephron and Molochite spanned the transition between the black months and the green, the astrological implications were clear enough, but still we had hope of restricting the depth of the cleaving. We aided the return of Suth with the expectation that the consequent election would fulfil the omens of conflict. The blood rituals of the subsequent Apotheosis would have closed the fissure by reunifying the twins in a new God Emperor. We first became

718

aware of a missing factor when Nephron disappeared. We searched frantically for him. When we detected his presence upon the Southern Plain, we devised careful counter actions. But, to our surprise, the perturbations, rather than diminishing, grew. We checked and rechecked our calculations and found no error. Exasperated, Legions decided to go himself to the locus of the disturbance to try to find the elusive missing factor. It was then we became aware of you. We began to wonder if it was possible that, somehow, your contribution had not been properly determined. Though we could hardly believe you important enough, we decided to eliminate you. Under examination, you revealed some suggestive aspects, but there were enough among us who did not believe these significant. We delivered you to Molochite. In spite of the imprecise analysis of trends, we were certain we had done enough to ensure Nephron's forces would be destroyed. His defeat would have truncated the amplitude of the disturbance. The system would settle down into a steady state that patient manipulation would, in some few centuries, restore to a stable equilibrium. His victory, we had not even considered. The probabilities of that were infinitesimal . . .'

Freed for a moment from the exposition, Carnelian regarded the Grand Sapient. Even through the conduit of the homunculus, Carnelian could clearly sense how deep had been the incomprehension of the Wise. He remembered the ancients they had lost in the Iron House. He had glimpsed the trauma of their loss.

Tribute's fingers came back to life around the neck of the homunculus. 'When you survived, we realized that, in spite of what our calculations insisted, you must be, somehow, the key disturbing factor. It was at that juncture we panicked and made the clumsy attempt on your life.'

Carnelian sensed how much this Grand Sapient recoiled from that action, but only because it was such an inelegant, unconsidered impulse.

'Having recast our calculations, taking into account your

719

true birth, everything at last makes sense. High-blood birth on the chaotic cusp incident on a God Emperor's death is a powerful enough input, but when combined with that of twins spanning a fault line, the consequences are catastrophic. Even then, had we known, had we had time to prepare, we could have avoided the abyss. We could have arranged it so that you would have succeeded your father and, with the sacrifice of the twins at your Apotheosis, we should have certainly healed the rift with minimal perturbation to the Balance.'

Carnelian floundered in this glimpse of timelines and how the past might have been rewoven to so profoundly change the present.

'But we believe, child, it is not too late. Though he whom the Gods protect none can harm, he has the power to harm himself if he wills it.'

Carnelian pondered this, his mind warring with his heart. He flinched when Tribute's homunculus came towards him and put out his hand, upon which sat an orb. Reaching out, Carnelian took it. Felt its leathery skin, gazed at its crown of spikes. He brought the pomegranate up to his nose. With inhalation came memories of being a boy in a fabulous, forbidden garden. For a moment he was lost in that miraculous vision. When he looked up, the Grand Sapient and his homunculus had gone.

'What's happened?' said Fern, alarmed. 'You look as though you've seen a ghost.'

'Is everything all right outside?' said Carnelian.

'Shouldn't it be?'

Carnelian could hardly believe that Tribute could have made it through his camp unseen. Though he remembered how easily the Wise could find their way through the perfect darkness of their Library and this place was as familiar to them.

The pomegranate was heavy in his hand. If it were not for that he could well imagine he had dreamed the visitation.

Why had Tribute brought it? Perhaps, with its red juice, it was a symbol of sacrifice.

Morose, he stood between two commentary stones, his cowl pulled down as much against the rain as to hide his face, as he watched the barbarian tributaries pass. Earlier, it had been huimur caravans, their domed backs rising above leather panniers, each larger than a man, which Carnelian had known must be stuffed with the bronze coins that were the taxes from the cities of the Commonwealth. Among the plodding beasts had walked deputations from the cities, their skins painted in imitation of the Masters, wearing elaborate, garishly dyed weaves, bearing upon their heads hats of outlandish design. This finery aped the pomp of the Masters, but was, in comparison, pathetic pantomime.

He had spent another night disturbed by dreams. Whatever they had to tell him, he was no longer prepared to listen. He had woken enraged at the notion that he might be the plaything of some god. Which god?

A hand clasping his shoulder made him jerk round with shock at being touched; at being caught unmasked. He heaved a sigh of relief when he saw it was only Fern.

'I've done everything as you asked.'

Carnelian had delegated to him the task of bringing in the tributaries. Not only had he been in no mood to do it himself, but also he had thought it a good opportunity to let Fern sit in a command chair. In the outer world, Fern was going to be his lieutenant.

'Everyone's in.' Fern waved his hand in the direction of the Forbidden Door, though it and the Black Field were hidden behind the standing stones. 'The dragons are arranged down both sides. I left them with clear instructions that under no circumstances whatsoever are they to light their pipes, nor move their dragons out of position.'

Carnelian thanked him, then both turned to watch the people filing past. Sodden, dragging their feet, women and old men, faces set against suffering, leading by the hands or carrying countless numbers of miserable, scared flesh-tithe children.

They stood watching the children until night fell, then they returned to their camp. Carnelian's voice sounded very loud when he ordered his people to stow everything for the journey into the Labyrinth. They set to it as if at a funeral. Through the darkness came the endless scuffling of the marching tributaries.

As Carnelian led them south-west, out of the Dance, he lifted his hand to touch the lefthand stone. Cold under his fingers, he stroked a worn pomegranate as if for luck. He frowned, remembering the fruit Tribute had brought him, his thoughts tinged by the dread in his dreams.

When they reached the outer ring, he gazed out. The terraces and windows of the Halls of Rebirth formed gashes and spots of jewelled light making the wall of the Plain there seem a window into a starry sky. Below lay the Black Field, its front edge twinkling with fires like a stopping place, its rear two-thirds in dense darkness. Shuffling towards this was a flood of shadowy heads.

With his back to the Forbidden Door, Carnelian gazed over the Black Field. Its nearest portion, lit by thousands of campfires, was made to appear a vast pebbled beach by the backs of the huimur. Beyond, squatting in the darkness, were the barbarians and their children spending one last night together without even the cheer of a fire. How long had he and Fern and his people had to wait for them to scuffle past? Long enough for hearts to grow heavy as stones, and legs to grow unsteady. Carnelian had made an attempt to have his people sit and wait it out but when he and Fern stayed standing so did they. When, at last, that miserable procession had ceased, they had followed the stragglers round, walking on the carpet of blue flames ammonites laid before them. They had skirted the Black Field with its sea of heads walled in by dragons, had endured the murmurous fear, the cries of the children, the weeping, the moaning bleak comfort of their mothers. Down the whole long side of that crowd they had walked, between the dragons and the Cages of the Tithe until, at last, beneath the malevolent gaze of the colossi, they had reached the Forbidden Door.

Carnelian turned from the outer darkness to regard the black maw of the Labyrinth tunnel with loathing, then, taking Fern's hand, he led his people into its throat.

APOTHEOSIS

Fire from heaven
Shatters even the sky.
(from the 'Book of the Sorcerers')

In the centre of the vast bed, Carnelian and Fern clung to each other like survivors of a shipwreck. They might as well have been upon a raft afloat on a dark, forbidding ocean. Having passed through gates and antechambers they had been glad finally to be able to close themselves away in this echoing chamber.

Carnelian stared blindly past Fern's shoulder into the darkness. He was remembering their long journey from the Forbidden Door, carrying in their hearts the misery they had left behind. Then that blinking emergence into a world of light. A miraculous field of stars spread away into the remote glooms of the Labyrinth by myriad lamps. Glowing pavilions hung from the columns like morning-dewed webs. He had recognized this as another Encampment of the Seraphim, though grander than the one he had witnessed in the Halls of Thunder. Indeed it resembled a stopping place, seen from afar, but if so, one made by angels descending from a midnight sky. Carnelian had seen how awestruck Fern was, how his people gaped who had never beheld such a spectacle before. When the Quenthas elected to lead them instead of the Ichorian guides, they had followed the sisters as if in a dream.

As they wound their way through the field of lights, the vision had soured. In the gloom around the feet of the pavilions, slaves huddled over lurid braziers, turning their faces furtively to watch them pass, some grovelling, others throwing themselves face down upon the ground. Above them, through the membranes of patterned silk, immense shadow Masters seemed to be caught in the act of pupating into monsters. Higher still rose the appallingly massive sepulchres that glowered down at them as the colossi in the Plain of Thrones were doing upon the miserable tributaries. It had been a relief to cross the Mirror Moat, then make the dizzying climb up the fiery steps of the Shimmering.

When they had reached the torn-down gate, they had turned their backs upon the Encampment that, from that height, had once more transformed into a dreamy vision, to enter the vastnesses of the Halls of Rebirth. A world more sombrely lit, haunted by sinister pillars of perfumed mist that drifted like ghosts through the endless halls. Everything moved, slowly, evolving. Everywhere countless aspects, bewildering: like trying to piece together a view from reflections caught in the flying fragments of a shattering mirror.

In the bed, Carnelian tightened the curl of their bodies. His heart quickened. He knew he must confess to Fern the decision he had made about the part he intended to play in the next day's ritual. Would Fern understand? Carnelian recalled the almost childlike expression of hope that had come over Fern's face when first he beheld the Labyrinth. He was sure that in its vaulted gloom Fern had seen some semblance of the mother trees and a yearning for the world he had lost. Heart aching, Carnelian felt sick with the misery that the one he loved might never be truly happy in Osrakum.

Osidian was beside the opening of the well that was the beginning of the Path of Blood. He looked up and Carnelian detected a change in the cast of his shoulders as he glanced past him to Fern. Carnelian gestured Fern and the rest of his entourage to halt and advanced alone towards Osidian. He opened his hand and offered him back the blood-ring Osidian had sent with his summons as a sign it truly came from him.

Osidian took it, frowning. 'After today, I will have no need of this.'

Carnelian nodded, understanding. That ring would become a lie once ichor flowed untainted in the new God Emperor's veins. Carnelian's gaze took in Osidian's guard in its new splendour. Marula, already forged into Ichorian collars of silver. Wearing breastplates of bronze. Shrouded in cloaks of silk patterned in green and black.

'They look handsome, do they not?' said Osidian.

Carnelian agreed with his hand, recalling the thought he had had the first time he set eyes upon Marula: that they were like the Chosen reflected in a mirror of obsidian.

'For the moment they wear the heraldry of the Sinistrals, but I have a notion to adorn them with scarlet. The colour would complement their skin. Does it not seem apropos to you, Carnelian, that they should combine the heraldry of both Ichorians?'

Again, Carnelian agreed.

'As today the Two are to be combined in my person, so shall the Ichorians of the left and right' – Osidian held his hands palm up – 'merge into a single Guard.' He brought his hands together, meshing his fingers.

Carnelian could see how the tattooed halves of the old Ichorians could be seen to find union in the black skin of the Marula.

Osidian regarded the warriors. 'From these, the Wise will make me syblings.' There was a glint in his eyes. 'Imagine how elegantly sombre such specimens would be, encased in iron.'

Unease arose in Carnelian. 'But you will help them rebuild the ladder down to the Lower Reach.'

Osidian made a gesture of dismissal. 'We shall send an expedition to retrieve from their land enough of their females to ensure an adequate breeding population here.'

'But what of your promise to Morunasa?'

'I have told him it is already too late. Their land is dying. Their only hope of survival is here. They will come to accept this soon enough. Why should they not? How could their noisome jungles compare to sacred Osrakum?'

Carnelian felt there was doubt caged within Osidian's certainty. 'But what of Morunasa. What of his god?' Almost Carnelian had said: What of your god?

Osidian's face took on a brittle cast. 'I have told him he and all his people can worship me. For is the Black Twin not the very same god they worshipped in the Isle of Flies?' His face betrayed something of the distaste Carnelian felt and a shadow of suffering seemed to be nesting under Osidian's brows. 'And is He not about to be poured into me?'

In Osidian's crazed eyes there was something of a child seeking reassurance. Carnelian gave a nod in spite of his misgivings. For a moment he teetered on the edge of despair. The solid ground of their agreement, of his hopes, seemed to be crumbling beneath his feet. He suppressed a desire to turn and find Fern. It was enough to know he was there. Enough that his people were in Osrakum. It was here the fate of millions would be determined. He had to cleave to the heart of power to do what he could to save as many as he could.

Osidian was gazing down into the blackness of the Path of Blood. He looked up, agony ageing him. 'I asked you here to say goodbye. This path I must tread alone.' His voice was low and tremulous. 'From this day forward, you shall never again look upon my face.'

Carnelian felt Osidian's loss and knew some of it was his own. It steadied him. He glanced round. If anything, Fern's face was grimmer now than when Carnelian had told him what he intended to do. There had been no arguments. Fern would endure this as he had so much else. Carnelian twitched a smile, then, turning back, reached out to touch Osidian's hand. 'Not alone.'

From distress, Osidian's face dissolved into horror. Carnelian grasped his hand. 'I have not chosen to die.'

'What then?'

'I will give of my blood to ensure yours is transubstantiated into ichor.'

Osidian took hold of Carnelian's hands as if they were all that was stopping him from tumbling into an abyss. He was trembling, tearful. 'Very well, brother, we shall do this thing together.'

Carnelian and Osidian approached the brightness at the end of the tunnel, hearts beating faster, still holding hands as they had done all the way through the darkness, like children. The opening swelled and they emerged, blinded, into the light. The air was filled with a sound Carnelian imagined could have been a locust swarm in flight. He lost hold of Osidian's hand. He looked up, his eyes narrowing behind the slits of his mask, sight returning. All around, a host of angels rose in serried ranks up into the heights of the cavern. Glimmering in stiff jewelled carapaces, crowned, their masks striping the Pyramid Hollow up to its black apex.

Carnelian's head fell, his soul chilled by the cold grandeur of the Chosen. Ahead the Creation Chariot was crowded. The Grand Sapients were sombre pillars erupting stellated crowns. Around them, barely reaching their waists, Oracles, feral teeth revealed in rictus grins, adorned in violent Ichorian greens, tamed by service collars of silver. From the midst of this assemblage a tower rose; its hollow interior, exposed, revealed the inner scaffolding of bird bones that held it up. Though these supports were more dense than any Carnelian had seen, he still had no doubt it was an immense court robe waiting to engulf its wearer.

Osidian stood transfixed. Only the slight glimmer of his eyes gave any indication there was a living man behind his mask. Carnelian followed the gaze of that perfect, dead face of gold and saw among the Oracles one whom he had not noticed: Morunasa, his yellow eyes popping as if he were being impaled, seeing only Osidian, to whom he gave the slightest of nods.

Carnelian had no time even to think about this, for one of the Sapients loomed up, each footfall on his high ranga causing the platform to shiver, walking with the aid of two court staves borne by ammonites. As Carnelian scried the cyphers the staves bore, the Grand Sapient released hold of them and allowed his hands to be drawn down to the throat of his homunculus.

'You have come to offer yourself, Carnelian of the Masks?' said the homunculus.

Carnelian looked up at the one-eyed mirror mask, knowing this was Tribute. 'Only enough of my blood to ensure proper ignition of the Lord Nephron's to ichor.'

The Grand Sapient felt Carnelian's reply through the muttering throat of his homunculus. Long it seemed until his pale fingers moved again, a period in which Carnelian felt the pressure of the chatter of the Chosen host.

'We accept the offer of your blood, Celestial,' sang Tribute's homunculus.

The Grand Sapient released the little man and, grasping his staves, swung aside, leaving a narrow path between him and the gaping, empty court robe. Carnelian glanced round and saw that, under the fierce gaze of the Oracles, ammonites were stripping Osidian. He walked round the court robe, then past the Grand Sapients' wall of purple brocade punctuated by pairs of Domain staves. He did not glance up, but was still aware of their masks reflecting light; and even more strongly, he felt he could sense the operating of the precise mechanisms of their ancient minds.

He emerged, it seemed, into a clearing and saw a naked man. Within the iron mould he lay spreadeagled. The circle of its turtle shell that his neck, his arms and legs crossed, gave the impression he was that creature's flesh exposed to the air. Carnelian ignored a murmur like distant sea, and gazing at the man felt reassured he was dead already, until he saw the chest rising, falling. Asleep? Or drugged? Carnelian shuddered. So pale he could see the blue tracery beneath skin that seemed too thin to withstand the slightest touch. By his beauty, one of the Chosen, no doubt from the House of the Masks. One of those members of whom Osidian had once spoken, who were bred for blood ritual. Panic surged in Carnelian that another was to die in his place. He was on the verge of rushing forward, pulling the man free of the iron frame, possessed by a vision of carrying him through the Wise, through the Marula, back into the safety of the tunnel. A childish fantasy, no more. The only way to save him was to take his place.

Carnelian heard again the murmurous sea and raised his eyes. What he saw stopped his breathing. On the plain below a multitude so numerous they seemed grains of sand. An expanse of sand stretching away almost to the ring of stones. He remembered the children that formed a substantial part of that multitude. In his mind he saw from where those children had come; he saw them chasing each other among the trees, free; their bright laughter, their innocence terminated by the coming of the childgatherers.

He forced his gaze back to the victim in the iron mould. He hardened his heart against the man. He would have to die. After all, he was only one among millions who would perish. Carnelian could not give his life for him, for it was not his to give, but belonged to those frightened children down there on the plain.

Two Sapients on lower ranga than their superiors unmasked Carnelian, then cut his sleeves away while their homunculi placed bowls of jade on either side of him near his feet. The Sapients were entrusting his arms to the gloved hands of ammonites, when a homunculus voice sang out. 'Gathered are we to reforge the covenant in blood, made here long ago between your fathers and the Two Gods . . .'

The voice soared up into the vault of the Pyramid Hollow, finding resonances that caused the air to reverberate.

'. . . in token of which They gave you victory perpetual over your foes . . . dominion unbroken over earth and sky . . . this They did, for you alone remained faithful to Them when all others had turned away.'

The last syllable rang, only slowly fading away.

'A narrow path of safety they gave you to walk in power absolute into eternity. This path is the Law and it must be obeyed. Shall you continue to obey it?'

Thunderous came the response from the serried tiers. 'We shall.'

The voices of many homunculi rose in eerie concert. 'What is this path of Law?'

'It is the tangling Labyrinth,' boomed out the wall of angels.

'It is the roiling sea,' sang the homunculi.

'It is the spiralling ammonite,' a multitude rumbled from somewhere beneath the platform on which Carnelian stood.

The homunculi sang out in unison again. 'Through the mystery of this covenant your Commonwealth shall be reborn anew.'

The Chosen thundered out the response. 'As it has been done, so shall it be done, for ever, because it is commanded to be done by the Law-that-must-be-obeyed.'

The voices of the homunculi rose up again, as one, but subtly timbred. 'When our Lords returned to Their realms They swore that though They would no longer dwell incarnate among the living, They would pour of Their dual essence into a vessel of your choosing, filling it brimful with ichor from whence you might all drink so that its fire might renew your blood.'

The Chosen roared out the same response. Carnelian gazed into the airy heights and it seemed their thunder was louder than the sky's. He became aware of light moving sinuously among those jewelled beings as their masks turned to gaze at a point somewhere behind the empty court robe.

'Is this the vessel you have chosen?' said a single homunculus.

'It is,' came the answer from the heavens.

Carnelian saw alabaster forearms and hands outstretched beyond the court robe. Osidian was displaying himself naked to them. The hands seemed to flash as they were retracted. The court robe quivered. From this side it was a spire of densely woven dull silver thread that Carnelian judged must be tempered iron. Running down its centre was an exquisite mosaic of cut gems, at once a rainbow, but also a glowing battle scene, a hunt, a view into a fabled garden. On its chest hung a great circular breastplate, something like a wheel, though eccentrically spoked. It had a thick rim of black stones above, of red below; there were hollows in the rim and more located on the spokes and in the hub. It seemed to Carnelian sinister, like some instrument of torture. His mind veered away from guessing at its purpose.

Osidian's perfect gold face appearing at the summit of the robe was a sunrise that woke him from nightmares. Osidian inhabited the robe, bringing it to life. His arms raised the ponderous sleeves and his pale hands, appearing at their extremities like doves, reached out to clasp the trees of two court staves. One smouldered with emeralds, peridots and jades, all feverish tendrils and growth, curling up into a monstrous crozier topped by a perfect youth that seemed water in the act of turning to stone. The other was of jet, adamants and mirror obsidian, gnarled with figures whose curves spoke of blades, whose contorted postures, of punishment and triumph, evolving up into a four-horned demon who gazed down malevolently upon the victim lying in the iron hollow.

A hush fell. The Pyramid Hollow became the cavity of an open mouth. That mouth spoke. 'In the beginning an ocean

732

seething, primordial, without boundary, without light, without thought, filling the void with its voiceless currents, its colourless eddies.'

The voices of the homunculi were one voice.

'Darkness concentrated birthed a seed, a mote, a single tear of jade. The Lord Turtle. The vast rivers in the sea he swam, arrowing the fathomless depths, cleaving the flood, scouring the abyss with his beacon eyes, searching the emptiness for another. Great heart pounding his straining flesh. Oar paddles threshing the black waters. Long he searched, but found he was alone. Until, at last, he began pouring forth, in song, his desolation.'

An eerie cry rose up that made the hackles rise on Carnelian's neck. Modulating, swelling, stretching its pitch, curling slowly, a sound equivalent to a rising blade of smoke. No human throat could shape such a song.

'One vast bell, the night-black ocean.'

The spiralling song seemed to have loosened some vast thing up in the dark apex of the Pyramid Hollow. He gazed up, but could see nothing. Then he felt a waft on his face from the air displaced as something massive moved. The next moment he would have snatched his hands up to cover his ears if they had not been held by the Sapients. Air avalanched with a thick reverberation that made everything shake, down to the marrow in his bones. A pealing so loud, he feared the crater of the Plain of Thrones must shatter and fall.

'Shimmering, shivering, shearing at the touch of the Turtle's song.'

Another ear-numbing peal.

'A shudder speeding towards the limit of the limitless.'

Clang.

'The ocean convulsed in agony and joyful exultation.'

Clang.

'Convulsed to this new-formed centre.'

Clang.

'Pressure beyond squeezing.'

733

Clang.

'Rage beyond violence.'

Clang.

'Passion beyond annihilation.'

Clang.

'And Lord Turtle was rent asunder,' shrilled the homunculi.

Carnelian cried out as pain leapt up his arms. He would have snatched them free, but the Sapients held them fiercely with their four-fingered hands. He looked down in shock. Watched the blood dewing from the cuts they had made. Running down his fingers to dribble into the jade bowls.

A sharp crack made him jerk his head up. A Sapient who was hovering over the victim in the iron hollow raised his hand gripping a cobble of black stone and smashed it down again upon the sternum of the prostate man. Ribs gave way like rotten wood.

'The upper shell becomes the dome of heaven,' cried the homunculi.

Other Sapients fell upon the victim; their fingers sheathed with blades tore at his chest like beaks. Prising the ribs loose. Snapping them back, one after another after another, hands gloved with blood. Carnelian flinched as some spat over his face. Reek of iron, the odour of his dreams.

'The lower shell becomes the foundations of the earth.'

The victim's chest was now a basket of bones like two splayed hands between which, in the seething cavity, his heart still beat. One of the Sapients reached in and plucked out the pulsing organ, pulled it up while others severed the vessels that the next moment were spraying blood everywhere. Carnelian's eyes followed the heart as it was carried to Osidian's court robe.

'Lord Turtle's heart becomes the mountain at the centre of the world.'

The heart was pushed into the centre of the wheel breastplate. Carnelian watched it convulsing there, dribbling

734

a trickle of blood to wind down through the jewel mosaic. Then it stopped. Soon the victim's liver was filling a cavity beneath the heart on the wheel frame, as it became the earth. The tongue went above the heart to be the voice of the winds of heaven. The eyes sat to either side as sun and moon. With brushes blood was spattered over the wheel as stars. The severed hands and feet were hung beneath it from hooks to be the lobed caverns of the underworld. More organs were harvested to adorn the wheel. The carcass of the victim no longer resembled a man.

When the great bell fell silent a grumbling chanting was heard. A burr in Carnelian's ears that he tried to dislodge by shaking his head. He felt his arms being raised. Blood trickled warm down his forearms. A grating sound near his feet made him glance down. Ammonites were carefully lifting the bowls that had been collecting his blood. He thought they had not been careful enough. So much seemed spilled upon the floor. The more he looked the more he saw. Blood everywhere as if a tide of it had washed in. He felt it licking at his toes.

A flash seemed to give his head a glancing blow. He looked up and saw four-fingered hands removing a mask. Osidian's face came into view. He was staring past the Grand Sapients, whose stellated crowns made them appear astonished. Carnelian focused on Osidian's face, which seemed translucent alabaster. His eyes were so intense. He knew what Osidian was gazing at, but refused to look too.

The rhythm of the chanting was speeding up, deepening. He watched a Grand Sapient dip a finger into a bowl held up to him and with it he dabbed a spot upon Osidian's forehead, covering his black birthmark. The smudge leaked a drop that found its way to the bridge of Osidian's nose. The Grand Sapient dabbed another spot to the left of Osidian's mouth, then one to the right. Dipping his finger again, the Grand Sapient raised it to Osidian's forehead, touched the smudge of blood there and then drew his finger down towards his left

735

eye, lightly over its lid, closing it, and on down to meet the smudge to the left of his mouth. Dipping his finger yet again, he linked that smudge with a trail across Osidian's lips to the smudge on the other side. With more blood he traced a track up Osidian's cheek to his right eye, closed it and reddened the lid, then up over the brow to close the triangle.

Carnelian frowned, not understanding what it meant, but feeling he should. Threads of blood had reached his armpits. There was a pounding in his head. Or was it? A drumming was swelling the chanting. A scraping sound of copper on copper. A rustling.

The Grand Sapient was painting Osidian's face wholly red. Carnelian watched the pale fingers dipping into the bowl and recognized it. The blood they were using was his. Osidian wearing his blood for a mask. Unease managed to seep up through Carnelian's numbness. In that red face he was seeing Akaisha's, bloated in death. All the women of the Tribe, their faces ochred for burial. It seemed a desecration to paint Osidian so, as if he was mocking the dead; but there was something else disturbing Carnelian about that red face. Then Osidian opened his eyes. Carnelian started, causing the Sapients to tighten their grip on his arms. His dreams were crossing over into his waking world.

'And it rained blood,' cried the homunculi.

Wet tearing sounds yanked Carnelian's gaze up the central stair of the Pyramid Hollow to see the long seed pods of the torsion devices that flanked it untwisting, swelling. Then they began to explode, not all at once, but in a long stuttering release, and the air turned red as if filled with rose petals. Carnelian gasped in shock as he was spattered. Warm, thick spots of it on his face and arms. Pattering on the platform, on the dark pinnacles of the Wise, on Osidian in his court robe. A great sigh went up from the tiers above that seemed one of sexual release. The Masters to either side of the steps were visibly reddened, though some gore reached them all. To

Carnelian, gazing up in horror, it seemed the stair was a gash in the cliff, even the vulva of some vast woman.

'Flesh, knit bone to bone, your withered earth . . .' the ammonites on either side were chanting.

The odour of freshly spilled blood was overpowering. Carnelian felt as if the tidal wave from his dreams had broken over them.

'Oh ancient mother, scorched tearless you await . . .'

The Wise were hooking a green face beneath the wheel breastplate. The face of a beautiful, radiant youth. It seemed the same face Molochite had worn in the Iron House, but that had been broken, so this must be a replica. Blood dribbling down its jade brow, cheek and lips from the liver and heart above made it seem as if the face had been freshly flayed from some youth. It looked, besides, incongruous, fringed as it was on either side by the amputated feet and hands of the victim.

Osidian with his scarlet face was being given some of Carnelian's blood to drink.

'The Sky Lord come to thunder . . .'

The Wise were holding up what seemed a face reflected in a mirror of night.

'Rumbling His stormy belly . . .'

The Wise held the obsidian mask over Osidian's face and he was transformed. Terrible he became, the very blackness of the sky incarnate.

'Heart-of-Thunder,' Carnelian heard the homunculi intone.

'Withholding Your urgent seed . . .' chanted the ammonites.

'Lord of Mirrors,' intoned the homunculi.

'Until You shall pierce her with Your shafts . . .' the ammonites sang.

'Father of Corruption, Lord of Pestilence, Prince of Plagues.'

'Quench the burning air . . .'

737

The obsidian mask was peeled away, revealing what seemed the raw meat of Osidian's face.

'Rill and pool her dusts . . .'

The jade mask was raised, the obsidian one hung below the breastplate in its place.

'Fill her wombs with spiralling jades.'

Osidian was drinking another draught of Carnelian's blood.

'Until her flesh swells up . . .'

The wise were dipping their fingers in the bowls of blood and sprinkling Osidian.

'In the midst of breaking waters . . .'

'Clenching for release . . .'

The jade mask was held over Osidian's face.

'Thrust forth are You, oh Green Child . . .' the ammonites chanted.

'Lord of Abundance, Lord of the Earth,' the homunculi intoned.

'Ten thousand times reborn . . .'

'Immortal One.'

'Squeezed into the air . . .'

'You who taught.'

'Enjewelled by the morning . . .'

'First and Last.'

'That You may dance again . . .'

'Lord of the Dance.'

'And once more breathe Your scents beneath the sky . . .'

'Life . . .'

The voices of the homunculi were drowned by a roaring fanfare.

With a lurch, the Creation Chariot began to climb the spine of the Pyramid Hollow.

'Our Lord leads the Faithful up from the sea.'

Carnelian reeled. They had resumed bleeding him into the bowls. It was an effort to stand. The vast, bloody apparition of the Black God was looming over them all. Carnelian had watched the Obsidian Mask replace the Jade. The glimpse of Osidian's red face had reminded him it was he beneath that carapace, but once he was wearing the black mask, there was nothing left of Osidian.

Carnelian gave his attention to the weird braided voice of the homunculi. He knew they were quoting from the Il Kaya, but it seemed they were describing the journey he, Fern and Osidian had made through the swamps. The horror of it, long forgotten, saturated their words. 'Then our Lord brings them up to the Land He had promised would be theirs . . .'

Carnelian recalled that first view of the Earthsky and smiled. His vision expanded to take in the sea of ferns and then the fragrant hill of cedars of the Tribe. He breathed deep, but the perfume of the mother trees had aged and was now laced with iron. Myrrh mixed with blood. Carnelian blinked and became half aware of where he was. The homunculi's talk of conquest cast a shadow over his heart.

'Men lower than beasts,' they said.

Carnelian shook his head weakly, anger rising in him. The Masters believed that, but he knew his Plainsmen and his beloved Fern were men. Desperate horror washed over him. Osidian, corrupted, corrupted them. Carnelian wept at what he had allowed him to do.

Shawms were braying. The banners that ammonites were carrying up the steps on either side fluttered like birds in flight. Among them glimmered the crescents of the Wise, the silver ammonite spirals of the Law. The music swelled, borne up on the growling of massive trumpets and a clattering and a constant shattering of glass. The ammonites were singing, joyfully, of peace. Carnelian's heart rose on the tide. He basked in this omen. Peace after war. A rebuilding, a remaking of the world, a new shape, a flowering of love.

'Their Commonwealth, to Heaven a perfect mirror,' the homunculi declared, and Osidian was once more jade-faced.

Carnelian watched a vast disc rising among the Wise like a

red sun. He frowned. Except that it was hollow, so that it was a vast glyph of death. An annulus of his birth stone polished to a mirror in which the world was reflected as if in blood. Still the ammonites sang of harmony and blessings but, through the red mirror's central hole, Carnelian saw the Wise were once more transforming Osidian into the Black God.

'But sin casts its shadow over their hearts,' cried the homunculi.

The shawms and trumpets shrieked in hideous cacophony. The red mirror shattered, shards gouging the bloody floor like talons.

'Brother falls upon brother. Canker spreads from flesh to flesh, carried upon the plague wind. Men fornicate with beasts. Mothers devour their children.'

Carnelian would have plugged up his ears, but Sapients were clinging to his arms. Defenceless, he was exposed to their descriptions of the destruction he and Osidian had brought upon the world. Famine and pestilence as the Darkness-under-the-Trees stalked the land.

'You He chose to be His own, for you alone held to your faith in Them.'

Carnelian relived the march on Osrakum, described as the Apostates coming against the Chosen. He relived the great battle in which the Chosen were defeated. He clung on, waiting for the hope there is even in despair. The hope of what he might yet do to heal the world with the power he had taken for himself, but the gloom of the symphony did not abate, but darkened further. The voices of the Wise were speaking of the Apostates coming with black hearts even into Holy Osrakum. In a great crescendo the last great battle was described, within the Valley of the Gate. The symphony of chaos rose to an excruciating pitch, then subsided as if tumbling into an abyss.

'Our Lord leading us, we are victorious. Joyously we bring Them hither for Their coronation.'

*   *   *

'You come with victory bright on Your brow,' sang the homunculi.

Carnelian was confused. They were speaking to the Gods and Osidian was Them, or possessed by Them, but Osidian had also come here from victory, a victory the Wise begrudged him.

'On the plain below You have written Your Law upon the twelve calendar stones. Upon this foundation stands the Commonwealth of the Chosen.

'Thrones You have erected here, upon which You will sit in judgement on the world. Here, now, as a symbol of Your mastery of the Three Lands, shall we crown You Emperor.'

The echo of the Quyan words reverberating round the Pyramid Hollow slowly died away, even as sistra began shaking out a bright, brittle rustling. One of the Grand Sapients was holding a hood of purple leather above Osidian's shaved head. As he lowered it, it flowed down on either side of the Obsidian Mask. Two long tresses of jewelled beadcord glittered and chinked as they snaked over the gory breastplate. Carnelian saw that the hood was bound to a silver diadem that sat now upon Osidian's brow. Emberous rubies ran round the circle of the diadem. By their spacing he judged there to be twelve stones and, though he could see only rubies, he was sure that, round on the side hidden to him, there would be two green stones and two black. It had to be a representation of the Stone Dance of the Chameleon. From what he could deduce of its orientation, it was as if the Black God, approaching the dance along the Rain Axis, had stooped to raise it and put it upon His head. It must signify His authorship of the Law. Carnelian expected some utterance from the Wise to confirm this, but they remained silent. Perhaps they did this as tacit acceptance of the new balance of power.

Carnelian was distracted by something rising into view that seemed an emerald glade. Hope of deliverance after stumbling lost through the glooms of some infernal jungle. It was a crown three Grand Sapients were holding above Osidian's head. From

741

a diagonal cross centred on a horned-ring of translucent jade, the crown flared down into a cobra hood that seemed to have been cut from the hide of some fabulous, bejewelled saurian. This hood split in two, and through the slit between the halves, Carnelian glimpsed delicate scaffolding, but his eyes could not long resist being drawn up to the verdant explosion above the horned-ring. A great shimmering nest set about by a thicket of quills sheathed with emeralds and peridots, malachites and prase. The whole thing shivered and glimmered like a thing alive. As this sank to rest upon Osidian's head and shoulders, Carnelian expected he would be unable to support its weight, but the structure of the robe held. The Obsidian Mask, framed by the flaps of jewelled leather, seemed a secret darkness lying at the heart of a fabulous forest.

'Behold the Green Crown,' cried the homunculi, 'symbol of Your dominion over the wildernesses beyond the Ringwall, over sward and jungle, over fernland and fen, dominion eternal over the savages who lurk there far from the light of Your countenance, who, in fear and adoration, bring to You as tribute their children to be Your slaves . . .'

The homunculi, reunited with their masters, turned outwards to face the plain and in stentorian tones cried out in Vulgate: 'Prostrate yourselves before your God!'

For a moment Carnelian was aware of the rustling and glimmer as the Chosen around him turned in their roosts to view the tributaries below. Vast trumpets blasting forth from beneath his feet made him turn too and gaze out. Along the edges of the multitude, the dragon towers were blaring a fanfare in reply. Smoke was drifting across the tiny figures so that for a moment Carnelian was breathless with terror that the flame-pipes were lit and that he was about to witness another incineration, but then, with a great sigh, the multitude subsided in abasement. He did not feel the pride he should have as one of the Chosen, but only shame.

*　　　*　　　*

Three of the Wise held aloft a hollowed globe, tapering upwards like a bud, or perhaps a half-scooped-out pomegranate, and indeed its inner surface was studded with rubies like sweet seeds and Carnelian realized it could be read as the glyph for 'womb'. Its outer shell, a rolling mosaic of almandines and pyropes, of coral, jasper and carnelian, made the swollen mass seem as if it had been freshly torn from a body. He watched as it was fitted into the emerald nest of the Green Crown.

'Behold the Red Crown,' the homunculi sang, 'symbol of Your dominion over the fertile earth of the Guarded Land from which the world draws sustenance . . .'

Carnelian frowned, remembering famine.

'. . . over its cities that teem under Your gaze, who, in fear and adoration and in gratitude for the protection You bestow unto them, bring You the tribute of their taxes in Your coin . . .'

Again the Wise turned to demand abasement from the plain, but Carnelian could not stop looking at the Red Crown swelling up from Osidian's head. As it had been lowered, Carnelian had noticed the bruising of purple leather at its base that could signify the Ringwall. An amethystine band edged the mouth of the hollow and if this were symbolic of the Sacred Wall, passage through which the Wise regulated with their Law, then the womb hollow it enclosed must be the crater of Osrakum. These deductions, for some reason, Carnelian found disturbing.

As the Creation Chariot neared the apex of the Pyramid Hollow, a single Grand Sapient held aloft a glinting shaft. Fluted it was, split in two from top to bottom by a lightning zigzag of gold. In form it seemed to be the Pillar of Heaven rising up from a horned-ring of midnight coral. Of jet and obsidian and adamantine were its ridges and planes.

The voices of the homunculi rose in unison. 'Behold the Black Crown, symbol of Your dominion over the Hidden Land of thrice-blessed Osrakum, where dwell the Seraphim who bask in the light of Your countenance and at whose heart now stands this vessel that You inhabit with Your double Godhead.'

The Grand Sapient lowered the Black Crown into the womb of the Red, and drawing back took his homunculus by the throat.

'Behold the Gods your Emperor,' cried all the homunculi. 'Prostrate yourselves, ye Chosen.'

Around the towering, triple-crowned apparition of the God Emperor, the Grand Sapients and their homunculi knelt. Carnelian was aware of the Lords in the tiers below making their abasement. A tide rose up of voices, drums and trumpets. Ever higher it rose until it seemed the world must be blasted to dust. Carnelian and the new God Emperor alone remained standing. He glanced down to the bloody floor. The purple robes of the Wise and the homunculi were soaking up the gore. He was certain his strength would fail him should he bend his knees, that he would topple head first.

The Sapients in kneeling had released his arms and he folded them, squeezing the wounds in his wrists closed across his chest. He gazed at the new Gods, transfixed. Their crowns grew upwards and outwards, a wheelmap in the round. At its root the Gods' face, anger of the skies; the night, the shadows under the trees crystallized into a visage of serene, sublime malice. What was there left of Osidian within that entity? Perhaps nothing more than a spindle of melting ice.

The chaos of sound beat upon Carnelian like a migraine. He struggled for consciousness. The beadcords running down past the cheeks of the Black God were like tears and Carnelian was possessed by a strange desire to reach out and touch them, to read them. His gaze climbed the jewel beads to the silver diadem. Nothing of the purple hood was visible and yet it lay between the Gods' head and Their crowns. Its purple membrane the power of the Wise separating the God Emperor from the Three Lands. How much the quills of the Green Crown looked like spears! If they were the legions that

744

had been kept from the God Emperor's control, then the Red Crown must surely symbolize the Great; its amethystine lip, the separation the Wise maintained between the Great and the House of the Masks; the Black Crown it held, the God Emperor imprisoned, isolated. Carnelian's eyes lost focus. The Crowns could be read as being the Three Lands, but also as the Great Balance. Dread saturated everything. Osidian was trapped behind the Mask, within the carapace of that robe bedecked with slaughter; crushed beneath the intolerable weight of the world the two of them hoped to rule. Shock forced its way through increasing horror. He would never see Osidian's face again! Carnelian sought hope, but this had flowed out of him with his blood. How ancient, how subtle were the systems of power the Wise wielded. Was it not insane to attempt to stand against their millennial patience? Even so might a rock hope to withstand the trickle of a stream.

CORONATION MASQUE

After the rain, a rainbow and then blue sky.
(fragment – origin unknown)

The world lurched to a halt. Carnelian felt that the narrowing walls of the Pyramid Hollow must come together somewhere above him in the gloom. Giddy, he felt his soul might, at any time, slip free of his leaden body. Vaguely he was aware that the Sapients were removing the wheel breastplate. The rainbow heraldry of the God Emperor's court robe, revealed, seemed barely dulled by dried blood.

Carnelian started as the towering apparition came to life. Oily shadows moved across the midnight lips of the Gods' face as They began to turn. The great volumes of the Crowns smouldered and sparked. The dense grey metal weave of the robe flickered a constantly knotting and tearing web of light that hurt Carnelian's eyes. The youthful Jade Mask came into view as the other Twin took His turn to gaze down upon the plain. A cloak pole was lifted and fastened to the shoulders of the tempered iron robe. A sweep of feathers was hung from it. Iridescent green and raven plumage interwove a bewildering tessellation as the God Emperor slid away from the platform. Morunasa and the Oracles enringed Them. The star-crowned spires of the Grand Sapients followed in solemn procession, the gory hems of their robes smearing a trail of blood. Carnelian managed to turn his head. Past the splayed-bone silhouette of the victim's erupted chest, down on the plain, the tributaries were in commotion where the margins of their multitude met glimmering borders of ammonites in the shadow of the dragons. The barbarians were paying their flesh tithe. Carnelian remembered Ebeny, one scared child among so many.

'Celestial?'

Carnelian sought the origin of the voice. It was a blinded ammonite offering him a square spoon heaped with a brown powder. He remembered watching his father inhaling a drug from such an implement.

'You are to draw it up into your nostrils, Celestial.'

Carnelian regarded the powder. He did not want to take it. It seemed the same his father had taken to gain a false strength when he had been wounded. It had broken his health.

This ammonite was an agent of the Wise. What if this were poison? Carnelian knew that, if anything were to happen to him, Osidian would slay the ammonite, but had not the creatures often proved they were prepared to die for their masters? He felt his consciousness wavering. He had made his decision. What else was there to do, but to trust to the new balance of power? He lifted a trembling hand, took the spoon, raised it beneath his nose and inhaled. The powder stabbed numbness deep into his head. Mucus dripped from his nose and down his throat, releasing a bitter, acrid taste. Vitality surged in. When it reached his head, it filled him with a merciless clarity.

Ahead. Carnelian had an impression of golden giants crowding in. Lamps like stars, like moons reflected in pools. He glanced back to get his bearings. The triangle of blazing daylight branded a headache into his forehead. It was the sudden blossoming odour of old myrrh that alerted him. He stopped just in time to avoid colliding with one of the Grand

Sapients. They stood like a copse of blasted trees. He moved round them until he could find a gap, through which he could see a ring of pale kneeling youths with eyes that seemed freshly gouged. Between their legs a slitted scar where their genitals had been. In their midst a figure encrusted with blood jewels and possessed of a girl's face of gold so achingly innocent Carnelian's breath caught in his throat. Yet this mask clung to a woman's head, shaved as perfect as an egg. A halo of rubies spread behind as if the head, cracked open upon a floor, had oozed a pool of blood. Pale hands, each bearing two Great Rings, confirmed what he already knew.

'I pay homage to thee, Deus, my son,' said Ykoriana, her syllables perfectly shaped. 'Where is my Lord Carnelian of the Masks?'

The golden girl mask searched for him, even though the eyes behind were stone. The Grand Sapients moved aside for him and he approached her.

Celestial, she gestured. Then the long fingers travelled round to her hidden, left side and drew out from behind her a porcelain doll. White as a lily, emerald-eyed, her ebony hair entwined around a nest of white jade pins. Her robe, leaf-green samite embroidered with olive peridots, buttoned down one side with watermelon tourmalines.

'The Lady Ykorenthe of the Masks,' Ykoriana declared. Her mask, gazing down, was frozen gold, but there was love in the hand that touched the child. 'Only the God Emperor has purer blood,' she said, pride lifting her Quya almost into song. 'Pay homage to your brother, little one.'

Ykorenthe knelt upon the stone. Carnelian glanced from her to Osidian, for he saw something of him in her face, but Osidian was not there, merely a looming idol, head aflame with greens and reds.

Ykoriana's hand urged the child to rise and then she caught hold of little Ykorenthe and held her close. 'We witnessed the ritual with the other Ladies of our House.'

'She watched it too?' Carnelian said, horrified.

Ykoriana's mask turned towards him. 'Why should she not? She has more right than any other.'

Carnelian's anxious gaze fell upon the little girl. Perhaps her innocence could not be spared. Was she not destined to become empress and the mother of Gods? His heart rebelled against this complacency. 'She is only a child.'

Ykoriana's hand tightened on Ykorenthe, who flinched. 'Do you question my role as her mother, Celestial?'

Carnelian was stung by the frost in her voice.

The God Emperor speaking turned all heads towards Them. 'Until she comes of age, the child is your concern.'

Carnelian looked at Them, wondering if it was the obsidian of Their mask that had deepened Osidian's voice or if he were truly possessed by the Gods.

Ykoriana shifted, her robe so stiff with garnets it clinked and formed prismatic folds and planes. It was hard to believe there was a human body in there, never mind the curves of a woman.

'We shall retire now to the Forbidden House, Deus.' She reached down and Ykorenthe stretched up to take hold of one of her fingers.

'I too must retire . . . Deus,' said Carnelian.

'You cannot, Celestial,' said Ykoriana. 'As Their viceroy you must show yourself at the coronation masque.'

Carnelian did not trust the crystalline strength the drug had given him, but saw there was political logic in what she said. Nevertheless, he shook his head. He raised his blood-stripped arms showing the meagre, slashed silk in which he was clothed. 'I am hardly dressed for the occasion.'

The God Emperor spoke. 'A robe has been made ready for you, Celestial.'

Carnelian acquiesced. This was the beginning of the life of duty he had chosen for himself.

After the ammonites had stripped him, he endured a cleansing that stung his wounds. They dressed him in undergarments of padded silk. They helped him climb onto ranga shoes higher than any he had seen. After many adjustments, they opened for him the chrysalis of a huge court robe. Of woven gold and bearing down its front his new heraldry of earth and sky. He walked into it and knelt. His fingers brushed against delicate bonework scaffolding as his arms found their way out through the sleeves. While they built the crown upon his head, muscles in his neck took the strain in a way that threw his mind back to a time that seemed several lifetimes ago. When they were finished, he rose and assumed the burden of the robe. He took a few steps, relearning the swinging rhythm of robe and ranga. Finally they produced three Great-Rings that they slipped onto his hand. His fingers, all but gloved by the three bars of jade, brought home the truth of his new, high blood-rank almost for the first time.

Emerging from the confines of the stairs into open space, he clutched at his court staves, reeling. Below was a drop spanned at many levels by bridges and staircases all alive with a glittering flow of the Chosen pouring from the Pyramid Hollow into this honeycomb behind.

An Oracle escort preceded him as he made to join the glimmering throng. With each ponderous step, the sibilant cacophony of chatter grew louder. His eyes were bewildered by the flash of their masks, the gleaming of their robes, the flutter and flap of their jewelled fingers as they accentuated their chatter with gesture.

They became aware of him, as of a stone dropping into their pool. Excitement rippled outwards, as they turned to greet him, speaking all at once, fawning on him. He looked down at them from the eminence of his ranga, unable to un-tangle their questions, aware of an odour undermining their attar of lilies. It was coming from the blood that had spattered their splendour.

*   *   *

They entered a chamber whose fleshy marble was banded with seams and filaments of coral. Ruby chandeliers filtered a bloody radiance over the Masters. Servants swarmed to meet them, their left sides dense with swirling tattoos. These Ichorians raised the skirts of some court robes to crawl under with bowls, while other Masters knelt on their ranga to allow their crowns to be disassembled and their faces to be unmasked. At the unexpected winter of their eyes, the snowy volumes of their naked heads, Carnelian almost cried out, but it was already too late. Throughout the chamber a blizzard of faces was already exposed to the gaze of the Ichorians. He tensed, anticipating massacre. When none came, he focused on the face of a nearby Ichorian, seeing how thin his lips were, how shadow ringed his untattooed eye. He glanced at another and another. All bore the same bleak expression. Carnelian was sickened, knowing in his bones that the prescribed punishment for this infringement of Masking Law was only being deferred. These Ichorians knew they were destined to lose their eyes and suffer other mutilations. As he watched them move among the towering Masters, Carnelian felt complicit, certain this was his House, the House of the Masks, choosing to display profligate extravagance.

Some of the Great within his hearing were venting irritation. He did not catch enough of what they said to know what it was they were complaining about, except that the object of their ire were the 'barefoot'.

He became aware that an Ichorian was kneeling before him. 'Does the Celestial wish to relieve himself?'

'No, rise.'

The man obeyed him.

'Does this happen every year?'

The Ichorian looked confused. 'Celestial . . . ?'

'This unmasking?'

'Only at an Apotheosis, Celestial.'

Carnelian frowned behind his mask. Behind this the

cunning of the Wise. How better to ensure the loyalty of servants, than by linking their sight and limbs directly to the continued life of the God Emperor whom they served.

'Come, unmask me and remove this confounded weight from my head.'

The man grimaced, arresting a shake in his head. 'There are Seraphim present, Celestial, to whom it is forbidden to look upon your face.'

Carnelian saw how, beyond the promontory of the Great, stretched a crowd of smaller Masters, the 'barefoot'. Lesser Chosen, most of whom were not entitled to wear court ranga and who, newly enfranchised, had been invited for the first time to a coronation masque. A sign of the new political balance, that, if the reaction of the Great was anything to go by, the new God Emperor was going to have a struggle making them accept. If the new order was to have any chance, the barriers between the Lesser Chosen and the Great must be cast down. It might be that he would have to spend much of the rest of his life behind a mask, but he did not want to have to wear it in the presence of the Lesser Chosen, many of whom would soon be serving him in the outer world.

'Nevertheless, unmask me.'

Looking scared, the Ichorian did as he was told.

Carnelian's act of defiance against the Law did not go unnoticed among the Great. It drew them to him as wasps to honey. He was finding their attention unbearable when trumpets and shawms began braying. He sighed with relief at the temporary respite. More Ichorians appeared, swinging censers high on poles. The serpents of smoke they loosed soon dissipated into acrid fog. Breathing it, Carnelian could feel it catching at his throat and knew it to be drugged. Even as he felt his thoughts fraying, there came a rustling like autumn leaves stirred to fury by a gust. A dense cloud of butterflies had taken flight. A symbol of rebirth, of sacred transformation. At their core, the God Emperor, upon a long dais, drifting among the Grand

Sapients with their cloven hands and staves, their skull faces. The Twins on Earth: a glittering, gorgeous apparition, like an idol carried in procession.

A surge among the Great carried Carnelian into a chamber of sardonyx dadoed with brown mottled turtle shell. Amber globes cast down a late evening light. More Ichorians circulated, carrying delicacies on plates of creamy jade. Gold beakers frothing over with bitter chocolate. Hollowed jewels holding exquisite liqueurs. Meats cooked and perfumed with flowers. Fruits like cut gems. Beasts, some entire, some still marginally alive, others dissected to form enticing symmetries with their organs, bones and plumage.

Carnelian found himself increasingly besieged by the Great. As he gazed on their porcelain faces, he struggled to order his thoughts. Perhaps it was the effects of the narcotic smoke that were dulling the brilliance of their conversation. He tried to listen, but was distracted by the flash of their eyes, the flutter of their hands. He feared the drug the ammonite had given him was failing; that at any moment his body, drained of so much blood, would collapse. He rallied sufficiently to begin deflecting their elegant flattery, their delicate enquiries about what the intentions of the new God Emperor might be. He could not tell them how the new political arrangements were to be enshrined in law. He could give them no insight into how much the God Emperor expected them to acquiesce in the erosion of their ancient privileges. He grew angry with them when they expressed anxiety about how the enfranchisement of the Lesser Chosen might affect the division of the flesh tithe.

He found himself in a chamber of beaten gold. Here the Masters were accompanied by vague reflections that made him feel he was watching murky, barely remembered scenes from his childhood. Pale summer light from citrine lamps shone down upon Masters dancing duelling pavanes with double-headed halberds. In time to stately music their ritual combat evolved with ponderous grace. Several young Lords invited Carnelian to demonstrate his puissance with them in a measure, but he declined, dizzied even by just watching the elegant gyrations.

He wandered into a more sombre chamber, violently striped with malachite and floored with speckled jade. Emerald columns filtered light like a forest canopy. In pits sunk into the floor frantic creatures, maws brimming with needle teeth, claws sheathed in bronze and obsidian, tore at each other, their screeching seeming to counterpoint the fierce symphony of horns and cymbals. Around these pits, Masters in a fury brought on by consuming juices harvested from glands being offered by Ichorian slaves demonstrated their wealth by gambling with each other on the bouts, using double-eyed iron coins.

He escaped to a dismal chamber in which sapphire rays lit contortionists undulating like denizens of the deep, coupling improbably while, around the walls, men sat with silver bowls upon their laps, running pestles round and round within their rims, producing pulsing, throbbing notes that sliced through Carnelian's head.

Here Masters were drinking potions Carnelian shunned for he did not wish to join their preying upon the sylphs who leaned here and there – languorous, half-asleep, it seemed – their skins of many shades, some patterned, tattooed, some with glimmering jewel eyes, others with their own half-lidded brown animal eyes. Sinuous, graceful creatures of different sexes, of none, giving themselves libidinously to the caresses of the Masters, sometimes until they bled.

He fled into an infernal chamber of midnight lapis lazuli. Mirrors of obsidian hung everywhere in which he glimpsed even more terrible shadow worlds. A haunting interplay of inhuman voices wove the misty air. Smoke curling in the voids was taking on the shapes of men, of monsters, of bizarre landscapes. He tried to shake his head free of these apparitions and managed to focus enough to see, in the shadows, figures completely sheathed in black, who were working the smoke rising everywhere in wavering streams. Stirring it, shaping it with strigils, blowing through tubes, sucking, as they conjured up their evanescent puppetry.

Carnelian could not long stop his mind from splintering and soon was lost in the chimeric visions. At first he was seduced by the shadows of what had been, then unease flared to terror as he saw what was to come. In full flight, he ruptured a slowly evolving nightmare.

In an amethystine chamber he found the hope of what seemed a silver dawn. Walls and floors writhed with nacreous loops and spirals. He started as the shadows coalesced into the shapes of men. Darkly clothed were they, with faces like a winter sky. They put his mask upon his face and doors opened for him and he staggered out onto a hillside aflame. A warm hand took his. Its clench anchored him. A familiar voice made him burst into tears. When the hand tugged, he followed like a child.

When Carnelian awoke, he felt his head was glass shattering. In the dim light he recognized a face. 'Fern,' he cried, drawing him into a desperate embrace.

Fern pulled free. Carnelian could see his mouth was moving, heard his voice, but could grasp no words. It was the sharp fear in Fern's face that brought his voice into focus. 'Can you walk?'

Carnelian stared at him.

'The Marula have come for you.'

OVERRUN

Ants fighting on the sand
Even as the tide comes in.
(Pre-Quyan fragment)

'What?' Carnelian was confused.

Fern's eyes were sharp with anxiety. 'Morunasa's trying to fight his way through to you.'

'To me?'

'Your people are even now fighting to hold him back. The Quenthas know a back way—'

'I don't understand.' Carnelian could not focus his mind. He felt so very weary.

A glistening, ebony face filled his vision: Sthax. 'Oracle come get you.'

A two-headed shape loomed up: the sybling sisters. 'This Maruli came to warn us.'

The pieces came together in Carnelian's mind. 'He has betrayed me.'

They were staring at him, waiting.

'I have to give myself up to him. To avoid bloodshed.'

Fern threw his head back, grimacing. 'You *know* how much that man hates you.'

'There may still be time to get you to safety, Celestial,'

said Right-Quentha, pointing towards a dark corner of the chamber.

'Into the depths of the Labyrinth where none will find you,' her sister added.

Carnelian regarded the sisters. 'You do realize it is the God Emperor Themselves you are intending to defy?'

Both faces set; indomitable. 'It is you we serve now, Celestial.'

That touched Carnelian, but he shook his head. 'How long could we hope to evade Their power? And to what end?'

A scuffing of footfalls in the outer chamber jerked their eyes towards the door. Fern and the sisters turned their gaze upon Carnelian in desperation. He pressed the heels of his hands against his temples. 'I need time to think.'

Fern gave a resigned nod. Sthax grimaced, his yellow eye following the Quenthas to the door. Carnelian turned, agonized, to the Maruli. 'The Oracle said nothing about who sent him?'

Sthax shook his head violently. Carnelian tried to pull apart the threads of the power play, but there was no way he could reweave them into anything that made sense. He groaned, desperate for clarity. Then he remembered walking hand in hand with Osidian along the Path of Blood and felt suddenly calm.

'He's not behind this,' he announced.

At that moment the Quenthas moved aside and Tain pushed into the chamber, eyes wild, blood spattered across his face. 'Carnie, they'll soon have the outer door down.'

'Get everyone in here,' Carnelian said. Tain stared, jerked a nod, then disappeared.

Carnelian rose from his bed, gripping Fern's arm when it reached out to steady him. He found the strength to stand on his own and indicated the bronze doors of the chamber. 'How long will those hold?'

Right-Quentha glanced at them. 'Long enough, Celestial.'

Carnelian had them bring him his green robe, his military cloak. He was already dressed when men crashed into the chamber, skittering on the polished paving, their chameleoned faces glazed with sweat and blood. Seeing him, they began to fall on their knees. Carnelian surged forward and plucked one up. 'Get up, you fools.'

Tain came in last of all.

'Anyone left behind?' Carnelian demanded. When his brother shook his head, Carnelian commanded they engage the door locks. Turning away, he saw a menacing shape looming against the wall: the glimmering carcass of his court robe. Glinting on the floor before it, cushioned in his neatly folded undergarments, a gold face, his mask.

Right-Quentha, catching the focus of his gaze, made her sister follow her as she went to scoop it up.

'No, leave it,' Carnelian said. The sisters frowned as they looked at him.

A thunderous clatter reverberated from beyond the locked gate. The patter of many feet. Something massive struck the bronze doors making them boom, but the locks held. Carnelian grinned grimly at the sisters, his blood up. 'Get us out of here.'

He did not breathe easily until they had finished the crossing of the Encampment of the Seraphim. Urging his people past him, he looked back. The column sarcophagi stood in sombre rows wreathed in a mist of smoke. The fires were now banked throughout the camp that lay sleeping at the feet of those hollow gods. He and his people had found a way through the camp in the golden twilight cast by the Shimmering Stair. Heads had risen as guardsmen had watched them pass, but it was not their place to challenge a party led by sybling guides.

Fern approached, bringing up the rear of the line.

'Is that all of them?' Carnelian asked, almost in a whisper. When Fern nodded, he put his arm round his shoulders and they set off after their people, into the forest of stone trees.

Openings in the high vaults let in the first grey light of dawn. They followed the sisters down winding stairs beneath the gaze of frowning colossi. For a while they moved along ravines flanked by their legs. Here, Carnelian managed well enough, only a few times having to lean on Fern, but when they began to climb countless steps, he found his legs leaden and they had to stop often to let him rest.

Fern gazed with knitted brows at Carnelian, who was wheezing, pain sawing his head in two. 'What did they do to you?'

'They bled me,' Carnelian said and his heart warmed when he saw anger burning in Fern's eyes.

As they climbed higher, he became aware the columns, though still massive, were more slender. Pausing to regain his breath, he gazed up into the shadows and saw that the stone stems swelled into pods that clung to the underside of the roof like the eggs of some monstrous moth.

At last they came up onto a road whose paving was raised here and there as if something had been burrowing beneath it. The vaults seemed a low stormy sky. Light slanting down revealed that the columns had the form of gigantic poppyheads upon whose spiked crowns the ceiling sat. Small as ants they moved off through this deathly, penumbral meadow. Here and there Carnelian could see the stems were graven with faces worn down to sketches of eyes and mouths. Glyphs that tattooed the stone were soft-edged, unreadable. Walking beside the Quenthas, he eyed these effigies, finding them familiar in a way he could not catch hold of. 'How do you know of this place?' he whispered.

'We used to come here as children, Celestial,' the sisters replied. Right-Quentha swept a hand round. 'This place was our playground.'

Such a name seemed to Carnelian incongruous for such a sombre place. 'The Labyrinth?'

'It is where we were born, Celestial,' said Left-Quentha.
'Our world,' her sister added.

They came into a green clearing where the vault between four poppyheads had collapsed. There a single tree reached up to the morning. From every crack fresh ferns sprang, uncurling their fronds all the way up the glyphed shafts of the columns. One of these had a verdant beard that showed where water trickled down to fill a pool nestling in some masonry tumbled at its feet. After the sterile wilderness of the Labyrinth, Carnelian was struck by unlooked-for joy at this haven of life. Beside him Right-Quentha smiled, half turning to her sister. 'It's still here.' She turned to him. 'This was our most secret place, Celestial.'

They formed a ring around the clearing. Carnelian had invited everyone, including the Suth guardsmen, who crouched, heads bowed. When one of them dared to glance up, Carnelian gave him a smile of encouragement, causing the man to blush and duck his head. He did not blame the man for being nervous in his presence and before his strange collection of friends, but the guardsmen had risked everything for him and he felt they had a right to be there.

'I've asked you all to sit with me because the decisions we're going to make will affect us all.'

There were nods around the ring; Tain and Fern fixed him with fierce attention. Carnelian began by asking Sthax what he knew about Morunasa's attack.

The man shrugged. 'I say.'

Tain shot the Maruli an angry glance, before returning his gaze to Carnelian. 'How can we trust him?'

'Didn't he just save us, Tain?'

Tain frowned. 'It could be part of their trap.'

Carnelian shook his head and, deliberately, looked Sthax in the eye. 'I trust him.'

Fern seemed to share Tain's anger. 'What need is there to

760

ask what's behind it? We all know the Marula are the Master's creatures.'

Carnelian re-examined his feelings, then shook his head again. 'In my bones I'm now sure the Master's not behind this.' He could see Fern was still not convinced. He turned back to Sthax. 'How much do you wish to go home?'

Sthax ducked a bow. 'You know.' There was both sadness and hope in his eyes.

'Why have you come over to me? What help could this possibly be to your people?'

Sthax's glistening forehead creased. His hands lifted as if trying to grab hold of the words. 'You know I follow Oracle. We follows Oracle. Oracle promise we peoples saves, Marula saves.' His eyes narrowed. 'We follows brings deaths. We peoples, Marula, in homes, suffers and we here' – he touched the silver collar forged around his neck – 'what we?'

Carnelian sensed how Fern, regarding the Maruli, was softening. Perhaps he was remembering he too wore a collar.

Carnelian turned his attention back to Sthax. 'The Oracle wears a collar identical to yours, Sthax. Is he a stupid man?' None around the circle believed that. 'Is he a coward?' Carnelian saw Fern's frown deepen and gaze fall. 'His promise to you, Sthax, was built on the promise the Master gave him. The Master told me himself he has no intention to honour that promise.'

Sthax's eyes narrowed further. 'You believe Oracle against Master?'

Carnelian nodded. 'Morunasa has taken the fate of your people into his own hands.'

Sthax looked incredulous. 'What good Oracle do?' He glanced round at the stone forest and shuddered. 'How Oracle control Masters?'

'There's another, greater power he might believe will give him the strength to conquer the Masters.'

Sthax's eyes widened with horror. 'Darkness under trees.'

761

Just as disturbed, Carnelian gazed into the gloom. 'This place is very like the Isle of Flies.'

Fern looked sick. Right-Quentha was registering the look on their faces. Her unease spread to her sister's face. 'We are not sure to what you refer, Celestial, but let us raise the Ichorians against this demon.'

'Would your brethren directly defy a command from the God Emperor?'

The sisters looked appalled. 'Impossible.'

'Well, the Ichorians have grown accustomed to seeing Marula around the Lord Nephron. If now, as a fully consecrated God Emperor, They choose to seclude Themselves behind these same Marula, who among the Ichorians would dare challenge this?'

From far away a murmurous sound came filtering through the Labyrinth.

'The Encampment of the Seraphim is waking, Celestial,' said Left-Quentha. 'Though they are much further away than the sound suggests.'

'So how . . . ?'

Her shrug spread to her sister's side of their body. 'Sound moves strangely through the Labyrinth, Celestial.'

'In one place, someone you can see directly,' said Right-Quentha, 'you cannot hear at all.'

'While in other places one can hear a faraway voice as if the speaker were close enough to touch,' said her sister, reaching out with her tattooed hand.

Right-Quentha smiled. 'For us, this was one of the chief attractions of this place. Several times we were alerted by the sound of the court preparing to migrate up to the sky.'

Both sisters nodded.

'Carnie . . .'

Carnelian turned to Tain.

'Why can't you raise the Masters against these—' He glanced at Sthax. 'They're all still there with their guardsmen.'

762

Carnelian looked at the Quenthas. 'Could that work?'

The sisters shook their heads. 'The Halls of Rebirth are a fortress, Celestial. Even with most of the Ichorians away garrisoning the Gates, our cohorts – the sybling cohorts – should easily hold off any assault.'

Carnelian nodded. 'At the very least there would be much blood spilled; at worst, it could ignite civil war.' A shadow passed over his heart. 'Besides, Osidian might be killed.'

'What of it?' said Fern. 'He deserves to die.'

There were gasps round the circle and wide-eyed fear at such sacrilege.

'If he dies now, most likely I would become the next God Emperor,' said Carnelian. He sensed more than saw the hope that entered many around the circle. 'Were that to happen, I'd be locked behind the Masks for ever.' He was aware of Fern's horror at this. 'Imprisoned here.' He extended his hands to take in the Labyrinth. 'Meanwhile, the world outside would sink into strife and famine.' He looked into Sthax's eyes. 'I don't know if I'd be able even then to save your people.' He shook his head, imagining it. 'The best I might manage would be to attempt to hold the balance of power here.' He glanced around the ring of faces. 'Be certain of this. If the Masters fall into fighting each other, they may destroy themselves, but they would take the world down with them.'

Everyone stared, consumed by their own vision of that calamity.

'What hope, then, is there?' asked Tain at last.

Carnelian felt some faint belief rising within him. He turned to Sthax. 'Do your brethren feel as you do?'

'We desperate.'

The Maruli looked at Carnelian as if he was a spar floating in a stormy sea. Carnelian would not refuse his hope. 'We'll do nothing to interfere with the Masters returning to their palaces. When Morunasa comes into the Labyrinth, we'll move against him.'

He did not reveal his relief when none there questioned

this. At that point, what he had stated was all the plan he had.

'How will we know when that happens?' asked Left-Quentha.

It was Fern who answered her. 'We'll know.'

The tree that inhabited the clearing was a pomegranate. Though laden with fruit, these were all still green. Right-Quentha had regarded them, disappointed, saying that she and her sister had hoped that the tree would be able to feed them at least for one night. On their previous visits, the fruit had been ripe, but then they had always come later in the year.

Even before they had thought to find some firewood, the sisters cautioned them against lighting a fire. Its smoke might betray their location to anyone searching for them. They made what camp they could within reach of the light. Fern made a bed for Carnelian from the fern fronds, but though they yearned for each other, they chose to sleep apart.

What little food they had was divided equally. As the day waned, they sought sleep as an escape from the darkness encroaching from the Labyrinth. Wrapped in his cloak, Carnelian lay listening to the murmur of the Masters' camp. Soon they would return to their coombs. What of Coomb Suth? Matters there were still unresolved. If anything were to happen to him or to his father, Poppy and the rest would be at the mercy of Opalid.

Another day of waiting, listening to the Masters' camp. When Fern went with the Quenthas and some of the Suth guardsmen to find some food, Carnelian remained behind with Tain. When the others returned, they had a couple of fish and a small saurian. Fern prepared them and they ate them raw.

*   *   *

Carnelian and Fern wandered off together. They had told the others that they would not be long and would stay within earshot of both their camp and that of the Masters.

'Are you sure you're up to this?' Fern asked.

Carnelian smiled at him. 'I feel much better.'

They walked along the road beneath the poppyhead columns, the silence deepening between them, until neither could find a way to words. It was Carnelian who spotted another clearing and headed towards it, though it took them away from the path. Even before he reached the clearing he realized it was much larger than the one around which they had camped. A column had collapsed, cracking others as it fell. A ragged hole had been left in the vaulting, through which light was flooding. The head of the fallen column lay half in light, half in shadow. Approaching the great bulb of stone, Carnelian reached out to touch it. Under his hand was the remains of the red with which it had once been painted. Like dried blood. He frowned, reminded of the funerary urns into which he and Osidian had been squeezed. His fingers found branching channels eroded into the stone. He gazed up into the light. This column had once stood naked against the elements. Long ago, perhaps, before the Labyrinth had been roofed in. He walked round to look at its spiky, poppy crown and saw the pod was cracked. A gash as if it had been slit to bleed its opium. He leaned towards it and detected a faint smell of ancient myrrh. He slipped his hand into the gash.

'What're you doing?'

Carnelian saw the anger in Fern's face. 'I just want to take a peek inside.' And, with that, he squeezed into the pod.

Inside, the air was musty. He stepped aside to allow light to filter in through the crack. It fell upon a sort of stalagmite angling up from the floor. But, of course, the whole pod had rolled over, so it was emerging not from the floor, but from what had been the ceiling. He reached out and touched it. It swelled into a spiral. Intuition made him reach out to the wall. His fingers found the buds, the seeds with which it was carved.

As much as he was inside a huge poppyhead, it was also a pomegranate. He could make out shapes piled up beyond the spindle. Cautiously he crossed the curving floor, using the spindle as a support. A mound of rubbish, of shards, a glimmer of metals and stones, among mouldering flakes and fibres of something else. He jumped when he saw the grin: a row of teeth in a skull skinned with thin, scabrous leather; a mummy, curled up as if in a womb, wrapped in brown cloth. There were others in among the heap. Bones held together by scraps of dried flesh. He grew uneasy, remembering the pygmy dead in their baobabs. He could hear again the crackle as they had burned. Caught by the stare of a dark socket, he shuddered, recalling the render the sartlar had made from pygmies they had killed. His eyes were drawn to a glinting profile. A beautiful face among the corpses. He leaned closer and saw it was a mask. Touching it, he found it was stone. The mummy to which it belonged was larger than the others, its wrappings paler bands of half-perished linen. Among these bands, the glint of gold. He stared, disturbed. This could be one of his fathers, his mothers. There was no sign here of an after-life, of resurrection. His thumb found the edge of the mask. The rest of his hand gripped across the bridge of the nose, into an eyeslit. He tugged and it snapped open like the lid of a rusted box. The face below had darkened, the eyes withered, the lips thinned, riding up the teeth, but it was still a Master's face. An adult face, but not much larger than a Chosen child's. Carnelian saw the hands crossed upon the chest, wedged behind the knees. He put the mask down and reached out to compare his hand with the mummy's. The mummy's was so much smaller. Perhaps embalming had shrunk it. Carnelian shook his head. The skull could not shrink.

At that moment the light was snuffed out. Carnelian turned, felt the tomb shudder, then a release of light dazzled him. 'Fern? Look here, this is a Master, but for some reason much smaller than I am.'

'Haven't you had enough of the dead?'

An edge to Fern's voice made Carnelian rise, shuffle back towards him. 'What's the matter?' he said, reaching out to touch him.

His hand was slapped away, stinging him to anger.

'What's going to happen?'

The almost childlike tone in Fern's voice cooled Carnelian's anger to sadness. 'I don't know, Fern, I don't know.'

'You must have a plan?'

'We wait for Morunasa and then—'

'You mean we wait for the screaming!'

Carnelian felt the grief leaching out of Fern connecting to his own. He remembered the nightmare in the Upper Reach. 'Yes, the screaming.'

'I can't bear it again.' The words a skin of ice over tears. Fern was reliving not the Upper Reach, but the massacre of his people. Carnelian felt panic rising in him. The memory of that horror came alive in him from where he had thought it buried.

'Tell me this time it will be different,' Fern sobbed.

Carnelian reached out, desperate to touch him, wanting to promise, but not daring to lest his promise should turn into a lie. 'I can't, Fern, but this time we'll fight to save what can be saved. This time, together.'

His hands reached Fern's face, felt his warm tears, his skin. They melted together, seeking life in the midst of death. Skin finding skin. Their mouths. Their hard flesh. Making love, at first violently, but then tenderly.

When they emerged from the tomb, they stood close enough to feel each other's breath. Eerie silence. Their cheeks grazed as they turned to look at each other. The Masters had left the Labyrinth.

The screaming began the following evening. Thin, bleak, harrowing sounds scratching the sepulchral gloom. Blood drained from the faces edging the clearing.

'What is it?' Tain asked in a whisper.

Fern closed his eyes as if he hoped that would close his ears. 'Morunasa feeding victims to his filthy god.'

Carnelian felt sick. 'Putting maggots in children.' As they all turned to him, he cursed himself for having said that aloud.

Heads angled as people listened to the pitch of the screaming. Fern licked his lips, looking queasy. 'The flesh tithe.'

Carnelian nodded. Tain jumped up. 'We must go now!'

Carnelian saw in Tain's face he was being haunted by what he had endured as a child.

The Quenthas shook their heads together, frowning, grim. 'It'll soon be night. If we attempt to find our way in the dark, we'll become lost.'

Carnelian, who had known that before the sisters said it, still felt angry at them for having taken from him any hope of action. 'Then we must sleep as best we can.'

He caught Fern's look of despair. How could they all endure such a night?

The first grey light found them awake, bleary-eyed, haggard. The screaming had kept them from sleep, or else mired in helpless nightmares. Carnelian glanced at Fern, saw how aged he seemed, as if it had been night for years. Memory weighed down on both of them. They had good reason to know the horror Morunasa had brought into the Labyrinth. Yet another scream sounded, a sort of lightning shrilling through their nerves. Carnelian had had enough. 'Let's go and end this.'

Everyone looked to him with hope; everyone save Fern, who did not look away fast enough to prevent Carnelian seeing his doubt.

Rain began to fall as they set off. They followed the sisters through the twilit Labyrinth. Above their heads the vaults hung like stormclouds. Water pouring in through openings hissed as it sprayed down.

*   *   *

They used one of the column sarcophagi as cover. Carnelian glanced back at the Shimmering Stair. No sign of life there. Dull, its cascade of steps seemed an approach to an immense tomb. Before it the moat was being turned opaque by water falling into it from the shadows above. Litter and mess was all that remained of the Encampment of the Seraphim. On higher ground, between two great pillars, stretched a line of sybling Ichorians. Beyond them, higher still, a darker cordon of Marula from within whose circle rose a particularly massive colossus shouldering flying arches and the high, shadowy ceiling. It was clear why Morunasa had chosen this vast sarcophagus, for it reminded Carnelian of the central trunk of the banyan of the Isle of Flies.

Somewhere near this colossus, a shriek rent the air, causing a shiver to ripple along the rings of Marula and syblings. All were fixedly turned outwards, no doubt fearing even to glimpse what was going on behind them.

Carnelian glanced round at his flint-eyed people awaiting his command. An attempt had to be made to stop that torture even if it should cost their lives.

As Carnelian strode towards the Sinistrals, he saw a party of Sapients addressing them. Fern, the Quenthas and Sthax were at his back. He had left Tain behind with the Suth tyadra.

The Sapients turned as their homunculi, muttering, watched Carnelian approach. Heart racing, he announced who he was.

One of the Sapients advanced. 'Celestial, please command these creatures to let us pass.'

It was as Carnelian had surmised: the Wise had lost control. The Sapient betrayed his agitation by the way he gripped the throat of his homunculus. The finial of his staff showed two faces turned to each other wrought in red stone. 'You are of Gates?' he guessed.

'The first Third of that Domain, Celestial.'

Carnelian scanned the finials of the other Sapients and it

seemed to him that, quite probably, all twelve Domains were there represented. He would test his hypothesis. 'Is it your masters, my Lord, have sent you hither?'

It was another homunculus who answered him, whose cypher of a cross Carnelian knew well enough was that of the Domain Legions. 'It is our masters, Celestial, we need to communicate with, urgently.'

An animal scream issued from up the slope. Carnelian fought to calm himself, to think. It seemed Morunasa had been cunning enough to realize he must control the Wise. 'Are all the Twelve within this cordon?'

Several four-fingered hands rose, making gestures of affirmation. It was as Carnelian had feared. Not only had Morunasa taken Osidian, but also the Twelve, thus decapitating the Wise. That only served to prove he was not dealing with a fool. He advanced on the Sapients, and they and their homunculi moved aside. Before him stood Ichorians armed with iron halberds, encased in armour and casques of the same precious substance. He threw back his hood and fixed one untattooed face with a glare. 'Do you not know who I am, Ichorian?'

The man ducked his head, even as his blind brother turned to him in consternation. His seeing half pulled them both down to kneel upon two of their three knees. 'Celestial,' he muttered. Raking their line, Carnelian caused them all to kneel, acknowledging him.

'Let me pass,' he said in an imperious tone.

Two heads rose from a forked neck. 'We cannot, Celestial.' The lips that spoke were baroqued with swirling black tattoos. Eyes in the darkened face were ovals of glassy obsidian. 'We have been commanded to let none through except at Their express instruction.'

'Did They communicate this command to you Themselves?'

Both syblings shook their heads.

'The Maruli, then?'

770

'It is not for us, Celestial, to question the choices of the Gods on Earth.'

'Celestial, may I address this centurion?'

Carnelian glanced round at the Quenthas and was glad to let them do what they could.

The sisters confronted the kneeling centurion. 'You know this is the brother of the Gods?' As the syblings nodded, the Quenthas continued relentlessly: 'From love of whom They changed the Law-that-must-be-obeyed. Do you imagine They will easily forgive this insult to Their beloved?'

'But the command—?' said the centurion.

'This command cannot apply to the Lord Carnelian,' said the Quenthas with steely authority.

The centurion ducked a bow. 'We dare not disobey divine command.'

'Was it given you in the angelic tongue?'

The syblings had to admit it had not been.

'How then can you be so certain of the precise nature of Their command?'

Carnelian could see the resolve of the centurion weakening and so could the Quenthas. 'Was it not delivered to you by a barbarian who traduced the holy will into a lesser tongue?'

Carnelian gazed down with haughty condescension. 'I shall vouch for you.' He scanned their ranks. 'For you all.'

The heads of the centurion turned inwards so that each caught the eye of the other. The syblings rose and, at their command, the line opened for Carnelian. Through the gap, he saw the darker ranks of the Marula. They would not be so easily cowed. He raised his voice to summon the Sapients to follow him, then he strode through the sybling cordon and on towards the Marula.

The Marula lowered their lances, their line buckling a little, bristling. They stared at Carnelian with yellow, feral eyes. He shortened his steps. Sweat trickled down his back. He was only too aware of the danger he was in, of the danger he was taking his people into. Earlier, the Quenthas had argued hard against this. Their counsel had been to subvert their brethren; to turn the Sinistrals against the Marula and slaughter them. It had been Fern's silence that had steadied Carnelian's resolve. Fern, who had reason to wish the killers of his people dead.

Carnelian glanced round at Sthax. They had made promises to each other. Hope lay in the trust between them. Sthax addressed the Marula. His voice carried with the clicks and throaty syllables of their speech. The Marula listened to him, their eyes flashing from Sthax to Carnelian, gripping and regripping their lances. When Sthax fell silent, Carnelian watched the Marula whispering among themselves. He recognized some of them. He remembered training them in the Upper Reach to fight in the formation they now used against him; he remembered fighting on the ground at their side against Osidian's mounted charges. Perhaps they too remembered this, because their lances began to rise as they moved aside.

Passing through the Marula Carnelian gazed up at the shadowy colossus to which they had been barring access. It was just another column of the Labyrinth, just another sarcophagus, in which lay the mummy of a God Emperor. It had the shape of a man, though one upon whose brow sat vaulting that seemed a stormy sky. It could have been the Black God incarnating as a column of smoke. Or was it the Darkness-under-the-Trees? The face of the colossus was hidden in the shadows of the roof, but Carnelian had the distinct impression he was gazing down with eyeless wrath. His arms crossed upon his chest reminded Carnelian of Legions in his capsule. The Standing Dead.

As he advanced, his gaze slid down the stone torso, the thighs each as mighty as a great tree. Between the ankles stretched what appeared to be a net upon which many fish were caught. His stomach clenched as he remembered the men hung up in the Isle of Flies.

Figures were emerging from between the feet of the colossus. Pallid creatures that seemed a mockery of the Chosen. He glanced to either side and saw with what terror the Marula warriors regarded the approach of these ashen men. Sthax said something to them in a soothing tone. He gave Carnelian a nod. The Oracles were close enough for him to see their ghostly faces. He wondered from where the ashes had come which they had rubbed upon their skin. They bared their sharpened teeth, eyes red with rage. They hissed at the warriors, spittle running down their chins. Carnelian felt the warriors begin to cower. Then, as a blur, someone sped past him, arm drawn back, and plunged the lance it held into one of the Oracles so violently the spearhead erupted out of his back. A look of surprise on the man's face as he plucked at the shaft jutting from his belly. Surprise too on the faces of his peers. Their ashen faces blanked with fear. Carnelian felt the warriors round him tensing. Their nostrils were distending as if they were smelling blood. They sprang. Soon the Oracles were encompassed by gleaming black flesh. Elbows made sharp angles and straightened as if, within their circle, they were pounding flour.

Carnelian moved on, the iron odour of fresh blood wafting in the air. The Quenthas were at his left, Fern at his right. At the feet of the colossus, more eerie figures were rising. Hanging on the netting above them, children pocked with wounds. Closer, Carnelian saw Oracles lying along the hollows between the toes of the colossus. Hearing the slap of pursuing feet, he turned to see Marula rushing up. His eyes found Sthax's. 'Can you control them?'

Sthax barked an order and Carnelian was reassured when the warriors slowed, though their eyes kept questing, hungry for more bloodshed. The Oracles confronting them looked terrified.

Carnelian half turned. 'Tell them their lives will be spared if they submit to me.'

Sthax stepped forward to harangue the Oracles. Glancing

back with shame, the ashen men crept forward and fell on their knees before Carnelian.

'Take care of them, Sthax,' Carnelian said, then stepped round the prone men, for, in the cave between the legs of the colossus, he had seen a single, pallid figure rising. He knew Morunasa by his proud bearing. As he neared the Oracle, Carnelian saw the ghostly shape of a Master lying naked on a bier at his feet. Even though the face was shadow, Carnelian knew it was Osidian.

Morunasa fixed him with crazed eyes. 'Come closer and I'll slay him.'

Carnelian glanced quickly to either side to make sure his companions knew to halt. He turned back to Morunasa. 'If you harm him, your people will surely die.'

Morunasa gave a dry laugh, his lips curling up to reveal his needle teeth. His head jerked up. 'What do I care for these traitors?'

'*All* your people will die.'

The cold grin died on Morunasa's face to be replaced by a haunted look. Carnelian felt his heart stirring for this man at bay. 'I've already promised him—' He glanced round at Sthax, who was approaching. 'Promised them all,' he said, with a gesture taking in all the Marula warriors, 'that I'll do everything I can to save those in the Lower Reach.'

He held Morunasa's gaze as the man tried to see into his heart. Morunasa seemed to find what he sought, for his head dropped and the tension left his limbs. He looked down at Osidian, who Carnelian realized was wearing the oily Obsidian Mask. Morunasa lifted his head, smiling defiantly, but Carnelian could see the man had little fight left in him. Morunasa raised his arms, bared his ravener teeth, then, with a lunge and a vicious twist of his head, he tore first one of his wrists open, then the other. His arms dropped, blood glistening in cords down his pale palms, to pour in skeins from his fingers. Instinctively Carnelian brought his own scabbed wrists together as if he were feeling Morunasa's pain.

He stepped forward, his foot slipping on the blood pooling around Morunasa's feet. He held the man's gaze once more, then knelt beside Osidian. His scrutiny took in the new wounds they had cut to put in the maggots, patterning the white flesh between the shadows of the old scars. He gazed at the gleaming, perfect black face that made it seem as if Osidian was one with the colossus towering above them. He reached forward to remove it, wanting to throw it away, to look upon Osidian's face.

'No! It is forbidden!' cried an unhuman voice.

Carnelian turned and saw a homunculus watching him, the figure of his master rising behind with his long silver mask. He considered for a moment defying the Sapient even as he questioned his fear at giving them back their power. He answered himself: Enough of the world is already broken. He became aware other homunculi were moving past him into the shadows beyond. Then he saw the frieze of what seemed skulls beneath the colossus. Grand Sapients. The Twelve slumped against the stone of the column, the odour of excrement and urine coming off them.

'Let's get him out of here.'

Carnelian saw it was Fern. They lifted Osidian between them and carried him out of the gloom. As they laid him down, Fern put an ear to his chest. He looked up. 'He lives.'

Carnelian nodded, but was watching the Grand Sapients being helped up by their homunculi. The ancients leaned upon them like infirm parents. But even as they rose, their hands quested for their children's throats. The homunculi began to make sounds, half-words, mutterings, as if their masters, drowning, through them were coming up gulping for air.

Carnelian looked up at the small bodies on the netting. They were covered with the fresh wounds into which maggots had been introduced. Some of them had their eyes open, glassy with terror. He left Osidian to Fern, called for Sthax and soon Marula were swarming up to free the children. Carnelian watched, agonized, as one by one they were released, passed down from hand to hand. As he caught a little girl, he winced at how cold and clammy she was; at the tremor in her tiny body.

Even as he helped, his attention was more and more being drawn to the Wise. They had regained their composure. The Twelve, in a line, were confronted by another line of Sapients. Between them, a double interface of homunculi. The Grand Sapients were reconnecting to their Domains. As Carnelian approached them, still reviewing his decision, he heard the rattling vocalizations of the homunculi. A constant, frantic stream of apparently meaningless syllables interspersed with the muttering of the Grand Sapients' receptive homunculi, through whose throats their masters were receiving who knew what volume of data. Carnelian glanced back at Osidian, lying inert. He refocused on the Wise. It was up to him. Should he try to take control of them? If he did not, how might they take advantage of the situation?

Suddenly, one of the Grand Sapients choked his homunculus silent and began prodding instructions into its neck. Soon others, terminating the receptive mode, were turning their homunculi to transmission. The homunculi that had been speaking fell silent and were soon murmuring an echo to the questions the Grand Sapients were voicing through their homunculi. There was a tension in the fingers of the Grand Sapients as they worked their voices' necks. Questions and answers shuttled back and forth, homunculi speaking all at once, so that Carnelian was amazed that anything coherent could be being communicated by means of such cacophony. Yet its frantic tone was infecting him with an increasing foreboding. The flow quietened to a murmur, then silence. The Twelve turned their empty eye sockets towards Carnelian. They nodded.

'Celestial?' sang one of their homunculi.

For a moment Carnelian could find no words, unnerved by their corpse stares. 'What news?'

'The City at the Gates is overrun by sartlar.'

Carnelian's stomach clenched. Some part of him had known this was what they were going to say.

'What happened to the legions dispatched to disperse them?'

The Twelve realigned in a row, facing him. Examining their staves, he deduced it was Tribute who now spoke to him.

'It appears, Celestial, contact with them has been lost.'

'This certainly seems to be the case,' said another homunculus at one end of their line. The staff it held bore a smouldering red cross. For a moment, Carnelian was shocked, then realized this was not Legions returned from the dead, but merely his successor.

'. . . we shall have to verify the integrity of our systems, Celestial.'

'Some degradation in their functioning is to be expected in this disorder,' Tribute said.

Carnelian fought his rising dread. 'What does "overrun" mean?'

The twelve homunculi echoed his words, murmurously.

'Sartlar are vermin,' said Tribute.

Carnelian did not consider this much of an answer. If they were still in the vicinity of Osrakum, the creatures must be desperately hungry.

'Additionally, these instruments of chaos must be destroyed.'

Carnelian wished they would shut up and let him think. 'Do you mean the Marula?'

'They have put unclean hands upon the God Emperor, upon us.'

Carnelian knew he must not give way to anger. He must think. Who knew how long it would be before Osidian regained consciousness? If Ykoriana discovered his condition, could she resist seizing power in the Labyrinth? He looked at the Wise. Dare he let them deal with the sartlar? No, he knew too well how pitiless were their methods. He must assume the agreement he had made with Osidian and Ykoriana would hold. The outer world was his responsibility. His father too would have to wait.

He raised his eyes to the Twelve. 'You will not touch the Marula. I shall take them away with me.'

'Away, Celestial?'

'To the City at the Gates. I shall also take the huimur in the Plain of Thrones.'

Tribute took Carnelian's words from the throat of his homunculus and then made it speak in the same garbled manner that they had been using before. Sound and murmuring interwove as the Twelve conclaved. At last they fell silent and Tribute's homunculus alone spoke. 'Will you accept our aid, Celestial?'

Carnelian considered this. At last he raised his hand in affirmation. He would feel better if at least some of the Twelve were where he could watch them. In truth, he was grateful for any help.

'Then Legions, Lands and Cities will accompany you, Celestial.'

Carnelian nodded, looking at Osidian lying on his bier.

'We shall take care of Them.'

Carnelian saw the children, Morunasa's victims, being carried by the Marula. 'I shall take these children with me too.'

The Wise voiced no objection. Carnelian remembered the thousands more out in tithe cages. 'Henceforth, you will consider all of the flesh tithe to be under my protection.'

Even as he spoke Carnelian realized these were the preserve of the Domain of Tribute. It could not help but be understood by all the Wise as a challenge to their leader's authority. So be it; on this issue, Carnelian would not back down.

'Your property, Celestial?'

'If that is what it takes.'

'Very well,' Tribute said, at last. 'We shall accept this. For now.'

Carnelian watched the children being led or carried off by syblings towards the cages of the flesh tithe. Other syblings, armed, escorted the few surviving Oracles, who had promised to oversee the children through their period of infestation. Carnelian had felt no need to threaten them; for, after all, most of what survived of their god was now contained in the tiny bodies of those children.

He frowned, remembering the long weary journey through the darkness. It had taken the fight out of him. The whimpering of the children had frayed his compassion, until it was replaced by disgust for what they harboured in their flesh. By the end, however unfairly, he was angry with them. He shook his head. They were just a place to put his anger. He glanced back at the Forbidden Door, uncertain what he was leaving behind. The Twelve were free. Osidian would, most likely, recover. Carnelian was glad that, when he had asked them, the Quenthas had agreed to remain behind to protect him.

He gazed at the Plain of Thrones. Flanking the edges of the Black Field the dragons remained in the positions they had held since the Apotheosis. The multitude they had menaced had all been driven out of Osrakum, leaving the Black Field a mired and stinking plain. He scanned the towered monsters. It would be best to lead them out on Heart-of-Thunder, from whose tower they were wont to take their commands.

Coming up through the floor onto the command deck, he was aware that the cloying, sickly smell pervading the tower was stronger here. As he stepped away to let Fern up, Carnelian became aware the air was being sewn by buzzing flights. Flies. His heart began pounding, his throat grew dry, as he searched the shadows at the back of the cabin. Somehow, Morunasa's god had found his way here. A bundle lay against a wall. Soft and tapering at both ends like some monstrous chrysalis. As he approached it, he became quickly

779

aware it was the source of the sweet odour. A smell of meat near rotting. He stood over it. Fluids it had oozed had stained the deck. Creeping horror claimed him as he realized the chrysalis had something very like a head. A bloated, leaking, swollen face. He stared with shock as he recognized it. He jumped when it moved. It was alive. Of course he was. Carnelian had seen enough corpses, had smelled enough, to know he was not yet dead.

'What is it?'

Carnelian looked into Tain's anxious face. He tried some kind of explanation. His brother's face twisted strangely when he heard the name. He did not seem to be listening to Carnelian's explanation of why this thing was there. As Tain gaped at what was left of Jaspar, Carnelian remembered what that Master had done to Tain when he was a boy. Carnelian wondered if the expression on his brother's face was the satisfaction of revenge. Disturbed, he looked away. There was a shape in the shadows he had not noticed before. Something like a child in a tight knot.

'You there.'

The knot tightened.

'I can see you there.'

The shape unbent and Carnelian saw its face and recognized it. 'You!'

Legions' homunculus cowered.

'What are you doing here?'

The little man indicated Jaspar with a shaking hand. 'Taking care of the Seraph.' Carnelian's frown of incomprehension forced more words out of him. 'Giving the Seraph water. Chewing his food for him.'

Carnelian stared at the homunculus, unable to understand why he should have chosen to prolong Jaspar's agony. Anger rose in him at the cruelty.

Then Tain cried out: 'He's looking at me.'

He stared in horror at Jaspar, whose eyes had squeezed into view between the bloated lids. Carnelian imagined how riddled Jaspar's body must be with worms. How long had he lain here? Tended by the homunculus just enough to keep him alive. Just alive.

Tain grabbed at Carnelian's arm, dug his fingers in. 'For the gods' sake kill him.'

Carnelian looked at him, not wanting to ask him, asking him: 'Do you want to do it?'

His brother stared at him as if he thought him mad. Tain shook his head, frowning, backing away. Carnelian became aware Fern was there, watching. He put his hand out, and Fern understood, for he unsheathed a blade and put its hilt in Carnelian's hand, who turned, crouched, then insinuated its point under the dewlap chins and, finding the root of an ear, punctured the flesh and sliced down. Then, rising, he watched a dark pool widening around Jaspar's head.

From Heart-of-Thunder's command chair, Carnelian gazed out to starboard, through the rain, at the ring of standing stones. Though he had had Jaspar's body removed, the deck scrubbed, the flies driven away, killed, the smell still lingered. He could still see the stains Jaspar had left in the deck. He looked round to the other side of the cabin to where Fern and Tain were sitting against the wall; Fern staring, frowning, grim; Tain still in shock, haunted. Further back, in the shadows, the homunculus. Carnelian felt like punishing the little man for his cruelty. Empathy quenched this impulse. How long had the homunculus been there, tending Jaspar's near-corpse? Abandoned without hope of rescue. Perhaps he had been cruel, perhaps merely lonely and terrified. Carnelian had to accept that it was he most of all who had abandoned the little man, had forgotten him.

A mutter at his feet made him turn, feeling the dragon beneath responding to his Left's whispered command. The view through the screen began sliding right until the narrow entrance to the Plain of Thrones came into view. He focused grimly on the task he had before him and wondered what he was taking them all into.

As they came off the Great Causeway, the downpour abated. On either side, the Turtle Steps cascaded down to the lake. Ahead, something smouldered. Staring at it, Carnelian felt a heaviness descend upon him. Though he knew it was the gilded Clave, it reminded him of the Iron House burning in the midst of a landscape of sartlar dead. Grimly, he contemplated that he was on a mission to inflict more carnage on the poor brutes.

When Fern coughed, Carnelian turned and saw him indicating Tain. His brother had the look of a terrified child, listening. Carnelian listened too. Beneath the shudder and rattle of the cabin there was a dull roaring. He glanced at Tain, then ordered Heart-of-Thunder onto the Cloaca Road. As the monster turned, a canal came into view, cut into the Valley floor, a spillway. Only a dyke separated it from the lake shore, through whose immense stone comb the Skymere poured into the spillway in many waterfalls. Carnelian recalled that Tain's ordeal in the quarantine had terminated somewhere near those falls. He glanced round at him. Clearly, the encounter with Jaspar had left Tain shaken. A solution occurred to him, not only for Tain – and for the homunculus as well, whom Carnelian knew he could not bring before the Wise – but for relieving another worry.

'Tain, you must carry a message to Father for me.'

Tain frowned, seeming to have difficulty in bringing Carnelian into focus. 'He'd not forgive me for leaving you unprotected.'

Carnelian indicated the homunculus. 'I also need him taken to safety.'

His brother gave a reluctant nod.

'Tell Father everything you've witnessed. Tell him I'm going to the City at the Gates to sort out some problems.' Carnelian could add no more. How long would it be before he was free to return to Osrakum?

Once Tain and the homunculus had disembarked, Heart-of-Thunder proceeded along the lip of the Cloaca, in whose depths storm waters roared.

The grey afternoon was waning when they reached the Black Gate. It opened for them and Heart-of-Thunder carried them into the Canyon. Nearby it was twilight, but further away, where the Canyon turned south, night seemed to have arrived already. Carnelian could only just discern the blacker clot of the Blood Gate. If they pushed on, he hoped they could reach the City at the Gates before nightfall.

'I wish to send a message ahead,' he said.

'A signal flare will have to be lit, Master,' said his Left.

As Carnelian waited he watched the cliffs on either side swaying in time to the cabin. The air trembled to a constant roar. It seemed a more dreadful sound than merely the rushing waters of the Cloaca reverberating along the Canyon. His Left announced the mirrorman was ready.

'Bid them open the gates, we're passing straight through.'

As his Left repeated his words into the command tube, Carnelian hoped this act of foresight would avoid any delays. He became aware of a blinking light that could only be coming from one of the towers of the Blood Gate.

'The outer gate cannot be opened, Master,' his Left said.

'Ask them why.' Carnelian waited impatiently as his message was transmitted. The Blood Gate signal resumed its blinking.

The Left turned to look up at Carnelian. 'They claim it is forbidden, Master.'

Unease stirred in him. He would have liked more information, but he was reluctant to carry out any further interrogation by signal flare.

A man-sized door opened in the cliff that was the closed inner portal of the Blood Gate. Several lanterns swung out, carried by a number of figures, each of whom seemed to have but half a face. These Sinistrals could not help glancing fearfully over Carnelian's head. He knew how menacing was the shape that loomed up behind him, for he had just descended from the monster's tower. The Sinistrals knelt, touching their foreheads to the stone. 'Seraph.'

'I am Carnelian of the Masks. Why have you closed this gate against me?'

They struck the stone with their heads. 'Forgive us, Celestial, we merely obey the Law.'

Carnelian could make no sense of this. 'The Wise have sent commands?'

As their eyes came up, he could see how confused the Sinistrals were. He did not want to terrorize them. 'Is there some kind of emergency?'

'Perhaps, Celestial, you might deign to see the cause for yourself?'

Carnelian almost barked: see what? Turning, he regarded the mountainous shadows that formed a line from the Blood Gate rock off across the massive bridge and down the Canyon. 'Fern, will you come with me?' he asked in Ochre. He waited for Fern's nod, then turned to his Lefthand. 'Please take my place in the command chair. Pass a message down the line. You are to wait for me.'

Carnelian turned to the Sinistrals. 'Show me this "cause".'

Carnelian was breathing hard. He had lost count of the levels they had climbed. Stair after stair past military gates, warrens and military engines of gigantic size. The chill on his face as a breeze caught his sweat was a relief. They had come out into the open at last. He became aware of the night, then, almost immediately, of a dull glowing on the underside of the clouds that capped the sky to the west.

'Dragonfire?' said Fern.

Carnelian shook his head, grimly. 'There're no flashes. The City burns.' He turned to the Sinistral commander. 'Is that what you wanted me to witness?'

'Not so, Celestial.'

Carnelian and Fern followed him to a parapet where the Sinistral pointed down. Carnelian sensed the vast spread of emptiness below. 'Can you see anything?'

Fern traced some vague outlines in the darkness. Carnelian was trying to work out where their eyrie was located, when he became aware of a murmur distinct from the throbbing of the Cloaca. The hackles rose on his neck. He knew that sound. Fern breathed the word that had formed in Carnelian's mind. 'Sartlar.'

BLOOD GATE

It is the will that conquers.

(a precept of the Wise)

Wandering lost through a forest of grey trees. His fingers, touching one, recoil. Cold, its bark degloves like corpse skin. Cracked bone revealed could be chapped lips. A baby there, nestling among desiccated, grinning dead. A boy he knows, but has forgotten. No, a girl. His mother? Which mother? He feels the tiny thing's need and scoops it up. His shadow has a horrible life of its own. A dark presence swirling the air. Itch in his ears. Fearing flies, he flees, cradling the child as if it were his own heart.

A wall crusted with spirals all the way to the sky. He feels its pulse. Puts his ear to the shell. Hearing the sea turns fear to rage. Plunging his spear in he tears a wound he squeezes into. Smothering flesh. Bursting into headache light. Up to his ankles in streaming blood. High banks bristling with bones. Thunder. The dark sea lap lap lapping at a beach of powdered bone. Salt wind murmuring in his face. Trying to tell him something he is desperate to hear, but he claps his hands over his ears in terror. The need in the child's eyes. No child belongs in the Land of the Dead! His cradling arms become a boat his shadow shoves into the swell. Another with him. Nuzzling the thither shore upon which looms a shape so terrible it blinds him. But he is undeaf to its roaring rage.

* * *

786

He woke in Fern's arms, sweating, heart hammering. There was comfort in Fern's warm strength, in his smell. The dread from the dream was slow to fade. Carnelian remembered the sartlar at the gate. That was something solid to worry about. He scanned the cell. Plain plaster walls. Some shelves. A wooden manikin, big-shouldered for wearing armour, mushroom-headed to take a helmet. A rack for weapons. An oblong of brass set into the wall, in which lurked a murky twisted world. A stone basin with a lead spout with a valve around its throat. The night before, the Ichorian commanders had offered to vacate some of their cells for his people. They had been aghast when he had told them he intended to occupy one himself. This chamber was the finest they had: that of the grand-cohort commander. It was certainly not intended for a Master, but he had slept in far worse places. It was clean and private and he found its simplicity soothing.

Thin light was filtering from somewhere at the foot of the bed. He was drawn to it. He kissed Fern and slipped out from his arms. 'I yearn to see the new day.'

'It's cold,' muttered Fern, getting up with him, his skin sliding against Carnelian's. He plucked a blanket from the bed and drew it round them both. Light was entering in through gaps in some shutters. They fumbled for the catches. As the panels opened they released more faint light and a shock of cold air. They stepped out onto a balcony that held them with no space to spare. Carnelian turned his head towards the light, squinting against the incandescent rind of the sun rising from a violet horizon framed by the Canyon walls. The dyke of the Black Gate provided a threshold to that view into Osrakum. Half occluded by one of the Canyon walls stood the dark apparition of the Pillar of Heaven. For a moment he was lost in memories of his time in its hollows.

He became aware Fern was gazing upwards and looked up himself. They were standing astride the ridge where two sides of the tower met. Above them, a thicket of flame-pipes ran in a triple band like a nest of snakes. Carnelian let his gaze fall, frowning. Below, two other balconies; a row of six more beneath those, many more in the next row and more and more, like the cliff-ledges gulls nest on; balconies erupting from the stone in a rash that widened then narrowed down the walls. He sensed this reflected the military hierarchy of the officers who occupied the cells below. The rash ran out as tiny blisters in the smooth masonry. This was rooted in rougher stone that went down and further down. His grip tightened on Fern's arm. They were high in an eyrie teetering on the edge of an abyss. There was a black gleam in the depths of the Cloaca.

'What is it?' Fern asked.

Carnelian silenced him with a touch to the lips. Just before Fern spoke he had become aware of a murmur that brought back the horror of his dream. He looked down the Canyon to where a vast bridge emerged from the gloom to touch the circular plain that stretched before the outer gates. It seemed covered with rust rough enough, he felt, to abrade his hand should he reach out to touch it. Subtle motion on that plain so far below made it clear the rust was a teeming multitude. 'Numberless as leaves,' he murmured in Quya.

'What?'

Carnelian turned to Fern, who had worry in his eyes. 'Something my father once said to me. It's not important.' He nodded towards the sartlar. 'I'd hoped I had dreamed them too.' He wondered if it was hunger that had driven the poor creatures this far. How difficult was it going to be to herd them back towards the City at the Gates?

Fern focused on their multitude. 'As placid as earthers cropping ferns.'

Carnelian remembered how violently earthers stampeded when they were spooked and foreboding sent a shiver through him.

Fern reacted to his shudder. 'Let's go back in.'

Carnelian was glad to follow him. The light revealed a design upon the wall. A grid, its boxes filled with red, black and green dabs forming diagonals across it. He did not need the colours running along the top and the twelve columns to know these were the months. Down the side of the six rows, pomegranates alternated with lilies, each having a number beside it. The six grand-cohorts of the Red Ichorians. The coloured dabs showed the month on which each grand-cohort was to garrison which of the three gates. It made him sad, this duty rota for men almost all now dead.

He looked away. He had his own duty. The previous night, as he and Fern had gazed down upon the sartlar, an ammonite had appeared, saying their masters had arrived at the Blood Gate and that they insisted he should attend a conclave with them immediately. He had been too weary, too disconsolate, to face them then, but he had promised that, at first light, he would meet with them.

Following the ammonite up into the open air, Carnelian was overwhelmed. All around him the Canyon walls rose up to challenge the majesty of the sky. Such vast space was a shock after the confinement of the military strata, whose spaces, though cavernous, were inhabited by engines of war, reeking of naphtha, around whose bloated brass Ichorians crept like ants around their queen.

Carnelian could see no threat and asked Sthax and his Marula escort to wait for him. His ammonite guide led him off across a plain that was the roof and summit of the Blood Gate tower in which he lodged and that was covered with a sparse forest of chimneys. They were heading for a promontory that curved up from a corner of the tower to a platform crowded with machines. As Carnelian climbed towards it he recognized some as heliographs, though larger than any he had seen before. As for the rest, he could not even guess their function. Sapients stood here and there, directing ammonites working the mechanisms. As he wound his way through the thicket of brass and bone, of lenses and louvred mirrors, he saw three taller figures at the platform edge and knew, from their staves, they must be Grand Sapients.

'Celestial.' It was the central homunculus of three who greeted him. Carnelian read the cypher of the staff he held. 'My Lord Lands,' he said, then reading the others, 'My Lords Cities, Legions.'

Their long masks gleamed as they slightly inclined their heads.

'Our link to the outer world is severed, Celestial,' said Cities' homunculus.

Carnelian could not see past them to the sartlar below. At first he thought Cities was referring to them, but then knew he was speaking of their heliographs.

'It is imperative we re-establish our link to the outer world,' said Lands. 'Without it, we are blind.'

'The huimur you brought hither, Celestial,' said Legions, 'must be sent to the Green Gate to restore the relay there.'

Carnelian was about to ask how they could know that there was where the problem lay – after all the City at the Gates was overrun by sartlar – but then he understood. 'The Green Gate is not responding to your diagnostics.'

'Just so,' said Cities.

'Can you be sure the watch-towers in the City at the Gates are still intact?'

'Even to a determined foe they would be nigh on impregnable,' said Cities. 'Besides, Celestial, a single link to the network is all we require to restore our vision of the Guarded Land.'

'A single link will allow our voice to be heard across the Three Lands,' said Legions.

Carnelian felt uneasy at the thought of the Wise reacquiring such power before the new political balance was in place to restrain them. This situation would have to be played carefully. He took a step towards them. Their homunculi were muttering even as they stood aside. He moved through the Sapients, aware of the dull, resinous odour of their crusted robes. Then he forgot everything except the vision that opened up at his feet. Though still in shadow, it was clear the Canyon floor was clothed with sartlar right up to the turn and beyond. He imagined the solid tentacle of flesh winding through the Canyon and out, spreading over the Wheel, to fray into the alleyways and causeways of the City. 'What of the sartlar?'

'They shall return to the Land.'

Carnelian turned to Lands. 'How do you envisage that this be done?'

It was Legions' homunculus who answered him. 'No doubt it is hunger that has driven them into the Canyon. That they have penetrated so far is only because of the breach made in the Green Gate by the previous God Emperor. With fire we shall quickly drive them back from Osrakum.'

Carnelian eyed the multitude below. 'Do they pose a danger to us?'

The Grand Sapient and his homunculus came to stand beside him. His master's fingers working at his neck, the homunculus raised a thin arm and pointed at the triangular tower across the circular plain below. 'That tower there, the Prow, has the firepower of three full legions.' Legions tapped the floor with his foot. 'This fortress has the puissance of another three. And, delved into the bedrock upon which these structures stand, there are tanks holding, under pressure, quantities of naphtha seventy-six times that which is held within a legionary fortress of the second class. Even were all our legions to rise up against us, they could not hope to overcome the power here. We are invulnerable.

'Fire will tame the sartlar brutes as it has always done. We advise that a firestorm should be unleashed from here to clear them from the approaches to the fortress. Issuing forth, the huimur will complete their rout. Be assured, my Lords, the link shall be restored before nightfall.'

Carnelian glanced round at the Grand Sapients, feeling as if he was beneath their notice. Were they attempting to assert their ancient authority? As much could their motives be focused on the internal struggle among them. Under his predecessor's rule, Domain Legions had been pre-eminent.

Perhaps the new Grand Sapient was merely trying to regain something of that lost standing. Carnelian gazed down at the sartlar. He remembered Fern comparing them to earthers. He remembered too the careful way the Ochre sent to fetch water had crept through the earther herds to the lagoons.

'Would it not be more efficient to merely walk the huimur through the sartlar? Surely they would move from their path?'

'Celestial, to open the gates without removing the creatures from the killing field would be to compromise our purity,' said Legions.

'The creatures are riddled with disease,' said Lands.

Carnelian remembered that the Ochre had given to the place where they had butchered the heaveners the name 'the killing field'. Remembering that bloody slaughter, pity rose in him for the sartlar, but he told himself that, if they did not return to the land soon, millions would die from famine. Even the destruction of all the sartlar in the Canyon was not too high a price to pay if it would lead to so many others being spared. 'I shall go to the Green Gate in the manner you prescribe, my Lord Legions.'

'My Lord has chosen the path of wisdom.'

Sitting in Heart-of-Thunder's command chair, Carnelian could not only feel the monster's power beneath him, but he was also aware of the other dragons, one on either side, framed by the bronze walls of the open portals of the eastern gate. Before him rose the unscalable cliff of the outer, western gate. Above that, the sky was choked with smoke from the lit ranks of flame-pipes that crowned the Blood Gate towers. His own pipes were lit. Everything was ready.

A vast voice roared; a horn blast that caught, echoing, in the throat of the Canyon, causing Carnelian to grind his teeth. The relief of silence filled him with a terrible anticipation that made him burst into a cold sweat. The air began to tear with high whinings almost beyond hearing. Then suddenly, with atrocious force, screams shredded the world, harsh enough, it felt, to skin him alive. A whoosh, dozens more merging into roaring, then he was near-blinded by continuous, flickering lightning. The portals ahead were shuddering as if being struck by an earthquake. Their bronze gonged. He did not hear this, but felt it through his chair, through the judder of the cabin. Black smoke rose turning day to night.

He endured the shaking, the shrieking that hysterically pulsed its daggers in his ears, as the towers round him lit up, flickering, reflecting the coruscating detonations of energy on the other side of the closed gates.

At last the pipes, spluttering, fell silent. The great gates throbbed and clanged as the opening mechanisms engaged. The firmament of bronze came apart to create a hazy slit that brightened as it gave a widening view onto unimaginable carnage.

He issued the command for Heart-of-Thunder to advance and they slid between the open portals of the outer gate. On the sides of his neck he could feel the heat the bronze walls were radiating. Involuntarily, his gaze was fixed in horror upon the charred meat encrusting the killing field. The stench of it assailed him, making him gag. A mesh of black and red and white and seething gold; of limbs and blackened torsos and heads, crisping. Glistening with bubbling fat. Rags and hair smouldering. And, through his chair, he could feel the delicate concussion as Heart-of-Thunder cracked skulls beneath his feet.

The ride smoothed out. Weak with horror, Carnelian became aware they were now moving along a shelf of the Canyon floor that seemed as clean as sun-bleached bone. All the way there their path had been carpeted with sartlar remains: even the bridge that they had crossed under the malevolent gaze of the Prow with its furious mane of smoke. Those sartlar surviving were ebbing away from him. Red they were, engrained with the dust of the outer world. He watched them with a weary, deepening hatred. All he wanted was to reach the Green Gate, fix the accursed relay, then return.

He was slow to realize the sartlar were no longer receding. Their mass solidified all the way to the turn in the Canyon and, no doubt, beyond so that it was impossible for them to move from his path. Filthy, stupid brutes, forcing on him the choice whether to trample them underfoot or to scythe a way through with fire. Lost in the loathsome contemplation of the decision he must make, Carnelian had to be alerted to their movement by his Left. They were surging towards Heart-of-Thunder. Instinctively he cried: 'Open fire.'

Soon screaming jets were splashing among the creatures, but he had delayed too long. Their vanguard was already within the minimum range of his pipes. They came on, mouths sagging open, so that it seemed the screaming of the incandescent arcs was their cries. He watched with a kind of paralysed fascination as their bow wave broke over the head of Heart-of-Thunder. Feverishly they leapt up, clambering on his horns. Soon his head was hidden beneath their writhing bodies. Even as his pain was communicated as a shuddering in the cabin, Carnelian saw the dragon's dark blood slicking the writhing sartlar and found his voice to order a retreat.

Back on the island rock and behind the Blood Gate, he gazed up at Heart-of-Thunder. The dragon's vast head seemed all raw flesh; his freshly gouged eye a bloody cave. It had been a brutal business cutting the sartlar off him.

As they were retreating, Heart-of-Thunder's agony had made Carnelian fear they might lose control of him. He was unresponsive to commands and could at any moment have run amok, plunging them all into the Cloaca abyss.

Incredulous with shock, Carnelian looked back to where more and more smoke was pumping up into the midday sky. The holocaust the Prow was pouring down had not proved enough to repulse their onslaught. Even now, enduring the firestorm, sartlar aflame were flinging themselves ineffectually against the bronze gate. The Wise had sent word that their frenzy must be allowed to exhaust itself upon the defences of the Gate.

From the balcony of their cell, Carnelian and Fern gazed down into the inferno. Each time a flame-pipe screamed they shuddered. A cry swooping from the sky would ignite into an arch of lightning that hissed as it kissed flesh. Shadows leapt feverishly. Blackness rolled across the incandescent arcs. Amidst the torment of fire and smoke, glimpses of undulating ground verminous with movement as the sartlar kept coming on. Why were they not even showing animal fear, but pushing on into the firestorm regardless?

All night, the whole tower trembled and shook from the barrage. Carnelian prayed that whatever instinct was driving the sartlar to self-destruction might lose its grip on them, but the screaming of the pipes never ceased.

The world contracted down to the womb of their cell. They lived a liminal existence between slumber and waking; between inner and outer night. Sometimes Carnelian believed he was back in the cabin, crossing the sea. Everything that had happened after that became nothing but a dream, at first bright as a vision of spring, but, inevitably, rotting down to nightmare.

A body stirred against him. Carnelian turned his head. At first he hardly recognized it was Fern. 'How long?'

In his eyes, Carnelian saw reflected his own despair. 'Days?'

He focused his hearing beyond the walls. It took a moment to resolve the raging into the scream of flame-pipes. Days? Revulsion woke him fully. He sat up. Days?

*   *   *

They rose and left the cell. Their legs seemed reluctant to carry them up through the entrails of the tower. They reached a high gallery overlooking a world upon which the play of liquid fire was migraine-bright. It was a while before their vision was able to discern a sort of choppy sea of smouldering ridges and troughs that swept up to dash a wave of corpses against the bronze cliff of the outer gate. Raising their eyes, they saw, beyond the smoke-enshrouded Prow, the shadowy throat of the Canyon disgorging a river that was steadily feeding more meat into the holocaust.

Higher they climbed. As they rose through the levels the air became as humid as breath. So much water had spilled down from above that floors were warped, doors jammed half open, wood everywhere swollen as if abscessed. Higher still the heat began. Air reeking of sweat and naphtha, furnace-hot. Floors awash with fluid as warm as blood. Ichorians laboured in the crevices between the machines. Blistered hands wrestled tubes and counterweights; dashed water from pails onto brass so hot it turned instantly into scalding steam. Mechanisms all around convulsed as if the tower were in its death throes. Carnelian and Fern watched the naked men servicing the engines. Some who saw them tried to get to their knees. All were red-eyed, confused, cruelly burned. Carnelian ignored them, searching until he found a purple robe. Not a Sapient, but only a sallow, gaping ammonite.

Your masters? Carnelian signed, certain his voice could not carry above the din.

They sleep, Celestial, signed the ammonite.

The man cowered when Carnelian frowned, incredulous. *Wake them!*

As the ammonite scrambled away, Carnelian watched the Ichorians. When he became aware his presence was a distraction that might make the poor wretches fall victim to the machines, he took Fern's shoulder and they left the way they had come.

There was a scratching at the door. Such a small, ordinary sound in a world of such monstrous cacophony. Carnelian rose and opened the door. An ammonite stood outside, silver face reflecting his pale body as a twisting curve.

'Celestial, Lord Legions, my master, will grant you audience.'

'He's here?' Carnelian tried to pierce the shadows behind the ammonite, but could see only his Marula slumped against the wall. When Sthax looked up, face wooden with terror, Carnelian gestured him to remain where he was.

The ammonite shook his head. 'Upon the roof, Celestial. He bade me bring you to him.'

Carnelian left Fern sleeping, then followed the ammonite up through the hollows of the tower. All the way, air sucked up from the lower levels rushed past them with ever increasing fury as if racing them to the roof.

As they came up onto the roof, Carnelian felt he was entering some vast forest. A canopy of sullen blackness hung above, fed by the trunks of smoke the chimneys were pumping up. Melancholy rain slapped against him in gusts and a snow of ash and soot that clung to everything.

The ammonite led him towards the edge, where some dark figures stood like burnt posts: Sapients, sheltering beneath parasols other ammonites were holding over them. As Carnelian drew nearer the screaming of the pipes grew so shrill he felt his bones must shatter. The plain below came into view, partially obscured by a steamy miasma. Pockets that seemed horrible chambers were lit here and there by the lightning flicker of the flame jets arcing back and forth. Through the murk he could see that a jerky, agonized scramble of sartlar were struggling to scale the crust of cooked meat that reared up against the outer gate. A flash, then screeching, as liquid fire slashed across them, baking them into the hill.

'Your plan has failed,' he cried above the din.

'To some extent, Celestial.'

Carnelian turned, startled by that angelic voice, serene in the midst of such chaos. He saw the homunculus who had spoken and the staff he held. Behind him his master, Lands, seemed just another chimney.

The Grand Sapient disengaged a hand from the throat of the homunculus and began signing. *Once they overran the City, there was always the danger this might happen. They have become like locusts that, once congregating in sufficient numbers, exhaust the food supply around them. Thereafter, they must move on, else perish. Whichever direction they choose they must maintain, for behind them lies only cannibalism.*

Carnelian saw the truth of this. He saw also that it was, perhaps, the initial attack upon them in the Canyon that had precipitated this carnage. Unable to retreat, they had surged forward against his incursion. Thereafter, like a siphon, the pressure of those coming on behind had been compelling those in front inexorably towards the Blood Gate and its killing field.

There was only one thing to be done. *We must punch through to the entrance of the Canyon and there deflect more from entering.*

It was Legions' hand that answered him. *Not so far, Celestial. We need only reach the Green Gate.*

Where a link can be re-established to your systems?

Once that is done, we can summon sufficient force to effect your deflection.

Carnelian regarded the Grand Sapients with the growing suspicion that they had engineered this crisis as the means to acquire control of the outer world and, with it, Osrakum.

'First you will have to remove this mound that blocks our gates, Celestial,' Cities' homunculus said above the din.

The three Grand Sapients seemed nothing more than protrusions of the tower roof. Such stillness on the edge of the abyss. Carnelian wondered what it was they were perceiving. Directly, perhaps all they could sense was the rain on their

798

hands, the whispering glancing tickle of ash. Through their feet, they would be aware of the vibration from the flame-pipes operating. But the infernal scene before them they could appreciate only from the throats of their homunculi, as nothing more substantial than a fairytale. Not for him such abstraction. The abomination spread out at their feet was screaming at all his senses. It had to be stopped at whatever cost.

Sitting in Earth-is-Strong's command chair staring at the locked gate, Carnelian was aware, with a prickly horror, of the mountain of carnage pressing against its other side. He glanced round at the two other dragons that stood close behind him as part of the wedge. The screech of the flame-pipes rising in pitch made him turn back. The Prow was initiating the furious barrage he had planned with Legions, in the hope of holding the sartlar flood back. Grimly he watched the massive crossbars on the gates slide away to both sides, groaning as the gate visibly quivered. Unlocked, the portals began to open. Shrieks of metallic agony came from either side as the mechanisms that opened the gates struggled against the weight they were holding back. A crack was widening between the two portals. At first he could see nothing. Then a dark stream began to pour through. A gush of corpses gradually increasing to a waterfall. An avalanche advancing towards him, one tumbling layer at a time, of things that looked like scraps of leather. A vast belch of fetid air struck them that made his officers recoil, moaning. Fluid welling in his mouth, in shock and horror, he gave the command and the beast beneath them lurched forward, lowering her head to form an immense ram. As the monster's head punched into the corpse avalanche, the cabin juddered, throwing Carnelian forward so that he was almost unseated. The cabin jerked erratically, yawing, pitching back and forth. He realized it was because the dragon's great feet were sliding. He tried not to imagine on what. Instead he fixed his attention on the monster's head as it clove like a prow into the wave of dead. Soon corpses were building up against the raised shield of her bony fringe, until they spilled over and poured out on either side, until her head was entirely submerged beneath the filthy carnage. His officers were soon retching at the stench. Grimly, Carnelian refused nausea, feeling through his chair Earth-is-Strong taking the strain, leaning her immense bulk into pushing the dead before her.

Before the gate was reclosed, Carnelian went out to make sure the way was clear for the next day's sally. He had just left Earth-is-Strong and the other dragons having wounds tended that their feet had sustained from embedded shards of sartlar bone.

His steps faltered as he came to the edge of the spread of paste the monsters had crushed from the corpses. He wound more turns of cloth across his mouth and nose and pushed on. The outer faces of the immense portals open against the flanks of the towers were coated with gore almost up to the top. The ground was slippery with fat and fluids. Banks rose up on either side that seemed of tallow. Up ahead the Prow rose with its mane of wavering smoke, on its brow its crown of thorns, whose brass throats were vomiting a juddering fury of fire that was keeping the sartlar at bay. A lone colossus amidst the thunder and shrill demonic screaming, it could not hope to keep that rate of firing up for long without being consumed by its own fire.

Carnelian had reached the first bridge. On the other side, upon the killing field, was the escarpment of corpses that had been left when he ordered the dragons back to the fortress. He made his way to the edge of the bridge, going as fast as he could, though loathing each step he took into the quagmire. The rock sloping down to the Cloaca was densely matted with the dead they had shoved over the edge. In the depths he dimly saw that a great mass of corpses now dammed the channel. If the other branch was also choked, the run-off from the Skymere might begin to pool behind it. Perhaps enough to raise the level of the Skymere. The coombs might be flooded. Unexpected rage welled up in him, driving hot tears into his eyes. So what if the palaces of the Masters should be washed into the lake?

'Celestial?' It was an Ichorian bleak with horror and disgust. 'An embassy has come demanding to see you.'

'An embassy?'

'Of the Great, Celestial.'

Carnelian watched them approaching, swaying on high ranga, immense in their black shrouds, their masks glinting from within their hoods like the sun through clouds. Ammonites scurried around them ladling a continuous carpet of blue fire before their feet. They came to a halt while still at some distance from him.

'My Lords,' he greeted them, coldly.

As they held up their hands to return his greeting, he saw the symbols painted on their pale skin. They were wearing the full ritual protection. One of them stood forward. 'I am He-who-goes-before.' He must have sensed Carnelian's incredulity at such a claim, for he added: 'Elected, yesterday, by the Clave in full session.'

Without the attendant command of the Red Ichorians, this honour seemed to Carnelian vainglorious. The Master raised his hand, pointing above Carnelian's head at the smog wreathing the towers of the Blood Gate; the flash and scream of liquid fire. 'For days all of Osrakum has watched smoke rising from the Canyon. Drifts of it have darkened the skies above the north-west coombs.'

Carnelian lost some composure as he realized that his father and his people must have been oppressed by these signs directly.

'We have sent demands to the Labyrinth, but They have refused to grant any audience, nor deigned even a reply. So we have been put to the inconvenience of coming here ourselves. What in the names of the Two is happening here, my Lord?'

Carnelian was aware he had not been addressed as befitted his new blood-rank. Such an omission could only be intended as a slight. Perhaps it was an indication of how these Masters were reacting to his appearance. Aloof on their ranga and with the decorum and precaution of their purity, they looked down upon him in his debased, tainted filthiness. He felt nothing but contempt for them.

'I came here in response to a report that the sartlar gathered outside Osrakum had swarmed into the City. When I arrived I found they had penetrated the Canyon. We do not know what drives them, but they pour towards our defences. Each day we destroy vast numbers of them, but there are always more. They are as numberless as leaves.'

Another of the Masters stepped forward. 'Why have the legions not been summoned, my Lord, to drive this rabble away?'

'All contact with the outer world has been broken,' said Carnelian.

Two more Masters shifted. 'All?'

The Master who claimed to be He-who-goes-before spoke before Carnelian could repeat his statement. 'How long, Celestial, do you expect it will be before contact is re-established?'

Carnelian saw no reason to tell them his plans and made a gesture of indeterminacy. 'The Wise have assured me the Blood Gate has enough naphtha to maintain the present levels of annihilation for many more weeks.'

'We do not have weeks, Celestial. Soon famine will visit Osrakum.'

This was news to Carnelian.

'It is inconceivable that these animals should pose such a threat to us,' said one of the Masters.

Another turned his shadowed face on Carnelian. 'Who brought this curse down on us?'

Carnelian wondered what the Masters would say were they to find out just how responsible he was for bringing the sartlar to Osrakum. 'Everything that can be done, my Lords, is being done. Return to your coombs.'

Turning his back on them, he walked away towards the Blood Gate. They called out to him. His eyes filled with the spectacle of fire and smoke, ears assaulted by screaming flame-pipes, he soon forgot them.

He woke, suddenly. It was the middle of the night. He could not at first locate the reason he felt so alert. Then joy flared up in him. Silence. It was so quiet he could hear Fern breathing. He rose carefully, not wanting to wake him, then padded over to the shutters. They creaked as he opened them. He stepped out onto the balcony. Perfect blackness. Gazing towards the killing field he thought he could make out the mass of the Prow like a cave in the night. The tang of naphtha was under-laid by the dull stench of cooked meat and rotting. He could hear a delicate rustling like a million ants pouring across leaf litter. A warm body pressed against his back.

'What's happening?' whispered Fern.

Carnelian hardly dared to voice his hope. 'The sartlar are leaving.'

'Why?'

'I don't know!'

Once more in Earth-is-Strong's command chair. The creaking of the tower, the mutter of voices remote on other decks, the clink of brass: all these sounds seemed strange, alien. Beyond their little world, a deafening silence. How long was it since the flame-pipes had fallen silent? His ears still felt raw. It was as if the screaming of the flame-pipes had worn deep channels in his head that now, empty, ached.

Dawn was casting the shadow of the monster and her tower upon the brazen cliff of the closed gate before them. Carnelian glanced round, glad to see Fern there. He gave him a nod and was rewarded with a grin. A grinding of brass teeth shocked him back to staring through the screen. It was only the mechanisms working open the gate. Morning spilling through the widening gap illuminated more and more of the edge of the plateau of dead, where everything was eerily still.

They emerged from the corpse quagmire of the killing field into open ground. The sudden drop of ground level to relatively clean rock almost gave him vertigo. Before them stretched the Canyon, still inhabited by the night. A sudden fear possessed him. What if this was a trap? 'Open fire!' Arcing incandescence drove back the shadow. The liquid light sputtered and dimmed, leaving glimpses of the empty Canyon burned into Carnelian's sight. As they lumbered on, he told himself his fears were groundless. A trap presupposed some strategic will directing the sartlar. He could not believe in that, even if he did not think them animals. But he could derive no hypothesis as to why they had left. Uneasy, he lit their way with sporadic bursts of naphtha burn.

They turned into another gloomy stretch. When at last they reached the second turn, Carnelian felt a hand on his shoulder and knew it was Fern come to stand behind him. He reached up to hold him there, even as the next section of the Canyon swung slowly into view. Its nearest portion was in darkness, but far away the morning slanted down to the Canyon floor, and there they saw, strung across the throat of the Canyon, the necklace of towers and curtain walls of the Green Gate. Carnelian felt Fern's grip tighten and his heart beat faster as fierce hope rose in him of freedom.

On the ground, the ripping of the breach from the fabric of the Green Gate seemed an act of wanton destruction. Though the Canyon beyond appeared to be free of sartlar as far as its final turn, he had plugged the breach with dragons. The smoke from their chimneys was hazing the upper part of the gap. The plug seemed flimsy in comparison with the massive torn masonry on either side. He took in the gaping hollows of exposed chambers. These had spilled the debris of their walls and floors in a scree up which the Marula were clambering in their search for any live sartlar lurking on this side of the wall. Dead sartlar were plentiful.

When a voice cried out, he looked up and saw a figure framed by the greater darkness of the cavern behind: it was Sthax. Carnelian could not make out what he was shouting, but could read his meaning in his shaking head. The place was empty.

'What killed them?' Fern said, gazing down through a grimace at a sartlar corpse long dead.

Carnelian rolled a reddish boulder with his foot. It turned out to be hollow. The interior still showed some unrusted black. It was an iron casque. 'The Bloodguard who garrisoned this fortress.'

Fern scanned the blood-soaked ground, which was scattered with more of these helmets and other armour and, here and there, a trampled cloak still showing a slash or spot of green.

'But where——?' Fern paled and Carnelian nodded grimly, gazing down at an empty cuirass of rusting precious iron: a shell from which a Sinistral had been extracted like an oyster.

Carnelian turned towards Earth-is-Strong and raised his hand in the prearranged signal. He could not see the message being relayed to the Blood Gate to say they had secured the Green. As he turned back, he glimpsed something strange in an alleyway that ran between the Green Gate proper and a tower that rose behind it. Fern followed him into the gap. As the blackness deepened, a foul stench swelled until they could go no further. An uneven wall rose, blocking any further progress. It was from this the stench was emanating. Craning, Carnelian saw this blockage filled the gap between the walls to a level higher even than the fortress wall and right to the very summit of the tower. Up there it was clear what composed this mound. Sartlar dead. Weary disgust gave way to unease. A desperation to find a way through the fiery holocaust might explain the mound the sartlar had piled up with their corpses against the Blood Gate, but here it seemed uncannily as if they had contributed their bodies to bridge the gap between the fortress and the tower.

The Sapients unfolded themselves from their palanquins. They had approached along a road of fluttering blue fire flanked by files of ammonites. A space had been cleared with billhooks; the corpses being dragged away like beached, rotting fish.

As the Sapients approached him on their ranga, Carnelian saw their leader was Legions. The Grand Sapient took his homunculus by the throat. 'You are certain the area is secured, Celestial?'

'We have found no living sartlar, my Lord Legions.' Since the discovery of the corpse bridge Carnelian had felt a need for urgency. 'We must hurry in case they should return.'

'Before it is possible to act, Celestial, it is essential to have a complete understanding of a situation.'

Carnelian felt irritation. What was there to understand? And then there was that word 'complete'. How could any situation be understood completely? He wanted to act and to act now. 'We need to know what is happening in the City, my Lord. I will take some aquar down the Canyon scouting.'

'This should be our last resort, Celestial. How much could you hope to see? Even were it possible for you to travel near and far across the Commonwealth your report would be nothing more than a single track through space and time.'

'You wish to reconnect to the heliograph system.'

'Even if a single device remains intact, it should be possible to achieve a link.'

Carnelian realized he had seen no sign of a heliograph. 'Where are these devices?'

Even as Legions' homunculus was murmuring an echo to these words Carnelian knew the answer. He was already gazing up to the tower that rose behind the fortress when the homunculus raised its arm to point to it.

Climbing the steps up onto the summit, Carnelian was immediately aware of the brass mechanisms around him: a double row of them running off to either side along the width of the narrow space. The military gates they had had to open all the way up through the tower had been closed from within, but evidence of bloodshed had been everywhere. Here on the summit was more blood and, scattered between the machines, discarded silver masks like the ones the ammonites attending Legions were wearing. As these men swarmed the machines, Carnelian wound his way to the edge, following his nose. There he found the corpse causeway. A ramp of the dead sloping up from the ramparts of the fortress. He felt a presence and turned to find Legions and his homunculus behind him.

'The devices are undamaged, Celestial.'

Carnelian glanced at the machines. 'So the link was broken when the ammonites were carried off?'

'Operators are not essential to maintain the link. The heliographs can be set up in pairs to relay signals, though there is an associated risk of degradation with this passive mode.'

'None were so aligned?'

'Either the operators had no time to set this up or else the devices were disturbed in the ensuing struggle.'

The homunculus must have reported Carnelian's glance at the corpse ramp to his master, for he said: 'Ants will cross a gutter on the bodies of their fallen.'

Carnelian glanced at the Grand Sapient's impassive mask and saw himself reflected there. Still disturbed, he gazed towards the last turn in the Canyon, wanting to know what was happening out there, but also dreading it.

'Celestial, may we make the attempt to re-establish the link?'

Carnelian turned back to the Grand Sapient. If he allowed this, the Wise would restore Osrakum's control of the legions and, with those, dominion over the Three Lands. In the present political situation, it would be their voice the world obeyed.

'We must re-establish a vision of the Commonwealth.'

'A vision of the Commonwealth?'

'An amalgamation of what has been and can currently be perceived from every watch-tower and fortress across the Land.'

'How long would that take?'

'Depending on how many channels remain intact, Celestial, little more than a single day.'

Carnelian stared. 'It would take a signal that long to go to Makar and return.'

'Still, it can be done.'

'From every watch-tower?'

'With a single command code, the entire system can be set into a seeing mode. All sources will supply data in a fixed, compact format along five channels. Of course, Celestial, to achieve a synthesis of the data it will all have to be relayed to the Labyrinth. We have not the facilities here to process it.'

Remembering the system of networked ammonites he had seen in the Halls of Thunder, Carnelian nodded. 'Ammonite arrays . . .'

There was a noticeable stiffening of Legions' fingers. 'Just so, Celestial.'

'What then, my Lord?'

'Our collective mind will possess a fully integrated temporal and spatial vision of everything that is happening in the Commonwealth.'

Carnelian tried to grasp what possessing such an understanding might be like. He failed. One thing was certain, though: thereafter, if they chose to act on this vision, they would be doing so trusting the Wise utterly. How, after all, could he or Osidian verify or question their analysis, never mind the vision upon which it was based? Carnelian yearned for the ride around that corner to look upon the outer world with his own eyes, but he could see only as far as a man could. There was no alternative.

'Re-establish the link.'

The heliographs were greased, swung round, angled back and forth. Ammonites pulled at the handles that caused their newly polished mirrors to louvre into strips. At last everything was ready. Five of the devices were chosen and, by means of sighting tubes, they were aligned towards points out on the far Canyon wall near the last turn. All five heliographs began sending signals. Several times they repeated the procedure. A while later a flashing began on the faraway Canyon wall. Another joined it and another, until five distinct stars were flashing signals that Carnelian knew must be coming from the watch-towers set in the gatehouses of the Wheel. Even as this was happening, five other heliographs had been aligned back into the Canyon and, soon, they too had obtained confirmation of a link back to the Blood Gate and, no doubt, on to the Wise in the Labyrinth.

It was some time later that the first signals started coming in from the outer world. At first it was only from one of the relay mirrors, but soon all five were flashing. Reports streaming in along the great roads from ever deeper into the Guarded Land. Two observers watched each channel and passed on what they were reading to the operators who were relaying the signals back into Osrakum. Watching all this, Carnelian imagined the minds of the Wise slowly filling with the light of landscapes far away.

He grew weary of the constant clattering of the heliographs and the muttering of their operators. With Fern, he descended into the accommodation strata immediately below the summit and they chose a chamber in which they could still feel the operation of the machines as a vibration in the walls. There he explained to Fern what it was that was happening above their heads. Fern looked unhappy. 'It is not for man, but only

809

the Sky Father to see all.' Carnelian had to admit that it was a strange, unnatural sorcery that enabled these blind men to see the whole world. Anxiety drove them into lovemaking; there was comfort and refuge in each other's arms. Later, at a small window, they watched the signals flickering on the Canyon wall. Ammonites brought them food. When darkness fell the signals continued to be sent using the light from naphtha flares. The vibration of the heliographs was unceasing so that, when Carnelian sank into sleep, he dreamed of the women of his household in the Hold weaving on a loom a fabric that became the world.

When he woke, Carnelian saw Fern's silhouette already at the window. He could feel the continuing chatter of the heliographs. He rose and slid his body past Fern's. His lover turned to kiss him, then cheek to cheek they both looked out. The sky above the blackness of the Canyon wall was a thinning indigo. In the blackness five stars winked.

They stood together, among the heliographs now fallen silent, watching a single star blinking on the turn in the Canyon that led into Osrakum. Legions and his Sapients were lined up along the summit edge, gently strangling their homunculi, who were reading the signals in a constant, wavering mutter.

The transmission had started a while ago. After breakfast, he and Fern had dressed and come up to watch the heliographs relaying the data from the outer world. The sun had passed its zenith when the streams had begun to fail. First one, then two more, then the fourth and, finally, the fifth. The heliographs transmitting these last signals to Osrakum had clattered on a while, then they too had fallen silent. A single signal coming back the other way seemed to blink in acknowledgement. Then, nothing. Eerie silence. The ammonites had found places to sit among the machines. The Sapients knelt upon their ranga and seemed like more devices. Carnelian and Fern had found a place to wait. A single signal had woken them all. It was then the Sapients and their homunculi had lined up along the summit edge, waiting. A short time later, the transmission from the Wise in Osrakum had begun.

The rising-falling murmur of the homunculi ceased suddenly, jerking Carnelian out of a stupor. The Sapients took their places in a wedge with the Grand Sapient at its apex, and a new murmuring arose from them. Carnelian could grasp no words. Something like a dialogue was going on between them, but rapidly, with no gaps in the streams of sound. After observing this process for a while, he surmised they must be checking the message between them to make sure it was comprehended perfectly. At last Legions moved away to stand on his own and one of his staff sent a homunculus to ask Carnelian to come and speak with their master. Eagerness mixed with dread as he approached the ancient.

'We have now a complete and perfect vision of the state of the Commonwealth,' said Legions' homunculus. 'Further, we have distilled from this an inescapable conclusion.'

Carnelian hesitated, wanting to know what this might be, but fearing it too. 'Can you describe this vision, my Lord?'

'It is an entity more easily apprehended through symbols than words, but I shall attempt to satisfy your request, Celestial.

'The cities in the south are beginning to run out of food. Supplies have been transferred from neighbouring granaries and we can arrange for a more extensive redistribution from further afield. No arrangement, however, can entirely avoid the shortage that will become universal within a few months. The parameters for the coming shortage are dependent on just how many provinces will fail to yield a standard harvest. Yield quotients are expected to be low to disastrous for the southern provinces. We do not have sufficient data to predict yields of the provinces in other zones. More positively, rumours of disturbances at the centre have not yet penetrated to the periphery. Negatively, all the peripheral provinces have been substantially denuded of their sartlar populations.'

'All?' Carnelian said, shocked.

'It appears that the summons issued from Makar has spread throughout the Guarded Land. We have no means at present to ascertain how this may have happened. What cannot be doubted is that all five radial roads are clogged with sartlar moving towards the centre. It is possible their entire population is coming here.'

Dread rose in Carnelian like a vast wave, threatening to break thunderously.

'Supporting this hypothesis is the observation that the density of the sartlar increases exponentially in proportion with proximity to Osrakum.'

Carnelian remembered the comparison the Wise had made between the sartlar and a locust swarm. Beyond the concentrating sartlar millions lay an ever widening ring of land from which they would have consumed everything edible. He felt a shadow fall across him and, glancing up, saw the clouds were closing over them again.

'The City at the Gates exists only as an empty husk.'

These few words were enough to stir to life a horrid vision in Carnelian's mind. As if from on high in one of the watch-towers that rose from a causeway, he saw the sartlar plague creeping through the tenements and hovels. What horror as the last scrap of food was devoured, with no hope of more anywhere, while every day brought ever more hungry mouths, ever more empty stomachs. 'They will devour themselves.'

'We cannot allow this to happen,' said the homunculus and Carnelian noticed how firmly Legions gripped the little man's neck. 'Without the sartlar to till and water it, the Land is already dying. Without the food the earth produces, the cities will die.' The Grand Sapient leaned forward over the head of his homunculus. 'But Osrakum will die first.'

Carnelian's breath stopped. Until that moment he had been an observer. 'How?' was all he managed to say.

'Within the Hidden Land there is less than a month of food. Before the sartlar consume themselves utterly, Osrakum will starve.'

A new vision crept into Carnelian's mind. A miraculous vision of the lake and its palaces, but this wonder was rotting at its roots. What would happen when the Masters began to starve? He snatched his mind's eye away from seeing more. 'What can we do?'

'Only one path remains open to us. The legions must be summoned to drive the sartlar back onto the Land; to save what can be saved, of the harvest, of the Land, of the sartlar, of the Commonwealth; to allow food to flow back into Osrakum. We must have the authority to transmit the command codes.'

Still caught in the coils of his dark vision, Carnelian took a while to appreciate what Legions was waiting for. 'Why ask me? Have you not communicated this to the God Emperor?'

'For the moment Their condition is beyond any remedy.'

Suspicion leapt into Carnelian's mind. Even in the throes of the maggot infestation it should have been possible for them to raise Osidian to enough lucidity to make this decision. Doubt ate away at this conclusion. He was remembering how weak Osidian had been, how spiritless. Morunasa had forced this new infestation on Osidian before he had fully recovered from the last. But Carnelian dare not trust the Wise. Nothing they did was free of the shadow of manipulation. Perhaps they feared that if Osidian were to make this decision it would confirm his absolute power, and what might they gain by passing the decision to Carnelian? Perhaps that any disasters consequent on the decision could be laid at his feet. A darker possibility occurred to him. If he gave the command, would he not appear in Osidian's eyes to be usurping the power rightly his? Did the Wise seek to cleave them from each other the better to control both? Then the thought came that perhaps the Wise wanted to summon the legions to use them to re-establish their Great Balance. Perhaps even to take power for themselves. What did he know about what was really going on in the outer world other than what he had just been told? He looked out along the Canyon, wishing he had followed his heart and ridden to where he could have seen things for himself. He shook his head. He was sinking into a quagmire of self-defeating argument. He knew in his bones the vision Legions had described to him must be true or close to the truth, but did it have to be he who made this decision? Was there time for him to return to the Labyrinth and raise Osidian himself? Then his mind began to drift again towards contemplating, almost as a whisper, what might happen in the palaces of the Masters should famine come to their coombs. There was no time to delay.

'Will the legions succeed?' he said, seeking some certainty.

The homunculus murmured and when he fell silent, his master's fingers began moving at his neck and throat.

'All animals fear fire. If they are given space to flee it, Celestial, the sartlar will flee.'

Carnelian nodded, wanting to believe it. 'How will we do it?'

'We shall bring the legions to a gathering point north of the City. When we have marshalled them, we shall guide them in, using our heliographs. We shall make it possible for you, Celestial, to observe everything from here.'

Carnelian paused for a moment, close to being unmanned by the ghosts of the many decisions he had made that had helped lead them all to this crisis. Then, with a heavy heart, he gave the Grand Sapient leave to transmit the command codes in his name.

Over the next two days, signals came in intermittently from legates acknowledging reception of the summons. Legion's Thirds oversaw the sending of detailed instructions that were intended to coordinate the meeting of the legions at the designated mustering point. The intention was to weld them into a single, massive, irresistible strike force. The

Thirds laboured constantly, providing each legion with a detailed route to the rendezvous so that all could be efficiently resupplied with naphtha and render. All this Carnelian discovered by talking to one of the Seconds, who also informed him that the legions coming to raise the blockade of Osrakum numbered twice as many as those that had fought at the Battle of the Mirror.

Carnelian woke into darkness hearing the sea that had troubled his dreams. Fern sat up beside him. 'What's that sound?'

'You hear it too?' Carnelian leapt from the bed and peered out through the porthole. Signals were blinking insistently on the faraway Canyon wall, but it was the susurrating sound that made the hackles rise on his neck. A lightning flash caused him to throw his hand up before his eyes. The screaming that followed stunned him. More brilliant, coruscating light revealing the Canyon floor filled from wall to wall with a tide of heads, into which the dragons he had set to hold the breach in the Green Gate wall were pouring fire.

In the corridor outside their cell, Carnelian and Fern ran into one of the Thirds overseeing the evacuation of his masters in their palanquins. The procession slid past his mirror face as he stood there holding the hand of his homunculus like a father with his son. Carnelian reached down and tore their grip apart, holding on to the Sapient's cloven hand as he tried to snatch it away and forcing it towards the homunculus. The little man saw what he wanted. At his touch, the Sapient calmed, allowing his fingers to be put around the little man's throat, who muttered something and, then, responding to his master's touch, said: 'This position is undefendable. You must cover our retreat, Celestial.'

'What about the heliographs?'

'Instructions have been given to leave them passively aligned. Then the operators are to flee with us so that the brutes will have no reason to go up there.'

Carnelian began to question this, feeling in his bones this was a mistake, but the Sapient had already disengaged and was shuffling off after his homunculus. Carnelian saw the panic banked in Fern's eyes and realized he had other responsibilities. 'We've got to get Sthax and his people out of here and see if we can't find a way to cover our retreat.'

Carnelian scrambled up the last ladder knowing Fern was just behind him. Clambering up onto the command deck, he ignored his prone officers and flung himself into his chair. The breach was a flickering screen set into the black mass of the Green Gate wall. The continuous firing of the flame-pipes there was a pulsing screech that made his eardrums feel as if they were about to rupture. Vast smoky shapes cavorted in the flash and dance of light that lit the cauldron on the other side of the wall. Carnelian had hoped that seeing it would inspire in him a way to extract his dragons. He was faced with the grim reality that they were a dam barely managing to hold back the flood. If he were to unplug the breach, the sartlar would gush through. As he sent a command to the rest of his forces for a general retreat, he tried to draw some comfort from the certainty that, whatever he did, the dragons in the breach were lost.

Once more upon the Blood Gate tower summit, Carnelian gazed past the Prow to where, just beyond the range of its pipes, the edge of the sartlar sea had reached. His retreat had been more orderly than he expected, though of the dragons in the breach there was no news. The heliograph relays had failed. Osrakum was once more severed from the outer world. Grand Sapient Legions had reassured him that the legions had received enough information to be able to operate without further guidance. It was always foolhardy to attempt to deduce what one of the Wise was thinking, but Carnelian had sensed the ancient was uneasy.

*   *   *

A black sky shed incessant rain. Carnelian gladly agreed with one of Legions' Seconds that the dragons should be serviced. Facilities were available at the nearby Red Caves and there was plenty of time. It would be nearly a month before the legions would reach the mustering point. Watching the dragons filing off across the bridge towards the caves, he was glad also for the relief the creatures would feel when their towers were lifted off them. They had been carrying them so long that the towers had worn sores into their backs. Other wounds needed tending. Mostly lacerations on feet and legs.

As the days passed, Carnelian would sometimes climb to the tower summit to gaze along the Canyon. The sartlar were always there beyond flame-pipe range, becalmed, as if they too were waiting. Rain soaking into his cloak sapped at his will and made him wonder what it must be like for them to endure such unrelenting exposure. Their hunger was likely to be a greater torture. He did not want to think about how they might be filling their stomachs.

Most of his time was spent in their cell with Fern. When they were not making love, they slept. In slumber Carnelian was haunted by floods: of dust, of water, of blood. Given his ever-present feeling of foreboding, it was strange that he would sometimes wake with a seed of hope in his heart, which he and Fern kept warm between them, as they whispered to each other of their hopes for the life they might have together when all of this was over.

Five days after his return from the Green Gate, with Legions at his side, Carnelian watched another embassy of the Great approach. Shadowy they looked, deprived of most of their pomp by the ritual protection. The only signs of their wealth were the jewels that sparkled and gleamed on their hands and the unearthly serenity of their masks. Because of the rain, Carnelian had chosen to site the audience in one of the Gate's chambers-of-returning. Pools spangled arches with wavering light. Man-shaped hollows stood round them in the brass walls.

An odour of camphor almost occluded Legions' aura of stale myrrh. They had agreed to confront the embassy together because they knew the Great were coming to complain. They knew also that whatever was said there would determine the mood that would prevail throughout the coombs. Carnelian feared panic spreading among the Masters at least as much as did the Wise.

Legions had informed him that the Clave had met the day before and had sent another embassy to the Labyrinth to beg an audience with the God Emperor, but had been turned away. To Carnelian's surprise Legions had answered his questions about Osidian. It seemed that, on the day they had fled from the Green Gate, Osidian had woken from a period of tortured dreaming, too confused and disorientated to deal with the Great. Carnelian had revealed to Legions what he knew about the maggot infestation: that, probably, Osidian would be in this state for some time and might then fall into unconsciousness from which he would emerge only when the worms came out from his flesh.

The Great were upon them, several of them speaking at once. Carnelian was made wary by their lack of decorum. Making no attempt to portray unity, they were complaining of how little food was left. Seventeen days. Less. He could feel that their hauteur concealed uncertainty, fear even. He watched them as the Grand Sapient explained about the mustering of the legions. They seemed to grow taller as they contemplated the fiery brushing away of the sartlar blockade. Carnelian noted that no mention was made of the broken heliograph link to the outer world. When Legions declared that there was no prospect of any immediate relief, the Masters drew back like cobras.

He continued: 'You should not expect the Canyon to be open again for at least a month.'

The Masters' hands sketched angry gestures. Their ire ignited into bitter complaint, but, again, underlying this demonstration, Carnelian could sense their fear and that increased his dismay at how they might vent this upon their slaves.

'There is another matter,' said one. 'The level of the Skymere rises.'

'By three hand-breadths,' said another.

'Four!'

'Many low-lying palaces will be flooded.'

'I myself have had to evacuate a suite of halls.'

'Are we now also to be washed from our coombs?'

Carnelian found their talk connecting to some core of unease inside him. The terrible, recurring forms of his nightmares seemed to rear at the edges of his vision.

'Clearly, the Cloaca is not draining properly,' sang Legions' homunculus.

'The corpses of the sartlar we cleared from before the Gate have dammed the flow,' Carnelian said. Even as his voice was making promises to do something about it he was brooding over how it was that Osrakum was being threatened with a flood by the dead.

Carnelian pulled a fold of his military cloak over the nostrils of his mask, but it was not enough to dull the miasma. To his right rose a bronze grille, acid green mottled with black, streaked with the excrement of the anvil-headed sky-saurians that roosted above it in the shadows. The grille was a defence against any attackers making their way up the Cloaca. Above, a stair scaled the ravine wall, becoming a vague scratch lost in the blackness lurking beneath the bridge that linked the killing field to the outer Canyon. Up there was a door from which a passage joined the supply tunnel that ran from the Blood Gate to the Prow. It was along that route they had come to this stinking sewer.

Barring the opening between the grille and the Cloaca bed was a massive portcullis clogged with filth. In slots cut into the walls on either side, Ichorians were greasing the tracks in which ran the counterweights that controlled the portcullis.

Eventually, it would have to be raised. Reluctantly, Carnelian looked upstream to where the Cloaca was choked by the immense corpse dam.

In the Cloaca, his feet squelched deep into a stinking putty. On the opposite wall, superimposed tidelines showed the levels where water had run. Through the portcullis, he could make out the Cloaca curving left, out of sight. He lingered, trying to resolve a feeling that he had seen this place before, then turned to face the dam. He began wading towards it through the filth, the fetor so thick it was almost a physical barrier.

The slope rising before him was like the midden mound beneath Qunoth, though immeasurably vaster. Of corpses, mouldering, mulching down to squeeze out their juices which were licking around his feet. He surveyed that mountain, judging the labour needed to release the waters it was damming. When he had stood upon the Blood Gate tower so far above, gazing down, it had seemed a simple thing to describe the opening they must make, as if with a single sword-cut. Sapients had described how, given a narrow channel through, the pent-up fury of the lake waters would quickly flush the whole mass away. Standing before it, Carnelian found it harder to believe their plan could work.

Around him, Ichorians, chins soiled with vomit, were trying not to see the limbs, the rotting faces in the mound they were going to have to dig through. Carnelian knew his impulse to work alongside them was inappropriate.

Climbing back up to the Blood Gate, he released more Ichorians and sent them down to the Cloaca. Thereafter, each day, standing among the mute heliographs, he watched them labouring far below in those sewers. Sometimes, when the breeze died, the charnel stench reached even his eyrie. Too slow the work, too slow for him so that, in desperation, he denuded the Gate of its garrison. Legions' Thirds protested that he was compromising their defences, but he held his ground, stating that the Prow could break up any sartlar surge long enough for the Ichorians to return to their posts.

Judging progress still too slow, Carnelian sent a command that work in the northern branch was to be abandoned and all effort concentrated on the southern. The Cloaca haunted his dreams. He longed to see its disgusting blockage flushed away as much as if it were a clot in his own arteries.

Infrequently, messages were heliographed from the Labyrinth. One reported that the God Emperor had slipped into a sleep from which he could not be woken. Knowing Osidian would soon wake, Carnelian wondered how he would react to what had been happening while he slept. In darker moments Carnelian brooded as to who it was who would emerge from such terrible dreams wearing the face of a god. At last, one of the Thirds came to inform him the God Emperor had taken up residence in the Stone Dance of the Chameleon. The Sapient had no answers for Carnelian's questions. He said only that Osrakum was now hungry. When Carnelian learned that Osidian had been deaf to the appeals of the Wise that the render in the Red Caves should be distributed to the coombs, he authorized it himself. That night, Fern and he stood on the summit of the South Tower in a world made frosty by a full moon. The only warmth came from the patch of gold that flickered in the Cloaca far below where the Ichorians had made their camp. Though both were starving, neither could stomach eating render.

One morning Carnelian woke feeling that a burden had lifted from his heart. He went to stand upon their balcony as had become his habit. Night still filled the Cloaca. He raised his eyes towards the open Canyon. His glance hardened to a stare of scrutiny. He called into the cell for Fern to join him. When he came, tousled, bleary-eyed, Fern confirmed what Carnelian already believed. Their spirits soared. The sartlar were gone.

Carnelian watched Ichorians scurrying along the Cloaca bed to clamber up into the counterweight slots. He could imagine how they were struggling to raise the portcullis. Filthy water was already gushing out of the channel they had delved in the corpse dam. As the stream widened, the edges of the channel crumbled into it like a sandbank into water escaping to the sea. The rush roared as it snagged more and more corpses and swirled them off along the channel. Carnelian felt it all as a physical release.

The sun falling beneath the clouds set them aflame. Light drained from the world, but the fire did not die in the west. Carnelian thought it was just another storm coming. It was Fern who recognized its true nature. 'Dragonfire.'

Carnelian caught hold of Fern and they grinned at each other like boys. It began to rain and they laughed as it ran down their faces. At last the legions had come to lift the siege.

The next day was dark and brooding. Even atop the Blood Gate, Carnelian felt as if there was no room for movement. Sounds were dulled by the thick air. The black, smothering sky felt close enough to touch. In the west, the cloudbase was reflecting the release of titanic energies. Masters started arriving. More and more came until, by nightfall, the summits of both Blood Gate towers were crowded. All profane eyes had been commanded to remain below, so that the host of the Great could look towards the west unmasked.

By the following morning the conflagration in the west had become a flicker. By late afternoon there was nothing except, now and then, a sudden, wavering discharge. By nightfall, the sky seemed eerily dead. As Carnelian left the roof, he detected the salty tang of render. Elegant voices rose and fell. The Masters, congratulating each other on their victory, talked greedily of the delicacies that would soon be flooding into Osrakum.

Cowled against the midday sun, Carnelian had been able to remove his mask to see better. Legions was beside him with his Seconds. Their homunculi, after having described to their masters what they could see, had fallen silent. The edges of the tower roof, west and south, were crammed with Masters. Every eye was fixed on the outer reach of the Canyon. It was some time since sartlar had appeared from around the corner and the sounds of consternation across the summits had had time to fade. Carnelian's mind had ceased to devise scenarios to explain them being there when he had been expecting towered dragons, or some aquar-mounted auxiliaries dashing ahead to bring news of her relief to Osrakum. Dread gripped him as he tried to pierce the intervening distance. Among their multitude, pale pyramids like bloodied ravener teeth, but large enough to rise above the dust of their march. Then there were the white grains that floated above the procession. He pulled himself back from the drop as terror possessed him. He could no longer deny what he was seeing.

THE FLOOD

Birth is preceded by a flood.
(a Plainsman proverb)

The dirty, pale pyramids the Sartlar were dragging, with their baroque hollows, were dragon heads stripped of flesh. Gouged-out eyes had left caves a child could curl up in. These skulls pebbled the slurry of sartlar creeping along the Canyon floor. Enough skulls to account for all the dragons of all the legions. Carnelian felt a pang at the loss of those colossal creatures, which, in spite of the terror they had brought, were just more victims of the Masters' lust for dominion. The feeling passed and he became eerily calm. The power of the Masters was broken and, somehow, he had known this was going to happen. The sartlar had wanted the legions summoned. Starving, unable to reach food, they had had the greatest store of living flesh in the Commonwealth come to them. With chilly certainty, he knew the pale standards the sartlar bore must be Masters, on frames, crucified. The commanders who had sat aloft, imperious, upon their ivory thrones, were now spreadeagled naked, alive or dead. He wondered whether the sartlar were carrying them in the hope the Masters would not hurl fire down upon them. More likely it was a terrible sign of their defiance.

Consternation was spreading like flames across the

summits of the Blood Gate towers. Carnelian turned from the sartlar victory procession to the Masters round him. Hands, frozen in gestures of disbelief and outrage, had lost their capacity for shaping words. Masks turning from the spectacle below gazed upon each other, as if hoping to deny the truth, or to return things to their proper compass: a time already receding when it had been the right of the Chosen to determine all things. Elegant voices strained like strings on an instrument overstretched. A strangely remote observer, Carnelian wondered if it was the silent ones in the midst of the cacophony that were causing his hackles to rise; for among the gathered Chosen were some who seemed turned to stone. No, it was something else that was scaring him. He identified it. The smell of fear; that familiar, sweaty odour that emanated as an aura from slaves in the presence of Masters. Except, this time, the smell was almost masked by attar of lilies. It was the Masters who were afraid. That realization shocked him awake. Always, they were dangerous, but Masters cornered, terrified – he would rather confront raveners.

He became aware of a homunculus staring at him, they all were. He felt a surge of hope: the Wise would know what to do. Then he saw how their fingers hung around the throats of their homunculi like the discarded moult of their living hands. Legions' fingers had let go entirely and were kneading each other in a slow, rolling motion. Carnelian shook his head to free himself of any hold the pleading eyes of the homunculi had on him. He backed away, turned and made for one of the openings that gave access to the strata below. In his mind there was but a single, beacon thought: he must find Fern.

On the balcony, Fern's body was stopping light from entering their cell. He turned as Carnelian approached. 'It's the end.'

Carnelian squeezed through to stand beside him. As they gazed down at the sartlar, he became aware of a gurgling sound rising from the blackness of the Cloaca. He thought he could see faint flecks of reflected light down there where that dark river ran, almost beyond the gaze of the living, as if it were in the Underworld. Snatches of his dreams seeping into his mind caused an idea to coalesce.

'There is nothing that can be done,' said Fern.

Carnelian raised his attention from the depths. It was hard to focus on something as close, as alive as Fern's face. Fern clearly was hoping to be contradicted. The idea was a seed of hope. 'We need to get to my father's house.'

'To die?'

Carnelian regarded Fern and, again, hope stirred within him, but it was yet too small a thing to admit into the light. 'To be with our loved ones, but we must move fast.' He threw his head up to indicate the tower roof. 'Soon the Masters will be flooding back into the Mountain.'

Fern's grim nod made Carnelian sure they both understood the danger. 'Let's go then. If we're going to die, I'd rather do it with other Plainsmen.'

Fern slipped back into the shadowy cell. Carnelian glanced down into the Cloaca, then followed him.

Sthax and some Marula were outside the door. Carnelian had been so focused on Fern that he had passed through them almost without seeing them. He realized how much he might have need of them. Besides, he had not forgotten the promise he had made to Sthax. If he commanded them to come with him, they might obey, though he could not imagine they would be eager to return deeper into the Mountain. But he would give no command: in what was coming they must have the freedom to determine their own fate. So he began explaining to Sthax what he knew. Describing the disaster made it rise more terrible before him.

Carnelian became aware of the lack of surprise in Sthax's face. 'You already knew this?'

The Maruli nodded heavily, his bright eyes never leaving Carnelian's face. Carnelian felt a thrill of cold fear. If Sthax knew, the Ichorians must know too. How far had the news spread its cancer through the fortress? He focused on Sthax. 'What will you do?'

'What you want we dos?'

Carnelian felt he was being tested. He explained that he and Fern were going to his coomb. 'Will you come with us?'

'You plan?'

Carnelian could no more answer him than he had been able to answer Fern. What he had was less than a plan, merely a course of action suggested to him by a dream. He was reluctant to even voice it yet. 'We're all trapped.'

Sthax nodded again, but distractedly, gazing intensely at Carnelian, who felt the man was trying to penetrate to what was in his heart. Sthax nodded, seeming satisfied. He consulted the other warriors, then turned back. 'We comes you.'

Carnelian was touched by Sthax's trust and reached out to grip his shoulder. Then he passed by him, through the rest of the Marula, making for the first flight of steps.

Approaching the dark cliff of the eastern gate, Carnelian came to a halt when an Ichorian challenged him. He pulled open his cowl so that they could see his face.

'Celestial,' they whispered as they knelt.

Carnelian regarded the obeisance with a kind of regret, sensing it had already become a courtesy from a lost world. He raised them with his hand. 'Have other Seraphim been here before me?'

As they shook their heads, Carnelian looked at them. He could sense nothing in their demeanour that would suggest the news had reached them. As, at his bidding, they opened a door in the gate, he considered giving them a command to let none pass: neither Chosen, nor of the Wise. He decided against it. These poor bastards would soon have enough to contend with. Why make them, unnecessarily, objects of wrath? He would have liked to have taken them with him, but it was already going to be nigh impossible to save the few he hoped to save. As he focused on who those were, he perceived his new identity to be no more than a disguise. His heart beat faster: he was going home, to see his father and Ebeny who were, in every way that counted, his parents.

They passed through the door into the vastness of the Canyon throat beyond, which was in shadow halfway to the Black Gate. The hidden valley of Osrakum seemed a bright, unattainable vision outwith the cares of the world.

As they walked away from the door, Carnelian focused on the solid reality of the camp that clothed the wedge of the Blood Gate rock as far as the two bridges. Though to call it a camp was to flatter it. Clumps of men huddling together among the pathetic shelters they had managed to improvise with their spears and cloaks. Their Masters had left them there without even a few sticks to make a fire. Anger flared in him against the mighty who had so thoughtlessly abandoned their own. He quenched his compassion: he could no more save these men than he could the Ichorians. They watched him and the Marula pass, with eyes that peered out between the bars and strokes of the tattoos that showed who owned them. Their world was ending just as much as was their Masters'. His blood ran cold when he thought what cruelties their Masters might inflict on them to assuage their own fear. Then he saw how numerous they were, that they had swords and fanblades, helmets and armour, and a different dread swelled in him. What kept these men subservient to their Masters' whims, other than terror of their power? He made an effort to keep his pace steady, his posture erect, imperious. All the time his mind raced: what now the power of the Masters was broken?

He was relieved to reach the left bridge without incident. Fear of what might happen in his coomb once the news reached there lent his pace urgency. They crossed, then hurried on. He could not help casting glances at the wall of the Canyon rising on his left. The stone red as if in token of some great slaughter. He glanced up to the barracks galleries. After that he could not rid himself of the feeling that the dead were gazing down from the countless windows, reproachfully. Almost he heard their voices: what has all this blood been shed for? He focused on the racks that now held erect his two legions' trumpet pipes that had screamed out so much fiery death. Behind them the dragon towers, smoke-blackened, battle-stained. Beneath and further back, the caves where Earth-is-Strong and Heart-of-Thunder lay wounded with the other dragons, all now the remnants of another vanishing race.

All the way he was aware of the gurgle of the Cloaca rising up from the abyss along whose rim they hurried. The Black Gate raised its wall before them. Beyond, the Hidden Land, soon to become a land of the dead.

Suddenly, their shadows leapt away in front of them as a great, flickering light sprang alive at their backs. As they turned, the air was strained, then shredded by the shrilling screams of the Blood Gate's flame-pipes. Coruscating energies reflected up the cliffs that flanked the towers. On the killing field was a boiling incandescence they had to squint at to endure. Carnelian turned away, printing blue images of that holocaust upon the blackness in front of him. Bitterness in his heart, in his mouth. How typical of the Masters that they should seek to salve their fear with senseless slaughter.

Judging it unlikely the immense dragon gates would open for him, Carnelian led Fern and the Marula towards the central portion of the black wall. There, a single door stood in the cliff of masonry: a door of oiled, precious iron. They came to a halt before it. He was reluctant to go this way: he remembered his previous passage; that first time he had entered Osrakum with his father. He was going to have problems with the ammonites that kept this purgatory. As he waited for the gate to open, the harsh ululating of the flame-pipes came echoing down the Canyon. Surely their approach had been noted? He caught Fern's eye and, glancing round, Sthax's and those of the leading files of the Marula. All bright, intense. Carnelian asked Sthax for his halberd. Its pole was crowned by an elaborate nest of iron blades and hooks. Striking iron on iron caused the door to give off a sonorous clang. Moments later it parted into two leaves that swung silently into the blackness within. Moist air swept out over them, intoxicating with myrrh. Carnelian shared the reluctance of his people to enter. The Marula recoiled as ghostly faces coalesced in the gloom. Carnelian held his ground, knowing them to be nothing more than ammonite masks.

'You must be cleansed, Celestial,' they sighed.

Uneasily, Carnelian eyed the dark behind the silver faces. Other odours wafting towards him made him recall the drugged smoke with which Legions had captured him in Makar. Even if it was nothing more than the standard narcotics employed during purification, he did not want his mind dulled. He wanted to see things as they were; to be entirely himself. Half turning away, he extended his arm to take in the Marula. 'I wish to pass through with these.'

'Impossible, Celestial. They must go through the quarantine. Would you bring death into the Land of the Everliving?'

Carnelian almost laughed, mirthlessly, and wondered if they could really be so ignorant of the irony. He peered past the disembodied faces, trying to determine how far there was to go and if he could find his way to the other side without their guidance. 'You know I am brother to the new God Emperor and that these men are his new Ichorians.'

'The Law does not bow even to Them.'

Carnelian lowered the halberd. 'But it will bow to me.' He advanced and the faces melted away into the darkness. He was glad to hear the shuffle of the Marula following him. Voices round him rose in a keening that had soon drowned out the Blood Gate flame-pipes. Even as he became aware of subtle revolvings in the air above him, he realized his focus was slipping. Gaps in the uncoiling smoke revealed the position of figures surrounding them. As he moved forward, apparitions slid towards him. He traced circles before him in the smoke with the halberd head to clear a path for them. It struck something with a sharp clap, even as one of the apparitions disappeared in a tinkle of shards. A mirror of glass as perfect as water. He was aware of the ammonites drawing back. He swung the halberd into another mirror and another and the ammonites faded, whispering, away.

His shadow died as he moved away from the light that was streaming through the open door behind them. He glanced round to make sure Fern and the others were still following him. By the time they reached an arch standing all alone, his eyes had adjusted to the gloom. He remembered seeing it before and put his hand out to touch it as he had then. Faces as vague under his fingers as they were to his eyes. The faces of corpses submerged in water. His hand recoiled. He could smell the blood rust on his fingertips and wiped them down his cloak. The ghost of an inscription ran around the iron curve. Unreadable beyond a vague whispering in his mind. He stood back. It was not an arch, but a ring partially embedded in the ground. If it were a glyph it would read as 'death'. He frowned. In Vulgate, his people referred to this fortress as Death's Gate. Reluctant to walk through it, he moved round it, gesturing to Fern, Sthax and the others to do the same.

They came at last to a barrier Carnelian knew must be the door that gave entry into Osrakum. As he placed his hand upon its cold surface, the whole world gave a shudder as if it had been struck by some immense hammer. Again, the sound shook the air and ground. A massive bell was tolling, that was soon joined by more, until it seemed to Carnelian the world must convulse itself to pieces. Clamping his hands over his ears, he sought some explanation why the ammonites were ringing the Black Gate bells in this cacophonous manner. Were they sending an alarum to warn of the imminent breach of Osrakum's sanctity? Or perhaps the warning was for their masters, the Wise. He shuddered as the feeling rose in him that the bells were announcing the ending of the world. Panic welled up in him, he felt trapped, buried alive. His hands fell from his ears and began feverishly scrabbling across the wall in front of him. Shapes stubbed his fingers, grazed his skin, but he kept on pulling, pushing, twisting, seeking anything that would free them from this tomb. His hand alighted on a wheel that turned under pressure. He forced it round and was rewarded by the quivering of some mechanism stirring into life. Several percussive shudders made him imagine counterweights rising, falling. A hairline crack divided the blackness to his left. It widened blindingly.

When his sight returned, he gasped. He heard other gasps around him. He forgot the bells. The Valley of the Gate fell away from them in a shadow that spilled out across the Skymere and the causeway to lap at the edge of a vision. Emerald shimmer and dance. An achingly beautiful dream – the Yden. For a moment Carnelian was lost again in that garden where he and Osidian had played as innocently as children. It seemed his heart had stopped at the beginning of the world. He dared not breathe out lest that should be enough to eddy that vision like smoke. His lungs forced the air out. The vision remained, but seemed changed. His gaze took in the whole vast lotus of Osrakum. Exquisite bloom that fed upon the life of millions. A flower whose roots had turned so many into corpses that soon it too must wilt and die.

The vision lost its hold on him. Fern at his side was real and solid. Carnelian reached out and felt the living warmth in him. His touch released Fern from enchantment.

Carnelian smiled and spoke, in a low voice. 'There's still much to do before the darkness comes.'

He led them onto the road that ran along the Cloaca rim. As they marched on, the clamour of the bells slowly dulled enough for them to hear the water rushing below. He stopped once to look over, but could see nothing other than a blackness that made it seem bottomless. Still, the sediment of his dreams stirred in him.

The roaring had been growing louder for some time when, on their right, the ground fell away into the immense spillway, upon which everything depended. He scrutinized its further edge where the dyke rose that held back the waters of the Skymere. The dyke was cut with many slots, from each of which tumbled a waterfall. In those slots were the sluices that were controlling the overflow of the lake into the swirling, threshing surface of the spillway. What Carnelian was interested in was the difference in height between that surface and that of the lake. He heaved a sigh of relief as he judged that at least part of his plan was possible.

Ammonites came to greet Carnelian as he walked onto the dyke. Most fell to their knees, but a few were brave enough to approach him, ducking bows. One spoke up, telling him, apologetically, that he must have come the wrong way; indicating with vague gestures where, behind him, flights of steps led down to the lake and the bone boats, but not daring the impertinence to tell him this, that all the Seraphim knew. 'This way, Seraph, lie only the sluices.'

'I have an interest to behold their operation.'

Reluctantly, they led him back the way they had come, towards the first pair of arches. As he followed them, a spark of light caught in the corner of his eye. Turning, he saw a second pulsing in the bright belly of the Labyrinth mound. Perhaps, as he had approached the dyke, these ammonites had had time to slip an alarm to their masters. He did not care. The Wise had more pressing matters to occupy their minds and, if they did not, then what matter? They would find out what he was up to soon enough.

Approaching the first slot, Carnelian was surprised how

much bigger it was than he had expected. He ignored an ammonite giving an explanation, and craned over the edge to look down. A bronze sluice at either end controlled the flow through the slot.

Everyone was watching him. He indicated to Sthax the cables that held the nearest sluice. 'Hack those through.'

The Maruli, frowning, nodded and, soon, paying no heed to the shrill protests of the ammonites, he and the other warriors were chopping at the cables. Carnelian returned to the edge. The first cable snapped with a twang, the second soon after. Ponderously, counterweights began to rise; squealing, the sluice fell, releasing a furious roar and gush that quickly abated as the slot emptied. The sluice at its other end was still holding back the Skymere. Carnelian turned to Sthax.

'Send your men to cut them all.'

From the top of the northern Turtle Steps, Carnelian gazed across the Skymere to where shadow, having consumed the Ydenrim, was eating its way over the lagoons. He swung the clapper into the bell and, as the sound shimmered the air, he narrowed his eyes, trying to see any sign of a bone boat answering its call. Twilight over the water hid any movement. Fern approached, Sthax and the Marula straggling in his wake. Carnelian's ears, recovered from the ringing, allowed him to hear the roar rising from the spillway, into which the Skymere was tumbling in a flood so violent that the more than twenty separate falls were uniting into a frothing foaming mass that ran the whole length of the sluice dyke. He frowned, imagining what chaos and destruction his flood would unleash upon the City at the Gates and its sartlar infestation. Now all that remained to do was to wait until the lake and the spillway reached a common level.

At last they pushed out into open water, Carnelian and Fern standing on either side of the bony prow. Ahead, shadow had killed the emerald shimmer of the lagoons and was beginning to edge up towards the Forbidden Garden and the Labyrinth. Soon only the Pillar of Heaven would rise gleaming from the blackness and even that must eventually succumb. Looking back along the length of the bone boat, Carnelian had to rid himself of the notion the deck was crowded with that same shadow made flesh. These Marula had been the agents of a malign force, but he was in no position to blame them for that. Whatever the Masters maintained, he believed the eyes anxiously looking at him were as human as his own.

He gazed past the stern. It must be because the lake was so immense that its surface showed no sign of the maelstrom where it was flooding into the spillway. The second boat was nudging away from the stepped slope. When the first boat had arrived, a kharon had told him that his vessel was not big enough to take them all. As they had waited for the second, he had imagined the one-eyed men struggling to launch the vessel from a boathouse. He recalled lying captive in one such boathouse with Osidian before they had been packed into funerary urns. It seemed some other life than his, but in his heart a desire stirred to see Osidian again. Only when the ferrymen had demanded payment had Carnelian realized he had no jade rings. At a loss, he had turned to the Marula, had considered using force, but then had had an inspiration. He had asked two of the warriors for their swords and given one to each ferryman. Even though they were masked, he had sensed their shock. Each of the iron blades in their hands was worth more than the boat they steered; probably more than all the boats of the kharon and their lives too. He was glad that such economics would not survive the Masters.

Slicing the dark mirror of the Skymere, the prow creased its water, mixing the lights from the coombs as sparks into the ripples. Carnelian watched Fern gaze at the palaces, entranced. Vague sweeps and outlines, heavy hanging masses all lit with what seemed countless burning jewels. As their eyes tried to grasp shape and form, Carnelian wondered what miracles of art and beauty lay behind those soaring façades. In his heart there was an ache for how much was going to be lost. For a moment, he perceived each of the myriad lights as a human life that must be soon snuffed out. His mind veered away from thoughts of atrocities in paradise.

The eerie silence was broken only by the sculling oars, the bow wave silkily slipping. He glanced back over his shoulder. Though the glory of the Yden was now muffled beneath a pall of shadow, the longer he looked, the more he saw the lagoons were still reflecting something of the blue sky, which its mirrors transformed into infinite, mysterious depths. Tearing up through the blackness, the double spire of the Pillar of Heaven. There at its summit, which was bathed in the last light of the sun, were the hollows where the glorious Chosen had gathered for sacred election. Beneath, the caverns in which the Wise had lodged the spooled beadcord of their library. He could not imagine all of that gone. Was beauty and wisdom then to perish from the earth?

His gaze followed the long back of the Labyrinth and climbed the slope of the cone that wore a crown upon its summit of molten gold as if to mark the place where, below, Osidian, the Gods on Earth, was camped at the heart of the Plain of Thrones. In spite of everything, some compassion rose in him for his once lover, now brother, imagining his despair. In seeking to possess Osrakum, Osidian had only brought it to utter destruction.

Carnelian was musing melancholically on these and other losses when he glanced up. They were sliding past a vast hollow in the Sacred Wall filled with a twinkling scree, among which he could discern a shadowy gathering of colossi. He recognized Coomb Imago and recalled his visit there; the tortured innocents dying on crosses. Other memories began to seep into his mind. The eyeless slaves living their life out in the dark like maggots, turning the wheels that lifted water up to cool the echoing palaces of his own coomb eyries. Then, in riotous recall, the death and maiming that was the lot of most in the outer world; the misery and fear. It was upon such suffering this paradise was built.

Shadow had now reached across the crater to turn the whole Skymere into an obsidian mirror. All around its rim the lit coombs formed a necklace of stars. Carnelian's hand rose, his fingers finding the scar that the slave rope had left around his neck. No less was this collar of palaces a scar about the neck of the peoples of the earth. Wonder died in him. Let the Masters and all their works perish.

FAREWELLS

What then do we make of an atrocity in Paradise?
(a Quyan dialectic)

Coomb suth was so much murkier than the other coombs they had passed that, as they slid towards it, fear gnawed at Carnelian that it had already become a tomb. A flickering thread of pinprick lights winding down towards the lake revived his spirits: people were coming to the visitors' quay to meet them. He searched within the arc of moving lamps for the carved pebble beach upon which he had landed on that first visit so long ago. He recalled a jade pebble, its spiral cracked in two. He could not remember if, then, he had seen it as an omen. A lurid red glimmer reflected from the sky showed the beach submerged. It seemed that, after all, news of a sort from the Blood Gate had reached here before him.

As the bone boat curved a course to present her port bow to the quay, Carnelian and Fern pushed through the Marula. Reaching the bow, he saw lamp-lit faces watching the boat nuzzle into the quay. He felt a burst of love. These were his people, and not only because they wore the chameleon that made him feel a child again, but because the faces beneath those tattoos were Plainsman.

He watched Fern's eyes and wondered if his frown meant he

838

was seeing his own, lost Tribe. Feeling the first touch of grief, Carnelian turned away from it, put on a smile, threw his hood back so the people on the quay could see his face. As they recoiled, he gasped, for an instant fearing he had done something wrong; realizing he had not, even as a familiar voice spoke up. 'Can't you see it's the Master's son?'

Carnelian located his brother among the guardsmen and relaxed as Tain led them to kneel upon the stone. The bone boat juddered as it touched the quay. Carnelian was surprised to see how far below the level of the deck it was, but thinking no further on it, swung himself round one of the mooring posts and jumped down onto the quay. As he landed, he realized that, of course, it was the lake that was higher. The corpse dam had raised its level further than he had supposed. He was going to have longer to wait for it to drain to the level he needed. On the other hand it might give him more time to sort matters out in the coomb.

He straightened, approached his brother and, stooping, drew him close and, to Tain's surprise, kissed him.

Tain, at first flustered by this breach of decorum, was soon grinning. 'Carnie.'

'Brother.' Carnelian told them all to get up and Tain's grin spread among them as he greeted those he recognized by name. Tain shocked them all by barking a command that brought everyone back into formal order. Though startled, Carnelian regained his smile: Tain had acquired something of the manner of their eldest brother, Grane.

'You'll be wanting to see the Master.'

Carnelian nodded, feeling a grimness come upon him, glad now that Tain had tamed the informality. Fern landed with a thump on the quay. Carnelian urged the Suth tyadra to move back from the boat, then motioned the Marula to disembark. He noticed Tain sending a messenger back up to the palaces. Further along the quay, the rest of the warriors were disembarking from the second bone boat. Carnelian asked Sthax to leave ten of his men, then to take the rest

839

and go with the guardsmen. 'Make sure you keep them under control. I'll send for you as soon as I can.'

The man gave him a sober nod. Carnelian put the ten selected warriors under Fern's command. He felt perfectly safe among the tyadra, but he wanted to make sure Sthax did not feel he and his people had been forgotten. No more did he want Fern to feel ignored, a barbarian, among the guardsmen. These arrangements made, he followed Tain away from the quay.

'When will we be receiving more food, Master?' said Tain.

Carnelian did not know how to answer that. 'How much hunger is there here?'

His brother shrugged. 'We've known for more than a month that resupply was likely to be delayed. Since then we've been rationing the stores. Still, things are getting tight.' He grinned, wanly. 'Those who suffered hunger in the Hold after we left keep saying this is nothing. The Master's made sure everyone's given a share appropriate to their need.'

Carnelian looked at Tain. 'Everyone?'

His brother nodded with satisfaction. 'The Masters too. Even himself.'

Carnelian saw the pain tensing Tain's face, but turned away. He did not want to learn more about their father just then. 'How tight?'

Tain made a face. 'For more than ten days we've had nothing to eat but that stuff from the "bellies".'

'Render,' Carnelian said and saw in Fern's face he was sharing their disgust. 'What about the mood of our people?'

Tain leaned closer. 'There's unease among the tyadra and between the households.'

Carnelian remembered Opalid's animosity. 'How secure are our people?'

Tain eyed him cautiously. 'From the others?' Then, when Carnelian nodded, 'Keal keeps guards on all the gates between our halls and theirs. We've turned ours into a fortress.'

'Ebeny? Poppy?'

Tain smiled. 'As safe as worms in an apple.'

As they walked on in silence, the warmth that came from the thought of seeing Poppy and Ebeny again was slow to fade. Their scuffling footfalls echoing back from distant walls made it seem they were creeping through vast caverns.

Carnelian jumped when Tain spoke. 'Why's the lake rising?'

'It's already falling.'

Tain nodded as if Carnelian had given him an extensive explanation. Carnelian sensed his brother was building up to something.

'More than a month ago smoke started drifting out from the Canyon right out over the water. A few days later we heard you'd taken control of the Blood Gate.'

'Who told you that?' Carnelian said, anxious that news of the disaster might have reached Coomb Suth already.

'Some Masters came to visit Father. We talked to their tyadra.'

Carnelian judged they must have come to ask his father to attend the Clave. What had they told him about what was going on?

Tain broke into his musing. 'The second time they came, Master Opalid left with them.'

'What happened when he returned?'

'He went straight to Father.'

Carnelian nodded. His heart sank. His father would know about the summoning of the legions, then, but it was he who was going to have to tell him about their destruction. And about the part he had played in all of this.

'How is he?'

Tain's face tensed again. 'Weak and spending most of his time alone.'

Carnelian nodded, sad. 'That's him all right.'

'Even Keal hardly sees him.'

'Ebeny?'

841

'Mother tends to him when he lets her.' Tain glanced at him. 'She'd love to see you.'

'I'll go to her after I've seen Father. And Poppy?'

Tain lit up. 'She'll be with Mother. It's as if they've known each other all their lives.'

Carnelian drew some much-needed comfort from that.

'Of course, if she's heard you're here, we might all be seeing her much sooner than we think.'

Carnelian saw the wry grin on his brother's face, then on Fern's, and all three burst into laughter that soon came swooping back from all directions out of the blackness as if the whole world was laughing with them.

They came to a guarded door where carved warding eyes gave warning they were about to enter the halls of the first lineage. The guardsmen looked uncertain, but began to kneel. He stopped them with his hand and advanced on one whom he recognized as Naith, who grew tearful recognizing his Master's son and kissed his hand.

The chambers beyond were warmed by light and a smell of home that brought tears to Carnelian's eyes. When far from prying ears, Tain asked him, bluntly, why he had come now and with the black barbarians.

That reminded Carnelian. 'Is the homunculus safe?'

'The little man? Safe enough.'

Carnelian saw his brother wanted his question answered. 'Difficult times are coming, Tain. I've a plan to save us all, but before I can speak of it, I must talk to Father.'

'Of course, Carnie,' Tain said, leaving Carnelian troubled by the trust in his brother's face, but also more determined.

At last they reached immense white doors. Carnelian saw Keal among some guards, and rushed forward to catch him by the arms to stop him kneeling. He kissed him. 'My brother.'

Keal blushed. 'He's expecting you,' he whispered, as if he wished not to wake some invalid beyond the doors. Carnelian eyed them with some faltering of his purpose. They looked so much like the doors of his father's hall in the Hold. Of course, he realized, it was the other ones that were a copy. His child's eyes had made those seem massive; these doors really were.

'Keal, are we secure from any outside attack?'

'We are, Master.'

There was a certain look in his brother's face, the same in Tain's, in that of the other guardsmen. All there were relating what was happening to what had happened on the island. Then the danger had come from Aurum and the other Masters arriving on their black ship. Though his people did not know it yet, the situation now was even more perilous.

Carnelian turned to Fern. 'Please wait here.'

Fern looked unhappy, but nodded. Carnelian cleared his mind and turned to the doors. They were an ivory mosaic of chameleons whose eyes were rusty iron rivets. He struck one of the doors three times with the heel of his hand. As the doors opened, through the gap between them he saw a fire. Beyond it, sculpted by its light, the shape of a Master. For a moment Carnelian felt the weight of time falling from him. He was a boy again, coming to tell his father of the approach of a black ship.

'Celestial.'

Carnelian hated his father greeting him thus. It was another barrier between them. As the old man removed his mask, his gaze alighted on him, before flicking away to take in the shadowy limits of the hall. Carnelian was sure he had seen in those grey eyes the love that his father found too difficult to express.

His father's frown crumpled further his lined face. 'You must find these palaces cold, unwelcoming, but as you surely know, Celestial, resources are at the moment restricted.'

He seemed very old, then. Coming alive again, he fixed Carnelian with his gaze. 'If only you had sent us warning of your visit.'

Carnelian grew angry. 'This is a lot more than a visit!' The anger left him. His father looked so vulnerable, but he had to know the truth. 'The legions have all been destroyed.'

His father's bones seemed suddenly to soften. He collapsed into a chair that the silk slopes of his robe had concealed.

'Father,' Carnelian cried, moving forward, but then was stayed by his father flinging up his hand in a barrier gesture. 'All?'

'All.'

His father sagged. 'Then it is over.'

Carnelian felt sick at heart with the need to help him, to touch him, to be touched by him. 'It is I who have brought this thing to pass.'

His father raised his eyes as if trying to make him out at some vast distance. 'You? Have you forgotten my warnings to you about the Chosen? How dangerous we are? It was only the Balance of the Powers that kept us caged. Without it, it was always fated we should fall upon each other like beasts. The Balance was the only thing keeping us from another internecine war that would lay the whole world waste.'

Carnelian was afraid that his father had lost his mind. 'That war was fought and, seemingly, won, but now the world *is* destined to fall into famine and ruin.'

His father lifted a bony hand shaping a contemptuous sign of negation. 'The Great will never submit to domination by the House of the Masks.' His gaze fell raptor-like on Carnelian, who desperately wanted him to make sense. 'You think you've seen a civil war, my Lord? You've seen nothing! If the Chosen are given the means to wage war upon each other, they will do so to the death.' His father's hand wavered in more negation. 'The Balance, bought at the price of the previous war, is our only hope to maintain the harmony of the Commonwealth. It is we, all of us, who have conspired to shatter its mirror.' His eyes dulled. 'But perhaps it is foolish to hope that the Balance should stand for ever. Who can hope to build a rampart proof against the sea?'

Carnelian felt lost. He had so much counted on his father's strength. The horror of what he had witnessed at the Gates piled onto that of the battlefield. It seemed as if he were succumbing to an avalanche of corpses. 'I broke the Balance!'

His father regarded him with a frown of incomprehension. 'Molochite . . .'

Carnelian was unable to dam the pouring out of a confession of his actions, of his influence on Osidian, of the influence on everything of his dreams and, as he did so, he was aware of his father's face softening and, when his father put out his hands, he hesitated, but laid his own upon his father's, whose thin fingers closed about them, tenderly. 'Son, dreams are the chief way by which the gods communicate with men.' He smiled. 'Perhaps not "gods", but those forces that move the world. Why did you follow your dreams?'

Carnelian frowned back tears, trying to find the words, eventually finding only one. 'Compassion.' A strange word; in Quya sounding almost shameful. His father smiled up at him, seeming suddenly very wise. 'It was your heart that listened.' He nodded, still smiling. 'Then you have done only what was necessary.'

Carnelian gazed down at his father, something of whose former beauty shone out from his wasted face. 'You say that, even though it has brought us all to ruin?'

The light went out in his father's face. He let go Carnelian's hands and folded his own together over his stomach as if nursing an ache. He gazed up, a strange, fearful expression in his eyes. 'In truth, my first reaction to your news was relief.'

Carnelian stared at him.

'It has lifted a burden from me. For a long, long time,' he sighed the words, 'I have thought of nothing but the succession here.' He lifted his chin to take in the vast darkness round them. 'Several times have you been taken from me. The last time, I knew the ruling of this House must pass to Opalid.'

'But I sent you word to reassure you.'

845

His father smiled grimly. 'The Maruli?' And when Carnelian nodded, 'It was not easy for me to believe you.' He laughed, grimly. 'How has it come to this: that I should find relief in the ending of the world?' His eyes fell bright upon Carnelian. 'You think me selfish?'

Carnelian did not know how to answer. It seemed so, but he too had a yearning to be free of the care of others.

His father's head dropped and he seemed to be watching one of his hands as it crushed the knuckles of the other. 'Whereas you have always followed your heart, I have striven to cut mine out.' There was fury in his eyes as he glanced up. 'As we teach and are taught to do.' He looked away. 'We face the world with our masks as proud and blind as the Sacred Wall. We raise these ramparts even between ourselves.' He turned back to Carnelian, haunted. 'Even on our island, far from Osrakum and the Law-that-must-be-obeyed, I told myself I must maintain this aloofness for your sake; for one day you must return here. Nevertheless, you know, to your cost, how poorly I prepared you to be Chosen.' His face twisted as if he had something bitter in his mouth. 'I lied to myself. It was for my own sake that I held onto my pride. In that remoteness, I was terrified I would cease to be Chosen.' His eyes grew bright with tears. 'You see, it became so difficult to believe that I was an angel. Even behind my mask, I was changing. I tried to blind myself to my degeneration by keeping before me always a vision of Osrakum and the manufactured hope and fantasy of return.' He closed his eyes and breathed deep. 'Powers and Essences forgive me, but when I saw in your face you were not of my blood, I seized on the danger to you as the excuse I needed not to return. In truth I did not want to return and we would not have, had the black ship not come.

'When it did, I turned against my heart; intoxicated by visions of a glorious return; telling myself I had to do it for your sake.' He looked up at Carnelian, tenderly. 'Truly, however misguided, for your sake.' He looked away into the darkness. 'I hid deep in my heart my fear, my grief. For all my vaunted pride, my world had shrunk down to the limits of that small island. And, yet, it did not feel too small. It was full and warm. Everything I loved was there. Still, I allowed it to be destroyed and brought all that I should have sought to protect, from safety, here to this terrible place.'

Carnelian reached down to take his father's hands. 'By not heeding your warnings before the battle, I have done the same.'

His father gave him a crooked smile. 'Well, it seems that everyone we love is now to die.'

Carnelian shook his head. 'There is still hope they can be saved.'

His father regarded him as if he feared him mad, but, as Carnelian explained his plan, that look left his father's face. 'Your dreams led you to this?'

'I think so.'

His father frowned. Carnelian was glad he did not go on to ask about how all the difficulties of his plan could possibly be overcome. What Carnelian was choosing to believe in was already the merest thread upon which to hang their hope, but it was all he had. 'We will have to survive here for several days.' Both knew that, once news got out that Osrakum was doomed, violent chaos would soon take possession of the coombs. Theirs would not be proof against it. As they talked, Carnelian sneaked sidelong glances at his father's wasted face. Some part of him was testing what he felt for this man, who was and yet was not his father, but gradually the tension in his stomach lessened. He knew that what he felt was love.

'You know Ebeny yearns to see you?'

Carnelian nodded. 'I shall go to her now.'

Emerging from his father's hall, Carnelian saw Krow between Tain and Fern. Carnelian smiled at him. He was not sure what he had expected back – certainly not Krow's frown and his refusal to meet his gaze. As the guardsmen sank to their knees, clumsily, Krow did so too, even though Tain and Fern remained standing. Krow was dressed in the same way as the other guardsmen and could easily have passed for one of them were it not that his face was free of the chameleon tattoo. Carnelian reminded himself of how long Krow had been here in this daunting world among the tyadra. It was foolish to have expected him to remain unaffected by the awe with which these men regarded their Masters. He glanced round to make sure the white door was closed before he commanded them all to rise. 'Fern, I'm going to see Tain's mother. Do you want to come with me?' Those words put pain in Fern's eyes, but he gave a nod. Carnelian was aware Krow had glanced up.

'Krow . . . ?'

When the youth looked again, Carnelian held his gaze. 'Do you want to come with us?'

Krow gave a nod, as Carnelian had hoped he would.

Tain brought them to a door and turned to Carnelian. 'I won't come in with you.'

Carnelian nodded.

'I'm not allowed . . . not allowed to enter,' said Krow.

Carnelian gave him a glance of concern, wondering why not: only Chosen women were subject to restrictive access. Clearly, Krow knew whose door this was, yet his tone implied he did not feel welcome there; but, if so, why had he agreed to come with them?

Fern's face arrested any more conjectures. He seemed to be on the crumbling edge of some precipice. Carnelian's pounding heart forced even this from his mind. Somewhere behind that door was Ebeny, whom he thought of as his mother. Almost he rapped upon the door in the special way that, in the Hold, had announced to Ebeny it was he. That had been another time. He gave the door a simple knock. Moments later it opened just enough to reveal a sliver of a face he recognized. The eye and mouth lit up. It was Poppy and he expected her to fling the door open and run to him, but she did not, instead biting her lip, half turning. 'It's Master Carnelian . . .'

'Well, let him in, dear,' said a voice in the chamber beyond. A voice that put a stone in Carnelian's throat.

The door opened fully and Poppy was there, looking past him, blushing. He was aware of Krow shuffling, but Carnelian's eyes were all for the small woman standing waiting for them.

'Krow's here, Aunty. Can I talk to him?'

The little woman gave a slow nod, her attention on Carnelian as he advanced towards her. She knelt before he could reach her. 'Master.'

Carnelian frowned, angry, upset, but respecting her wish for decorum, in some ways welcoming it as a way to keep his feelings under control. His instinct was to rush forward, to kneel before her, to kiss her, but he was no longer a child. Looking down at her bowed head, he saw with a kind of anguish how grey her hair had become.

'Please get up,' he said and stooped to help her rise, her smell stinging his eyes with tears.

She gazed up at him. She was so much smaller than he remembered, but with the same dear face, a little more lined, and the same bright eyes shining out between the legs of her tattoo. He stooped again, embraced her, resisted the desire to pick her up, to show her his strength. Now, that felt inappropriate. He kissed her face and she kissed his, then, as he unbent, she took his hands and lifted them to her cheek, stealing wet-eyed looks at him. They nodded at each other, little nods to punctuate their taking stock of each other.

'It seems we've both survived.'

He grinned through his tears at her. 'Yes, little mother.'

She warmed at his words, even as they both settled back into the comfort of their love for each other. Then he remembered Fern. Turning, still holding Ebeny's hands, Carnelian saw him standing stunned. 'This is—'

'Fern. I know . . .' she said. Carnelian saw the pain in her face. At first he was confused, then it became clear: of course Poppy had told her everything. Ebeny knew they had come from the Koppie, the home the childgatherer had torn her from. She knew of their years there, of the massacre of her tribe, of Akaisha, her sister.

She squeezed his hands then released them, moving past him, approaching Fern, tears glistening down creases in her cheeks. 'Sister's son,' she whispered, in Ochre, opening her arms for him.

Fern gazed at her, a forlorn child. Carnelian made himself blind, not wanting to see him so vulnerable. Fern knelt as he entered her embrace. She turned enough for Carnelian to see her eyes, wild, speaking to him. He gave a nod, slipped away, aware of her small body trying to comfort Fern's sobbing.

While he waited for Fern, Carnelian summoned the homunculus. When the little man arrived, he confirmed he had enough knowledge of the metallurgy of the Wise to help restore the ladder to the Marula's Lower Reach.

Fern emerged from his meeting with Ebeny transformed. He smiled, he laughed a lot and cried too in Carnelian's arms. He seemed much more the man he had been before grief had overwhelmed him.

Carnelian had need of him in the days that followed. He and his father made plans for the attempt to escape Osrakum. No one would be forced to go, and only those who had been with them on the island would be invited. Carnelian asked many himself. Tain and Keal approached the others. Most of the older people chose to stay, claiming the Master and the household were the only world they knew. When the young lit up, eager for the adventure, their parents exchanged sad glances with each other, and with Carnelian. As well as they, he knew how quickly innocent hope could be crushed by bleak reality. Still, they put on smiles, so as not to take the light from their children's eyes, urging them to go, comforting them when they realized they were going to be leaving their grandparents behind.

Carnelian had guessed what Ebeny's choice would be. That

same determination was in her face as when he had begged her to go with him across the sea. His father would not go, and she would not leave him behind. Carnelian bowed his head, accepting her decision. When he looked up again, he saw her tears through his own. They clasped hands as if holding off for a moment their final separation.

The pain of the coming partings spread through the household. It was as if those who were leaving were already on the boats; those left behind lining the quay holding their hands, grips tearing as the boat pulled away. His brothers too would be losing their father and also their mother without hope of seeing either again. Child and man fused in each one of them. One wanting to cling, the other knowing he had to pull away. The unbearable had to be borne. Their burden was made lighter when Grane announced he would stay behind to look after their parents. He did not have to tell them why: they could see his stone eyes.

Inevitably, these partings, the gathering of stores that the Master had had the foresight to set aside, all this brought back to many the destruction of the Hold and the famine that those who had been left behind had had to endure. Still, even those who had known terrible hunger gladly gave up what food there was for their children to take with them.

The first morning after Carnelian had appeared at the coomb, he and Fern had watched the boats bringing the Masters back from the Gates. After that, nothing disturbed the eerie calm of the Hidden Land except, sometimes, a torn banner of smoke drifting across the sky from the Valley of the Gate.

On the third day after they had reached the coomb, Fern spotted a pale grain where the carved pebble beach touched the Skymere. Something had washed up on the mud.

The two of them, alone on the mud, an immense white corpse at their feet. Already bloating, its greasy marble was slashed with blue-lipped wounds. The hands had been hacked off, the face sliced away, leaving a mask of blood. Carnelian recalled, with a deep resonant horror, the red faces in his dreams. It was a Master.

He gazed out across Osrakum. A beautiful morning. The sapphire waters of the lake. The emerald Yden. The jade hump of the Labyrinth. The pure green slopes that concealed the Plain of Thrones. To the north, coombs were revealed by the rising sun as jewels.

At his feet, the water level had fallen enough to reveal a band of greened-black rock that edged the Skymere as if it were a vast well. He shuddered at what might be revealed were the lake entirely to drain.

He looked once more upon the corpse. It shocked him to the core, this mutilated Master. It was not just that he felt in his gut horror at the tortures the man had had to endure, but at who it was must have done this. He gazed back at the palaces piling up behind him, porticoes and friezes and, among the columns and pierced marble, all kinds of openings, each seeming as blind as a Sapient's eyepit. Yet, from any one, a Master could be looking down; worse, one of their slaves.

Carnelian removed the blanket he had thrown on and covered the corpse with it. Its border was quickly darkened by the stream winding down from under the skirt of carved pebbles. He watched it washing the noisome liquids leaking from the corpse down to pollute the lake.

There were signs that the drop in water level was slowing, but they dare not set off until it stopped altogether. The sky was a clear blue, untainted by smoke. Though he had been expecting that for days, it still seemed shocking.

'The attacks on the Blood Gate have stopped,' Fern said.

Carnelian nodded. 'Soon it'll be time to go.' He saw the relief on Fern's face and allowed himself to see past his grim determination to follow his plan, through to the hope there was in this sign. He glanced up towards the Plain of Thrones. Was Osidian still there, in the Stone Dance of the Chameleon?

He became aware Fern was looking at him, but decided not to notice. He was not clear enough about how he felt to talk about it. He indicated the corpse with his chin. 'We need to do something about this.'

That night, one of the coombs on the far shore of the Skymere lit up, luridly, as if it were a fire in a grate. When morning came a lazy column of smoke could be seen uncurling into the sky. More smoke seemed to be rising from a neighbouring coomb, but its origin was concealed from them by a buttress of the Sacred Wall. Bloody rebellion was spreading around the shore of Osrakum.

Later that day, Opalid headed an embassy from the Second Lineage to their Ruling Lord. Carnelian stood with his father as he lied to them, telling them he did not know what was happening, but that, the moment he did, Opalid would be the first to be informed. When the Masters left, Carnelian told his father that he felt Opalid had not believed him. His father nodded, grimly. 'I have faith the tyadra will remain loyal to me.'

Carnelian wondered for how long, once he had left with half the household and all of its remaining supplies, but he locked his doubts away. He felt like a child, harbouring hope that a thing unsaid could not come to pass.

Lying with Fern in the dark, Carnelian finally came to a decision.

Deliberately thinking no more about it, for he knew that, however he phrased it, he was going to hurt Fern, he said: 'I have to go and see the Master.' He felt Fern tense beside him. 'I could tell you that this is the most certain way to get the boats we need, which is probably true, but I will not try to deny that I want to say goodbye to him.' He might have added that Osidian was his brother – but Osidian was also the murderer of Fern's people.

Fern stirred against his side. 'Will it be dangerous?'

Carnelian felt an overwhelming gratitude for Fern's level tone. 'It could be.'

'Is it your dreams that drive you to this?'

Carnelian shook his head. 'No.'

And they left it at that.

Overnight the level of the lake had hardly changed at all. A bell sounding again made him glance up at the main palace quay, which was stranded by the falling water. The summoning bell was up there, but it would be down here on this muddy shore that the bone boat would have to pull up. His father seemed huge in a cloak much grander than Carnelian's black military one. Ebeny beside him, tiny, yet his bulk could not eclipse her beautiful, brittle smile, her sad eyes. Fern was frowning. He knew Carnelian was going into peril.

'Are you sure you want to go alone?' said Keal.

Carnelian nodded. They were none of them happy about that. Grane's frown was causing his eyelids to ruck against his stone eyes. 'This is our final goodbye, then, big brother.'

The blind man ducked a nod, 'Master,' then would have knelt except that Carnelian held him up and embraced him. He felt Grane soften in his arms, lean into him, a little, for a moment accepting the love Carnelian was giving him. Then they drew apart, Carnelian frowning back tears. Ebeny's eyes seemed bright glass. His instinct was to fall before her, clasping her round the waist, putting his head where she could stroke it, comforting him, but he was no longer a child, though the child was still there within him. He stooped to put his arms about her. Felt her wet face slide past his cheek. 'Mother,' he whispered into her ear.

'My son,' she whispered in his.

Gently, he disengaged, smiling through his tears at her, holding hands, until these too let go.

His father's mask seemed a furtive fire in the hood of his cloak. A Great Lord among his servants. Carnelian's eyes fell, drawn to a movement. A pallid hand, all bones and sinew. The

Suth Ruling Ring back in its place like a swollen joint. The hand rose and for a moment seemed about to speak. The other joined it and, together, they moved into the shadow of the hood to release the mask. Carnelian was compelled to turn by a sudden, startled movement. Keal stood back, a look of horror frozen on his face. His instinct was that he was facing blinding; nevertheless he did not look away. Panic stirring in Carnelian was stilled by his brother coming alive with wonder. Their father gazed with love upon Keal, a son who had never before seen his father's face. Suth turned his eyes to Carnelian, who could not bear his father's look of aching sadness. Carnelian approached him, wanting to say something, but his father spoke first. 'You are my son too, Carnelian.'

Carnelian embraced him. 'You are my father.'

They stood together thus for some time, Carnelian feeling how weak his father was in his arms. Fearing that, should he let go, his father would fall broken upon the ground. Then he felt strength coming into him, and his father pushed him away. 'The boat approaches.'

Carnelian put on his mask for fear of terrifying the kharon. The bone boat slowed, shipping her port oars as she sought the rocky shore. His father was again a Master wearing an imperious face of gold.

Carnelian turned to Fern. 'I'll see you tomorrow.'

Fern gave him a nod. They had already said their goodbyes.

There was an inky space between the bone boat and the muddy rock upon which he stood. The kharon ferryman was below upon the deck, his bony crown rising up like gnarled fingers. He extended his whitened hand for his payment. Carnelian took hold of it with his left hand, held it as the ferryman attempted to jerk it back. It relaxed in his grip. After some hesitation, the man helped jump him aboard. Soon oars were clunking against the rock as they pushed the boat away from the shore.

To keep his people in sight, Carnelian moved back along the bow towards the stern as they slid away. He stopped short of the ferryman and leaned out upon a bony rail. He saw his father and his mother holding hands, seeming no longer to care to whom they announced the truth of their relationship. For a moment Carnelian managed to hold onto Fern's dark eyes.

Losing sight of them, Carnelian turned to the ferryman. Against the stern post he stood, the black and white design of his robe a furious dapple uncomfortable to look upon. His white-washed hands steady on the steering oars provided a quiet counterpoint. The turtle glyph was like a saurian egg in the nest of his crown, but it was his sinister ivory mask that made it seem he was gazing away off over his shoulder. Carnelian was close enough to smell his stale sweat; close enough to see through the slit to the gleam of his single eye. 'Didn't you fear bringing your boat to my coomb?'

As the ferryman shook his head, his crown rustled. Carnelian gazed at him, his eyes finding the edges of the delicate mosaic that formed his mask. Not ivory, then, more probably it was made from the same bone from which the boat was wrought. Carnelian realized he had never before heard a kharon speak. For all he knew, they, like the Wise, might have been lacking tongues as well as an eye. He tried again, this time in Quya. 'Did you not fear coming to my coomb?'

'Seraph,' said the ferryman, 'we are into your service bound.' His Quya was husky, thick, sounding strangely antique.

'But you must be aware of the disturbances?'

The ferryman bowed his crowned head.

'Still you came . . .'

'No troubles did we observe in Coomb Suth, Seraph.' Then as, Carnelian considered this, he added, 'We hoped it would be thee, Seraph, who summoned us.'

Carnelian was taken aback by this. Confused. 'You know who I am?'

The crown rustled again. 'Seraph Carnelian of the Masks.'

'How do you know that?'

'We carried thee to Coomb Suth, Seraph. You paid us with sky-metal.'

Carnelian regarded the ferryman with a more acute eye. These kharon were more aware of things than he had guessed. Clearly, they communicated among themselves. He tried to imagine how recent events might have appeared to them. Though each was possessed only of a single eye, between them they had enough to observe everything. The gentle sculling of the oars impressed itself upon Carnelian's hearing. How many kharon were there beneath his feet? And there must be women of their kind, and children. He mused for a moment on how their society formed a ring along the shore of the Isle.

'Why didst thou, Seraph, break the sluices?'

Carnelian heard the tremor in the man's voice. He was brave to be so bold. Carnelian considered rewarding him with an answer, but his heart misgave. It was too soon and now it occurred to him that what he must ask of the kharon must be asked of all of them at once. He considered this for some moments before speaking. 'If the kharon wish to know what is happening in Osrakum and the world beyond, then you must send an embassy into the Plain of Thrones.'

Lurching, the boat betrayed the ferryman's reaction. 'Impossible,' he sighed.

'There is a good chance you could talk to the God Emperor Themselves.'

The whitened hands curled tighter round the oars. 'We are permitted only the Inner Shore and the Shadowmere.'

Carnelian wondered at how strangely the ferryman named the lake, even as he tried to find a way to persuade him to do what he was now even more sure he needed. Again he thought hard before speaking lest he should lead them into peril. He glanced up at the Sacred Wall. The peace within its circle was an illusion. How could these people hope to survive what was coming?

'You say you know who I am,' Carnelian said.

'Carnelian of the Masks,' said the ferryman.

'Then you must know that I am brother to the God Emperor, who went with him into the outer world, returned in triumph and who survived his elevation.'

The nest crown inclined and Carnelian was certain the kharon not only knew this to be true, but understood the implications. 'Even as I have defied the Law, so must you. Upon my blood I swear I shall answer for your coming before the God Emperor my brother.'

For a moment Carnelian felt the ferryman's eye peering at him, until at last he inclined his head. 'Thy command shall be sent around the Shore.'

Relief washed over Carnelian. 'One more thing I would ask of your people.' Without thinking he put his hand upon the ferryman's arm. At his touch, the man shuddered, but his steering grip held firm. 'At dawn tomorrow, send three boats to Coomb Suth. There embark my people and their baggage and bring them to the Quays of the Dead.'

'As you command, Seraph,' the ferryman said and Carnelian drew his hand back, thanked him, then turned to walk along the deck, gazing at the vast green slope rising before them from the lake, within the summit of which lay the Plain of Thrones.

Carnelian clambered up onto the quay, his robe and cloak mired up to the knees with mud. He looked up the steps and let his gaze follow the path as it narrowed up into the cleft that led eventually into the Plain of Thrones. A long climb and at the end of it, what? It was only now he was facing the reality of seeing Osidian again; of having to confront him one last time. His heart was uncertain. Then there was the dull ache of fear. He had no idea how Osidian might be taking the failure of all his dreams. Fern had been right to worry about the danger. That was why Carnelian had insisted on coming alone.

858

He glanced back at the trail he had left in the shelf of mud as he had struggled up from the new shore. The bone boat was already moving off. That sight hardened his resolve. He had to prepare the way for the kharon. He turned back to the steps and began the climb.

He paused to get his breath, looking back the way he had come. The endless shallow steps. The scrape of his footfalls echoing off the rock walls had given the ghostly procession graven into them an eerie life. He was glad of the light up ahead. Only a few more steps and he beheld the Plain of Thrones spread out: a bright vision. The Pillar of Heaven seemed a vast shaft of light stabbing down from the morning sky. Beneath it, the jewel of the Pyramid Hollow and the gleaming rank of the funerary colossi. There was a glinting on the plain. It took him some moments to recognize the Cages of the Tithe. Recalling the myriads of children there, his heart failed. He had forgotten them. Then he became aware of some thick smoke rising from the western edge of the plain. The House of Immortality where the children of the Great were being prepared for their tombs. He gazed at the heart of the plain. Squinting, he gained the distinct impression the Stone Dance of the Chameleon was a lot wider than it should be. There appeared to be a slight hazing above it. Grimly, he began to walk towards it.

Coming closer, he saw that something like a small town had engulfed the standing stones. Smoke was spiralling up from many different locations among innumerable emerald pavilions.

As he came into the camp, he saw that the campfires were mostly located on the road where it split to encircle the Stone Dance of the Chameleon. It was covered with people who began to rise as he approached, turning their half-black faces towards him. Such a great gathering of Ichorians suggested the God Emperor must be near. Two gatestones rose behind them like sentinels standing guard on a dark wall where the outermost stones of the Dance were supposed to be. Somehow reminded of the shadowy eaves of the Isle of Flies, Carnelian shuddered.

Figures came through the Ichorians, pulling on helmets. As they approached they knelt before him. From their silver collars he knew they were centurions. He gave them his name and, when he told them he had come to see the God Emperor, he detected a flicker of fear in their eyes. There was something else there: hope. That drained him even more. What was it they were hoping he would save them from? He did not ask, but followed them along the right-hand fork as if he and they were a funerary procession. He distracted himself from this ill omen by observing the Dance, deducing it had been covered up to form some vast pavilion. The ghosts of the stones could be seen pushing through the midnight brocade that clothed them.

They came at last to a second pair of gatestones: those that stood opposite the road that led off to the House of Immortality, from where smoke was still belching ominously. The Ichorians around the two stones were syblings. They knelt. Carnelian waited as his guides communicated his words to them. His gaze became enmeshed in the black wall that rose behind them. Chimeric visions wrought into the silk were picked out with green and yellow jewels like feral eyes. Jade cameos hung here and there from which peered monstrous faces as if up through stagnant water. He tore free to look outwards. The quarter of the camp lying between the Immortality Road and that which led to the Forbidden Door was formed of purple pavilions spotted with silver spirals. He searched for ammonites or a glimpse of one of their masters, but the camp of the Wise seemed lifeless, abandoned. Ill omens were everywhere.

*　　　*　　　*

'Celestial?' said two voices he knew. He almost exclaimed with relief at seeing it was the Quenthas.

The sisters seemed to have aged, faces wasted, the dark tattoos sinking into Left-Quentha's cheeks; Right-Quentha's eyes were haunted by some terror. Twitching a smile, she begged him to follow them. He was drawn past flaps of the black samite into the gloom beyond in which a myrrh fog revolved ponderously in monstrous curls. Pale wraiths haunted the twilight. Were it not that this place was much more confined, he could fancy he had been transported into the Labyrinth. The pale slabs of the second ring of stones formed a broken ring that seemed lit by some dying moon. His mask was smothering him and, knowing he could, he removed it. 'Are They here?'

Grimly, the Quenthas nodded. Left-Quentha clapped her hands. Slaves approached, naked, cringing. As they converged on him, Carnelian protested.

'All here must be unclothed, Celestial,' Right-Quentha said. She and her sister divested themselves of the robe they were wearing. Carnelian was fascinated by their joined body half dipped in the shadow of tattoos; by their small breasts and, for a moment, his gaze lingered on the strange form of their nearly joined sex. He himself removed his military cloak, bundled it up and gave it to the sisters. 'Keep this for me.' He could see they thought it strange he should care about such a rough, muddy garment, but they took it in their four hands. Then he submitted to the blind slaves. They stripped him, shaved his head, his face, his body. They cleansed him with pads. Through the sharp menthol he could still smell their sweaty fear.

Even through feather rugs Carnelian could feel the bony network of the pavement that linked the ghost stones to their commentaries. Like worms burrowing just beneath skin. In the gloom, pale flesh huddled to pale flesh, jewel eyes glinted furtively. A whispering like a breeze made him feel he was following the sisters through some enchanted forest haunted by the spirits of the dead.

When they came to a gateway guarded by more naked syblings, Carnelian became aware of a small group of lost children. No, homunculi, twelve of them, their faces hidden by their blinding masks.

'You alone can save him,' Right-Quentha whispered in his ear. 'Prepare yourself,' her sister said.

They opened a wound in the blackness through which light flooded. Carnelian put his hand on the stone lintel to steady himself. He felt the spiral under his hand. Then he let go of it and stepped into the blindingly bright heart of the Stone Dance of the Chameleon, still open to the sky, even as his stomach clamped, spit welling in his mouth at the charnel stench.

He almost crumpled under the assault of fetor. He would have run, if he had known where to run to. His eyesight returning allowed him to see a pale figure sitting stiffly on red earth. The knobs of its backbone, the shoulder blades seeming ready to tear through the sallow flesh. Skin disfigured with countless angry-looking, blue-lipped wounds. Bands around the swelling of the shaved head showed it must be wearing a mask. His arm across his nose and mouth, Carnelian was for a moment shocked that one corpse could so much pollute the air, but then he saw the stones that walled in that place; saw the things sagging, rotting in the man-shaped hollow in each stone. Green-black. The heads lolling back into the hollows were already more skull than face. Gashes over their bodies showed where the blood must have trickled down their skin, to gather in the hollows and dribble down the channels into the red earth. The slits left by their castrations had been torn open like vulvas by swellings forcing themselves out like babies' heads, so that it seemed that the Grand Sapients had died in the act of giving birth.

'Why did you do this?' Carnelian breathed.

'They lied,' said the dead man at the centre of the Dance. 'I had to force them to tell me the truth.'

With disgusted fascination, Carnelian crept round, wanting to look into Osidian's face. He stopped when he saw the black, glassy profile. 'What truth?'

The Obsidian Mask turned its distorting mirror to Carnelian. 'That the sartlar *are* the Quyans.'

THE STONE DANCE OF THE
CHAMELEON

Flesh endures longer than iron.
(sartlar proverb)

'The sartlar are the Quyans . . . ?' repeated Carnelian, stunned.

'The Wise have always known this,' said Osidian, his voice wintry. 'But, obsessed with their computations, they missed the real threat.'

'They lacked the factor of my true birth.'

The Obsidian Mask turned its malice towards him. 'Do not flatter yourself, my brother. Even once they had that factor, they found there was another, far greater, missing from their mosaic. Even as they died they held to their certainty. It was the inability of their simulations to predict the uncurling of events that made them powerless to effectively oppose them. What could explain the sartlar behaving as if directed by a single mind? Why, suddenly, are they capable of overthrowing their animal fear of flame that, for millennia, we have used to tame them?'

Carnelian shook his head. 'But— if they are the Quyans—'

The dark mirror mask slid away, distorting in reflection a

hideous corpse in a hollow. 'Even the Quyans in their glory could not have withstood our legions.'

'How . . . ?' Carnelian was struggling to grasp this shift in the bedrock of his reality.

'When the plagues of the Great Death humbled them, we issued forth as conquerors. Perhaps it would have been better had we slain them all, but the land needed to be tilled and we desired to make them our slaves. To ensure our dominion over them, we forced them to build the roads that would contain them; the watch-towers to keep unsleeping vigilance over them. We raised the legions and perfected them. But, most of all, we wrote here the Law-that-must-be-obeyed.' Osidian indicated the grim stones enringing them. 'Its codicils described a system, independent of the hearts of those who would come after, that, relentlessly and without pity, would grind them down into such abject bestiality that it would become impossible for them to regain their previous state.'

Though Carnelian had felt something of the weight of the Law, had suffered himself and witnessed more suffering than he could bear to remember, he could not even begin to grasp the immensity of horror that had been inflicted upon the sartlar by the Masters and their Law.

His mind recoiled. It was too much. He veered away, protecting himself. 'But does not this Law weigh down also upon the Chosen?'

Unexpectedly a chuckle came from behind the Obsidian Mask. 'Chosen?' It turned a little towards him. 'It was not enough that the Quyans should forget what they had been; we too had to forget. So we hid this history even from ourselves, appointing these' – he indicated the corpses around them – 'as its guardians, and in a few generations we had forgotten it utterly.'

'Why? Surely it is from our ignorance the current disaster has sprung?'

'You don't understand,' Osidian said, with what seemed a

groan of pain. 'What we sought to forget was not their glory, but our shame.'

'That our blood runs in the veins of the sartlar?'

Osidian hunched forward as if he bore the whole weight of time and disaster as a yoke across his neck. 'Even when I excruciated them' – his hand feebly indicated the corpses – 'they would not tell me, until at last I prised open their minds with one of their drugs. You see, Carnelian,' his tone strained, appeasing, 'we were not always as we have believed ourselves to be.'

Carnelian felt desperate curiosity. The black mask gazed westwards to where smoke was still rising from the House of Immortality. 'The Quyans brought their kings here. Within this circle they evoked the Creation through blood sacrifice. There, to the west, they entombed them to await their reawakening.'

As Carnelian grasped at what Osidian might mean, bleak realizations dawned on him. Death's Gate, the Shadowmere, the Quays of the Dead. 'This *is* the Isle of the Dead.'

Osidian's head dropped again, as if the weight of the stone mask was too much for him to bear. Carnelian watched the smoke fraying into the morning sky. There, in the Quyan tombs, the House of Immortality, the Chosen mummified their own dead. He remembered that Quyan treasures were the most prized possessions of the Chosen. 'We robbed their tombs.' He frowned. 'But then who are we?' Revelation came upon him. He muttered the words he had once spoken in the Labyrinth: 'Where do we get this obsession with death?' The most secret books in the Library of the Wise were on embalming. 'We were the keepers of the dead.'

Osidian nodded. 'Glorious Osrakum was the necropolis of the Quyan kings.'

Carnelian, who had lived through the filth and horror of preparing the dead, was left, by this knowledge, feeling more unclean. 'We are not descended from the Gods? Our forefathers were outcasts?'

'Untouchables,' Osidian spat out. 'Chosen we were from among the people of the outer world. Those who were as pallid as corpses; who had the pale eyes of the people who long ago had come up from the sea seeking the Land of the Dead; who were sent here to tend the dead.'

Carnelian felt Osidian's madness seeping into him. Disgust and shock and a feeling of coming adrift, of losing his footing in a flood. 'But, still, we conquered them.' This said still in some hope that the Gods had seen fit to raise the lowly to angelic heights.

Osidian groaned with anger. 'The plague had brought our masters low.'

'But why were we spared its ravages?' Still Carnelian was casting around for some sign that providence had chosen them for greatness.

Osidian sank his head again between his shoulders as if he were some carrion crow. 'The procedures for processing corpses had made us skilled in protecting ourselves from putrefaction.'

Carnelian recalled the elaborate precautions the Masters took before exposing themselves to the outer world. 'The ranga, the ritual protection, our masks.' He saw the links with the Law. 'Wearing a mask was not only a precaution against contagion, but a means of separating us from and terrorizing the survivors.'

'The Quyans wore masks only in death. To them it must have seemed as if the Dead themselves had risen from the Underworld to enslave them.'

Carnelian gazed at Osidian wearing his stone mask. Why was he still wearing it who could no longer have any illusions of his divinity? Carnelian's heart answered him. There was perhaps another reason the keepers of the dead had worn their masks, as Osidian was doing: to hide their shame not only from their former masters, but even from themselves. Weariness and blackness overwhelmed him. 'It is all a lie then.'

Osidian sprang up. 'One that, had Legions confided it to me, I could have saved the Commonwealth!'

Carnelian understood then the real reason why Osidian had killed the Grand Sapients. 'Search your heart, Osidian,' he said, compassion softening his voice. 'Even had he told you everything, would you really have turned back?'

Osidian stood for a moment, as if turned to stone, then sagged back to the earth. Even now Carnelian could not be certain that Osidian had faced up to what they had done. It was a flaw in him that he inflicted upon others what, in his heart, he really wanted to do to himself. Carnelian looked round at the twelve hollows. Not that the Wise were innocent. 'Knowing this, why did they not fear the sartlar more?'

Osidian's voice sounded like a boy's when he spoke. 'Because nothing that was happening made any sense to them. They believe— they believed their blindness protected them against the seductions of this world. For them, sight revealed only the mendacious surface of things and not the flows of reality beneath. It was these currents they sought to study and control.' The black face came up. 'For centuries they had been attempting to stop a power rising again; a power they had thought was, if not slain, at least in chains.'

Carnelian regarded him, feeling a tide rising in him. 'What power?'

'The third God.'

'The third God?' Carnelian asked, knowing already what Osidian would answer.

'The Lady of the Red Land.'

Her red face broke into Carnelian's mind with the shock of revelation. 'The Mother,' he breathed.

The eyeslits of the Obsidian Mask seemed to be scrutinizing him. 'The Wise said that you would know Her; that you were one of Her major pieces in the game.'

Carnelian felt faint, knowing it to be true.

Osidian indicated the stones around them. 'Those are the

Black God's; those the Green God's. The eight red stones are Hers.'

And the eight red months and the ground upon which he sat that was a portion of the vast red land outside the Sacred Wall that was no longer guarded. Other impressions flashed into Carnelian's mind. 'Her pomegranates everywhere.'

'What?' Osidian said.

'We shared one in Her Forbidden Garden.'

Osidian's shock was revealed by the cast his shoulders took. 'Her garden?'

'Forbidden to men.'

'Except, perhaps those who serve Her.'

'The urns,' Carnelian gasped. Everything seemed so sickeningly clear. 'The *Three* Gates.'

Osidian nodded. 'The Quyans believed Osrakum to be her womb. The Pillar of Heaven the cord with which she nurtured the sky.'

Carnelian gazed up to where its bright shaft was lost in the morning light. 'Why did we forget Her?'

'Her power was great in the Land. When we closed the Gates we turned our back on Her. We feared Her. We feared Her revenge and so we built the Gates to keep Her out. Not just spatially, but in our minds. Of this even the Wise are not certain. It seems, perhaps, there was in Osrakum already alive a vestige of an ancient heresy of duality.'

Carnelian contemplated how the Father and the Son might have become the Twins. Osidian and Molochite. He, as the third brother, made the Two once again Three. Carnelian felt a rush of emotion that almost choked him. 'She was always there in my dreams. She brought me here.' He saw the angry red scar about Osidian's neck and felt his own itching and touched it. 'She brought us both here.'

He clawed at the red earth. It had been black. He looked to the edges of the Dance and saw there what remained of the moss and black earth that had covered up the red.

He sank to Her ground. 'What now?'

The black mask glanced round at the stones. 'They tried to buy their lives with a vision. That, taking their elixir, I might escape with them into the far future. The sartlar threat will subside naturally. Those the famine does not destroy might, perhaps, become true men again, but, if so, far from here. The Red Land will become a terrible desert that shall protect Osrakum more completely than the Sacred Wall. Eventually, they believed, the Land will come back to life. When the time is ripe, we would emerge from the chrysalises of our millennial sleep.'

Osidian's voice had grown stronger as he spun this vision in Carnelian's mind, the words reverberating from the stones. In the silence that followed, Carnelian hung half entranced, half in horror.

Osidian, shaking his head, brought them both back to earth. 'Though I sought to conquer the world, I will not countenance lingering like a ghost, rebuilding with infinite patience the world I helped destroy.' He reached behind his head and loosed the bands that held his mask on, then leaned forward to rest it in his palm. Carefully he laid the mask on the red earth. The pale face revealed, Carnelian hardly recognized. Lines of suffering had aged it; its eyes were as lifeless as stones.

'You may not believe this, but I did seek to build; even though all I have ever done is to destroy; even those things I most loved.' His sad eyes fell upon Carnelian.

Osidian frowned. 'I choose to die with the only world I know or wish to know.'

Carnelian was overcome by a surge of rage. 'Not everything or everyone needs to die! Can you think of no one but yourself?'

Pity cooled his anger. Osidian was a broken man. But he still had some power left. Carnelian sat down beside him. 'Will you help me save something from this?'

As Osidian gazed at him, lost, Carnelian began explaining his plan of escape. Osidian seemed puzzled as if he could not

870

grasp it. Carnelian did not need his understanding, only his compliance. He was about to explain to Osidian the part he would have to play, when he found himself recalling the homunculi he had passed when he entered the Dance, huddled like abandoned children. The flesh-tithe children! He felt again the ache he had always felt when Ebeny had told him of when she had been such a child. He lived again the agony of the Tribe beneath the Crying Tree as they said goodbye to their children. How many hearts in the greater world ached for their lost children? Then his heart swelled up as he became possessed by a mad, glorious yearning. Logic fought against it, but he could not, would not, let it go. He saw Osidian, weary beyond measure, like an old man, all his failures crushing him. 'Help me save the flesh-tithe children.'

Osidian frowned at him as if he was unsure he could mean what he had said.

'Help me take them with me.'

Osidian looked incredulous. 'All of them?' As he saw that was, indeed, what Carnelian meant, he began to list the obvious and insurmountable obstacles to such a plan. Carnelian took Osidian's hands in his, looked into his eyes. 'The dreams I have followed are not yet wholly spent.'

There was a hardness of doubt and failure and horror in Osidian's face. His heart seemed almost to have turned to stone, but something of love passed between them and Osidian began to cry, and Carnelian cried too, for the hope there was in Osidian's eyes of at least that much redemption.

Carnelian stood with Osidian in the shadow of one of the red stones of the Dance. He had slept in the pavilion a dreamless sleep and, when he had returned into the Dance, this time clothed, he had found it fresh and fragrant in the cool morning air, the corpses having been removed from their niches and everything cleaned up.

He glanced at Osidian, once more the God Emperor, his wasted face concealed beneath the mirror-black perfection of the Obsidian Mask. His huge form was shrouded by a vast cloak of samite blacker than the shadows, but worked through with murky green stones that could have been the eyes of lizards.

Movement across the red ground drew Carnelian's gaze to the two green monoliths glowing in the sun. Figures were coming through between them, heads averted, arms hooked up to shield their eyes from the light. They wore the eye-mazing robes of the ferrymen, but, without their ivory masks or crowns, they seemed almost headless. Only their necks were painted white like their startled hands. Their narrow faces were sallow, stubbled, each with a narrowed left eye, but the right a staring orb like an egg. At first he thought their expressions haughty and proud, but quickly realized they were struggling to hide the terror that their trembling hands betrayed.

When perhaps a hundred of them had entered, they opened up a path in their midst along which women came, older than the ferrymen, wearing the same black and white designs, weighed down with gleaming pectorals that Carnelian could see were made from jade rings; the same, no doubt, the Masters gave them as payment for passage on their boats.

Once these women had taken their place in front of their men, the crowd parted again to allow not more than twenty ancients to hobble forward, each walking with a staff surmounted by a crescent that, for a moment, seemed to be in imitation of the Wise, until Carnelian saw these upturned curves were not silver but of ivory, and not representing the moon, but rather their boats. However, it was another detail that, for a moment, seemed to stop his heart. Each of these old men and women had a great mane of snowy hair whose dreadlocks threaded more of the jade rings so that they resembled the Elders of the Tribe.

A muttering arose among them. Some, bowing, pulled those beside them down as they became aware of the two Masters in the shadows. Osidian and Carnelian advanced until the

Obsidian Mask emerged into the light. Behind the elders, the crowd, moaning, fell to the ground as if their legs had been scythed through. Shaking their heads, staring at the ground, the elders slid slowly to the red earth, their effort squeezing out groans. Once on their knees, they laid their staves flat, then all pushed their faces into the earth.

'Rise,' Osidian said, using a Quyan imperative.

Only the elders did, erecting their staves, pulling themselves up into standing position, heads bowed, visibly shaking.

'We have something to ask of you,' the black mask said.

'Speak, Holy One, and we shall obey thee.'

As Carnelian saw with what cruel power the Obsidian Mask regarded them, he felt a sickening unease. This was not what he wanted. He had not brought them here so as to exploit their fear and awe to force them to do his bidding.

Osidian raised his arm and took in the stone around them. 'Here you are within the very heart of the Law, but here, within its circle, as within the greater circle of the Sacred Wall, I tell you now that Law has been irrevocably broken.'

The elders half glanced up, frowning, licking their lips.

'Do you know what has come to pass at the Gates?'

One wizened woman dared to speak. 'If it pleases thee, Holy One, those of the outer world have risen again, as they did once before, and have come here seeking to destroy the Inner Land. But, as before, thou shalt not let them enter in and shalt hurl them back into the darkness.'

Carnelian stared at them, stupefied. Did they have some understanding of what even the Chosen had long forgotten? 'Who is it you think they are?'

The woman turned to him. 'Do you test us, Holy One?'

'Answer him,' boomed Osidian, his voice causing them to quiver like autumn leaves.

The elders ducked three bows in quick succession. 'The Dead, Holy One, they are the Dead.'

Carnelian's stare was deflected by an unexpected sound, Osidian laughing. This terrified the elders even more and they

873

began slumping once more to the earth, but were drawn back up by Osidian's commanding hand. 'They are as much flesh and bone and blood as you or I, though you speak in part the truth: they do come to finish what they once began, but this time we shall not vanquish them.'

A moaning leaked from the elders, which found a bleak echo in their people behind them.

'Soon they will break in and Osrakum will be laid waste, but there is still a chance for you and your people to escape this destruction, if you leave Osrakum in time.'

Again, the legs of the elders gave way beneath them and they collapsed to the ground, their staves wavering like saplings in a gale. The moaning was now broken by gasping so that Carnelian feared they might be expiring from the shock. 'Did you not hear there is a way you can escape?'

Another of the elders lifted her head. 'Why do you banish us, Holy Ones; how have we displeased you?'

Carnelian did not know what to say. He glanced round, sensing Osidian's exasperation, fearing it. The Obsidian Mask let forth a long sigh. 'Very well. Prepare yourselves.'

One of Osidian's hands rose to cup the chin of the Mask. The other slipped back past his ear, into the shadow of his cowl. Carnelian's heart leapt; Osidian was unmasking. He looked from him to the kharon. Whatever Carnelian's feelings, it was nothing to their agony, as they writhed in the earth covering themselves in its rust. Their staves toppled as the elders covered their faces with their hands.

Osidian was regarding them with gloomy eyes, his wan face like worn ivory. 'Look upon me,' he commanded.

Carnelian could not very well remain masked when the God Emperor's face was bare and so he too removed his mask.

'We dare not, Holy One,' panted one of the elders.

'Do as I say,' Osidian said, his voice softening. 'Upon my blood I swear no harm will come to you from it.'

Slowly the elders uncurled. Carnelian watched as their faces came up, eyes and mouths twitching, anticipating what?

He remembered what once he had expected: a blast of light that would make them blind.

Osidian threw back his hood. 'Look well. See, I am as you are, made of the same stuff as are all men.'

These words sliced like a shard of ice through Carnelian's heart. He saw Osidian's quiet acceptance. A shadow of shame was upon his face, but also a clean sanity; and a remnant of the nobility of the boy he had once fallen in love with.

Osidian's gaze ranged over them. 'I could have commanded you, but this thing you must choose for yourselves. If you choose to follow him, my brother will lead you out.' He looked with love upon Carnelian. 'And you can take all the children with you.'

Carnelian's heart could not reject him and he smiled.

'Children, Holy One?'

They both turned and saw the old woman regarding them wide-eyed as if she beheld them in a vision.

'The flesh-tithe children,' Carnelian said. 'We wish to return them to their mothers.'

As the elders frowned, Carnelian explained his plan to them. He watched with what difficulty the details sank into their minds. He slowed, answering their questions with care, trying to coax them past the inconceivability of it all, into some understanding. When he was done, he suggested they discuss it among themselves and they retreated into a huddle.

As they waited Carnelian gazed sidelong at Osidian, who was staring, frowning, at the mask of obsidian in his hand. His face was lined with suffering and the shadows around his eyes and at the corners of his mouth still showed the lingering effects of the maggot infestation. His eyes seemed chips of cloudy jade. The fire in them had gone out, but what if in his heart a spark still burned that could once more set him alight? Could he risk it? Compassion overcame wariness. 'If they agree, why don't you come with us?'

Osidian shook his head slowly, looked around the ring of

stones, then up to the gleaming spire of the Pillar of Heaven. Carnelian looked too, as if he hoped to see through to the Halls of Thunder. Somewhere up there were the honeycomb hollows of the Library of the Wise where they had met. Carnelian glanced at Osidian and infinite sadness welled up in him.

Osidian gazed at Carnelian. 'This is not your world, it never has been, but it is mine and I will die with it.'

Carnelian felt grief, but also deep relief; if Osidian had chosen to come he was sure to bring the poison of the Masters with him. The pain in Osidian's eyes made Carnelian aware that his face had betrayed what he was feeling. He was going to say something, but Osidian reached out to touch his lips and smiled, shaking his head. Carnelian nodded. Things were as they were, however much either of them might desire them otherwise.

A youthful brightness had come into Osidian's eyes. 'I shall remain here and we shall see if I cannot find the means to make the end of the Chosen glorious.' He smiled, letting his manufactured vision take him over. 'I will muster the Great. We still have some huimur left at the Gates. We shall open those and let the sartlar in and fight them in a great battle in the Valley of the Gate and, who knows, perhaps we shall pull it off again?' He smiled warmly at Carnelian. 'It might even help to cover your escape.'

Then quickly he leaned in and kissed Carnelian. He pulled back, melancholy already returning. 'We were magnificent, were we not, brother?'

Carnelian did not know whether he spoke of the two of them or of the Chosen as a whole, but he nodded nonetheless. There was no time for more talk: the kharon were coming back.

The ferrymen agreed to follow Carnelian and to take the children in their boats, but then, stealing glances at Osidian's face, they pleaded that they might return. Carnelian examined their faces, certain nothing in their hearts had changed. In spite of the evidence of their eyes, they still believed Osidian a god. He felt compassion for them. 'You may not want to try to save yourselves, but please consider letting your children come with me.'

The elders nodded, though he did not believe they would consider it at all. 'Meantime, Holy One, we shall go and ready our boats and be at the Quays of the Dead by morning.'

Carnelian told them that he would not be ready until the following evening and hoped to leave the morning after that. The kharon bowed and, with due decorum, left the Dance.

Carnelian turned to Osidian. 'I shall go and begin preparing the children for the journey.'

Osidian gave him a sombre nod.

'I will come back when I can.'

'Very well,' Osidian said and looked again at the hollow face in his hand.

Carnelian looked at his own mask. He turned it so that it was looking at him. The face his father had worn upon their island. It was a dead thing, no more than a discarded shell. He glanced round at the standing stones, stooped and laid the mask as a sort of offering on the red earth. As he was leaving the Dance, he looked back. Osidian was a shadow in the shape of a man and no more substantial than the sacrificial hollow in the red stone that rose behind him.

The Quenthas were waiting for him. 'Your people are here, Celestial.'

He followed the sisters through the gloom and out into the morning. Joyfully, he saw it was Fern and Tain. He was about to greet them when he saw the anger on Fern's face. 'The boats are here as you asked.'

Fern's anger sparked his own. Most of it was irritation at himself; he had forgotten he had asked them to come that morning.

Fern looked exasperated. 'What did you expect us to think when you weren't there to meet us?'

Carnelian's anger drained away. This was love speaking. They had become fearful for him and why not? How daunting it must have been for them to come up here not knowing what might confront them. He asked Fern to relate everything that had happened. As Fern described their arrival and the discussion they'd had about what to do when Carnelian had not appeared, he grew gradually calmer as his body registered that everything was all right.

'And the homunculus?' asked Carnelian.

'We left him down by the boats,' said Tain. 'He didn't want to come up here.'

'Why's he important?' asked Fern.

As Carnelian explained, they nodded.

'Well, everything's ready, Carnie,' said Tain.

'We're not going just yet.'

'Why not?' asked Fern.

'Because we need to get the flesh-tithe children ready.'

'Ready?' said Tain, frowning.

'To come with us.'

Fern stared at him. 'All of them?'

Carnelian smiled. 'All of them.' As he explained something of what he had in mind, he watched tears well in Fern's eyes.

'Surely it will be impossible . . . risky?'

'A risk worth taking?'

Tain grinned broadly. Fern slowly nodded. Carnelian watched a frown deepening on his brow. Fern was seeing all the difficulties. Carnelian needed to talk to him alone.

'Tain, can you return to the boats and bring everyone here?'

'Here? Even the Marula?'

'We need all the help we can get.'

Tain gave a nod and set off. Fern was still frowning. 'How're you expecting to get us all past the sartlar?'

'We'll manage it,' Carnelian said, trying to cover up his own gaping uncertainty.

Fern nodded, though Carnelian could see he was not convinced. 'What do you want me to do?'

'We will—' Carnelian changed his mind. He glanced at the sisters to see that they understood, then back to Fern. 'Go with the Quenthas. They'll get you some Bloodguards to help you fetch the children from the cages. I've got matters to attend to here.'

Fern gave a curt nod and left with the syblings.

Fern and the Ichorians channelled a river of children back from the cages. Though Carnelian tried not to show it, their numbers stupefied him. They huddled together, so thin he thought their hanging heads must break their necks. He fought panic. Had his need for atonement led him into terrible folly? How could they hope to get these frail creatures halfway across the world through uncountable dangers? Fern came to stand beside him and they watched the Ichorians herding them to an area of the plain just beyond the encampment. They looked at each other.

'Each one of them is going to have to carry his or her own food,' Carnelian said. Then to stop Fern voicing his objections, 'How long do you think it'll take us to get to Makar?'

Fern grimaced. 'On foot?' When Carnelian nodded, Fern shrugged. 'Fifty days.'

Carnelian's heart sank, discouraged, even though he had known the answer himself. 'The road will be entirely ours.'

'They're only children.'

They looked grimly at each other.

'They'll just have to manage,' said Carnelian.

'What about water?'

'We'll have to find enough on the way . . .'

Fern smiled wryly. 'You've got it all worked out, haven't you?'

Carnelian could not help smiling; that made them both

feel better. This was a fight they were both prepared to take on.

'One step at a time,' said Fern.

'Can you devise some packs for them?'

'Out of what?'

Carnelian pointed at the abandoned ammonite camp. Fern sized it up and gave a nod.

'Besides, it'll get them to lift their heads . . . having something to do together.'

Fern gave him another smile and went off. Carnelian walked towards the pavilion and Osidian.

The Quenthas stood before the entrance into the heart of the Dance.

'I want to see him.'

The sisters shook their heads. 'The God Emperor has commanded that none may pass.'

Carnelian frowned. 'Surely he'll see me?'

'Not even you, Celestial,' said Right-Quentha.

Carnelian's impulse was to push past. He calmed himself. He and Osidian had already said farewell. What more was there left to say? But Osidian had so long been at the centre of his life that it was wrenching, as if he were leaving behind a part of himself.

'We shall stay with him until the end,' Right-Quentha said, tears in her eyes.

'Die with him,' added her sister.

Carnelian regarded the look of determination in their faces. 'You know there is a place for you both at my side?'

Both smiled. 'This is our world.'

Carnelian knew he had to respect how they felt and accept this further loss. Tenderly, he kissed them both, then, glancing towards the entrance they guarded, he walked away.

Bonfires spangled a corner of the plain beyond Osidian's camp. Carnelian sat with the heat of one full on his face. Fern was on his right, Poppy and Krow on his left. With the darkness all around, it was possible to believe they were already in the Earthsky. Children completed the circle round the fire. Mostly they were eating, ravenously, but there was also the sound of strange languages and even a little laughter. That even a spark of the natural joy of childhood had returned to some of their eyes strengthened Carnelian in his resolve. Making the knapsacks together had loosened the grip of the many days of fear they had endured. The adults had done what they could to communicate to the thousands of children what they planned to do. People who themselves had come from the flesh tithe had struggled to recall snatches of the tongues they had not spoken since they were the same age as these children, but finding other speakers among the throng had proved hopeless. The best results had been achieved by finding those among the children who knew Vulgate and asking them to pass the news on to whoever else they could. Still, many, perhaps the majority, had no idea what was going on, but were, it seemed, just glad to have been released from the cages.

Nearby, around one of the other fires, sat Sthax and the surviving Oracles with the infested children. They would have to be carried until they recovered. Movement caused Carnelian to glance at Poppy, who had a smile on her face as she leaned into Krow, her eyes narrowed against the dazzle. Carnelian looked into the incandescent heart of the fire, hunching his cloak up so that its hood came down a little more over his face. He could feel the night behind him and, massing in the blackness, all the fear of what they would soon have to confront in the outer world. What made him believe he could lead them to freedom? He lay down, curled up, blind and naked without the certainty of his dreams.

Black water at his back, he shrinks away from the tree. Vast, it ensnares the sky in its branches. Its roots bind the earth, and his limbs; entwine his iron spear. He reels, gazing skywards, mouth agape, pouring a moan. His eyes misty blue cataracts.

On the pit rim, he grips the earth with frantic fingers for fear of falling in. The world tree's roots snake down to feed upon the Underworld. Roots awrithe with worms. O false strength! Terror that it will topple on him, tearing the sky from its circle; uprooting the earth. A small door lies open in its trunk. Strange he has not noticed it before. He and his shadow hold hands as they enter.

Alone in the tomb. A seed crushed in a withering pomegranate. A baby in a dried-up womb. He sees the huskman. No, a woman, arms outstretched, desiring to hold him. He is willing, for she is the mother of his mother he has never known. He offers her a baby. Puzzled, he knows it is himself. Glancing up, he sees her unfleshed, eyeless face and knows she is Death.

He woke, gasping, terrified, the dream more real than the night. He sat up, aware of the shapes of his loved ones sleeping around the fire. Silence beyond, pregnant with the multitude of children. He focused on the embers blushing with each shift of air. He had asked for a dream, for certainty. Now his heart was registering its bleak meaning. He quietened his fluttering mind. There was no room for doubt. Some part of him had known it all along. Still, it had been a long struggle to accept it.

Brooding, he was watching the food being distributed to the children that many were already packing away for the journey, when a slave shuffled into view. The slave's painted eyes flinched as it caught sight of his face. It fell trembling to its knees, but not before Carnelian had seen its mutilation displayed within a frame of ivory.

'Please, will the Celestial Lord deign to follow me?' said the eunuch.

Carnelian noticed two scarlet palanquins some distance away and signed agreement. As he approached, he saw more of the eunuchs in gorgeous costumes of verdant silk ribbed and studded with jewels, but his focus was on the palanquins: boxes lacquered the colour of fresh blood. He had a premonition of whom they might contain. In a whisper his guide urged him to kneel before the first of these. Frowning, Carnelian obliged. A panel sliding back released a dark perfume of mummified rose. A glimmer like a fish in the gloomy interior made him lean forward. Inside, curled up as if in a womb, an apparition smothered in scarlet damask, a mask in her lap, her pale beautiful face staring at him with two angry, eyeless pits.

'My Lady,' he said.

'Lord Carnelian,' said Ykoriana. Her head inclined a little as if her empty sockets were giving him a sidelong glance. 'What is it I have been watching from my palace?'

He saw no point in not telling her the truth. When he was done she dipped her chin. 'It is as I had thought. The world is finished then?'

'This world is.'

'And what hope have you for life beyond, Celestial?'

Carnelian considered the dark promise of his dream. 'For those I lead, certainly not the life they might have lived here, but one lived freely beneath the sky.'

Ykoriana nodded, her brow creasing, sadness in her face. Her brow smoothed. 'You know why I have come?'

'I have an idea, my Lady.'

One of her hands slid out from a sleeve and, opening like a lily, reached out to him. Carnelian took it. Though it seemed porcelain, it was soft and warm. 'Take your niece with you.'

He was touched by her plea, but felt in his gut the danger of taking with him a child from which could be grown a brood of imperial progeny.

Ykoriana pulled her hand free. 'Do this not for my sake, but for hers.'

She made a sign of summoning that caused the eunuchs around the second palanquin to kneel. One opened its panel, then all touched their foreheads to the ground as a tiny figure emerged into the light. A divine doll wrapped in a dark robe. The very plainness of her costume only served to accentuate the beauty of her face; the emerald slivers of her eyes.

'She has had no reason yet to become cruel.'

Carnelian returned his gaze to Ykoriana, who had retreated back into the gloom of her palanquin. He was remembering that the girl had witnessed the bloody rituals of the Apotheosis. Ykoriana was putting on a mask. Unhuman beauty frozen in gold. A hard brittle smile, but it was the eyes that startled Carnelian. Not slits, but solid staring ovals with irises of icy sapphire. The mask made Ykoriana appear as if she was in terror of some horror just behind Carnelian. It was an act of will for him not to turn to look for it. As the little girl tottered towards them in response to her mother's call, Carnelian leaned towards her. 'Let her see you as you really are.'

Ykoriana shook her head violently and her staring mask made her seem as if she was crazed. The little girl was there beside him, on tiny ranga, gazing up at the mask. Carnelian's heart ached as he saw the barrier this mother felt she must put up between herself and her daughter.

'This is your uncle, Carnelian. Do you remember, Ykorenthe?'

The little girl looked at him with solemn eyes and gave a nod.

'Carnie,' he said and she rewarded him with a smile.

'Carnie.'

He gazed at her, entranced, then turned to Ykoriana. 'She would be raised as a barbarian.'

'But she will be free?' said the staring mask.

Carnelian frowned. 'I make no promises. We may never even win our way to any kind of safety.'

Her hand found his again. 'Promise me you will keep her close to you.'

Carnelian looked upon the beautiful child again. 'I will if I can.'

Ykoriana let go of him. 'That is enough. The Gods love you.' Her hand found the child's face, caressing her chin, then sliding up her cheek. 'My delight,' she murmured.

Carnelian, watching this, was touched and considered once again urging her to unmask, so that at least she could kiss her daughter one last time, but the Dowager Empress was already receding back into her palanquin. 'I shall pray for you both.' With that, she slid the panel back. Soon it rose into the air, turned, then began the journey back towards the Forbidden Door.

Carnelian felt a tiny hand slipping around one of his fingers. He sensed the little girl's anxiety and, scooping her up, rose and turned to carry her back to the camp and the other children.

Standing in the entrance to the Plain of Thrones, Carnelian turned to look back. Beyond the river of children, the shadow of the western cliff was beginning to creep towards Osidian's camp. Above the tomb colossi were the galleries of the Halls of Rebirth where, at that very moment, Ykoriana might be standing having the scene described to her. Behind her the incomparable marvel of the chambers honeycombing the rock and opening out into the underworld of the Labyrinth. Rearing above its roof, the Pillar of Heaven, its flank gilded by the sinking sun. He felt a deep melancholy at all that was to be lost, even though those wonders had fed on misery and injustice and lies. He turned away to look down the steps cascading all the way to the turquoise waters along whose new muddy shore an armada of bone boats was pulled up like so many seeds. He smiled at Poppy who was holding Ykorenthe's hand. It gladdened his heart that Poppy seemed to like her; that she was prepared to see Ykorenthe as a child first, a Mistress second. He caught Fern watching him. Carnelian put his arm about his shoulders and grinned. 'Let's go home.'

BONE BOATS

And through this second birth
He created himself.

(from the myth 'The Tale of the Three Gods')

Carnelian turned side-on to the breeze. A band of blackness separating the glory of the heavens from its murky reflection in the Skymere was relieved only by a few pricks of light. He focused on one, telling himself it must be coming from a chamber in which his father and Ebeny were together and he sent them a benediction. Then he pulled his cloak about him, suddenly chilled by the thin light of the stars.

Carrying Ykorenthe, Carnelian led a group of children along the boardwalks the kharon had laid across the mud to their boats. He was seeing his way by means of the indigo of the dawning sky. He turned to make sure the children were keeping up. They were only the tip of one of many teeming fingers splaying out from the quay. Judging they would soon catch up with him, he set off again towards the pale hulks of the bone boats that seemed the remains of monsters washed up on the shore.

Mud up to his knees, water slapping at his waist, Carnelian handed Ykorenthe up to a man creasing a chameleon tattoo into a grimace. Carnelian had to bark at him to take a firmer hold of her, nervous as the guardsman was to touch a Mistress. An urchin was perched on the end of the nearest board, squinting with fear at the water. Carnelian waded over to him with lolloping lunges, trying to reassure the boy with a smile, cursing as one foot plunged deeper than the other, lurched free, scooped the child up, grabbed his arm to tighten his hold on his pack, waddled back with him, handed him up. He paused, panting, looking along the shore where other boats were being held bow-on to the strand. Across the mud foreshore, a deluge of children was flowing towards them whom Suth people and Marula were steadily lifting up to the boats. He frowned; this was going to take much longer than he had hoped. When he went back for the next child, he had to remember to smile.

Standing with his arm around the trunk of the prow, Carnelian looked back along the deck dense with little heads, adults rising as sparse fences at the edges. He craned over the side. The water was lapping just below the oarlocks. They were riding low, but he was sure the steersman would have said something if he thought it unsafe. He looked back towards the kharon, with his crown, standing like a startled puppet against the sternpost. Carnelian raised his arm. A moment later he heard the port oars begin to thresh the lake and, ponderously, the prow swung away from the strand.

Slowly they ran parallel to the shore. As other boats turned into open water, more slid in to take their place. He had counted more than a hundred in all, perhaps a third of which were already laden with children. Nevertheless, their throng still stretched unbroken up into the Plain of Thrones. The kharon had promised him they would manage to load them all. Carnelian had made sure Keal understood that his was to be the last boat. Still, he fretted, reluctant to set off, anxious not to leave even a single child behind. His hesitation was increasing the danger of boats fouling each other. Already, there were too many of them near the shore and these heavy and sluggish. A collision was the more immediate peril and so he gave his steersman the prearranged signal. The oars began digging into the water. They picked up speed, heading east. Leaning over the side, he saw Fern waving as his boat curved its course to follow. Several more were carving the lake to enter their wake.

As they came round the green flank of the Plain of Thrones, a view of Osrakum opened up that Carnelian had never seen before. The eastern face of the Sacred Wall rose sheer, carved with coombs wider than those he was familiar with, but all consumed by the shadow that still spilled out towards them across the water. Those dark pits showed no hint of being inhabited. In truth nowhere was there a sign this world had ever been touched by human hand. A melancholy settled over him, the threshing oars seeming to become his heartbeat as they carried them all through this empty landscape. What a strange, silent, wild place this would become once men ceased to live here.

His mood of contemplation was broken by the vast barrow mound of the Labyrinth rising from the Isle. His thoughts were haunted by the dark womb that belly concealed, by imagining its fate. The column sepulchres would fall one by one like forest giants. Light and rain would pour in, enough to nurture seedlings to uncurl and grow. Slowly the stone roof would crumble and fall to be replaced by a swaying, breathing green canopy.

He spotted some tiny figures winding down to the Ydenrim shore. No doubt kharon come to watch their boats pass. His gaze returned to the vast, black mass of the Pillar of Heaven. It appeared much wider from this side and more immense than he had seen it since Osidian and he were together in the Forbidden Garden. His gaze lingered on the cleft that seemed to threaten to divide the Pillar in two from its brow to where its feet were lost in the tiny forest of thorn trees. The ladder was there in that cleft, that they had used to visit the Yden. Carnelian closed his eyes and breathed in the earthy perfume drifting towards him across the water. A flashing vision played before him of that bright, innocent time. He opened his eyes and felt the mountain was scowling at him. He relived that second, fateful descent to capture, and expulsion from what they had both then thought paradise.

They gradually passed along the Ydenrim whose gleaming edge held back the green mirrors of the lagoons. Here, the southern sweep of the Sacred Wall was inset with coombs blazing with snowy palaces and the verdant jewels of gardens. Then Carnelian saw the scythe of the lake narrowing off towards the gape of the Valley of the Gate that squeezed up to the Canyon throat. He wished then that they could have left Osrakum along the Canyon floor, but his flood had made that impossible. Squinting, he tried to make out the row of sluices he had broken. From a distance, his plan had seemed reasonable, but the closer they came to its reality, the more it seemed madness.

The nearer they drew to the sluice slots in the cliff edge of the Valley of the Gate floor, the thicker became the slurry of debris floating on the water. Carnelian was at least relieved to see no evidence of flow. As he had hoped, the Skymere had found a level with the outer world.

He watched the prow cleave the thickening mat. Broken branches scratched along the sides of the boat. All kinds of rubbish bobbed past in a sort of procession that sedated him. A thump against the hull shocked him alert. A raft of bodies, bloated, their heads punching the hull, mostly dark-skinned servants bearing wounds so deep it was almost as if attempts had been made to butcher them for meat. A shock of paleness in that dark expanse. The corpse of a Master; two more. Carnelian watched one slumping as its shoulder dragged along the hull. Water welling over a ruined face into which the heraldic cypher of a House had been cut with a knife.

The boat edged towards the sluice, which appeared to be least choked with debris.

'There's room enough?' Carnelian asked the kharon who had come to stand beside him.

The man nodded, 'If we ship oars, Seraph.'

Carnelian felt the knot in his stomach ease a little. He looked up. In the casements on either side of the slot, counterweights were hanging almost at the bollards. A wooden arch spanned each end of the slot. The cables he had had cut free from them now wallowed beneath the surface like water snakes. Deeper was the murky upper edge of the fallen sluice gate. It was seeing this that caused the kharon to turn to shout something back to the steersman. The boat slowed almost to a halt, as the oars backwatered. The kharon fed a pole down into the water until it touched the sluice gate. Then he lifted it out, dripping, strung with weed, until he had inverted it, so that the steersman could gauge the clearance depth. Carnelian watched the steersman and had a long time to wait for his reluctant nod. Carefully sculling, the banks of oars aligned the boat towards the gap. The oarheads raised, dipped and Carnelian felt their push against the water. The boat slid forward. With a rush and clatter the oars retracted into the hull just in time to avoid the leading ones being snapped off. For a moment he thought they were going straight through, then he was thrown forward as her keel bit into the sluice. A judder as slowly she scraped forward over it. Kharon at the bows slapped their hands out against the rock and pushed against it to keep her moving. Carnelian moved to help them. His hand against the chill of the basalt, shoving, recalled to his memory the entry of the baran into the Tower in the Sea. The children in the bows also tried to help with their tiny hands. The keel struck the second sluice gate and they really had to struggle against the rock on either side to keep the boat juddering forward. Slowly, she edged out. Then, suddenly, everyone was thrown back as she slid free.

As they turned and began moving down the spillway, another bone boat was emerging from a sluice. Carnelian had to believe they would all be able to get through. Ahead, the mouth of the Cloaca was coming slowly into view. Dark it was and, as they curved in towards it, a waft of its fetid breath broke over them and he felt his resolve cowering, for he knew what lay in wait for them.

A movement made him turn to see the kharon next to him unmasking. The man's single eye peered into the shadowy ravine. As Carnelian watched him lick his sallow lips, he remembered what it was like to behold something heard of, but never before seen. Another stinking waft made the kharon grimace, then smooth his face when he became aware Carnelian's eyes were on him.

'This will bring us out,' Carnelian said and almost began explaining the stench lest the man think it characteristic of the outer world, but what was the point? They would all be witnessing the cause soon enough. He gazed back over the boat and saw how the taller children were straining to see where they were going. Each waft from the Cloaca creased their little faces with fear. He considered making a speech to try to reassure them, but how many would understand his Vulgate? Besides, he could only guess what lay ahead. He looked up at the widening grandeur of the Sacred Wall. This world was going to die: only outside was survival possible. He gave the steersman a signal. The man's bony crown tilted forward in acknowledgement, then the oars began rising, falling and, slowly, as if the boat herself was reluctant, they slid towards the Cloaca's stinking mouth.

*   *   *

It seemed a long time they had been creeping along. A breeze was streaming the fetor past them. The steersman threaded the boat along the channel so narrow that often an oarblade would graze the rock wall. Carnelian could feel the inward pressure of the black rock that rose sheer and unscalable.

Then he sensed the shadow falling upon the upper northern wall. His hackles rose as he felt the presence of some vast malevolence looming over them, eclipsing what little blue there had been above them. His eyes resolved battlements. It was only the Black Gate. The Death Gate, a voice within him said in Vulgate. And, though he now knew it was Osrakum that was the Land of the Dead, it seemed to him he was in a funerary barge carrying them all to damnation.

The fetor swelled into a miasma moist with decay. Approaching the fork in the ravine, they were too close to be able to see the Blood Gate that he knew was rearing its bulk somewhere above them. He glanced round at the cowering children. Mucus clung to their upper lips; vomit from their chins. Beyond them, the steersman seemed carved from the stern post. Carnelian raised his arm, amazed that the foul air should provide so little resistance, and indicated the left fork.

The sound the oars were making dulled as the water became as thick as treacle. They were coming to where the corpse dam had been. Still piled against the walls was a mouldering scree composed of filthy bones. Hissing, a torrent of flies broke over them. Carnelian swallowed a cry as he, the kharon and the boat all became encased in the itching, buzzing plague. Behind him the screaming of the children turned to choking. Then he was thrown forward as the hull struck something. He only just managed to catch the bow to stop himself falling into that soup of putrefaction. Flailing at the flies he glimpsed the mound of matter upon which they had run aground.

* * *

With poles they delved into the filthy stuff beneath the prow. In an agony of disgust, convulsed by dry heaving, they painfully gouged a channel. Squinting back through the swirling plague, feeling the writhing nodules of the flies with each blink, sneezing them out of his nostrils, Carnelian watched the kharon along the bow shove their poles into the soft weeping mounds on either side, loosening chunks that plunged into the pools, causing the splashed to whimper.

They slid free into the shadow of one of the bridges that spanned the Cloaca. Carnelian sank his head in despair as he saw, ahead, a bronze grille barring their way. On either side angled the slots with the counterweights. They edged the boat as close as they could, then Carnelian scrambled over with a couple of Marula. More clambered into the slot on the other side. After a struggle, the counterweights began to slide down their ramps, even as the grille rose, shedding lumps, streaming fluid.

The bone boat passed under the toothed edge of the grille. The channel ahead was clear. The kharon rowed them so fast they snapped some oars on the ravine wall. Everyone feeling with each push of the oars they were edging away from the horror. Soon they were emerging from the bridge shadow. The fly plague thinned and, as they reached the joining of the channels, they all gazed up the edge of the Prow, drinking in the clear air, the blue beauty of the sky, crying tracks down their gory faces.

They waited to see that the next boat was following, then continued down the channel. By the time they reached the first turn in the Canyon, the Cloaca walls were noticeably less lofty; the stream of the sky was widening to a river. By the second turn they had begun to feel they had escaped death, that they were fully alive beneath the filth whose stench came off their bodies and the boat, so that they hardly noticed the miasma fading in the breeze. Following the turn they saw the Green Gate rising to bar their way. Carnelian tensed as he realized how much the water level in the Cloaca had risen. What if the boats were unable to pass under the fortress?

The bone boat slowed as the first structures of the Green Gate loomed up before them. The Cloaca continued under the masonry along a barrel-vaulted tunnel. It was obvious there was not enough clearance for the prow and stern posts. Carnelian saw that here the walls of the Cloaca were not much more than twice his height. The stone was smooth, but they might be able to rig up some kind of ladder, or netting, to scale it. Though he could not see out, he was sure they would be able to reach the leftway that ran all the way from here to the Wheel, round it and then alongside the south road. The whole route must lie above the flood level, at least until it reached the section Molochite had had demolished. Could the flood have reached that far? That first doubt caused his vision to unravel. There were so many places where the leftway might have collapsed or been torn down. All it would take would be for one of the bridges that spanned the gates of the Wheel to be broken and they would be stranded without any means to go further. He looked again at the sloping Cloaca wall: even if he took the risk of trusting to the leftway, it was hard to imagine how they could get the thousands of children up that. He shook his head and instead examined the elaborate mosaic of limb bones from which the prow post was shaped. His hand reached out to touch it. They needed these boats. He peered down the tunnel. It seemed clear all the way through to the oozing daylight beyond. He picked his way back along the deck. What was going to have to be done would be best put to the steersman.

Kharon were hacking into the bones of their forebears. As Carnelian stood in the stern watching the prow post splinter under the Ichorian blades they had borrowed from the Marula, he remembered the columns of his home being felled at the insistence of Aurum and the other Lords. He was glad to be distracted by the approach of another boat, Fern in the prow, who raised a gore-encrusted arm in salutation. Carnelian returned the greeting, then gestured him closer so they could talk.

The splintered, butchered stump of the prow post still stood higher than Carnelian, but, as they moved into the tunnel, it was a good forearm's length short of the vault. He leaned forward to help spy out their way. The confined space muted the thresh of the oars. He noticed all manner of holes in the vaulting that led up into the fortress. So it was he could not miss the serrated edge of a portcullis pulled up into the roof just before the tunnel end. Of course there had to be something to bar entrance, otherwise the Cloaca would have perforated the defences of the Green Gate. What a relief that it was raised. It would have been a major undertaking to find the mechanism that opened it. Unease soaked into him as he questioned who had opened it.

Just then the boat carried him out of the tunnel and he forgot everything else, mesmerized. Before them the Cloaca flowed on, seeming to rise until, in the near distance, it over-flowed to fill the Canyon with a lake that shimmered all the way to where the Wheel colossi stood gazing out upon a world of blinding, dazzling light.

When the boat reached a point in the Cloaca where its walls were level with the bows, they began helping the children to disembark onto a portion of the dry Canyon floor still above the flood. Fern's boat arrived before they were finished. Carnelian confirmed with him the details of the plan they had agreed earlier. Leaving him to muster the flotilla as it appeared from under the Green Gate, Carnelian set off down the Cloaca, his boat lighter and swifter.

* * *

Reaching open water, the boat leapt forward as if in delight at winning her freedom from the Cloaca. Carnelian too felt elation as they sped down the flooded Canyon. They slowed as they passed the ankles of the colossi. Kharon came forward to stare in wonder at a world they knew only from stories. Before them the drowned Wheel seemed shimmering glass. Carnelian could just make out the ring of punishment poles standing at its centre; the backs of the six bridges rising like huimur from the water. He gazed round the outermost edge of the lake. The five pairs of gatehouses still seemed intact, but the rim of tenements and towers that had once made the Wheel a shallow bowl seemed rotten, crumbled, broken. Beyond he thought he could make out something that might have been the ruins of the city; further still, nothing but an ominous haze that could have been the very edge of existence.

They rowed towards the Wheel, staying above the Cloaca channel in case the water covering the Canyon floor was too shallow. When they reached the moat that defined the edge of the Wheel, they decided to follow it sunwise, reluctant to move out over the submerged pavement for fear of running aground. One of the bridges that linked the Canyon to the Wheel they drifted over without mishap. Carnelian gazed at the lake, sad at how still the place was that once had been such a ferment of humanity. Soon they were approaching the southern lip of the Canyon where twin gatehouses rose from the water embossed with quincunxes. As they passed over the bridge these towers guarded, there rose on their right the vast, once dazzling brass gates, tarnished, as if sucking the blue-green up from the water. On their left the beginning of the Great East Road had become a stagnant canal clotted with mounds and debris; flanked by mouldering half-collapsed tenements like a long jawful of rotting teeth. The kharon stared, their wonder turning to horror. Carnelian shared their relief when this view was hidden by the rim wall. This too was decaying. The buildings that had once formed its smooth jigsaw were coming apart. Ramparts buttressed with brick, though bulging, still stood; but in many places reinforcing beams, charred, shattered or swollen, had torn wounds in the mudbrick walls. Leprous plaques of shattered plaster covered the façades that looked ready to shed them dangerously onto the boat slipping past below. Sewer mouths had ruptured, dribbling filth to corrode cavities into the cliff. The whole curving wall seemed a dance of giants, rotting as they staggered and threatening to collapse. The further the boat went the more nervous everyone became of the ruinous overhangs. Some looked so precarious that the waves their oars sent lapping at the foundations might bring the whole lot down on them.

At last they steered away, between a pair of crooked cranes, out over the pavement of the Wheel, eyes half closed, anticipating a grinding of the keel even as they tried to spy out a clear channel. Carnelian became aware that they were following the dark serpent of the Dragonway, sinuous beneath the water, but at that moment the steersman turned their prow back towards the rim. They were moving round the back of the second pair of gatehouses to avoid the brass posts where once guards had demanded tolls. Soon these were swept from view by the bulk of the Gate of the Sun. They slowed behind it, floating above its bridge, as they turned towards the Great South Road: another gloomy canal hemmed in by ruined, leaning walls. Its path of water in some places seemed merely a linked string of wounds gouged through the corpse of the city.

Carnelian's heart sank into his stomach. How could they find a way through that? As he looked round, past the gatehouses, the Wheel seemed seductively open and free. Perhaps the next road would provide a clearer route to the Gatemarsh; but shadows were lengthening. If he did not find a way now, they would have to try again the next day. Could the children spend a whole night crammed on the boats? Perhaps they could all disembark in the Canyon. He imagined how long it would take; the chaos. His plan had been to disembark them on the road south before nightfall. That was still the best plan. Reluctantly, he gave the steersman the command to take them into the rotting city.

They poled the boat from one pool to the next, having to coax her keel through the narrow channels that linked them. The flooded road was shoaled by the mudbrick walls that had collapsed into it, then softened into shapeless mounds. In places they had to lower themselves over her bows and struggle to find a footing in the slime as they pushed and dragged her hull through the sucking mud.

Once, Carnelian wandered away into what had once been a courtyard. The place stank of mildew and sodden plaster. The walls defining the chambers that opened into the court were now vague, crumbling boundaries. Here and there a patch of stucco still showed a snatch of ochre, of blue, of yellow that spoke of a room in which people had lived. Mostly everything was blotchy with mould or succumbing to a creeping dingy green scum. The angled, swollen, charred stumps of immense beams seemed bones ruptured for their marrow. Peering round at the blackened shells, he saw how conflagration had brought floors and walls down. The tumbled ruins seemed the remains of half-burnt, half-eaten corpses.

Slowly they dragged the bone boat along the road. Most of the alleyways branching off on either side were choked with fallen debris. Those that gleamed with water were too narrow for the boat. Carnelian grew morose, feeling the rot of the place invading him. All around them, torn and exposed, were homes where once families had eaten their meals, loved, slept. Where humble treasures had cheered busy lives. What fire had not consumed was sodden and as mouldy as old bread. The spaces seemed haunted by voices and laughter and the roar of the multitude that had once poured down this thoroughfare. The relentless decay drew even these imagined vestiges out of him until nothing was left but ruin and a silence that pressed in on them. For they were clearly the only living things in that dead city. He could not deny the growing, uneasy realization that they had not seen the slightest scrap of any of the millions that had once inhabited this termite mound, nor yet of the sartlar hordes. Away from the gory boat, there was not even the slightest odour of a corpse.

Then, just as they came within sight of the burnt stump of a watch-tower, brightness ahead showed where there must be a wide gap in the buildings. As their ragged prow slipped into the light they saw, to the right, a flight of submerged steps that had once led down to the lake. The water above them formed a channel easily wide and deep enough to accommodate the boat. They scrambled back onto her deck and her oars propelled her between collapsed towers out into open water turned to liquid gold by the late afternoon sun. Across the water they saw the gilded tumbled tenements that flanked another of the raised roads running off towards the west. The flood stretched as far as the horizon. If it had not been so still, Carnelian might have imagined they had reached the sea.

They rowed west for a while so that they could look down the ruin-clustered flank of the Great South Road. At last Carnelian called out for them to halt. As the oars backwatered, he peered south. He nodded, certain that the tiny spike he could see there must be what was left of watch-tower sun-three. He pointed and asked the nearest kharon. The man confirmed that there was a thread running from that tower away to the southern horizon. There the road surface rose from the flood. Carnelian gave the order to turn about. They must return to the Canyon as fast as they could if they were to have any hope of guiding the flotilla back and so reach that road before night fell.

When Carnelian's boat slid out from behind the gatehouses of the southern gate, he saw the rest of the flotilla coming towards him out from the Canyon mouth. A figure standing in the prow of the lead boat waved and he waved back, certain it was Fern. When close enough, Fern called out that all the boats had made it through unscathed and that they had picked up the children Carnelian had disembarked. Carnelian passed this news to his steersman and, soon, his boat was turning back towards the ruined city.

The sun was low, the flooded lake copper when Carnelian's boat cut into it again. Down the flank of the long island they rowed, Carnelian turning to watch with satisfaction as one boat after another emerged into open water. When they reached the end of the island, he saw the road emerge, running south across the flood, but so little raised above its surface that the wake of the boat washed right over the road to lap against the leftway wall.

By the time they were passing the stump of watch-tower sun-three, the road had risen above the water by perhaps half Carnelian's height. He urged the steersman on until the road was standing higher than the bows. At his signal the boat began to slow, angling slightly towards the road. The port oars were shipped as they closed. Her hull struck the stone, scraping along it as he and the kharon reached up to the lip of the road to try to bring her more gently against it. Scrambling up, Carnelian was stunned for a moment by the vast expanse of limestone whose paleness showed here and there through the filth. As the kharon in the boat cast ropes up, Carnelian walked over to the ditch that ran between the road and the leftway wall. There he found a basket that he loaded with rubbish and dollops of mud. He handed this to a kharon who appeared at his shoulder. He himself salvaged a wheel with a broken hub and rolled it back towards the boat. With these and other salvage they made her fast.

As other boats drew up along the improvised quay, more were approaching from the north. He frowned. It would be dark before they got them all anchored. He gazed back towards the watch-tower, tiny in the distance. He wondered if any-thing survived there with which they could make some light. He doubted it. The realization came to him that, now he had safely brought the children out from Osrakum, he must follow his guiding dreams to their bleak conclusion. He looked to-wards the sun. Its gory gaze from the horizon made the world seem drowned in blood.

In the afterglow he strolled north along the road, watching the shadow boats disgorge a flood of chattering children. There were cries of frustration, shouting, but also laughter as everyone managed as best they could in the near darkness. He halted and peered down the road. It was impossible to see if all the boats were there. Soon it would be impossible to see anything. Then it would be time for him to leave.

He lay on his back looking up at the stars. Their frost seemed to be chilling the air. He wrapped his cloak more tightly round him and snuggled closer to Fern. In the dark they had all fumbled some morsels out from their packs. Water had been drawn from the flood lake and bowls of it passed from hand to hand so that everyone got a sip. It had been his decision to set no guards. He had argued that there was little they could do if they were attacked, but he had other reasons. Then, finding what comfort they could, they had huddled together and lain down to sleep. He had even dozed a bit himself. He had wanted to make sure everyone was asleep before he left.

Awake now, he found doubt was gnawing at his certainty. In this darkness, at the edge of a frightened multitude, it was a lot harder to believe in the truth of dreams. Reality seemed as cold and solid as the stone beneath his back. Here they were with no possibility of defending themselves, exposed to who knew what horrors.

Fern's warm body called to him, but Carnelian feared to touch him lest he should wake him. He knew he must go before his courage failed. He listened. At first all he could hear was the lapping of the waves; the small sounds rising from the sleeping children. Then he managed to focus in on Fern's breathing. Carefully, he rolled away, all the time listening to that breathing. Hearing no change in its rhythm, he pushed himself up onto his knees, then stood. Nothing indicated Fern or anyone else had noticed. He gazed at the black road ahead of him. He knew there was no one there. He had made sure of that. One step. Two. Another and another and another. He imagined it would get easier, but it did not. He was leaving behind all that was left of what he loved. His heart felt as if the night was drawing the life from it. He concentrated on feeling the edges of the paving stones with his feet.

Suddenly a touch on his shoulder made him spin round. A shadow man was there.

'Where're you going?' it whispered in Ochre. It was Fern.

'To make water.'

'Why not just go to the edge of the road?'

Carnelian thought of making up a better lie. Then he felt an overwhelming need to confess to Fern and it all poured out in an urgent whisper: his dream, its promise of salvation in return for his sacrifice.

'I knew you were up to something.'

'Then you'll let me go?'

'Yes, but I'm coming with you.'

Panic tightened Carnelian's chest. All kinds of objections came to him, but all he said was: 'You can't.'

'What if you've not understood the dream properly?' hissed Fern.

'What do you mean?'

'Are you so sure the shadow is Osidian? Couldn't it be me?'

Carnelian wanted to deny this, but the dark vision of his dream held him back. Or, desperate to have Fern with him, was he just fooling himself?

'Do you think I feel less for these children than you do?' Fern said.

Carnelian thought his decision to go on alone weakening. Fern reached out for him. They clung to each other.

Carnelian felt Fern mouth the words against his neck: 'I'm not going to let you die alone.' He felt suddenly safe and, almost, joyous.

Black road beneath their feet. To their right, an infinite field of stars into which Carnelian kept kicking things to ripple the mirror and thus destroy the vertiginous illusion that kept making him lean towards the water. They had tried walking nearer the centre of the road, but away from the lake it grew so dark they stumbled all the time. In that direction rose the impenetrable black band of the leftway and its evil-smelling ditch. Apart from their scuffling footfalls and the curses as they stubbed their toes against the edges of paving stones, the only sound was the lapping of the water.

Where the watch-tower should have been was nothing but stars. Tumbled into the ditch amongst a mound of rubble that blocked the lower door they could just make out the spars that had held up the heliograph platform. Carnelian tried to see if they could at least scale the mound to get up onto the leftway, but it did not reach even halfway.

Fern called to him, softly, as if the night might be listening. He went to stand beside him, gazing south. 'Look there.'

Carnelian saw Fern's arm against the water starfield, pointing. 'What—' he began, then saw it himself. A narrow band of blackness between the stars in the lake and those in the sky. Their first glimpse of land beyond the flood.

Suddenly, the leftway came to a ragged end and they saw, spreading out before them, the flood mirroring the stars of heaven. From the water rose a lonely watch-tower. It seemed to Carnelian they had been walking lost, without any certain destination, neither uttering a sound, for fear words might dent their resolve, but he knew in his bones that that watch-tower was what they sought.

'Let's climb it,' he said and Fern agreed, adding: 'The edge of the flood must be close to where the Iron House lies ruined.'

Uneasy at that thought, they set off towards the shadow tower.

Posts rose up on either side of the road that they realized must be the remains of the massive outer gates of Molochite's camp. Carnelian hesitated. The posts seemed guardians; like the colossi that guarded the entrance into Osrakum. He knew that he and Fern stood upon an earthbridge; on either side the military ditch had become a moat.

'What's the matter?' Fern asked.

Carnelian sensed that, once they crossed the drowned ditch, there would be no turning back.

'Come on, it's not far away,' Fern said in an angry tone Carnelian sensed was really fear.

They walked along the road that cleaved the mirror of the flooded camp where once Molochite had marshalled the might of the Masters. With each step the tower grew larger until they could see its arms spread wide against the stars. Carnelian felt the visceral shock even as Fern whispered: 'It's like a tree.'

Chilled to the bone, Carnelian said nothing, but just kept walking. They came to the stumps of the gates that had once opened into the Encampment of the Chosen and passed through, aware they were entering another circle. A ring within a ring, like the Stone Dance of the Chameleon, except that this circle was cut directly into the body of the earth. And then Carnelian saw that it was as if they were penetrating to the heart of some infernal mockery of the Koppie, except that in place of its mother trees there stood a lone, gigantic black tree. Like a baobab, he thought, with deepening foreboding. The impression grew stronger as they came closer and it spread its branches above them. Then they were standing before the doorway at its foot and Carnelian shuddered, for its reflection sent roots down into the Underworld and he knew in his marrow that this was the fulfilment of his dreams.

'Now what?' Fern whispered.

Carnelian summoned up his will. 'We climb.'

Together they approached the doorway and offered themselves up to be swallowed by its absolute darkness. Dank the air, thick with an animal stench. Carnelian sensed the fingers seeking his and clasped Fern's hand. Slowly, he felt his way along the clammy wall until it brought them to the first ramp. Their feet found the ridges in the slope and they began climbing. They followed the wall round to the next ramp; breathing stinking air; starting each time the body of the tower creaked above them. Both wanted to go down, to flee into the starry night, but they had accepted it was their fate to climb higher. Ridge after ridge after ridge. Another turn. Until, at last, they shuffled out onto a smooth floor, their free hands fingering the blackness, a cool, sweet breeze in their faces. They followed it, hoping to reach the exposed section of leftway remaining outside. Then their grip clenched as they heard movement on the ramps below. They turned, aware of the animal odour swelling. Padding footfalls. They drew closer, wanting to face the brutes together.

MOTHER DEATH

The heaviest burdens are carried in the heart.
(Plainsman proverb)

'We're unarmed,' Carnelian said into the darkness that he sensed was filling with bodies. 'We've come to offer ourselves up to you, willingly.' He had not managed to keep his voice steady. The scuffling grew louder. He could smell their sweat, their filthiness, the foulness of their breath that seemed a contagion he wanted to shrink from. He stood his ground, however, drawing what reassurance there was in feeling Fern against him, but he did not fool himself. He was afraid. If this was the fulfilment of his dream, it was not how he had imagined it. What had he done? How could he have brought them to such a squalid end?

The scuffling ceased. The smell of fear was sharp in his nostrils. At first he thought it was rising from his own body, or from Fern's, but then he realized it laced the stench wafting towards them. This sharpened the panic to an insistent throb in his temples. Frightened, the sartlar could be as dangerous as raveners.

Sudden light stabbed his eyes. He threw his arm up to shield them. Gasps were followed by the sound of the creatures in the darkness recoiling. Carnelian lowered his arm slowly, squinting. He could make them out, a shapeless mass crowding the chamber; all hair and rags. A single crooked, bony arm holding aloft the light. He glanced round at Fern. Each saw the other's fear. The skin around Fern's eyes creased. Carnelian read this as a sign of acceptance. It calmed his heart a little. Disengaging from him, he turned back to the sartlar and raised his arms, pressing the wrists together in a sign of submission. 'We'll not fight you.'

Heads lowered, the sartlar shuffled closer, some edging along the walls to surround them. Carnelian could not help searching through their manes for their eyes, seeking the light of any humanity that might have descended to them from their Quyan forebears, wanting to find that part of them that was like him; but they ducked as his gaze fell on them, wincing as if he were hurting them.

Suddenly, with a shriek, one of them lunged towards him, swinging at him. Carnelian raised his arm, but not fast enough. Something hard crashed into his temple. Next thing he was on his knees, groaning. Fern's anguished cry made Carnelian try to focus. He became aware of them pounding Fern with their clubs. He gaped at him falling to the ground bleeding, certain he must be dead. A groan from Fern caused Carnelian's paralysis of grief to melt into tears. He fought down rage and an urge to violence and allowed his arms to be wrenched behind him. He bore the cruel binding as if his forearms had been someone else's. He watched them trussing up Fern. What hope was left in Carnelian died as he saw them tie a rope around Fern's neck, so that he hardly cared when one was put around his own.

Sartlar shoved and yanked them down the ramps like sacks of roots. It was easier once they tumbled out onto the road. Then they were marching, stumbling at each tug of the ropes around their necks, crashing to their knees to be jerked up again. Remotely, Carnelian remembered his last slavery upon this same road. This time there could be no Fern riding to the rescue.

Lurching along, Carnelian fell against one of the sartlar, who threw him off. They had come to a halt. The sartlar growled words to each other he could not make out. Though he could just see their shapes around him, it was their stench that gave them a more solid presence. There was a sound of footfalls running off along the faint road. Trying to make out the runner, he found instead a black mass cut out from the starry sky. At first he could not imagine what it might be, then he knew. Half off the road, what else could it be but the Iron House?

A slackening of the rope at his neck distracted him. He sensed the sartlar around him relaxing and took the opportunity to shuffle towards where he guessed Fern to be. His shoulder touched something that shuddered, but then pressed back against him. As their point of contact warmed, Carnelian felt a little safer. His gaze returned to the malevolent mass of the Iron House. Was that odour of blood oozing from its iron skin? He gave a shudder and looked away, soothing his fear with the view into the water below the road, with its dusting of stars. He became aware its southern margin was dull. Squinting, he could see nothing but darkness in that direction. A susurration came across the water as if they were near the sea. He shivered, turned back to the brooding blackness of the Iron House. That the flood should have reached here and no further seemed an evil omen. Then he remembered something and turned to search for the edge of the road near him. Sure enough, a curve of shadow rose there, so close that, had his arm been free, he imagined he could reach out and touch it. It was the upper edge of Molochite's fallen standard leaning against the road. It had given them shelter the first time they had made love. He chose to see in this a more hopeful omen.

'Follow,' said a voice in the darkness. Carnelian had heard the footfalls approaching. The rope jerking at his throat forced a groan. Through the rage surging into his head he was aware Fern behind him was crying out. There was a struggle.

'Just you,' said the sartlar.

Carnelian's anger froze to fear. He would never see Fern again! It was no good. They had both chosen this. He let go of hope and followed the sartlar into the darkness.

A torch flared. Its light revealed a shallow slope of sharp-edged undulations, one side of which was wedged into the road. He recognized the hinged, partially lowered flight of steps that gave entry into the Iron House. Its leaning wall of scales faded up into the night. Becoming aware of its bulk haloed by stars, for a moment he was certain it was toppling towards him. Someone was behind him. The bindings on his arms fell loose. He brought his arms forward, rubbing at his wrists as he felt the prickle of blood returning to his fingers. He was shoved forward. A sartlar holding aloft a torch was negotiating the steps. The man seemed to be leaning so much to one side it looked as if he must fall. Carnelian followed, slipping his feet into the angle of the steps.

The torchlight defined the leaning rectangle of the great doorway. The darkness of the Iron House swallowed much of the light so that Carnelian stumbled several times reaching the sloping floor within the doorway. The tang of old conflagration made him remember what had happened here. To his right the sartlar was climbing a flight of steps that leaned towards him precipitously. Carnelian followed, edging towards the wall so that his feet would not be in the sartlar's shadow.

Concentrating on not slipping from the angled steps, he was not immediately aware of the other odour. Dry, dusty with a sickly meaty tang. Slowly he came up into cavernous space that seemed partially open to the sky. The floor sloped up towards a wall, but the light was moving the other way. Carnelian turned and looked down the slope of the throne-hall and stared. The place was crowded. On either side of the raised central walkway, dark figures packed together leaned with the slope of the chamber.

It was their stillness that convinced him these were not living men. In the wavering light of the torch that was moving steadily away from him, he saw what seemed expressions shifting as the shadows ran across the hollows of their faces. Sunken cheeks, gnarled dark skin. At first he thought they must be barbarians of some kind, but then he realized how, even standing in the pits on either side of the walkway, they dwarfed the sartlar shambling through their midst. Chosen, then, in some way mummified. He became aware that those he could see had empty pits for eyes. Scared, he hurried down the slope after the edge of the torchlight aware of the corpses' stares.

By the time he reached the steps that rose to the throne dais, the sartlar was already climbing them. The light stopped moving and the man returned down the steps without the torch. Carnelian stepped aside to let him pass. He listened to the footsteps receding behind him. Soon an eerie silence descended, made thicker by the delicate guttering of the torch up on the dais. The shadows of the crowd of Standing Dead slipped up and down the walls as if they were bobbing in some solemn dance. He began to climb the steps. Slowly the throne came into sight. The two gods rose behind it, their faces sinister and glowering. He stepped up onto the dais that sloped down to the throne, empty save for a mound of discarded rags. Carnelian's heart jumped as a voice spoke from their midst.

'Master.'

Among the rags, Carnelian located a pair of eyes; eyes that were gazing at him from within the ring scar of a deep branding. A face whose wrinkles seemed a continuation of the folds in the sacking that clung to the head. Carnelian was trapped in a waking dream, gazing upon that red face.

The eyes widened. 'You?'

910

He stared back. 'Kor?' Could this be the same sartlar woman? He tried to remember when he would have last seen her. Had she even made it as far as the Leper Valleys? He peered at the mutilated face beneath the coating of red ochre. The obscene nasal cavity in her skull had widened, but her eyes had a glint of cunning that was familiar. Was it a vestige of the Quyan humanity millennia of subjugation had crushed from her kind?

He froze. Unlikely as it was that she was here, it was his dreams that had brought him to her. Was it possible that she was the answer to all the riddles; the factor missing from the calculations of the Wise? Was hers the single mind behind the swarming sartlar? Her red face was certainly an echo of his dreams and there she sat upon the throne of the Gods. They stood behind her, Father and Son. Her face marked for the Mother, she completed the Triad. He sounded again the Quyan word for death, 'kor'. He swallowed past a parched throat. This, then, was where he must offer himself in exchange for the children. He sought mercy in her face, but all he could see in its ruin was a leathery indifference. Any life there had been in her eyes had been murdered by what she had seen.

'Why have you come here?' she said.

Carnelian tried to find something artful to say, but only the truth came out. 'I'm following a dream.'

Her brows eclipsed her eyes as she frowned. Her lower lip consumed the upper. Carnelian wanted to catch her emotion before it sank beyond reach. Frantically, he tried to sort images in his mind. She was slipping away from him. 'The dream came . . .' he said, saw her red face, read the branding, 'from the earth.'

As her face uncrumpled, the brand became circular again. 'All are clay in Her hands.'

Enough tension left Carnelian's chest for him to be able to take a deep breath. It was a start. He regarded her, trying to find the next step. 'What brought you here?'

Kor squinted at him. 'You.'

Carnelian thought he could see a path. 'You mean, because I freed the sartlar from the land?'

Kor's mouth sagged open, leaving Carnelian uncertain of his footing. He explained the dream that had led him to free the sartlar. As he spoke her head sank into her chest. He realized something. 'You didn't know it was me.' Why should she? All she could know was that a command had come to her people from a watch-tower.

The sartlar raised her head and Carnelian saw a glinting in the grooves around her missing nose. Was she crying? His shock that she might be made him realize he had still been thinking of her as some kind of animal. It made him angry at himself that, in spite of everything that had happened, he was still that much a Master. However mutilated, this was a woman.

'Clay in Her hands,' she said.

Carnelian sensed his news had somehow lightened her burdens. 'What did you mean . . . before?'

'Your blood,' she said, grimacing away the tears.

'My blood . . . ?' He was confused.

She frowned. 'You don't understand? We believed you to be the Dead.'

'The Dead . . . ?'.

'Our Dead, whom the Horned God had led up from the Underworld to enslave the Living.'

Carnelian stared at her. 'The Masters—?' Seeping insight overtook his tongue. Her words were a shadowy reflection of the revelations Osidian had given him in the Stone Dance of the Chameleon. The same events seen, murkily, from the point of view of the sartlar, from that of the Quyans.

'When you appeared unmasked . . .'

As Kor gazed at him in wonder, he glimpsed the child she might once have been.

She squeezed her eyes closed, grimacing again, shaking her head. 'The *monstrosity* we imagined you hid behind

912

your masks from shame.' Then her eyes opened. 'But such beauty . . . ?'

Carnelian was struck by the irony: those that the beautiful considered monstrous, believing the beautiful monstrous. Of course the sartlar had been right in so many ways.

She was scowling. 'Clouds darkened my mind. The world had been turned inside out. When you claimed to be angels, we had had no doubt that you lied.' She appraised Carnelian. 'You even showed compassion. I came to believe that perhaps it wasn't you who were cruel, but the overseers and their masters.' Her blistered lips curled into a sneer. 'The other Master showed me otherwise.'

Carnelian knew she meant Osidian.

'He proved to me that your beauty was indeed a lie; that, though you had the power to take on a pleasing form, beneath it you were being consumed by worms. Things became once again as they had always been. And how could the Living ever hope to fight the Dead?'

Understanding broke over Carnelian like an icy wave. 'My blood.'

From under her brows, Kor regarded him with baleful eyes. 'I tasted it.'

'You discovered we were just men.'

Her voice flat, clipped: 'I discovered you could be killed.'

So much seemed clear to Carnelian then. The purpose of the Law, the Wise, what the true Great Balance had been. He saw in his mind's eye how the world had whirled into destruction. He was appalled. 'From a single drop of blood?'

'It took more than that spark to ignite our rebellion. When I came up to Makar, of those of my people I found there, few believed me. As for our multitudes across the Land, they were beyond my reach. Generations it would've taken to pass on this new creed.'

Carnelian saw what he and Osidian had done to make the disaster inevitable. Gathering the sartlar together. Marching them to the heart of the Commonwealth, and there destroying not so much the legions as the Masters' aura of invincibility.

'When, in obedience to the Mother, you gathered up Her Children, my creed found many willing listeners.' Her face became a dead mask. 'Those who opposed me, we fed upon.'

Carnelian must have shown his disgust, for she lashed out: 'Does the Master forget who it was taught us to feed on man-flesh?'

Hatred rose in him against the ugly, filthy creature. 'What do you mean?'

'You *really* do not know?'

It was her surprise that tamed him. His hatred was a defence against the realization rising in him with the vomit: that render was sartlar flesh. He struck the floor with his knees, pumped his stomach out in acidic convulsions.

'So you've eaten from the same pot,' she said, gleefully. 'Did you really believe it was only the barbarians who paid you flesh tithe?'

Carnelian wiped his mouth, recalling the mounds of render sacs, glimpsing something of the scale of horror she was re-vealing to him. Looking up he watched her rage cool until she seemed to be wearing a leather mask.

'I was born in the rendering caves. It was well after I grew into a woman that I first breathed the Mother's sweet air. Mostly it was the old who were sent down to us, but also "troublemakers", rebels, any and all who showed any spirit of defiance. The overseers even sent us children.' Her glassy eyes slid to meet his gaze. 'We tried to drug them before smashing out their brains with rocks.' Her nose cavity changed shape. 'I'm never free of the stench of their cooking.'

Carnelian cradled his stomach, tears and phlegm running together down his face. He withstood the contempt in her eyes.

'How did you expect us to stay alive on the march to the Mountain? And on what do you imagine we feed now?'

He wiped his eyes, his nose, lost in horror, desperate to find light somewhere. 'The meat from the dragons?'

Kor stared at him, then threw her head back and let forth a raucous coughing noise he realized was laughter. The convulsions slowed, and she lowered her head, shaking it. 'That was barely enough to provide each of us with one meagre meal. Even the City's inhabitants only fed us for a single day.' She frowned. 'We can't escape hunger, nor do we wish to. Our Mother's dying. She's been dying since you enslaved us. Only our love and care have slowed Her decline. Still, each year She's given us less.'

'Surely some of the Land can still be saved?'

Kor glanced at him with a misery beyond sadness. 'Too late. She turns to dust. Once we've consumed what lies here at Her heart, our dust will mix with Hers.'

'Surely you must want something to survive? What about your children?'

As she turned away, he glimpsed a gleam of madness in her eyes. 'We consumed them all,' she whispered. 'I, their mother, made my people do it. I asked them why they didn't wish to spare their little ones more suffering.' She gave him a desperate, furtive glance. 'I feared they were so tired of killing, of dying, that they might give up, settle down to starve to death or attempt to find survival' – her huge hands flailed the air – 'somewhere.' Her gaze fixed predaciously on Carnelian, her face filled with disgust. 'So I stoked up their hatred. Now they hate me, but they hate you more.' She leaned closer and spat words at Carnelian with her filthy breath. 'We shall all die, but first I'll rid the world of your cancer.'

She subsided, became just a strange, misshapen, mutilated woman. Carnelian was too weary for strategy and so let his heart speak. 'But what will be left of that world?'

Her madness abated; Kor gazed at him with human eyes. She shrugged. 'The lands beyond?'

'The barbarians . . .'

Kor shrugged again.

Carnelian put his trust in his certainty that she was a woman, with a woman's heart. 'I have their children here.'

She looked at him, strangely still.

'I brought their flesh tithe out from the Mountain. Thousands of children.'

Tightness had spread to buckle the upper curve of her branding. He held her old woman's eyes. 'Let them go.'

Kor chewed her upper lip, her eyes lensed with tears. He watched her face, breathlessly, as it betrayed the turmoil in her heart. Then, at last, she nodded and joy burst out through him as tears.

She turned. 'Take them with you.'

'Me?' He had expected to pay for this boon with his life.

She gazed at him, seeming blind. He dared more. 'Some of my people came with me.' She was not saying no. 'And some Marula . . .' Her frowning made him quickly add, 'whom I freed from their masters the Oracles.'

'Take them all,' she said. 'The Children of the Earth shall show you mercy who have never been shown it themselves.'

Her eyes turned to glass and Carnelian judged his audience was at an end. He rose, turned away.

'Master?'

Heart beating, he looked round.

'How did you arrive here?'

At first Carnelian was confused, then he remembered the boats, remembered the water gate they had had to leave raised. His instinct was to lie, but it was a price that must be paid. He hardened his heart against the people in Osrakum. 'We came by boat from the lake within the Mountain.'

Kor stared as if she could see that far. 'Our legends speak of water the Dead have to cross.'

Carnelian waited a little, then turned away. His joy at what he had achieved was leavened with horror at the fate of those he had delivered to Mother Death.

*   *   *

916

'Is that you, Carnie?' came a voice from a clump of shadows on the road. He told Fern it was. Lumpen shapes surrounded Carnelian. 'She's let us go,' he said to them. They grumbled and for a moment he did not believe they were going to let him through, but then they shuffled aside.

'What's happening?' demanded Fern.

Carnelian closed in on his voice, gripped him, felt Fern tense then relax as he embraced him, found his mouth and kissed him. He threw his cloak around them both.

'Aren't you going to tell me?' Fern said into his neck.

Feeling his warmth against him, Carnelian decided there was no reason to burden him unnecessarily. 'They're going to let us pass.'

'How?'

'They don't care about us.'

'All of us, the children too?'

Carnelian heard the incredulity in Fern's voice and hesitated before answering with a nod. His encounter with Kor already seemed an implausible dream. He remembered her tears. 'All of us.'

Carnelian came awake, shivering. Cold had penetrated to his bones. He smiled as Fern snuggled into him. The sky was greying in the gap between the sombre, leaning mass of the Iron House and the vague blackness of the Sacred Wall. He regarded that mountainous mass. Within lay the Land of the Dead. He frowned, trying to focus on what he had left back there, but it already seemed a fairytale. Even the mist rising from the water in front of him seemed more substantial. He watched the pale edge of dawn. A new day with hope of life that raised his spirits so that he no longer cared about the cold.

His muscles tensing must have woken Fern. 'What . . . ?' He saw the intense look on Carnelian's face, slipped his chin free of the edge of the cloak and followed his gaze. The flood-lake shore curved away, the dry land beyond was textured by a vast encampment. Between it and the water the shoreline was encrusted with rafts and all manner of makeshift boats.

On the edge of the road they sat hunched and shrouded though the sun was still low and they welcomed its heat. Carnelian in particular wanted to conceal his height, his pale skin. He did not want to needlessly provoke the sartlar. He gazed at his feet, kneading his toes. When he had decided to stay by the Iron House, he had been relieved that Fern insisted on remaining with him. They had reassured each other that, finding them gone, Keal, or Tain, or Poppy, or Krow would have the sense to march the children south towards them. Carnelian had not wanted to go and fetch them because he feared that what hope there was for them all depended on him; depended on his tenuous link with Kor.

His gaze was drawn back to the Iron House, as shocking now as when the rising sun had revealed it. Molochite's black chariot was now a furious red. It was hard not to believe it a sign that the Mother had claimed the chariot for Herself. An angry marker at the very edge of Her earth defiant against the flood, but also the place where the Horned God had died with the children of the Great. The womb tomb in his dream.

He watched the crowd milling its duller reds around the rusty ruin and pouring in and out of its door in a constant, frantic, anthill activity. It soothed him to watch, for he needed to believe that this red tower was the centre of their swarm. For if Kor were not their queen . . . ? He shuddered and curled forward until his chin nearly touched the stone. His slitted eyes slipped eastwards from the broken wheel of the chariot. Water clotted with debris lapped at the feverish raft-building along the shore. Everywhere, trails of sartlar were filtering down to the water edge, filling pots, staggering back burdened with the filthy stew. To quench the thirst of . . . Carnelian could not help following the water carriers away from the shore. His heart raced. As far as the horizon, the land teemed

918

with spindly life that seemed to him not people, nor even sartlar, but only a voracious plague of man-eating vermin.

As the sun rose higher, they grew increasingly worried about the children. Fern was the first to rise to gaze north. Carnelian joined him, feeling too tall. At first they could only see the heat hazing above the road, then, far away, that something was dulling its incandescence.

Three figures came ahead of the children. By their face tattoos, Carnelian recognized two of them as of his tyadra and guessed the man shrouded in their midst must be one of his brothers. All three seemed to be staring at the sartlar multitude. Carnelian did not greet them, but waited until they came close before opening his cowl.

'Carnie,' exclaimed the central figure, pushing back his hood so that they could see it was Tain. 'Thank the Gods,' he said, his eyes flicking anxiously back to the sartlar.

'I've arranged safe passage,' Carnelian said.

His brother stared at him, frowning. 'How— ?'

Carnelian interrupted him with questions about the dispositions of the children and the others. He nodded as Tain explained.

'There's nothing like enough of us if things should turn nasty,' said the youth.

Carnelian nodded. 'We can't do anything about that. What we can do is keep them under control. We need to get through as quickly and quietly as we can.'

Standing alone in the shadow of the Iron House, Carnelian watched them file past, shuffling, scuffling. Sometimes a child's voice would rise, but would be quickly hushed. Children filled the road from side to side, except where they had to pour around the chariot. The ant tide of sartlar clambering in and out through its door had been pushed into a narrow corridor running to and from the nearest ramp. He hardly

919

breathed, longing for the march to reach open road. Fern and the vanguard were already lost in the haze to the south, but the river of children still stretched back as far the other way.

When the last children walked past, Carnelian sighed in relief, then left the bloody aura of the rusting chariot and attached himself to the rear of the march. Sthax was there with a couple of Marula herding the children with the hafts of their lances, all the time their yellow eyes darting fearful glances out over the sartlar-clad earth.

The children did not need to be told to be quiet. Dread spread from those on the edge of the road into the heart of their march. All eyes able to look out could not help doing so. Sartlar smothered the land like locusts. Stick women wound their way through the squatting multitudes, bowls of brackish water on their heads that looked as if they must snap their necks like twigs. Men huddled around pots from which steam billowed, wafting a stench of cooking meat towards the road, mixing with the odour of shit and urine, of rotting, of indescribable filth. Many of those passing on the road above were fighting nausea. Below, among the multitude, some rose to watch them pass with enormous eyes. Their sagging, disfigured faces might have been angry, or sad, or in shock. Few looked as if they would survive the day, but Carnelian remembered the rafts and he shuddered at the thought of this army of the near-dead, determined to force their way into the Land of the Dead. He sought solace in the healthy faces and bright eyes of the flesh-tithe children. For moments at a time he managed thus to avoid being aware of the sea of despair and hatred through which they were winding their thread.

They came into a region of pink dunes. Dazed with horror, Carnelian thought for a moment they must have reached some sea shore. Then he saw how pallid were the ridges and knew they were composed of the piled-up remains of the sartlar dead. Upon that battlefield, the matrix of their bones was ensnaring great drifts of ruddy sand. The road carried them through that eerie landscape in whose valleys sartlar crouched, in places having delved hollows in which they hid like crabs. Here too cauldrons bubbled their noisome stench. Carnelian slipped into a dream rhythmed by the movement of his legs, in which everything in the world was or had been a body that they were crossing on a causeway of human bone.

He became aware the world was turning red. A clean, dry russet red. He looked around. At last they were leaving the sartlar camp! Behind them Osrakum was lit from the west. How low the sun was. He squinted against the glare from which the road emerged: the flood-lake, around which there lay a stain that merged with the Sacred Wall to form a black ring. Kor, the sign of death. He turned away and saw their march like a bleeding cut in the raw meat of the Land. Gently, he began to push his way forward through the children.

Shadows were long when they reached a watch-tower. Carnelian glanced up and saw, beneath a disc, a bar and four spots. Nine. He stared, stunned. Watch-tower sun-nine. This was where they had received the Wise. Where he had met his father and brothers. Where he had deserted Osidian. He could make no sense of that memory, nor of the intervening time. That other, Chosen reality no longer seemed credible. Just a story in which he had imagined he had played a role.

When Tain came up to him, Carnelian asked him to get the children settled down for the night; find places for them to sleep, draw as much water as they could, light fires where possible.

Carnelian caught hold of Fern's arm. 'Come with me.'

Fern was about to ask where, but when he saw Carnelian was looking up at the watch-tower, he nodded.

*   *   *

Standing upon the heliograph platform, they gazed south. A vast land spread out before them, shapeless behind drifting red veils of dust.

'It'll all soon be desert,' Fern said and turned anxious eyes on Carnelian. 'How can we hope to get them all through?'

They both gazed down at the stopping place overflowing with children. Carnelian set his jaw. 'We'll have to manage somehow, there's no going back.'

They looked round. Osrakum was a sombre crust rising from the rotten heart of a land that soon would die. Death would pursue them all the way to the Ringwall. Carnelian felt Fern's arm around him. They smiled at each other, then together peered south as if trying to glimpse the Earthsky.

CODA

Suddenly the red fog clears. Carnelian stares. he lifts Ykorenthe down from his shoulders because he fears his legs might buckle. If he were not so desiccated, tears would be running down his face. The verdant vision hurts his eyes. Green veined with silver. Intimidating colours. Hues so strange, so unreal. A vast stretch that in his dreams would have been the lush water meadows of the Leper Valleys. Everything was turned upside down. Could the dust ocean of the dying Land really have washed them up on this wet and smiling shore? Unbelievable glitter of free, running water almost enough to quench the thirst that long ago had dried up his mouth and eyes. On his tongue the ever-present taste of death.

Slowing his heart against the fear he will lose his vision, he dares to look away. He gazes at Fern beside him and finds some confirmation he is not mad in the look of wonder upon his sweet face. Poppy is there in Krow's embrace as they gaze, gaping. His brothers grin like idiots. Sthax and the other Marula, frozen in a stare. The homunculus, his eyes gauging, judging; he alone seems to be certain what he is looking at is real. All around them their children, encrusted in the red dust of the Land that has slowly been drawing the living moisture from their flesh; each sandstorm hiss and scrape progressing their mummification. Every eye blinks red in a red face. Breathing is coughing that barely flutters each pair of blistered, thinned lips. Love for them rises, threatening to overwhelm him. It seems he has been witnessing their struggle along the road all his life. Trudging on through a red world. Driven south and ever south along the empty road by the screaming, gasping fury of the Land in Her death throes. Cowering in the feeble shelter of their rags and arms and bodies; huddling together against the raging dust. Sipping the trickles that they found in cisterns, or delved for in the black honeycombed depths of wells.

Carnelian gazes back at the long, long column of children that is swallowed up into the red smoky throat of the Pass. Moments ago he was putting one foot in front of the other, seeing nothing, deaf to the scratching air, following the memory of a desperate hope that, somewhere, something of life has survived the death of the world. Makar is up there, a piling-up of the Land's bones snaring Her red dust so that, along its duned road, they had walked almost at the level of the rooftops. Its people had abandoned the lost city as if it were a ship run aground. That he had seen no evidence of violence anywhere in the houses, or the alleys, was the first sign that had stirred hope in him.

He turns back to the vision and laughs joyously when he finds it is still there. Fern is grinning at him, offering him his hand. Carnelian smiles back, lighting up at the happiness releasing the beauty in Ykorenthe's face. He lifts her back onto his shoulders, grips Fern's hand and, with a smile to his family, leads them down onto the sward, drinking the clean, bright air until it hurts, eyes narrowed against the shimmer of the beckoning streams; the blaze and mercy of the clear, blue sky.

THE CHOSEN
Stone Dance of the Chameleon
by Ricardo Pinto

'Pinto writes with an almost Donaldsonian/Feistian grip'
Anne McCaffrey

Carnelian is of the Masters, cruel beings who rule their kingdom from an earthly paradise hidden in a crater that is the navel of the world. Soon after he is born, Carnelian's father takes him across the sea to an island in the colourless north. Far from the Crater's rituals and pomp, their household is allowed to become a family to the boy and the world of the Masters fades to alluring fairy tale.

In deepest winter, years later, a ship comes riding before the gales, three Masters her only cargo. As these giants remove their masks of gold, Carnelian is awed by the light that seems to radiate from their skin. In formal conclave they ask Carnelian's father to end his exile and return with them to oversee the election of a new God Emperor. His father's agreement feeds Carnelian's longing for the world beyond the sea, but as the days pass Carnelian watches with growing horror as the ship's needs devour his home. The Masters are indifferent, imperious, concerned only with their blood politics, their majesty. As his father becomes strangely powerless, Carnelian strives to save his people, but when the ship turns her prow towards the stormy sea he knows that he is abandoning them to famine among the ruins of his former home.

This is the beginning of Carnelian's journey. The terror of the tempest yields to the weary grind along the road, the climb up the forboding cliff wall to the Guarded Land and then the frantic rush into the deep south. Carnelian's education, which began with the starving of his people, proceeds with bitter lessons in bloodshed, intrigue and betrayal. When they finally reach the Canyon of the Three Gates, which leads into the Crater, Carnelian finds both love and treachery, but it is here within the Heaven Wall that he will set in motion the concluding events in a story already ten thousand years old.

'Boldly conceived and intelligently written . . . Lingers in the memory like a strange and disturbing dream'
Interzone

9780553505818

THE STANDING DEAD
Stone Dance of the Chameleon Volume II
by Ricardo Pinto

'The groundbreaking *Stone Dance of the Chameleon* trilogy . . .
is that rarest of things – a deeply original fantasy'
SFX

In desperation, the Ruling Lord Suth searches within the sacred
walls of Osrakum for Carnelian, his son, and Osidian, the God
Emperor elect. He suspects the Empress Ykoriana is behind their
disappearance and knows that if they are not found soon it is her
other son, Osidian's brother Molochite, who will rule – with
fearful consequences for the Three Lands.

Captive of the tribes of the Earthsky, Carnelian is – for the
moment – safe. Succumbing readily to the seasonal rhythms of
tribal life, he is convinced by unexpected discoveries that it is
fate that has brought him there. He grows to love these simple
people and hopes for sanctuary among them. But the dark forces
Carnelian helped unleash in Osrakum begin to cast their shadow
over his adopted home. He is witness to the awful oppression that
the Masters – whom the tribesmen call the Standing Dead – have
been inflicting on them for millenia. But even more terrible is the
presence Carnelian has unwittingly brought with him.
Potent and terrifying, it threatens everything he now
holds dear in this new-found world.

With *The Standing Dead*, Ricardo Pinto gives us a tumultuous new
chapter in the acclaimed *Stone Dance of the Chameleon* trilogy
and confirms his place as one of fantasy's most singular
and literate voices.

'Panoramic, riveting and stimulating . . . a majestically
structured and vivid piece of fantasy writing'
Starlog

'Beautifully written . . . challengingly complicated . . . highly
original . . . brilliantly realized . . . totally believable'
SFX

9780553812855